Modinha,
composed by Dorival Caymmi,
for Tereza Batista:

They call me missy Tereza
Perfumed with rosemary
Fill your mouth with honey
Before you talk of me
                    Flowering hair
                    Flowering me
                    River and sea

TEREZA BATISTA

Home from the Wars

JORGE AMADO

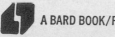 A BARD BOOK/PUBLISHED BY AVON BOOKS

Originally published in Brazil as *Tereza Batista cansada de guerra* by Livraria Martins Editora S.A., São Paulo
Copyright by Livraria Martins Editora S.A.

AVON BOOKS
A division of
The Hearst Corporation
959 Eighth Avenue
New York, New York 10019

Copyright © 1975 by Alfred A. Knopf, Inc.
Published by arrangement with Alfred A. Knopf, Inc.
Library of Congress Catalog Card Number: 74-21313
ISBN: 0-380-01752-0

First Bard Printing, September, 1977

BARD TRADEMARK REG. U.S. PAT. OFF. AND IN
OTHER COUNTRIES, MARCA REGISTRADA,
HECHO EN U.S.A.

Printed in the U.S.A.

for
ZÉLIA
home again in Bahia,
by the sea

Plague, famine, war; love and death,
Tereza Batista's life is a ballad to sing in the streets.

"Que ta coquille soit très dure pour permettre d'être
très tendre:
la tendresse est comme l'eau: invincible."

Let your shell be so hard that you can be really gentle:
Gentleness is like water: invincible.

ANDRÉ BAY (*"Aimez-vous les escargots?"*)

The last time I saw Tereza Batista was on enchanted ritual ground last February at the fiftieth anniversary celebration of Menininha de Gantois's induction as a holy daughter of Oxossi. Dressed all in white, with her round full skirt and lace chemise, the queen of Bahia's iyalorixás knelt to ask a blessing; so for that and many other reasons I put her first on my list of the friends young Tereza and the author shared. After her come Nazareth and Odylo, Zora and Olinto, Inas and Dmeval, Auta Rosa and Calá, little Eunice and Chico Lyon, Elisa and Alvaro, Maria Helena and Luiz, Zita and Fernando, Clotilde and Rogério—all friends from both sides of the ocean. But Mother Menininha and the author are the two who have come the farthest—from the Kingdom of Ketu, from the sands of Aioká. We two belong to Oxossi and Oxum. Axé.

JORGE AMADO was born in 1912 in Ilhéus, the provincial capital of the state of Bahia whose society he portrays in such acclaimed novels as *Gabriela, Clove and Cinnamon*; *Dona Flor and Her Two Husbands*; and TEREZA BATISTA, HOME FROM THE WARS. His father was a cocoa planter, and his first novel, *Cacau*, published when he was nineteen, is a plea for social justice for the workers on the cocoa estates south of Bahia. The theme of class struggle continues to dominate in his novels of the Thirties and Forties; but with the Fifties and *Gabriela, Clove and Cinnamon* (1958), the political emphasis gives way to a lighter, more novelistic approach. It was in that novel, published in the United States when Amado was fifty and enthusiastically received in some fourteen countries, that he first explored the rich literary vein pursued in TEREZA BATISTA.

When people heard I was going back there, they said to find out what on earth was happening to Tereza Batista— to see if I could clear up a few things. There sure is plenty of curiosity in the world, ain't there?

So I poked around here and there, at markets in little backwoods towns and down on the dock; and with time and nosiness to spare, after a while I got pretty much up to date on some queer stories and tales, some funny, some sad, each one funny or sad in its own way, depending on how you look at it. I gathered together all bits and pieces I heard and could make sense of—anecdotes, tunes on the harmonica, dance steps, cries of desperation and moans of love, all jumbled up together—and brought them back to tell to people who wanted to know about that copper-colored girl's ups and downs, and all her wanderings. It still doesn't add up to an awful lot: folks in these parts aren't what you'd call real talkers, and the ones who know the most say the least. Nobody out there hankers to get a diploma for telling tales.

Some of Tereza Batista's adventures happened out in the country along the Real River, where Bahia and Sergipe meet, but inland a good way; and some happened in the capital. Out there the people are all halfbreeds and high yellows and black Indians, folks who act quicker than they think, except for those funny mulattoes in the capital, who sing and beat the drums. When I say "capital," all of you understand of course that I'm talking about the city of Bahia, sometimes called Salvador. Nobody seems to know why. And anyway, who cares? The name of Bahia has traveled all the way to the French court and the frozen land of Germany, not to mention the coast of Africa.

You'll forgive me for not telling you the whole story just

*the way it happened. I don't because I can't. Is there any-
body in the world who knows the whole truth about Tereza
Batista—the times when she was down and out, and the
spells of easy living? I can't believe there is.*

Tereza Batista's debut at the Aracaju cabaret

or

Tereza Batista's gold tooth

or

Tereza Batista and how she gave the usurer his due

1

Well, since you ask me so nicely, young fellow, I'll tell you this: all bad luck needs is a start in life. Once it gets going there's no holding it; it spreads and it flourishes. Talk all you like, bad luck's a product for mass consumption if ever there was one. Now happiness, on the other hand, is a mighty finicky kind of plant, old pal. It doesn't last long, and while it does it doesn't cast much shade; it doesn't thrive in full sun, or in the rain, or where it's windy; it needs feeding every day—just the right amount of fertilizer and soil that's not too wet and not too dry; it's a hot-house flower for rich people with plenty of money to throw around. Happiness is preserved in champagne; all rum can do is ease your misery a little, maybe. Yes, sir; bad luck's a hardy shoot: just stick it in the ground and forget it. It'll grow all by itself, don't you worry, and be putting out leaves in no time alongside of every road. There's always plenty of it in a poor man's yard, friend, even if there isn't another green sprig to be found. If the sun hasn't burned his skin to leather, if he hasn't a strong back and calluses inside and out, he can go to the voodoo man all he wants to, but there isn't a spirit that can help him. I'll tell you another thing, my friend, not that I want to brag about how big and strong us hillbillies are: it's just the pure and simple truth that it's only poor folks who've got toughness and pride enough to stand up under such a load of misfortune and go on living. Well, now I've got that off my chest without you contradicting me, tell me, brother, what do you want to know about Tereza Batista's hard life for? Do you think you can change anything that she went through a long time ago?

Tereza had a hard row to hoe, no doubt about that. Not many men could have pulled such a load; but she stood it all and kept going, and nobody ever heard her complain or *ask anybody to feel sorry for her. When somebody helped her once in a while, it was out of friendship and not because of weakness on her part; everywhere she went she chased sadness away. She just didn't pay much attention to bad luck, brother; she thought happiness was all that was worth bothering about. Would you like to know whether Tereza was made of iron and had a heart covered with armor plate? From the pretty color of her skin, you'd think she was made out of copper instead of iron, but her heart was made of butter or maybe honey: the Doctor who owned the mill—and who ever knew her better than he did?—always called her by one of the two names he'd given her: Sugarsweet Tereza or Tereza Honeycomb. That's all she inherited from him.*

Bad luck was an early bloom in Tereza's life, old friend; I wonder how many men could have survived what she went through in the Captain's house.

What Captain, you say? Why Captain Justo, or rather the deceased Justiniano Duarte da Rosa. Captain in what army? An army whose weapons are a rawhide strap, a knife, a German pistol, cheating, and beastliness: the rich man's army, the landowner's. Not so rich and not owning so much land that he could wear a colonel's stripes, but too much to be a mere civilian instead of a military man. It was Emiliano, the oldest of the Guedes brothers, the owner of the sugarmill, who had enough land to be a colonel— leagues and leagues of green sugarcane; but once he had earned his lawyer's ring and diploma, he never used any title except doctor, although he never practiced. Times are changing, pal, but don't be fooled too much by that. Titles change—a colonel calls himself a doctor now, an overseer is a manager, a plantation is a "business enterprise"—but it's only the title that's different. Rich is rich, and poor is poor, with plenty of bad luck still to go around.

One thing sure, friend: Tereza Batista had a fine start in life—I don't think. Not many sinners in Hell are suffering what that little orphan went through, father and mother dead, all alone—all alone against God and the devil, as the saying goes: not even God took pity on her. But confound the girl, by golly she crossed the worst piece of swamp all by herself, the very worst patch, and came out safe and sound on the other side, and with a smile on her face. Well, I don't know for a fact that she was smiling, but that's what I've been told. If you really want to know for certain all about Tereza Batista's beginning, just take the Leste Brasileira train to where the outback begins. That's where she had her start, and maybe the folks who still live there can tell you the details about how it was.

The hardest thing Tereza Batista had to learn was how to cry. She was born to laugh and have a good time. Nobody wanted to let her have fun, but she was stubborn as a mule, little Tereza Batista. Maybe that's a bad way to put it, friend, because there sure wasn't anything mulish about her but her stubbornness. She wasn't mannish, or a dyke, or dirty-mouthed—Oh, how her mouth smelled of perfume—or shrewish, or a slut, or spoiling for a fight; and if anybody told you different, he was either kidding you or he didn't know Tereza Batista, one. The only time she ordered anybody around was when it came to love: I told you before she was made for love and when it came to loving she didn't fool around. Then why in the world did they call her Tereza the Fighter? Well, pal, she was a good fighter; there was nobody like her for courage and pride and a heart full of sweetness. She hated a roughhouse and never tried to stir up trouble. But maybe because of what she went through as a child, she never could stand to see a man hit a woman.

2

So that some necessary dental work could be done on the star of the show, Tereza Batista's much-anticipated debut at the Gay Paree Cabaret, in the building called the Vatican, near the Wharves of Aracaju, territory of Sergipe del-Rey, had to be postponed. Naturally this meant a loss of revenue for Floriano Pereira, commonly known as Flori Pachola, the owner of the cabaret and a stalwart son of Maranhão, but Flori took it like a man, without complaining or blaming anybody else, as people usually do.

The debut of the Incandescent Star of the Samba (Pachola hadn't a peer as coiner of catchy phrases and publicity slogans) had aroused a great deal of interest, of course, since Tereza Batista's name was common currency, especially in certain quarters: among traveling salesmen, in the marketplace, at the port, in the red-light district. It was Dr. Lulu Santos who had brought Tereza Batista to Flori's attention. Poor people gave him the title of "doctor," but actually he was just a practicing amateur of the law who was famous all over Sergipe for his defenses before juries, his biting epigrams, his witty sayings (his admirers credited him with every funny remark ever made), and for his equal competence in courtroom or bar. In fact, he spent his afternoons in the Egypt Café and Bar interviewing clients, laughing at fools, and cracking jokes, all in a cloud of smoke from his eternal cigar. His legs were shriveled from infantile paralysis, and Lulu Santos hobbled on two crutches; but his good humor was unalterable. He had enjoyed a long friendship with Tereza Batista. It was he, in fact, who had traveled to the interior some years before, hired by Dr. Emiliano Guedes, owner of a sugarmill straddling the border between Bahia and Sergipe, now dead (and in what an enviable way he died!), to quash a lawsuit against Tereza Batista. The suit was illegal, in any case, because Tereza Batista was still a minor; but none of that concerns us here except that a friendship grew up between the girl and the lawyer, an amateur worth a whole raft of licensed lawyers with their degrees and diplomas, speeches, and caps and gowns.

A full house, a lively crowd, a festive and convivial milieu. The Midnight Jazz Band is playing its heart out, the customers are buying beer, rum, and whiskey very freely. According to the prospectus lavishly distributed around town, "the gilded youth of Aracaju find entertainment at a reasonable price at the Gay Paree"—the gilded youth of Aracaju consisting of clerks and office workers, students, municipal employees, traveling salesmen, José Saraiva the poet, the young painter Jenner Augusto, a handful of university graduates, and an equal number of bums and professional men of varying ages, some of whom were prolonging their gilded youth past the age of sixty. Flori Pachola, a stocky mulatto with a gift of gab, had spared no pains to publicize the debut of the queen of the samba and the *maculelê*, and to make of Tereza's first appearance on the dance floor of the Gay Paree a memorable event. Memorable, indeed unforgettable, it was.

Tereza Batista was very self-possessed on opening night—
a little nervous, of course, but managing not to show it as
she sat at a table discreetly off to one side of the hall. She
was waiting until it was time to change for her act, talking
to Lulu Santos and laughing at his amusing remarks about
the customers. She knew hardly anyone in town, having
just come, but the amateur lawyer knew everybody.

Despite the dim lighting and their out-of-the-way table,
Tereza's attractiveness did not go unnoticed. Lulu drew
her attention to a table next to the dance floor where two
pale young men were drinking new cocktails. One was
pale from illness; the light skin and deep-set blue eyes of
the other, a native of Sergipe, made him look like a for-
eigner.

"The poet can't take his eyes off you, Tereza."

"What poet? That young fellow?"

The sickly-pale youth had stood up and raised his glass
in a toast to Tereza and the lawyer; he held his hand on his
heart as a way of openly expressing his friendship and devotion. Lulu Santos acknowledged the compliment by
waving his hand with the cigar in it.

"There you have him: José Saraiva, as talented as anyone in this world, an honest-to-God poet, if ever there was
one. It's a shame he has so little time left."

"Why, what's wrong with him?"

"Tuberculosis."

"Why doesn't he take care of himself?"

"Take care of himself? He's killing himself, that's what
he's doing—staying out all night, drinking and carousing.
He's the worst night-owl in Sergipe."

"Worse than you?"

"I'm nowhere compared to him. Oh, I like a few beers
once in a while, but he doesn't know when to stop. You'd
almost think he wants to die."

"That's bad, when you want to die."

The jazz musicians, after a few minutes' intermission to
gulp down a beer, returned to the attack with redoubled

energy. The young poet got up and walked over to Tereza and Lulu.

"Brother Lulu, present me to the goddess of the evening."

"My friend Tereza—the poet José Saraiva."

The poet kissed the girl's hand. He was a little drunk, and the sadness in his eyes belied the free-and-easy air he tried to assume.

"Why such a squandering of beauty? These eyes behold beauty enough for three fair women, with grace and loveliness to spare. Heavenly vision, shall we dance?"

As they went toward the dance floor, the poet Saraiva stopped at his table to down the rest of his rum in one gulp and to show Tereza off to his companion.

"Artist, here for you to admire is the supreme model worthy of Raphael and Titian."

The painter Jenner Augusto (for this was who the young man at the table was) looked at Tereza's face and never in his life forgot her. Tereza smiled politely but in a distant kind of way; her heart was empty, shut and bolted; she had no interest in male glances, bold or shy; she was at peace at last and little by little putting herself together again.

Tereza and the poet began to dance. Perspiration sprang out on the young man's tired forehead, though he was leading the most skillful of partners, the lightest of ladies with the keenest of ears. Dr. Guedes had taught her to dance; she danced to perfection and loved to do it, forgetting the world to the rhythm of the music, her eyes closed in bliss.

It was a pity to have to open them and pay attention to the poet. Poor poet—along with his amusing words, a faint, persistent whistle issued from his consumptive chest.

"So you are the blazing comet of the samba! Do you know that Flori's ad is a poem? But of course you don't need to know; your only obligation is just to be beautiful. When I read the leaflet about your performance I asked myself: Now José Saraiva, you know everything; tell me what on earth got into Flori Pachola to make a poet of him? I know the answer now but that isn't all. Now I can write dozens and dozens of poems—not doggerel like Flori's, but real poems."

He yearned to improvise flattering and exalted verses in jazz rhythm, then and there on the dance floor; and he undoubtedly would have done it if an incident had not occurred just then a few feet away from them, setting off the powder train that exploded in the fight.

A couple was gyrating nearby, cheek to cheek and clutched in a tight embrace. The gentleman was a traveling salesman, judging by his brand-new clothes, the padded sports jacket and loud tie, not to mention his brilliantined hair and the insinuating compliments he was murmuring into the ear of the chubby, cross-eyed girl with the interesting profile. Although she listened eagerly to the salesman's honeyed words, obviously fascinated by his elegance and good manners, the girl's eyes betrayed inner tension as she continually darted uneasy glances at the entrance door. Suddenly she gave a cry:

"Oh, God! There's Libório!" She slipped out of her partner's embrace and turned to flee, saw there was nowhere to go, and burst into tears. Libório, whose appearance in the nightclub with three friends was the cause of the girl's panic, was a long lean individual dressed in funereal black, with swollen eyelids, slick hair, stooping shoulders, and a flaccid mouth—taken all together, hardly an object of beauty, looking as if the funeral he'd come from was recent. He headed for the dance floor, planted himself in front of the girl, and raised his nasal voice:

"So you went to visit your sick mother in Propriá, you little tramp?"

"Libório, for God's sake, don't start a fuss."

The traveling salesman, who had been badly burned in earlier encounters of this kind, didn't want to add another black mark to his professional dossier at the pharmaceutical firm he represented in Bahia, Sergipe, and Alagoas ("an excellent salesman, competent, aggressive, and honest; but with a weakness for women and night life; has been in trouble in nightclubs and bawdy houses, and has even been arrested"). He quietly removed himself from the scene even as his colleagues and table companions rose to their feet, ready, if it came to that, to back him up.

The poet was about to shrug off the incident and resume his dancing and improvisation where he had broken off— outraged cuckolds are a common breed around nightclubs —when the crack of a slap drowned out the jazz music. Tereza stopped where she was just in time to see a large hand strike the girl's face for a second time, and to hear the lanky individual's nasal voice say what she'd heard all too often in days gone by: "I'll teach you to have some respect for me, you bitch!" The voice was different but the words were the same old ones, and so was the sound of the man's hand striking a woman's face.

Tereza Batista instantly disengaged herself from the poet's arms and marched over to the couple:

"A man who hits a woman isn't a man at all, he's a coward . . ."

By this time she was looking him straight in the eye:

". . . and I never hit a coward, I spit in his face."

No sooner said than done. Tereza Batista, trained from infancy in games of cowboy and Indian and in fighting fleet-footed boys, prided herself in her unerring aim; but this time the target was so high that she missed his rheumy eye and the spittle lodged on his chin.

"Son-of-a-bitch."

"Come on and hit me if you're a man!"

"Damned right I will, you bitch!"

"Come on, then!"

She didn't wait for him to do it but sent a kick at his lower regions, aiming for the groin but missing again. The fellow had legs like stilts. Tereza lost her balance; one of the coward's companions went behind her and seized her arms, leaving her face defenseless. Not content just with hitting a woman, Libório had on his brass knuckles, and the blow gashed Tereza's mouth.

Saraiva the poet fell upon the varlet who had dared lay hands on the incandescent star of the samba, and the three fell to the floor in a tangle. With a bound, Tereza was up again and spat in her opponent's face for a second time; this time blood and a piece of tooth accompanied the spittle. Reinforcements came up on both sides: on one hand the offended cuckold's other henchmen; and on the other Jenner Augusto, biting his lips in rage, and the traveling salesman who had prudently abandoned his dancing partner to her fate—that girl he'd never seen had done what he should have done himself. Losing his head and forgetting what remained of his damaged reputation, but regaining the respect of his colleagues in the process, he entered the fray. The musicians were still playing but the dancers had left the floor, clearing it for the combatants. Someone who was standing on a table with a twenty-cruzeiro note in his hand bellowed a challenge:

"Twenty on the girl! Who'll take me?"

Tereza had managed to get a grip on the greased pole's scanty hair and pulled out a handful. He tried to reach her with his brass knuckles to knock out another tooth, but Tereza feinted agilely, almost in a dance step, eluded him while managing to kick his shins and spit in his face, always on the alert for a chance to aim a kick at a more strategic spot.

The customers were standing in a circle around the dance floor so as to get a good view of the thrilling show; and the cross-eyed girl, the cause of it all, followed each jab from a distance as she wondered which man she'd be going home with.

A new arrival on the scene of battle, a vigorous *caboclo* with sun-bronzed muscular build and windburned complexion, watched for a while and then remarked for everyone to hear:

"Holy Virgin, I never saw a better woman in a fight in all my days."

Just then two civil guards came into the hall, attracted by the uproar. Evidently they knew Libório and his friends, for they raised their night sticks and started for Tereza with the obvious intention of showing her how many ways there are of skinning a cat.

"Yansã! here I come!" was the *caboclo*'s war cry. No one knew why he called on the African goddess of war, Yansã. Perhaps he meant to honor Tereza by giving her the name of the indomitable voodoo divinity, bravest of all; or perhaps he was informing his guardian spirit that Captain Januário Gereba, her *ogan* in the Bogun *candomblé*, was ready for a fight.

He made a good start. The two policemen flew through the air in opposite directions. Then the *caboclo* intercepted an attempt by one of the beanpole's unsavory sidekicks to wipe the sole of his shoe on José Saraiva's face, as the weak-lunged poet with the brave heart lay speechless on the floor of the arena. Like a whirlwind the *caboclo* lifted the poet to his feet and kept on slugging. The police came back for more—

As one of Libório's police buddies pulled out a revolver and threatened to shoot, the lights went out. The final picture to be seen was Lulu Santos, his cigar in his mouth, balancing himself on one crutch and whirling the other around him like a windmill. Libório the cuckold bellowed in the darkness; Tereza had finally landed a kick in the right place.

Needless to say, no debut took place that night. No queen of the samba made her debut, at least, but Tereza's first public appearance on the dance floors of Aracaju was a never-to-be-forgotten one all the same. The dental surgeon Jamil Najar, the man who had laid the twenty-cruzeiro bet, refused to charge any fee for the gold tooth he deftly inserted in the upper left side of Tereza's mouth, where her lip had been cut by the brass knuckles. Any payment he might have asked for would certainly not have been in money.

4

Flori put his place back in order and held his breath while he waited for the dental surgeon to give him the signal to set a new, fixed, and unshakable date for the more-than-ever eagerly awaited debut of Tereza Batista at the Gay Paree. Dr. Najar was spinning out the treatment as long as he could: My dear Pachola, work in gold, *any* sort of work in gold, takes art and pains, skill, and above all plenty of time, especially when you are making a gold tooth for a celestial mouth: you can't hurry it, you can't do it any old way—it's a delicate task for a gallant man. Flori kept pushing him: Yes, yes, I understand your scruples, you mender of shattered teeth; but please let's get a move on and stop spinning our wheels. While he waited he outdid himself on new publicity.

At each of the four corners of Fausto Cardoso Plaza, where the governmental palace stands, colored billboards announced the imminent appearance of "The Blazing Empress of Samba," or "Miss Samba Herself," or "The Marvel of Brazilian Samba," or, finally, "Brazil's Number One Samba Star." These were clearly exaggerations, though praise which in Flori's opinion paled before the actual physical merits of the star concerned. On the long list of the remarkable samba dancer's ardent admirers the

nightclub owner's name naturally took precedence over
those of an unlicensed lawyer, a dental surgeon, a poet, or
a painter, if for no other reason than because he was paying all the bills and shouldering the losses of Tereza's
aborted, though glorious, debut.

All the men's heads were turned. Flori, grown gray in
his dealings with artists, preached the necessity of daily
afternoon rehearsals while the dental work was in progress
and Tereza's split lip slowly grew together. She must not
risk losing that indispensable sway of the hips, that samba
swing. Ideally, these should have been rehearsals *à deux,*
with no one present but the dancer and her accompanist—
in this case Pachola himself, a man of multiple talents:
piano, violin, mouth organ, blindman's laments. But how
to keep out Tereza's throng of admirers—the dentist, the
poet, the painter, the lawyer—every one of them after her,
interfering with rehearsals and upsetting Flori's sly
schemes?

More than a decade before, Flori had come to Aracaju
as manager of the mortal remains of the Jota Porto & Alma
Castro Variety Show, the company responsible for three
hundred performances of the musical review *Pepper
Where It Burns* in the Recreio Theatre in Rio de Janeiro
but a good deal less fortunate in its long (and let us call it
triumphant) tour of the North. When Flori, who was
young and enthusiastic at the time, joined the company in
São Luís do Maranhão, his vocation as business manager
and impresario was yet to be revealed, for he had had no
experience whatever. Experience he was soon to have,
however; record problems, in record time, throughout the
tour: from São Luís to Belém, Belém to Manaus, and
back again. What first revealed his vocation to him was a
fulminating and fully requited passion for the madcap
Portuguese actress Alma Castro, for whose sake he left his
job in a palm-oil export firm, a job lacking in surprise or
excitement. The diva caught his eye, and when he heard
that the company's pianist had treacherously taken French
leave, he instantly offered his services. No sooner offered
than accepted, and he immediately took over not only the
pianist's job but also that of assistant in all practical matters to the impresario and male lead Jota Porto: arrangements with theatre owners and lessees, transport
companies, hotel proprietors, and other creditors. In each

new town the cast dwindled and the number of acts in the
spicy, sparkling revue grew smaller. By the time the show
reached Aracaju there were so many gaps that it was
barely long enough to fill an intermission at the movie
house. In fact, by that time the tottering roadshow was reduced from the Jota Porto & Alma Castro Variety Show to
Alma Castro's Little Theatrical Company. It was in the
main square of Recife that Jota Porto, his eyes filled with
tears, gathered up the company's last few nickels and took
his leave. Alma Castro he kissed chastely on the forehead,
but Flori he kissed on both cheeks and in a very equivocal
fashion; that matinee idol, who made little girls lose their
sleep, was suspiciously limp in the wrist. Flori found himself stranded in Recife with the scenery, the wardrobe, one
violin, and four actors including Alma Castro; he didn't
have a plugged nickel. Promoted to impresario, the new
general manager swiftly scaled the peaks of his theatrical
career, showing what he could do by getting the group engagements in Maceió, Penedo, and Aracaju. It was in
Aracaju that Flori volunteered to remain as a hostage
while the others sailed for Rio de Janeiro, the understanding being that Alma Castro would send money, as soon as
she reached Rio, to release her new manager and ex-
boyfriend, along with the props, from the durance in which
they were being held by Marosi, the owner of their hotel.
In Rio Alma had innumerable friends to whom she could
turn for bed and board, foremost among them the loyal
Comendador Santos Ferreira, an important and generous
member of the Portuguese community and the fraternity
of "Alma Castro's old friends," all of whom were rich, senile, lavish spenders, eminent, and impotent. Not a dime
did she send Pachola.

After some time had gone by, the good Marosi began to
realize that he was only compounding his losses by detain-
ing his unwilling guest, who occupied a double room and
ate enough for three. So he gave his money up for lost and
put finis to the incident; he even offered to pay Flori's passage in order to get rid of him; but Flori, who had become
fond of the pleasant and hospitable city, chose to stay on.
Sticking to the fringes of the theatre so as to make the most
of his stage sets and his experience, he managed to carve
out a career for himself, successively, as nightclub employee, manager, partner, and owner of several cabarets:

the Eiffel Tower, the Miramar, the Ouro Fino, La
Garçonne, and finally the Gay Paree.

Tereza rehearsed and danced in a costume that had
once been part of the company wardrobe: turban, short
skirt, and lace overblouse. A considerable part of her was
bare, but what of that? Melancholy Flori, seated at his
piano, cursed the never-failing literary, artistic, occasionally juridical, almost always odontological court at Tereza
Batista's feet. However, he was both persistent and clever,
and had long since learned patience; after all, he was
owner of the nightclub and the star's employer; who was
better placed than he?

All the men trailed her, Lulu Santos no less than the
others; he had a reputation as an inveterate womanizer,
crutches and all. All were in love with her, each one farther gone than the next. Saraiva the poet proclaimed his
passion publicly in a copious outpouring of lyric poetry.
Tereza was the inspiration for his best poems, the whole
"Copper Girl" cycle; it was he who coined the epithet,
Tereza, Girl of Copper. The hot Arab blood of Jamil
Najar, the dental surgeon, boiled with a determination to
make Tereza happy, as he held her mouth open and fitted
her gold tooth; and the painter gazed at her out of his
deep-set blue eyes, silently tenacious, silently painting her
likeness on colored paper. Those watercolors done on per-
ishable poster paper were the first portraits of Tereza
which Jenner Augusto painted. He was to paint many
more, mostly from memory, though some years later she
did consent to pose for him in his Rio Vermelho studio for
the prize-winning picture he did of her, standing all copper
and gold, a glorious woman in the full flower of her years
and beauty, and wearing the costume of the old Gay Paree
days: the Bahian turban, gaily colored flounced short skirt,
bare legs, and gleaming thighs.

Tereza laughed gently and politely at all of them, grateful and pleased to be enfolded in loving attention and
madrigals; she had so much yearned for true affection,
been so thirsty for human warmth. And yet she could not
give of herself easily, perhaps because the only jobs she
had had up to then were as domestic help (slave, more accurately) and as prostitute and mistress, jobs in which she
had lain with many men, at first out of fear and then to
earn a living. Later, when she was awakened to physical

desire and gave herself ardently and unstintingly, it was only for love. Liking was never enough. Neither the crafty Flori, nor the gallant dentist, nor the caustic Lulu Santos, nor the silent painter with the piercing eyes, nor the poet—that was a pity!—none of them had the power to touch her heart and light the spark hidden within it.

If Lulu Santos had said to her: I want to sleep with you, my dear friend; I want to so much that if I don't I can't stand it, Tereza would have gone to bed with him as she had so often done before with other men in order to earn her living—distant, indifferent, plying a trade. She was in the lawyer's debt and if he demanded her body in payment, she would not tell him no; it would only be one more tiresome obligation to fulfill. If José Saraiva should come, clearing his throat and then coughing convulsively, with that whistle in his chest, and tell her he couldn't die happy unless he had lain with her first, she would lie with him. She would have gone to bed with the unlicensed lawyer out of gratitude, to pay a debt; or with the poet out of compassion. But to give herself joyfully—that she could neither do nor pretend to do; it was impossible. She had paid a high price in the hard coin of misfortune for being true to her own nature.

Neither the lawyer nor the poet asked for such a favor; they only showed their affection and waited. Both wanted her but neither as charity nor in payment of a debt. As for the others, whether they asked her or not (and Flori often had—begging, groaning, imploring), they got nothing for their pains. Even if she had been offered a shower of money for her nest egg, she was not interested. She still had a little money in her purse and she hoped the public would like her dancing. She wanted to be her own mistress, for a while at least.

When she first came to town and was boarding, on Lulu's recommendation, at old Adriana's house, she had had a proposition made to her by Veneranda, proprietor of the most elegant and expensive "castle" in Aracaju. Looking like a madam from a prosperous southern city with her commanding figure, her luxurious silks, and her high heels, Veneranda did not show the age registered on the birth certificate she kept carefully concealed. When she was still a child, Tereza had heard the Captain refer to the elegant bawd, and Veneranda was then already at the top of her profession in Aracaju. Having heard her old customer Lulu Santos mention Tereza's name, no doubt, or perhaps because she was aware of certain episodes in Tereza's past, Veneranda had come in person to have a talk with her.

Spreading open her fan, Veneranda seated herself and dismissed the curious old Adriana with a cold glance.

"You're even prettier than they told me you were," she began.

Veneranda described her domain: a vast colonial mansion, nestled among trees on an estate surrounded by high walls, its enormous rooms subdivided into cozy modern bedrooms; a waiting room on the ground floor with a phonograph and records, where drinks were served and available girls displayed; on the second floor a large front room where Veneranda received politicians and literary men, factory owners and industrialists; the dining room; the garden. Tereza could live in the house if she liked. This offer of a place in the establishment itself was a mark of high favor shown by Veneranda to only a few chosen women, usually foreigners or southerners who only came north for a season (when the grain was harvested, they went south again); but Tereza deserved to have an exception made in her case. Or, if Tereza preferred, she could go to the "castle" only in the evenings and at night, the busiest times; and she could either serve whoever paid the price charged by the house or entertain a few customers exclusively. In fact, in Tereza's case, the wily Veneranda was prepared to build up a select clientele of men of substantial means, on a more or less regular schedule, a clientele that would be very lucrative and not at all tiring. If Tereza turned out to be as competent as she was pretty, she could earn money very easily; and if she was sensible enough to keep clear of gigolos, she would have built herself a nice little nest egg before long. At the castle she would meet Madame Gertrude, for instance, a Frenchwoman who had bought herself a house and land in Alsace with the money she had earned there, and who proposed to go back to her own country the next year, to marry and have children—God willing, and with His help.

As Veneranda fanned herself, a strong, musky perfume hung in the hot air of the summer afternoon. Tereza listened to the whole proposition in silence and showed a courteous interest in its various enticing options. When

Veneranda had finished, and her lips curved in an en-
couraging smile, Tereza said:

"Yes, I made my living that way once, I won't try to hide
it. And I may have to go back to it someday. I don't have
to just now, but thank you anyway. Maybe someday . . ."
She had learned manners from Dr. Guedes, and when she
was taught a thing she didn't forget it: her teacher in elementary school, Miss Mercedes, had often praised her
quick intelligence and love of learning.

"Not even once in a while, with good pay and no daily
chores, just as a special favor for someone high up? You
know, don't you, that the best people in Aracaju come to
my house?"

"Yes, I've heard about it, but just now I'm not interested. Thank you just the same."

Veneranda bit the tip of her fan in annoyance. A novelty like this, with a gypsy air to her singular beauty and
heralded by a piquant history—oh, she would be a morsel
of angel-food cake for what teeth certain carefully chosen
customers had left, or for their dentures. And she'd be
money in the cashbox; money galore.

"Well, if you change your mind, just come and speak to
me. Anyone can tell you where it is."

"Thank you very much; I'm really sorry."

At the door Veneranda turned:

"Did I tell you I knew the Captain very well? He was
one of my best customers."

Tereza's face darkened, as dusk fell like thunder over
the town.

"I never knew any captain."

"Oh? Didn't you?" And Veneranda laughed and went
out.

5

Alas! No man can touch her heart, none can awaken the
dormant desire nor kindle the hidden spark! As friends she
gladly accepts all of them—lawyer, poet, painter, dentist,
nightclub owner—but as a lover, none. But what man can
be satisfied with a beautiful woman's friendship? Who is

there who understands the ways of the heart? Who can explain them?

In all the immensity of Aracaju, where does the giant walk? The dark *caboclo* who rose from the waters, burned by the sun, burned by the wind, oh where is he? He had been scarcely perceived, barely glimpsed, in the uproar of the fight and then over a celebratory drink in a bar at the end of the street, just as night ended. He vanished at dawn, in the first intimations of light just before daybreak; the dawn and the man were the same color, made of the very same stuff, and the giant dissolved with the coming of day. Through the window of the taxi, Tereza saw him, enveloped in the dim glimmer which is night's end and day's edge intermingled. His toes touched the ground, his arms touched the sea, his hair was a cloud, curly with rain in the indigo sky. He had promised to come back.

Like the expert *capoeira* wrestler that he was, he had put an end to the fight single-handed, laughing and shouting, addressing the bystanders and his friends, those present and those absent, real people and spirits alike. When the policeman had pulled out his gun and threatened to shoot, Flori had pulled the fuse, and responsibility became collective and therefore nonexistent. Who can be a witness to what happens in the dark? As the lights went out the *caboclo* spirited away the gun as if by magic, and if the policeman's ugly snout hadn't made such a thud as it hit the ground, you could have sworn he did it without using his hands or his legs, deftly, delicately, by pure sleight of hand. He seemed to hang suspended in the air, a giant, muscular bird, Januário Gereba—doesn't the name Gereba come from Yereba, the giant? Isn't Gereba the condor, the grandest high-flyer of them all? That was how Tereza knew him, and that was all she had to know.

With the lights out, the confusion grew and spread—more than one customer who had nothing to do with the fight took a sporting dive into it, just for the fun of the thing. But it didn't last long; the water never really came to a boil. At a warning cry of "Here come the cops!" from the street below, the contenders scattered just as the police reinforcements, called in by one of the civil guards, arrived on the scene. Tereza felt herself lifted off the ground by two powerful arms and carried downstairs and out into the street; they doubled around corners and darted into alleys and out again at a silent run. The giant's chest smelled of salt. . . . She was finally set on her feet many blocks away on a quiet street corner. Before her stood the smiling *caboclo:*

"Januário Gereba, at your service. Captain Gereba's my name in Bahia, but my friends call me Janu."

The world was filled with peace as he smiled.

"The reason I hustled you off so fast was to get out of sight of the cops. I don't go for cops, here or anywhere else."

"Thank you, Janu." Liking isn't bought, isn't sold, it can't be forced on you by a knife at your heart, and it can't be dodged either: liking just happens.

He reminded her of someone she knew, but she couldn't think who. A sailor by profession, captain of a fishing boat; his port was Bahia, washed by the Bay of All Saints and the River Paraguaçu; and he had left his boat, the *Waterflower,* at anchor by the Market Ramp.

He wasn't really a giant, as he had seemed to be during the fight; but a few more inches and he would have been. His keel-like chest, his laughing eyes, his great callused hands, everything about him breathed tranquillity as he stood firmly on his feet but let the breeze sway his body slightly. Or not tranquillity exactly, Tereza corrected herself: he was certainly capable of unexpected reactions, of explosions; no, it was a sense of security, of definite certitudes. Who *was* it he reminded her of, this man risen out of the sea?

The resemblance was not a facial, a physical one, but he somehow reminded Tereza of someone she had known very well. Standing next to him in the street, Tereza no longer looked anything like the indignant girl who had started the fight. She listened quietly as he explained how he had come into the Gay Paree just in time to see her spit in the impudent cuss's face and stand up to him, the sort of brave little gal a man takes off his hat to.

"Brave, nothing—I was scared. It's just that I can't stand to see a man hit a woman."

"Any man who hits a woman or goes after a child isn't a man at all," the giant agreed. "But I didn't see how the tail-pulling started. So that's how it was."

It was mostly chance that had put him in Aracaju—doing a favor for a friend, the owner of the barque

Ventania, whose mate had taken sick and let him down on the very day he had to sail no matter what. The owner of the cargo was in a terrible hurry and wouldn't hear of waiting any longer. Caetano Gunzá, barque owner, was Januário's compadre and of course turned to him in his difficulty. That's what friends are for, isn't it, or else what's the use? He had left his fishing boat at anchor, and they had had a good crossing with a fair wind and a jolly sea. They had docked the afternoon before and would stay in port just long enough to unload the rolls of tobacco from Cruz das Almas and to pick up some cargo so as to make a little profit on the voyage. They would only be in Aracaju a few days; a vacation, you might say. His friend had stayed on board, but Januário was tired of working and had come ashore to look for a place to dance, something he loved to do. Instead of a dance, though, he had found himself a fight, and a good one.

They walked in a desultory way, in no particular direction and in no particular hurry; there must be some little place still open in this town where we can have a drink to celebrate winning and getting acquainted, Januário said. And so they strolled along, he doing the talking and she listening, listening to the waves and the wind in the billowing sails, and the sea calling in the conch shells. Tereza knew nothing about the sea. It was the first time she had found herself so close to salt water. The ocean was right out there beyond the bar, just outside Aracaju; and she felt the sailor's swinging gait at her side, the sailor whose chest was bronzed from the sun and the gentle sea breeze, and buffeted by the storms. Januário lit a clay pipe. There were all sorts of things in the sea: fishes and castaways, black octopuses and silver rays, ships from the other side of the world, and sargasso plantations.

"Plantations? Out in the ocean? How can that be?"

Before he had a chance to explain, they came out again into the area around the Rua da Frente, close to the black bulk of the Vatican, where the multicolored lights of the Gay Paree's marquee served as a landmark for couples looking for a bed for the night or for a half-hour. Every so often, now here, now there, a dim light would flicker weakly in one of the countless cubicles of the ancient house; in a half-hidden doorway lurked the ageless

pimp, Alfred the Rat, collecting payment in advance for
Seu Andrade, the landlord. They heard the lawyer's
voice and the sound of his crutches nearby:

"Hey, you two! Wait for me!"

Lulu Santos had been looking for Tereza, afraid she
might have fallen victim to some trap set by Libório or
his friends. Santos knew every bar in Aracaju and took
them to one not far away for a celebratory glass of *cachaça*. Tereza barely touched the glass to her lips—she
had never learned to like the white firewater, even when
it was of superior quality like this *cachaça* with its woody
bouquet. The lawyer drank his in dainty sips, savoring it
as though he were tasting a fine liqueur, old port, sherry,
or French cognac. Captain Gereba downed his in one
gulp.

"That's a wicked drink. Yep, *cachaça,* the worst drink
I know. People who drink *cachaça* are no good." He
laughed and ordered another.

Lulu brought fresh news from the battlefield. When the
police finally got there, they found no one in the dancehall except Lulu, Flori, and Saraiva the poet, sitting and
drinking a beer, as peacefully as you please. Libório, king
of the bad guys—what a rotten stinking piece of garbage!—had made his getaway. And guess in whose company? Why that silly little girl's, of course, the bone of
contention, the one he had slapped. Since the traveling
salesman was nowhere to be found (by that time all the
customers were halfway home), when the girl saw the
cuckold bellowing that he was crippled for life, with both
hands on his balls and bawling for a doctor, she forgot
all about being slapped and hauled the guy off down the
stairs. They were two of a kind all right: she was used to
playing tricks and getting knocked around for it, and he
was used to catching her at it and giving her what for.
Lulu Santos summed it up: a couple of pissing assholes.

Saraiva had urged him to go along to Tidinha's place,
the best address in Aracaju for topping off an evening;
but the lawyer was too worried about Tereza to go. The
poet went off by himself, with his hoarse cough and his
whistling chest.

After the drinks, the three said good night. The lawyer
took Tereza home in a taxi, since Libório, that piece of
crap, ate and slept with the police and you couldn't be

too careful. She looked out of the car window and saw Captain Januário Gereba walking toward the pier where the barque was anchored. He was dawn-colored and he soon melted into the dawn.

Her heart throbbed wildly. The meeting had left her timid, helpless and unresisting, feeling as she had so many years ago in the warehouse when she saw Daniel, the painted Angel of the Annunciation, come to life. Dan with his imploring eyes. Who did the *caboclo* sailor look like? No, it wasn't anyone he looked like, but someone to whom she had been very close that he reminded her of. It was just as well that he didn't remind her of an angel in a painting, come down from heaven. Ever since that long-ago day, Tereza had been suspicious of men with angel's faces and sorrowful voices and supplicating mouths and equivocal beauty: they might be good in bed but were sure to be weak and false.

Home and alone at last? She took leave of Lulu Santos with a good-night and a thanks-so-much, you're-a-friend! all without letting him get out of the car; if he did he might want to stay. . . . In her bare, undecorated room, with its narrow iron bed, as she closed her eyes and tried to go to sleep, she finally realized who the fishing-boat captain reminded her of: it was Emiliano Guedes. Though unlike in every way, one white, aristocratic, rich, and learned, and the other a dark mulatto toughened by the sea wind, poor, and almost illiterate, the two were in some sense kin. They had a family resemblance. Maybe it lay in their self-assurance, their vitality, their goodness. Both were real men—that was it.

Captain Januário Gereba had promised to come and show her the port, the barque *Ventania,* and the place where the ocean began, out beyond the harbor. But he hadn't kept his promise. Where could he be?

6

Lulu Santos dropped in to invite her to the movies; he was crazy about cowboy films. He lingered to talk on the open veranda with its breeze from the river, and old Adriana offered him a choice of mangoes or sweetened cornmeal gruel or both. First he would have the mangoes, his favorite fruit; the donkey-tea could wait until they got back from the movies. Radiant with pride in her back-yard, a veritable little orchard, Adriana displayed her finest, most fragrant mangoes: swords, pinkies, charlottes, oxhearts, and bleeding hearts.

"Shall I slice them for you?"

"Thanks, Adriana, I'll slice them myself."

While he smacked his lips over the fruit, Lulu re-galed them with his version of current events:

"Tereza, you are simply incredible. You no sooner get to Aracaju than some people are swooning over you and others are up in arms."

Old Adriana loved a bit of gossip:

"I know at least one of the swooners"—she cast a side-long glance at the lawyer—"but how could anyone not like such a good girl?"

"This afternoon I was talking to someone who said: That Tereza acts awfully high-and-mighty, but she's one foolish girl all the same."

"Who was it?" Tereza demanded.

"Veneranda, our illustrious Veneranda, who runs the most famous meat market in town. She swears every bit of merchandise is filet mignon, but today she tried to fob me off with a French tidbit that had already begun to stink."

Before opening her little grocery store—fruit, vegeta-bles, charcoal—old Adriana had been in the same line of business as Veneranda. Right there in the house she in-herited, she gave hospitality to furtive couples in search of a temporary roof; occasionally she still granted such a favor to a friend, although these days she preferred to rent her rooms by the month to some girl who worked in an office or to a discreet free-lance hooker, someone's mistress, if possible. That way at least she had company. She still harbored a certain resentment against Vene-randa, who even in the early days had been aloof, su-perior, self-important, always putting on airs and looking down her nose at her more modest colleagues.

"That what-shall-I-call-her was here, all right, trying to hook Tereza with her greasy bait. I said to Tereza: Now honey, you be careful; that woman's up to no good."

"But what did I do?" Tereza wondered. "All that happened was that she wanted me to go work for her and I said no."

Old Adriana was bursting with curiosity and full of questions:

"Who else doesn't like Tereza? Tell us what you know."

"Libório das Neves, for one. He's mad as all get-out. If it were up to him, Tereza would be rotting in jail this minute. Lucky for her he was scared to blab. He lives such a filthy life, he won't dare fool around with any friends of mine, even if he does have police protection. And especially not now, when he knows I'm bringing suit against him."

"Seu Libório—" Old Adriana pronounced the name with a certain awed respect. "He bosses plenty of people around."

"He's a piece of shit," said the lawyer; Libório obviously stuck in his craw. "There's nobody around here, but nobody, who's worse than that louse, that shit-head, that son-of-a-bitch. The thing that's driving me up the wall is that I've argued two cases against him and lost both times. Now I'm working on case number three and I'm about to lose again."

"You, Lulu? You lose a case with a jury?" exclaimed the old woman. "Everybody says you can't lose."

"It's not before a jury; it's a civil case. The rat's had plenty of practice rigging things to suit him. But I'll catch that hyena by the toe one of these days; see if I don't."

"What does he do?" Tereza wanted to know.

"What doesn't he do? I'll tell you all about him some time. It's a long story and we'll have to hurry if we want to catch the movie. Tomorrow or the day after, I'll tell you all about Libório das Neves, the number one hood of Aracaju, the man who steals from the poor." He reached for his crutches and stood up. "Adriana, my beauty, thanks for the mangoes. Yours are the best in Sergipe."

The breeze stirred from the harbor, from the Isle of Palms, softening the heat and dampness of the sweltering night. So quiet, so peaceful, and that starry sky, just right for story-telling. Why shut themselves up in that oven of a movie? Besides, what if Januário should come?

"No, Lulu, let's save the movie for another time. I'd rather stay here where it's nice and cool, and listen to you talk, than suffocate at the movies."

"Anything you say, princess. All right, we'll see the movie tomorrow instead, and I'll tell you who Libório is. But you'd better hold your nose; he stinks."

Lulu Santos set down his crutches and lit a cigar. He never had to buy anything; his friend Raimundo Souza sent the cigars to him free from the Walkyria factory in Estância. In fact, Lulu was always being given presents: things to eat or drink, all kinds of gifts. Other things he bought on credit and forgot to pay for; how could a poor man's lawyer like him keep body and soul together otherwise? More than once he had paid court costs with his own money instead of asking a fee. As he puffed on his cigar, he began to describe Libório das Neves's life and times.

"We're stirring up the crap, honey; I warned you." He began to pull out all the stops, as if he were accusing a criminal or pleading before a jury, growing inflamed with excitement, raising his voice, clenching his fists, seized by turns with indignation and pity, and larding his speech with four-letter words and popular sayings.

To summarize, the lawyer explained that Libório had gotten his start as a banker for the animal game; but an animal-game banker, as everyone knows, has to be absolutely honest or he doesn't last long as a banker. Since Libório was constitutionally incapable of honesty, he failed the very first test, ratted out, and refused to pay off. There was hell to pay. A few of his indignant customers got together under the leadership of a soccer player named Mulefoot, who was famous for his powerful kick, and they went after the crooked banker. It is worth pointing out that Mulefoot had no personal interest in the affair, since he had never played the numbers. He took up the cudgels in defense of his neighbor Auntie Milu, who was almost a hundred years old and who spent the livelong day plotting her bets in groups, ten and a hundred and a thousand; modest bets, but tricky. The old lady would follow one animal for months at a time, betting a ten, a hundred, a thousand. Once in a while she won a little bit, and she'd never had the slightest trouble getting her money. Then she had changed bankers for some reason; the then-youthful, smooth-talking Libório had induced her to give him a try. She picked the dog and stuck to it through the 10, the 910, the 7910. And she wasn't the only one; a lot of people bet on the dog that day because the day before a little boy had been rescued from drowning by a mongrel dog off the coast by the lighthouse, and the story had been given a big play on radio and in the press. The dog it was, and Auntie Milu won her hundred and her thousand. As for Libório, he vanished in a puff of smoke. As the biggest winner, the old lady took his absconding as a personal insult. Bent double and leaning on her cane, she called on God and man to help her lay hands on the prize money that was due her. Mulefoot, with his fierce kick and his tender heart, made his neighbor's cause his own and led a group of other victims in search of the banker until they tracked him down.

They tried to collect the money by using arguments and threats. At first Libório tried to weasel out of it by putting the blame on somebody else and inventing a partner who had disappeared with the winnings; but after Mulefoot had pushed him around a little, he promised to pay up in forty-eight hours. Human credulity is great; even a popular soccer player's credulity is great—even when he has a cannon in each foot, as the sports-writers claimed Mulefoot did. Mulefoot had no other talents to speak of, however, and even his soccer-playing left much to be desired; it was only his powerful kick that kept him on the team, for there wasn't a goalie alive who could block a football he had aimed. When he wasn't in training, he spent his time ambling along the street, stopping in every bar along the way and kibitzing in the pool halls. In other words, he was a bum.

Forty-eight hours passed without a sign from Libório. Mulefoot went into action: he knew his hometown and its suburbs by heart. He ran the thief to earth in a side street out near the salt-pens. Libório was quarreling over a game of backgammon with the owner of the house, a Syrian moneylender, when Mulefoot, without stopping to clap his hands or for a by-your-leave, made his way into the house with four of the creditors. The Syrian, making a play as a he-man, showed a knife; the attackers took it away from him and distributed some punches between the two, the larger share—as was only fair—going to Libório.

Having no more time to spare, Mulefoot's four companions contented themselves with that; having taught the thief a lesson, they went away satisfied. Libório, too, considered the chapter closed and congratulated himself on having come out ahead; he had exchanged his debt for a few punches, he thought. But unlike the others, Mulefoot had all the time in the world, and since he was representing Auntie Milu, he could hardly let the false banker off. It was fine for Libório to get knocked around a little, but he ought to be knocked around and pay up besides. When pressed a little further, Libório paid some of his debt, a little over half, on the spot, promising to pay the rest the next day. But the little old lady insisted on full payment that very day. Highly indignant—who ever heard of an animal-game banker refusing to pay?—she called for her money and didn't propose to wait.

Libório went into hiding a second time, but the good Mulefoot kept looking for him and found him again a week later right in the middle of town, on the Rua do Méio. He was walking down the street, bold as brass, as if he owed no man a penny, and talking fast into the ear of a hayseed about some dubious business having to do with false jewelry. Then he bumped into Mulefoot. He lost his animation, acknowledged defeat, and handed over the rest of Auntie Milu's money. The old lady finally got every last cent that was due her, and Mulefoot must have earned admittance to the Kingdom of Heaven, for only a few days later he was killed in an accident. The regular soccer team and a few substitutes were on their way to Penedo by bus for a friendly match. The bus turned over, and three people died; Mulefoot was one of them. Never again did such a powerful kicker play soccer for Sergipe, and never again did such a softhearted bum walk the streets of Aracaju.

The day the bank broke in the animal game marked Libório's debut in the business world. From then on he was mixed up in every shady deal of the next twenty years. Twice before civil judges, Lulu Santos represented clients whom Libório had robbed. One case had to do with false gems. For some time Libório had traded in diamonds, rubies, and emeralds, one real stone for each fifty imitations. Lulu lost his case for lack of proof. Libório grew rich and important in the underworld and the red-light district, and made friends among the police by bribing detectives and cops. The poor were his favorite

prey and usury his main source of income. He lent at exorbitant rates of interest and took all his victims possessed for unredeemed debts. He was said to work with
Seu Andrade, owner of the Vatican, in exploiting the
prostitutes who rented rooms for a night or an hour; and
on the last few days of the month he bought up, heavily
discounted, the future salaries of municipal employees
who were desperate for cash. It was when defending one
of these poor devils that Lulu Santos was outsmarted by
Libório for the second time.

Libório—who was a backer, naturally, of gambling
dens full of loaded dice, marked cards, and crooked roulette wheels—had discounted three months' advance
wages for a municipal employee who was an inveterate
gambler, though an honest man, and who had given him
a notarized IOU for the amount. The careless borrower
was so anxious to lay his hands on some cash, that instead
of writing out the IOU he signed a blank sheet of paper
on which Libório typed in the terms to suit himself: he
put in six months' wages instead of three. There was no
way on earth to prove it was a fraud: the poor man's signature, duly notarized, was on the document. It was no
use for the amateur lawyer to swear that Libório had
bought only three months, and not six, of the man's meager wages, in exchange for a few roulette chips. It made
no difference that the victim was an exemplary employee,
an honest man, a good husband, the fond father of five
children—a pity he was also addicted to gambling—or
that Libório was a known swindler who was continually
called before the bar of justice but never convicted.

Lulu Santos was carried away by his own narrative as
he recalled how that so-and-so Libório had pretended to
be ever so humble and persecuted. Oh, how he had longed
to forget the respect due the judge and the court and
throw his crutches in the rascal's face! Tereza couldn't
imagine how it had done his heart good to see her spit in
that cuckold son-of-a-bitch's face. Yes, cuckold, cuckold,
a hundred times over; he was used to those public scenes,
used to hitting women to show what a brave man he was.
He only hit women; he wasn't man enough to face one
of the many, many guys who had put horns on him. He
would get even with them behind their backs if he could,
of course, using his fearsome reputation and his friends

among the police—and now the spitting image of an all-round, complete, honest-to-God son-of-a-bitch . . . had been spat upon!

The case Lulu was working on now and which was on next week's docket was even worse than the last. It was already a lost cause, and that was too bad! At the very thought of it, Lulu was beside himself with rage. His eyes flashed.

"I'll tell you about it so you can see just how far the son-of-a-bitch will go." He pronounced each syllable distinctly. Lulu called everybody an SOB, most often affectionately; but Libório was a Son-Of-A-Bitch, with all four syllables enunciated loud and clear.

In a truck garden and orchard full of mango, cashew, jackfruit, and hogplum, sweetsop, cherimoya, sugar apple, and biriba trees, lived and labored the widow of a Portugese, an elderly black woman named Joana França, or Joana das Folhas. Senhor Manuel França, the Portuguese, an old acquaintance of Lulu's, was the first to plant lettuce, big tomatoes, kale, cabbage, and other southern vegetables in Aracaju, along with the bitter *jilós*, gherkins, pumpkins, and sweet potatoes that already grew in the fertile soil of his little farm. Soon he had steady customers for his small-scale but prosperous business. At sunup he was already digging in his fields, the black Joana beside him; lovers at first, they were married by judge and priest when their only son grew up and Seu Manuel's heart began to give out on him. But the son didn't wait for his father's death; he stole his savings and ran away from home. His defection was a mortal blow to the honest Portuguese. From him Joana inherited the farm and some money which his friend Antônio Minhoto owed her husband; and never was an inheritance more deserved. Joana was as strong as she was black, a good, honest woman who worked like a dog and worried about her son. She hired a man to help her work the farm, and to deliver the lettuce, tomatoes, and kale to her customers.

"Don't tell the rest until I get back," begged Adriana as he paused for breath. "I'm just going to get the *mungunzá;* I'll only be a minute."

"Lord!" burst out Tereza. "What a no-good hound that Libório is."

"Wait till you hear the rest and you won't think I'm good for much either."

The night breeze swept in from the harbor. Lulu Santos talked about Manuel França the Portuguese, his wife Joana das Folhas, and their wandering son; and all the time Tereza was thinking of Januário Gereba and wondering where he could be. He had promised to come and take her to see the barque; they were going to walk on the bar where the sand dunes lie and the real ocean begins. Confound him, why didn't he come?

The *mungunzá* was served in bowls with a spoon—a tempting mixture of cornmeal and coconut, cinnamon and clove. Momentarily the lawyer even forgot the brilliant theatre of his accusation of Libório das Neves. Ah, if only he could take his case before a jury!

"Adriana, this *mungunzá* is heavenly, there's no other word for it. If only it were a jury case . . ."

—Gentlemen of the jury, approximately six months ago, the widow you see before you (who is not only a widow but orphaned as well, for she has a son who ran away to the South and never returned) received from this son, first a letter, then a telegram. Her husband, she knew, was at peace in an upper circle of Paradise, this consoling and definite news having come to her through Dr. Miguelinho, a spirit from the beyond, who manifested himself to the Peace and Harmony Spiritualistic Circle where he has effected several miraculous cures. In that quarter, she knew she had nothing to fear. If only the same could be said of her son! He lost his head in Rio, managed to get himself into debt, and the letter said he would soon be in jail if he didn't pay back several thousand cruzeiros in a matter of days. He appealed to his mother in the cruelest possible way: if she did not send him the money he said he would do away with himself, he would shoot himself in the heart. That was sheer conscienceless blackmail, of course; he had no intention of doing anything of the kind. But the poor, long-suffering, illiterate mother of this one beloved child nearly went out of her mind with worry. Where on earth could she put her hands on the eight thousand cruzeiros the boy said he had to have? The neighbor who had read her the letter and telegram as a favor had heard of Libório and got hold of his address. And in this way the widow fell into the clutches of a scoundrel who lent her the eight thousand cruzeiros on her promise to pay fifteen thousand in six months. Take note of the unheard-of, astronomical interest, gentlemen of the jury! Libório wrote up the agreement himself: if Joana could not pay in full on the date fixed, she was to forfeit the little farm which was made security for the debt—a farm worth at least one hundred thousand cruzeiros, gentlemen of the jury!

Since the widow could not read or write, nor even sign her own name, one of Libório's lackeys, Joel Reis, signed for her as proxy. Two more of the racketeer's jackals signed as witnesses. When she incurred the debt, Joana was perfectly easy in her mind: her compadre Antônio Minhoto, an upright man whose word was his bond, owed her ten thousand cruzeiros which were to be paid in four months, and she could easily save the remaining five thousand cruzeiros in the six months allowed her by the agreement. She had kept all her husband's customers.

And almost everything happened as she had anticipated: her compadre paid her what he owed, and when he had said he would; her savings came to more than five thousand cruzeiros; and she went to Libório to liquidate her debt. And then—what do you suppose he said to her? Can you possibly guess, honorable gentlemen of the jury?

"Why, what *did* he say?"

"That she owed him not eight thousand cruzeiros but eighty thousand."

"What?"

"When Libório wrote out the document he had been careful to write the amount of the debt in numbers only, without spelling it out as well. And as soon as Joana left, the wretch added a zero to the number. With the same pen, the same ink, and at almost the same moment. And this poor abused woman? Where, I ask you, is she to get eighty thousand cruzeiros? Where, gentlemen of the jury? Libório has petitioned the court to put her farm up to be sold at auction, with the undoubted intention of picking it up himself for a song.

"Just consider! What is to become of this woman, who has toiled all her life on that little farm? Now, overnight,

she is to be driven off her own property and reduced to
begging for her bread. Do you fully understand what that
means? Naturally, I'll beat my breast, I'll shout, I'll
clamor that justice be done; but what will all that ac-
compish? If her case were being tried before a jury of
her peers, that might be another story. But this case goes
up before a civil judge. I have nothing against this particular judge. He knows all about Libório; he knows quite
well that the document has been altered and he would
rule in Joana's favor and slap Libório with a countersuit
for tampering with a document with intent to defraud, if
only he could. But how can he, I ask you? How can he,
when the paper is right there before him, complete with
witnesses' signatures and nobody to prove that the zero
was added?"

He stopped to take breath. The indignation burning in
his face made it almost handsome.

"It's common knowledge that this is another of Libório's dirty tricks. And there is not one solitary thing
we can do about it. He'll swallow up Manuel França's
truck farm, and Joana will have to live on charity. I just
hope her miserable bastard of a son does put a bullet
through his chest. It's exactly what he deserves."

Silence fell like a stone. For a few moments no one
spoke. Tereza was looking off into the distance, but now
she was not thinking of Captain Januário Gereba, known
to his friends as Janu, nor was she thinking of the sea
breaking on the sand. She was thinking only of black
Joana das Folhas, Mrs. Joana França, bent over the
soil first at her Portuguese husband's side and then all
alone, planting, harvesting, living by the labor of her
hands, with her son off having a high old time in Rio, demanding money, and threatening to kill himself. If they
took her farm away from her—? If Libório won the
suit—? What would happen to Joana das Folhas then?
How would she earn her own bread, much less save anything for her no-good son to waste on himself?

Old Adriana picked up the plates and went out to the
kitchen.

"Lulu, tell me one thing. . . ." Tereza brought her
thoughts back from far away.

"What?"

"Would that paper still be legal if Dona Joana could read and write her name?"

"What do you mean, *if* she could read and write her name? She can't, and that's all there is to it. She never went to school, and her parents were illiterate too."

"But if she could? Would that document still be legal?"

"No, of course not. If she could sign her name, then the document with its proxy would have had to be forged. Unfortunately, though, that's not the case."

"Are you sure? Don't you think it might have been forged? What makes you so sure? Where would Dona Joana have to go to prove that she can sign her name? Before the judge?"

"What are you talking about? What's all this about proving she can sign her name?" Then suddenly he saw what she meant and broke off. "A forged document? Sign her name? Am I hearing what I think I hear?"

"If Dona Joana could read and sign her name, she could go to the judge and say: 'That paper's no good. I can sign my own name. I mean, you're the one who would say it, aren't you? All she'd have to do would be to sign?"

"And who the devil is going to teach Joana das Folhas to sign her name in a little over a week? It would have to be someone we could trust absolutely."

"That person is sitting right here, at your service— When is the hearing, exactly?"

Lulu Santos began to laugh like a madman, and old Adriana came running in alarm.

"What's gotten into you, Lulu?"

Finally the lawyer recovered enough to say:

"I can't wait to see that Libório's face when it dawns on him that he has been had. Tereza, Doctor Tereza, I dub you lawyer *honaris causa, summa cum laude!* I'm going home now to mull over the whole business for a while, but I think you've hit the nail on the head. Lovely Adriana, who serves up a *mungunzá* fit for the angels, I'll see you tomorrow. Set a thief to catch a thief, as the saying goes. . . . All I ask is one good look at that shit-pot's face when he catches on—It'll be the happiest moment of my life!"

Tereza stayed out on the porch. She had forgotten Lulu Santos, Joana das Folhas, and Libório das Neves—all of them. Where *could* he be, confound him? He had promised to come, with his claypipe and his windburned skin and his chest like a keel and his hands that lifted her into the air. Why didn't he come?

7

Lonely, mortified, hurt in her pride, Tereza combed the sleeping city and the deserted port for Januário Gereba. Maybe he was away or sick and hadn't been able to come. But he could have let her know; he could have sent someone with a message. He had promised to come that evening so that they could have a supper of fish stew on the barque, the way they made it in Bahia—when it comes to palm-oil cooking, I'm your man!—and then they'd take a look at the real ocean, with real waves breaking outside the bar. The real ocean and not that tame bay. Oh, the Cotinguiba was a nice river, he didn't deny that, the way it hugged the Ilha dos Coqueiros in its ample waters, gentle on the bank where the town was, and with a good anchoring place for big sailboats and little cargo ships. But the ocean, now—you'll see, you just can't compare them, they aren't the same thing. Oh, the sea is a road that never ends, it's too strong ever to be tamed; it can brew terrible storms or be as gentle as a lover, when it turns itself into foam on the sand. . . . Why didn't he come? He had no right to treat her like some common, ordinary woman; she hadn't asked him to come.

For the past several days, even when he was busiest unloading the barque and scraping it clean for the next cargo—sacks of sugar—Cap'n Januário had managed to find time to visit Tereza and to sit with her on the Emperor's Bridge. He told her tales of fishing boats and crossings full of adventure; of storms and ship-wrecks and interesting things that happened on the docks; and of voodoo ceremonies, with fishing boat captains and *capoeira* wrestlers and spirit guides and the spirits themselves, the *orixás*. And he told her about all the holidays; in Bahia there seemed to be a holiday for every day in the year. There was Good Jesus of the Navigators on January first, celebrated on the ocean near Boa Viagem, with the fishing boats escorting the gondola carrying the

image on its way out and back, and after that the samba,
hot and heavy, day and night. There was Our Lord of
Bonfim from Sunday to Sunday of the second week in
January, with its solemn washing of the church on Thursday. The mules, horses, and donkeys laden with flowers
and the Bahianas carrying pails and earthenware jugs of
water balanced on their hips, waters of Our Father Oxalá
cleansing the church of Our Lord of Bonfim, one a black
African, the other a white saint from Europe—two different saints rolled into one to make one real Bahian
saint. The Ribeira festival came right afterward, like a
foretaste of carnival; and Yemanjá's Day in Rio Vermelho, on February second. The presents for the Mother
of Waters—Yemanjá, Janaína—would keep piling up
in big straw baskets (combs, perfume, perfumed soap,
trinkets, rings and necklaces, a profusion of flowers, and
letters pleading for calm seas, good fishing, health, happiness—and always, love), from very early in the morning until the hour of the evening tide; then the fishing
boats would put out to sea in Janaína's procession, Cap'n
Flaviano in the lead carrying the biggest present of all,
the fishermen's gift. And the Queen waited down in the
depths of the sea, dressed in transparent blue shells and
with her scepter in her hand: *odóia, Yemanjá, odóia!*

He told her all about Bahia too: how it was born in the
sea and climbed up onto the mountain on steep little
streets. And about the Market, and Agua dos Meninos, and
the Ramp and the wharves; and the *capoeira* schools,
where he had fun on Sundays wrestling with Mestre
Traira and Cat and Arnol; and the sacred voodoo ground
of Bogun, where he had been raised up and confirmed as
an *ogan,* a spirit medium for Yansã and just by the way,
it was Janu's considered opinion that Tereza must be a
daughter of Yansã; they had the same courage, the same
fearless temperament. Yansã was a woman, but she was
the bravest spirit of them all, just the same; she fought in
battle beside her husband Xangô, and wasn't afraid even
of the spirits of the dead, the *eguns.* It was Yansã, in fact,
who welcomed and saluted them with her war cry:
Eparrei!

Just last night on the Emperor's Bridge he had touched
her lips with his fingers to make sure the brass knuckles
hadn't left a scar. The gold tooth wasn't in yet, but that

was all. Januário had stopped with that light touch of the fingers, which had been enough to open her completely. Instead of going on to make certain of the healing by a deeper examination of them with kisses, he had taken his hand away—as if the contact with Tereza's moist mouth had burned him. He had brought her a magazine from Rio with colored pictures of Bahia. There was a two-page spread showing the Ramp leading to the Market and the *Waterflower* anchored right there in front, just back from a crossing with its sky-blue sail unfurled. And standing at the tiller, in patched trousers and with his chest bare, was the captain of the fishing boat, Januário Gereba, Janu to Tereza. That's what my friends call me, Janu.

Tereza walked down the Rua da Frente, hoping to see the giant loom up with his sailor's rolling walk and the coal of a clay pipe lighting his way. She could see the shadow of the barque, the *Ventania*, tied to the worm-eaten wooden pier not far from the Vatican; its lights were out and nothing stirred on board. If anyone was there he was certainly asleep, and Tereza hadn't the courage to go any nearer. Where was Cap'n Gereba? Where had the giant of the sea lain his head? Where had the condor, the mighty flying bird, flown?

On the second floor of the Vatican, the strings of colored lights—red, green, yellow, purple, blue—enticed strangers and the gilded youth of Aracaju into the Gay Paree dancehall. Why, Januário might be cavorting on that dance floor this minute with a pretty girl in his arms, some cheap little piece from the port. Dancing was his weakness; he had been looking for a place to dance the night he went up the steps to the cabaret just in time for the free-for-all. Oh, I just wish I could walk through that door and up those steps, thought Tereza, and burst into the room like Libório das Neves; stalk straight over to the dance floor, plant myself in front of him with my hands on my hips as he was squeezing his loving partner, and say: So—this is the way you call for me tonight like you said you would!

Flori had forbidden her to come to the cabaret at night; he wanted to keep Tereza's fighting image intact for her debut. Everyone had seen her and talked about her; but if she began to go out at night, and to dance and chatter with this customer and that, the club's habitués would for-

get how she had risen up in fury to spit in Libório's face
and defy the world. No, sir; they shouldn't see her again
until the big night when the Queen of the Samba appeared
in her short skirt, chemise, and turban. Besides, there was
her swollen lip and missing tooth. Speaking of teeth, Flori
wondered suspiciously when Dr. Jamil Najar intended to
put the finishing touches to his masterpiece. No dental
and prosthetic surgeon had ever before taken so long
to put in one gold tooth. Calixto Grosso, a swaggering,
handsome hunk of man, a mulatto who was the long-
shoremen's leader in Aracaju, had a passion for gold teeth
and counted seven in his mouth all told—four on top and
three below, with one, the prettiest of all, right smack in
the middle on top. And most of them had been put there
by Dr. Najar without any fooling around at all. One time
he had set in three at once, three great big teeth, and it
hadn't taken him half as long as it was taking him to fit
one little old gold tooth in Tereza Batista's mouth.

It was not because she was forbidden, though, that
Tereza didn't go into the Gay Paree; nor even because
she was snaggle-toothed. It was because she had no right,
none in the world, to call the Captain of the fishing boat
to account, whether he was dancing, flirting, spooning,
feeling up, or rolling on the bed with some hot little
piece. She had no claims at all on him yet, not even as a
sweetheart. Nothing but quick glances out of the corner
of his eye—he always looked away when Tereza caught
him eating her up with his eyes. True enough, she called
him Janu, the nickname people who liked him called him
by; and he in turn called her by various Brazilian, Indian, and African terms of endearment: Tetá, angel,
muçurumim, iaô. But that was as far as their intimacy
went. Tereza waited, like a proper woman; it was up to
him to say the first meaningful word, the first word of
love. He seemed happy enough to be with Tereza, all jol-
lity, laughter, and talk; but the affair stayed strictly
within platonic limits. It was as if there were something
checking a warmer tone of voice, a word of love, a tender gesture; something holding back Cap'n Januário
Gereba's plain desire.

And then he hadn't kept his promise after all; he hadn't
come for her; he had kept her waiting since seven o'clock.
Lulu Santos had turned up and invited her to the movies,

and then they had stayed home talking instead; and the lawyer had told her about Libório das Neves and what a sordid, revolting worm he was; and then he'd said good night a little after nine, delighted to think he'd discovered, with Tereza's help, a fine way to get the better of the beast in this miserable business of Dona Joana, and on his own stomping ground, too, the courtroom. Tereza had said good night to Adriana and tried to go to sleep, but she just couldn't. Finally, she covered her head and shoulders with the Doctor's last present to her, a black mantilla embroidered in red roses, and leaving the house, walked toward the port.

But not a trace of Cap'n Gereba, not a sign of giant Janu could she find. All she could do was go back home again and try to forget. Cover the hot coals with ashes, put out the fire before it was too late. Foolish heart! Just when she was at peace with herself at last, calm, untroubled, finally ready to get her life back on the track, her restless heart had gone off on its own. It's so easy to fall in love; it just happens when you least expect it. A look, a word, a gesture, and the flame leaps up, burning out your heart and lips from inside. And it's so very hard to forget, longing goes on devouring you as long as you live. Love is no pimple you can squeeze, not even a tumor you can cut out; it's a lingering wayward pain that goes its own way and kills from within. Tereza started for home, wrapped in her Spanish shawl. Tears did not come easily to her; instead of weeping, she felt her dry eyes burn.

There was someone coming after her, almost running. Tereza supposed it was some fellow looking for a girl to take into the Vatican through the doorway guarded by Alfred the Rat.

"Hey! Lady! Wait for me, I've got to talk to you. Please wait."

After one glance back Tereza's first thought was to quicken her steps, but the man's rolling gait and the worried note in his voice made her stop. It was because of his troubled face and that disturbing scent, just like the smell of Januário's chest—that sea smell, though Tereza knew nothing about the sea except what little she had heard these past few days from Janu's jolly talk—that, and his skin tanned by the wind, which reassured her. Even before he spoke again she knew who he was and felt a pain constrict her chest: Oh, no, something awful had happened.

"Good evening, ma'am. I'm Cap'n Gunzá, Januário's friend. He came to Aracaju in my barque just to help me out of a tight spot."

"Is he sick? He had a date with me and didn't show up, so I came out looking for him."

"He's in stir."

As they walked on, Caetano Gunzá, master of the barque *Ventania,* told Tereza what he'd managed to find out. Januário had bought a fish, palm oil, lemons, red pepper, a bell pepper, coriander—all the vital ingredients, in short. He was a lavish cook and that day he had out-done himself on the fish stew. Caetano knew because when he realized that it was after nine and he was start-ing to get hungry, without his friend and her showing up, he'd tasted a little of it. Not long after seven, Januário had left the pan simmering on a low charcoal fire and gone to pick up Tereza, saying he'd be back in half an hour. That was the last Caetano had seen of him. At first he hadn't been worried, thinking the two of them might have gone for a stroll, or to dance awhile, Januário being a great one on his feet. But then, as he said, nine o'clock had come and he had helped himself to some of the stew. He hadn't eaten much, though, because by that time he had begun to get really worriéd. Putting down his plate and fork, he started out to look for Januário, but he hadn't found a trace of him until he'd walked a long way and came to an ice cream parlor. Some young fellows who were hanging around told him the police had caught a criminal (and a very dangerous one, according to the cops). In fact, it had taken ten of them to drag him away; the guy really was tough; he'd beaten up three or four cops. A big, hefty guy, a *capoeira* wrestler; he looked like a sailor. There couldn't be any doubt who the prisoner was. The police had had it in for him ever since the night of the free-for-all.

"I've been all over town trying to find him. I've been to two police stations, and to headquarters, and nobody will tell me a thing."

Oh, Janu! To think that I tried to forget you, to cover the embers with ashes and put out the flame that burns in my breast! I'll never, never forget you, not even when the *Ventania* crosses the bar again with you at the tiller or hoisting the sail; I'll never forget you. If you won't take my hand, I'll take yours, your big hand that felt so light as it touched my lip. If you won't kiss me, my lips will find your burning mouth and the salt of your breast, and oh, if you won't love me . . .

8

It wasn't until about two in the morning that the fish stew was finally served on the poop deck of the barque; and a lip-smacking stew it was. Lulu Santos carefully licked each little bone and then asked for the head, the best part, to his way of thinking.

"That's how you built up all that gray matter in your noggin, doctor," said Cap'n Caetano Gunzá sagely; he was an authority on scientific truths. "Anybody eats fish-heads gets as smart as a whip; everybody knows that."

In those few crowded hours, the master of the *Ventania* had become an unconditional admirer of the empiric lawyer. They had waked Lulu up and dragged him out of bed in the modest little house with garden on Santo Antônio hill where he lived.

"I know where Dr. Lulu lives," the taxi driver had boasted, though there was really nothing to boast about; everybody in Aracaju knew the address of the poor man's lawyer.

A tired, resigned female voice responded to the taxi horn and Cap'n Gunzá's handclaps. In spite of the lateness of the hour, when they said the matter was urgent, that they had to get someone out of jail, the voice became cordial at once.

"All right. He'll be right down."

And sure enough, almost at once, Lulu put his head out of the window and called down:

"Who is it? What do you want?"

"It's me, Dr. Lulu. Tereza Batista." The "Doctor" was for the benefit of Lulu's wife, whose protective shadow loomed behind Lulu's figure. "I'm sorry to bother you, but I'm here with the captain of the *Ventania*. It's about his friend. . . ." How could she explain that she was talking about the giant who had fought such a grand fight in the Gay Paree and carried her off just in the nick of time? You know who I mean. . . ."

"You mean the one who hit the cops and the detective the other night at the Gay Paree?" Tereza so cautious and gingerly, and Lulu speaking right out about the nightclub! That was just like him.

"Yes, that's the one."

"I'll be down in a shake."

A few minutes later he joined them in the street. They caught a glimpse of his wife closing the gate and heard her resigned voice warning him, "Watch out for the nightwatchman, Lulu." He climbed in the taxi and told the driver, "Drive straight ahead, Tião." Tereza told him the whole story. Caetano was laconic:

"I said to Januário: Compadre, I says, where'd you leave your brains? Don't you know plainclothesmen are worse than snakes? They'll stick a knife in your back every time. Paid me no mind. That's the way he is. Walks right into things."

Lulu yawned sleepily.

"It's no use making the rounds of all the precincts. We'd better go right to the top, to the chief of police. Dr. Manuel Ribeiro's not a bad guy; he's a friend of mine."

He gave them a rundown of Dr. Ribeiro's good qualities, not to mention the budding talents of his writer son. A bookish man with a law degree, highly educated, and brave besides. Though not the kind to stand for any lip, he wasn't the kind to tolerate injustice or unwarranted persecution either—except, of course, for political opponents, enemies, people who were against him. But even in such cases he felt no personal animus; he was only carrying out the responsibility he was charged with of keeping public order; he was just a man doing his job.

Despite the lateness of the hour, lights were on in the chief's den, and there was a bustle and stir around the building. An MP guarded the entrance, lounging against the wall and dreaming nostalgically of his former career as a holdup man. But when the taxi braked to a sharp stop, he straightened up in an instant, his hand on his revolver. When he recognized Lulu Santos, he relaxed at once into his sloppy pose and smiled:

"So it's you, Dr. Lulu? You want to talk to the Man? Go on in."

Tereza and Captain Caetano waited in the car. To soothe her fears, the sympathetic taxi man said, "Just relax, lady; Dr. Lulu'll get your husband out."

Tereza laughed to herself without answering. The driver went on talking about Lulu. Now there was a fine man, who would drop whatever he was doing to help somebody who was in trouble. And when it came to brains—well, when Dr. Santos defended a case before a jury no prosecutor in town had a chance of winning. And none in the whole state. He had defended people accused of felonies even in Alagoas and Bahia, and not just in the backwoods but in the capitals. An inveterate jury-watcher, the cabby described in exciting detail the trial of a badman called Mãozinha, one of the last to roam the backlands with rifle and cartridge belt. He had come from Alagoas with Lord knows how many notches on his gun, and had dispatched a few of his neighbors from Sergipe to a better world. The judge had appointed Lulu Santos to defend the fellow—for free, of course, since the outlaw didn't have a penny to his name. Man alive! Nobody who hadn't watched that trial from beginning to end —forty-seven solid hours of rejoinders and rebuttals and summations—could know what a really smart lawyer with brains could do. Just listen to how he opened his defense: it was the neatest thing you ever saw. He began by pointing his finger at the judge, then at the prosecutor, then at the jurymen one by one, and finally at his own chest, talking all the time, the way he knows how to do, with every word more biting than the one before: The real culprit, the man who is really guilty of those murders the prosecutor blames on Mãozinha here is really you, your honor; my honorable colleague there; you, and you, and you, worthy gentlemen of the jury; it was I, it was all of us, it was our society. I never heard anything like it in my life. I still get gooseflesh just telling about it; imagine what it was like to hear him!

A long time passed and then Lulu appeared in the doorway, smoking a São Felix cigar the chief of police had given him and laughing heartily at some sally made by the upstanding PSD party member who had accompanied him to the door.

"Headquarters, Tião," he told the driver.

When the taxi stopped, Januário was just coming out of the door. Tereza flung herself out of the car, ran to him with outstretched arms, and threw them around the giant's neck. Cap'n Gereba smiled into her eyes. The unshakable vow he had made in all good conscience and all good faith was broken, but how could he help kissing her now, when she was hanging on his lips? Even so, it was a hasty kiss, lasting only as long as it took the others to get out of the car. The cops had to just look on from the door of police headquarters; it was their hard luck that the chief's orders were unequivocal: Let the man go, now, at once; and if you lay a finger on him, you'll have me to answer to.

They had laid more than a finger on him already; that was plain from the sailor's black eye. The fight that began in the street had started all over again when they'd got him in the hoosegow. He had the hometown and the fans against him, but Cap'n Gereba hadn't done too badly even so; he had taken plenty but he'd dished it out, too. When the bunch of cowards had finally left him, promising to come back later for what they quaintly called "the breakfast round," the sailor was battered and bruised but still all in one piece; and a cop named Alcindo and a sergeant named Agnaldo were a good deal the worse for wear themselves.

Back at the *Ventania,* everybody had some fish stew, including the cabby, who at first refused to charge anything for the interminable run, but finally accepted the fare so as not to offend Cap'n Gereba, who was very touchy about money. It was Lulu who revealed a hidden facet of the friendly driver's talents: Tião composed sambas and marches, and had won first prize in more than one Carnival.

They drank *cachaça* along with the fish. As usual the lawyer drank in measured sips, popping his tongue after each one; Januário and Caetano poured the rum straight down their throats, and the taxi driver followed suit. Tereza sat next to Janu, eating with her hands. How many years had it been since she had eaten a meal that way, molding the food with her fingers to make a ball of fish, rice, and manioc flour, and then dunking it into the sauce? When they first went on board she had bandaged the cut under Januário's eye, ignoring the big fellow's protests.

The first bottle of rum was soon finished, and they opened a second. Lulu was beginning to show signs of fatigue; he had eaten three full plates of stew. Feeling expansive, after all the fish stew and *cachaça* he had consumed, Tião, the driver, invited the whole party to a beanfest the next Sunday, out at his place on the Rua Simão Dias. He said he would sing and play his latest songs on the guitar for his friends. His was a poor man's house, without luxuries or frills, he added in his peroration, but they would find no dearth of either friendship or beans. Having accepted the invitation, Lulu at once curled up on the deck and went to sleep.

It was four in the morning, and a faint dimness was beginning to seep into the still-powerful darkness when Januário and Tereza set off for Watchtower Beach with the cabby, who by that time was feeling no pain. The taxi proceeded in zigzags; Tião had downed a good deal of rum.

A capella—without the accompaniment it loses an awful lot, he explained—Tião sang the samba he had composed in honor of Lulu Santos's sensational defense of Mãozinha the outlaw:

> You killed him, Mr. Big,
> Don't you try to deny it.
> It wasn't the nigger, he just pulled the trigger.
> You it was who killed him
> You, the judge, and the jury.
> It was hunger that killed him.
> It was you and you and me,
> And man's injustice to man.

He flung out his arms in a wide gesture to give emphasis to the words. As his hands left the steering wheel, the car went out of control, skidded, and almost turned over. But nothing disastrous could happen that night, for it belonged to Januário Gereba and Tereza Batista. Well, now, a marriage like that, thought Tião, precursor of the protest singers to come, when a husband and wife are that crazy for each other, might really be worth the trouble. He got the car under control, and off they went down the narrow path, Tereza snuggling flirtatiously close against Januário's chest in the cool breeze that springs up just before dawn.

Suddenly, there was the sea.

9

Oh, sighed Tereza. They lay on the sand, the waves broke over their feet, and day broke, the color of Januário. At last Tereza found out where the smell came from that clung to the big man's chest. It was the sea's perfume. He tasted and smelled like the sea.

Why don't you love me? Tereza had asked as they ran along the beach hand in hand, away from the car and the driver's triumphal snores.

Because I do love you and want you. I fell in love with you; that's why I don't dare come any closer, why I run away and put a lock on my hands and my lips, and smother my heart. I want you for my whole life, not just for a few minutes. Oh, if I could only take you away with me to our very own house, put a wedding ring on your finger and take you with me forever! But I can't!

But why can't you, Captain Januário Gereba? With a ring, without a ring, I don't care; in our very own house and forever—Yes! I'm free; I have no ties and you are all I want in the world.

But I'm not free, Tetá; I have fetters on my feet. I have a wife. She has a cruel sickness and I can't ever leave her. I took her away from her father's house, where she had everything, and from the owner of a store she was engaged to. She always did right by me; she never complained when times were hard but went right on working and smiling; she smiled even when we were hungry. It's thanks to her that I could buy my boat; she scrimped and saved for the down payment, wearing out her health at the sewing machine, day and night, night and day. She never was very strong, and pretty soon she got a weakness in the chest. She wanted a baby and couldn't have one, but not a word of complaint ever passed her lips. All I earn with the boat goes for medicine and doctors to make the sickness last longer. It isn't enough to cure it; we'll never have enough money to make her well. When she ran off with

me I wasn't anything but a wharf rat, a bum without a
grain of common sense. The girl I loved and wanted, the
girl I stole from her family and the rich fellow who was going to marry her, was a healthy, happy, pretty girl. Now
she's sick and unhappy and ugly; but I'm all she has: she
has nothing and nobody else in the world, and I won't run
out on her. I don't want you for a day, or a night or an
hour in bed; I want you forever and I can't have you. I
can't give you anything. I have chains on my feet and
handcuffs on my hands. That's why I've never laid more
than a finger on you, why I never called you the love of
my life. The only thing is that I didn't have the guts to run
away for good and never come back. I wanted to be able
to keep your Indian copper face in the back of my eyes,
your warm pretty color, the feel of your hand, your slim
tallness, the curve of your hips. So that the thought of you
could nourish me on lonely nights at sea. So that I could
look at the ocean and see you in it.

You've treated me straight, Januário Gereba. You're
the way a man ought to be; you tell the truth like a man.
Janu, my Janu in chains, what a shame it can't be once
and forever, in our very own house until death do us part.
But if not forever, then let it be for a day, for an hour,
for a second! One day, two days, less than a week—for
me that day, those two days, that less than a week will be
as long as life multiplied by all the seconds and hours and
days of love, even if I go crazy afterward with longing and
desire and loneliness, even if I dream of you every night
and torture myself with impossible dreams. It will be worth
it, even so. . . . I want you now, this minute, now, let's not
wait any longer, now, now, now! now and tomorrow and
the day after, Sunday and Monday and Tuesday, morning,
noon, and night, any time; in the nearest bed, on the nearest mattress, the ground, the sand, the bottom of a boat,
the seashore, just anyplace where we can die in each other's arms. I don't care if I go to hell for it, I want you just
the same. I have to have you, Januário Gereba, you Captain, you giant, you king condor, you bad, no-good sailor
from Bahia.

There was the infinite sea, now green, now blue, blue-
green, now light, now dark, chiaroscuro, indigo, sky-blue,
fat oil, and clear dew. And as if the ocean wasn't enough,
Januário Gereba had ordered a gold and silver moon, a

lantern hung high in the sky above the two bodies entangled in an eager loving embrace. It was two who came, two became one, as a wave higher than the rest washed over them on the sand.

Tereza Batista, drenched by the sea—in her mouth, her streaming black hair, her erect breasts, in the star of her navel, in the shell of her sex, black pasture, flower of seaweed—I am dying, my love, on the edge of the sea, your Sargasso Sea, your sea of missed meetings and shipwrecks, and who knows? Someday I may die in your ocean in Bahia, on the deck of your boat. Your mouth tastes of salt, your chest is like a keel, I am the sail furled round your mast. I've been born again on the deck of the waves. I'm a mermaid, a fisherman's bride and his widow, seafoam and bridal wreath, veil of my longing, my love from the sea.

10

No, my fine-feathered friend, I can't tell you much about Tereza Batista's African origins. There are some awfully smart fellows around who specialize in such things, some at the university, some on fellowships; and they've got a knack for digging up ancestors to please the customers. Authentic or not, I don't know, but as long as the grandchildren are happy . . . Why I even know one fellow with so much gall that he goes around introducing himself as a descendant of Ogum, the war god, himself! Just think what a crackerjack of a genealogical expert had to look up his family tree! Maybe he did the research himself, though; that's probably the best way. You can't really trust a stranger in an important and delicate matter like that. After all, it's a family affair.

As you no doubt know, honored friend, a mixture of every tribe under the sun went to make up the Brazilian nation. An expert who really knows his business can find clues in the way a person walks, or the look in his eye, or his way of doing things, so that he can tell you who his great-great-grandparents were and what specific kind of mongrel he is. Why, it wouldn't surprise me none if that boaster really did turn out to be first cousin to Ogum, even if he is a bastard. You know how Ogum and Oxossi, the

god of the forest, weren't above paying visits to certain little fillies in Barroquinha. And go complain to Carybé, the
painter, if you think I'm making all this up. He's the one
who spreads all that gossip about the spirits, with Oxossi
right at the front of the pack. And it's only natural to act
that way, after all.

As for Tereza Batista, since Your Honor seems to be so
interested in her, there are a lot of stories about her, but
don't expect them to be consistent. People go on arguing
forever about Tereza over their bottle of cachaça, just for
the fun of arguing. She's been identified as malê, muçurumim, and haussá by men who wanted to make her. Others
have seen something gypsy about her—she could read
palms, she was a horsethief and childstealer, with gold
hoops in her ears and gold bracelets, and dancing feet.
Others thought she was half Indian because of her features
and straight black hair and a sort of standoffishness when
you weren't expecting it. And Africa—she was nagô, Angola, gêge, ijexá, cabinda? She was as lithe as a Congo-
lese, but where did her copper blood come from, and when
and how did it mix with all the other kinds? One thing's
sure: she was smeared with Portuguese honey, like everybody else around here. You see how black I am? Well, sir,
the first man to lie in my grandmother's bed was a Portu-
gee soldier.

I do know one thing for sure: a peddler was friendly
with Tereza Batista's grandmother Miquelina; but when I
say peddler, I hope you won't ask me to narrow it down
to Arab, Syrian, or Lebanese—they're all Turks anyway.
The state line passes through the back country just about
where Tereza was born, and that makes it hard to be sure
who's from Bahia and who's from Sergipe, especially a
traveling salesman with an eye for the farmer's daughter.
As far back as anyone can remember, the women of that
family have been eye-filling enough to raise a dead man's
tool, and they kept on getting better and better until they
got to Tereza. Even so I've heard more than one loudmouth swear that she was really homely, and clumsy too,
but that with witchcraft and the devil's help, she put a
spell on men. So, my friend, you see how many contradic-
tions there are in this story. And to think that some of us
still go on believing what they call eyewitness accounts,
and the made-up stories in the history books.

Just a few days ago I was taking my ease here in my stall, and eating a few pancakes, when a damn fool came along and began to run off at the mouth to a bunch of visitors from São Paulo, and there was one little rosy paulistinha, a morsel for a rich man's mouth, all smiles and dimples, and man oh man, if I wasn't a happily married man . . . Well, as I was saying, before that cute little gal from São Paulo interrupted my train of thought, the silly loudmouth, one of these modern kids who can't even tell a straight lie, was trying to impress the strangers by telling them that Tereza was a chubby blonde. The only thing he didn't take away from her was her spunk, and that was just because he wanted to ruin her reputation and show what a big man he was, the fool blowhard. He said that one time when she was making a fuss about something he put a stop to it right off, just by frowning and raising his voice. If you can swallow a tale like that, you'll believe anything. Right here in the Model Market, pal, you can hear things that stop you dead in your tracks—lies that ought to be fastened up on the wall with a Russian hammer and a nail a foot long.

If I was you, my well-meaning friend, I'd leave off worrying about Tereza's tribe. What earthly difference does it make whether she has malê or Angola blood in her veins, or whether that Arab peddler had a hand in it, or it was some gypsy who camped out in the fields? A fellow from back yonder told me one time that a lady named Magda Moraes got her sisters to testify to the police that Tereza was just an impudent little nigger. Can you beat that? And the woman's sisters swore up and down that it was true. From blonde to black, from gorgeous to a homely runt, Tereza goes from mouth to mouth in the marketplace. I stay put in my stall and listen to it all, but I don't say a word. And yet, who do you think knows more about her than I do—didn't she ask me to be her compadre?

Well, I reckon that's all I have to say about Tereza's ancestry. I don't claim she is Yansã in the flesh, but she may be a twin sister or some kind of cousin, like the fellow who claimed he was kin to Ogum. And as for your tribe, friend VIP, I don't have to work very hard to make a pretty good guess. Underneath that white skin of yours I can hear the tom-toms beating. You belong to the tribe of light mulattoes, milord, and a mighty fine tribe it is. Cama-

*feu de Oxossi belongs to it; and he's Xangô's high priest,
whose stamping ground is the Model Market, in St.
George's Tent, in the city of Bahia, navel of the world.*

11

Those were hectic days for Tereza as she hurried back and
forth from Joana das Folhas to Flori Pachola and the Gay
Paree to Cap'n Januário Gereba to the breeze's caress, the
cooing of doves, the murmur of waves, Tereza's loves. Her
retinue of admirers, the time spent at the dentist's, and
Veneranda's insistent solicitations kept her busy in what
time was left.

At about ten in the morning Tereza would get off the
bus at the door of Joana's little house, a special stop for
her made by the driver of the crowded bus. By that time
Joana had finished most of her daily labor—her young
helper caught the first bus in the morning to deliver the
baskets of vegetables to the customers who lived out in
the residential sections. After having been busy since
sunup, digging in the fields, tending to the orchard, picking fruit and vegetables, planting, fertilizing, Joana would
come into the house and wash her hands.

Every morning they sat down at the dining-room table,
determined and stubborn, with pen, pencils, inkwell,
book, and notebooks before them. Tereza was not altogether a novice at this task; out in the quiet street in
Estância where there were hardly any passersby, she had
begun teaching Lulu's and Nina's children the alphabet.
Little friends in the neighborhood began to join them, and
soon there were seven pupils in all, sitting on their heels
in a circle around Tereza, whose laughter and scoldings
were like a mother's. There wasn't very much that she
could teach in those days of quiet happiness during which
it was Tereza herself who was learning. What she knows
today she owes to those years—which, because they were
useful, productive ones, weigh as much in her mind as
the bad years of suffering which preceded and followed
them. (We're not forgetting, of course, the little school
where Dona Mercedes Lima taught, the country schoolteacher who didn't know much more than Tereza but

was just as dedicated.) The daily classes she held from ten to eleven in the morning, except when the Doctor was in town and at home, were a combination of school and picnic. Tereza taught the children their ABCs and the multiplication tables and penmanship, and she stuffed them with cookies and bread, cheese, homemade jam, fruit, chocolate bars, and soda pop.

Her little urchins were almost without exception bright as quicksilver, just as Tereza herself had been in Miss Mercedes's class. A few were little blockheads, but none gave her half as much trouble as Joana das Folhas did. Not that Joana was dull or stupid; quite the contrary. When Lulu Santos explained the plan of battle, she grasped it at once and only hung back a little because of her innate honesty. She would much rather have paid the swindler his eight thousand cruzeiros plus the interest she had agreed to, exorbitant as it was; but the lawyer persuaded her that it had to be all or nothing. If Joana wanted to pay what she owed she would have to recognize the validity of the document she had signed by proxy. She could accuse Libório of altering the figures, but how was she to prove it? There was no way in the world to prove such a thing. No, the only feasible course to take was to deny that she had signed by proxy; to disown the document and accuse Libório of having falsified everything from beginning to end because he thought she was illiterate, friendless, and isolated on her little farm. She had never borrowed a penny in her life and owed nothing to anyone. She could read, she could write, she could sign her own name; and she was ready to prove it by writing her signature on the paper in front of the judge. All Lulu asked in return was to see Libório's filthy mug when she did it.

She could do either one of two things, but she had to choose which: she could acknowledge that the document was valid, in which case her farm would be sold at auction and delivered to Libório on a silver platter—remember, there's absolutely no way we can prove that he changed the figure. In that event Joana das Folhas could look forward to working as Libório's servant on her own land or go begging in the streets of Aracaju. On the other hand, if she chose the other alternative and declared the document a forgery, her farm would be safe and she would be free of debt at the same time. The scoundrel wouldn't get his paws on a penny. That was the ideal solution. Joana let herself be persuaded but wanted to give Lulu the money she'd save, as a fee—though I can never pay you enough, *seu doutor*, for your goodness in taking my case without expecting to get anything out of it. None of that, my dear woman; the court costs and fees will come out of the swindler's own pocket, if the sentence is as fair as it ought to be. In her heart Joana was not sorry to have the confidence man taught a lesson. She had all a country-woman's shrewdness, and that helped her grasp with comparative ease the alphabet, the syllables, and the general concept of reading.

Her poor hands, though, had none of the agility of her mind, so quick to perceive subtleties and strategy. Joana's hands were two great calluses, two lumps of dried earth, her fingers twisted branches. Those hands were used to handling a spade, a mattock, a hoe, machete, or ax; how could they now manipulate a pen or a pencil?

She broke the points of a thousand pencils, splayed out quantities of pen-points, wasted reams of paper. But Tereza's patience never wavered during that heroic marathon against time and those awkward hands; and Joana, entirely convinced by Lulu Santos's arguments, was determined to win the battle, cost what it might. At first Tereza would hold the gnarled hand in her smooth one and guide it so that it could learn the movements more quickly.

Stopping only for a quick lunch, she labored with Joana's hands until three in the afternoon. It was really hard work but rewarding too: taking note of every tiny sign of progress, never letting hope flag, rising up after each failure, always resisting the temptation to take the easy way out and give it up as impossible. And Joana? What a mighty effort she made! Sometimes she prayed to Manuel in heaven for help; sometimes she bit her hands as if to punish them; and her eyes filled with tears when she finally traced a legible J.

Tereza caught the three o'clock bus to the dentist, then went on to rehearse at the Gay Paree, where Januário would meet her at the end of a day that had been full of hard work for him too: moving cargo, scouring, painting, mending sail, everything to make the *Ventania* seaworthy again. The plotters had taken him into their confidence, and he knew all about the fraud and counterfraud. His comment was that there's nothing better than fooling somebody who's tried to fool you. No one else was in on the secret, not even Flori, who continued to urge the dentist to finish his work, while he watched all his plans for bed and board with the Incandescent Star of the Samba crumble into dust: the sailor had taken the fort by storm, and Tereza was all languishing eyes and laughter. But as we've said before, Flori Pachola, a man of broad worldly experience and knowledge of women, did not give up easily. One day, sooner or later, when all the sacks of sugar had been loaded, when the sails were unfurled and bellying in the wind and the anchor raised, the barque *Ventania,* that light seagoing cockleshell, would put off from the quay and set sail for Bahia. As he beat out a samba rhythm on the piano, Flori looked without rancor at the giant at the head of the stairs. Go on, warm up the bed for me; no one hops to it in bed like a woman who's been left all alone.

When Januário appeared on the scene, poet and painter made their exit. The poet's quest was nothing but an illusion, a frustrated idyll, an ephemeral dream that would live forever in the poems born of the copper girl, those poems of passion and death. As for the painter, he was silent. His deep-set eyes seemed to look both at what was visible and what was within, taking possession of an image he never forgot, of every fleeting expression, of all that was contained in the past, all the vitality and élan: the dancer, the woman with cyclamen, the country girl, the woman of the port, the gypsy, the samba queen, the daughter of the people—in how many paintings, with how many titles, was Tereza's haunting face to look out of his canvases?

When the rehearsal was over, about six, Tereza went back to the farm with Januário, and the lesson began again. It was an exhausting but exhilarating time, without a second of leisure. During these feverish days, Joana and Tereza grew to be friends. The black woman told Tereza about her husband, a strong, fine-looking farmer with the best heart in the world, whose only sorrow in his life was his son. He had hoped to see him working the soil, tending the fruit trees, the garden, the customers—turn-

ing the little place into a real farm. He couldn't forgive
the boy for running away. Manuel was handsome and
lusty, and loved to bury his thick moustache in the back
of his wife's neck. He had never looked at another
woman; he had his black Joana. When he died, Joana
had just turned forty-one, and twenty-three of those years
she had spent at Manuel França's side. At her husband's
death her periods stopped; she was now as dead to sex as
he.

When Lulu Santos could get away from the bar or the
forum, he would turn up at the farm to encourage Joana
and see how she was coming along. At first he was terribly discouraged; Joana das Folhas's hand, he thought, was
a hand for tilling and fertilizing, for the spade and hoe,
but it would never be able to write out the letters of
Dona Joana França's name. Time was growing short; the
hearing was right around the corner, and Libório's lawyer, a nosy parker and no better than a jailbird himself,
was putting pressure on the judge. But as the days passed,
the poor man's lawyer plucked up hope again, and all his
old optimism returned. The nib of the pen no longer tore
the paper, there were fewer blots. Tereza had worked a
miracle, and letters began to bloom under Joana's hands.

The gnarled fingers no longer needed to be guided, and
when Tereza said good-bye at eight (she and Januário
kissed scandalously in the crowded bus, anticipating their
night of lovemaking), the black woman would go on
scratching at the paper, writing the alphabet over and
over, and then the same words again and again, her own
name innumerable times. The illegible scrawl became
writing, the scribbles clearer, firmer, more intelligible.
Joana das Folhas was fighting for everything she possessed: the little garden she and Manuel had made into
an Eden of shade trees and vegetables, an orchard of
prize fruit; her daily bread; the inheritance her husband
had left her, the fertile seedbed that yielded what she
needed for her modest living, besides a little luxury for
her prodigal, ungrateful, much-beloved son.

12

"Young girls these days are just so flighty. They don't have the sense God gave a goose. Never give a thought to tomorrow," opined old Adriana to Lulu Santos, shaking her gray head.

"Crazy, that's what she is—throwing away a grand prize like that—" The grand prize was a senator and captain of industry. The old woman poured out her heart to the lawyer, who had come to see Tereza.

"Tereza's never at home any more. She goes out the minute breakfast's over and spends the whole day and night running after that confounded fisherman."

A girl who carried a figure like Tereza's the way she did could set her own price in a place like Aracaju, where there were plenty of fine married men with position and money to spend, ready and willing to set up and keep a gift of God like Tereza.

Not that she, Adriana, harbored any great love of Veneranda. Lulu knew she had every reason to dislike her; but just the same she had to give the devil his due: this time the stuck-up old busybody really had done the handsome thing. She had sent a message to Tereza, proposing a discreet tête-à-tête in her castle with—guess who! Lulu would never guess! She lowered her voice as she revealed the name of the banker and industrialist, who had the added luster of being a senator. For one afternoon in Tereza's bed, just one afternoon, he was offering a small fortune. It seems he had had his eye on her ever since the old days in Estância; an old pash, a hard-on cooked over a slow fire (Lulu must excuse the expression; she was just quoting Veneranda). The madam had sought out Adriana to act as go-between and promised her a decent commission. It was a piece of cake for Tereza; but even more important, there was always a chance that the generous plutocrat would take such a shine to the way the girl moved her hips (and the chance was almost a sure thing) that he would set her up in a fine little nest of her own. Tereza could be lying on a bed of roses and Adriana, her bosom friend, could pick up some crumbs. That was all she asked—just a crumb or two. Tereza, is your head screwed on at all? Not satisfied with just saying no, when Adriana still tried to persuade her—after all, she had to keep her promise to Veneranda—Tereza threatened to move somewhere else. It made no sense, it was just ridiculous, to turn down the richest man in Sergipe for a good-for-nothing freshwater sailor. Did you ever hear of anything so silly in your born days? I just don't know what's come over girls today. The featherbrains think of nothing but putting out, all right, but not with anybody worth the trouble. No, they lose their heads over the first silly boy they see and forget all about the important thing. It's money makes the world go round, and they'll all end up in the poorhouse, you just mark my words.

Relishing the old woman's despair, Lulu Santos teased her about the tip Veneranda had promised. So—his esteemed friend Adriana, a woman of principle and tradition, and discreet to boot, had turned procuress for the most notorious madam in Aracaju in her old age! Where was her pride?

"Lulu, times are hard, and money doesn't smell."

Adriana, old friend, for goodness' sake leave the girl alone. She knows the value of money, all right; make no mistake about that. But she knows life and love are worth more. You don't think the senator's the only one who's after her, with his billfold in his hand and a peeing hard-on? (Pardon the expression; I'm quoting Veneranda too.) There's a poet full of verses who's dying for love of her, and every one of his poems is worth the tycoon's millions. If she didn't put out for the poet, why should she for the textile magnate? Why, she wouldn't even have me, Adriana, and I taste as sweet as coconut candy to the ladies of Aracaju. The only one she wants is the one who touched her heart. Leave Tereza in peace during the little time of love and happiness she has, and be ready to take care of her lovingly and comfort her like the true friend you are tomorrow or the next day—it won't be long now—when her sailorman sails off and the long, long time of bitter despair is upon her, when she's so unhappy she's ready to gnaw on the chamberpot (once again you'll pardon the vulgar expression; it's borrowed from our fine lady Veneranda).

Yes, of course Adriana would promise. She'll be a sis-

ter and a mother to Tereza and dry her tears (Tereza's
not one to cry over nothing, old friend). Even if the silly
girl did bring it all on herself, Adriana will offer her sympathy and a shoulder to weep on. A fleeting ray of hope
lit up Adriana's eyes: once the big fellow was gone and
she could think again with a clear head, maybe Tereza
would see reason and decide to take the father-of-his-
country up on his offer. Adriana would be content with
the crumbs.

13

Don't tell me until the day before, begged Tereza. I don't
want to know which day you're leaving until the time
comes. Let's act as if we were going to spend our lives
together, as if we were never to be parted, as if the
Ventania were going to stay at anchor forever in the port
of Aracaju. They lived out their festive holiday in a
frenzy and filled Sergipe with their sighs of love—on the
sandy beach, under the coconut palms, in hidden spots on
the island, in Tereza's room, in the bottom of the boat.

Januário shared every hour of Tereza's life. At rehearsals he showed her *capoeira* feints, darting movements suited to her flexible body, enhancing Tereza's
still-timid samba with daring, elegance, and grace. Master seaman and master *capoeira* wrestler, master Carnival dancer that he was, Janu knew every samba trick
there was to know.

Tense with interest, he followed every step in Joana
das Folhas's progress, laughing with pleasure when he
saw she had finally tamed her stubborn hand and made it
guide the pencil or pen—scratching the paper still but
no longer tearing it, splattering ink but no longer making
illegible smudges of the letters. During each evening's
lesson there was always at least one moment when all
three shared a smile of triumph: Tereza, Janu, and Joana
das Folhas.

Janu and Tereza kissed on the streetcar, held hands as
they strolled around the port, sat and talked on the Emperor's Bridge or on the deck of the *Ventania*. One night
Januário took her out in a rowboat, and then, dropping the

oars, took her in his arms in the rocking boat, both of them fully dressed, in a confused splashing of water and laughter, as the light boat drifted down the river. Then he landed on the Ilha dos Coqueiros, and they circled the island to find love nests. And one night on Watchtower Beach they followed the moon in the sky, only the two of them on the vast stretch of sand, shedding their clothes, plunging into the sea, Tereza giving herself to him in the midst of the waters, all sea-salt and foam.

"You're not Yansã any longer; you're only Yansã when it's time to fight. Now you're Janaína, the queen of the sea," Janu told her out of long familiarity with the *orixás*.

Tereza very much wanted to ask him about his fishing boat, the *Waterflower*, about the crossings, the Paraguaçu River, the Island of Itaparica, the harbors where he landed, what life was like down there in Bahia. But since that first night at the Watchtower when he had told her the most important thing of all, they had not spoken again about fishing boats, or the Paraguaçu, or Maragogipe, Santo Amaro, and Cachoeira, or the islands and beaches, the city of Bahia, the Bay of All Saints. Instead, they talked about Aracaju and its affairs: about Joana das Folhas's imminent day in court, the day for the hearing having been set by the judge; about the Gay Paree and her dance numbers, and her debut which was not far off now either; about her gold tooth at last taking form under Jamil Najar's chisel—say, is that guy a dentist or a sculptor? An artist at dental prosthesis, he would have replied as he exhibited his masterpiece. They talked lightly about such topics as these, just as if they would never part, as if life had stopped when love came to them both.

On Sunday they went to cabby Tião's for lunch with Lulu Santos and Cap'n Caetano Gunzá, as they had said they would. The bean-and-pork *feijoada* was beyond all praise—worthy of all the superlatives and exclamations it evoked. It was a large and lively party; among the guests were taxi drivers, amateur musicians with their guitars and flutes, a first-class mandolin player, and some neighborhood girls, lively, saucy friends of Tião's wife. They ate, they drank, they sang, and finally they danced to a phonograph. Everyone treated Janu and Tereza as if they were truly married.

"That pretty gal's the big man's wife."

"He's a sailor, you can tell."

"She's a mighty fine-looking piece."

"Yes, Cavalcanti, she's a peach. But you'd better not fool around with her; she's married to that guy."

A sailor's wife, as everyone knows, is soon a widow. Either her husband dies at sea or he sails away and doesn't come back. A sailor's love lasts as long as the tide. Knowing her joy to be ephemeral, Tereza clung to Janu.

A life of mourning was a heavy price to pay, but the dawn of love was worth it, even so. However high the cost, it could not be too great.

14

When the clerk motioned them to do so, everyone in the courtroom rose to his feet: the solemn moment for the verdict had arrived. As he stood up, the judge glanced at Lulu Santos out of the corner of his eyes. His Honor Judge Benito Cardoso, a jurist with a brilliant career behind him, was not deceived in the least by the empiric lawyer's sober face, which still expressed his disgust at the treachery, the fraudulence, the thievery, the crime he had denounced. For his essays, articles, and judicial opinions as published in the São Paulo *Court Review,* the judge had earned the definitive accolade bestowed by an illustrious colleague, Professor Ruy Antunes of the University of Pernambuco, whom a complicated question of penal law had brought to Sergipe: "In Dr. Cardoso, profound knowledge of the law is linked to an admirable knowledge of humankind."

In the depths of the lame lawyer's eyes, Judge Cardoso perceived a glimmer of malice. The hearing had been nothing but a comedy of errors from start to finish, but if it took lies and mockery to unmask the thief, blessed be the mockery and lies. Lulu Santos, the sly fox of the forum, totally without false pride or squeamishness as to means, had succeeded at last in trapping the most outrageous usurer in town, a fellow who embezzled under the very eye of justice, forever bending the law to his purposes and forever going scot free. How many times had

Judge Cardoso been forced to acquit him for lack of proof, though knowing full well that he was guilty? Four times in all, if memory served. Lulu, your defense was impeccable and your witnesses played their parts to perfection. This time you gave me everything I needed to render a proper verdict for once. But the judge decided he would ask Lulu to clarify one small point, just to satisfy his curiosity, once the courtroom was clear.

He raised his eyes and fixed Libório das Neves with a severe, disapproving gaze. At the usurer's side Silo Melo, a shyster little better than a felon himself, read in the judge's face that he was defending a lost cause—even his lean and hungry client's toothy countenance suggested that of a thieving rat. His honor cleared his juridical throat and read out the sentence. At the slow, solemn tones of the whereases that preceded the verdict, Libório das Neves slowly crumpled, like an inflated bag that's finally been pricked. Lulu Santos's eyes followed each step in that long-awaited crumpling: yes, he was an empty bag, a measly sackful of shit. Judge Benito Cardoso's voice was grave as he enunciated each syllable, each letter of each word seeming to grow more emphatic as he neared his peroration:

"For the foregoing reasons, and others set out in the court proceedings, I judge the suit brought by Libório das Neves against Joana França to be without basis and the document on which that suit rests to be null and void. Furthermore, since the document is fraudulent, this verdict is to be without appeal. If any appeal is attempted, a true copy of this decision is to be sent to the appropriate bureau of the Prosecutor's Office so that responsibility for the fraud can be fixed by the proper authorities and sanctions applied under the penal law currently in force. The plaintiff shall pay double the amount of the court costs as penalty for bringing suit in bad faith, and an additional twenty percent penalty over and above legal fees. May justice be done."

On the memorable evening in Adriana's house when they had settled on their plan of battle, Lulu Santos had told Tereza Batista: All I ask is the chance just to see Libório's face. Now he not only saw Libório's face break out in a cold sweat but heard his nasal voice cry out in agony. Lulu felt richly repaid for all the hard work—his, Tereza's, and Joana das Folhas's.

"I object, your honor! I object! I've been framed! It's a plot! They're robbing me blind!" wailed Libório, beside himself with despair.

The judge had not yet adjourned the case. Still standing, he brandished a threatening finger.

"One more word and I'll have you taken into custody and booked for contempt of court. Court adjourned."

The convicted scoundrel pulled in his protesting tongue and his horns, and Silo Melo, with his rodent's face and dullard air, still bemused by the turn the trial had taken, dragged his client out of the courtroom. The audience filed out, and also the court clerk, carrying under his arm the big black book in which the decision had been inscribed. Alone together, the judge shed his robes, and the people's lawyer picked up his crutches. The two were old friends. Lowering his voice to a confidential whisper which was scarcely audible, the judge queried Lulu about the one point which still puzzled him; everything else seemed clear enough:

"Tell me, Lulu, who taught that black woman to sign her name?"

Lulu Santos measured the judge with a suddenly suspicious eye:

"Who taught her? Why, Dona Carmelita Mendonça. She said so, right here in this room, just now, and under oath. The most honest, upright woman imaginable, respected by everyone in the state of Sergipe, teacher to us all—your teacher, too; a woman of unblemished honor and unquestioned word."

"And who's refuting her word? If I had wanted to question it, I'd have done so during the trial. You're right: she was my teacher, and yours too. You were her favorite because you were the smartest and . . ."

". . . and because I limped," laughed Lulu.

"Well, yes. Listen, Lulu, now that the verdict has been handed down, let's admit that you and I both know Dona Carmelita never laid eyes on that black woman before she came into this courtroom. She came because you told her the facts of the case and persuaded her that it was the right thing to do. That Libório is a disgusting fellow and had to be taught a lesson—not that I see much chance of his taking it to heart. He's one branch that grew crooked from the start. But for heaven's sake, Lulu, tell me who the genius was who taught those hands—have you ever really looked at your client's hands, Lulu?—to write her name legibly and without a single mistake."

The lawyer looked at the judge again, smiling now, his eyes clear of any lingering doubt or suspicion.

"If I told you it was her fairy godmother I wouldn't be far from the truth. If your honor weren't such a respectable judge I'd invite you to come with me next Friday to a nightclub down in the red-light district called the Gay Paree, and I'd introduce you to the girl."

"What girl? You mean she's a prostitute?"

"Her name is Tereza Batista. She's a rare beauty, old man. And she fights even better than she writes."

With that, Lulu walked out of the courtroom, leaving the judge to ponder on how surprising and sometimes absurd life is: that trial, which was nothing but a tissue of lies, had led to truth and justice. Lulu hurried along on his crutches to catch up with Silo Melo, who was waiting for him, chastened and humbled and anxious to make friends. As soon as he got out of the courtroom, the amateur lawyer threw back his head and laughed. Oh, what a rare treat it had been to see Libório's face turn to shit.

15

As his honor had said, the trial was a comedy of errors, a farce in which every member of the cast was satisfied with his role except the author-plaintiff, Libório das Neves, who had gone from wan to livid and lost his temper at the wrong moment. The lawyer vented the euphoria of victory in rhetoric: innocence had been proclaimed in the courtroom and the guilty man punished. Justice had been done.

It had been worth all the hard work, including the visit to his venerable teacher Carmelita Mendonça, and the soft soap he had had to apply to persuade her to act as his accomplice.

"Teacher dear, I've come to ask you to testify before a judge and bear false witness."

"False witness, Lulu? Are you still as crazy as you used to be? I've never told a lie in my life and I'm not about to tell one now. And in court, too—"

"Miss Carmelita, I'm asking you to commit perjury in the cause of truth, to unmask a criminal who wants to reduce a poor, hardworking widow to misery by robbing her of the little she owns. And to try to save herself from penury, that woman, who is almost fifty years old, has learned to read and write in ten days. . . . I've never seen anything like it."

Lulu recounted the whole story from beginning to end, in very dramatic fashion. After retiring from public-school teaching, Miss Carmelita had dedicated herself enthusiastically to the problem of adult illiteracy and had soon become an authority, the author of much-quoted essays and studies on the subject. She listened to the narrative with growing interest, and the vision of the black woman bent over the paper, trying with all her might to master pen and ink, won her over to Joana das Folhas's cause.

"You can't have invented that story, Lulu; it's bound to be true. Yes, you can count on me. You come for me the day of the trial, and I'll say anything you want me to say."

The judge knew that Lulu's weapons of counterattack were the very ones used by Libório—lies and perjury—when he denied the validity of the document presented in evidence of the latter's claim. He declared it was a forgery from the first letter to the last; that his client had never borrowed money from the plaintiff; that she owed him nothing, he could prove in the clearest, most irrefutable way: since the defendant could read and write, she had no reason to sign by proxy. Why, the document was a monstrosity; it was as false as Judas, your honor.

He had advanced an entirely new version of the affair: Yes, Mrs. Joana França had needed eight thousand cruzeiros to send to her only son, who resided in Rio. Since she did not have the money, she had sought out the usurer Libório das Neves in order to borrow the amount from him. The moneylender was only too glad to make her the loan provided that she agreed to repay fifteen thousand cruzeiros at the end of six months. In other words—and you may well be amazed, your honor—an

annual interest rate of more than 150 percent, 12 percent
a month! Faced with such an outrageous rate of interest,
Dona Joana gave up the idea of borrowing the money.
Since she was to receive in six months the repayment of
a sum lent by her husband before his death to his good
friend and compatriot Antônio Salema (familiarly known
as Antônio Minhoto), she appealed to Antônio to advance
her the eight thousand cruzeiros she needed so urgently.
This he immediately did. Knowing that the widow was
hard-pressed, and having learned, how and through whom
we do not know, that she had signed her marriage papers
with Manuel França by proxy, she being then illiterate,
the foxy Libório plotted to cheat her and so take possession of the defendant's little farm, just as he had used
equally illicit means to entangle other unhappy victims in
his snares on earlier occasions. Thus, he forged the legally
recorded document as grounds for claiming that the
woman had borrowed not the relatively modest amount
she had really asked for but a sum ten times as great, his
covetous eye being cast on the land which the Franças'
own hard work and care had transformed into a beautiful
little orchard and truck farm. But when the swindler laid
his felonious plans so craftily, one very important detail
had escaped his notice. Not long after their marriage—
that is, more than fifteen years ago—Manuel França became ashamed of the fact that his legitimate wife was
illiterate, and hired Miss Carmelita Mendonça to teach
her to read and write. Dona Carmelita certainly needs no
introduction from me. She has taught whole generations
of eminent citizens of Sergipe, including some of our
state's most illustrious public servants, His Honor Judge
Cardoso among them. After months of unremitting labor
and the application of all her vast knowledge of the subject, Miss Carmelita Mendonça, that capable woman who
is the glory of Sergipean pedagogy, rescued the good
Dona Joana from the darkness of illiteracy and illumined
her spirit with the torch of letters. That was exactly
fifteen years and four months ago, your honor.

Clever devil, that Lulu Santos, reflected the judge as he
listened to his argument. He had got Dona Carmelita to
teach Joana das Folhas to scrawl her name, and here
he is proclaiming that she has been literate for fifteen
years—what a monumental coup! But no sooner had that

delightful octogenarian entered the courtroom—the glory of Sergipean pedagogy, the spiritual mother of so many of us, in the lawyer's emotion-charged phrases—than the judge realized she had never in all her long life laid eyes on the robust and silent Negress sitting beside Lulu Santos. Only he and Libório das Neves noticed the old lady's almost imperceptible hesitation. Who *had* taught the defendant to read and write?

Yes, she said, Joana França, to whom she had taught the alphabet and the rudiments of writing fifteen years before, was the same woman who was sitting there, looking older, of course, and now wearing mourning. Who could have the temerity to question Miss Carmelita Mendonça's word? Lulu Santos was a demon, a regular devil.

And then Antônio Salema, known as Minhoto because he was born in Póvoa do Lanhoso in Portugal's province of Minho, also recited his piece to perfection. Lulu had gone out to Laranjeiras with Joana to enlist the Lusitanian's help and to school him in what to say. He confirmed and supported the amateur lawyer's story: Yes, he had advanced his comadre the eight *contos* she had asked for; and in answer to Silo Melo's question as to whether the defendant was literate, and if so, how long ago she had learned to read, Antônio said he had never known his comadre to make a mistake in her accounts, and so much the worse for anyone who tried to cheat her!

The *coup de grâce* was a no-show, the nonappearance of the third witness summoned by Lulu Santos: Joel Reis, thief and pickpocket, known as Joel Cat's-Paw in state prisons and the lowest criminal circles. Subpoenaed by the judge, as soon as he received and had signed the summons, he ran away from Aracaju rather than explain in court why he had signed the document attesting to that false debt as if by proxy for Dona Joana França—this not at her request, of course, because he had never laid eyes on her in his life, but under orders from his protector and patron, Libório das Neves. Who had got Cat's-Paw out of jail in Aracaju by using his influence in a certain police milieu in which criminals and police fraternize and it's almost impossible to distinguish one from the other? The plaintiff, of course. For whose benefit had Joel Reis carried out certain sordid tasks, such as collecting from prostitutes for the squalid rooms they rented? Who meticulously prepared marked decks of cards? Now, your honor, for whose benefit could he do all that? Whose but that of the honorable, unblemished, immaculate Libório das Neves the thief, your honor!

Yes, it really had been worth all the hard work: the long talk with Miss Carmelita, spoken with the catch of emotion in his voice; the trip to Laranjeiras; the threats made to Cat's-Paw, coupled with a second-class ticket on the Eastern Railroad and the small gratuity: take your choice, clear out or rot in jail.

He had been richly repaid. There was Joana das Folhas's signature spelled out five times on the snowy white paper before the judge, and without a single blot or a single error—the clear, unmistakable signature of Joana França, your honor, and in a very fair hand.

16

Without making a single gesture, like a stone statue carved on the moldering pier, Tereza Batista watched the barque *Ventania* make ready to sail. The anchor was raised, the unfurled sails began to flap in the breeze, and the Captain and First Mate, Gunzá and Gereba, stood in the poop and prow, at sails and tiller. A few minutes earlier, Januário had swarmed up the mast like a circus acrobat, a king condor, high flier, giant bird-of-the-sea, O Janu, my man, my husband, my love, my life, my death: Tereza's heart shrank within her and her slender form began to tremble as if the statue had been stricken.

As they were sitting in the Egypt Bar and Café the day before, waiting to hear the result of the lawsuit brought against Joana das Folhas by Libório das Neves, Januário had told her: It'll be tomorrow, with the first tide. Taking Tereza's hand in his big one, he had added: Someday I'll be back.

Not another word was said, but Tereza's lips were suddenly pale and cold, the warm afternoon breeze turned to ice and the sun to ashes, like harbingers of death. Hands clasped hands, eyes gazed into the distance, sure of what absence would bring. Just then Joana and the lawyer

burst in from the street, bubbling with the joy of victory:
Let's celebrate!

What a contradictory world, joy and sorrow all mixed
together. In Joana's house, when the table was laid and
bottles opened, Lulu offered a toast to Tereza. May she
have health and happiness! Happiness! What a mess life
was!

On the farthest beach she nestled close to the chest of
the man she had been born for but had found too late.
Violently, she let him take her; with the bitter taste of
separation in her mouth she bit and scratched him, while
he clasped her to his breast as if longing to burrow inside her very skin. On the last beach, on their last night
of love, she strangled her sobs. No, she mustn't cry. A
wave came and covered them, the sea came and took him.
Sailor, farewell.

Januário leaped from the barque to the pier next to
Tereza and took her in his arms. His last kiss rekindled
her cold lips. A sailor's love lasts as long as the tide, and
the *Ventania* sailed south with the tide, to its dock in
Bahia. Tereza had so longed to ask what life was like in
Bahia, but what use would that have been? Sails unfurled,
anchor lifted, the barque drew away from the pier,
Caetano Gunzá at the tiller. Parched tongues, voracious
teeth, desperate mouths, burning the distance away and
fusing life and death with the fire of a kiss, Tereza
marked Januário's lip with the gold tooth.

The fiery kiss came apart, leaving a drop of blood on
Januário's lip, a remembrance of Tereza Batista, tat-
tooed on the corner of his mouth by a gold tooth: Sea and
river, river and sea, I'll come back to you some day
even if it rains knives and the sea turns to sand, I'll come
on crab's feet walking backwards, I'll come in the storm
like a castaway seeking a harbor, the tender stone of your
breasts, the waterjug of your belly, your conch shell of
mother-of-pearl with its copper seaweed and its bronze
oyster and its golden star, sea and river, river and sea,
stream of farewell, tide of nevermore. The sailor jumped
from the pier, from Tereza's arms to the deck, the leaping giant with his salt smell, his odor of the sea, and the
handcuffs on his hands and the fetters on his feet.

Tereza stood motionless, a statue of stone with dry
eyes. The sun swung in the ash of the sky, and then there

was a sad purple twilight, and then a night empty of stars, and the moon was useless forever. The quick breeze sprang to the sails and the conch shell, calling the wind, mourned hoarsely in Cap'n Januário Gereba's mouth in a poignant farewell. Good-bye, Tetá *muçurumim*, moaned the deeptoned voice; good-bye, Janu best-beloved, answered a heart already torn by the agony of absence. Waters of farewell, sea and river, farewell; good-bye to the crabfeet, good-bye to the castaway's wake, forever and ever, good-bye.

The giant stood on deck and the conch tore a path through space, commanding the wind. The barque *Ventania* left the dock of Aracaju, in Sergipe-del-Rey, with Cap'n Caetano Gunzá at the tiller and Januário Gereba at the mast, a bird with clipped wings, a prisoner in an iron cage, with fetters on his feet. Where the waters of the river met those of the sea, riversea, *riomar*, the giant raised his arm and with his hand waved good-bye.

Tereza Batista stood stock still on the time-rotted boards of the pier, a stone statue with a dagger thrust into her breast. The night stole around her and drenched her with shadows and emptiness, longing and absence, the sea and the river, my love, my love.

17

With her gold tooth and her icecold heart, Tereza Batista, Incandescent Star of the Samba, Blazing Empress of Swing and Sway, finally made her debut at the Gay Paree, on the second floor of the Vatican, in the red-light district of Aracaju, facing the harbor where Caetano Gunzá's barque had been anchored. The quay still echoed with the deep sound of the conch shell blown in farewell by Cap'n Januário Gereba, who had come to help out a friend and to make someone die of love—just when that someone was finally easy in her mind and at peace in her heart, making a new life for herself at long last. It was Januário, the chief merrymaker in Carnival, the samba dancer par excellence, who had taught her those Angolan gyrations.

Not since that other festive first night had the Gay

Paree dancehall been so packed to the roof with the
lively, flashy, gilded youth of Aracaju. Couples struggled
for space on the dance floor to the strident sound of
the Midnight Jazz Band. At the crowded tables there was
a hearteningly brisk consumption of beer, rum cocktails,
Brazilian brandy, adulterated whisky and, for the snobs,
wine from Rio Grande do Sul. The battalion of lovers
was there in full force: the painter Jenner Augusto, with
his deep bedroom eyes; the poet Saraiva, with his heart-
rending verses, his consumption, and a flower for Tereza
which he had picked on the way; the dental surgeon,
Jamil Najar, the prosthetic magician; the victorious lawyer for the defense, Lulu Santos; and the happy host and
aspirant to the star's favors, Floriano Pereira, Flori
Pachola, biding his time and joining to the enviable condition of employer that of suitor.

Besides the aforementioned quartet, there were at least
two dozen others with beating hearts, and three dozen
more with hard-ons throbbing on the altar of the Divine
Shepherdess of the Samba (the epithet they read on the
colored posters). This is not to mention those who were
constrained by discretion from appearing in person at the
nightclub to applaud the debut of Miss Samba (Flori's
posters again). But one, at least, sent a representative.
This was the senator and captain of industry, the richest
man in Sergipe, according to old Adriana and the tax col-
lectors. Veneranda, surrounded by a bubbling cortege of
her girls, lent the honor of her presence to a ringside table. She had been given carte blanche by the plutocrat to
offer whatever it took to get the comely wench to dally
with him for an afternoon in the quiet of the castle.
Later on, if he took a fancy to her, if she turned out to be
as tasty and delicious a morsel as she looked, the great
man was disposed to honor her with his protection: rent,
food, charge accounts in the shops, and all the luxuries
of a mistress—chocolate bonbons, a gold watch, a diamond
ring (a small one), even a gigolo if she insisted on having one.

The barque *Ventania* sailed on the back of the sea off
Mangue Seco, lashed by waves and south wind. Oh Janu,
best-beloved, all I can think of is time and the tide, and
the road to perdition, and the dark, empty night. I want
no offers, no applause, no purse full of money to spend,

no colonel to protect me, and I hate gigolos. I don't want the poet's verses; I want your chest like a keel, your sea smell, and the salt and ginger taste of your mouth. Oh Janu, never more.

At eleven sharp the lights were dimmed, the drums rolled a fanfare, and trumpets heralded the Incandescent Star of the Samba. The red glow of a spotlight fell on the dance floor, lighting up Tereza Batista. She was dressed in a short skirt and a Bahiana's chemise, sandals, necklaces, and bracelets left over from the Jota Porto & Alma Castro Variety Show, all of which set off the dusky, gypsy-Indian-African beauty of the national *mulata* in all her sensual pride. There was a storm of applause and whistles and cheers; Flori brought an armful of flowers, the gift of the house; José Saraiva, a faded rose and a fistful of poems.

For all that, the long-awaited debut almost turned into a debacle again, and for the very same reason as before. As luck would have it, just as the clapping died down, a sharp argument became audible at one of the tables between a weary old hooker and a smart-ass young rake showing his teeth for the first time in his career as a pimp.

As Tereza curtseyed a thank-you for the flowers, verses, and applause, the ruffian's bullying voice was heard, producing a whimper from the woman:

"Shut up or I'll smash your face."

Taking a haughty stance, with her hands on her hips and a sudden dangerous glint in her eye, Tereza said:

"Go ahead and do it, little boy. . . . Go ahead; I'm watching you. Smash her face, if you've got the guts to do it."

Nervous expectation swept the crowd: would the bum take her up on it? Would the debut have to be put off again? Would there be another fight like the one they still remembered, with another gold tooth to be molded daintily to order by Najar, the dental surgeon? However, the bully didn't rise to the challenge. He was simply dumbfounded, and didn't know where to put his hands or hide his face. Tereza had spoken, and that was enough.

A wild ovation drowned out his words, and Tereza swept into her dance on that sea of applause. Now she was a samba star—one more career for someone who had had so many and was destined to have so many more, she who wanted nothing from life but to be happy with her man at sea.

The day before she had gone to the law courts with the lawyer, at his request; and in one of the civil courtrooms she was introduced to Judge Benito Cardoso, to some lawyers, prosecuting attorneys, court clerks, and other notables: Tereza Batista, star of the stage. She was shy for a star and smiled bashfully, a little embarrassed; what a pretty thing she was! They all thought her a new conquest of the lame, woman-chasing lawyer. Only his honor knew about the good deed, or rather miracle, that the novice teacher had performed with Joana das Folhas as beneficiary—that farmwoman getting along in years and with hands like roots. The eyes of the judge were soon brimming with admiration and desire. Ah, if only he were a judge on the State Court of Appeals, he could offer her a home and heart; but the stipend of a lower-court judge was barely enough to feed his legally wedded wife and his children. He could hardly afford to keep up his civilian household; there was no use in thinking of a "military home" with a friend, mistress, or concubine in it.

Tereza Batista, the artiste, was swept along on a sea of applause, beginning another career of ups and downs, but off to a triumphant start. Her heart was frozen, an oyster enclosed in itself. Oh, if she could only cry—but tomboys don't cry and neither do sailors. She saw waves on a sea of absence, shipwrecked love. Where is Cap'n Januário Gereba, best-beloved Janu, on his voyage to the port of Bahia?

Meanwhile she let her ass fly the way he had taught her, her buttocks like deep sea waves, her undulating belly, the seed of her navel, the stem and the flower. Cold heart, icy distance. Oh, Januário Gereba, giant of the sea, king condor flying over the waves in the storm, when will I see you again, taste the salt and the sea on your breast, and die in your arms, and drown in your kiss? Oh, Januário Gereba, Captain Janu best-beloved, oh love, when, when, when will you come to me again?

The girl
who bled
the Captain
with a jerky knife

1

*You've been around some, me lad, and I don't doubt
you've seen a thing or two, but I ask you if you ever saw
a Christian marked with the pox, his flesh eaten away to
one big open sore, sewn up in a sack on his way to the
pesthouse. You tell me if you've ever carried a man in the
last throes of smallpox on your back for a good league
to the pesthouse, the pestilence stinking up the air and pus
running off the burlap like honey. I'm telling you, comrade, you should have been there to see it.*

*Believe it or not, like it or not, below God the Father it
was the whores and nobody else who faced the smallpox
when the black, rotten thing went on the rampage out
there. "Below God" is just a manner of speaking, just a
saying: God never got that far. That wasteland at the end
of the world is what you might call godforsaken, and if it
hadn't been for those poor miserable women from Soft
Chancre Street, there wouldn't have been hide nor hair
left of any living creature to tell the tale. God's got enough
to do hearing masses and things like that. With all the fine
places there are in the world for Him to rest His eyes on,
why should He bother about looking after the smallpox
victims in Buquim? Somebody did look after them, though:
none other than our own Tereza Batista, nicknamed
Tereza Knifecut, Tereza Wiggle-Hips, Tereza Seven Sighs,
and Tereza Tread-Softly. She earned every one of those
names, and one besides: Omolu's Tereza—Omolu's the
god of smallpox, you know. The voodoo worshippers gave
her that name just as the pestilence died down and people
started going back home. Tereza bit a leg off the smallpox,
chewed it up, and spat it out. She chewed it with those
filed-down teeth of hers and the gold tooth the dentist in
Aracaju put in her mouth for free—and a mighty pretty
tooth it was, too.*

That was something to see and remember, comrade. I, Maximiano Silva, called Maxi, King of the Black Gals, watchman at the Buquim Health Center, survivor and witness, I can close my eyes and to this day see Tereza, the prettiest thing you ever saw, lifting that sack up off the ground, and inside the sack young Zacarias, groaning and praying, nothing left of him but one rotting sore. I can close my eyes and see it all: there she goes, bent under the weight, shifting it onto her shoulder and walking toward the pesthouse. Tereza Ain't-Afraid-No-More, that's another name they gave her. Maybe that was the very first nickname she got a long time ago. Do you want to know how and why?

2

Tereza Batista was not quite thirteen when her aunt sold her for fifteen hundred cruzeiros, a supply of victuals, and a ring with a flashy glass stone. She sold her to Justiniano Duarte da Rosa, Captain Justo, whose reputation as a rich man, a brave man, and a bully had spread all over the back country and beyond. Wherever the Captain went, with his fighting cocks, his pack of mules, his saddle horses, his truck and fishwife, his bundle of cash, and his bodyguards, his reputation went ahead of the truck, preparing the way for good business deals.

The Captain was quick to lose his patience in an argument. What he liked to see was visible evidence of the respect his presence imposed. "They're scared shitless," he would whisper happily to Terto Cachorro, his driver and gunman, an outlaw on the lam from Pernambuco. And when Terto pulled out his knife and a roll of tobacco, fear did visibly grow around him. "It's no use trying to argue with the Captain. The more you argue, the more you lose. A man's life's not worth an ounce of strained honey to him." There were tales of ambushes and dead men and of fixed cockfights; of doctored bills sent out by his drygoods store and collected too, in return for a clout or a cuff by Chico Half-Sole, another of his thugs; of land bought under duress for the price of a hand of bananas, at rifle point or knife point; of girls raped before they were ripe—Justiniano Duarte da Rosa had a weakness for little girls. How many girls under fifteen had he deflowered? Well, under the Captain's shirt, between his fat breasts, a necklace of gold rings went jingling down the road like a rattlesnake's tail. Each ring was a little girl, every one of them less than fifteen years old; the older ones didn't count.

3

Justiniano Duarte da Rosa, all dressed up in his white suit, leather boots, and panama hat, jumped out of the cab of his truck and extended two condescending fingers to Rosalvo but his whole hand to Felipa. Wanting to show some politeness to the woman, he smiled all over his round face:

"Well, how are you, comadre? Do I deserve a glass of water?"

"Sit right down, Captain, and I'll make you some good fresh coffee."

The Captain looked out of the dirty parlor window and narrowed his greedy eyes as he stared at the girl running free in the tall grass of the meadow, climbing the guava trees, running and playing with a mongrel dog. Now she was in the top of a tree, biting into a guava. She looked like a boy, with her slender figure, her breasts hardly budding under the calico blouse, her skirt halfway up her long thighs. She was so tall and thin, and still so far from being a woman, that the neighborhood boys, who were hardly backward in their adolescent urges, who were, in fact, permanently on the lookout for likely girls to kindle their precocious desires for lascivious touching, kissing, and fondling, never paid Tereza that sort of attention. They raced with her, played cowboys-and-Indians and war games with her, and even let her be their leader, she was so agile and daring. She could beat them all in a race; she was not only faster than any of them but would climb to the highest treetops. She was still an innocent, too, lacking even the curiosity to go down to the river with Jacira, the albino girl, and fat Ceição, to spy on the boys in the swimming hole.

The Captain's eyes followed the girl as she climbed from branch to branch. Her agile movements lifted her skirt to reveal muddy drawers. Justiniano Duarte da Rosa's little eyes squinched together even tighter, the better to see and imagine; and even Rosalvo's dull tired eyes, rheumy from *cachaça* and usually staring blankly at the ground, came to life at the sight of Tereza, and moved upward along her legs and hips. From her place near the stove, Felipa did not fail to catch either Justiniano's stares or those of her husband; if she held back for even a little while longer, Rosalvo would be after the girl himself. Felipa had seen through her husband's plans for his niece long ago, and that was another compelling reason for humoring the Captain's obvious wishes. Three visits in two weeks, and all there was to show for it was a lot of jawing and beating around the bush. It was time he laid his cards on the table and got down to brass tacks. In Felipa's opinion, the preliminaries had dragged on long enough. She knew the Captain was rich, powerful, and well guarded; she knew what he wanted and knew that he could have it—why didn't he speak out and be done with it?

Or is he thinking he can have that tasty little morsel as a gift? If that's what he's thinking, he doesn't know Felipa. Captain Justo may own land and farms and cattle, and the biggest store in town; he may be an outlaw chief and widow-maker; he may be violent, wicked, anything you like; but that doesn't mean Tereza belongs to him. It wasn't Captain Justo who fed and clothed her for four-and-a-half years. If he wants her, he'll have to pay for her.

No, it hadn't been the Captain nor Rosalvo either, that rum-swilling father of indolence, old Mr. Lazybones himself, a wet rag of a man, deadweight carried on Felipa's back. They would never have taken the wretched orphaned girl into their home in the first place if he had been the one to decide. Now, though, just look at him lick his chops when she walks by. Look how greedily he watches the filling out of her figure, the budding breasts, the new curves of the buttocks; just the same way as he watches the pig getting fat in the pigsty. Pipsqueak of a man, no earthly use to anyone. All he knows how to do is eat and sleep.

Who takes care of the house, buys manioc meal and beans and jerky, the clothes on their backs, and even Rosalvo's *cachaça*? Felipa, that's who, by the work of her hands—planting, raising the animals, and selling the produce at the market on Saturdays. Not that Tereza had cost them much; actually she helped around the house and on the farm. But whatever it had cost, much or little, to buy her food and clothes and school notebooks so she could learn her ABCs and multiplication tables, the one who had paid for it was her Aunt Felipa, sister to her mother Marieta, who had been killed with her husband in a bus accident, going on five years ago. Now that she has the men after her it's only fair that it should be Felipa who pocketed whatever was to be made out of her.

Maybe she was still a little green yet; the right time hadn't yet come. If she could only be left to ripen another couple of years, then she'd be just right. It was downright wicked to turn her over to the Captain while she was still such a child, no getting around that; but Felipa would have had to be crazy to wait any longer or to try to raise objections—wait until she found the girl in bed with Rosalvo or out in the bushes with some fool boy? Make objections, stand in the way, until Justiniano hauled her off by main force, without paying a nickel? After all, Tereza would be thirteen in a few days. Felipa hadn't been much older when Porciano paid her the honor, and that same week his four brothers and his father climbed on top of her. And as if that wasn't enough, old Etelvino the grandfather, already smelling of the grave, had had a lick at her. And she hadn't died or even been any the worse for it. She had been married in church, with a priest's blessing and all. Although, to be truthful, there was no other man around with Rosalvo's vocation for growing horns. The born drunkard was also a born cuckold.

She would have to lead the conversation in such a way as to squeeze as much as possible out of the Captain; she was in urgent need of a little extra cash. She wanted to go to the dentist and fix herself up a little, buy herself some clothes and a pair of shoes. Time was going by and she was getting as ugly as a barbed-wire fence. Men didn't buzz around her any more on market day. If they stopped to look in her direction at all, it was to calculate how long it would be before Tereza was ready.

If the Captain wanted the girl, he'd have to pay a good price, not tumble her for free like he did all the others. When he found one to his taste as to greenness and prettiness, he'd hang around her parents' house pretending to be friendly, sometimes bringing a packet of coffee, now a pound or two of sugar, some pralines or molasses candy wrapped in blue paper, sweet-talking the girl with little presents of chocolate candy or a ribbon bow, and promises, promises. None more generous and open-handed than Captain Justiniano Duarte da Rosa with promises. And promises were all he ever gave.

One day without warning he'd load the girl into his truck whether she wanted to go with him or not, and just laugh in her parents' faces. And who was brave enough to protest or to file a complaint? Who was the political boss in these parts? Who picked the sheriff? Weren't the soldiers in the place just the Captain's gunmen, maintained at state expense? As for his honor the judge, he bought on credit at Justiniano's store and owed him plenty. Nothing too peculiar about that, when he had a wife and three children still in school and all living in the capital, while he kept a free-spending mistress here in this dreary hole; and all on a magistrate's puny salary. I ask you, what else can he do?

One time a complaint was filed by a certain Venceslau, the father of a girl with a pert bosom, named Diva. Justiniano had stopped his truck at their door, beckoned to the girl, and driven off with her without a word of explanation. Venceslau ran to the judge and the sheriff, full of big talk about crippling and killing. The judge promised to investigate and found that the girl had been neither ravished nor deflowered; whereupon the sheriff, who had promised fast action, acted fast: he threw the plaintiff in jail for disturbing the peace by slandering honest citizens, and in order to curtail Venceslau's taste for threats and impose respect for the law, ordered him whipped with a knife to teach him a lesson. But then again, when he was let out of jail next day the afflicted father found his daughter Diva waiting for him at the door of their house, a little mussed up by the Captain. She had already been penetrated a long time ago, the little bitch.

Felipa had no intention of making a fuss or filing any

complaint; she would have had to be out of her mind to set herself against Justiniano Duarte da Rosa. Besides, she knew perfectly well that Tereza would take up with somebody else sooner or later; that is, if she didn't run off into the bushes and come back with a full belly after some fool kid had knocked her up, if not Rosalvo himself. Yes, Rosalvo, the shameless old cuckold. And for free.

Felipa only wanted to bargain and make a little on the deal. Tereza was the only capital she had left. If she had only been able to wait a few more years, she could have made a better deal, no doubt about that; the girl was developing in a very promising way, and the women in the family were all beauties, fatal and fought over. Yes, even Felipa. Even now when she was almost ready for the trash heap, she still had a trace of her old proud bearing, a reminiscent swing of the hips and flash of the eyes. If it only hadn't happened so soon! But the Captain had made up his mind. There was nothing Felipa could do.

4

Felipa broke the meaningful, calculated silence.

"Tereza!" she called. "Come here, confound you."

"Did you call me, Aunt Felipa?"

The girl swallowed the last piece of guava, swung down from the tree, and came running into the house, her coppery face glowing with perspiration, joy in her eyes and on her lips.

"Come and serve the coffee."

Still smiling, Tereza went to get the tin tray. In the hall her aunt gripped her by the arm and turned her this way and that, showing her off as if accidentally.

"Where are your manners? Don't you see we have company? Ask the Captain for his blessing first."

Tereza lifted the pudgy, sweaty hand and touched her lips to the fingers laden with gold and diamond rings. She especially noticed the prettiest one of all; it had a green stone in it.

"May I have your blessing, Captain?"

"God bless you." The hand touched the girl's head and then slid to her shoulder.

Tereza bent on one knee to Rosalvo.

"Your blessing, uncle."

A gust of anger swelled in Rosalvo's throat, strangling the breath out of him. Ah, that dream he had cherished for so many long years as he watched her grow and develop day after day and guessed at the rare beauty to come, when she would be a more perfect replica of what her mother Marieta had been in all the splendor of her beauty, of what her Aunt Felipa had been in her heyday, so ravishing that Rosalvo had rescued her from a life of sin and married her. How long had he held in his impatience, letting his eagerness build up, and craftily laying his plans? And now suddenly he saw it all slipping away from him, like water flowing downstream. The truck waited at the door with Terto Cachorro at the wheel. At the time of the Captain's first visit, Rosalvo had seen the writing on the wall. Why the devil hadn't he acted then? Why hadn't he put ahead the clock, the almanac, the calendar of death? Because it was too soon, she hadn't even reached puberty yet, as Rosalvo knew very well. Who knew better than he? Hadn't he spied on her often enough at dawn? She's not ready for a man yet, Felipa. How can you sell a niece, the orphan child of your own dead sister? I've waited patiently and longingly, Felipa, all those years; and you know good and well the Captain's house is a hellhole. Your own sister's child, Felipa. The thing you are about to do is a sin, a mortal sin. Aren't you afraid God will punish you?

"She's getting to be a big girl," commented Justiniano Duarte da Rosa, moistening his thick lips with his tongue, a yellow gleam in his small porcine eyes.

"She's a big girl already," Felipa declared, opening the negotiations.

But that's an out-and-out lie and you know it, Felipa, you damned heartless old whore. The days of the moon haven't come for her yet, she hasn't bled yet, she's still a child and your own niece by blood——Rosalvo pressed his hand to his mouth to keep from crying out. Ah, if she were a big girl and ready for a man I'd have made her a woman by now. I've done everything but dig your grave, you miserable merciless stone-hearted woman, bargaining away your own niece. Rosalvo lowered his head; his disappointment was less than his rage and his fear.

The Captain stretched his short legs, rubbed one hand against the other and asked, "How much, comadre?"

Tereza had vanished out the kitchen door. She reappeared in the yard, playing with the dog, both of them running and rolling on the ground. The dog barked and Tereza laughed, a country animal herself, and just as healthy and innocent. Captain Justo touched his necklace of maidenheads, his small eyes almost squinched shut.

"Tell me your price."

5

Justiniano Duarte da Rosa took a packet of bills from his pocket and began to count them out, slowly, reluctantly, one by one. He never did enjoy saying good-bye to his money and felt an almost physical pain whenever he absolutely had to pay it out, give or return it.

"This is only out of consideration for you because, like you say, you brought the girl up and fed her and gave her an education. But I'm only helping you out like this because I want to. If I took a notion to just carry her off, who do you think would stop me?" He shot a scornful glance at Rosalvo and moistened his finger with his tongue so that he could separate the bills more easily.

Rosalvo sat with his dull eyes fixed on the ground. He was filled with rage, fear, and impotence as he heard the money changing hands. He'd never even see the color of the money that devil of a woman he was married to had finagled so skillfully—not unless he could manage to steal it, and that would be a risky business. Oh, why had he kept waiting around, when he had had the plan worked out in his head, step by step, such a long time ago? It was simple, easy, and quick. The hardest part would be digging the hole to bury the body in, but he had counted on Tereza's helping with that when the time came. After all, Tereza would benefit more than anybody from Felipa's death. Wouldn't she be free of domestic tyranny, promoted to be Rosalvo's wife and the mistress of the house, the farm, the chickens, and the hog? For months and months, as he watched his niece growing into a woman, he had elaborated and perfected his scheme. He had noted the budding seeds of Tereza's nipples, the sprouting of the first hairs at the base of her golden belly. Ah, to think of the day when she would be a woman, and ready! On that day of jubilee he would bring what he needed from his cache in the woods and that night he would finish the job. A hoe is a tool of many uses; it would serve to do away with Felipa and dig her grave besides—a shallow one without cross or epitaph. Damn her, she didn't deserve them. Rosalvo had stolen the hoe at Timoteo's farm more than six months before. More than six months ago he had made up his mind to kill Felipa as soon as Tereza reached puberty.

It had never occurred to him that their neighbors and acquaintances might be puzzled by Felipa's disappearance and start asking questions that would lead to an investigation. Much less had it ever entered his mind that Tereza might protest or stick up for her aunt; that she might refuse to help him or not want him as a man. So many contradictory possibilities were too much for Rosalvo's mind to contain. It had been more than enough for him just thinking about stealing the hoe and a rope, and working out the details of his plan to put the quietus on Felipa, when the she-devil was asleep. Trying to do it while she was awake was obviously impossible; then somebody else would be the corpse. As he lay in bed beside his wife, Rosalvo could see the hoe smashing in her skull and face. He could see her battered features, a mass of blood in the black night: go get you a man in hell, you dirty old bitch. He could hear the sound of the hoe splintering bone and cartilage in the stillness of the nocturnal countryside, and he trembled with joy. But Rosalvo had not ventured beyond plots and imaginings. They more than filled his empty days, giving his *cachaça* a better flavor and putting some hope into his existence. Life and death would spring together from Tereza's first bleeding: life for Rosalvo, death for Felipa.

And now the Captain's hands were crumbling those plans and dreams to dust, and with Felipa to thank for it—that woman so full of evil that she was ready to sell her own orphaned niece, her sister's daughter, who had no one else in the world. Why, why hadn't he carried out his fine scheme before now? Why had he waited for Tereza's blood to run down and dye her little gold rose, waited for her to be ready and willing? Why hadn't he acted? Why hadn't he hurried on the hour of living and dying? What would have been the harm in that? Now it was the Captain who would do it. Felipa had just sold a child, a little girl, a baby; her niece and an orphan. It was a mortal sin.

"Well, who would have stopped me?" Justiniano turned toward Rosalvo. "Would anyone have had the guts to stop me, Rosalvo? You, for example?"

Rosalvo's voice came from out of the ground, from the dust, from the caverns where fear cowers:

"Nobody, sir. Me? God forbid."

Now that the seal had been made and the crucial moment when the money was to be paid over had come, Felipa relaxed a little into cordiality, but remained cautious and firm even so:

"Now, I ask you, Captain, where could you find a handier girl? She can do most any kind of work around the house and farm, she can read and figure, there's nobody like her at selling in the market, and pretty? Is there a girl in this town who can touch her for looks? You'd have to go to the capital to find anybody to compare with her, and even there you'd have to look hard. And who's going to have all the good of her? It's you, Captain, isn't it?"

Slowly the money changed hands. If only he doesn't back out now and renege on his bargain! If only he keeps his word!

"I'm telling you, Captain, somebody's already been here wanting to marry Tereza; and not a nobody, either, but a fine upstanding young man, believe it or not."

"Wanting to marry her? And who was that, may I ask?"

"Seu Joventino. I don't know if you know him, a young fellow with a corn and manioc farm about three leagues from here, over towards the river. A fine, hardworking man."

Rosalvo remembered him, all right. On Saturdays at the Market, when he had sold his wagonload of corn, manioc root, yams, or flour, Joventino would come over and strike up a conversation with them, telling anecdotes and commenting on the events of the day. Wouldn't leave them alone, in fact. Felipa puffed herself up, thinking all this flattering attention was for her, but Rosalvo had seen what he was really after: he wanted the girl, of course. What he wanted to do was to send the fellow packing, but he couldn't find any excuse; Joventino was a model of discretion who limited himself to an occasional meaningful glance or word. Besides, he always stood Rosalvo to a drink, and offered beer to Felipa and *guaraná* to Tereza. And when he was around, Felipa swung her ass just like old times.

Then one Sunday Joventino turned up at the farm, all slicked up with a necktie and all, and began to talk marriage. Well, it really had been funny; Rosalvo couldn't help laughing. Felipa was as mad as a wet hen. She had spent half an hour primping in her room while the boy sat in the parlor with Rosalvo and shared a bottle of rum; and when she finally made her appearance, all dressed up and smelling sweet, instead of a gallant admirer, what she'd found was a suitor for her niece's hand. She almost kicked the young man out the door. Was that any kind of proposal to make? Who ever heard of marrying a twelve-year-old baby? Why, she's not even half grown! It's ridiculous! Oh, what an indignant, outraged aunt she'd been.

"I'll be back," Joventino announced as he took his departure.

But Joventino wouldn't be the one to enjoy her. Oh, no! and neither would Rosalvo. Finally the Captain finished counting the fifteen hundred cruzeiros for the second time. It's a lot of money, Dona Felipa.

"Here's the cash. Count it again if you want to while I make out the order."

He tore off a sheet from his little notepad, laboriously scratched in the sum, and signed with an elaborate signature full of curlicues, of which he was very proud.

"Here's an authorization for what you can buy at the store. You can either use it all at once, or a little bit at a time. But a hundred cruzeiros, remember; not a penny more."

Rosalvo raised his eyes and looked at the money. Felipa folded the bills, put them carefully inside the paper on which Captain Justo had scribbled the order, and secreted the packet in the waist of her skirt. She held out her hand.

"What do you want?" asked Justiniano Duarte da Rosa.

"The ring. You said you'd throw in the ring."

"I said I'd give it to the girl. It's her dowry." He laughed: Justiniano Duarte da Rosa didn't leave anybody out in the cold.

"I'll keep it for her, Captain. A girl that age has no sense of what things are worth. She'd only lose it or forget where she put it. I'll keep it safe for her. After all, she's my own niece. She's got no father or mother."

The Captain stared at the terrible gypsy standing before him.

"That was part of the bargain, wasn't it, Captain?"

He had brought the ring along to give to the girl, to help win her over. It was just a piece of junk, gold-colored tin with a glass stone. He took off his finger the imitation gold, the glass emerald, the showy green stone. After all, he didn't have any more need to make up to the girl. He'd paid the price put on her, and now she was his.

Felipa rubbed the ring on the hem of her dress, put it on her finger, and looked at it against the light with satisfaction. There was nothing she loved better than necklaces, bracelets, rings. Every scrap of money she could save she spent buying gewgaws from the peddlers.

Captain Justo stretched his legs and stood up. The necklace of gold rings, the virgins' rattle-gourd, jingled on his neck. Tomorrow there would be a new ring, made of eighteen-carat gold.

"Well, call the girl, and I'll be on my way."

6

Still admiring the ring, Felipa called out:

"Tereza! Tereza! Come here quick!"

Girl and dog appeared at the door expectantly.

"Did you call me, Aunt Felipa?"

Ah, if only Rosalvo weren't chained to the floor, if only a spark were to kindle in his heart, bringing him to his feet to confront Felipa, the lord and master, as a husband was meant to be! Rosalvo locked his lips on the curses and insults that were choking him. Felipa, that woman with no soul, no bowels of compassion; that heartless, un-natural mother! One day you'll pay for your monstrous sin, Felipa; God will call you to account for selling an orphan niece brought up as a daughter—our daughter, Felipa, sold like a four-footed beast. Our daughter. You're a plague-ridden, filthy beast yourself, woman.

Still enthralled by the ring, Felipa spoke in an almost affectionate tone:

"Tereza, go get your things together, all of them. You're going away with the Captain to live in his house. The Captain will bring you up from now on. You'll have every-thing there you could want; you'll live like a lady. The Captain's a good man."

Tereza did not usually need to be told anything twice. At school Miss Mercedes, her teacher, had always praised her quick understanding, her keen intelligence and powers of reasoning. She had learned to read and write in a flash. But this piece of news was something Tereza couldn't understand.

"Go live in the Captain's house? Why, Aunt Felipa?"

It was Justiniano Duarte da Rosa himself who an-swered in a masterful voice. He stood up and stretched a hand out toward the girl.

"You don't need to know why. No more questions now. With me, to hear is to obey, remember that. You'd better get it in your head once and for all. Now come on."

Tereza retreated from the doorway but not quite quickly enough; the Captain caught her by the arm. Stocky and stout, not very tall and with a round neckless head, Jus-tiniano was nonetheless agile and strong, light and fast on his feet, a good dancer who could also break a brick with one blow of his fist.

"Let's go." Tereza lashed out at him. "You're coming with me."

He was about to push her in front of him when the girl bit his hand as hard as she could, out of sheer fury. Her teeth left blood on his fat, hairy paw. The Captain let go and she was off like an arrow into the woods.

"She bit me, the god-damned little bitch. She'll pay for that. Terto! Terto!" he shouted at his bodyguard, who was snoring in the cab of the truck. "Over here, Terto! And you two"—he turned to Tereza's aunt and uncle—

"you come on and help me catch that damned tomboy. I don't have any more time to waste."

Along with Terto Cachorro, he and Felipa started into the yard.

"What's Rosalvo think he's doing, just standing there?" Felipa whirled round toward her husband.

"Ain't you coming? I know what you're after and you've got your nerve, you shameless old mule. Come on and get a move on before I really get mad."

What a rotten hopeless life. What could he do but join the rest? But not because I want to. What a terrible sin. This sin isn't mine, Lord, you know it isn't; it's hers, the old whore's; it's that she-devil's sin. She knows good and well that the Captain's house is hell on earth. Rosalvo trailed along with the others to hunt for Tereza.

The hunt lasted an hour, maybe more—the Captain neglected to check the time on his chronometrically accurate wristwatch—and they all had their tongues hanging out when they finally cornered the girl in a tangled thicket. Rosalvo tiptoed around behind, and the mongrel dog, on the watch for the strangers, didn't bark at him. Rosalvo touched Tereza for the last time. He clasped her in his arms, pressed her hard against his chest and legs, hugging her to him before delivering her over to her enemy.

Terto aimed a vicious kick at the dog, leaving it stretched on the ground with a shattered paw, and went to help Rosalvo. He seized Tereza by one arm, and Rosalvo, white-faced, undone with pleasure and fear, held the other. She struggled and tried to bite them, her eyes blazing. The Captain came up quietly, stopped in front of her, and hit her face with his big, fleshy open hand. Once, twice, three times, four. A trickle of blood ran from her nose, and Tereza choked back a dry sob. She didn't cry. Leaders don't cry—she'd learned that from the boys when they played war.

"Come on, now!"

He and Terto dragged her to the truck. Felipa went into the house, flashing her green stone in the sun. At first Rosalvo stood stock still, exhausted; then he walked over to the dog. The animal whined from the pain of its broken bone.

On the running board of the truck, gay, blue-painted letters said: STEP UP TO FATE. Justiniano Duarte da Rosa

slapped her again, hard, to make her get in. And so
Tereza Batista set off to meet her fate: pestilence, famine,
and war.

7

They threw her inside a room and latched the door on the
outside. When they got out of the truck, Justiniano and
Terto had had to drag her by her arms and legs. The dark
little room at the back of the house had only one window
(too high up, darn it) through whose panes a little light
and air filtered. On the floor was a wide double mattress
with sheets and pillows, and a chamber pot. On one
wall hung a reproduction of an Annunciation, with Mary
and the Angel Gabriel in color, and a rawhide whip.
There had once been a bed, but since the slats had twice
given way during first-night skirmishes—once with black
Ondina, a very devil on the rampage, and a second time
with Gracinha, so scared and crazy she belonged in a
madhouse—Justiniano had decided to dispense with the
bed. A plain mattress on the tiled floor was more convenient and a whole lot simpler.

In the Captain's house in town, behind the store, there
was another room just like this one in the farmhouse.
Almost identical, both were dedicated to the same enjoy-
able purpose: Captain Justo's nuptials with the maidens
he gathered on his quests and errands. He preferred very
young ones, the younger the better, and they must be
guaranteed to have their maidenheads intact. They should
be girls under fifteen, still smelling of milk, as Veneranda
had said when she confided Zefa Dutra to him (Veneranda kept a high-class whorehouse in Aracaju and had
literary inclinations). Zefa still smelled of milk all right,
but she'd been earning her living in the oldest profession
for more than a year. What Veneranda needed was a good
beating. Girls under fifteen—if they were really virgins,
that is—deserved the honor of a link in the gold chain.
In that particular, Justiniano Duarte da Rosa always acted
with the strictest punctilio. Justiniano collected girls just as
some other people collect stamps—thousands and thousands of people all over the world, in fact, from the late

King of England to Zoroastro Curinga, a clerk at the post office and a shrewd rascal; and others collect daggers, like Mílton Guedes, one of the sugarmill owners; or, in the capital, some people collect old worm-eaten statues of saints, or matchboxes, or porcelain and ivory, or even clay figurines—the kind they sell at the fairs. Justiniano tracked down and captured quarry varying in color and age; some were even over twenty-one and their own mistresses. But the only ones who counted in his collection were the real children, the little girls who "smelled of milk." The honor of being a gold ring on the necklace was reserved for children under fifteen.

Many were the girls he'd tumbled, on the farmhouse mattress and on that other one in town. A few of them, usually the older ones, were used to necking and fooling around and knew more or less what was coming, but most of them were fearful, if not terrified, and tried to escape by hiding in corners where the sportive Captain could give chase. Once one of them had wet herself with fear when he caught and grabbed her. The piddle had run down her legs onto the mattress; it was crazy and exciting. Justiniano still got gooseflesh with pleasure when he thought of it.

Sportsman that he was, the Captain naturally preferred girls who offered some initial resistance. The easy, more-or-less knowledgeable and practiced ones, did not give him the same exultant thrill of power, of victory, of arduous conquest.

Timidity, shame, resistance, rebellion, anything which obliged him to resort to violence in teaching the proper fear and respect due their master, lord, and lover; kisses wrung from them with blows—these added new dimensions to pleasure, making it deeper and more satisfying. Usually the thing ended well enough, with a few slaps, a few blows, sometimes a spanking, but almost never a real beating with a belt or the rawhide strap. It was the strap, though, that made Ondina open her legs. By the time a week or two had passed, at most, the lucky girl was drooling over him and couldn't think of anything else. Some of them were so crazy about him they got to be a pain in the ass, and those didn't last long as favorites. That Gracinha, for instance; she'd been so terrified he had had to beat her unconscious so that he could enjoy her in peace.

And not a week after that bitter night when she learned fear and respect, she began to sigh with impatience, and even had the nerve to chase after him when he wasn't in the humor.

On his frequent business trips to Aracaju, Veneranda would laugh mockingly as she propositioned him about some new girl who was supposed to be a virgin but who had almost always had a tumble or two in the hay. Veneranda's house was a luxurious chateau which enjoyed semiofficial status, frequented as it was by numerous politicians, the noble governor himself at the head of the band. (It was, in fact, the best government department in the state, according to Lulu Santos, who could always be found there on his crutches.) Judges of the lower and upper courts were habitués also, and bankers and entrepreneurs; it also had police protection. (To quote the aforementioned authority again, it was the most decent, orderly place in Aracaju, including the homes of the best families.) No one could remember more than one occasion when the tranquil atmosphere so necessary to the comfort and performance of its eminent clientele was shattered; and the man who shattered it was Captain Justo, trying to demolish everything in the room where he had discovered that the old pumice trick had been played on him to make him think a new girl from the interior still had an intact hymen. Once his rage had subsided and all the uproar had died down, though, the Captain and Veneranda became friends; and from then on the madam, with her literary turn of mind, always referred to him as "the wild man from Cajazeiras do Norte, the great explorer of virgin forests." The best thing in Veneranda's castle was the gringas imported from the South, French girls from Rio and São Paulo, Poles from Paraná, Germans from Santa Catarina, all platinum blondes who would do anything. The Captain was not one to scorn gringas. On the contrary, he appreciated their talents to the full.

The suburbs, the slums, neighboring villages and towns, and above all the poverty-stricken countryside—why, the whole place was running over with girls whose families wanted to sell them. Raimundo Alicate, a tenant farmer on land owned by the sugarmill, provided the Captain with girls in return for small favors. A fellow who went to all the parties, a drummer who knew a lot of *caboclos,* Raimundo had a flair for smelling out good-quality heifers; and when he said "She's a virgin," that's what you could bet she was. Then Gabi, who ran a little whorehouse in town, managed to turn up a fair piece of goods from time to time. You had to be careful of the old bawd, though; she'd sell you something shopworn whenever she could. More than once Justiniano had threatened to close her place down. It didn't do any good, though; the old fraud always went back to her old tricks.

The best girls were the ones he found for himself—on farms, clerking at stores, at country dances, and on his travels hither and yon with his fighting cocks. Often they cost very little; they came to him cheap, for nothing almost, in exchange for a trifle. A few came higher, and had to be paid for in presents and even cash. So far Tereza had cost the most, if he didn't count Doris.

Should Doris be on the list? Things had been different with her; he'd had to get himself engaged and married before both a priest and a judge to get her. And she hadn't been deflowered in either one of the two dark little bedrooms, but in her own virginal chamber in the house on Cathedral Square. When the civil and religious ceremonies were finally over, "the lovely, beaming bride who sets her feet today on the flowery path of wedded bliss," as Father Cirilo had put it so poetically, went to change her diapers for a traveling dress in which to board the train for her honeymoon. My God! She had a dress for every hour of the day, every one as expensive as they come!

No, he hadn't fucked her for the first time on a mattress in a cubicle with no bed, nor yet in the elegant room of the Hotel Meridional in Bahia, where they spent their honeymoon. He had done it right there in her bedroom, with only a wall between it and the parlor full of all the convivial guests Justiniano's mother-in-law had corralled to demolish the houseful of food and the fountains of liquor he'd provided. Right then and there the Captain had started getting his money's worth for all the extravagant expense he'd been put to.

He followed Doris into her room and began at once to undress her, tearing off her veil, wreath, and bridal dress in his impatience to crunch her frail bones. The finger on his lips warned her to be silent: all the most important people in town, the crème de la crème, were

guzzling as greedily as rats in the next room. The house
was full of them; Doris couldn't make a sound without
their hearing her.

Buttons leaped from her bodice and Justiniano Duarte
da Rosa's heavy hands tore the lace of her panties. Doris's
eyes grew wide and she crossed her arms on her tubercular chest. She could not suppress a convulsive shiver. Her
one desire was to shout, to cry out in such a loud voice
that the whole town would come running. The Captain
saw her trembling, her eyes distended, her arms crossed
on her birdlike chest. Her fear and excitement were so
great that the grimace of her lips as she stifled her sobs
was like a smile. He licked his lips as he tore off his coat
and his brand-new trousers. That girl had cost him a
fortune: credit at his drygoods store, dresses and parties,
all sorts of miscellaneous expenses, a paid-off mortgage,
and a wedding besides.

8

Justiniano Duarte da Rosa had already had his thirty-
sixth birthday when he was united in holy matrimony to
fourteen-year-old Doris, only child of Dr. Ubaldo Curvelo, deceased, former mayor, leader of the opposition,
and physician, whose death was lamented throughout
Cajazeiras. Besides a mortgaged house and a pile of his
patients' unpaid bills, all he left his wife and twelve-year-
old daughter at his death were a revered memory and a
reputation for honesty and administrative ability as a politician, and skill and compassion as a doctor: "The brain of
a great diagnostician," according to the pharmacist, Trigueiros; "God's gift to the poor," according to a consensus
of those who knew him.

As long as the doctor was alive, they managed well
enough. As director of the largest clinic in a town where
four doctors were struggling to make a living, he had been
able not only to support his family but even to indulge
Dona Brígida in the little ostentatious luxuries that were
her due as the community's indisputable first lady, and to
buy and pay for a house on Cathedral Square. True, a
good many of his patients were poor devils who didn't

even own enough land to be buried in. Many walked miles and miles to consult the doctor. The more prosperous paid with yams, manioc root, a pumpkin, or a jack fruit, while others could not even afford that but could only murmur an abashed "God will repay you, Doctor." He even gave some of them the money to buy the medicines he prescribed, for in that border country there is no limit to the poverty. But with all this and Dona Brígida's taste for luxury besides, the doctor might have left them at least a small nest egg, if he had not gone into politics at his friends' behest and out of respect for his wife, whose father had once been elected to the town council.

He was left a defeated, disillusioned, penniless man as a result of three successive demands: first, his mayoral campaign, contributions to his party, and then the years when his public duties left him little time in which to run the clinic; second, mortgaging his house to cover up and repay funds embezzled by Cintra, treasurer of the Quartermaster Corps and a staunch party member, to whose efforts the doctor's election was largely due; and third, a second campaign, in which he suffered ruinous defeat.

He came out of the electoral race with shattered nerves and a heart like a heavy stone in his chest. His former joviality had been eaten away by his troubles, and he had become a sad, impatient man. He would not have been able to leave behind him even his reputation for kindness and charity if he had not died soon afterward of a coronary occlusion. When Dona Brígida was able to dry her tears long enough to look at the inventory of their possessions, she found that she had nothing except a pittance of a pension as widow of a public-health physician, and the patients' uncollectible bills.

Two years had passed since Dr. Ubaldo Curvelo's memorable funeral, in which all of Cajazeiras—rich and poor, members of his party and his adversaries, the members of the government and the out-of-power, elementary-school pupils and high-school students—had followed the procession from church to cemetery. Now Dona Brígida and Doris could no longer keep their heads above water: the mortgage was going to be foreclosed, they could not live on the monthly pension, and they could get no more credit. Dona Brígida could keep up appearances no longer, for all her mending of dresses and frantic efforts to hide their pitiful economies and vicissitudes. Storekeepers began to insist on cash. The doctor's blessed memory began to grow fainter, then to fade away with the passage of time until not enough of it was left for them to live on.

Dona Brígida realized that she was about to be deposed as Queen Mother. First Lady of the township as long as her husband presided as mayor, his death had not made her lose her majesty; in fact, she had become even more haughty and arrogant. One of the old comadres of the town, Dona Ponciana de Azevedo, a notorious gossip worthy of a wider field in which to exercise her talents, had dubbed Dona Brígida "Queen Mother" during a meeting of the patronesses of Our Lady St. Anne's Feast Day; but she had wasted her time and venom. Dona Brígida liked the new title and felt it suited her.

She continued to cling aristocratically to her mantle and scepter even when hard times came upon her, but no one was fooled. One quiet night the vengeful, persistent Dona Ponciana slid a newspaper clipping under Dona Brígida's door: "Queen of Serbia Starving in Exile; Pawns Jewels." Jewels—in the old days she had owned a few good pieces of jewelry, but she had sold the last rings to a Turk from Bahia, a haggler who went from house to house buying gold and silver, dilapidated statues of saints, the antique furniture that had newly come into style, even procelain chamber pots and spittoons. Neither she nor her daughter had quite felt the pangs of hunger yet when Captain Justo's unexpected generosity, coming just when the other merchants had cut off their credit, saved them in the nick of time.

Generosity was not quite the right word, perhaps. A man of limited refinement, Justiniano Duarte da Rosa was not one to make delicate hints or beat around the bush. One day he stopped by the window from which Dona Brígida commanded a view of the street, and without so much as a good-day, came rudely and directly to the point:

"I know you've been having a rough time, ma'am, and there isn't a store left where you can buy on credit. Well, from now on you can buy anything you want, and

as much as you want, in my store. The doctor had a
grudge against me but he was a *prócer* all the same."

The Captain had learned the word *prócer* on a recent
trip to the state capital. Someone had introduced him to
a member of the secretariat as they were walking by the
city hall by saying: "Dr. Dias is a *prócer* of the government." Justiniano had relished the term especially because
his acquaintance had applied it also to him: "Your Excellency, Captain Justiniano has a lot of prestige up there
in the *sertão*. He'll be a *prócer* too, before long." He
quite happily treated the fellow—a sometime journalist
hoping to cadge a meal—to beer and cigars; and setting
vanity aside, asked:

"What the devil *is* a *prócer?* Some of those foreign
words, I don't always know what they mean—"

"A *prócer* is a civic or political leader, an important
personage, a man of eminence of proven worth—for
example, Rui Barbosa, J. J. Seabra, Goes Calmon, Colonel Franklin. . . ."

"Is it French or English?"

"German," said the charlatan, adding even more luster to the word as he ordered another beer.

Prócers have certain obligations toward one another,
unless they are on opposite sides in a political campaign.
And even such differences are erased by death: what has
been said is now unsaid, offenses are buried with the
dead. The doctor had been a *prócer,* and that was that.
Your credit is good at my store, ma'am.

Such an offer was too good to be true, of course, and a
few days later Dona Brígida discovered what was behind
the Captain's proffered credit. She all but fell to the
ground in a dead faint—No! Impossible! She couldn't believe the evidence of her senses. It was a boundless, unthinkable absurdity, and yet it was also a patent, inescap-
able fact: the Captain had his eye on her Doris and was
hanging around her skirts.

Short skirts and low-heeled shoes: Dona Brígida had
not promoted her daughter to the status of a young lady
in spite of her fourteen years and the onset of her periods.
She kept her a child because it was cheaper, and more
appropriate to her situation and lack of prospects. It
had never once crossed Dona Brígida's mind—that was
the stark, naked truth—that anyone could ever be

interested in Doris. Silent, uncommunicative, a difficult temperament, wrapped up in herself, without friends, Doris thought of nothing but church, masses, and novenas. "That one's cut out for a nun," the old wives always said, and Dona Brígida voiced no objection. As far as she could see, there was no other course, no better solution.

Doris had inherited her father's nerves. She was easily wounded, cried over nothing, and lurked sulkily in corners, rosary in hand. Then there was her utter lack of physical charm, a point on which Dona Brígida preferred to remain silent. Not that Doris's face was unattractive, with its large, light, startled eyes and blond bangs; but her figure was a calamity—a bundle of bones, with legs like twigs, a flat chest, and nothing to her breasts. She had never had a boyfriend. Dona Brígida, whose maternal love no one could presume to doubt, used to clasp her daughter to her opulent Queen Mother's bosom and exclaim dramatically: "My poor little Cinderella!" Yes, all the signs pointed to Jesus as the enchanted prince for this backwoods Cinderella; the nuns at the high school and the hospital nurtured her undeclared vocation, and her cruel schoolmates called her Sister Skeleton.

And now, if you please, here came the Captain! No schoolmate, not even a boy in the street, had ever looked into Doris's eyes with either tenderness or lust; none had ever tried to take her behind the hill, the classic lover's lane where most of the girls went after school to learn the rudiments of another kind of knowledge. Doris only knew of such things by hearsay. The other girls took sadistic pleasure in confiding, with much exciting detail, their tales of kisses, clutchings, and heavy petting. In their vanity they showed her their bitten lips and the purple marks on their necks. Doris heard them out in silence, without a change of expression, a laugh, or a comment. No boy had ever invited her to walk around the hill with him.

And here was the Captain, a rich, mature man, a confirmed bachelor supposedly, who couldn't take his eyes off the skinny girl. Whoever would have dreamed such a thing could happen? Captain Justo, with his bad reputation—his terrible reputation, in fact; it would be impossible to have a worse one. He was respected, of course, thanks to his money and his bodyguards, but in the final analysis he was nothing but a shrewd little local boss, albeit an overbearing, violent, and anguinary one. Even Dr. Ubaldo, who had never spoken ill of anyone before he entered politics and was, if anything, too tolerant of other people's shortcomings, had despised Justiniano, whom he called "that monster." One reason the doctor had been elected, though he belonged to the party out of power, was his courage in speaking out publicly in condemnation of the unholy alliance against the town, consisting of the Captain, the former mayor, and the sheriff. So many scandals were brought out into the open that the Guedeses, who constituted the town's unofficial guardians, were roused to the point of withdrawing their decisive support of the "shady clique in power." Once in office, however, the doctor found he could do little or nothing against the men he had accused; he had neither solid proof of malfeasance nor the solid support of the townspeople. He had to be content to govern honestly; too honestly, from the point of view of the Guedeses. Everything should have a limit, even administrative honesty; and a politician incapable of recognizing the subtle distinction between "honest" and "too honest" is doomed to a brief career in public office. From their distant plantations, from the big house at the sugarmill, the Guedeses first elected, then defeated Dr. Ubaldo Curvelo, that intemperately honest man. Captain Justo had been kept on a tight rein during the doctor's term of office and had received the affront of having two of his gunmen arrested at a cockfight. At news of Dr. Ubaldo's defeat for reelection, Justiniano Duarte da Rosa galloped his horse across the main street and plaza, firing his pistol in the air. Horses' hooves and gunfire imposed a new reign of terror before the new mayor even took office.

And now, here was Justiniano Duarte da Rosa, better known as Captain Justo, coming along the sidewalk eyeing the girl. He had even been seen in the cathedral at vespers, his little pig eyes fixed on Doris there in the twilight.

Dona Brígida put her hands to her temples—Good Lord, what should she do? She longed to run to Father Cirilo or her friend Teca Menezes, or else to Trigueiros the pharmacist, to talk it all over; but prudence held her back. Before discussing the matter with anyone, she must work things out in her own mind; there was more than enough material to give her food for thought.

After supper the widow and her neighbors brought their chairs out to the sidewalk to enjoy the cool of the evening while they indulged in their favorite, unrivaled pastime of cutting people to ribbons. Doris listened in silence. There was no forgiveness and no immunity from the gossip mill: all storekeepers were thieves, all husbands philanderers, and all girls shameless, not to speak of the adulterers and complaisant cuckolds.

The Captain's footsteps were heard, and a nervous, expectant silence fell on the group. All eyes were on Justiniano, and his eyes were on Doris. Dona Brígida had an impulse to rise and usher her daughter ostentatiously indoors, slamming the door behind her. But once again prudence held her back. She answered the monster's greeting civilly, and smiled.

9

Dona Brígida passed many bitter, sleepless nights and tormented days, weighing the pros and cons, analyzing the situation and speculating about her daughter's future. All the calculations and decisions were up to her; the innocent girl lived in another world, and her only real interest was church. She paid no attention in school, was the worst possible company for any kind of party or fun, and it was no use even talking about boyfriends or flirtations, poor little thing.

One might say Doris was born an old maid: she was predisposed that way by temperament and disposition, and it was difficult enough at best for any girl to get herself engaged and married in that little whistle-stop of a town, with its plethora of marriageable girls and scarcity of suitors. The boys no sooner began to grow pinfeathers than they headed south in search of opportunities their hometown couldn't afford. The city budget was supported almost exclusively by taxes paid by the sugarmill, the property of the Guedes family. They owned banks in the capital and all the really fertile land along the river where the sugarcane grew, their green fields in vivid contrast to

the desert around them. The mill gave employment to a
few privileged men; the puny local trade—small shops
and grocery stores—made room for a few others; and
the rest took the train south. The girls fought bitterly over
those that remained. To the delight of the gossips, every
so often some girl would drag her family's good name in
the dirt by stepping out arm in arm with some traveling
salesman who was married and the father of a family;
anything was better than going quietly mad as an old maid.

The Guedeses were rarely seen in town. The three
brothers, with their wives and children and other kin,
came and went directly from the capital to the sugarmill,
boarding the train at a special stop in the middle of the
canefields. Their townhouse on Convent Square was closed
up all year, and no one but Seu Lírio, the gardener and
watchman, wandered about under the ancient trees. Once
in a great while, every two or three years perhaps, one of
the brothers would bring his wife and family to town to
celebrate the Feast of St. Anne, the patron saint of their
family as well as the town. Windows would be thrown
open, laughter echoed through the rooms and corridors,
and guests from the capital would fill the house. The local
girls would buzz with excitement; the visiting boys were
like bees in clover. The party would last a week or ten
days, two weeks at most. Kissed and squeezed and pawed,
virgins still but on fire, the girls would be abandoned just
when the fun was at its height, to go back to their unin-
teresting schoolmates and insignificant salesclerks, back to
their homes and the church socials, old maids at twenty.
Even if they had wanted to lie on the Captain's mattress,
they were too old and experienced to interest him.

What on earth could Doris hope for, growing up in that
dull place? Once in possession of her diploma from the
convent high school, she could do one of two things: by
dint of much begging and using her position as Dr.
Ubaldo's orphan daughter, she might be able to wangle a
miserable job as a schoolteacher in one of the few public
elementary schools, or she could take her vows and go
into a convent. Primary schoolmistress or Sister of Charity;
there was no third option that Dona Brígida could see. A
husband? Marriage? Impossible. If other girls better en-
dowed physically and financially, pretty, healthy, willing
daughters of farmers, businessmen, and government em-

ployees, languished hopelessly at windows, what earthly chance did poor skinny, awkward, homely, bashful, tongue-tied, sickly, poverty-stricken Doris have? It would take a miracle.

The miracle came like a bolt from the blue: Captain Justo showed obvious interest, the old wives were soon abuzz, and a feast of gossip began. The women who came in groups of twos and threes, and Dona Brígida's intimate friends, who came each one alone, dressed in black and fanning themselves, all lit into the Captain. They repeated the most horrifying things: "They say . . ." "The person who told me was there himself . . ." "Just the other day I heard . . ." Dona Brígida listened to the appalling stories and shook her head noncommittally; the Queen Mother was a sphinx. The comadres swarmed around her like cockroaches—up the street and down, at mass, at vespers, in the long, long idle hours. Dona Brígida kept her own counsel, as mum as if the affair had nothing at all to do with her.

But at night, in the silence of the locked house, where the gossips' venomous whispers couldn't be heard, Dona Brígida lay awake, worrying about her problem and telling the endless rosary of the Captain's wickedness.

When one considered the matter calmly and impartially, the list of misdeeds grew considerably shorter, she found. The old wives emphasized most the Captain's womanizing, his iniquitous career of lechery. The parade of girls and even children deflowered in his bed, the orgies in cheap hotels and brothels, the ignorant girls who were raped, beaten, and forced into a life of sin. After all, the Captain was single, and what bachelor hasn't sown his wild oats? Unless he was abnormal, that is, a pervert like Nenen Violeta, moviehouse usher and official town queer. One of Mílton Guedes's sons was said to be of doubtful virility, too, but his parents had packed him off to Rio de Janeiro.

Justiniano's past did seem rather lurid, but who could come out whole when the old gossips began to tear into him? Not even the most respectable married men were exempt. The gossips even whispered things about Dr. Ubaldo—a saint, as we know—and two of his patients, the Loreto sisters, single girls who had inherited a house and a little money. Though there wasn't a shred of evidence for such a tale, the comadres hinted that the doctor had been the lover of both women. No one could escape censure in a place where there was so little to do and so many old maids with endless twilight hours to try to fill.

Dona Brígida admitted to herself that naturally the Captain was not a model of chastity to hold up to a Sunday-school class. Wealthy and unattached, he was unlikely to lack feminine company. There were enormous families springing up on every street and in every country field; platoons of girls on the highways, festoons of foolish virgins at every window, and all to be had at a very low price. After all, they had no choice: girls from so-called good families soon withered into sour spinsterhood except for the very few who got married or ran away. As for the others, among the common people, the great majority of the womenfolk—an army of them—plied the oldest profession from a tender age, either in bawdy houses or as "girl scouts" on their own.

The Captain was a bachelor and had a perfect right to amuse himself, Dona Brígida decided. Any exaggerations should be attributed to his vigorous health and appetites. Besides, some people say the men who have lived the most disreputable lives make the best husbands. Having sown their wild oats before marriage, they're ready to devote their minds and everything else to being exemplary family men, once they settle down.

To the old women the Captain's scandalous, debauched sex life weighed more heavily in the balance against him than all his other sins put together. His dishonest bookkeeping, for which there was ample evidence; his brutality; the money he extorted by threats; his quarreling and cheating at cockfights; his arm-twisting tactics to gain the advantage in real estate deals; the crimes he had masterminded, even murder—none of that seemed to bother the old gossips much. His gross carnality was the unforgivable thing—how vile he was! And if the Captain was not to be forgiven, neither were the unfortunate girls he had seduced; they were judged and found guilty as soon as accused. There were no victims in that chapter of the Captain's life. He, the pervert, was guilty, and so were the girls he led astray, those lost women, those tramps.

However, Dona Brígida pondered longer before making up her mind about other aspects of the Captain's behavior, weighing the accuracy of the stories—often hair-raising ones—she had been told. As far as the false bookkeeping and forcible collection of money were concerned, what storekeeper could not be accused of dishonesty? Woe betide the merchant who failed to use any means in his power to put the squeeze on his debtors; an overscrupulous man would probably not be paid at all and would leave his family without a roof over their heads, like the dear departed Dr. Ubaldo, a man who was incapable of presenting a bill, much less of putting the screws on a debtor to pay it. What he had left her was a whole flock of debtors, people he had diagnosed and treated for years. Many of them owed him their lives, but not one had sought out his destitute family in mourning to cancel out his debt of honor. The creditors, on the other hand, lost no time in showing up; and they had been very rough in their demands.

During those sleepless nights, as Dona Brígida tried to be objective in sifting facts and accusations, Justiniano Duarte da Rosa's image gradually began to take on more human shape: the monster became less of a bogeyman. Not to mention his other good points, he was rich and single.

But were impartiality and goodwill enough? With all the goodwill in the world Dona Brígida found it impossible to ignore certain sinister *terrae incognitae* in the Captain's murky life, suspicions that had never been laid to rest: echoes of shots from ambush, visions of graves dug by night. At the inquest held after the Barreto brothers, Isidro and Alcino, were murdered in their sleep, one of the killers, named Gaspar, had pointed to the Captain as the man who had ordered the killing. His responsibility was never proven, however; the day before Gaspar was to testify, he hanged himself in jail—out of remorse, no doubt.

When she thought of these things, Dona Brígida shuddered. What she desperately needed was to clear the Captain completely. How else could she be at peace with her conscience in persuading Doris to marry him? The silly child was only fourteen. Alien as she was to such complexities, indifferent to gossip and with her eyes always on the ground or turned up to Heaven, probably Doris was not even aware of the Captain's advances.

Dona Brígida longed to bring in a favorable verdict and labored all night to do so. Doris's marriage to Justiniano Duarte da Rosa was the Heaven-sent, perfect solution to all of their problems. And yet—those vague, fleeting shadows continued to haunt her and fill her with fear; she kept postponing a decision and the frank talk she must have with her daughter.

Dona Brígida knew how difficult that talk would be and kept putting it off from one day to the next. She dreaded the reaction of her nervous, crybaby daughter when her mother revealed the controversial *prócer*'s interest in her. How could a young girl who was preparing for mystical union with sweet Jesus of Nazareth in the quiet of the cloister consider for a moment the Captain, with his brutal reputation? Why, Doris would never agree even to discuss his offer. For all that she was a frail, lachrymose bundle of nerves, no one could be more obstinate when she chose. She was quite capable of locking herself in her room and refusing to budge out of the house.

In the sleepless dawn Dona Brígida, most loving of mothers, weighed feelings and duties in the balance. She knew she could never bully Doris into marrying Justiniano Duarte da Rosa if the girl put her foot down and said no. Force would never do. But that being so, how in God's name to persuade her?

10

The talk took place that afternoon, most unexpectedly, as mother and daughter were returning from a social call on Dona Beatriz, a perfumed lady from the capital who was the judge's wife. She had come to spend the holidays with her husband, and had brought with her her seventeen-year-old son Daniel, an ethereally beautiful adolescent, a little dandy, with a face worthy to be stamped on a medal. They found other people of importance in the town engaged in elevated, ceremonious talk in the front parlor, but they did not stay long.

Once out of the house, Dona Brígida remarked to the dreamy, self-absorbed Doris:

"What a handsome young man! He looks like a picture."

With her usual faint drawl, Doris said:

"Young man? A silly little boy tied to his mother's apron strings, that's all he is. I can't stand spoiled little boys."

Dona Brígida was surprised at such an opinion, expressed in so scornful a tone.

"To hear you talk, honey, anybody would think you knew something about boys and young men," Dona Brígida teased. "You call him a silly little boy, but I call him a wide-awake little boy. He kept staring at Neusa's cleavage the whole time, if you can call that a cleavage. I call it shameless myself, letting her bosom hang out— didn't you notice? But you never notice things like that." Suddenly the words were out of her mouth. "I'll bet you haven't even noticed that Captain Justo has his eye on you."

"Yes I have, Mother."

Dona Brígida felt a shock, a blow in the solar plexus.

"You have? When?"

"Oh, a long time ago, Mother."

They walked a few steps in silence while Dona Brígida attempted to rearrange her ideas.

"A long time ago—and you never said a word."

"I was afraid you wouldn't like it."

"What?"

Doris laughed a strange, unnerving laugh. Dona Brígida put her hand to the heart in her panting bosom. Good Lord in Heaven!

"Do you mean you . . . Do you mean . . . you're not mad at him . . . you don't . . ."

"Mad at him? Why should I be mad? We're engaged, Mother."

Dona Brígida felt her heart flutter wildly. She urgently needed her smelling salts and a chair to sit down on; the summer sun was blinding her, and her other senses were affected too. Could she be hearing what she thought she heard? Was this really her poor, innocent daughter Doris walking beside her down the street and declaring that she was the Captain's fiancée in the same low, languid, almost inaudible voice in which she told her beads—or was this whole dialogue a hallucination?

"Darling, for Heaven's sake, tell me everything before I suffocate."

That laugh again. Was it a laugh of triumph?

"He wrote me a note and sent it—"

"Sent you a note? Where? Who gave it to you?"

"He sent it to school. I got it in the morning, on my way to school. It was Chico, his clerk, who brought it. So I answered it and he wrote me again; and I answered again. Chico gives me the notes on my way to school and waits for my answer when I go home. He wrote day before yesterday asking me if I wanted to be his fiancée, and said if the answer was yes, he'd speak to you about it."

"Well? Did you give him an answer?"

"I answered him the same day, Mother. I told him that as far as I was concerned, I already considered myself his fiancée."

Dona Brígida stopped short in the middle of the street and stared at her skinny daughter in her skimpy little-girl's frock and low-heeled shoes, her emaciated face innocent of makeup, her bosom almost nonexistent, a foolish, innocent schoolgirl. . . . Ah, the fire that was consuming her!

11

His honor Dr. Eustáquio Fialho Gomes Neto, district judge, was also, in his leisure hours, the poet Fialho Neto; he had had sonnets published in Bahian newspapers and magazines, and while he was still a student, his "Garden of Dreams" had won an honorable mention in a competition sponsored by *Fon-Fon*, a little magazine published in Rio de Janeiro. Obviously he was a person of some importance among the town's intelligentsia and he defended, in all seriousness and with the best arguments he could muster, a surprising thesis: he was firmly convinced that Justiniano Duarte da Rosa was inflamed with a deep and sincere love for Doris Curvelo, a love destined to endure. Love, he said, in the broadest sense of the word, containing in it all the joys of paradise and pains of hell.

"You certainly have an extraordinary concept of love,

no doubt about that. . . ." In the opinion of Marcos Lemos, bookkeeper at the sugarmill and another devotee of the muses, the judge, like the wag he was, was amusing himself at his friends' expense.

"Dr. Eustáquio has a fondness for paradox," temporized the district attorney, Dr. Epaminondas Trigo, a blubbery, unshaven, careless dresser, with five children to bring up and a sixth in his good wife's belly—and he not yet thirty. His membership in the local culture-loving elite owed less to his law degree than to his skill at solving puzzles. A nullity as an attorney, he was a blazing talent when it came to deciphering cryptograms. Since the judge was his superior in rank, Epaminondas did not venture to dispute his opinion.

"What a cynic you are!" laughed a fourth member of the group, Aírton Amorim, myopic and crewcut, a stamp collector who read Portuguese novelists like Eça de Queiroz and Ramalho Ortigão, and a close friend of the judge. "Love is a noble sentiment . . . the noblest of all."

"Well, what of it?"

"Captain Justo and noble sentiments don't match."

"Besides being unfair to our dear Captain, Aírton, you're a lousy psychologist. This is love, true love, and I'll give you facts to prove it."

Not only the intellectual elite but the whole town puzzled over the engagement, the marriage, and other aspects of the Captain's inexplicable behavior. A few days before the mortgage was to be foreclosed he paid it in full, thus relieving widow and orphan of the greatest threat to their security: that of losing the property the doctor had sacrificed so much to buy.

"Isn't such generosity, nay, munificence, sufficient proof of love?" his honor argued, this time with concrete facts to back up his case.

And what about Doris's trousseau? Who had paid for all the silk, linen, cambric, lace, and ruffles? Who had paid the seamstress? Was it perchance Dona Brígida, with her state pension? No, indeed; it had all come out of the Captain's pocket. The same Captain who was usually so stingy, such a miser, had suddenly turned into a big spender who paid without a murmur. Once again Dona Brígida had credit in the shops and queened it over the clerks, who now bowed and scraped before her—the same miserable wretches who had plagued her with bills just a little while before.

If it wasn't love, then what was it? How could the Captain's generosity, his spending, his kindnesses—yes, his kindness—be explained if he wasn't doing it all for love? Why on earth (asked the judge, pointing a finger to emphasize his point) would the Captain want to get married if he wasn't in love? What did Doris have to offer but her own skinny carcass? Property? She didn't have a place of her own to drop dead in. Of course, she had her father's honorable name; but what use could the name, the honor, the memory of Dr. Ubaldo Curvelo be to Justiniano Duarte da Rosa? Only blind, ardent love could explain it.

"Especially blind," Aírton Amorim interrupted jokingly.

As his honor Dr. Eustáquio saw it, nothing but a blind and ardent love could explain such an engagement and marriage, accompanied by such favors and such largess. His judicial and poetic opinion was listened to respectfully but shared by few. It was a period rich in debates, in contradictory arguments, and in rude, whispered jokes. The ever-inventive Dona Ponciana de Azevedo reaped great success with one of her precise quips: "It's the union of a washboard with a pig the right size." A cruel comparison, but none could deny that it was apt.

Whether love or, as the gossips would have it, some other, unknown motive was to blame, Captain Justo did seem to have lost his wits. He scarcely resembled his old self. When one of his fighting cocks suffered an ugly defeat, Justiniano neither disputed the verdict, said he'd been robbed, nor punched Renato, the barber who owned the winning cock, in the nose.

Meanwhile, Dona Brígida was unable to free herself entirely from the shadows that haunted her nights. She had got into the habit of weighing deeds and gestures, expansive generosity, against miserly restrictions. True, the Captain had saved them from having the mortgage foreclosed by the bank, but the lien had not been canceled in the registry nor did the widow have the receipt. She had simply become the Captain's debtor. When Dona Brígida brought the matter up as tactfully as possible, Justiniano stared at her out of his little eyes as if he were insulted. Weren't he and Doris getting married? Wouldn't it all stay in the family? What need was there to spend money at the registry on receipts and such foolishness?

In the shops, too, she sometimes met with an apologetic excuse:

"I'm sorry, Dona Brígida, but we'll have to consult the Captain about a large purchase like this. . . ."

Pettiness in the midst of plenty; Dona Brígida felt she was treading shaky ground. A fragile crust of generosity and kindness overlay treacherous badlands, steep cliffs without shade or water. Doris's trousseau was not lacking in anything really necessary, and everything was of good quality; but it was not by a long shot the grand, rich, unforgettable, incomparable trousseau of Dona Brígida's dreams. And so her dreams and her satisfaction were marred by doubts and shadows, but not to the point of making her doubt Justiniano Duarte da Rosa's real interest in her daughter. After all, he had proclaimed his love to the world.

The engagement lasted three months, the necessary minimum for the preparation of the trousseau. At the time of the proposal Dona Brígida had suggested a reasonable wait of six months. *Six months?* Just to sew a few dresses and cut out some sheets? Ridiculous; the Captain wouldn't hear of it. If he had had his way they would have become engaged one day and been married the next. If Doris had had her way, she'd have been married the day before.

Justiniano Duarte da Rosa had asked Dr. Eustáquio and the mayor to accompany him to the house on Cathedral Square for the ritual of asking for Doris's hand. Dona Brígida had invited Father Cirilo and a few of her intimate friends and had prepared meat tarts, cakes, and assorted sweetmeats. The gossips were out in full force, and many other people too. A crowd gathered in the square. When the white-suited, panama-hatted suitor appeared, flanked by judge and mayor, a loud murmur rose.

The Captain stopped and looked around. A new man, a man of peace, he raised neither his fist nor his voice; he did not call for Terto or Chico, did not draw his revolver. All he did was look around, but that was enough. "You'd think they never saw a man get engaged," he growled to the mayor. "If it weren't for my respect for the family I'd teach those yokels a lesson."

Several times during the brief engagement he was all set to "teach some yokel a lesson" and restrained himself only with an effort. When he took Doris and Dona Brígida to the movies or to church, and someone gave them an obviously curious stare, the Captain's first impulse was to explode. He did boil over once, when, not content with staring, a couple exchanged remarks in an undertone. "Haven't you ever seen me before, you son-of-a-bitch?" snarled the Captain, ready for the attack. Blood would certainly have been spilled if husband and wife had not taken to their heels. "Calm yourself, Captain!" Dona Brígida implored. Imperturbable on her fiancé's arm, Doris said nothing.

The curiosity, debate, expressions of opinion, astonished stares, ill-timed visits by the comadres to the parlor where the engaged couple sat and courted, jokes, sniggers, and witty remarks—all came to an abrupt end, once and for good. On one of her nocturnal sallies, when she was setting out to push under the judge's door an anonymous letter in reference to what his wife was doing in the capital and his honorable concubine under his very nose, the crafty Dona Ponciana de Azevedo was accosted by Chico Half-Sole, one of the unsavory characters who took orders from the Captain and saw to it that debts to him were paid up. Chico took out a knife and pricked her lightly with the sharp tip. Dona Ponciana had just time to reach her house before falling into a fit of hysterical weeping. She stayed behind locked doors for a week, recovering from the worst attack of nerves of her lifetime. The story spread: Dona Ponciana had been stabbed. Peace descended on the town.

And so the three months of the engagement dragged by. Dona Brígida tried to establish a bond of trust and friendship with her future son-in-law but found him unresponsive. Justiniano Duarte da Rosa was a man of few words; and during his daily after-dinner visits he limited his conversation to the bare essentials: talk of the indispensable arrangements for the coming wedding and nothing else. For the rest, the happy pair remained seated on the parlor sofa in silence. Dona Brígida would try to start a conversation, but it was a waste of her Latin and her time. All she elicited from the Captain for her pains was a grunt or two; from Doris she got not even that.

The couple waited in silence for Dona Brígida to go to the kitchen or dining room on the pretext of making fresh coffee or bringing in some banana, jackfruit, or cashew dessert. No sooner had she turned her back than the sweethearts began to kiss and grab at each other, mouth to mouth, busy hands. Would the three months never come to an end? Dona Brígida didn't know what to do or where to look. Hadn't Doris actually had the nerve to criticize her for staying in the parlor all the time to watch them instead of just leaving them alone once in a while? Weren't they engaged, for Heaven's sake?

A woman conceives, gives birth to, suckles, rears, and educates a daughter, all with the tenderest care, following the precepts of our holy religion and thinking she knows everything about the child. And all the time she knows nothing; nothing at all, Dona Brígida thought sadly from her seat of exile by the window, where she had to face the curious stares from the street in order to turn her back to Doris and her fiancé.

Her days were divided between joy and fear: the delight of lace and embroidery, nightgowns and petticoats, shopping expeditions and fittings, the concoction of sweets and liqueurs, along with the bustle and excitement of the preparations for the wedding; and in contrast, her concern over the fiancé's ardor, the fear of an explosion by her son-in-law-to-be, that contumacious user and abuser of violence. Dona Brígida had a horror of violence, and during that tumultuous period she was never really at ease for a single moment. And yet, she could not repress a certain thrill of pride and exultant taste of power when she heard how Dona Ponciana had almost died of fright when she felt the point of the knife between her ribs. That viper had gotten exactly what she deserved, and it would be a good lesson for the rest of them. Learn this lesson once and for all, dear friends and zealous gossips, and forget it if you dare; from now on this is how it is going to be: anyone who annoys Doris or Dona Brígida takes his life in his hands. Anyone who thinks he wants to can play the fool—and pay the price. She spent a whole euphoric afternoon listening to at least ten different versions of Dona Ponciana's adventure; but with nightfall the dark shadows and the fear crept back.

That engagement was as precious as the finest cut glass, and as fragile. She worried about her son-in-law and his secretive, subterranean nature; and she worried even more about Doris, as she languished and burned. Rages, a short temper, longings, impatience, and a total lack of interest in anything outside herself: where was the timid schoolgirl, fresh from the hands of the nuns? She had never had much appetite, but now she barely picked at her food. Black shadows under her eyes, stooped, skinnier than ever—she was literally skin and bones. Less than a month before the wedding she woke one day with fever and a persistent cough. Dona Brígida called in Dr. David. After examining her—ear to her back, taps on her ribs with his knuckles, "Say thirty-three"—the doctor advised a trip to the capital for lab tests. It wouldn't be a bad idea to have some X-rays taken too. It would be wise to postpone the wedding. "She's awfully weak—too weak—and the tests are a must."

Dona Brígida felt the ground give way beneath her feet.

"Does she have a bad chest, doctor?"

"No, I don't think so. But she will if she goes on like this. She needs rest and nourishment. Just see that the lab tests are made and put off the wedding for a few months."

Dona Brígida, Queen Mother and a woman of character, recovered her poise. Household remedies broke the fever, the cough dwindled to an occasional clearing of the throat, and no postponement of the wedding was even considered. The tests could wait until they went to the capital on their honeymoon, as they would surely do. The matter was not mentioned again. Dona Brígida swallowed toads and lizards to protect and preserve that fragile crystal, that delicate cut glass, the precious engagement. She was afraid, so afraid.

12

As she sailed into the sheltering harbor, the final anchor-
age of the wedding day, Dona Brígida fairly glittered.
Majestic she was in her haughty gait, in the rustling silk
of her long dress and in her hat covered with artificial
flowers; majestic as she fanned herself; majestic in her
sense of mission accomplished. Gone forever was the
threat of penury; they were no longer beggars in disguise.
She had done her duty as a mother and received congratulations with a smile of condescension.

Doris was in her bridal gown with its thousand frip-
peries, copied from a Rio magazine, the Captain in his
brand-new blue suit, all the guests in their Sunday best.
They were celebrating the most talked-about wedding
ever to take place in Cajazeiras do Norte: first the religious ceremony in the Cathedral, complete with maternal
tears and a sermon by Father Cirilo; then the civil ceremony in the bride's house, embellished with a touching
speech by Judge Eustáquio Fialho Gomes Neto—poet
Fialho Neto—which was studded with elegant metaphori-
cal descriptions of love: "sublime sentiment that calms
the tempest, that moves mountains, that illumines the
shadows' gloom," and so forth; most inspired.

The town turned out into Cathedral Square en masse.
Even Dona Ponciana de Azevedo was there, now quite
over her spell of nerves and ready for fresh battles; but
with all due respect, of course, for the Captain and his
new family. "There never was a bride as pretty as Doris;
believe me, dear Brígida." Dona Brígida, delighted but
maintaining her dignity, accepted the flattering praise of
the comadres as her due.

The Queen Mother presided over the festivities with
a watchful eye, attentive to the serving of food and drink,
giving meticulous orders to the waiters and maids. She
saw Doris go to her bedroom to change and the Captain
follow her—bold as brass, right at her heels. Good heavens, how could he do such a thing! Did he have to be in
that much of an almighty hurry? Couldn't they have
waited a day, or a few hours, even, until they were on

the train or in a hotel bedroom? Why did they have to do it here, of all places, practically where the guests could see them?

Yes, mother, where the guests can see us; with the whole town looking on. And all of the girls, every single one of them, the ones who used to go to the grove behind the school, the ones who smeared themselves with schoolboy kisses and sperm, the ones who did it with rich boys in the Guedes's garden or behind the counters with shop clerks on empty afternoons. Yes, right in front of them all. The ones who told her how they kissed and hugged and sighed and moaned, about breasts caressed and open thighs; the ones who made me feel envious and humiliated and called me nun, Sister, Mother Superior. And let all the other women in town come and look, too, and lump it, married women included: the faithful and the adulterous, the crazy old maids in the yards, the gossips at their windows or in church, the nuns in the convent, the prostitutes in Gabi's house, and the free-lance hookers, let them all take a good look, all of them, every one.

Arms crossed on her consumptive chest, eyes starting out of her head, her frail body swept by convulsive shudders, Doris longed to cry aloud. Let me shout, Justo, why do you make me be quiet, my dearest? I want to cry out so they'll all come running and see poor Doris stark naked, and beside her on the bed, ready to take her, take her maidenhead and enjoy her, panting with desire—a man. Not a stupid schoolboy, not a tailor's apprentice with his scissors and tape measure, hurriedly masturbating with one hand on her breast and one at his crotch—hurry up and run, someone's coming. No, a man, and what a man! Justiniano Duarte da Rosa, Captain Justo, known as a he-man, famous as a macho, the biggest macho there is. And every bit of him belongs to Doris. He is her man. Do you hear? Her man, her husband, all hers, on the bed in the bedroom right next to the parlor. Come on, girls, come and have a look!

13

To fight with a mortal man, that's not such a hard thing to do, your honor, if you'll excuse my saying so. I've seen a lot of good fights like that. Once I saw a nigger named Pascoal do Sossego face a whole platoon of soldiers; he was a crackerjack Angola cupoeira wrestler, and he showed them plenty. That was a real fight to the finish.

And if you've got a gun or something, why then it's a pushover. Anybody's brave with a revolver in his hand; there ain't no cowards left in the world then. If I shove a firestick into some guy's chest, it's a cinch I'll be promoted to outlaw chief or police lieutenant, ain't it, whitey?

But seeing's believing, and one thing I'd like to see is a man with balls enough to stand up to a ghost. Yes, sir, a real sure-enough ghost, a spirit who roams the dark woods at night, snuffling out fire from his nose and the holes where his eyes ought to be, and with his claws dripping blood. Hoo-eeh! You know how big a werewolf's teeth get, your honor? And his fingernails? They're sharp as a razor and cut you from a long way off.

Once upon a time I was taking a shortcut through the woods at night, and when I got to the crossroads I heard the Headless Mule's hoofbeats. I'm telling you the plain truth. I no more than caught sight of that critter, with fire where his head ought to be, than I got so scared my feet stuck to the ground and I couldn't move an inch. All I could do was pray to Father Cícero, my patron saint: Help me, Father Cícero, deliver me from evil. Amen! I owe my life to Father Cícero and to this bulletproof scapular I've got hung around my neck. That ghost demon passed me by not three hundred yards away, and all around me was just nothing left. Everything was scorched and charred, brush and grass, trees and rattlesnakes, manioc and sugarcane—everything. You just listen to me, your honor: mention ghosts and that's all it takes to scare a strong man shitless.

Tereza Batista was the only one with the spunk to face

*up to an evil spirit; Tereza, that gal I've told you about
before, and that's my answer to that funny question of
yours about whether she was really as brave as people
say. She looked an evil spirit in the eye and fought it too
—and if you don't believe me, just ask anybody who
was there. She didn't run and she didn't cry quits; and
if she yelled for help when she was getting the worst of
it, it's a sure thing nobody came; she just had to save
herself the best she could. No gal on this earth was ever
so alone and so forsaken by God and man. That was the
way Tereza Corpo Fechado sealed her body against bullets, knives, and snakebite.*

*Well, I'll say no more about it because I've heard this
true story told in a lot of different ways. Everybody sees
it his own way, and takes things out and put things in
and changes it around and adds whatever fancy touches
he has a mind to. A ballad singer down from Alagoas—
that's a long ways off, and I reckon he couldn't believe
the thing happened the way it did and had to try and
find some way to make it make sense to him—this fellow, he said Tereza sold her soul to the devil when she
was just a kid. And plenty of people believed him. But
another ballad singer who's famous all over Brazil, Luis
da Câmara Cascudo his name is, when he saw how
Tereza had to suffer all alone, he put a flower in her
hand and said it was flower to go with sorrow, flower
to go with love.*

*Each one tells the story the best he can, but they all
agree about one thing: no demon out of purgatory was
ever seen around those parts again. The way I look at
it, the living have troubles enough without being scared
out of their wits by souls in torment roaming around the
world when they ought to be six feet under.*

*I know nothing's impossible, I won't swear to any-
thing, I don't answer questions, nothing surprises me, I
don't doubt what you say, I won't take sides, I'm not
from around here anyway, I'm a stranger here myself.
But you see, your honor, my distinguished friend—the
long and the short of it is, there's an awful lot of mystery
in the world. The Tereza I knew and can swear to was
called Tereza of the New Moon, and she had the color*

and the sweetness of honey, and she sang modinhas *in a
low, gentle voice and was as tender and loving as she
could be.*

14

Talking to herself, Dona Brígida came up from the creek,
shadows all around her. When she was halfway up the
slope her dreary monologue was broken into by shouts.
A few more steps and she saw the girl being held by her
arms and legs as she struggled in the grip of the Captain
and Terto Cachorro.

She hid behind a mango tree, clutching the child to
her breast, as she cast her eyes heavenward and whispered curses. One day God is bound to look down, and
when He sees such wickedness He will punish it, some
day when her penance has come to an end.

The shouting explodes in her breast and makes her
heart race. Her eyes dilate, her mouth becomes dry, her
face changes. Dona Brígida has been metamorphosed,
and the world around her as well. It's no longer Justiniano
Duarte da Rosa, her son-in-law, who is gripping the victim's arms; it's the Evil One, the Devil, the monster, Hog.
He feeds on little girls; he sucks their blood, gnaws their
young flesh, crunches their bones.

And Jackal helps him do it. The skulking vassal, the
leader of the accursed pack, sniffs out and flushes game
for his abominable lord and master. False and vicious,
he would devour the little girls whole if Hog's back were
turned. But he's a coward, too, and must be satisfied with
the leavings. At such moments Dona Brígida could see
into the heart and divine thoughts; that gift she had been
granted a long time before.

There were other beasts almost as terrifying as Hog
and Jackal. It was hard for Dona Brígida to sort them
out in her poor confused mind, but as soon as one appeared at the farm to peddle fresh meat or carrion she
at once recognized it. Headless Mule, for instance: the
carrion-seller.

She could put on any disguise she liked—Great Lady,
Fairy Godmother, Courtesan—but she would never fool

Dona Brígida again. When she came to the gate the first time, about ten days after Doris was buried, the Captain had ridden off to a cockfight and it was Dona Brígida herself who let her in and entertained her in the parlor. Dona Gabi had come in leading a girl by the hand, like a protective godmother. She explained that the Captain had said they needed someone to help take care of the orphaned baby, and so she had brought along this very suitable girl. This well-mannered, pleasant-spoken elderly woman, obviously a person of some education, was the most sympathetic visitor a grief-stricken mother could wish for.

They were so engrossed in conversation, as confidential and intimate as if they were old friends, that they did not at first realize the Captain had come back. When they looked up, the Captain was standing in the doorway, pointing his pudgy finger at them and shaking with laughter. Justiniano Duarte da Rosa's belly shook with his uncontrollable mirth. Such laughter was not a pleasant sight to see in Captain Justo, who rarely laughed at all. He tried to speak but words and guffaws came out together:

"Look at the two hens—Haw! Haw! Haw!—thick as thieves! Who'd believe his eyes—Haw! Haw!"

Embarrassed, Dona Gabi jumped to her feet and began excusing herself awkwardly.

"I just stayed to offer my condolences. . . ." She turned to Dona Brígida. "Good-bye, ma'am."

She made as if to leave the room, pulling the girl along with her by the hand, but the Captain stopped her.

"Where do you think you're going? We have some talking to do, and we'll do it right here."

"Here? I don't think this is a good place—"

"This is where we'll talk, I said. Spit it out."

"Well, you see—I brought this little thing right over, thinking she could help take care of the baby—" She stole a glance at the widow, who was wiping away the obligatory tears she had shed when thanking the other woman for her expressions of sympathy. The procuress lowered her voice: "And for the most important thing you'll find she's first-rate."

The Captain guffawed even louder. Gabi did not know whether to laugh from fright or weep for pity.

"Well, I'll find out tonight. If she's what you say she is, I'll stop by tomorrow and pay you."

"Please, Captain, can't you pay me part of it today? The woman who brought her came from a long way off and is waiting for her money. I really need to have it."

"You won't get money out of me in advance, not today or any other day. Haven't you got that through your skull yet? Do I have to give you a little reminder? If there's anything to pay you'll get it tomorrow. Come and get it if you want to, and then—Haw! Haw!—you can keep my mother-in-law company. That's a good one: keep my mother-in-law company!"

He shook with laughter again. Gabi begged:

"Please, Captain. Please give me a little something now."

"You come back in the morning. If I find her gourd intact, I'll pay you cash on the barrelhead. If I don't . . . well, I wouldn't come around, if I were you."

"But I can't take the responsibility for that. When they said she was a virgin, I brought her right to you, Captain. You know when I get hold of something good I always save it for the Captain."

"So—you can't take the responsibility, can you? Trying to fool me again, were you? So you think I'm a fool just because I didn't give you what you deserved last time? Didn't wipe that rat's nest of yours clean off the face of the earth? Get out of here. It won't hurt you to wait for what's coming to you."

"Can't you give me back at least what I'm already out of pocket for?"

For answer the Captain began to interrogate the girl, turning his back on Gabi and well within earshot of his mother-in-law.

"Are you still a virgin? Don't you lie to me if you know what's good for you."

"No, sir, I ain't."

Whirling on his heel, Justiniano seized Gabi's arm and shook her, hard.

"Get out of here before I punch you in the jaw."

"For Heaven's sake, Captain, don't shout like that! What's come over you?" Still not understanding either her son-in-law's laughter or his anger, Dona Brígida tried to intervene. "For Heaven's sake don't shout!"

"Don't you stick your nose into what's none of your business. Just stay put in your corner and count your blessings."

He was overcome by another fit of laughter when his mother-in-law defended Gabi, saying, "Why don't you leave the poor soul in peace?"

The Captain thought he'd die laughing.

"Do you know who this poor soul is? Oh, you don't? Well, I'll tell you. Haven't you ever heard of Gabi, the Priest's-Mule? The one who shacked up with Father Fabrício and opened up a whorehouse after he died, with the money he got saying masses?" He had laughed so hard that he ached from his mouth to his guts. "Haw! That's a good one—'poor soul'—Haw! Haw!"

"Oh, my God!"

Gabi Priest's-Mule had to trot off down the road with her tail between her legs, but when the girl started after her, she was stopped by the Captain.

"How long has it been?"

"Yessir, a month ago."

"Only a month? Don't you lie to me."

"Yessir, a month."

"Who was it?"

"Dr. Emiliano, up at the sugarmill."

Goddamn it, he should have beaten the dirty old whore to a pulp for trying to fob off leftovers from the Guedeses' table on him. The three brothers gave him plenty of competition, especially Emiliano Guedes. No girl ever came out of his sugarmill in one piece. Not a solitary gold ring on the Captain's necklace had come out of the Guedes canefields.

"Where's your bundle?"

"Don't have none, nossir."

"All right, go on inside."

Dona Brígida stared at her son-in-law, trying to find words strong enough to damn him with, while the Captain was overcome again with helpless laughter, repeating over and over, "Poor good soul, Haw! Haw! Haw!" as he pointed at his mother-in-law. Dona Brígida fled from the room and rushed headlong into the forest through the doors of Hell.

The Captain showed her not the slightest respect. She might as well not exist. That night, after a gloomy sup-

per by murky lamp-light, he looked for the new girl in
the nursery where the baby was sleeping and told her to
pick up her ass and come on. There at the end of the hall,
in the red smoky gleam of the kerosene lamp, Dona
Brígida saw Hog for the first time, monstrous, filthy, unspeakable, and knew him for what he was.

Even before Doris died, she had become a little un-
balanced, and now she shut herself up with her tiny
granddaughter. The Captain's heavy breathing could be
heard rooms away. Damn that son-of-a-bitch of a Guedes,
he'd penetrated her fore and aft.

During the next year and a half the Headless Mule
came often to the farm, always leading a goddaughter by
the hand; but Dona Brígida knew who she was all right
the minute she caught sight of her at the gate or in the
lane. And at the first glimpse her world became an inferno teeming with demons. Dona Brígida was paying for
her sins while she was still alive.

Headless Mule, priest's concubine, sacrilegious whore.
Hog wasn't fooled by her either. His bellows of rage
withered the leaves on the vine, killed the lambs in the
meadow and the birds in the forest.

"Don't you bring me any of your crap! You know
damned well I don't eat anybody else's leavings—I'll
smash your face in, you bitch!"

Cries, groans, the whack of blows, the whistle of the
rawhide whip, a little black girl howling all night long, a
chain of little girls hanging around Hog's neck. And the
biggest ring of all, the one that was pure gold, was Doris.
Dona Brígida's thoughts oppressed her more and more,
were a wearier and wearier burden. Sometimes she was
in the world and sometimes she was in Hell, but which
was worse?

Where had that majestic lady, Senhora Dona Brígida,
gone? The First Lady, widow of the estimable Dr.
Curvelo, Queen Mother presiding at the wedding of her
only daughter? Things got jumbled up in her mind; her
memory and judgment weren't to be trusted. She became
negligent in her dress and took to spending the whole
day in a dirty skirt and blouse, her slippers runover, her
hair unkempt. She forgot when things had happened, confused details, forgot facts. Her mind alternately dimmed
and brightened, became blurred and untrustworthy. For

days at a time she was completely self-absorbed, talking
to herself and tending the child automatically. Then, suddenly, the slightest incident would plunge her into a hal-
lucinatory world where monsters pursued her, Hog
leading them all, the abominable devourer of her daughter who one day would eat his own.

The only thing about which she always remained perfectly aware was the enormity of her crime. Yes, she,
Dona Brígida Curvelo, had fed Hog just as Gabi Priest's-
Mule did. Just like Terto Cachorro Jackal, she flushed
game for Justiniano Duarte da Rosa, Captain Hog, Devil,
Father of Lies. She had handed him her daughter so that
he could suck her blood, crunch her bones, feast on her
meager flesh.

Don't let's say she was an innocent victim of circumstances who naturally mistook the Captain for a human
being and confused a sordid bedroom affair for a noble
marriage. No, for her sins and the crime she committed,
she deserves all her suffering in this life. She had known
the truth from the first, had seen it in the Captain's lascivious eyes. She was never deceived, no, never; and it
was during all those sleepless nights that she developed
her gift of second sight, learned to read minds and to
foresee the future.

Oh yes, she had known. She just refused to admit to
herself that she knew. She just held her tongue, swallowed toads and lizards and every sort of affront, hid the
tubercular lesions in Doris's chest under one hand and
blotted out the light with the other, applied a sponge of
amnesty to the Captain's past, and led her child to the
altar and then, at the wedding feast, to her virgin bed.
And Hog ate her for lunch, dinner, and breakfast; swallowed her one piece at each meal. If it hadn't been for
her pregnant belly, there would literally have been nothing left of Doris. By the time they laid her in the ground
there was almost nothing to bury.

As punishment for this monstrous crime, God Almighty
had ordained that Dona Brígida should pay for her sins
now while she was alive, here in her son-in-law's accursed house, on land that was stolen and peopled by
starving tenants, iron-spurred fighting cocks, gunmen with
knives and rifles, and defenseless children. Children, girls,
once in a great while a woman. How many since Doris

died? Dona Brígida had lost count, and even if she had
been able to add up all those on the farm there were as
many in the room behind the store in town.

Many things she forgot entirely and others she remembered through a haze. She entirely forgot Doris's own eagerness, her delirium. Even if Dona Brígida had opposed
the marriage, Doris, in her arrogant, obscssivc wanton-
ness, her cynical debauchery, would have run to the bedroom on her own two feet, hand in hand with her
bridegroom. Dona Brígida had wholly expunged from her
memory the sight of Doris in the parlor with her fiancé,
lost to decorum, all depraved hands and tongue. She
brought back to life her daughter as she had once been,
the innocent, artless schoolgirl with her lowered eyes, af-
fianced to Christ, rosary in her hand, prayers on her lips,
a mystical vocation in her heart: the sacrificial victim of
her mother's ambition and the Captain's lust.

She also rooted out entirely the recollection of Doris as
the enamored, humble wife, a slave at her husband's feet.
The marriage and Doris's thin, feeble blood had lasted
ten months: ten short days for her passion and a thousand
years of humiliation and insults for Dona Brígida.

There never existed a more ardent, devoted wife. Doris
spent those ten months in unremitting heat, giving thanks
to the Captain. She came back from her honeymoon with
a stuffed belly and an unholy elation which never left her
till the day she died, having lived just long enough to give
birth. She hung on her lord and master's every whim,
begged for a glance, a gesture, a word, a lay. On their
rare excursions to the movies or into town she swelled
with pride on Justiniano's arm. Dona Brígida overthrew
her reason in the terrible effort to wipe out of her memory the shameful sight of Doris, crouching before a basin
of water at night, washing Hog's feet and kissing them,
one toe at a time. Now and then, out of sheer playful-
ness, the Captain would thrust his foot in her face,
making her lose her balance and fall over backward.
Struggling to hold back her tears, Doris would try to
laugh—it's just his way of joking, Mother. That was the
Captain's way of showing his affection.

God in Heaven! The ignominy! But Doris took pleasure
in humiliation. All she wanted out of life was to go to

bed with her husband and hold him between her poor little toothpick legs.

Full of plans and self-interested projects at first, Dona Brígida had tried to establish an *entente cordiale* with her son-in-law by engaging him in conversation. She set forth modest proposals over dinner—wouldn't it be nice to have a place in town, a house of their own, rent-free, on Cathedral Square? They'd have to keep it up in some style, of course, as behooved people of good family like themselves, but it needn't cost much since most staples would come from the Captain's store. As for servants and a servingwoman, those people worked for practically nothing—just what it cost to feed them, really.

They'd have a place to entertain their friends and all the local people of importance. And she knew how to do things properly on very little money. The Captain laid his knife across his fork and licked the beans from his fingers:

"Is that all? Sure you don't want anything else?"

Not another word did he say to clarify what he meant, and the conversation died away in uncertainty. A few days afterward the widow learned that the house on the square had been rented to a protégé of the Guedes family, a man who owned a rum distillery. When she heard the news, Dona Brígida, still trailing clouds of glory, mounted her high horse and abandoned dialogue for argument and plans for demands. Why, the very idea of renting her house right out from under her without so much as a by-your-leave! Where would they live, she'd like to know, when they wanted to stay in town? Did her son-in-law imagine that Dona Brígida intended to rot here in the backwoods forever? Or that she'd be willing to sleep with his clerks and hired thugs in the shack behind the store? How could the Captain think he could treat her like this? She wasn't a nobody.

But the argument was no sooner begun than it was settled, once and for all. As Dona Brígida rattled on, carried away by her own indignation, the Captain exploded:

"Fuck you!"

Dona Brígida's mouth fell open, her hand still in the air. The Captain's little eyes looked daggers at her. What the hell did she think she was talking about—*her* house? Who paid off the mortgage? Get down off your high horse, you shitty uppity dame; it's about time you woke up. Yes, I said shit. A sackful of shit is what you are. Not a room of your own to drop dead in. The only reason you've got food to put in your mouth and a roof over your head is that you're Doris's mother. And if you want to leave, get the hell out. If you want to live in town and go hungry on your measly pension, the gate's wide open. Get on out, who needs you? But if you want to stay here and keep on living off of me, you'd better stick your tongue up your ass and never raise your voice to me again.

And where was Doris in that hour of outrage? Did she support her mother and give her weapons to fight with? She did not; she took her husband's part, as she always did.

"Mother, you're getting to be impossible. I really don't know how Justo can be so patient. He has enough problems already without your nagging at him all the time. For heaven's sake, stop talking about it and let's have a little peace."

One day, when she heard her mother complaining to a friend who was visiting from town, Doris sprang to her feet and stood over her mother angrily.

"Mother, stop that once and for all if you want to go on living here. You're living on charity and still have the nerve to complain."

The queen's throne crumbled; a cord snapped in the shitty, uppity dame's brain. She became glum and eccentric. She clung to the last shreds of her dignity by ignoring her son-in-law and speaking to Doris only when strictly necessary. She began wandering in the woods, talking to herself.

As for Doris, she hadn't a vestige of dignity, shame, or self-respect left. She was putty in the hands of her husband, who had completely reverted to his old habits and disposition. He often stayed in town until dawn, and mingled with the sweat that soaked his blubbery chest was the smell of other women, cheap perfume, telltale odors, and visible traces, none of which it ever occurred to Justiniano Duarte da Rosa to conceal from his wife. Just as he was, straight from another woman he'd taken at Gabi's house or in the room behind the store, he'd give Doris a tumble for dessert. On these occasions the skinny girl outdid herself. No harlot could equal her, and that was the truth.

Sometimes the Captain was so tired that he would skip the foot-washing ritual, spurn warm water and caresses, and with a "Go to hell and leave me alone," would fall heavily asleep. Then Doris was in despair and would spend the hours crying, or rather whimpering to herself so as not to wake him. Maybe when he woke up? First thing? She was sure to be waiting at his feet, like a faithful dog.

Never once did she dare to remonstrate or open her mouth to complain, not even when the Captain cursed her in one of his brutish, irascible moods. It was Dona Brígida who ate her heart out, and the bitter resentment she was forced to hold in corroded her mind. Once when Doris was a little slow in fetching a jacket he'd bawled out to her to bring, Justiniano hit her in the face before her mother.

"Didn't you hear me call you, you slut?"

Doris wept silently but would not hear of leaving, as Dona Brígida, in a first flush of rebellion, begged her to do. "It's nothing to get upset about, just a little slap. I *did* take too long. It was all my fault."

Somehow or other, by this trick or that, Doris did succeed in keeping the Captain's interest in her alive. Maybe it was because the fire of consumption burned in her flesh; but however it was, no one was her peer—and the Captain knew what he was talking about. Two days before Doris gave birth and died, he covered her like an animal because of her belly, and Doris gave herself as ardently as that very first time, on the single bed in her room in the house on Cathedral Square, where she'd gone to change out of her wedding gown. Yes, indeed; the love of this wedded pair was as deep and enduring as the wise judge had thought.

Doris's malady was diagnosed as galloping consumption in the last week of her pregnancy. The cough of the prenuptial period had developed into a chronic, racking cough after the wedding; the hollows under her cheekbones and collarbone deepened, but she did not spit blood until a few days before her confinement. The truck was sent for Dr. David. He reminded them of his earlier advice: "Well, I warned you; don't say I didn't. You should have postponed the wedding and given her the tests. Now it's too late. Not even a miracle could save her now."

When she saw her daughter spitting blood and wasting away before her eyes, more cords snapped in Dona Brígida's mind. She forgot all the insults, the harsh words, the indifference; she blotted out the lewd images of Doris as sweetheart and wife and recovered intact in her failing memory the biddable little girl who obeyed the nuns at school, the pure young Doris with downcast eyes and the rosary looped around her wrist, a stranger to all the world's wickedness and well advanced on the road to her novitiate. Once her daughter was restored to sanctity, Dona Brígida, for her sins, began her descent into Hell. She was just lucid enough to be able to care for the baby.

Death followed on the heels of birth that rainy night. Under the hands of Noquinha, the midwife, a plump, healthy little girl came into the world; and soon afterward Doris expired in the hands of Dr. David. The doctor had arrived too late for the birth but in good time to write out the death certificate.

And what were the Captain's sentiments? It was later learned in town that as soon as the doctor was dropped off in front of his house, Captain Justo drove the truck to Gabi's house, where four night-owls were desultorily drinking brandy with Valdelice, a strapping girl who was ashamed of her job. Having contracted to spend the whole night with one of the four men, the girl waited in yawning patience for the customers to finish boozing and arguing about soccer. Arruda, the waiter, Gabi's pet and a tough and competent bouncer, was snoring on top of the counter. The Captain walked in the door, picked up the bottle of brandy without a word, and downed it in one draught. Arruda roused himself for a fight, recognized Justiniano, thought better of it, and pulled in his horns.

For lack of anything better, the Captain made do with Valdelice. When the girl, being already spoken for, hung back at the Captain's "Get a move on!" he gave her a couple of resounding slaps and pulled her by her tousled hair into an adjacent room from which he did not emerge until midmorning.

In the meantime, news of Doris's death in all its scarifying details had brought the comadres out in full force to the courtyard of the church while the cocks were still crowing. They were there in plenty of time to see Captain Justo cross the street from the direction of Cuia Dágua, where the prostitutes plied their trade. Heavy, somber, slow-footed, sinister, mute, he looked more than ever like some dangerous wild beast.

Once her daughter was dead and buried, Dona Brígida expected to come into some sort of inheritance; and in a supremely reckless act of daring courage, she raised her voice to demand an inventory. The Captain laughed in her face. Appointed executor by his honor the judge, he consented, as a great favor, to continue to allow Dona Brígida to occupy the back room and to care for the child.

As days and girls came and went during that endless eighteen months after Doris died, Dona Brígida, a ragged, dirty, harmless madwoman, lived with the monsters of popular ballads: Hog, Jackal, Headless Mule. Never free of a torturing sense of guilt, perpetrator of an unforgivable crime against her naive, defenseless daughter, she lingered in that living Hell, expiating her guilt.

But all the time she knew that when her sentence came to an end, when the penalty ordained by the Lord had been fulfilled, an Angel of Vengeance would descend from Heaven. In her endless conversations with herself, Dona Brígida joyfully anticipated that day of liberation. An angel from Heaven, St. George probably, or St. Michael, or else the crazed father of a girl who had been raped, or a sharecropper cheated out of his due, or the owner of a fighting cock done out of his winnings, or a hired killer, or just some poor miserable wretch—maybe even Jackal, the arch-coward himself—would come to Hog, and bleed him.

Then Dona Brígida, redeemed from sin at last, and rich and free, would ensure her granddaughter the life due her lineage. Oh, let it be soon, before the infant grew into a girl to catch the Captain's eye and be forged into a ring for his golden chain.

Hidden behind the mango tree, child clutched to her breast, hair disheveled and dressed in rags, Dona Brígida saw the beasts carry the girl out of sight. Demons were abroad, filling the countryside, the fields, the woods, the house, the world.

The struggling form was forced inside the room and
the door locked from the outside. The Captain spat on his
palms and rubbed one hand against the other.

15

The Captain turned the key, opened the door, went in,
locked the door from inside, and set the oil lamp on the
floor. Tereza stood with her back against the wall farthest from the door, lips parted, watching him intently.
Justiniano Duarte da Rosa didn't seem to be in any hurry.
He took off his jacket and hung it on a nail between the
rawhide whip and the oleo of the Annunciation, took off
his trousers and untied his shoelaces. He would do without warm water for his feet, just for tonight—tomorrow
the little tomboy would wash them for him in the basin
before the show began. In shorts and unbuttoned shirt,
belly hanging out, rings on his fingers and chain around
his neck, he picked up the lamp to inspect the plate and
mug provided by old Guga, the cook. The plate was un-
touched, but some of the water had been drunk. Then, by
the dim, murky lamplight he inspected his purchase. His
merchandise had cost him a pretty penny, one thousand
and five hundred cruzeiros, plus the chit for his store.
Well, he didn't regret it; it had been money well spent—
a pretty face and a good figure, which would be even better when she grew up a little and her bust and hips looked
more like a woman's. As a matter of fact, though, nothing
was more to Justiniano Duarte da Rosa's taste than the
greenness of girls like Tereza who still smelled of
mother's milk, as Veneranda would say. Veneranda was
a sassy old bitch, but she was smart, all right: she knew
all sorts of lewd tricks and words with double meanings,
and she brought foreign women to Aracaju, experienced
gringas who would do anything you could name. But, here
—this was no time to be thinking about Veneranda. She
could go to hell and take her protector and sweetie-pie the
state governor with her. Felipa had told the truth: you'd
have to go to the capital, to Bahia that is, to find a prettier
girl. In Aracaju you'd never find such perfection—that
deep copper color, that black hair hanging down her

back, those long legs—she was a real picture. Just like
some paintings of a saint, like that one right there on the
wall. Oh, she was worth what he'd paid for her, all right.
She'd cost him a good round sum, but she wasn't over-
priced; there was a difference. The Captain ran his tongue
over his lips as he set the light on the floor, throwing long
shadows onto the walls. Lie down! he ordered. Lie down!
he said again. When he reached out an arm to make her
obey, the girl slipped away from him, still keeping her
back against the wall. Justiniano let out a short laugh:
Want to play blindman's buff, do you? So you're afraid of
the fox between my legs? All right, I don't mind; I'm
game if you are. A little chase fires the blood. The Captain liked to meet with some resistance; girls who opened
legs and cunts without putting up a fight never stayed in
his good graces long. Doris had been the only exception,
but then she had been his wife—and how could Doris
have resisted anyhow, there in her bedroom off the parlor
where she couldn't make any noise? She'd swallowed her
terror and lit a fire in her guts until not a whore in Veneranda's stable—French, Polish, or Argentine—could hold
a candle to her for ardor and skill. The Captain loved to
ride roughshod over resistance and fear, the more fear the
better. To see terror in some young thing's eyes was as
good as an elixir, as good as strong drink; it really set the
Captain up. You can yell all you want to: there ain't nobody around to hear you but a crazy old woman and a
kid. You can sob and scream your heart out, and not a
soul will pay you no nevermind. Come on, pretty! As the
Captain stepped forward, Tereza dodged but not in time
to avoid a blow which caught her across the nose. The
Captain laughed a second time. She'd cry now; he'd
looked forward to that. Crying warmed Justiniano's heart
and made his blood run faster. But instead of crying,
Tereza responded with a kick. Trained in fights with boys,
she landed it square on the Captain's shin, and her big
toenail broke the skin. It was just a scratch and bled
scarcely a drop, but Tereza had drawn first blood. The
Captain bent over to have a look at his wound and as he
stood up he let fly at the girl's shoulder with the full force
of his fist. Tereza, the little outlaw, the good soldier, the
ringleader in fights with the boys, Tereza had learned that
fighting men don't cry, and neither would she. But she

couldn't hold back a cry of pain because the blow had dislocated her shoulder. Well, did you like that? Have you learned your lesson? Are you satisfied, or do you want some more? Lie down, damn you! Lie down before I break every bone in your body. By this time the Captain was burning with lust. The girl's resistance, more effective than any herb or Spanish fly, had hardened his tool, stirred his blood, inflamed his appetite. Lie down! Instead of obeying, the stupid girl tried to kick him again. The Captain retreated. You'll be sorry for this, you cheeky brat! He dealt her a thumping blow on the chest which made her totter and open her mouth to catch her breath. Justiniano Duarte da Rosa saw his chance at last and seized her in his arms. He crushed her against him, kissed her on the neck and face, and tried to kiss her on the mouth. When he relaxed his arm a little the better to embrace her, Tereza whirled, escaped from his clutches, and dug her fingernails into the fat face close to her own. Why, she might have put the brave Captain's eyes out! Captain, oh Captain, who's scared now? Tereza's eyes showed hatred and nothing else. I'll teach you to scratch my eyes out, you bitch. No more fun and games now. As Justiniano advanced the girl evaded him; the shadows came and went; suffocating red smoke from the lamp filled the contenders' nostrils. Mad with rage, the Captain planted a blow like the thump of a bass drum on Tereza's rib-cage. She lost her balance and fell between the mattress and the wall. Justiniano's face was on fire. The damned little bitch had tried to blind him. He bent over the girl, but she wriggled along the floor, caught hold of the lamp, and the Captain felt the heat of the flame in his testicles and groin. Criminal! Murderess! Put the lamp down this second or you'll set the house on fire and I'll kill you. Tereza stood up and the lamp rose in her hand and went forward. The Captain retreated, this time to protect his face. With her back against the wall the girl moved the light to spy out the enemy's position, showing a bold, perspiring face as she did so. Where was the fear, the mad fear all the others had shown? There was nothing but hate. He had to teach her a proper fear and respect for the lord and master who had bought her from those who had the right to sell her. After all, he owned her, didn't he? What was the world coming to if there was no respect? Suddenly the Captain filled his cheeks with air and blew with all his might. The flame trembled and went out, plunging the room into darkness. Tereza was lost in the blackness, but it was clear as day to Justiniano Duarte da Rosa. He could see the girl against the wall, eyes filled with hate, the useless lamp in her hand. He had to teach her to be afraid; he had to educate her; it was time for the lesson to begin. Tereza received the slap from his open hand full in the face, she didn't know how many times. Neither she nor Captain Justo kept track. The lamp rolled on the floor. The girl tried to shield her face with her arm, but it wasn't much use; Justiniano Duarte da Rosa had a heavy hand, and he hit her with the back of it and with the open palm, all his rings on his fingers. Tereza had drawn first blood—a foolish little drop. Now it was the Captain's turn; his hand was stained with blood from the child's mouth. You'll learn respect for me, damn you. You'll learn to do what I say. When I tell you to lie down you lie down, and when I tell you to spread your legs you'd better spread them quick and be proud to do it. I'll teach you to be afraid. You'll be so afraid you'll guess what I want before I tell you, just like all the others, and even quicker. I'll stop hitting her, I guess she's had enough; but why won't the god-damned little bitch cry? Tereza tried to squirm out of his grasp but couldn't; the Captain held her and twisted her arm. The little girl gritted her teeth and pressed her lips together as the pain shot through her. The bully was going to break her arm but she mustn't cry, fighting men don't cry, not even when they're dying. A ray of moonlight came through a hole in the latticed window and into the attic room, too small to hold so much abuse. Tereza slowly yielded to the pain in her doubled arm. She fell on her back. Have you learned your lesson or do you still think you're smarter than I am? Standing over the prostrate girl, dripping with sweat, a scratch on his leg and his face afire, the Captain laughed in triumph. It would have been better if he had cursed; the Captain's laugh was fatal. He let go of Tereza's arm. Vanquished, she was no longer a threat. But in his rage the Captain had ended by hitting for the sake of hitting, abusing her for abuse's sake: in his indignation he had forgotten what he was about, and instead of being aroused, he had come out of the combat with a shriveled

prick. The ray of moonlight shining on her bare thigh rekindled Justiniano Duarte da Rosa's lust. He narrowed
his squinty little eyes, pulled off his shorts, and swung his
balls over the girl: You see, honey? It's all yours. Come
on and take off your dress. Hurry up and take your dress
off, that's an order. Tereza reached out a hand toward the
hem of her dress. The Captain followed the gesture,
thinking the she-devil's revolt was over. Come on, hurry
up and take your dress off. Obedient, that's the way I
like to see you, get a move on! Instead, Tereza, supporting herself with one hand on the floor, sprang to her feet
as nimbly as a boy and fled to a corner of the room. The
Captain lost his temper: I'll show you, you devil-bitch!
He took a step forward and felt Tereza's foot in his nuts.
God! The pain! the worst pain there was. He let out a
terrible bellow, writhing and in contortions. Tereza
reached the door and beat on it with her fists, crying for
help, for the love of God, somebody come before he kills
me! There and then she felt the first bite of the rawhide
—a whip made to order, with thongs of plaited, greased
rawhide, ten knots to a thong. Maddened, made wild by
the unendurable pain, the Captain's only thought was to
beat the girl within an inch of her life. The leather struck
Tereza on her legs, belly, breasts, shoulders, back, buttocks, thighs, face; and each lash of the seven thongs,
each bite of the knots left a slash, a gash, a trickle of
blood. Leather makes a sharp knife. The whip hummed
in the air. Panting and blind with fury, the Captain
flogged as he had never flogged before; not even little
black Ondina had had such a bad time of it. Tereza tried
to shield her face with hands that were open wounds. She
mustn't cry, but the cries and tears sprang out and rolled
down her bloody face against her will. Willpower was not
enough: Tereza howled with pain, oh, please, please
stop! From a neighboring room came Dona Brígida's futile curses; they didn't calm the Captain, didn't console
Tereza, didn't wake the neighbors or the wrath of God.
The Captain was tireless. After Tereza rolled on the floor,
half-dead in her blood-soaked dress, the Captain went on
beating her for some time. Had enough, you bitch? Nobody crosses Captain Justo, and anyone who does soon
wishes he hadn't. This is how I teach fear and obedience.
Justiniano Duarte da Rosa bent down, the whip still in his

hand, and touched the prostrate body, the childish flesh. A flicker of desire returned to his throbbing testicles and rose through his body, hardening his member, restoring his pride and self-respect. He felt a cold, thin remnant of pain down below, but it wasn't worth bothering about and it certainly wasn't going to stop the Captain from starting to make good on his fifteen hundred cruzeiros. The child let out a groan, the whining little she-devil. Justiniano put out his hand and ripped her dress from top to bottom. There was blood on the cloth and blood on the tense, firm flesh. He touched the nipples of breasts that were hardly breasts but only budding forms, barely rounded, like her buttocks. She was just beginning to be a woman; she was still a green and tender girl, just the way the Captain liked them—what could be better? She's a hellhound but pretty as a picture all the same, fit for a king, no virgin so virgin. The Captain's hand touched the few silky black hairs below her little belly, ran his tongue over his lips, put a finger to thrust into the mystery of the budding rose. Having overcome his pain and rage, the Captan felt as much desire as before. Now he was ready and willing and his prick was erect; the show could begin. But the she-devil crossed her legs and tightened her thighs. Where did she find the determination and the strength? The Captain tried to uncross her legs, but no human power could do that. Again Justiniano Duarte da Rosa, pursued by the Hound on his nuptial night, brandished his whip in fury. He stood up and began to beat Tereza in earnest. He whipped in desperation, he whipped to kill. If there's no obedience, what in hell is the world coming to? The howls of pain died away in the forest, where Dona Brígida had finally fled, her grandchild in her arms. The beating went on until Tereza's cries stopped and she lay still, an inert piece of flesh. The Captain rested for a minute, dropped the whip, uncrossed her legs, and touched the secret mystery. The girl made a feeble movement, but a couple of slaps across the face settled her down. The Captain, who loved to deflower green maids who smelled and tasted of milk, deflowered Tereza, who tasted of blood.

16

When a lusterless predawn light struggled through the chinks in the latticed window, Tereza, broken in two with pain, aching in every particle of her being, dragged herself to the edge of the mattress and gulped down the water that was left in the mug. She sat up with an effort, the Captain's snores making her shudder. There were no thoughts in her head, only hate. Until then she had been a playful, laughing child unusually merry and sociable, a sweet girl who was everybody's friend. In one afternoon and night she had learned to hate. Fear was still to come.

On hands and knees she crept to the chamber pot, groaning with pain as she squatted down. The Captain woke up as she used it. He wanted her awake, not a lifeless hunk of flesh. He wanted to watch her receive his member, her body thrilling with rebellious pain. It excited him beyond measure to hear her urinate.

"Lie down and let's have some fun."

He caught Tereza by one leg and pulled her down beside him, biting her mouth. Desire won out over the persistent, dull pain in his testicles. Spread your legs if you don't want me to beat you to death. The blasted girl not only locked thighs and lips, she did something worse: she gave his gold necklace a tug and the rings rolled around the room, each ring a maidenhead, gathered green. Damnation! Forgetting the pain in his balls, the Captain bounded to his feet. Pain in his tail and pain in his heart. Nothing in the whole wide world—person, animal, or object—was more precious to Justiniano Duarte da Rosa than that chain of hymens: not his little daughter, nor his gamecock Claudionor, of pure Japanese stock, nor his German pistol. His balls and his necklace the same night! The girl was a demon! So you haven't learned yet, she-devil bitch-of-a-bitch! By God, I'll teach you! You'll pick up those rings one by one to the tune of the whip. Get going! Let's have the rings, one by one! Whip in hand, blind with rage, nagging discomfort in the groin!

This time the flogging was enough to kill a horse. A little more of it would have killed Tereza. Packs of dogs in the distance echoed her howls: take that, god-damned little cockteaser, and that. And let it be a lesson to you. He beat her unconscious, but it was the Captain who picked up the rings.

Captain Justo was a weary man by the time he had found them all. His arm ached; he had almost dislocated his wrist, and there was still that persistent heavy feeling in the groin. He had never beaten anyone so hard before. He liked to beat people; it was fun. But this time he had gone too far; the damned little rebel was too hard to tame. In trying to break her will he had broken her body. The Captain was pretty battered himself, but he was not ready to show the white flag yet, not by a long shot. No one could say he wasn't a man. He mounted his untamed, golden-assed prize.

When the cocks crowed he dismounted. His nuts ached, damn that stubborn little bitch. But you can bend even iron if you hit it hard enough.

17

Fear branded on a girl's face at the moment of truth stimulated the Captain's libido, giving sexual desire a deeper dimension and an exotic flavor. It was pure delight to him to see his quarry terrified and fainting with fear; and when a girl left him no choice but to take her by force and by blows, that was pleasure fit for the gods. But that so-and-so of a Tereza—Hah! no fear to be seen yet in her eyes. He had beaten her to her knees, all right, the first night; but all he could see in her was fury, rebellion, hatred. Of fear not a trace.

Justiniano Duarte da Rosa was known—and respected —by all as a sportsman who raised fighting cocks and bet like a king. Now he made a bet with himself: he'd gotten across Tereza's threshold all right, and broken another gourd for his collection, but he would not set foot in Abdon Carteado's jewelry store in Aracaju to order the commemorative gold ring until he had taught that little bronco some fear and respect and had her broken at his feet, attentive to his every command and caprice— an abject suppliant, ready and willing to spread her legs when he gave the word, and then to beg for more. He would teach her all those tricks the gringas in Veneranda's castle knew. Doris had learned in no time at all to out-whore the whores; too bad she was so skinny and homely. Now Tereza, here, she was the picture of a saint, and the Captain intended to get double his money's worth out of her, one cent at a time, even if he had to whip her ten times a day and ten more a night. He *would* see her tremble with fear before him. And then—but only then—off he'd go to Abdon's jewelry shop in Aracaju to order the gold ring.

Nothing much had happened for the next few days, except for one attempted escape; the Captain was confined to bed with a swollen testicle, the result of Tereza's kick. If the damned girl had had shoes on she would have put Justiniano out of action for the rest of his natural life. Twice a day old Guga the cook unlocked the door and brought in a plate of beans, jerky, and manioc and a jug of water, and took away the chamber pot. When Guga appeared with breakfast the first morning, Tereza was so battered and helpless she didn't stir from the mattress. Guga sniffed the scent of blood in the dark room, picked up the whip, and shook her head, talking all the time:

"Tain't a bit of use crossing the Captain, you better off doing what he wants right off the bat. What you got you want to keep so bad? What's the use? You just a baby, just a bitty thing to make such an almighty fuss. You better do what he wants you to. He whupped you and whupped you like he'd never stop. I heard you hollering all night. You think anybody going to help you? Who? Old crazy woman? You crazier than she be. Now you stop your fussing and let folks get some sleep. We too tired to listen to you holler all night. What you do to the Captain to make him stay in bed? You ain't got no sense at all. No, you can't go out. You can't leave this room till the Captain say so."

You can't leave this room till he say so—Just see if I can't. When the old colored woman came back toward evening Tereza was ready for her, and without giving Guga time to come in, she darted through the door and made her escape, wrapped in a sheet. From where she was in the parlor, Dona Brígida saw her rush past like a soul in Purgatory, some more remains of the Captain's prey. Oh, God would punish him one day. She crossed herself, she too a captive in a living Hell.

They didn't find the runaway until the middle of the night, way off in the brush. Terto Cachorro was in command, the Captain having to direct the expedition and capture from his bed, where he lay soaking his shapeless sack in an infusion made from cigar-box tops—a sure cure for orchitis. The Captain's pack scattered over the countryside. It was Marquinho, an expert at tracking strayed cattle, who found her asleep in a thicket of thornbushes. The Captain's strict orders were that she must not be hurt or mistreated in any way. No one else was to lay a hand on her; he alone could administer punishment.

They brought her into his room, still wrapped in the sheet. Propped up against pillows in his bed, the Captain wielded the big heavy ferule from slavery days, one of much better quality, of course, than anything made nowadays. The bullyboys held Tereza while the Captain gave her four dozen blows, two dozen on each palm. She thought to herself, I mustn't cry, but from halfway through the ordeal to the end she wept quietly, stifling her sobs as best she could. Then she was locked into the little room at the back of the house again.

After that, one of the bodyguards stood by the door whenever Guga came in. On the second day, when her hunger was too great to bear, Tereza gave in and cleaned the plate. I mustn't cry—and she cried; I mustn't eat—and she ate. Shut up in the room, all she thought of was how to get out.

Nuts back to normal, the Captain returned to the battlefield of the bedroom. Guga appeared one day at an unaccustomed hour and with her was one of the guards, carrying a basin and a pail of water. The old woman gave Tereza a piece of soap and told her to take a bath. Not until after she had bathed and old Guga came back and hung a lantern between the picture of the Virgin with the Angel Gabriel and the cat-o'-seven-tails still stained with blood did Tereza understand the reason for the bath. Guga delivered a peace-offering:

"He say for you to put it on. It belong to the one who passed away. You try and see if you can keep quiet tonight—not bawl and keep folks from sleeping."

It was a batiste nightgown trimmed with lace, a fine piece of lingerie from Doris's trousseau, slightly yellowed now. Why don't you put it on? You just ain't got good sense.

By the cheerless murk of the lamp, the Captain shed his trousers and shorts. He took off his necklace and hung it on the picture frame, just in case. Why didn't you put on the nightgown I sent you, you ungrateful little hussy? Isn't my present good enough for you? The battle was renewed, blows succeeded by cries in monotonous succession. Dona Brígida fled again to the woods, clamoring for Divine Justice—punishment for the monster and punishment for his shameless victim. Who was she to yell her head off and let herself be thrashed within an inch of her life? Who did she think she was, playing so hard to get? Did she think she was better than Doris? Back she went to her living Hell.

Methodically, stubbornly, step by step, the Captain went on with the treatment that had always worked so well before. Tereza would learn fear and respect in the end, and she'd learn obedience too, by God, the obedience that makes the world go round. Hit the iron often enough with the hammer and it bends.

Tereza was beaten for more than two months. No one could keep exact count by the calendar, but it was long enough for people to get used to being lulled to sleep by her cries. What's that awful screaming, asked a curious traveling salesman. Oh, that ain't nothing. Just a crazy woman the Captain's taking care of. Tereza held out for two months. Each time the Captain took her he had to fight for her. Each new trick was learned slowly and by dint of brute force. Suck, the Captain ordered, and the disobedient vixen clenched her jaws tight and he hit her on the lips with a belt buckle. Open up, you bitch! until she did. Each lesson took long nights to learn, and the teaching aids were slaps on the face with the open palm, blows on the chest with the fist, belt, ferule, and whip. Tereza would finally become so exhausted that she let him have his way or did what he wanted. Clotted blood, the stink of urine, bellows of pain initiated Tereza into the art of the bedchamber. Turn around, ordered the Captain, and get down on all fours. In order to take her from behind like an animal Justiniano Duarte da Rosa almost wore out his fine rawhide whip with its seven thongs, ten knots to a thong.

The Captain was obstinate and he had made a bet with himself: Tereza would have to learn fear, respect, and holy obedience. And she learned them. What else could she do?

18

Tereza learned. But not before trying to run away a second time, when she found that the thugs had been taken off guard duty in the hall during Guga's comings and goings. The Captain thought, no doubt, that two months of intensive treatment had made her submissive and bent her to his will.

Once sure the guard was gone, Tereza made her escape, clad this time in Doris's nightgown, swift as a forest creature. She did not get very far: Guga's cries summoned the Captain and two of his gang, who cornered her outside the house and brought her back. This time the Captain ordered her to be tied up and thrown, a helpless bundle, back into the room.

Half an hour later Justiniano appeared at the door and laughed his short dire laugh, a sentence of doom. In his hand he held an old-fashioned iron full of coals. He raised it to the level of his mouth and blew into it. Sparks flew up and live embers glowed. He touched a finger to his tongue and then to the bottom of the iron. The spittle hissed.

Tereza's eyes widened, her heart shrank within her; finally her courage had failed her and she knew the color and taste of fear. Her voice quavered out a lie:

"I swear I wasn't going to run away. I just wanted to take a bath, I'm dirty all over."

She had endured the beatings and never begged for mercy; endured silently, except for her sobs and cries. She had never cursed him nor called down anathemas on his head, but as long as she had the strength she had not surrendered to him. True, she wept and did what he commanded, but she had never begged to be spared. Now the end had come:

"Don't burn me with the iron! Oh, please, don't do it! for the love of God. I won't ever run away again, please forgive me! Forgive me! I'll do anything you want, please forgive me! Don't do it, for your own mother's sake! Oh, forgive me! Please forgive me!"

The Captain smiled when he recognized real fear in Tereza's eyes and voice. Well, it was about time! Everything comes to pass in due time if you pay the right price.

The girl was laid belly up on the mattress, bound as she was with cords. Justiniano Duarte da Rosa sat down, Tereza's bare feet in front of him, and applied the iron first to one sole and then to the other. There was a smell of burnt flesh, a sizzling of skin, unearthly screams, and then deathly silence.

Once he was done, the Captain untied her. Cords and vigilance, a guard in the hall, the lock on the door—none of this was needed any longer. The course in fear and respect was over, and Tereza had learned obedience at last. Suck! and she sucked. Hurry up and get down on all fours! and she quickly got down on hands and knees. Alone and afraid, Tereza Batista was now a ring on the Captain's chain.

19

Tereza Batista spent just over two years in Captain Justo's company, sometimes in the country and sometimes at the store in town, as—what shall we say?—his favorite? The Captain's new mistress, people called her; but was that the right word? The condition of mistress, concubine, "other woman," "friend," implies the existence of an understood agreement between the chosen one and her protector: a body of mutual obligations, rights, privileges, and advantages. A perfect liaison calls for expenditures of money and generous, sympathetic understanding. Now Belinha, lady friend of his honor the judge, was his mistress in the fullest, most accurate meaning of the word. The magistrate had installed her in a house in a discreet dead-end street, where she had a yard full of cashew and mango trees with a breeze and a comfortable hammock; her furniture, curtains, and rugs were

simple but decent; and she was provided with a little
money for extras, over and above the necessities of food
and clothing. Even married ladies were envious when
they saw Belinha on her way to her dressmaker, beautifully turned out, eyes demurely lowered, with her maid
in attendance. She had a maid whose duties included not
only the housework but also going with her to dressmaker, dentist, shops, and the movies; for a mistress's
honor is fragile and must be guarded at all times. In exchange for these advantages, Belinha had undertaken to
offer her distinguished lover the complete intimacy of her
charming person, to outdo herself in loving little attentions, to be a pleasant companion, and—this above all—
to be faithful. Any violation of one or another clause in
this tacit contract for good living was only to be ascribed
to the fallibility inherent in the human condition. Take
Belinha, for example: the paradigm of the ideal mistress,
but incapable of fidelity, just a congenital lack in her delightful nature. His honor, understanding and twice-
burned, closed his eyes to the visits of Belinha's "cousin"
while he was in court, out of respect for family feeling.
If his own wife in Bahia rejoiced in a whole tribe of
masculine relatives, how could he deny one furtive, solitary cousin to dear, temperate Belinha, who had to spend
so many hours by herself when he was dealing out justice
in his jurisdiction? The judge was a veteran cuckold by
vocation; such resignation is indispensable sometimes if a
perfect liaison is to remain perfect.

No, Tereza could not be called the Captain's mistress,
even if she did sleep in the double bed at the country
house and in the antique bed in the town house. That privilege did raise her above the level of the others, consign-
ing her to a special category in the unending roll of girls,
flames, protégées, who followed one another in Justiniano
Duarte da Rosa's life. A significant privilege, no doubt,
but the only one, unless you counted the hand-me-down
dresses from Doris's trousseau, a pair of shoes, a mirror,
a comb, and a few peddler's trinkets. As for the rest, she
was a servant like the others. She worked from morning
to night, first in the farmhouse and then at the counter in
the store, after Justiniano discovered that she could figure
accurately and had a legible hand. As servant and favorite
Tereza enjoyed the privilege of the double bed for two

years and three months. She had rivals and competitors
but they all stayed in the little back room. None graduated from the straw mattress to a bed with clean sheets.

No woman had ever remained for so long in the Captain's good graces; he was a man who liked variety and
change. Females by the score—children, young girls,
young women—lived for a season in one or the other of
Justiniano Duarte da Rosa's two houses. Since they were
always available, the Captain's attentions, intense at the
start, dwindled to nothing in a matter of days or weeks,
or on very rare occasions, months. Then the wretched
girl was out in the world. Most of them headed for Cuia
Dágua, the local district for women leading "the life," as
it was called; a few of the physically more attractive
took the train for the larger markets of Aracaju or
Bahia. For more than twenty years the Captain had furnished the centers of consumption with a constant and
abundant supply of varied raw material.

According to Aírton Amorim, a different sort of collector altogether, such a mania for variety had the scientific name of impotence. Impotence! Epaminondas Trigo,
the district attorney, protested the use of the word. He
had had enough of Aírton's paradoxes; taking advantage
of his friends' good faith by spinning nonsense seemed to
be his favorite pastime.

"There you go again with your crazy ideas. He must
have a hard-on like a studhorse to take on so many
women; that's what I say."

"Surely you don't mean to tell me that an educated
man like you hasn't read Marañón?"

The bibliophile was fond of showing off his erudition:
Yes, Gregório Marañón, the Spanish scholar and professor at the University of Madrid, had established the fact
—and with authoritative proof, my dear fellow—that the
more women, and the more different kinds of women, a
man has to have, the less virile he is.

"Marañón?" Marcos Lemos, the bookkeeper at the
sugarmill, expressed surprise. "I've heard of that theory,
but I thought it was Freud's. Are you sure it's Marañón's?"

"I've got the book in my bookcase if you don't believe
me."

"Well, I sure as heck wouldn't mind being impotent

like that, screwing a different dame every night. That guy breaks their gourds one after the other and you call him impotent! That's really one for the books." The attorney remained unconvinced.

Aírton lifted his arms to heaven and then let them fall: "Lord, what ignorance! That's precisely the point! A man with five years in the university and a law degree, and you didn't know that? When a man has to have a different woman every night to arouse his libido and keep his potency, he's not much of a man, is he? Are you aware, Mr. District Attorney, that the most impotent man in history was Don Juan, the Great Lover, the man who had a thousand women? And I'll give you another prime example of impotence: Casanova."

"Oh, come on, Aírton, that's too much even for a paradox."

The judge, however, not liking to appear less learned than his friend, affirmed the existence of the disputed Marañón and his far-fetched theory: whether true or not, the theory had been advanced and debated. Hotly debated, in fact. As for Freud, that was something altogether different: his theory of dreams and complexes, and that tale about Leonardo da Vinci . . .

"Leonardo da Vinci? You mean the painter?" Dr. Epaminondas had seen the name in crossword puzzles. "Was he impotent, too?"

"Not impotent. Queer."

Subject matter for endless disputation: stallion or impotent? It depended on who was arguing the point. But whichever he was, the Captain sometimes formed an attachment to one or another of the bounteous sea of girls at his disposal. Nearly always it was a little girl still in diapers—to quote our knowing Veneranda again, an authority on sexual matters equal to Freud or Marañón and much less controversial. But if you added to the prerogative of the double bed—the surest proof of the Captain's favor—the cheap dress, some sandals, a pair of earrings, or a bow of ribbon, you pretty much summed up all the privileges accorded a favorite. The Captain had never learned to be a spendthrift. That sort of thing was all very well for his honor the judge; nothing comes easier than spending other people's money.

There was never an affectionate word or sign of tenderness; no compliments, no caresses. Nothing but ever more furious diligence in bed. Sometimes, at the most unpropitious moment, he would give Tereza the signal— Hurry up and hop into bed!—raise her skirt and unburden himself as if by unpostponable necessity, then send her back to work.

This strong partiality of the Captain's never kept him from frequenting other women. Sometimes he would have two female guests besides Tereza, one in each of the twin rooms in the country and in town, and would serve them all the same day. A studhorse and a stallion, that's what he was; and that joker of an Aírton Amorim calling him impotent! Well, not even the corroborative testimony of the Judge could persuade the attorney that that fellow Marañón, whoever *he* might be, was anything but an ass.

When Tereza Batista came from the farmhouse to the store in town and was installed behind a little desk to keep accounts, curious townsmen began to drop in for a glimpse of "the Captain's new girl—she's a real looker!" Justiniano Duarte da Rosa's town girls were discussed in the old wives' parliament and in the causeries of the professional men. One of the girls, Maria Romão, had caused quite a stir when she was seen arm in arm with the Captain outside the moviehouse, gyrating her ample rear and superb bosom. Soon it came out that an account had been opened for the mulatto girl at Enock's drygoods store, an unheard-of event, worth printing in the papers. She was tall, dark-skinned, straight-haired, a regular statue. Oddly enough, she was not very young—already nineteen when Captain Justo picked her out of a crew of backlanders from the Northeast on their way south to work on the *fazendas*. Captain Neco Sobrinho, a soulmate of Justiniano Duarte da Rosa, dealt in backlanders, rounding them up in the drought-stricken North and selling them later on in Goiás. It was impossible to lose on the deal, and he usually made a good profit. But finding himself temporarily short of cash and in need of fresh supplies as he went south, he had traded Maria Romão for jerky, beans, manioc, and brown sugar. Maria Romão was the first girl for whom an account in a store was opened, and the last. The Captain had a violent crush on her and thrust her shamelessly under the noses of the townspeople, but the flaming passion lasted less than a week.

The Captain was not given to confiding in anyone; on the contrary, he was secretive and reserved by nature, an enemy of all prying meddlers. Nevertheless, when he had sent Maria Romão packing, he made no objection to making a clean breast of the whole affair when his friend Dr. Eustáquio Fialho Gomes Neto questioned him about the truth of the tale circulating around town. The judge, new to the district and with his family living in the capital, had a social position which precluded his frequenting houses of ill fame. Naturally, he was looking for a girl to set up housekeeping with and thought Maria Romão might just suit.

"Is it true what people are saying, Captain? That the Romão girl is no longer in your company?"

"Yes, it's true. I traded off that good-looking puss of hers for a rickety little job Gabi got from the textile mill in Estância." He paused, and then added: "Gabi thinks she sold me a bill of goods. But the man or woman who can sell Captain Justo a bill of goods ain't been born yet, judge."

"Traded her off, Captain? What do you mean exactly?" The judge was eager to learn about local custom and the Captain's methods.

"Oh, me and Gabi like to do a little bargaining, judge. She lets me know when she's got something new in stock, and if I take a shine to it, I buy it, trade for it, rent it, make some kind of a deal. When I get tired of the goods, we start doing business all over again."

"I see." The judge didn't see, exactly; but no doubt he would understand in time. "You mean then that the girl is free if anyone should want . . . ?"

"You talk to Gabi. But if you don't mind my asking, why are you so interested?"

The judge explained his problem: he could be frank with the Captain, to whom he had been given an introduction by important friends. With the children at school in Bahia, his wife spent more time there than with her husband. She came back and forth a good deal, and so did he, but . . .

"Must cost you a hell of a lot," remarked the Captain, whistling between his teeth.

It certainly did. . . . It didn't bear thinking about, but what could he do? Educating children means making sacrifices, Captain. And a man like you can understand my position as magistrate. It would hardly do for me to frequent back alleys and houses of prostitution. It would be much more suitable to find some trustworthy girl who appealed to his senses. Now he had heard that Maria Romão was free, and if the Captain was no longer interested . . .

"I wouldn't advise it, judge. A pretty face, pretty figure, but rotten inside."

"Rotten . . . ?"

"Leprosy, judge."

"Leprosy? My God, are you sure?"

"I can tell by a person's shadow, and hers has started to bloom."

In the course of time the judge learned a good deal about local customs and the Captain's methods. Having a number of things in common, they became associates and did each other favors. People murmured that what they really had in common was membership in the same brotherhood of scoundrels, an unholy quartet made up of the mayor, the chief of police, the Captain, and the judge. Dr. Eustáquio prided himself on knowing more than anyone else about Justiniano Duarte da Rosa's real feelings. Within the intellectuals' circle, when both learned and lewd matters were being discussed, as on dreamy afternoons in the warmth of Belinha's bosom, the Judge held forth freely on the sentimental and sexual life of the respected *prócer*. Love worthy of that exalted name, the Judge declaimed, love strong enough to lead a grown man of long-established principles to commit real follies, true love, had been felt and suffered but once by Justiniano; and the object of that great passion had been Doris. What follies? What proof of blind love, mad love? What evidence of love sublime? Why, my dear colleagues, my sweet friend, the folly of marrying such an unattractive creature as that poor consumptive. Folly of follies! Love, sublime or sordid, as you will, but love, true love. The Captain had never confessed to love for anyone before he met Doris nor ever felt love again—all the rest was flames, crushes, whims, in vulgar parlance a yen for a lay, lasting a sometimes longer, sometimes shorter time, but usually shorter.

Tereza had no account in Enock's store nor was she ever seen on the Captain's arm before the movie started; on the other hand, she was the only one to occupy the matrimonial bed and enjoy Justiniano Duarte da Rosa's favor for more than two years. Two whole years and three months, and who knows how much longer it might have gone on if what happened hadn't happened?

The honorable judge, a profound student of psychology, contumacious debater, and persistent bard (he had dedicated a whole lascivious sonnet sequence in the style of Camoens to Belinha), not only refused to let Tereza follow Doris on the Captain's roster, but he balked at even calling her the Captain's mistress or favorite, as everyone else did. Favorite? Who? *Tereza Batista?* The fact that his honor was to some extent involved in the denouement of the affair may certainly have diminished his impartiality and adversely affected his muse, blinding him to certain distinctions between love and hate, fear and courage. He saw everything in terms of victims and a villain, innocence and guilt. Every actor in the drama, including the Captain, was a victim except Tereza, who was the deep-dyed villainess of the piece—so young, so perverse, her heart hardened to stone by vice.

There were those, of course, who held a diametrically opposite view, individuals of anomalous status, neither jurists nor littérateurs like Dr. Eustáquio Fialho Gomes Neto (Fialho Neto to the muses), nobodies who understood neither metrics nor the law. But in the end the matter remained unsettled, due to the unexpected and decisive intervention of Emiliano Guedes, patriarch of the Guedes clan.

20

What Justiniano Duarte da Rosa's true feelings were toward Tereza, to keep her so long in his favor and daily renew his interest, remains an unresolved question, learned men not being able to agree among themselves.

As for what Tereza felt, there is little dispute; her only feeling was fear, pure and simple.

In the beginning and as long as she was able to resist his power with all her might, Tereza's hatred kept her strong. After that she was afraid and nothing else. As long as she remained in Justiniano's house, Tereza Batista was a submissive, attentive, diligent slave, at work and in bed. She never waited for orders but was active, quick, painstaking, unwearying as she went about her chores. She had been given the hardest, dirtiest tasks and toiled all day long at washing, ironing, scrubbing. Hard work gave her strength and endurance. No one looking at her slender figure would have believed her capable of lifting hundred-pound sacks of beans and great bundles of jerky.

She had offered to help Dona Brígida attend to her granddaughter, but the widow would not even let her approach the child, much less care for her. Tereza was the enemy, the traitor who slept in Doris's bed, wore her clothes (the tight dresses provocatively emphasizing her developing figure), and tried to pass herself off as Doris, the better to rob Dona Brígida of daughter and inheritance both. No matter how far she plunged down into the abyss peopled with monsters, Dona Brígida always retained the glimmer of rationality that told her her granddaughter was sole heir to the Captain's property. On the day the Avenging Angel would descend from Heaven, the child would be rich and the grandmother would be ransomed from Hell to live again in opulence and in the Grace of God. Her granddaughter was her hostage to fortune, the charter of her emancipation, the key to her salvation.

And now this creature, dragged in from Hell by the Headless Mule or Jackal to join Hog's pack of hellhounds, this intruder masquerading as Doris, was trying to close off her only exit to freedom, to steal away her granddaughter, her property, her hope. Whenever she caught site of Tereza coming toward her, Dona Brígida would disappear with the little girl.

If only they would let her look after the child! It wasn't because of the doll that she wanted to, or at least not only because of the doll; Tereza loved animals and children and had never played with dolls. Dona Beatriz, the Judge's wife, chosen by Doris as godmother when first she knew she was pregnant, had brought the doll from Bahia as a birthday present. It could open and shut its eyes and say "Mama," had blond ringlets and wore a white bridal gown. It was usually locked away in a closet, but on Sundays the child was allowed to play with it for a few hours. Tereza had held it in her hands once, before Dona Brígida snatched it away from her.

Tereza didn't mind the work, not even emptying slops, scrubbing the latrine, tending the open sore on Guga's leg, or washing dirty clothes; but she did suffer keenly from the widow's open dislike of her and the prohibition against touching the baby. She watched from a distance as the child tottered on unsteady legs. It must be nice to have a baby, or even a doll.

She suffered even more from her duties in bed—to serve as the Captain's mount, to satisfy his whims, to give herself docilely at any hour of the day or night.

After dinner, when he was at home, she would bring a basin of warm water and soap and wash his feet. She did it to imitate Doris, Dona Brígida thought; but Doris had been happy to do it, had worshiped the Captain's feet and kissed his toes, feverishly anticipating the coming performance in bed. For Tereza the task was full of risks and uncertainties; she would a thousand times rather have been washing Guga's festering sore. Remembering Doris, or perhaps out of sheer meanness, the Captain would sometimes push her over with his foot: Why don't you ever kiss me or try to please me, damn you? Better women than you have done it. He would shove his foot in her face: Damned prideful piece of shit! The shoves and kicks were entirely gratuitous, bestowed out of sheer malice, for whenever the Captain demanded it, Tereza would swallow her pride and repugnance to lick his feet and the rest.

Never once had Tereza felt the slightest pleasure, the least eagerness or desire; every physical contact with Justiniano Duarte da Rosa was a nauseating burden and it was only out of fear that she gave herself to him and satisfied his demands, and made herself be what he wanted—a female who was always ready, willing, available. At that time in Tereza's life, whatever had to do with bed or sex signified only pain, blood, filth, resentment, and servitude.

It never even occurred to her that such a business might hold the joy of reciprocal pleasure, or indeed pleasure of any kind. Tereza was simply the vessel into which the Captain relieved himself, emptying his semen into her as he emptied his urine into the chamber pot. That sexual intercourse could take any other form, that there might be affection, caresses, joy, never crossed her mind. She could never understand why on earth Aunt Felipa should have wanted to shut herself up with a man. Passion, affection, longing, joy—none of these existed for Tereza.

She never asked for anything: a prideful piece of shit, though unconscious of her pride. Justiniano gave her dresses from Doris's trousseau, a pair of shoes from Enock's store, one or two cheap baubles on feast days when one of his cocks left an adversary dead in the ring, torn by the iron spurs. None of these rare gifts altered in the least the strong sentiment in Tereza's breast, that of fear. When she sensed anger in the Captain's voice or gestures, she at once felt death in the soles of her feet, the same icy terror that had gone through her when she saw the iron in his hand, the sparks flying. He had only to raise his voice, shout an ugly name, laugh his chilling laugh, and ice-cold death gripped Tereza's heart and branded her feet again with the red-hot iron.

21

Did Captain Justo know that women can feel pleasure just as men do? He knew it perhaps, but the matter did not particularly interest him and he had never bothered to share pleasure and passion with a bed partner. Mutual possession, reciprocal sensations, pleasure shared with another—all such stuff was the silly talk of sissies who could talk up a storm but not do much about it. The female animal was for mounting and that was the end of it. In the Captain's eyes, the woman who was good in bed was the one who awoke his lust, either because she was a timid, green, inexperienced virgin or because she was a professional who knew plenty of tricks. As was public knowledge, he preferred them young and shrinking; the necklace he wore to symbolize the gourds he had broken was proof of that.

What the Captain wanted from women was pleasure, and all for himself. He couldn't help noticing, of course, that some women were more ardent, more eager and responsive than others. Doris, burning with fever, for one; not even among the gringas in Veneranda's castle had he found any harlot who loved harlotry more. Feminine ardor and desire satisfied the Captain's masculine pride and were a tribute to his virility. After all, wasn't he a macho who could spend a whole night deflowering a virgin and then ride out the morning with a competent whore? His passion was not aroused by any pleasure or fondness shown by his partner. On the contrary, he easily became annoyed when any girl more coquettish than the others gave herself passionately and then claimed any sort of reciprocal affection or attention. What kind of tomfoolery was that? No real man sucks up to a woman.

What happened, then, between the Captain and Tereza? Why did she sleep for so long in the big double bed? Why didn't Justiniano tire of her after a while and get rid of her? Two years is an awfully long time. Every time he laid eyes on Tereza, desire welled up from scrotum to chest. Tereza was not forgotten when he was off on a trip and enjoying fancy women in the capital. More than once on the farm, he deflowered some new girl on the mattress in the back cubicle, then climbed into the double bed and entered Tereza while he was still smeared with the other girl's blood.

Why? Because she was so tall and so pretty, a pretty thing everybody coveted? One afternoon, when news of fresh prey had brought him to Gabi's house—this one I'll vouch for, I'll put my hand in the fire for her, if she isn't an out-and-out virgin you don't have to pay me a penny —Gabi seized on the Captain's obvious interest to propose that he give her Tereza in exchange; a face like hers was just what the establishment needed.

"I have a list of candidates already waiting in line."

The Captain, needless to say, never allowed any loose talk with or about any woman of his: How could anyone have forgotten what happened to poor Jonga, who was once a prosperous sharecropper? He had lost his crops and the use of his right hand, and if he escaped with his life it was only thanks to the doctor at the charity hospital —and all because he struck up an innocent conversation with Celina when she was on her way to the creek. The words were no sooner out of Gabi's mouth than she swallowed her smile; Justiniano Duarte da Rosa was tearing up the parlor in a rage.

"List? You show me that list! I want to know the names of the bastards who had the nerve to—Where's the god-damned list?"

The peace-loving customers vanished. Gabi had a hard time of it soothing the mettlesome Captain: There wasn't any list, that was just a manner of speaking, of complimenting him on the girl's prettiness.

"I don't want any compliments."

Whether he wanted them or not, the girl went on being complimented and praised, and new names were secretly added to the list, in order of precedence. No other girl around was so comely or so much desired. The Captain's vanity was flattered by being the owner of a jewel that had caught the eye of Emiliano Guedes, the millionaire hidalgo himself—and Emiliano Guedes was hard to please. Justiniano showed off Tereza at cockfights; and when some planter came to visit him in the country or a drummer showed up at the store, he would call her in to serve coffee or rum so that he could enjoy to the full the covetousness of his visitors and the pleasures of being an envied proprietor. But with all that he was not nearly as proud of Tereza as of Claudionor, his unbeaten champion and ferocious killer cock.

The Captain was not particularly sensitive to beauty except when it was time to negotiate, to bargain, and to sell; then a girl's face and figure, her charm and grace were worth good hard cash. In bed other qualities weighed more with him than beauty. Homely, sickly Doris had lasted as long as she lived. But if it wasn't her beauty, then why did Tereza sleep so long in that double bed?

Who can say? Maybe it was because the Captain had never once been sure she was wholly and completely his. Yes, she was submissive and obeyed him in everything; she ran to serve him and carried out his whims and his orders without a murmur; but he knew she did so only to avoid punishment, the ferule, the belt, the rawhide whip. He gave the orders and she obeyed them, but she never took the initiative, never offered herself. She lay down, spread her legs, opened her mouth, got down on all fours; but none of it was really her doing. Doris had melted in bed, made provocative suggestions before he even thought of them: "I'm going to suck your prick and your eggs." Not even Veneranda's gringas went that far. Tereza was silent and efficient, carried out orders. So much submission was a source of satisfaction to the Captain, of course; he had taken a good deal of trouble to teach this rebellious kid to be afraid, and he had finally tamed her and broken her will. He was an expert at breaking young mares. For just that reason he liked to wield the ferule or the whip on any pretext at all, or even with none, just to keep the notion of respect for him alive and prevent rebellion from again raising its ugly head. If there weren't any fear, the world would come to an end.

Could it be that the Captain was waiting until he had brought her completely under subjection and had her at his feet, amorous, melting, suppliant, provocative, as he had so many others, from Doris on, before he considered sending her away or trading her off to Gabi or Veneranda? Really she was good enough for Veneranda's castle, a fitting morsel for the exigent palates in the capital. Was Tereza some sort of challenge to him, another bet he had made with himself? No one could be sure, when the Captain was so reserved, so little given to confidences.

Most of the townsfolk, including the comadres, his honor the Judge, and the local intelligentsia, were content to attribute such a long-lasting affair to just one thing—Tereza's increasing beauty as she neared her fifteenth birthday: hard little breasts, a round derrière, and that deep copper color, that golden skin. Peach skin, said the bard/Judge poetically; too bad so few people could appreciate the image, never having seen or tasted the foreign fruit. Marcos Lemos, bookkeeper at the sugarmill, preferred to compare Tereza to cane-sugar syrup and sapodilla pulp. Marcos Lemos's name headed Gabi's list.

What was Tereza to the Captain? A wild colt? If that's what she was, he had tamed the bronc, and he rode it with bullwhip and roweled spurs.

22

The free, uninhibited, happy girl who had climbed trees
and run races with a mongrel dog and fought with boys
whose respect she won with her fighting arm, who had
laughed with her schoolmates and been praised by her
teacher for her intelligence and good memory; that smiling, sociable, friendly little girl had died on the mattress
in the back room, under the rod and the whip. Gnawed
with fear, Tereza kept to herself in her corner, put a lock
on her feelings, and made friends with no one. She was
always just on the edge of panic; her tenseness never relaxed except when the Captain went to Aracaju or Bahia
on business two or three times a year.

She expunged from her memory the carefree childhood
days on her uncle's farm, at Dona Mercedes's school,
with Jacira and Ceição, or in mock warfare with the
boys, or enjoying the weekly holiday at the Saturday market. She tried to forget all of that so as not to remember
the day Aunt Felipa had sent her away with the Captain:
The Captain's a nice man, you'll have everything your
heart desires when you live in his house, you'll be a lady.
And Uncle Rosalvo had taken his eyes off the ground and
come out of his chronic stupor to help them round her up;
he had been the one who caught her and gave her away.
The ring had sparkled on her aunt's finger. What did I do,
Uncle Rosalvo? What crime did I commit, Aunt Felipa?
Tereza longed to forget everything. It was bad to remember, it made her hurt inside. Besides, she was always half asleep. She got up at day-break, Sundays and
holy days included, and at night there was the Captain.
Sometimes he was at her all night without giving her any
peace at all. When he went off on a trip or decided to stay
in town, what holy, blessed nights those were! Tereza
could sleep and have a respite from fear. Lying in bed
she wiped away her dead childhood, but the mongrel dog
kept her company as she slept like a log.

Even if Tereza had wanted to make friends with the
sharecroppers and outlaws and the few women around
them, it would not have been easy. She was the Captain's

girl and she slept in his bed; that was enough to drive everyone away from her out of fear of Justiniano Duarte da Rosa's all too easily aroused anger. It wasn't healthy to go around grinning at any favorite of his, or to talk to her any more than you had to. Some of the tenant farmers had seen what happened to Jonga, and all the others had heard about it. Jonga had escaped with his life; he was a lucky bastard. Celina had paid for talking and laughing on the edge of a knife; when she finally ended up at Cuia Dágua, it made you feel sorry for her to look at her. The Captain's women were deadly danger, contagious disease, snake poison.

Twice the Captain had taken her to cockfights on the croup of his horse. He was proud of his gamecocks and his pretty little strumpet; he wanted to show Tereza off to the others and make them envious. Packets of money for bets in his pockets, his bodyguards around him, the flash of knives and revolvers, and the bloody cocks in the ring, iron spurs, feathers torn from their breasts, heads sprinkled with white rum. Tereza shut her eyes tightly so as not to see, but the Captain made her look: This is the most exciting thing in the world, they say bullfights are even better but I don't believe it! I'd have to see that with my own eyes. Both times the Captain's cocks lost badly—inexplicable, unprecedented defeats. There was bound to be some explanation; it had to be somebody's fault. Tereza's, of course, with those accusing, pitiful eyes, and her anguished cry when the cock fell, twiching convulsively, chest spurting blood. Anybody who raises cocks knows that a crybaby in the audience, man or woman, is fatal when a champion's getting ready to fight. It's a hoodoo, sure as shooting. The first time Justiniano contented himself with some cuffs and curses to teach Tereza to appreciate and applaud the fighting cocks. But when it happened the second time he beat her good, to take away the jinx and make up for the money he'd lost on bets and his disappointment at losing. He never set her behind him on the horse again and forbade her ever to go to a cockfight—nobody that lily-livered deserved such a treat. Tereza thought the beating a cheap price to pay for her unexpected freedom. She would much rather spend her rare idle hours catching Guga's fleas and killing nits.

So Tereza, in almost constant panic, saw two years of her life wear away at the Captain's farmhouse. One day he surprised her scribbling on a piece of paper with the stub of a pencil. He took paper and pencil away from her.

"Whose writing is that?"

Tereza had written out her own name, Tereza Batista da Anunciação, and the name of her school, Tobias Barreto Grammar School, and that of her teacher, Mercedes Lima.

"It's my writing, sir."

The Captain recalled having heard Felipa praise the girl's reading and writing at the time of the sale, as a justification for the high price she was charging; but all he had been thinking about then was her gourd and he hadn't paid any attention.

"You know how to add?"

"Yes, sir."

"And subtract and multiply and divide?"

"Yes, sir."

A few days later Tereza was transferred to the town house and her bundle deposited in the Captain's room. She did not miss the farm, not even old Guga and her fleas. In the store she took the place of a boy who had gone south, the only one who had known how to do all four operations in arithmetic. Chico Half-Sole, a completely trustworthy fellow, knew the stock by heart, and woe to anyone who thought of pinching anything! But this indispensable collector of unpaid bills, with all his teeth and his fishknife showing, could hardly add two and two. A couple of half-grown boys, one named Pomp and the other Flycatcher, were strong at putting their thumbs on the scales but weak in arithmetic. Tereza kept a record of deliveries, totaled receipts, acted as cashier, and kept the monthly accounts. Justiniano watched her closely for three days and pronounced himself satisfied. The customers peered at her out of the corner of their eyes and took note of her pretty figure and general good looks, but none of them dared to speak to her. Remember: Captain Justo's women are a fatal disease, snake poison, death.

23

One time when Tereza still lived on the farm, Emiliano Guedes appeared to sort out some business concerning a few head of cattle. Justiniano Duarte da Rosa, a man with his finger in many pieces, bought and sold a little of everything, buying cheap and selling dear, which is, of course, the only way to make money. He had bought a drove of cattle a few months before from a fellow named Agripino Lins on the road to Feira de Sant'Ana. The herd was ruined, the animals nothing but skin and bones; one of the cowpokes had come down with typhus and some of the stock died, so the cattle dealer had sold the rest for what little he could get. When it came time to pay, Justiniano deducted, from the amount agreed on, the value of one cow that was dead when the herd reached his land and two others that were more dead than alive. When the drover tried to protest, the Captain threatened him: Don't you raise your voice to me and don't call me thief. That's something I don't let anybody do. Take your money and vamoose, you bastard, if you know what's good for you. And he gave orders to turn the cattle out to pasture to fatten up.

Coming to look at the cows and pick out a few for his herd, Emiliano Guedes sprang down from his black horse —silver spurs, silver bridle, silver-mounted leather harness—and Justiniano greeted him fawningly, in the way befitting the chief of the Guedes clan, eldest of the three brothers and real lord of those lands. Rich Captain Justo, of whom so many men were afraid, was a nobody by comparison, an insignificant cur with none of his insolence and bluster showing.

In the parlor, still holding his quirt with the silver handle in his nervous hand, the visitor caught sight of Dona Brígida, looking very old and as if she were in some world of her own, shuffling in her slippers after the baby girl—why, he would hardly have recognized the poor woman.

"She hasn't been right in the head since my dear wife died. She's just let herself go, pays no mind to anything any more. I keep her here for charity's sake," the Captain explained.

Dr. Guedes gazed after the widow as she wandered off into the woods and murmured:

"Who could have imagined it? She was such a distinguished lady once."

Tereza came into the room with the coffee, and Emiliano Guedes forgot Dona Brígida and the way the world turns. He stroked his moustache as he appraised the child. He was a connoisseur and he could hardly conceal his astonishment: God in Heaven!

"Thank you, my dear." He stirred his coffee, his eyes on the girl.

Emiliano Guedes was a fine-looking man: tall and spare, with graying hair and a full moustache, aquiline nose, piercing eyes, and well-tended hands. Tereza was serving coffee to the Captain, her back to Emiliano; he sized up her good points, her thighs and buttocks squeezed into the other woman's dress. What a truly lovely thing she was! And still malleable. If she were properly molded, with love and affection, what a marvel she would blossom into someday.

When the two men had finished their coffee, they mounted and went to look at the cattle. Emiliano picked out the best cows and a price was agreed on. Back at the house with all the details of the deal settled, Emiliano checked his horse at the Captain's door and, thanking him, refused an invitation to dismount.

"Thank you, I haven't time today." He raised his whip; but before flicking his horse and galloping off, he stroked his moustache and said: "Would you consider adding to the lot the little heifer you have here at home? If you will, name your price. Your price is mine."

At first the Captain did not understand him.

"The heifer I have at home? What do you mean, Dr. Guedes?"

"It's the girl I mean—your maid. I need a servant at the sugar-mill."

"Oh, that girl is my ward, Dr. Guedes. She has no parents and I'm bringing her up, so she's not mine to give away. If I could, she'd be yours. I'm sorry I can't accommodate you this time."

Emiliano lowered his hand and flicked his thigh lightly with the silver-handled quirt.

"We'll say no more about it. You'll send me the cows, then. Good-bye."

His was the ancestral voice of command. He touched his silver spurs to the horse's belly and reined it in until it rose on its hind legs, superbly, and made it whirl about as it reared. The Captain instinctively retreated a step. Guedes waved a curt farewell, and the horse's hooves kicked up the dust. Patience! If that child belonged to him, he wouldn't part with her either, not at any price. He had glimpsed the flash of her eyes, the flash of an uncut diamond waiting to be polished by a gemcutter who knew his business. Such a jewel of many carats was a rare and precious thing. He caught sight of her again, walking down to the river with a bundle of clothes on her head and a graceful sway of the hips; her rump was beginning to lead a life of its own. Well cared for, surrounded by affection and plenty, she would reach perfection and be a gift of God. But Justiniano, that brute with the lowest kind of instincts, was incapable of perceiving that; he could never polish such a diamond and bring out its facets, or value at its true worth the gem that had fallen to his lot by a freak of capricious fate. If she belonged to Emiliano Guedes he would make her a jewel for a king: do the thing well, and take pleasure in doing it. The flash of those black eyes! Yes, fate was capricious.

Captain Justo watched from his porch as the fiery horse galloped off into the distance. It was a thoroughbred stallion, and just now, when it reared on its hind legs, it had frightened him—and that arrogant rider decked out in silver. Justiniano Duarte da Rosa played with his gold necklace, each ring a gourd gathered green. Tereza's had been the most difficult one of all; he had had to beat her senseless to take her. Tereza had cost him fifteen hundred cruzeiros, plus credit at his store, Tereza when brand new, not yet thirteen, Tereza smelling of milk, with the hymen of a child. And if he wanted to sell her, deflowered and all, he could do it and make a good profit on the deal. If he wanted to sell her.

Dr. Emiliano Guedes, chief of the Guedes clan, lord

of wide leagues of land and serfs without number, would
pay a high price for the Captain's leftovers. No, he
wouldn't sell her. Not yet anyway.

24

The winter rains freshened the parched land, seeds quickened and sprouted, and the fields bore fruit. Girls
chanted the old songs on festive saint's-day novenas, drew
lots to see who they would marry, and made promises to
the saints; harmonica tunes filled the country roads when
there was a dance in the neighborhood, rockets burst in
the sky—and after the prayers and the vows to the saints
came the shuffle dances, the liquor, the firewater, the
cane-sugar rum, the flirtations, the pairings off, the girls
tumbled in the woods among protests and laughter. It was
the month of June, the month of corn, of oranges, of green
sugarcane, the kettles of corn syrup, of corn fritters and
cornbread and fruit and genipap cordials. Every table
was laid for a party and altars blazed to Anthony the marrying saint, to God's cousin John, to Peter, patron saint
of widows. School was out and women were pregnant.

Lights were on in the front room of the house belonging to his honor the judge, Dr. Eustáquio Filho Gomes
Neto, the ardent sonneteer Fialho Neto; all the chairs
were occupied by visitors come to welcome home Dona
Beatriz Guedes Marcondes Gomes Neto, the wife who
was almost never there, the loving, anxious mother who
spent all her time in the capital taking care of the children, "because these days you can't leave children all by
themselves alone in a big city, with all its lures and temp-
tations."

For Dona Beatriz, too, the winter rains had proved
beneficial. In four short months, between her last flying
visit in February and this one in June, she had grown at
least ten years younger. The skin on her face was smooth
and taut—no more wrinkles, no double chin—and her
breasts stood firm and high on a slender figure. All in all,
one would have said she had lived through thirty fiery
springs at the most. My God, how shameless can you be,
as Dona Ponciana de Azevado, she of the spiteful phrases,

grumbled indignantly to her friends after she had paid her call. "That so-and-so is the walking glorification of modern medicine." To Dona Ponciana, plastic surgery was a crime against propriety and religion. To change the face God gave you, to cut your skin and sew up your breasts and God knows what else—anathema! Mariquinhas Portilho disagreed; she couldn't see that it was a crime or a sin; she wouldn't think of doing it herself, of course; had no reason to, since she was poor and a widow, but the judge's wife lived in the capital and went about in high society. . . .

"High and low society, comadre, and low more often than high," Dona Ponciana cut her off implacably. "It's been a long time since she saw forty, and now she turns up trying to look like a girl, and Chinese at that."

This was a reference to the new almond eyes for which Dona Beatriz had traded in her old ones—large, melancholy, suffering, imploring, an important factor in her previous successes, but unfortunately puffed up in a sea of wrinkles and crow's-feet and no longer a novelty.

"Is she really over forty?"

Yes, of course she was. She had married late in spite of being an heiress from a good family. It had taken an intrepid dowry-hunter indeed to turn deaf ears to the universal clamor: Dona Beatriz, when single, had been a very easy lay. Why, her son Daniel, who had come with her this time, must be almost twenty-two, and he was the second son. The firstborn, Isaías, was almost twenty-seven —between the two there had been a girl who had died of croup—and would graduate from medical school in December. Yes, and let me tell you, Mariquinhas, since you always take her part—those innocent children she's watching over in Bahia, while she leaves her husband here to take up with that trollop Belinha, are a pair of grown men, and Vera, Verinha, is twenty, if she's a day, and she's on her third engagement, even if she is still marking time in high school. So Madame lives it up in Bahia, playing cards and sleeping around, and all the while she's not ashamed to pose as the noble wife giving everything up for her children, as if *we* were a pack of crazy old women with nothing better to do than criticize the way other people live. And isn't that exactly what we are? laughed kind Mariquinhas Portilho. The other women, however, agreed with Dona Ponciana Azevedo, who seemed to be kept so well informed about the Judge's family by acquaintances of hers and neighbors of Dona Beatriz: eyewitnesses, ladies! Every single afternoon that loving mother goes out to play bridge with other women as shameless as she is or to meet Dr. Ilírio Baeta, the professor at the university who's been her lover for the last twenty years; in fact they say he was the one who did her the favor, when he was a student. It isn't enough for her to put horns on the judge; she cuckolds the good doctor, too, because she's crazy about young men. That's why she absolutely had to do something about her face and figure, get herself half-soled—whole-soled, I'd say!—squinch up her eyes and sew up her bosom and God knows what else. The comadres' own bosoms swelled with envy, and envy left a residue of bitterness in their mouths and hemlock on their tongues.

Momentarily alone with her husband in a breathing space between bunches of callers—that flock of vultures, that pack of venomous old witches, all they come for is to poke each other and whisper—Dona Beatriz gave vent to the melancholy impression she had come away with from her visit to Dona Brígida and her godchild the day before.

"The poor woman's living in filth. She's just left to her own devices, with nobody to talk to but the child. It's a shame to watch her going downhill the way she has these past few months. And she still tells those awful stories that give you gooseflesh. If there's a grain of truth in the dreadful tales she tells, your friend Justiniano, our compadre, is the world's worst monster."

The judge repeated to his wife the explanation he always gave; he had to defend the Captain after every one of his wife's visits to her goddaughter, and stick up for him to many other people too, friends of the deceased Dr. Ubaldo Curvelo and Dona Brígida:

"She's crazy, poor thing. The death of her daughter unhinged her mind. She lives that way because she wants to; she won't listen to anyone who tries to tell her to take care of herself. What do you think the Captain should do?" Send her to the madhouse in Bahia? To São João de Deus? You know in what dreadful conditions the inmates live there. No, our compadre keeps her with him on the farm, sees to all her wants, and lets her take care of her granddaughter. She really is fond of the little girl, you know. It would be easy for the Captain to pull strings and get the asylum to make room for her, and then he could wash his hands of the business." He added: "I beg of you, my dear friend, to avoid any comment that smacks of disrespect when speaking of the Captain. Whatever faults he may have, he is our compadre, and has been an obliging friend to whom we owe a great many favors."

" 'We,' my dear friend?" (putting in her voice the same faintly ridiculous solemnity that had been in his honor's). "*You* do . . . you owe him money, I believe."

"Yes, money for expenses. Or do you think a judge's salary is enough for people like us to live on?"

"Don't forget, my dear friend"—in the same mocking tone—"that I pay my personal expenses with the income I inherited, or rather, the small part of it that I managed to hang onto by a miracle before you could throw it away."

Whenever his honor had that money thrown in his face —and it was often—he reacted in the same way: by raising his hands to Heaven and opening his mouth to protest vehemently; except that he did not protest but said nothing at all, as if, a victim of the most crying injustice, he was abstaining, in the interest of conjugal harmony, from annihilating his antagonist with an unanswerable explanation.

Smiling slightly, Dona Beatriz rested her almond eyes —everyone in Bahia said they suited her very well—on her long, manicured nails, away from her poor wretch of a husband and his effort at the same old act, the worn-out, silly gesture. She felt sorry for Eustáquio, with his rustic concubine, his mask of respectability, and those verses, the song of a young cock and an old cuckold. And he was putty in the hands of the Captain, who was the worst sort of scoundrel, eager to serve him and cover up the beast's outrages and crimes. It was lucky for them there was no chance of a political upset; lucky that she, Dona Beatriz, a relative of the Guedeses on her mother's side, was a guarantee of immunity. It was thanks to the Guedeses that Eustáquio had been appointed a magistrate twelve years before, when seeing herself in danger of losing her inheritance through a marital fiasco, she had imposed that solution in order to fend off divorce and dishonor. She shrugged her shoulders; no use thinking about that; and anyway, Dona Brígida's problems didn't really interest her very much. She had gone to see her to fulfill a social obligation, just as she had come to spend a few days with her husband in the interests of social duty and her own interests too; after all, her children would not approve of her divorce or separation from her husband, and her Guedes cousins certainly would not. This world is full of tiresome obligations; those are the rules of the game, and you have to follow them; no one can ignore them.

No, not even Daniel, her favorite child, the picture of his mother, walking into the room just then with his permanent seductive smile on his face. Hadn't Daniel had to come up here to spend a month's vacation with his father, so as to place distance and absence between himself and the sixty years of Pérola Schuartz Leão, the millionairess? He was fed up, of course, with the senile old thing's rings and necklaces and sobbing and scenes of jealousy. For all his pose of dissolute cynicism, Dan was just a little boy at heart.

Sensing the tension in the room and having a horror of dissension, arguments, and frowns, Daniel tried to lighten the charged atmosphere:

"Well, I've been out exploring the burg. Pretty sad, don't you think? I'd forgotten what a one-horse town it is, but then I haven't been up here for ages. I don't know how you can stand it all year round, Dad, only going twice a year to Bahia. Too much! I'll get my law degree if you want me to, but I hope you won't ever ask me to be a small-town judge; I couldn't take it."

Dona Beatriz smiled at her son.

"Your father was never very ambitious, Dan; he's a poet. As intelligent and well read as he is, writing for the newspapers and all, and with my family's prestige, he could have had a political career if he'd wanted one; but he chose to be a judge instead."

"Everything has its compensations, my boy." Again his honor wrapped the toga of respectability around him.

"I believe you, Father," Dan agreed, his thoughts on Belinha, whom he'd just then seen in the street.

"I can study in peace here, and I have plenty of time

to work on both of the books I am writing, the one on penal law and the book of poems. After I retire, I am thinking of submitting my name to the faculty selection board at the university. Academic life tempts me as politics never did; for politics I feel only repugnance!" The judge, newly invested in a mantle of moral dignity, had fully recovered his usual self-importance.

Dona Beatriz decided to change the subject. Eustáquio's solemn affectations grated on her nerves. Heavens, what a bore he was!

"Well, Dan, how many grand passions have you inspired? How many hearts have you set on fire? How many husbands are threatened, how many respectable homes endangered?" Dona Beatriz was an understanding confidant who got a kick out of her children's love affairs and was a laughing accomplice whenever Daniel was mixed up with one of her card-playing friends.

"I'd say the selection of local womenfolk is meager but aggressive, Mater. They're all in heat; I never saw anything like it—every window's full. Not much to tempt me though; not so far, at least."

"Nothing that appeals to you? They may be country girls, but I've heard they're not hard to get." She turned to her husband. "This son of yours, Eustáquio, is Bahia's number one heartbreaker."

"Don't believe her, Pater; maternal love exaggerates. Oh, I've had a little luck with old ladies and inspired a few romantic crushes, that's all. Small potatoes."

The judge gazed in silence at his wife, who was concentrating on her fingernails, and his son, whose mouth was open in a yawn. They were so much alike, and both such total strangers to him. What did he have in life, after all? Talkfests with the local geniuses, problems of metrics, afternoons and evenings in Belinha's sheltering warmth. Dear gentle Belinha, so sweet, so attentive, so discreet, and a cousin; surely that was a venial sin.

Hands clapped at the door—the distinguished wife of the mayor to call on the judge's illustrious lady. Daniel slipped away to haunt the Captain's store.

25

"I'm an incurable romantic. What can I do?" complained Daniel, the old ladies' pet Dan, to his friends in the law school courtyard.

A law student with a Ph.D. in loafing and seduction earned in nightclubs, brothels, and stews; tall, slender, languid, a handsome boy with great soulful melting eyes like Dona Beatriz's before she turned Oriental; bedroom eyes, his classmates called them; fleshy lips, curly hair, and a rather equivocal beauty that was frail rather than effeminate—all this made Dan the darling of the girls in the cathouses and the elegant society ladies at the end of the trail where plastic surgery could do nothing more for them. He accepted presents and money from both sets of ladies—ties, belts, watches, yardgoods for suits, thousand-cruzeiro notes—which he then displayed ostentatiously to illustrate the piquant anecdotes with which he enlivened dull classes.

Surreptitiously, so as not to hurt his feelings, Zazá Sweetmouth introduced a substantial part of her daily earnings into his jacket pocket. Dan would pick her up at Isaura Maneta's castle at dawn and they would stroll in a lovers' idyll down São Francisco Street to her well-kept little room with its sweet-smelling surinam cherry leaves on the cement floor and its bed with clean sheets perfumed with lavender. Along the way, Zazá would discreetly, delicately find an opportunity to slip the money in Dan's pocket without his noticing it—ingenuous Zazá Sweetmouth.

"All I have to do is look absentminded and she stuffs the bread in my pocket," said Daniel, "without wounding my sensibilities."

Now Dona Assunta Menéndez do Arrabal, a lusty dame of forty whose aging husband owned a string of bakeries, would lay out gifts and money on the bed, praising the merchandise and telling him how much it cost. This cost me a fortune, you pretty boy (but she got good discounts in shops belonging to her husband's friends); this is British worsted, pretty boy, contraband, of course.

Libidinously she hung neckties on Dan's penis and covered his belly with greenbacks: Just look how much your old lady spends on you, you pretty boy!

Yet for all his perfect gigolo's physique, his seductive ambiguous air—sentimental libertine, or cherub steeped in vice—for all that he possessed the necessary skills to ply his noble trade, for he was competent, persistent, a smooth dancer, and a smooth talker, had a facile tongue and a somnolent voice that was soft, warm, intoxicating, was good in bed (I'm the best little cunt-sucker in Bahia, in the whole Northeast, maybe the best in Brazil)—not all these sterling qualities put together could make a real professional out of him, as he confided to his fellow students:

"I'm an incurable romantic, that's the trouble. I fall in love like a silly calf, I give myself away for nothing, I even spend my own money! Whoever heard of a decent self-respecting gigolo throwing money away on a woman? I'm just an amateur."

His school friends laughed at such shamelessness. You couldn't do a thing with Dan; he was a hopeless case; his cynicism was beyond all bounds—although his close friends bore him out by saying that he really was given to sudden consuming passions that induced him to abandon rich protectresses and comfortable old flames. His luck in love had become proverbial in the student and bohemian milieu; whole clusters of love affairs were laid at his door, many times the real number. From a tender age he had earned money from women and spent it on them too, the precocious pup.

The judge's children rarely came out to the country to visit him. Dona Beatriz, ever watchful of good manners and the conventions, resorted every so often to arguments and promises to induce one of them to go with her on these visits to their husband and father—tiresome, no doubt, but indispensable to the family's good name. It was five years since Daniel, the most rebellious and the least available, had embarked on the tedious journey on the Leste Brasileira train. Why should I bury myself in that hole for a month, Mater? I can see old Dad when he comes to Bahia, and besides, I've already made my vacation plans. On the other hand, he had been quite willing to go to Rio, São Paulo, Montevideo, and Buenos Aires

in the company of devoted women who were only too
happy to pay for his physique, his talents, and his time.
This time, however, Dona Beatriz had neither had to argue with him nor to butter him up; Daniel had unexpectedly offered to go himself—Mater, I need a change
of air! It was the only way to be rid of Dona Pérola
Schuartz Leão, that dodo pickled in cosmetics and jewels,
a pitiful caricature of a girl who could not even laugh naturally any more, the skin on her face had been pulled
tight so many times. A sexagenarian widow from São Paulo
with piles of money and a strong smell of garlic, she had
come to Bahia to visit the churches, caught sight of the
baroque, celestial young Dan in São Francisco, lost her
head and her decorum, rented a house on the beach, and
poured out the contents of her fat purse in his lap. Her
textile fortune went straight into pay for the whims of a
vain little mulatto girl named Tânia, a newcomer to
Tibúrcia's castle who had turned Dan's head for a time.

He had grown sick and tired of both women at the
same time. No surgery could attenuate the garlic smell
Dona Pérola gave off, and money and satisfied caprices
spoiled Tânia's artlessness and made her demanding and
too uppity for her own good—Dan's passions were fired
by kindling that was very quickly consumed. Since flight
seemed the only option, he went off with his mother, out
to the frontier of the state where his father dealt out justice and wrote love poems.

Verinha, his sister, newly elected Student Princess—
she had missed being Queen only because of evident partiality on the part of the jury—had called her brothers' attention to some of their father's sonnets, which had been
published in the literary supplement of *A Tarde:*

"Get a load of this, boys! The old man must have got
himself something pretty neat in the way of a woman to
write aphrodisiac poems like this. They're all about
breasts, belly, love couches, ravening lust. I like them,
they're great. Isaías, you're a brain; what in the world
does he mean by *fornizian coitus?*"

Isaías, the eldest, almost ready to graduate from the
University of Bahia, engaged to the only daughter of a
prominent politician and with the promise of a job in the
Department of Public Health, neither knew nor cared to

know the meaning of *fornizian:* to set his face in a mask of indignation, simple *coitus* was enough.

"The old man lacks a proper sense of decorum. After all, he's a judge. We may do certain things but we don't have to proclaim them to the world, not even in verse." Isaías was the image of his father, in character and looks: a little chip off the old block, Eustáquio spat and shat, Dona Beatriz used to say bitterly; he may fool you but he can't fool me, I know my folks.

Dan, who resembled his mother, didn't agree with Isaías: why couldn't each act as he thought best and leave everyone else in peace? If Dad got a kick out of praising his hillbilly muse in erotic verse, that was his affair; why criticize him for it? Living all alone in that dead little burg, without even his wife and children to keep him company, if he whiled away his exile counting syllables and working out hard rhymes—why not? And what the hell was *fornizian?* (You might know: we don't even have a dictionary in this house.)

The sonnets piqued his curiosity, and as soon as he arrived in Cajazeiras he tried to discover who had inspired those ardent paternal effusions. It was Marcos Lemos, who held a high position in the office of the sugarmill and was a literary colleague of the judge, who enlightened him concerning Belinha, and once his tongue had been loosened, told him about Tereza Batista as well.

The last time Dan had been out in those parts as a lad of seventeen, he had rubbed up against a few frantic girls and felt the salient breasts of a matron with plunging cleavage as he passed her in the hallway, and that was all. But now, as he crossed Cathedral Square and went down Main Street, he noticed that the windows filled with smiles, glances, damsels by the dozen. And all doomed to celibacy, to the "keg"—a malignant word: the younger girl has one foot in the keg, the other's gone all the way in and pulled the lid down—that is, they were under sentence of over-devoutness, hysteria, madness. Daniel had never seen so many devout women, so many madwomen, so many females begging for a male. The government, he remarked to Marcos Lemos and Aírton Amorim when he took his seat in the assembly of educated men, if it really cared about the population's health and well-being, ought to hire half a dozen husky athletes for the benefit of the desperate masses of females. Aírton Amorim jokingly applauded the idea:

"That's a good thought, young man, except that our little community would need two or three dozen stout champions, at least."

If Dan chose to spend his month's vacation feeling up virgins in doorways, he had a plentiful supply at hand. He could take his pick, but he would have to be very careful indeed not to make a fatal slip and there goes her cherry. They were dying for that to happen, of course, so they could tell the world—Help! help! he made me do it, I was a virgin, now I'm pregnant, bring a priest and a judge—that he was a vile seducer and prime candidate for a shotgun wedding. He, Daniel? The judge's son? Not on your life. Virgins weren't his type anyway; he preferred experienced women, married, shacked up with somebody, or free of entanglements. Very few married women in that sluggish place were worth a second glance; they soon lost any charm they might have had in domestic labor, continual pregnancy and childbirth, and the monotony and tedium of daily life. Daniel had scarcely recognized the one whose opulent breasts he had felt in that momentary encounter five years ago; now she was a fat matron with a flaccid bosom, who had taken on the color of a cloister. One rather pretty little thing, with a mischievous face and darting Arab eyes, exhibited a toothless mouth as she responded to Dan's bedroom look. Snaggle-toothed! How they neglected themselves! It was a shame the way they let themselves go.

Besides, there was the danger of scandal. Imagine some outraged husband with brand-new horns accusing him, Dan, the judge's boy, of destroying a happy Christian home, of casting mud at the sacred institution of the family! And he might do worse than that: he might threaten death and vengeance and light out after him with a gun. And Dan had always been allergic to any kind of violence.

He couldn't play a dirty trick like that on his dad, nor could he lay himself open to the rustic zeal of primitive backwoodsmen who might as well have been living in frontier days when soiled honor could be washed away only with blood. Deceived husbands didn't shed blood in Bahia, except in the so-called under-privileged classes and even then only rarely; above a certain income, if a husband's fury was great because his love had been great he gave his wife a beating to teach her a lesson; or if his skull was simply too thin-skinned to bear the weight of horns, he could always get a separation and start all over again with someone else. The vast majority simply resigned themselves to cuckoldry, and the richer they were the easier resignation was. Daniel was an authority on all ramifications of the subject, to be sure. But, way out there in the land of outlaws and ranchers where civilization was still only a word, it was the better part of valor and a proof of common sense, too, to give a wide berth to married ladies as a mark of respect to lawful families.

On the other hand, there were always those women who were living with someone—kept women, mistresses, light-o'-loves, paramours, concubines, friends. Since those arrangements held no implication of commitments of honor solemnly sworn before a judge and priest, but only love and money changing hands, the danger of scandal was almost nil and violence was inconceivable. Why should anyone stir up a storm over a mistress, or kill for a concubine? According to Daniel's code, in those circumstances, no one could argue that a home had been destroyed or honor offended.

A cursory inspection of the kept women in town revealed the deplorable standard of bad taste that prevailed: the excessively high value set on fleshiness as an element of beauty and the demand for various household skills, cooking foremost among them; a good concubine was expected to have a light hand for pastry. Dan found only three women worthy of his attention, and one of those could hardly be called by the sweet name of ladyfriend or any of its synonyms; she was really nothing but a servant girl who slept with her master when he took a notion.

The first of the three was a fine, creamy mulatto girl, full-fleshed but firm, with light skin and negroid features, a greedy mouth in a calm face, and definitely good in bed —you could tell by the lazy way she moved her hips. She had been Aírton Amorim's true wife for more than five years, for his other wife was paralytic, imprisoned in a wheelchair. It was hard to imagine that she would even consider jeopardizing the excellent position she had

earned and the prospect of appearing before the priest
and the judge, whenever it might please Our Lady of Ó, of
whom she was a fervent devotee, to carry Amorim's present wife up to a better world than this. Mother of God, if
you have to spend your whole life in a wheelchair without being able to move or even talk or do anything but
stare all day at a sunbeam moving down the wall, you
might as well not be living at all. Why didn't the silly
woman die and be done with it?

The second concubine, also visibly competent, had a
flavor of incest about her, for she was none other than
Belinha, the judge's muse. Marcos Lemos had pointed
her out a little distance away, coming down the street
with her maid and her sunshade, going to the dentist, perhaps. As Daniel caught up with her for a closer look, she
quickened her graceful steps and raised her shy eyes for a
better look at the judge's boy. Daniel smiled at her charm-
ingly and asked for "your blessing, mamma." She didn't
answer, but laughed in gentle amusement and went her
way, swinging her derrière a little, eyes again cast down.
She consoled herself with a cousin when his honor was
away.

These domestic liaisons might well have tempted a university student on holiday from the maddening round of
life in the capital if the Captain's slavey hadn't been a
dream of a girl. Next to her the others were nowhere.
How had such a marvelous flower taken root in that harsh
soil? Marcos Lemos, showing off as cicerone to the nice
young fellow, could not resist telling him all about the
Cinderella who was the Captain's sweetiepie (he had
given the title of Cinderella to a madrigal inspired by
Tereza). Well, not sweetiepie, exactly; just another one
of Justiniano Duarte da Rosa's many flames.

Daniel took one look at her and went out of his mind.
His flames were invariably roaring bonfires.

26

The Captain's reputation could hardly have been worse.
It seemed he was splenetic, violent, turbulent, with a
black heart and perverted instincts. But, for all his cau-

tion and dislike of trouble, Daniel was not particularly alarmed when Marcos Lemos told him all this, for he laid it down to exaggeration on the part of his new friend. Dan trusted in his lucky star, which had never failed him, and in his long experience, and could not believe that the blustering bully would care very much about the behavior of one of his, what shall we call them, Daniel? Let's say, just one of his sleeping partners, for he cares so little about her that he actually sleeps with two or three others at the same time, on the farm, at brothels, in back alleys, even there in back of the store, right under the girl's nose.

And anyway, why the devil should the Captain ever know? Prudence and caution were called for, of course; but then Daniel had his Ph.D. in prudence and caution. And besides, this time circumstances were all in his favor, and Dan's lucky star never let him down.

Right across from the Captain's store was one of the finest mansions in town, the Moraes house, where four sisters lived who were the last of a once-powerful clan, the inheritors of rented houses and government bonds. Good-humored, pretty, well provided for, perfect housekeepers, had they lived in the capital, they would certainly not have lacked for suitors to their hands and fortunes. In Cajazeiras, though, the eldest at twenty-eight and the youngest at twenty-two were withering on the vine, fated to end their days in the keg, with no prospect before them but church festivals and novenas, Christmas crèches, and the baking of cakes and cookies. Of course, that had been before the June holidays and the appearance of Dan on the sidewalk across the way.

Magda, the oldest, plunked away at the piano (she had studied with the nuns); Amália could recite "When I Was Eight Years Old," "The Doves," and "In Extremis," with much feeling; Berta copied landscapes in pastel and watercolor to adorn the walls of their own house and those of family friends; and Teodora had had an affair with a famous Greek juggler from the Great Oriental Circus. The two had exchanged kisses and engagement rings in the dark and the moonlight, and Teodora had first said she'd elope and then, when her gallant lover was hauled off to the police station to explain himself, said that she'd kill herself (Magda had secretly instigated the investigation, but God forbid that anyone should find that out; if news of her sister's meddling ever reached Teodora's ears, she'd pull the house down). With his back to the wall and in imminent danger of a flogging, he admitted that he was a Brazilian and married, though betrayed and abandoned by his wife. Despite his whining confession, Teodora might have sent the family honor to the devil and followed the unlucky trapeze artist down the beckoning sawdust trail if the Athenian from Cataguazes had not ridden his mule out of town in the dead of night without waiting for the circus tent to be pulled down.

This romantic episode had stirred the town. The idyll was brief but intense; the loving pair took no pains to conceal their emotions. Teodora was deaf to scoldings and good advice, but her dream of love ended in an anecdote for local gossip. The comadres' astuteness was baffled on one point and remains so to this day: Had the international king of the jugglers (as he was touted on the circus programs) done Teodora the favor of relieving her of her maidenhead, or had she remained *virgo intacta,* technically pure? Not even her sisters, who were dying to know, could find out, for Teodora herself, who should have been the first to proclaim herself to be immaculate, pure, and intact, fanned their lingering doubts by replying with ambiguous words, dubious giggles, or deep sighs to all their hints and attempts to clear the matter up.

She had alarmed Magda no end by threatening suicide after the circus had left:

"You know, Magda, I'm worried. Don't say anything to the others."

"Worried? Why? Tell me everything, Teó, by our mother's soul!"

"It hasn't come yet. If it doesn't come, I'll kill myself, I swear to God."

"Don't talk silly. What hasn't come? Tell me, for the love of God."

"The curse."

"How many days late?"

Several days and her breasts hurt; telltale symptoms, Magda. Magda called a secret convocation of the other sisters. Teó's pregnant, sisters, what a tragedy, what shall we do? She's saying she'll kill herself and she might do it, too, she has so little sense. If it happened to somebody else, said Amália, I'd say it served her right; she's had her fun, let her pay for it; but since it's Teó, we'd better call in Noquinha the mid-wife, the best angel-maker in town. Noquinha? She's an expert all right, but her tongue is hung in the middle, she'd never keep it quiet, objected Magda; wouldn't it be better to have Dr. David, the family physician? Neither Noquinha nor Dr. David, was Berta's opinion; Teó's just playing the fool, trying to make us think that thing really happened. Well, do you think it didn't? Yes, that's just what I think: it didn't, she didn't, he didn't. That's enough, said the eldest; we'll wait then.

The suspense didn't last long, the curse came; but Teodora still maintained her air of ambiguity, distant and grave, with the superior air of a woman with a past and a secret; her sisters remained unenlightened and envious and couldn't stop talking about it. Neither could the town; people still wonder. Teodora sighs and languishes at the window, gazing into the distance, the most fascinating of all the riddles of Cajazeiras do Norte.

Captain Justo's store was a constant source of diversion to the four sisters as they sat at their first-story windows, where they could see who went in and came out and how much they bought, acknowledge greetings, and kill some of the infinite time stretching before them to the end of their lives. Business had picked up lately; there were more male customers than before. Magda went shopping with the excuse that the maid had some work to do that couldn't be put off; Magda made that very clear. She realized what all the stir was about as soon as she went in. Everyone was curious about the Captain's new girl, who was adding up the bills. Just a slip of a thing with a frightened face and her hair hanging down, Magda told her sisters; and the description was a good one as far as it went. Curiosity about her diminished in time, and only Marcos Lemos became a steady customer, buying cigarettes in the morning and matches in the afternoon on his way home from the office.

When they first saw Daniel scrutinizing their venetian blinds, the four sisters were shaken to their roots. Magda sat down at the piano and filled the air with waltzes; Amália practiced her elocution; Berta mixed her watercolors; and Teodora planted herself at the window in a party dress and high hopes. No gentleman could have been

handsomer or more distinguished! And well educated, of
course; after all, he studied in the capital and was the
judge's son, and even if he hadn't been . . . When timid
Amália appeared in the doorway to rescue her cat Mimoso
from the perils of freedom—the cat was altered and obese,
but loved the street and its debaucheries; had turned ho-
mosexual, in fact—Daniel cut off the fugitive's flight and
handed him over to the swooning Amália. Long-drawn-
out greetings, smiles, and glances greeted Magda and Berta
when they appeared at the windows, and he acknowledged
in a poet's words the glass of cool water requested of the
maid and served by Teodora's own hands. By a coincidence, Captain Justo drove in from the country just then
and jumped out of the cab of his truck just in time not to
miss the exchange of smiles and polite words; Teó—Teó
bending over a little to show off her bosom framed by a
low neckline, and Daniel gallantly kissing her hand.

"Hi there, Captain."

"Well, how's our town treating you, boy?" and as Daniel
came up to shake hands, the Captain lowered his voice
and said craftily: "I see you're not wasting any time. All
ready to pounce, eh?"

Daniel did not contradict him. He took the Captain's
arm with a smile of complicity, his eyes first on Teó, still
offering her bosom in the doorway and then moving to
the first-floor window where Magda, Amália, and Berta
each garnered a smile, a bow, and a nod. He couldn't
have dreamed of a better cover than those heaven-sent
old maids; God was watching over him, all right. That
younger one, now . . . if there hadn't been so many com-
plications, she was well worth a tumble or two, not ready
for the trash heap by a long shot. But how could he think
of another woman when that dazzling little girl of the
Captain's was within reach of his hand? Justiniano Duarte
da Rosa ushered Dan into his store.

27

All at once Tereza felt a pair of eyes staring at her. She
raised her own and saw it was that young fellow talking
with great self-possession to the Captain. Between indif-

ference and fear, Tereza was not usually inclined to trade
glances with customers. Naturally she noticed the comings
and goings of Marcos Lemos, with his smiles and his avid
eyes; he was there every day. A gangling awkward fellow
who looked older than his fifty years, Marcos sometimes
made signs to her and winked. The first time it happened,
Tereza had burst out laughing to see a grown man with
white hair winking and blinking like a boy in the street.
After that, she paid no attention to him but kept her eyes
on the notebook where she set down the prices shouted
out by Pomp or Flycatcher, or by Chico Half-Sole when
the trusted gunman came in to give the clerks a hand.
(Chico took care of the outside jobs: unloading the merchandise that arrived by train or on muleback, dealing
with porters, teamsters, muleteers, collecting payment
from customers who paid by the month and dunning those
who were late; so he rarely clerked at the counter.) Marcos Lemos would take a long time to light his cigarette,
hoping to catch Tereza's eye and see her laugh again.
Finally he would take his leave, momentarily discouraged
but conscious of his privileged place at the head of the
line: first name on Gabi's list, and no one had got in
ahead of him at the drygoods store. When the Captain
shut the girl out in the cold and she found herself all
alone, she'd remember him. He felt that his position was
good.

Tereza lifted her head again at the sound of guffaws.
The boy was looking at her over the Captain's shoulder,
as the Captain bent over, his belly shaking in one of his
uncontrollable fits of laughter. The boy was smiling at her,
one hand on the counter, lips parted, eyes melting and
soulful, hair in ringlets, a gentle expression on his face;
why was he so familiar, since surely she had never seen
him before in her life? That smile, and his grace . . . suddenly she remembered the Angel of the Annunciation on
the wall of the cell in the farmhouse; he was just exactly
the same. That painting was the most beautiful thing
Tereza had ever seen in her life; and now she was looking
at the angel in person. As she lowered her eyes, she smiled
in spite of herself.

Flycatcher dictated the prices of parcels: a kilo and a
half of jerky at fourteen hundred cruzeiros, three pounds
of flour at three hundred, a pound of beans at four hun-

dred, a gallon of *cachaça,* two hundred grams of salt. Then
the Captain's voice between chuckles:

"Tereza, when you've finished adding up the bill, go in
and make us some coffee."

Daniel was well into a long spiel about the brothels and
cabarets of Bahia, complete with names, dates, circumstances, and delicious anecdotes. Justiniano Duarte da
Rosa liked to keep up-to-date on the doings of all the
women in the red-light district so that he didn't feel out
of things on his trips to the capital; and the fellow sure
knew how to tell a funny story.

Tereza set the tray with the coffeepot, the little cups,
and the sugarbowl down on the counter, and as she served
the coffee she heard the boy tell the Captain, without
withdrawing his suppliant, insistent gaze from her own:

"While I lay siege to the fortress, Captain, will you let
me use your store as a redoubt?" The fragrant smell of the
coffee rose, and Dan took a sip. "Delicious! Do you think
I might deserve a good cup of coffee like this once in a
while?"

"Store's open from seven in the morning till six in the
afternoon, at your service, and when you want a cup of
coffee you just ask." He turned to Tereza. "When my
friend Daniel here comes around—and I think he'll be
coming around pretty often"—he laughed and nudged the
young man in the stomach with his pudgy finger—"you
just make him some good fresh coffee. If you're busy he'll
wait; he's not in any hurry, are you, young fellow?"

"No, Captain, no hurry at all. I'll be devoting all my
time to that one thing exclusively, from now on." His eyes
held Tereza's, as if he were speaking to her and about
her.

Tereza disappeared with the cups and coffeepot and the
Captain explained to Daniel:

"The story is that Teodora—did you know her name
was Teodora? Nickname's Teó. Well, there's some who
say she's got nothing left to lose, the road's wide open; a
circus artist did her the favor when he was traveling
through. I don't believe it if you want to know what I
think. Hugging and kissing, sure; I could see them from
here, glued together, saying good night on the doorstep.
There was a lot of heavy petting, all right, but that was
all. Where the hell could they go? Cajazeiras isn't Bahia,

and it isn't the country either, with a lot of woods all
around. Besides, nobody lets you get away with a thing in
this town, you'll find that out before long. There's only
one person in this place who couldn't care less and does
just what he has a mind to, and that's your humble servant. I have my fun and I go my own way and they
can talk all they want to. It's true I stay clear of highfalutin' dames like those ladies across the road. The only
time I got mixed up with high society was when I got
married. I like small game myself; no trouble, no head-
aches. Speaking plainly, I'd say that the circus guy loved
the gal up a little, but if she felt the weight of his tool
it was just in her hand; it's foolishness to think anything
else. Anyhow, whether her cherry's been picked or not,
she's a sweet little piece."

Daniel raised his voice as Tereza returned, gazing at
her over the shoulder of Justiniano Duarte da Rosa:

"She's the prettiest girl I ever saw in my life."

"Hey, what are you talking about? Don't get carried
away. Not just that she's a little long in the tooth for my
taste—I don't have anything against her, though I like 'em
a little greener myself; but there's lots of better ones
around. I know some she couldn't compare with. In
Veneranda's castle in Aracaju there's a gringa, a Russki
or a Polack, I don't know what the hell she is. What I
do know is that she's blonde from her head to her toes,
every bit of her, from the fuzz on her arms to the hair on
her ass. Her hair's so blonde it's white. She says hair like
that has a special name where she comes from, *plata* or
something."

"Platinum blonde," said Dan.

"That's right. She isn't blonde the way our high yellows
are; it's something else, much better. I'd like to go to
Europe just so I could buy me a little bitty gringa with a
little bitty blonde white ass, all in one piece."

Daniel pretended to be listening while his eyes melted
all over the girl. For her part, Tereza Batista had never
seen anyone so good-looking. Never? Well, maybe the Doctor, the owner of the sugarmill; but that was different. She
looked at Dan wonderingly, hardly knowing she did so;
and her lips parted in a smile.

28

She smiled wonderingly, for no reason that she knew, and looked without meaning to look at the young man on the prowl, as he walked up and down the sidewalk and into the grocery store. Making an excuse to talk to her, he would ask for a glass of water. Wouldn't you like a cup of coffee? I'll go inside and make some, Tereza would say awkwardly, embarrassed, in a trembling voice. While he waited, Daniel would give the clerks contraband American cigarettes. The two lads didn't suspect a thing, convinced as they were that the plot of the movie was quite a different one, with Teodora as the heroine. With open envy they watched the villain from the big city as he laid his snares for the innocent victim—he was a very nice villain, though, and the heroine wasn't as innocent as all that.

Teodora, and sometimes Tereza, had lain many times on the iron bedstand with its straw mattress in the cubbyhole where Pomp slept, kissing his greasy, pimply adolescent face. He had enjoyed both of them in the palm of his hand, inventing exciting movie plots as he went along. He had slept with countless movie stars and local girls besides, but his favorites were Teodora and Marlene Dietrich. On the wooden-slatted bed where dark, thick-lipped, kinky-headed Flycatcher lay at night, his dreaming callused hand made Teodora swoon with delight, along with her three sisters, several customers, Tereza and—sorry, Dan—Dona Beatriz, whom he had seen more than once with practically no clothes on during her last visit. That was when Flycatcher was an errand boy for the judge before he went to work in the Captain's store. After her bath, Dona Beatriz would linger in her dressing room surrounded by creams, cosmetics, and perfumes, with only a skimpy face towel concealing her abundant nudity. On lucky days, through a crack in the door, the youth could feast ecstatically on her opulent flesh. What a beautiful clean lady; she even puts perfume on her ass! Teodora, however, the equivocal Teó, was still way out in front; Flycatcher could just see himself in the circus, doing daredevil deeds on the flying trapeze and laying Teó.

Teodora came into the store once in a while to buy something, usually in a floating dress that displayed the curves of her breasts to advantage. The two boys tossed coins to see who would wait on her and feast his eyes on her snow-white bosom. While pretending not to notice, she'd take part in the clerks' little game, making up her mind what to buy very slowly and resting her elbows on the counter to show a little more of her décolletage; she always just happened to have left off her bra. Along with her purchases she took away the poor tribute of the admiring youths; on nights when she couldn't sleep, the rapid, covetous glances of the two dun-colored clerks fed her dreams. As soon as she turned her back, Pomp spat into the palm of his right hand and lit out for the latrine; Flycatcher saved the thrilling vision for a night of love.

They both thought the affair was clear as day: if Daniel hadn't given Teó a lay by now it wouldn't be long before he did. It never occurred to them that the student might be interested in Tereza, not only because they thought he was in love with Teodora, but because Tereza belonged to the Captain; only a madman would have had the nerve to want her, except as a deep, dark secret, spitting on his hand in the dark.

Tereza didn't always stay at the little desk doing sums: she had to look after the Captain's room and his clothes. The house and store and latrine in the yard were given a lick and a promise by the two clerks early every morning. Chico Half-Sole, who had learned how to cook in jail, would make stew for dinner, throwing in beans, jerky, pumpkin, cassava root, sweet potatoes, and a hunk of sausage. At noon when there weren't any customers, Chico and the two boys would go out back to eat their dinner, leaving Tereza alone in the front of the store in case a customer should happen to come in. When the Captain was in town, Tereza set the table with a tablecloth, plates, and knives, forks, and spoons and served him *cachaça* before lunch and beer with the meal. Justiniano's meals, a great variety of piping hot dishes, were brought in from Corina's boarding house. The Captain enjoyed his meals, helped himself to heaping platefuls of food, and drank all he wanted without turning a hair. Chico Half-Sole was allowed a glass of *cachaça* at lunch and another at dinner, no more than one, drunk down at a gulp. But he made up for it on Saturday nights and the day before a holiday or religious festival, when he drank until he flopped like a stone onto his cot or in some fifth-class hooker's room. When the Captain was gone, Tereza put no cloth on the table and dispensed with knife and fork, eating Chico's grub with her hand as she crouched in a corner.

Dan soon learned the habits and customs of the store by heart from the answers the clerks gave to his casual questions as they gleefully watched him make eyes at the four sisters, who hardly left their windows at all.

The sisters were in an agony of impatience and bewilderment. What could such absurd timidity mean? After all, he came from Bahia and he had a reputation as a bona fide ladykiller, a terror to all decent husbands, and even a gigolo—Dona Ponciana de Azevedo, hearing that Dan was hanging around the Moraes house, had lost no time in coming to tell them all about the scandalous young man—and yet the handsome youth still kept his distance in an extraordinary display of discretion, without even trying to approach any nearer; still wasting time with preliminaries, and what was even more inexplicable, seeming to be equally interested in all of the sisters, lavishing his ingratiating smiles and hints impartially on all four. Why, maybe that was it! Maybe his puzzling bashfulness stemmed from the very fact that he couldn't make up his mind which one to court! The youngest, the heroine, took it for granted that she and she alone drew the student to the house before lunch and at twilight. The other sisters objected that he liked them too—he waved good-bye to me today, Magda pointed out; he threw me a kiss, announced Berta; he made a gesture as if he were clasping me to his bosom, Amália declaimed. Teodora said nothing; she knew who he was after. All four threw themselves into a battle of dresses, hairdos, and makeup, of silk and lace unearthed from trunks and smelling of mothballs and mold. They had lived in harmony, but now they clashed and jangled in an atmosphere of mistrustfulness and quarrels, or sharp words and scornful laughs. Each sat at her own window, and Dan stood below on the sidewalk and smiled. Once, twice, three times he walked up and down, in the noonday sun or the late-afternoon breeze, before retiring into the store. Sighs rose from the sisters at their balconies and Berta went running to the bathroom; just watching him go by made her feel cold underneath, and she had to hold herself in not to weewee.

The Captain, too, wondered why Daniel didn't make more progress.

"Well, when are you going to have a taste of the forbidden fruit?"

"Not so fast, Captain. I'll tell you when I do."

"All I want to know is whether she's a virgin or not. I bet she is."

"I hope you're right, Captain."

And the two men would strike up a lively conversation with one invariable theme: life in the stews of Bahia, a subject of unending fascination to Justiniano Duarte da Rosa. Dan had won his confidence, and the two of them had gone to Gabi's house to have a beer and look at the girls. As he leaned against the counter in the store, critically dissecting the state of the local demimonde, Daniel trailed his wing before Tereza, right in the Captain's face, in a mute language of smiles and glances, each laden with meaning, preparing the ground.

"Third-class material, Captain; pretty lean pickings at Gabi's house. Mediocre, in fact."

"Now don't tell me you didn't like that girl; she hasn't been in the life more than three months."

"She wasn't much. Captain, next time you show up in Bahia, you let me be your guide and I'll show you what a real woman is. And don't tell me again that you know Bahia like the palm of your hand; if you haven't been to Zeferina's or Lisete's you don't know Bahia. And don't start in with that Polack in Aracaju because I'll show you a real blonde, a real natural platinum blonde and a humdinger! Tell me something, Captain, did anyone ever give you the Arab bouché?"

"The bouché? Thousands of times. That's one thing I really like. Any woman who lies down with me has to know how to wiggle her tongue. But I don't know what you mean by Arab. The way I heard tell it, bouché's a French thing."

"Well, you don't know what's good. That blonde I was telling you about specializes in that very thing; she's an Argentine and she'll make you sit up and take notice.

She's a tango singer, Rosalia Varela. I like her better in bed; she sucks better than she sings. But that Arab bouché . . . yummy, yummy."

"Well, what the hell is it?"

"If I tell you, that'll spoil it. But Captain, I promise you this: once you've tried it, you won't want anything else. But with Rosalia it's got to be tit for tat."

"What do you mean, tit for tat?"

"I mean just what I said: tit for tat—vice versa—in a word, the well-known sixty-nine."

"Oh! Well, forget it. Me, suck a woman? One that asked me to do it once, a tramp who came around here reading people's fate in the cards, I smashed her face in for her so she wouldn't have the nerve to ask again. It's all right for a woman to suck a man, that's a law of nature; but a man who sucks a woman's no man, he's a lapdog. I'm sorry if it makes you mad, but that's just what he is: a little French lapdog." He had learned the expression from Veneranda and repeated it with pride.

"Captain, my friend, you haven't entered the modern world. I'd give anything to see you once Rosalia gets hold of you, doing whatever she wants you to—and I'll tell you something else, you'll go down on your knees to her and beg her to let you do it."

"Who, me? Justiniano Duarte da Rosa, Captain Justo? Not on your life."

"When are you planning a trip to Bahia, Captain? You set the date and I'll bet on Rosalia, ten to one. If she lets me down, the party's on me."

"The trouble is I'm going to Bahia in just a few days, right after the holidays. I got an invitation from the governor for the reception in the palace on July second. A friend of mine on the police force got it for me."

"Will you be there long? Maybe I'll catch up with you."

"I don't know myself, all depends on the judge. I've got a suit pending at court. While I'm there, I'll look up some friends in the government bureaus. I have a lot of friends in Bahia, and after the Guedeses, I'm the one who runs things around here, so I have a lot of business to attend to. I'll be there a good two weeks or so."

"I guess I won't catch up with you even so. I promised my old man I'd spend the month with him, not to mention our little neighbor over there; I've got to clear up that business and find out for sure if she's a virgin or not. It's a point of honor with me. Why don't we do this: I'll give you a letter for Rosalia, and you just look her up at the Tabaris and mention my name."

"You mean the nightclub? I've been there."

"Well, she sings there every night."

"All right then, you give me the letter and we'll see about that Arab *bouché*. But you tell her to respect me; she can do it to me and that's all, if she doesn't want a beating."

"I've made my bet, Captain. Rosalia's going to turn you inside out."

"The woman who gives orders to Captain Justo ain't been born yet, much less the woman who makes him into a little French lapdog. No he-man would stoop to a thing like that."

"A *conto* of mine to a hundred of your cruzeiros says Captain Justo licks Rosalia and asks for an encore."

"Never repeat that, not even if you smile. And I won't take your bet. You write to that dame and tell her I'll pay her what she asks, but she'd better not try to make a fool out of me. When I get mad, watch out."

For all his bluster he's just a clown, concluded Daniel. What else can he be when he wears a necklace with gold rings to remind him of all the poor little country girls he's laid? Belching machismo while Daniel was seducing Tereza in front of his nose.

Seducing Tereza. In spite of herself, without knowing why, against her will, Tereza responded to his gaze—what melancholy eyes, what fatal blue eyes; and his red mouth, and his curly hair; a fallen angel. When the two men went off down the street, still deep in their endless talk, Tereza hid in her bosom the flower he had brought. Daniel had held up the faded rose behind the Captain's back, kissed it, and laid it on the counter. He had picked it and kissed it for her. On the greasy counter lay a red red rose. A kiss.

29

At the end of a week passed in nervous uncertainty,
Magda, assuming her authority as the eldest sister, brought
up the problem for discussion at the dinner table.

"It's time he spoke up. Whichever of us he wants to
marry, we'll all agree to it, the other three will just make
the best of it, and we'll all help with the trousseau. But
he can't have all four of us; there's only one of him."

"I think he could have two of us, at least . . . there's so
much of him!" Amália spoke up timidly, willing to try
any sort of arrangement.

"Don't be ridiculous. That's just idiotic."

"It's more ridiculous for an older woman to run after a
younger man."

Magda was so on edge with nerves that she burst out
weeping: "I'm not running after him; he's running after
me, and I'm not old; I'm in my twenties just like you,"
her words interspersed by sobs.

Amália, instantly repentant—Oh honey, I'm so sorry;
I'm just so nervous!—embraced her sister, and they wept
together.

"Why do you want to make him speak up when things
are so nice the way they are?" put in Berta, the plainest
one, content with little—half a loaf was better than none
and she was enjoying it all so much. That young man
walked up and down on the sidewalk and she felt that
little chill in her bladder just looking at him. "If you all
start in spoiling things he'll go away and never come
back."

Oh! that would be the end of all their hopes—and then
back to the tedium, the bitterness, the senseless fits of
weeping, the resentment, the blues, the spiteful little slaps,
the hypocrisy, the spats, the sour, thankless life old maids
lived. Yes, Berta was right, we'd better not set deadlines
and push him to make up his mind. And so Magda
made a vow to St. Anthony, patron saint of marriage;
Amália looked up Áurca the fortune-teller, unrivaled in
counsels of love, and paid her for an infallible fortune
in advance; and Berta went to black Lucáia in a back

alley and bought some of her herbs and bath powders, which were equally infallible.

Teodora just smiled and said nothing; she had experience and knew a sure thing when she saw it. This time, dear hated sisters, this time won't be like last time. He won't get away; I'll have him even if it takes all my money to do it, even if I have to sell the Treasury bonds and the rented houses. Don't people say he takes money from married women, and even from fallen women? Dona Ponciana says so and she can prove it—a jealous girl in Bahia made a terrible scene right in the middle of the street, yelling out just how much money she had given him and when. Well, all right then: Teó's willing to spend money too; she has some put away, besides what she gets every month, and if she has to steal her sisters' savings, she'll do it with pleasure, Dan.

By talking, asking a few questions and prowling around, Daniel had made sure of the ideal time. When Chico Half-Sole and the two clerks were having their dinner at noon, Tereza sat at the counter by herself in the store, just in case by some miracle a customer came in. One more proviso would ensure the success of the plan: the Captain had to be away, either out of town on business or out at the farm. Daniel watched and waited his chance.

After a few days of impatience had passed, he gaily refused the Captain's invitation to go with him on an outing. They were to leave in the morning to see a cockfight in a nearby town across the border in Sergipe and return the same evening. It was ten leagues off over a bad road during the rainy season, but Terto Cachorro was a good driver and could get them there in two hours, and those fighting cocks were sure worth the trouble. This was a good chance for the Captain's new friend to win a little money by betting on the Captain's cocks. What a shame, but Daniel had to say no; he had a rendezvous for that very day, in a very secret place, and this might be his only chance to hold his lovely neighbor in his arms and discover the whole truth—what a shame, Captain.

"Well, that's a good reason, so I won't insist; you can go with me some other time. You take a good look now and tell me if I'm wrong: for my money the girl still has her cherry; he may have spilled some on her legs but that's all." The Captain was already seated in the truck next to Terto Cachorro. "I'll be on my way, I've got to stop by the farm. So long."

Before lunch, after his customary penance in front of the Moraes house, Daniel drank fresh water from the earthenware jug, taking the glass from Teodora's hands and catching sight of her breasts framed by a low-necked dress—a thousand thanks for slaking a poor pilgrim's burning thirst, now I'm going home to slake my hunger, until this evening, fair water nymph.

"Won't you have lunch with us, isn't pot luck good enough?" Teodora's blandishments were hard to resist.

Some other time I'll be proud and eager to accept, but today my parents are waiting for me and I'm late as it is; first things first, Teodora; later on, maybe, on my next vacation. Today I'm going to taste divine ambrosia, manna from heaven, so good-bye; I'll tell the Captain I found out you were a virgin and left you your maidenhead because I was afraid of the consequences, but only your maidenhead and nothing else; I'll tell him I enjoyed everything else and had me a banquet of thighs, tits, and ass.

When the windows were empty and the street was deserted, Daniel retraced his steps from the corner to the grocery store. When Tereza saw him come in she stood stock-still and dumb, unable to stir or make a sound. She had never felt that way before, her heart had never beat so fast—if it wasn't fear or repugnance, what could it be? Tereza didn't know.

Neither of them uttered a single word. He took her in his arms and pressed his hot cheek against Tereza's cold one. The youth's breath was like perfume, and made her dizzy. It came from his hair, his skin, his hands, his half-open lips. The Captain stank of burning sweat and reeked of *cachaça*—real he-men don't wear perfume. Without stepping back from her, Daniel lifted both hands to Tereza's face, framing it in his fingers, and gazing into her eyes, approached his half-open mouth to hers and kissed her. Why didn't Tereza turn her head away, if she hated kisses so and felt nausea when the Captain's mouth touched hers, sucking and biting? Fear was greater than nausea. But she wasn't afraid of the young man; why did she let him do it, why didn't she avert her face, why didn't she tell him to go away?

Tereza's mouth yielded little by little to Dan's mouth, lips, tongue, to that long, delicate caress, until suddenly something burst in her breast, and her eyes, drawn to the angel's celestial eyes, filled with tears. Were there other reasons to cry besides someone's hitting you, or impotent hatred, or overpowering fear? What else was there in life? She couldn't say; she had always had to eat the rotten part. Pestilence, famine, and war had been Tereza Batista's life.

A distant rattling of plates and tin knives made Tereza start. They broke the embrace and the kiss. Dan hastily kissed her wet eyes and was off down the windswept street. Seeds quicken under the winter rain, the green shoots sprout, and the wild, dry, harsh earth bursts into blossom and fruit.

When Pomp came into the store, closely followed by Fly-catcher, Tereza still stood in the same place, dreaming in another world, so different and strange that that rainy night both clerks, one on an iron bedstead, the other on a wooden cot, betrayed their beloved Teodora in secret and took Tereza in the palm of their hands.

30

Dan kissed her on the eyes, then on the mouth, his right hand sliding downwards from her back to her hips, the left entangled in Tereza's hair. Four days had gone by since Dan had given her that first kiss, but Tereza still felt it whole on her lips when he gave her the second. His hot voice lit a fire in her breast:

"Tomorrow is St. John's Eve," said Daniel, "and the Captain told me he's going to a party that lasts all night long and into the next day . . ."

"I know, he goes every year, it's out on Seu Mundinho Alicate's farm."

"Be at the back door at nine tomorrow night, at nine o'clock sharp. We'll celebrate our own feast of St. John."

That mouth again, and that kiss. Tereza lightly, fearfully touched Dan's ringlets, as soft as lamb's wool. Tomorrow we'll have our party, without fail.

31

Not even to Doris, his lawful wedded wife, much less to Tereza, who was nothing but a maid of all work, had the Captain deigned to communicate his comings and goings, nightly wanderings, plans, and decisions; no woman of his had ever had the nerve to inquire where he would spend the night—at home with her or in Gabi's seraglio drinking beer, trying out a new boarder, or at a cockfight or off on some business of his own—a man with proper self-respect knows how to keep a woman in her place.

Tereza never found out about longer trips, to Bahia or Aracaju, until the night before, just in time to pack his suitcase—the beautifully starched shirts, the white suits gleaming with spermaceti. Sometimes she'd overhear snatches of conversation between the Captain and Chico Half-Sole, and that was how she'd happen to learn that he was planning to stay out at the farm to get the work started; or go to Cristina to have a look at black Batista's little store (the Negro's in name only; money and merchandise belonged to Justiniano); or spend a night out here or there, at a party at some friend's house, at some farm or little town. He was an enthusiastic dancer, and those country shindigs were the best spots for recruiting girls just green enough to suit the Captain. Those were nights when Tereza could rest.

Tereza knew about the St. John's Eve party in Raimundo Alicate's house, on a distant plantation belonging to the sugarmill, because the Captain never failed to go; he was the guest of honor every year. This Mundinho Alicate, a protégé of the Guedeses and a crony of Justiniano's, was a popular personage in the district. Besides tilling his canefields, he sold various kinds of white rum, some said to be aphrodisiacs, as well as herbs with the same purpose—*catuaba*, answer-stick, raise-the-dead, eternal youth—and on days of obligation he received the *caboclo* spirits in a shed at the back of his house, the *caboclo* Trailbreaker at their head. For this reason he was known also as Raimundo Trailbreaker, or Mundinho de Obatualá, for he claimed to have been made a spirit guide in Bahia by the deceased *babalorixá* Bernardino do Bate-Folha. Besides all this, he rounded up girls to supply to the Captain and other distinguished people (reserving the most attractive ones for the sugar-mill Guedeses, as local gossip had it), Gabi's little establishment, and the other stews in Cuia Dágua. He was an indefatigable party-giver. In June there were shindigs at his house all month long to hail St. Anthony, St. John, and St. Peter in the *caboclos'* shed behind the house. St. John had the biggest party, with great bonfires, mountains of corn, the red glare of rockets, booming mortars, bombs exploding, and the dancers' feet flying. People came from miles around, on horseback, by oxcart, on foot, in trucks and Fords. Raimundo Alicate would kill a hog, a kid, a lamb, hens, and chickens; there was always a good spread at his parties. Mandolins, harmonicas, and guitars played waltzes, schottisches, polkas, mazurkas, fox-trots, and circle sambas, and there was music and dancing all night long. The Captain loved to square dance; his feet never rested, neither did his fork and neither did his eyes, ever on the lookout for fresh material to his taste. When he had made his mind up, Raimundo, who knew which side his bread was buttered on, would flatter him and jump to do what he asked, and so the matter would be quickly settled. The Captain never left those parties empty-handed.

Tereza had starched the white suit, the blue shirt. The clean ironed clothes lay on top of the bed, and on the edge of it the Captain sat naked. Tereza washed and dried his feet and went out to empty the basin, shivering with fear. Today it wasn't the old fear of blows and ill treatment; today she was afraid he'd do what he usually did: tell her to lie down, spread her legs, and empty himself in her before getting dressed for the party. Dear God, not today! It was always an unpleasant, painful duty, and Tereza submissively performed it nearly every day, knowing she'd be punished if she didn't. But not today, my God, not today! Make him forget it!

If the Captain did order her to do it, she'd have to obey; there was no way to say no. It wasn't even any use to lie and say she had the curse; Justiniano loved to have her on those days. It excited him to see the bruised menstrual blood flowing. This is war! he would cry as he threw her down. *Vive la guerre!* (Another expression learned from Veneranda.) It had been that way since her life's blood had flowed for the first time, making her a woman. This is war, dirt, and disgust, and duty was even harder on those days of the month. But God in Heaven, today would be even worse.

When she went back into the bedroom, oh my God! The Captain had moved the freshly ironed garments from the bed to the chair and was stretched out full length, his stocky trunk and fat flesh waiting for her, with nothing on but the string of gold rings on his plump chest. Tereza knew her duty: if the Captain lay down she had to lie down too, without waiting to be told. It was unthinkable not to. But in a panic of fear as she was, the fear of being beaten that never left her, Tereza went to pick up the clothes as if she hadn't seen him.

"Where the devil are you going? Why don't you lie down?"

She walked over to the bed on leaden feet, feeling sick inside, worse than when she had the curse—but there was no help for it; she took off her panties with a reluctant hand.

"Hurry up, damn it!"

She lay down on the bed and the heavy hand touched her thigh, parting her legs. Tereza shrank away. There was a lump in her throat. She was always reluctant, but never so much as today; today it was just too hard; it was another, greater kind of suffering that made her heart ache. When he mounted and covered her, she resisted him inwardly to the point of sealing the doors of her body that he had broken down by force more than two years before.

"Have you gone back to being a virgin again or did you get hold of some pumice to rub on yourself?" That was Veneranda's trick with young spoiled virgins; she rubbed pumice in their cunts to fool fools.

This was almost as good as a new hymen to the Captain. Tereza felt hard and tense. Her body was no longer amorphous, supine and inert; now it was stiff and difficult and held back—so she was finally reacting, thought the Captain with satisfaction. He felt as if he were conquering the child's rebellious nature all over again; no macho could hold a candle to him.

He was so excited at the moment of climax that he took possession of her mouth. It tasted of gall.

In his hurry to get dressed, the Captain didn't bother to wash; when Tereza came back with the basin full of water, he had already put on his shorts after wiping himself with the end of the sheet. Tereza put on her pants. If only she had time to take a bath! She had had one earlier, after she had finished up her chores in the house and the store, pumping water from the well for the little tub in the bathroom. Tereza knelt to help the Captain on with his shoes and socks and then passed him his shirt, trousers, tie, and jacket one by one, his knife and his revolver last.

Terto Cachorro was already waiting at the wheel of the truck in front of the store: driver, pistolero, and partyloving pal, a nifty harmonica player and ready to kick up his heels any time. Chico Half-Sole was already off and running. In his epic St. John's Eve marathon, weaving from house to house, full of white lightning, brandy, and cordials—genipap, cashew, cherry, jurubeba, it was all the same to him. Toward dawn he would drag himself off to his cot in one of the cubicles at the back of the house, with its jumble of sacks of salted fish and dried meat, its muddy floor and swarms of flies; that is, if he wasn't sacked out in some girl's room in the lowest cathouse in Cuia Dágua.

Garbed in white as fashion decreed, a rainmaker, a *prócer,* as he knotted his necktie, the Captain considered for a moment the possibility of taking Tereza with him. She could put on one of Doris's dresses that was almost as good as new, and she'd look as pretty as a picture for him to show off at Mundinho the Trailbreaker's dance. When Dr. Emiliano Guedes was at the sugarmill on St. John's Eve he always stopped by at Alicate's for a little while with his relatives and guests to show the visitors from the capital "a typical June festival dance in the country." They never stayed long, just time enough for a drink and a fling on the dance floor and then back to the luxurious comfort of the plantation house, but the Doctor would stroke his moustache and inspect the womenfolk with the eye of a connoisseur. Raimundo, alert to the least sign of interest, would do whatever was needed to make the chosen woman available to the master of those lands.

The Captain would have liked to flaunt his gal Tereza for the eldest Guedes, the lord of Cajazeiras do Norte to see and envy. But Dr. Emiliano had just left for a pleasure trip abroad and would not be back for months. Even so, the Captain, after measuring Tereza approvingly from head to foot, half-opened his mouth to order her to fix herself up for the party.

Tereza guessed his intention and was seized with panic for the second time, not disgust or fear of mistreatment this time but a still greater fear: if the Captain took her with him, the boy would be kept waiting out in the rain at the back door, and they'd never have the party he'd promised, and she'd never again feel that flame in her breast, or the soft fleece of his hair, or the mouth that tickled her.

Dr. Emiliano was off having his fun with the French whores in Paris, and besides, what if some cute little gal at the party caught the Captain's eye and he wanted to take her back to the farm? What would he do with Tereza? Send her back in the truck by herself with Terto Cachorro? No woman of Justiniano Duarte da Rosa's was going to run around at night with another man. Terto might be his right-hand man, but he hadn't been gelded so far as the Captain knew, and Satan attacks in the dark. Even if the worst didn't happen, people would say it had, and who could prove different? Justiniano Duarte da Rosa wasn't born to be a cuckold, whatever else people might say of him and did say, behind his back. They called him a cruel bandit, seducer of minors, lecher, land thief, swindler at weights and measures and accounts, cheater at cockfights, criminal assassin—behind his back; who would have the nerve to call him any of those things to his face? One thing, however, no one could ever accuse him of: no one had ever said he wore horns, was a devotee of St. Cornelius, or had ever been tricked by a woman. Neither cuckold nor queer nor cunt-sucking hummingbird. That young fellow Daniel with that doll's face of his and his dirty talk and his drooling eyes and his gigolo's reputation, now he might be a one to lick cunts—and he sure as hell was, unless the Captain was very much mistaken. No self-respecting man would stoop to such nastiness, but those kids from the capital couldn't even stand up to a woman. Hadn't Daniel shut himself up for a whole morning with that Moraes girl—anyway, that was what he said—without eating her cherry because he was afraid of what might happen? But he had done all the rest. What rest? Now Captain, what a question; haven't you ever heard of thighs and ass and fingers and tongues? Sure, he must have done it with his tongue, like a dirty French lapdog. As for him, Justiniano, if he found a cherry to his taste he wouldn't care who it belonged to; thighs and ass could come later and tongue not at all, he was no gringa's little mutt. He wouldn't bother taking Tereza, she'd been filled up for today.

"When I go out, turn off the light and go to sleep."

"Yes sir," Tereza breathed again; Lord, how many different kinds of fear she had felt, and St. John's Eve was just beginning.

Captain Justo strode into the store and opened the street door. It was raining outside.

32

The backyard opened off a narrow alley, all backs of houses, where the truck and the oxcarts unloaded merchandise which then went straight to the storerooms in the house so as not to clutter up the store. On his travels, the Captain bought up remainders and articles on sale at a good price—whole crops of beans, coffee, and corn. Since he had liquid capital with which to pay cash, he got special discounts from wholesalers. Buy at a profit and sell at a profit, that was his motto—not very original, perhaps, but it worked.

The rain had put out the bonfires in the street, made puddles of water in the alley, and turned the ground to mud. Daniel, wearing a waterproof and standing in the corner of a gate across from the wall of the store, peered into the darkness, ears alert to any slight sound, eyes trying to pierce the curtain of rain and blackness.

That day after dinner he had asked Dona Beatriz:

"Old lady, do you think you might have some little knickknack, nothing valuable, but something kind of pretty, that you could let me have to give to a lady? The local stores don't have anything worth buying."

"Dan, I don't like you to call me an old lady and you know it. I'm not as old and broken down as you think."

"I apologize, Mater; I was just showing my affection. You're a Balzacian beauty at the height of your form, and if I were Daddy-o here I wouldn't leave you all by yourself at loose ends in Bahia." He laughed good-humoredly, thinking himself both intelligent and entertaining.

"Honey, your father doesn't much care what I do. I'll go see if I can find some little gewgaw you can have."

When father and son were alone in the room, the judge spoke admonishingly:

"It has come to my attention that you are spending a good deal of time in the neighborhood of the Moraes house, perhaps with Teodora in mind. You've no doubt heard whispered gossip and tales. Don't believe them: the girl is *virgo intacta,* it was nothing but a silly flirtation. I'd be careful if I were you; those girls come from a fairly good family, and any scandal involving them would have very bad repercussions. After all, the town is full of free, unattached girls without entanglements and rigmarole."

"Don't you worry, Pater, I'm not a little boy and I won't stick my hand in a beehive. I didn't come here to make trouble for you. They're nice girls and I like them, that's all. As a matter of fact, I like them all equally well."

"Who is the present for, then?"

"For a free, unattached girl without entanglements and rigmarole. You don't have to worry."

"Another thing: It's for the sake of you children that your mother lives in Bahia. I would rather she lived here, but she can't leave your sister alone."

"Verinha?" Daniel laughed. "You'd better believe me, daddy, when I tell you that Verinha has more brains than anyone else in the family. She's made up her mind to marry a millionaire and you can consider that a *fait accompli.* What Verinha wants Verinha gets. Don't you worry about little Vera."

Daniel's cynicism was a little too much for his honor's respectability. Dona Beatriz came into the room with a little *figa* set in gold. Will this do, honey? That's perfect, Mater, *merci.*

Standing in the alley, leaning against the gate, Daniel played with the amulet inside the pocket of his raincape.

He lighted one more cigarette, gusts of rain washing his face. The Moraes sisters' big bonfire on the next street over was dying out; the servants had stopped feeding it with bundles of firewood. On the miraculous Eve of St. John the four sisters waited too, all alone in their house before a table set with cornbread and cornmeal gruel, fritters and cordials. The heavy rain kept visitors away: comadres, distant cousins, a few friends. What about Daniel? Several families were giving parties; at which one was he dancing? Or did he have an invitation for Raimundo Alicate's fandango? Daniel thought of the sisters, at the impatient limit of dying hope. He liked all four, and the youngest was still desirable, with her bosom that burned to the touch. He would certainly call on them the next day, try their cornmeal mush and flirt shyly with all four, Magda, Amália, Berta, Teodora, his perfect cover. Rain ran down the boy's face. If the taste of Tereza were not still in his mouth, if he had not felt her slender body tremble against him and seen that sudden flash in her tear-filled eyes, he would have left long ago.

At last the sound of the truck's motor, running outside the store, made him prick up his ears; the Captain was getting off to a late start, the bastard. The truck's headlights soon shone at the corner, cutting through the darkness, and disappeared in the rain. Daniel smoked one more contraband American cigarette, then left the shelter of the gate to come closer and see better. Unprotected from the rain, his curls were soon sopping wet. The door to the backyard of the store opened a crack, and Daniel saw the wet face, the straight hair dripping water, the countenance of Tereza Batista.

33

Some folks set no store by miracles, but I ain't one of 'em. You can pay no mind to what I say, or a whole lot, just suit yourself. Here you come, snooping around with a bagful of questions, each one slyer than the one before—and people who talk soft and sweet are the worst kind, they can wind you around their finger and make you swear to things you never saw. I knew a deputy sheriff like that

*once; nobody bothered about him at first 'cause he didn't
yell at you or hit you, nobody he put in jail ever got
beaten; it was just nice talk, now won't you tell me this,
won't you tell me that if you please, picking the fruit off
the tree just as easy as pie. I know, I know, you're not
from the police. I don't mean to insult you, don't get me
wrong—but when you want to know so much about Tereza
Batista, we can't help being suspicious, thinking that where
there's smoke there's fire. If you ask, it's because you
want to know, and why do you care so much? Just to tell
the folks down on the docks all about it when you get
back home? Well, if you want to know so much you can
buy more than thirty different ballads about Tereza
Batista right here in the market, all in verse, with plot and
rhyme. Each one costs a penny. That ain't money, that's
giving 'em away. Just think, in this world where prices are
out of sight and everything costs more and more all the
time, the only thing that poor people can still afford is
living poetry. You can hand over a penny and learn what
Tereza is worth.*

*Getting back to what folks has told you and sworn to,
all I have to say is that miracles do happen. If this country weren't full of blessed miracle-working saints, what
would become of us all? There's Father Cícero Romão,
and Blessed Melânia from Pernambuco, and Blessed
Afonsina the Virgin, and that saint from the slums in
Propriá who had leprosy, Arlindo das Chagas was his
name, and Our Good Jesus of Lapa is beatified too; he
can cure any sickness you name. If it wasn't for those
saints of ours who stop drought and plague and flood and
cure people's hunger and diseases and help us hillbillies
out here in the brush make the best of our bad luck—
well! If it wasn't for them, I say, you tell me what would
become of us all, my fine friend. You think we should
expect the doctors and colonels and governors to help us?
Don't make me laugh. If we counted on the government
and the big shots to help us, Lord, everybody out in the
backlands would have died ailing or starved to death a
long time ago. I tell you, if we're still alive at all, it's a
miracle.*

*They say it was the Angel Gabriel who worked this
particular miracle, because he was an eyewitness to what
that innocent little gal Tereza went through when she was*

forced and raped and dishonored and spat on and shat on and pickled in blood, but don't be surprised none if you find that Blessed Afonsina the Virgin had something to do with it. After all, she went through the same kind of misery: eighteen outlaws busted her gourd one after the other, and the very last one was Berilo Lima, who had such a dreadful big tool they called him Berilo the Gatepost, but Berilo died right afterwards of a cramp in his bowels. And, when the fun was over, Afonsina was all in in one piece, just as good as new. Well, anyway, whether it was the angel or the Blessed Afonsina who worked the miracle or both of them put together, what everybody knows is that whenever Tereza Batista gets her a new man she turns into a virgin again, with a brand-new gourd and her hole stopped up; and she's gained a lot by it, too.

It's a funny kind of miracle, young fellow, I agree with you there; but a lot of folks have thought it was a real fine one, as you'll find out if you listen to blind Simão das Laranjeiras on the road to Sergipe:

> *Come hear me sing*
> *Of a wonderful thing*
> *A miracle true*
> *That Tereza can do*
> *Bust her gourd at night*
> *Next day she's closed tight.*
> *If my old bag knew how*
> *I'd be humping right now.*

Some folks set no store by miracles, but I ain't one of 'em.

34

That night that began in the backyard, under the rain, was a hundred years long. Once Tereza was in his arms, Daniel kissed the eyes, cheeks, forehead, mouth of her face. How could something bad turn into something good, how could misery turn into joy in less than an hour? In bed with the Captain, stiff as a board with a lump in her throat and a knot in her stomach, filled with nausea and repugnance inside and out, when he let go of her at last and she went out of the room to get the basin of water, Tereza had spat out a sour gush of vomit.

With her chintz dress clinging to her body as Daniel held her to his breast—a hesitant hand touching her bosom, rainwet lips traveling over her face—Tereza was assailed with feelings and sensations unknown to her: her legs trembled and went slack, she felt cold at the pit of her stomach but her cheeks were burning, and suddenly she felt sad, as if she would cry, as if she would laugh, and she hadn't felt so happy since she took hold of the doll at the farm—Let go that doll, confound you!—she felt eager and anxious but knew everything would be all right, it was all mixed up together, and oh, how wonderful it was!

As soon as she heard the truck start up and the sound of its motor fade away in the distance, she had run to clean up a little, using the water she had brought in the basin for the Captain and that he hadn't used because he was in such a hurry to get to the party. It was late when he finally went out the door; he was still getting dressed when the church bells struck nine. Nine o'clock sharp, the angel had said, and there wasn't time for Tereza to pump water from the well for an honest-to-goodness bath. She washed the Captain off her as well as she could in the handbasin that Justiniano used for washing his feet before bed: washed off his sweat, his mucus, his spit, his sperm trickling down her legs. But she still felt him making her dirty inside.

Out in the yard by the gate the rain washed her and cleansed her. Tereza's heart throbbed against Dan's as she gazed at the countenance of the Angel Gabriel, come down from Heaven. His lips took possession of her mouth and the point of his tongue tried to open her lips. Tereza, passive, let him do as he wanted, but she was still entirely passive, still a prisoner to her own fear and disgust. Out there in the yard, as that immensely long night began, when Daniel opened her lips and with tongue and teeth invaded her mouth, the old hate was reborn in Tereza, the emotion that had given her courage to defy the Captain for two whole months, before terror had made her a slave. Tereza was still afraid, but now she had her hate back, her first spoils in that night of return. For an instant, hate took possession of her, overwhelming sadness and jubilation together and making her so tense that Daniel sensed something strange in her and paused in his caresses. The rain kept him from seeing the lightning flash in the girl's eyes; if he had seen it, could he possibly have understood it?

Without suspecting what he was doing, Daniel passed between fear and hate. He kissed her lips, her eyes, her face, sucked at her tongue and her earlobes, and Tereza gradually yielded, stopped thinking about the Captain, found that her heart was at ease. When he stopped for a moment to let her draw breath, she smiled, a little abashed and said:

"He won't be back before daybreak. We can go inside if you want to."

And so Dan picked Tereza up in his arms, and holding her against his chest, carried her in the rain from the garden gate to the door of the house, just the way bridegrooms carried brides on their wedding night in the old movie magazines Pomp and Flycatcher read.

He set her down inside the house, not knowing where to go. Taking him by the hand, Tereza crossed the living room and led him down the hall to a door at the end which opened into a stuffy little room crammed with bags of beans, ears of corn, canned goods, sacks of jerky and salt pork, and a cot with wooden slats. Daniel stumbled over the corn in the dark:

"Hmm. Is this where we're going to stay?"

She nodded. Daniel felt her trembling; she must be afraid.

"Is there a light?"

Tereza lit a lamp hanging from the ceiling. By its dim, lugubrious light, Daniel could see her apologetic smile. Why, she was just a little girl.

"How old are you, pretty?"

"I was fifteen day before yesterday."

"Day before yesterday? How long have you been with the Captain?"

"Going on two years and a half."

Why did he ask so many questions? Rain dripped down from Daniel's waterproof and Tereza's dress, gluing it to her skin, and made puddles on the tiled floor. The last thing Tereza wanted was to talk about the Captain and remember the past, all of it bad. It had been so nice out there in the quiet and the dark at the gate of the back-yard, nothing but lips and hands touching her. What did it matter to the Angel whether Justiniano was the first and the only man, why did he stand there and question her, dripping rainwater and cold? Yes, he was the first and only one, there hadn't been any other, the Angel in the picture knew that; he had seen it all. She stopped pay-ing attention to the questions in her ears, only the music in his voice, even more soulful than his eyes, a nocturnal voice, a lazy bedroom voice (when I hear your voice I can't wait to go to bed; so Madame Salgueiro, a society woman in Bahia, had defined its effect) filling her ears. She answered none of his questions: how did you end up in the Captain's house, don't you have any relatives, father and mother, sisters and brothers? Without realizing what she was doing, lulled by that soothing voice, she copied Daniel's gesture from the first time they had been alone in the store: she framed his face with her hands and kissed him on the mouth. Dan's experienced lips gath-ered the first kiss ever given by Tereza Batista's unskilled mouth and held and prolonged it to infinity.

"I guessed it was your birthday and I brought you a present," he told her, giving her the *figa* set in gold.

"How could you guess? I'm the only one who knows." She smiled gently and happily as she looked at the little amulet. "It's beautiful, but I can't take it. I haven't got anyplace to keep it."

"You just hide it in a safe place, and some day you can wear it." A damp smell of meat and salt pork rose from the floor. "Tell me, isn't there someplace else we could go?"

"There's his room, but I'm afraid."

"What for, if he won't be back for a long time? Before he comes back I'll be gone."

"I'm afraid he'll know somebody's been in it."

"Isn't there any other bedroom?"

"Yes, but it's just like this one. It's full of all kinds of provisions, and Chico sleeps there, and his bed and his things are in it. Oh yes! there's the one with the mattress."

"Mattress?"

"There's one here and another one just like it on the farm. It's where he . . ."

"I've heard about it. Let's go in there, this one stinks."

Many girls had lain on that mattress, some raped, others not, most of them practically children. Of all the girls who had been beaten and groaned and struggled and been taken by force with loud words and slaps and blows and beatings (there was a wide leather strap in the room, but it didn't have seven tails like the one on the farm), the only traces that remained were bloodstains on the discolored mattress and rings on the Captain's chain. The sheet was still sweaty from the last girl who had lain down on the mattress almost a month before, a poor demented creature who had started to pray aloud, going down on her knees and calling on the saints and the Virgin when her eyes beheld the vision of Justiniano Duarte da Rosa naked, with upraised prick. St. Sebastian! she called out in ecstasy, setting him off on one of his uncontrollable fits of laughter. The Captain took her in the middle of her litany. Prayers and invocations of the Virgin's holy name mingled with howls, guffaws, and the child's weeping— Satan or St. Sebastian? Tereza, alone in her bed on the other side of the house, could get no rest on her free night. Mercifully, this lasted only four days. The Captain soon had a bellyful of prayers and lamentations, and since Gabi's establishment had no place for a crazed girl, he sent her back to her parents with a ten-cruzeiro note and a little bundle of provisions.

35

Well, at least here there were no sides of bacon or sacks of jerky and salted fish. Daniel hung his raincoat, jacket, and tie on a nail in the wall. He whistled when he saw the leather strap, and shuddered at the thought of the welts a whipping with that strip of rawhide would raise.

"Take off your dress, darling, or you'll catch cold."

He took it off himself, and with the dress came the bra, so that all that Tereza had on was a pair of flowered chintz pants; the flowers were a faded red. Tereza had lapsed into expectant silence again. Her breasts stood erect and she made no move to conceal them. Good Lord, thought Daniel, doesn't she know anything at all? She acts as though she had never been alone in a room with a man she intended to lie down and make love with. And yet, surely she does know, she must; after all, she's been living with Captain Justo and going to bed with him for more than two years . . . or else, what kind of animal is that Justiniano Duarte da Rosa, with his leather strap?

Daniel, the old women's darling, Daniel the society ladies' pet, Daniel, gigolo to prostitutes, had sometimes come across married women (some of them had been married for years), mothers of children, who might as well have been virgins for all the pleasure they had ever felt. They belonged to a man and he had made them pregnant and that was all. At home with one's wife all was duty, respect, and modesty in the bed in which children were made; outside the home, with a prostitute or a mistress, all was pleasure, refinements, libertinage in the bed of debauchery—that was how many a pious family man divided his behavior. Hungry women, meeting a lover for the first time, were overcome with shame and remorse and wept like sinners: "Oh, my poor husband, oh, wretched me, I must have been out of my mind, oh, what shall I do? I'm not an honest woman anymore!" But Dan was very good at his profession, a first-class consoler of fallen women, the best possible comforter to wipe tears away. He took it upon himself to lead these victims of their consorts' strict moral code up every step of the broad staircase of pleasure. And they were quick to learn— dazzled, grateful, insatiable, absolved of all guilt, cleansed of sin, free of remorse, and every one of them with good reasons to spare for turning adulteress. How should you treat a husband who, whether from masculine prejudice or lack of imagination, treats his wife like a thing, a vessel, a lifeless form, or a piece of meat? Why, by adorning his eminent forehead with a fine pair of horns, burnished by pleasure taken like his, outside the bed of matrimony.

With Tereza it was different. She was neither wife nor mother, neither kept woman nor light-o'-love, but only the Captain's slavey. What respect could he possibly feel for her? Yet there she stood waiting, in silence. She didn't even know how to kiss; her mouth was hesitant and unsure. She didn't cry or show signs of remorse, didn't play hard to get or look as if she felt sorry for herself, but just stood there and waited. Her fifteen-year-old body was still not quite formed, but she was getting prettier all the time and in some ways she seemed older than her years. It would have been hard to say how old she was if she hadn't told him. Years of suffering don't show on the calendar, certainly not to the eyes of an inconsequential young man from the capital like Daniel. To the beautiful, frivolous Dan, the old ladies' darling, spoiled by too many easy conquests, Tereza was a dark, indecipherable mystery.

But he had eyes to see and appreciate the beauty of her face and figure. Tereza was all copper and coal, and the coal was her eyes and long hair. Her breasts were two river stones with water running over them. She had long legs and thighs, a firm belly, full hips, and glorious buttocks, adolescent and opulent. Only the rose planted in the vale of copper was hidden under the flowery cloth, and Daniel chose not to unveil it for the moment. He would gather the hidden rosebud in good time. But what about the rest, Daniel? Tereza silently waited.

For once in his life, Daniel couldn't find the right words.

He stripped off his shirt and trousers. Tereza's black eyes grew tender at sight of the Angel, the hair on his chest, the smooth belly, the muscles of his legs. When Daniel took off his shoes and socks, and she saw his thin feet with their carefully clipped nails, she thought how she would love to wash them and cover them with kisses.

They stood face to face and Daniel smiled, still with no words for Tereza. He knew a great many words, all of them fair ones, words of love and flaming passion, even some of His Honor's own torrid verses. He had worn them all out by repeating them to so many old ladies, fiery matrons, and romantic hookers and dancehall girls. None of them were right for the girl standing before him. He smiled and Tereza gave him an answering smile; he went to her and embraced her, body to body. Daniel's hand descended to her waist, but before stripping her of the flowered cloth, his fingertips felt a scar. He bent down to see what it was: yes, it was the old scar of a wound with a deep hole in the middle, as if someone had driven a nail into her flesh. How did this happen to you, darling? Why do you want to know so much, why do you spoil everything with questions, when this night is so short and we may never have another one again? It was the point of the belt buckle, one time when he beat me. Did he beat you very often? With that rawhide strap? He still does, but why do you want to know that, why do you back away, why do you stop touching me and look at me like a puzzled angel? Why are you so surprised? If you didn't already know, you wouldn't be able to believe it; but the angel in the picture in that other room in the farmhouse saw it all happen, saw the whip and the iron. Yes, he still beats me for the least little thing or just to punish me for no real reason: a mistake in addition and he brings out the rod; but what use is it to tell you if there isn't anything we can do about it? Don't ask me anything else, the night won't last long. Before long they'll put out the bonfires, put away the harmonicas, and stop dancing— and just before sunup the Captain will be back to climb into his bed and onto his slave, Tereza.

Carried beyond his selfishness and inconsequential juvenile effrontery, beyond the superficial sentimentality with which he had launched himself on another trivial amorous adventure, Daniel was actually touched. He knelt—imagine that!—and kissed the scar on Tereza's belly. Oh, love! she said, pronouncing the word for the first time in her life.

36

During that century-long, brief night, all was repetition, and yet the repetition was new, a discovery. Dan, still kneeling, lifted his hands to her breasts, while his lustful mouth drifted from the scar to her navel, into which his tongue darted, a dagger of a caress. His hands slid from her breasts down her torso to her waist, groping along the curve of her hips, the plateau of her buttocks, the columns of thighs and legs. On her feet the copper took on the greenblack patina of bronze. Dan's hands rose again to take Tereza's and make her kneel down. They embraced as they knelt face to face, the girl's lips parted imploringly. They lay down as they kissed, and their legs intertwined; stone breasts throbbed against a velvety thicket; soft thighs were clasped between the youth's taut muscles. Dan's impatient hand felt inside her pants and reached the black garden where the golden rose was asleep and languishing—in that mystery of mysteries the copper turned to gold. Oh, love! Tereza said to herself again, still too fearful to repeat it aloud. The girl's unskilled hand timidly touched the angel's ringlets, then with gathering courage moved down his face, then across his neck and shoulder, to end up triumphantly in the down of his chest. Daniel squatted in front of Tereza and slipped off her last flowered garment, covering with one hand the garden of black hair concealing the coffer and the rose. He stood up and pulled off his shorts; Tereza looked up at him as she lay and contemplated the Angel drawn up to his full height in celestial splendor: the sweet meadow of tawny ringlets and the sword upraised. Oh, love! He lay down again beside her, the weight of his thigh on hers, the hair on his chest like ermine, plush and velvet to Tereza's playful fingers, as Dan's left hand wandered from one breast to the other, squeezing the swelling nipples, which swelled still more when his mouth sucked at them before greedily devouring the whole breast, crushing the stone in the suction of a kiss and then with intoxicating words: Give me your milk, I'm your baby and I want to suckle at your breast. Daniel found the right words then, probably the same worn words he had always used, but now they were spoken without artifice, without hypocrisy, without cunning, and became new again in the simplicity and sweetness and shyness of that peerless night: My love, pretty doll, little girl, silly little thing, my life, *menina, minha menina*. His mouth whispered tender things into her ear, his lips touched her earlobe and his teeth bit into it, I'm going to eat you up, every last bit of you, his tongue went into the feverish shell of her ear, and how many times did Tereza think she would faint? Tereza's hand clutched his arm and shoulder and plunged into the hair on his chest, her mouth learned how to kiss and her tongue throbbed voraciously. Daniel's right hand was still in possession of the black tuft where the coffer with the golden rose was concealed. One finger, his index finger, escaped from his hand and fled inside Tereza, penetrated her subtly, tenaciously; oh, love! Tereza sighed and shuddered again; how could deadly duty be transformed into such happiness? The girl's hand moved awkwardly, irresolutely over the Angel's willowy body, and he led it to the soft, tawny field, to the gleaming sword. Tereza touched it with her fingertips. It was made of flowers and steel . . . she grasped it in her hand. Daniel unveiled the mysterious coffer and its rose blossomed in the warmth of a lighted ember, the first. The sparks spread to her nipples, her panting lips, her bitten ear, along her thighs, to the vale of her belly and the fold of her buttocks. The flower throbbed, the sword flamed. Tereza opened her legs, the thighs of a girl who was a woman at last. It was she who untied the knot, she who offered and gave herself. No one told her to do it, for the very first time, and she was not afraid. Daniel bestowed a kiss on the tuft of black hair before setting off with the girl toward the revelation of life and death; it would have been bliss to die then when St. John's Eve was consumed in the bonfires of love and Tereza Batista was born again. Oh, love! she repeated in the beginning, at the end, oh love.

37

Tereza started out that night as one person and when it was over she was someone else—at the end of that night that flew so swiftly, measured minute by eager, swooning minute, but was a hundred years long in joyful revelations and rewards.

When she recovered and woke with a sigh from that first moaning climax, violent, prolonged, and heartfelt from the tips of her toes to the roots of her hair, Tereza felt Daniel stir by her side, put his arm around her waist, and draw her grateful body closer to his.

"You're my own darling little woman, my dear little girl who doesn't know anything yet. But you'll learn how nice it is, I'm going to teach you one thing at a time, just wait and see," as he kissed her lightly.

Tereza smiled weakly, unable to reply. If she had had the strength she would have told him to start right away without wasting any time, because they had only a few hours left and could never be together again. The only firm date on the Captain's calendar of revelry was this St. John's fandango at Raimundo Alicate's house. He might go back there on St. Peter's night, but then again he might just go to Gabi's house and sit around drinking beer with the girls, and there was no telling when he'd be back—it might be late, it might be early, there was just no way of knowing. So, hurry up, Angel, hurry up, we can't waste a minute, she would have said if voice and courage hadn't failed her.

No sooner was she snuggling up against him again, breast against breast, leg against leg, thigh against thigh, than her newly awakened desire, young and demanding, lighted a fire in her again. Saying nothing, she ran her hand over Daniel's body, touching every inch, stretched out her arm to reach his feet and caress them. She lingered longest over the hair on his chest, thrusting her hand into it with open fingers; and then she ran her fingers through the curls on his head, over and over. Little by little she was learning. Her mouth grazed Daniel's lips. My darling doesn't know how to kiss, but I'll teach her. Daniel, a born gigolo by vocation and almost by profession, felt real pleasure in the pleasure of his bed partner, whether she was a young and eager prostitute or a snobbish old rich woman. I'm going to make you feel things no woman ever felt before—and he always did his best to keep his side of the bargain, whether he was paid for it or did it free when some short-lived passion took hold of him. Tereza was learning to kiss with lips, teeth, and tongue, as Daniel's hands multiplied disturbing, delightful sensations in her most hidden parts, in the wet well of her womb and the narrow ravine between the cliffs of her buttocks. Tereza's hands found other favorite places: the hair on his belly, like a fluffy skein of wool, and the sleeping bird that awoke at her touch. Their mouths mingled avidly, his knowing just where to find the spring of hidden excitement, hers revealing itself eager and audacious though a novice at kissing.

Soon the bird, under Tereza's fingers, rose impetuously in its dizzy flight, while Daniel's fingers found dawn's honeydew in the well where the golden rose opened its petals impatiently. No longer able to endure such long preparation, the clever apprentice—that girl's a fast learner, she's as clever as she can be, you only have to tell her once, as Miss Mercedes used to say in that long-dead time—slipped out of Daniel's embrace and positioned herself expectantly on her back, legs parted, the nest of coal and gold waiting for the plunge of the bird.

Daniel burst out laughing and said no. Why do what
we did before, darling, when there are so many different
ways to do it, each with its own special name, each better than the last? And I'll teach you all of them. He laid
her on her side again, against his chest, lifted her thigh
and took her from the side. Their bodies intertwined and
without anyone having to teach her, Tereza caught him
by the waist, legs twisted together, and they rolled on
the mattress. Blind and mute, hungry and thirsty, Tereza
was learning. No virgin was ever so virgin; she had a
thousand maidenheads; everything she did was done for
the first time. Daniel had never felt anything like it; it
was all new to him too. He held back his own orgasm
when Tereza was aroused, but his impatient partner was
behindhand with pleasure; she pressed forward to climax
and he couldn't hold her back. Faint and exhausted, closing her eyes, Tereza relaxed the knot of their legs, but
Daniel persisted, ever so slowly and artfully went back
for her again, caught her up again in the bird's flight,
and yes, this time both together they attained God's
grace. Tereza Batista's bonfire was lit on the Eve of St.
John, and once Daniel had lit it he was consumed in it
too. The fire was new and trembling, but it spread swiftly
in a crackling of sighs and smothered moans, and none
excelled it in high, hot leaping flames.

After that second time, Daniel took a cigarette from
his jacket pocket and smoked it with his head in Tereza's
warm lap while she gently scratched his head. Let me
catch your lice, she said, and they both laughed. That was
the only endearment Tereza knew; she had learned it as
a baby from her mother before she had died in the bus.
Daniel put out the cigarette with the sole of his shoe and
hid the butt in his pocket. He laid his head on the girl's
stomach again, and she felt the blond curls against her
black tuft, tickling her gently; as she scratched his head
Daniel fell asleep.

Tereza watched over the Angel's rest. He was even
more beautiful in real life than in the colored picture.
She thought about a lot of things while he slept. She remembered the mongrel dog, Ceição, Jacira, the mock
battles and cowboy-and-Indian games with the boys, her
aunt who took strangers to bed with her, Uncle Rosalvo
with his rheumy eyes, how they had all run after her

through the woods and her uncle had handed her over, Aunt Felipa with the ring on her finger, how they had driven away with her in the truck, that terrifying little room in the farmhouse, her attempts at escape, the rod, the whip, the belt, the iron. Suddenly, all of that was behind her, as if it were just some tale of a soul in torment, some ghost story told by Dona Brígida, some crazy foolishness the poor old widow had made up. That rainy night had moistened the dry, cracked earth; joy and tenderness had blossomed on top of the old hurt and panic fear. She would not let the Captain hurt her again for anything in this world.

Now she could die; she wouldn't die missing things, sadly, all alone and in fear. It was far better to die than to go back to the Captain's sweaty, sticky bed. On the farm Tereza had seen a girl, Isidra, one of the maids, hanging from a rope in the door to her room, her black tongue half out of her open mouth, her eyes starting wildly out of her head. She had hanged herself when she heard that Juárez, her man, had been stabbed in a drunken brawl. There was plenty of rope in the storeroom. Between the time the Angel left and the Captain came back, she would have more than enough time to knot the noose.

38

On that immeasurable night without beginning or end, that night of meetings and partings and successive dawns, Tereza, doomed to die, escaped from the gallows by galloping away on a horse made of fire.

Daniel slept and she watched over his sleep; he was an angel come down from heaven. But she longed to be in his arms one more time, press him again to her breast before a last farewell. She touched his face, fearfully. Angels come down to earth to carry out their appointed missions and then go back to make a report to God: that was what Dona Brígida said, and she knew all about angels and devils. What bliss to be able to die in his heavenly arms; but Tereza'll die all alone; she'll hang in the doorway, with her tongue sticking out.

Daniel woke up when he felt the girl's hand groping

uncertainly, and saw that she was sad. Why are you sad, darling, didn't you like it, wasn't it good? Sad? No, I'm not sad, I'm as happy as I've ever been or ever will be. There's never been such a joyful night as this, such a first night of infinite happiness; only there won't be a second time or another time or a next time, and I'd rather die than go back to being a slave and being beaten and taking that basin full of water back and forth and getting into that double bed with Justiniano Duarte da Rosa and his stinking breath. There's plenty of rope in the store, and I know how to make a knot.

Darling, for heaven's sake, silly little darling, why shouldn't there be other nights like this one or even better? Surely there will be. Daniel sat up, and now it was Tereza who rested her head in his lap, feeling the warm bird and the tickling soft skein against the back of her neck. You just rest, darling, and listen to me. The Angel's hands covered her breasts, pressing them tenderly; his divine voice erased her unhappiness, opened new horizons, saved Tereza, doomed to die, from the noose. Didn't she know the Captain had a trip to Bahia all planned? He was going on business and pleasure. There was the governor's invitation to the July-second reception—the idiot doesn't know it's a public reception and anybody can go; the printed invitation's just a formality; all it's good for is just so that guy from the police can score a few points with our yokel from Cajazeiras do Norte who thinks he's so smart but is just a clown—and then he has a case at court, and calls on government officials and wholesale suppliers, besides an introduction to Rosalia Varela, a tango singer at the Tabaris who's a mouth specialist and a whiz at the Arab bouché. One day I'll teach it to you, darling, there's nothing like it—when the Captain's away in Bahia and we can have a party every night.

The main thing was just to be patient and put up with the Captain's demands and his rudeness for a few more days, be as docile as ever and not show any change. But she knew he'd want to sleep with her and she just couldn't do that, ever again! Why on earth not? It was nothing to worry about provided Tereza kept aloof as she always did and didn't cooperate, didn't take part, didn't come in the Captain's arms. Tereza suffocates with disgust in the Captain's arms, believe me. Well, then? Just bow your head the way you've always done; it'll be a whole lot easier now. You'll be putting up with the stupid bully so you can take revenge for everything he's done to you. We'll decorate him with the biggest horns in the district, we'll give the Captain a pair of antlers fit for a general.

Having had plenty of experience and also being very persuasive, Daniel told her just what she ought to do. Why, the very next day he would make himself go to the Moraeses' house and eat cornmeal gruel and drink cordial and be cordial; it was tiresome, but he had to do it. The Captain was convinced that Daniel was after one of the sisters, the youngest one. It was thanks to that little fib that he was able to spend so much time at the store, seeing Tereza all he wanted to without arousing suspicion. And besides, who's to say we won't have another chance to meet before the Captain goes away? On St. Peter's night, for example? Now, no more talk about killing yourself. You're raving, girl, and the world belongs to us, and even if the big fool should happen to catch us someday, don't be afraid—I'll teach him a lesson he won't soon forget. Daniel would teach the Captain to wear his horns with all due courtesy and jubilant modesty.

Of all that she heard, ony one thing really meant anything to Tereza: the Captain was going away! He was going to the capital for at least ten days and maybe two weeks, and that meant ten nights of love, maybe even fifteen. She seized Daniel's hands and kissed them gratefully. It was Chico Half-Sole who worried Daniel the most. What should he do? Buy him off with a fat tip? No, Angel from Heaven, not a tip. No tip could buy away Chico's fidelity to Justiniano, but luckily Chico wasn't a problem: he slept in the store when the Captain was away and left the rest of the house to Tereza. If Daniel came in the back way and the lovers went to the master bedroom, the farthest away from the store, Chico would never know about it. You see? Everything works in our favor. All you have to do is make sure that Justiniano suspects nothing. Nothing, Tereza, do you understand? She understood: she wouldn't do anything to make him suspicious, she'd find the courage somehow.

During the latter part of their talk, Daniel's hands began to run over her again, lingering on each hollow and swelling curve in a long, continuous caress, a subterranean arousal.

Still made uneasy by his words and her own thoughts, Tereza had withdrawn into herself and opened again in fear, hate, despair, hope, and love. Having said what he had to say, Daniel brought his mouth to Tereza's breast and traced its contours with his tongue, up her bosom to her neck, around the nape to her ear, and then to her lips. And it all began again. We'll begin again a thousand times, darling; I'll never be tired of you; there'll be lots of other nights, you'll see. I'm so glad, love! said Tereza.

Daniel wanted her to mount him. Tereza had never done that before, since the Captain had never told her to —he wanted no woman riding him; no self-respecting male turns himself into a jackass for a woman to ride. Mounted on her ardent steed, Tereza Batista left the noose behind and rode to freedom. She looked down on her Angel with his smiling face, his hair in ringlets, his melting eyes, his incandescent face. She galloped over the fields of night toward the dawn. When she rolled onto the mattress, dissolved in pleasure, she could still smell the inebriating scent of her perspiring steed—horse, angel, man, her man!

39

Daniel said good-bye at the gate at daybreak, in a kiss of tongues, teeth, and sighs. After she had gone back into the house alone, Tereza went to pump water for the wooden tank in the bathroom and washed Daniel's perfumed sweat off her body with coconut soap. She would have loved to leave that fragrance on her skin, but the Captain had a hunter's nose, and she had to fool him to be worthy of another visit from the Angel. She stripped herself of his perfume, but the taste of the youth clung to her mouth, her breast, her earlobes, her belly, the black tuft of hair, the depths of her body. Even before she bathed, Tereza had swept the narrow cubicle and changed the sheet, leaving the door open so the morning wind could blow away the odor of tobacco and the echoes of that festive night—over the sordid mattress of unhappy memory, a rainbow had arched full-blown.

Words, gestures, sounds, caresses, a world of memories;

lying on the big double bed in the Captain's room, which was still dark, Tereza remembered every single moment. Lord, how could anything that had been so terrible be so good? When Daniel penetrated her, after awakening her senses and kindling her desire, when he took her and gave himself to her and they moaned in unison—only then did Tereza know why it was that when Uncle Rosalvo went to drink rum and push dominoes around in Manoel Andorinha's grubby little store, Aunt Felipa, out of no duty nor obligation but for nothing and happy to do it, shut herself up in the bedroom with other men she had met at the market or neighboring farmers or just passersby. She used to threaten Tereza: if you tell your uncle I'll give you a beating that'll make your head swim and I won't give you any dinner; you stand in the door and watch, and if you see him coming you come running and tell me. Tereza would climb the mango tree and look far up and down the road. When the bedroom door opened and the man went his way, Aunt Felipa, now all smiles, would tell her to go and play. More than once, she had even given her brown sugar candy. All the time she lived in the Captain's house, whenever she thought about her old life on her aunt and uncle's farm—she had tried to forget it, but on nights when she was alone, nights when she could sleep and get some rest, a medley of people and events rose up before her and kept her from going to sleep —Tereza wondered what the reason could be for that strange habit of her aunt's. She had to do it with Rosalvo, she guessed; after all, they were married and a husband has rights and his wife has duties. But to do something that hurt so much with somebody else? No one made her do it or beat her with a leather strap. Why, then? Now she finally knew why: it could be awful or so nice you could hardly stand it; it all depended on who you lay down with.

The Captain did not return until afternoon. When he got down from the truck in front of the store—closed because it was St. John's—he heard laughter coming from the Moraes house. He looked up at the window; the big parlor was open and there inside in the midst of the four sisters was young Daniel with a liqueur glass in his hand, making himself agreeable by telling them amusing society gossip from the capital. Justiniano waved a greet-

ing to the merry company. He would have to tell the boy
to take certain precautions so Teó would not have a baby,
if he did decide to eat her cherry. She was old enough so
that if he did it carefully, he wouldn't get her pregnant. If
he did, she'd yell to high heaven and insist on their being
married and there'd be the devil to pay, his being the
Judge's son and all. The Moraes girls belonged to an old,
conservative family, and that Magda was tough as a turkey neck—just ask the juggler if you don't believe me,
he had to sweep up at headquarters and was threatened
with a beating besides. The Captain shrugged; that young
squirt wasn't one to stick his neck out for the sake of a
hymen; thighs and creases and finger and tongue were
good enough for him, that cunt-sucker, that French poodle
for virgins.

Tereza was starching clothes in the dining room, while
Chico Half-Sole recovered from his hangover in the store
—he never stayed alone in the house with Tereza when
the boss wasn't there. He was a husky *caboclo,* and a
few hours of sleep were enough to cure him after his
inevitable Saturday-night and holiday drinking sprees.
Even so, he couldn't hold a candle to Justiniano Duarte
da Rosa, who was capable of drinking steadily for four
days and four nights without sleep, laying a broad every
night, and then riding off on his horse to wherever he had
to go. He was made of iron. While Chico lay snoring,
dead to the world, the Captain was as fresh as a daisy.
No one could have believed that he'd drunk and danced
all night long and then gone out to the farm when the
sun was high in the sky, driving the truck himself—Terto
Cachorro was so drunk he had rolled under the bench
where the musicians had sat—a homely little spring chicken
with a silly red face sitting in the front seat beside him.
At the party, when Alicate had seen him coming, he had
come running up to welcome him, towing the silly little
girl who didn't dare even raise her eyes in his wake.

"Lift your head up so the Captain can see your mug,
perdition take you."

Yes, she was a green young'un, just right for the Captain's chain. If she's a virgin, that is.

"I've been saving her just for you, Captain; she's still in
swaddling clothes, the way you like 'em. Now I won't
try to fool you by telling you she's still in one piece, 'cause

she ain't; she comes from out by the sugarmill and you know as well as I do that virgins from those parts don't last very long. But she's fresh and clean and she ain't been passed around much, and she ain't diseased. She might as well be a virgin, almost."

Those Guedes bastards. You might know. There was always one of the three on duty at the sugar refinery while the other two lived it up in Bahia or Rio or São Paulo when they weren't in Europe or the United States. They took turns looking after the business and picking virgins as they got ripe. Of the three, the most effective in business, the one who really ran things, was Dr. Emiliano; and he was also the hardest to satisfy when it came to looks. He wouldn't take just any little girl; he was picky and choosy. Even if he had been at the refinery instead of spending his money on Paris whores, he wouldn't have taken that snub-nosed, red-faced little girl to bed. He was a mite too particular for that.

"Who did you the favor?"

"Seu Marcos . . ."

"Marcos Lemos? Son-of-a-bitch!"

When it wasn't the owners, it was their underlings. Even the bookkeeper's leavings, chawed-up cane from the sugarmill, raw brown sugar, molasses tailings, were served up to the Captain to eat. But never mind, in town, in his own house, he had a high-class girl, with a face and figure that no one could find fault with, the prettiest girl for miles around. She didn't have her equal anywhere in town, on the farms, or at the mill, rich, poor, or in debt, maid, wife, or whore. Not that the Captain made a point of a woman's being pretty; good-looking or homely, if they were young enough it was all one to him; but it gave him pleasure to know that Dr. Emiliano Guedes, the head of the family, the landowner, the tribal chief, so high and mighty sitting up on his black horse with its silver trappings, was willing to spend good money to have her, he didn't care how much. His perfect manners and the insolence in his voice—Don't you want to sell that little heifer?—could not conceal his covetous interest: your price is mine. Who does that pretty girl belong to that everyone wants, with a waiting list at Gabi's pension and a parade of clients gaping at her in the store? Why to none other than Justiniano Duarte da Rosa, known as Captain Justo because he owns wide fields, herds of cattle, a well-stocked drygoods store, and fine fighting cocks. One day, when the acres have broadened to leagues, when he has unlimited credit in the banks and even more rented houses and political prestige than he does now, he'll be Colonel Justiniano, a real *prócer*, every bit as rich and as influential as the Guedeses. And when that day comes, he'll be able to talk to them as an equal, discuss heifers and hymens and even trade girls with them, without tasting the bitter flavor of leftovers in his mouth. Some day; not now.

"Come here, Tereza."

She heard him call, the iron upraised in her hand. Oh God, could she bear it? She was still wrapped in fear like a sheet, the sheet she had wrapped around her when she tried to escape the first time. Why not run away with Daniel, anywhere to escape from that double bed, from the Captain's voice and his presence, from the rod, the whip, and the iron? From the branding iron, the one he branded cattle with and would brand any woman who dared to deceive him, though who would ever dare? No woman could be that crazy. Tereza had been crazy enough to dare. She set down the iron, folded the garment she had been ironing, and girded up her loins.

"Tereza!" his threatening voice.

"I'm coming."

He held out his feet and she untied his shoelaces, took off his shoes and socks, brought in the basin of water. Fat sweaty feet, dirty toenails, callused soles, and they stank. Daniel's feet were wings to rise in the air and fly away on—slender, clean, dry, perfumed feet. It was no use to think of running away with him. He was the Judge's son, he came from the big city, he was a student, almost had his law degree; she would be no use to him, either as concubine or servant. In the capital he had heaps of women to choose from, he could take his pick. But he had said my love, my darling, I never saw such a pretty girl, I'll never get tired of you, I want you with me all my life long. Why would he say it if it wasn't true?

She washed the Captain's feet quickly and efficiently. She had to keep him in the dark, without a glimmer of suspicion. Otherwise, he'd cancel his trip to Bahia, put his thugs on her trail, bring in the iron for branding steers, cows, oxen, and cheating women. Tereza had once heard him remark at one of the cockfights he had taken her to, to show her off:

"If some crazy broad ever tries to cheat on me, not that any of them ever will, before I put the damned lying bitch out of her misery, I'd brand her in the face and the rump with the branding iron I use for cattle, just to teach her her master's name. She'd learn it, all right, before she died."

The Captain took off his jacket and drew the knife and gun from his belt. That St. John's Day he had eaten leftovers from the sugarmill. The silly girl knew how to move and clearly enjoyed it. Sassy little redface, she was all right for an hour or two of fun, just for a change. Change was the best part of the game. But she wouldn't do for the double bed, night and day and any old time, for years on end. Some day, when he got tired of his gal Tereza, and it was sure to happen sooner or later, he would make a gift of her to Dr. Emiliano Guedes, a gift from *prócer* to *prócer*—here you are, Dr. Guedes, I hope you enjoy the Captain's leavings, and *bon appétit*. Not now, though. He was still a nobody compared to the Guedeses, and then, tired as he was, home after a night of nonstop dancing and drinking, topped off by a morning on top of a greedy little girl who knew a trick or two, he no sooner clapped eyes on Tereza Batista than his prick lit up and his balls started to itch.

"Hop into bed, quick."

He pulled up her dress, pulled off her panties, unbuttoned his fly, and mounted Tereza. What was she up to? Was she a virgin again with a brand-new gourd? She had stayed tight as it was, a rare virtue; there was nothing worse than a woman who was loose. He didn't care if a girl had a homely face and a graceless form; it took more than that to make the Captain retire from the battlefield. But he couldn't stand a woman with a wide nozzle, door to a freight car, twenty-gallon jug. A tight passage, a difficult entry, a tiny crack in the door—that was Tereza. But now the door was shut all the way; not a crack, not a crevice was open; damned if she didn't have her maidenhead back. The Captain knew what to do with a virgin and plowed right ahead, thinking that Tereza deserved two gold rings on his necklace. He didn't see the flashes of hate in her fearful, coal-black eyes.

40

Days of anguish and impatience preceded the Captain's trip to Bahia. Only once could Tereza exchange a hasty kiss with Daniel at noon, when he told her to keep her chin up; the trip was still on. The day before, he had left a faded flower on the counter, and its dying petals kept Tereza alive during five mortal days of waiting.

Daniel came to the store every day, almost always in Justiniano's company, the two of them talking and laughing like old cronies. Her heart beating fast, Tereza hung on the heavenly apparition's every gesture and look, hoping to surprise a loving message. When the Captain wasn't with him, the youth came in on one foot and left on the other, just time to say hello and good-bye, with American cigarettes for the clerks and a melting look for Tereza, along with a pout of the lips that meant a kiss, all too little for her awakened, demanding hunger.

Daniel was more fortunate, in one way at least: he partook of an early supper with the Moraes sisters every evening at their table spread with luscious desserts, the best in the world—sweetmeats made from cashew fruit, mango, mangaba, jackfruit, guava, currant, coromandel, gooseberry—to list them from memory is to be inevitably unjust; one simply can't remember them all—pineapple, for instance, and bitter orange, Lord, how delicious! and sliced banana—and all the variations of corn, from the whole roasted ear to fritters and cornmeal mush, not to mention the cinnamon-flavored pudding and coconut custard, traditionally served in June; and ciruela jam and genipap jelly and slices of angel food cake with coconut milk, curds and whey, hog plum and wild cherry juice, and all the fruit cordials. Just a little snack, the sisters said; a fairy banquet, Daniel retorted gallantly and greedily. In the drawing room, the piano covered with a Spanish shawl, a memento of better days, groaned under Magda's fingers as she pounded out the notes of "Prima Carezza,"

"The Turkish March," and "Lake Como," a select repertory and mercifully a short one. Berta tried to copy his profile with her colored pencils—did he think it looked like him? A very good likeness, you're an artist. Applause for Amália, the elocutionist: willing to go to any lengths, Daniel recklessly asked for an encore after she recited, trembling with emotion, the words from "In Extremis": "the lips that kissed your ardent lips." On the pretext of giving him a manicure, Teodora held the youth's hands, with her knees touching his and her bosom permanently on show, and even bit the tip of one of his fingers. Her sisters unanimously reproved her for the false manicure, which they considered an unfair, not to say indecent, subterfuge. Teó, very self-possessed with her nail scissors, nail file, and bottle of acetone, said she had never felt such soft hands.

Powdered and painted and fragrant with perfume and cologne, the four girls were almost beside themselves. The town comadres were divided into two factions: one party was sure the engagement of Daniel and Teodora would soon be announced, that the poor boy had fallen into the snare set for him in the mansion by the terrible sisters; the other wing, marshaled by Dona Ponciana de Azevedo, laughed knowingly and laid their bets on Daniel: look at that Teó, giving herself to him on a silver platter along with the jam and the fritters; and if he isn't guzzling down the other three too, it's because he doesn't want to. The Captain, an eyewitness who was friendly to the fun-loving, garrulous student, in spite of certain bad habits he had—no real man licks a woman's ass—had warned him against getting Teodora pregnant. In reply, Daniel had narrated a series of priceless anecdotes on the problem of avoiding children, each one funnier than the last. The Captain had almost died laughing. The impudent rascal could tell a joke like nobody's business.

On the morning of St. Peter's Day, Justiniano went to the judge's house to take Daniel with him in the truck to a cockfight. They took lunch out in the country and didn't come back until late in the afternoon. Tereza still nourished the hope that he might go to Raimundo Alicate's shindig, and then, oh then, she and Daniel would have the night free to make merry. But the Captain didn't even change his clothes; dressed just as he was, he went off for a beer or two at Gabi's and came back early. Tereza washed his feet with a heavy heart. She felt like running out to look for Daniel in the streets, at the judge's house or the Moraes mansion, and begging him to take her with him to the end of the world. She was so disappointed and unhappy that at first she didn't take in the sense of what Justiniano was saying to her: I'm taking the train to Bahia tomorrow, see that my clothes are packed. I'll do it right now, she said as she wiped his feet. No, not now. Tomorrow morning'll be time enough. When she came back from emptying the basin, there he was, lying in bed waiting for her. The Captain had never been so attached to that big double bed, Tereza's bed. No other woman had ever appealed to him for nearly so long as she had; it had been more than two years now, going on three, and his interest in her had grown instead of waning. Was it because she was pretty? Tight? Young? Difficult? Who could say, if the Captain didn't know himself?

Every St. Peter's Day during the ten years she survived her husband, Dona Engrácia Vinhas de Moraes, who had loved her husband and loved parties too, had gone to church in the morning to pray to St. Peter, patron saint of widows, and given a party to honor him in the drawing room of the mansion that night. They would build an enormous bonfire in the street, and a lavish table would be spread for their distinguished relatives, numerous friends, and the young men who danced with the daughters of the house, the four marriageable girls, Magda, Amália, Berta, Teodora. The single daughters, almost old maids now, kept up their mother's devout tradition: they went to mass and lit candles before the image of the Apostle, and threw open the doors of the mansion at night. Some poor relatives came, a few friends, no young men. But this year the St. Peter's Day celebration took a new lease on life: the gossip-hungry comadres came in droves, and Daniel was there with his bedroom eyes and moist laughter, his mind wandering to the other side of the street where Tereza needed every bit of courage she could muster, up there in Justiniano Duarte da Rosa's big double bed.

The next day Tereza packed the Captain's bag, putting in, as he had ordered her to, the dark blue suit of fine wool that he had had made for his wedding day and practically never worn since. It was his suit for big oc-

casions—he would wear it to the July-second reception at
the governor's palace. She also packed several white suits
and his best shirts, a whole stack of them; it looked as
if he was planning to be away for a long time.

Before he left for the station he gave Tereza and Chico
Half-Sole their orders: Take care of the store and keep
an eye on those clerks—with the cat away the mice might
want to steal for their own benefit instead of the boss's,
and take a bundle home every day. As usual when the
Captain was away, Chico Half-Sole had orders to sleep in
the store on a cot, partly as a security measure, to make
sure the merchandise was safe, and partly, no doubt, to
make the house itself off limits to him at night, with no
possibility of his running into Tereza.

As for Tereza, she was forbidden to set foot outside
the house or the store or to let the customers talk too
much; she was to speak only when strictly necessary.
When supper was over, Chico was to lock himself in the
store and Tereza in the house. The Captain didn't want
any woman of his wandering around loose, and whether
he was right or wrong made no difference to him.

Without a word of farewell—good-bye, see you soon—
or a wave, he went off to the station, with Chico Half-
Sole carrying his suitcase. In his jacket pocket, next to the
governor's invitation, was the letter of introduction to
Rosalia Varela, the *porteña* who plied her trade in Bahia,
the cabaret singer who specialized in Argentine tangos and
games with the mouth, so justly celebrated in words and
music: "Depraved woman, with your lewd and sensual
mouth . . . ."

Just before he left, when he was changing his clothes,
seeing Tereza Batista with her back to him next to the
wardrobe, the Captain felt the familiar itch in his balls,
pulled up her dress, seized her from behind, and took her
like an animal, as a parting gesture.

41

They spent exactly eight nights in the Captain's double
bed, and one of them lasted well into Sunday while Chico
Half-Sole slept off his Saturday-night hangover. He had

drunk two full bottles of *cachaça* the night before, but he had drunk it in the store—while the boss was away he wouldn't, for anything, have left the merchandise entrusted to him unguarded.

Every night as soon as the bell of St. Anne's struck nine, curfew for sweethearts and the girls' *paseo* in the plaza, Daniel was at the back gate. Just before the sun rose, he was off into the lingering darkness. In the afternoon (he slept soundly until lunchtime), he went for high tea with the Moraes girls, stopping by the store with the excuse of asking Chico for news of the Captain—no, he still hasn't sent us a telegram yet saying when he's coming back, *doutorzinho*. He always had American cigarettes for Pomp and Flycatcher and a nickel for Chico, and for Tereza a melting glance. He was gaining weight on all that corn pudding and jam, and bewildering the four sisters with his reticence and ambiguous gestures. The three eldest sighed, and Teodora was on the verge of dragging him off to bed—if Tereza hadn't kept him in such a turmoil of emotion, Daniel might have let Teó have her way and done her the favor; she was pretty and giddy enough to deserve it.

But the man who mounted Tereza and let her mount him, the man who lifted her across the portals of happiness and taught her what color the dawn is, could not think of anyone else. Raped two and a half years before, taken by the Captain almost every day, she had withdrawn deep into her fear and had kept herself innocent, pure, and credulous. Suddenly awakening and finding that she was a woman, those few nights that went by all too swiftly were enough to open a well of infinite pleasure in her, and she blossomed into beauty. She had been a pretty girl with the simple grace of an adolescent, but now the rich oil of pleasure bathed her face and body, and sheer happiness and joy of love lit that fire in her eyes of which Emiliano Guedes had seen the spark months before. What else? She had learned a few tender words, variations on kissing, and the secret of certain caresses. Though much to one who had had nothing before, it was really very little. Everything had happened much too quickly, and Dan's youth had kept him from mastering his art completely. He lacked the most subtle art of all: the finesse to spin pleasure out to infinity, possession by inches, ccstasy that was the more intense because it came slowly. Daniel was too impetuous and eager for that, and he knew (as Tereza did not) just how short his holiday fling would be and how little time they had left. Tereza didn't know and had no desire to try to guess, to argue or clarify things. To have him beside her, to roll on the bed locked in his arms, to be mounted by him and to mount him, to satisfy his desires and be paid in the same coin herself, his slave and his queen, what more could she want? To go away with him, of course; but since there was an agreement between them on that score, the discussion was closed; there was really no more to be said. Daniel was an Angel from Heaven, a baby Jesus—perfection.

He had promised to take her away with him and free her from the Captain's yoke. Why not do it right now, while Justiniano was away? He was waiting for some money from Bahia, but it would be here soon. The promise was vague and the excuse even more so, but his brave words were definite enough: Just let the Captain try some of his tricks with me and he'll soon learn which of us is the real man and the difference between courage and empty boasts.

The plans for escape and their future together did not take up much time during nights that were all too short for the joys of bed. Tereza never doubted the boy. Why should he lie to her? On the first of those eight nights, when they were still recovering from the first mad gallop, and the panting Daniel had laid his head on Tereza's moist belly, she said to him with deep feeling: "Oh take me away from here. I can even go and work for you, I don't care what I do, but I never want to be with him again." Almost solemn for once, Daniel gave his promise: "Yes, I'll take you to Bahia, don't fret about it anymore," and sealed the promise with a kiss in which their tongues entwined greedily.

All the things that had been dirty and painful with the Captain were heavenly with Daniel. He didn't say, Suck! as the Captain had, brandishing the rawhide whip with its seven thongs, ten knots to a thong. On the second night —oh, why not the first, Dan?—he made her lie on her back. Now lie still, he commanded, and began with the tip of his tongue on her eyes. Then her ears, inside and out, around her neck, on the nape, the nipple and contour

of each breast, down her arms—his teeth biting her arm-
pits, for teeth and lips had their part in this caress—then
her stomach, the navel, the black tuft of hair, then her
legs and thighs and at last the secret entrance between
her thighs, the flower that thrilled to his touch; mouth
and tongue sucking her, oh, Dan, I'll die! That was the way
he asked her to do something, by doing it first to her.
Tereza took hold of the gleaming sword and at last they
did it together. Then Tereza understood that the hour of
death had come; so be it!

Half dying of ecstasy, her head fallen against the Angel's belly, she said: "I thought I was going to die; just
now, I wish I had. If I don't go to Bahia I'll kill myself,
I'll hang myself from the doorpost, but I'm never going
to sleep with him again. If you aren't going to take me,
tell me so, but don't lie to me."

For the first and last time she saw him angry. Haven't
I already told you I'll take you? Do you doubt my word?
Do you think I'm the kind of man who lies? He told her
to be quiet and never to question him in such a way again.
Why did she insist on mixing gloomy threats with the
joy of that moment? Why lessen and spoil their night
of pleasure by talking about death and unhappiness? Every
subject had its time, every conversation its place. That
was another thing that Tereza Batista learned from the
law student Daniel Gomes, and she never forgot it. She
did not ask him any more questions about the elopement
they had planned, or think any more about hanging herself
with a rope.

Daniel never said, Get down on all fours, like Justiniano
Duarte da Rosa, beating her with the belt buckle until
she bent to his will; Tereza still had the scar. On one
of those resurrection nights the Angel marked out on the
ample territory of her hips the borderline that joins earthly
paradise to the kingdom of heaven; flying up from the
golden well which had been its resting place, the spirited
bird found another nest in the bronze ravine. My love!
said Tereza.

She had died with the rod, the belt, the whip, the iron,
but now she was born again. The taste of gall and the
marks branded by pain and by fear were all wiped out,
one by one. In possession once again of every particle
of her being, when the test came, without a trace of fear,

but in all her beauty compounded of sweetness and valor
in equal parts, the famous Tereza Batista rose to her full
stature.

42

Neither Daniel nor anyone else noticed when Berta, the
homeliest of the four sisters, led Magda, the eldest, to
the window of the darkened drawing room in the mansion and peered with her through a crack in the blinds as
the bells in the church tower struck nine.

"Look, here he comes," said Berta. She knew it with
liquid certainty, for no sooner did she sense his presence
than she felt a chill in her lower regions and an almost
irresistible need to urinate.

Hidden behind the curtains, they watched his figure go
down the street and turn the corner, his muffled footsteps
dying away in the alley.

"Now he's at the gate. He must be going inside."

Yes, Magda was tough as a turkey neck. Convinced
of her responsibilities as the firstborn, she watched until
dawn and recognized Daniel, looking handsome and very
pleased with himself, coming back from his night with
Tereza just before daybreak. The cad had used the four
sisters as a screen, as a solid, unimpeachable cover in
order to conceal from Justiniano Duarte da Rosa and the
town his unspeakable orgies with that girl from the store,
the fatuous Captain's tart: No woman's ever going to fool
me. Naturally the scoundrel must have bought Chico Half-
Sole's complicity with a few cruzeiros for *cachaça*—only
an imbecile like Justiniano would trust his woman and his
goods to a hired bandit—and to ensure himself total impunity, he had abused the good faith, the friendship, the
sentiments, and well-spread table (even more well-spread
than usual when he came to see them), of the four sisters,
Magda, Amália, Berta, Teodora. And now their names
were on everybody's tongue; the comadres were cutting
them to ribbons, and that girl was enjoying herself in bed.

Magda had won prizes for her handwriting at school,
but for a certain type of correspondence she preferred to
print, following Dona Ponciana de Azevedo's sensible ex-

ample. From the whole scandalous affair she derived only one pleasure, the gloomy pleasure of an old maid: for once she could write down all those wicked words that young girls and proper ladies were forbidden to use: cuckold, horns, shit, two-bit gigolo, whore of a servant girl, oh, that whore of a servant girl.

43

Tereza had fallen asleep after ascending to Heaven. As he smoked a cigarette, Daniel considered what would be the best way to break the news of his imminent departure for Bahia, the law school and the nightclubs, his classmates and bohemian companions, the old ladies and romantic hookers. "I'll send for you later, darling, don't feel bad and don't cry, for heaven's sake don't cry and don't torment yourself; as soon as I get there I'll see what I can do." He foresaw a bad quarter of an hour ahead of him; how tiresome it would be. Daniel had a horror of all scenes, ruptures, leave-takings, weeping and laments. Their whole last night would be spoiled, unless he waited until the last minute to tell her, at dawn when they said good-bye at the gate after a deep kiss with lips, tongues, and teeth.

Maybe it would be better not to tell her that night at all. He could stop by the store the next morning to say a general good-bye to them all——he had had an urgent call from the law school, there was no help for it, he had to go; if he didn't he'd lose credit for the whole year. He was leaving on the very next train, but he wouldn't be away long, a week at most. But what if Tereza didn't believe him? What if she realized she'd been duped, and started yelling and making a scene in front of Chico Half-Sole and the clerks? How would the faithful pistolero react when he found out that somebody had put horns on his boss and protector right under his nose? Chico had killed men before, and he had told Daniel himself that he owed the commutation of his life sentence to the Captain's efforts in his behalf. No, the best thing was to leave without telling her at all. It was a dirty trick to play, no doubt about that, a very dirty trick; the simple, credulous girl, blinded with passion, thought he was an Angel from Heaven, and here he was stealing away, without a word of apology or farewell. But what else could he do? Take her to Bahia with him as he had promised her he would do? It was not to be thought of; such a crazy idea had never crossed his mind. He had only mentioned the possibility to keep her from weeping and wailing and talking about hanging herself.

The voice of Justiniano Duarte da Rosa yanked Daniel out of bed with a bound and awakened Tereza. The Captain was standing in the doorway, the wide leather strap hanging from his right wrist, the knife and the German Luger visible under his open jacket.

"You cheating little bitch, I'll settle accounts with you in a little while. You won't lose anything by waiting. Do you remember the iron I used on you before? Well, this time it'll be the branding iron, and you'll heat it yourself." He laughed his curt, biting laugh, a sentence of death.

Daniel, livid and trembling, stood against the wall, too frightened to speak. Turning his back on Tereza—he had all the time in the world to take care of that little tramp, the red-hot branding iron would give her enough to think about for the moment—the Captain reached the boy in two strides and struck his face twice with the flat of his hand, making his mouth bleed—Justiniano Duarte da Rosa's heavy hand was laden with rings. Daniel, aghast, wiped the corner of his mouth with his hand, saw the blood, and blubbered.

"You son-of-a-bitch, you gringa's lapdog, you cunt-licker, where did you get the nerve? You know what you're going to do for openers? For openers," he repeated, "you're going to be a cock-sucker for once instead of a cunt-sucker and I'll make sure everybody hears about it, in this town and in Bahia."

He opened his fly and took out his privates. Daniel wept, his hands clasped imploringly. The Captain gripped the handle of the rawhide strap and landed a blow at his kidneys. The whiplash left a red stripe as a fearful howl rose. The youth bent double, his knees buckled, and he wet himself all over.

"Come on, you fairy: Suck!"

He raised his arm again and the rawhide whistled

through the air—are you going to suck me or are you not, you son-of-a-bitch? Daniel swallowed convulsively, the rawhide whistled in the air, and Dan was about to obey when the Captain felt a knifeblade in his ribs. The blade felt cold and his blood felt hot. He turned and saw Tereza standing with upraised hand, her eyes flashing, her beauty dazzling, her hate boundless. Where was the fear and respect he had taught her and that Tereza had learned so well?

"Put down that knife, you she-devil, aren't you afraid I'll kill you? Have you forgotten already?"

"Ain't afraid no more, Captain! Ain't afraid no more!"

Tereza's free voice made the welkin ring over the town and echoed for leagues and leagues, ran like wildfire along the roads of the *sertão,* and the echo resounded on the fringe of the sea. In the prison, in the reformatory, at Gabi's house they started calling her Tereza Ain't-Afraid-No-More. She was given many nicknames in the course of her life, but that was the first.

The Captain saw her but he didn't know her. Yes, it was Tereza, but not the same girl he had tamed and bent to his will with the whip, not the one he had taught fear and respect, because if there's no obedience what's the world coming to, can you tell me that? This was another Tereza, just beginning a new life, Tereza Ain't-Afraid-No-More; and it was strange, she looked taller, as if the winter rains had made her blossom. She was the same and yet she was different. He had seen her a thousand times without her clothes on and had had her to the tune of blows on the mattress, in the wide bedstead at the farm and right there in that double bed, but her nudity was different now. Now Tereza's copper body gleamed, and Justiniano Duarte da Rosa had never touched that body, never possessed it. He had left her a girl and found her a woman, left her a slave to fear and now there was no more fear. How had she dared to deceive him? She would have to die, after he had branded her with the intertwined letters of the branding iron. Blood bubbled from the wound in the Captain's ribs, an uncomfortable, burning itch. He felt desire flicker in his groin, flare up, and rise to his chest. He must have her one last time, or was it the first?

Justiniano Duarte da Rosa, Captain Justo, called Hog

by Dona Brígida—Hog, the most dreaded of all the specters of Hell—left Daniel and started for Tereza. The peeing coward saw his chance to flee and burst into the Moraes house, weeping convulsively and stark naked. Justiniano came forward to grab the damned girl, throw her on the bed and break down that last, eternal maidenhead of hers, penetrate to the depths of the narrow crevice, slash his way to her very womb, brand her with his own iron inside and wring her neck, kill her at the moment of climax; and he bent down to do it. Diving underneath him, Tereza Batista bled Hog, the Captain, with the jerky knife, once and for all.

A B C
of
Tereza Batista's
war
against the
black smallpox

A

*Amigo, you're a honey-fucking friend let me tell you,
dingdonging in our ears all day without stopping, picking
our brains; you go down as easy as a swallow of cachaça
but you sure do ask a lot of questions. Have you ever
thought that maybe some people like to be left alone to
live their own lives in peace?*

*A good housewife? I should think so. Born free and then
sold as a slave, the day she had her own house, with a
living room and bedroom and a flower garden and shady
trees and a hammock in the backyard, it would have done
your heart good to see how well Tereza Batista kept house
and saw to every little thing. It was a nice, clean, well-
furnished house to begin with, and while Tereza was in it
there was happiness and good eating, crickets chirping
and wild cherry trees to perfume the air. There wasn't
a house to compare with it in all of Estância, and
Estância's a place where people know how to live.
That's what I think anyway, and a lot of other people
agree with me; anyone would who knew her when the
Doctor was alive. That's my opinion and you're welcome
to it, friend; I won't charge you anything for it unless you
count these few little swallows of cachaça you've treated
me to. But maybe I ought to tell you that lots of people
are beginning to think you're asking a sight too many
questions for an outsider, and they may start to clam up
'cause they don't know what you have in mind. My old
lady's got it into her head that you want to proposition
the girl and that's why you keep poking your nose under
dead leaves. Maybe so, but if that's what's in your mind
you'd better give the idea up and leave Tereza Batista
alone.*

*Do you think she'd say yes to a stranger when she said
no to a moneybags who was a hardheaded businessman*

*and a bigwig in politics too? After the Doctor's polite ways
and his kindness, how could she put up with the foolishness and selfishness and bad moods of some pompous ass
of a big shot, even if he is a banker, a captain of industry, a father-of-his-country and rolling in dough? A word
to the wise, you know, and if you're wise you'll take my
friendly advice not to go ahead with any plans you may
have, otherwise that firecracker'll go off in your hand. No,
the only thing that could make her forget the goodness and
politeness and interrupted companionship she enjoyed for
so long, the only thing that could make up to her for losing
all that, would be the mantle of love, my friend; it's just
like a poem written by a girl I know who works in a
nightclub in Ilheus, where the cacao comes from and everyone's a poet in their own rough way even if they have no
booklearning. "Love is a velvet mantle that covers man's
imperfections." Covered in a velvet mantle, Tereza Batista
earned respect, and everybody thinks well of her now; so
you'd better just leave her in peace.*

*The only thing about housework she never learned was
how to order servants around, keeping a proper distance
and treating them with the kindly condescension that's
reserved for domestic help and poor people in general.
The Doctor taught her a lot of things, but she taught him
something too by showing him, as time went on, that any
and all differences set up between people because of
money and social position are false and worthless. You can
only tell the difference by a real yardstick when it's a
fight to the finish on a bare field. In that kind of a fight
you're either a real man or you ain't, and that's the only
thing that counts. Nothing else is worth a damn, whether
it's a question of money or book-learning. Who's inferior?
How? Tereza was the equal of any rich man or poor man;
she could eat with perfect manners off silver plates or
pick up her food with her hand, which is the way it tastes
best. The Doctor gave her a man to be a doorkeeper and
look after the yard (and to look after loyalty and honor,
too, in the beginning, until he saw that she knew better
than anyone how to act), and a maid to cook and do the
housework, and called her his queen and surrounded her
with affection; but even so, the one who worked the most
around the house was Tereza. She never lolled around on*

a sofa like a fine lady, giving orders and getting fat off her lord's gifts.

So if you're thinking about propositioning Tereza, friend, you'd better quit right now. Just let her be forgotten by the world in her mantle of love. There's only one kind of perfection for each thing, each moment, in this world, and it never comes twice—Tereza Batista didn't even try to repeat that perfect companionship without marriage; the memory of those happy years with the Doctor had to be enough.

And speaking of doctors, friend, that other little doctor they told you about was never her lover, goodness no; he was just a holiday companion, you might say. It was just a kind of agreement they made, to kill a little time and get Tereza away from a would-be protector who was breathing down her neck. And that little half-pint doctor reminds me again how right Tereza Batista's ideas about rich and poor were: it's when they're scared that you can measure, weigh and compare one with another, using truth as yardstick and scales. Yessir, the fellow with the doctor's diploma was the one who ran away when his duty as a doctor was to be out in front and take command, but if you think he did that you've got another think coming. When the smallpox swooped down on Buquim, the only ones to fight it were the ladies of the evening, sir, commanded by Tereza Batista. She had been Tereza Honeycomb, Tereza the Zephyr before; but after that she was Omolu's Tereza, Tereza of the Black Smallpox. She had been covered with honey; now she was covered with pus.

B

Ball of Fluff, Sweet Ass, Maricota, Fairy Hand, Gregória the sexagenarian, and Cabrita the Kid, a little girl of four-teen who had been in the business since she was twelve —yes, comrade, a bunch of whores—stared down the black smallpox all alone out in Buquim where that pitiless murderer was on the rampage; and leading the fight, on the side of the people, was Tereza Batista.

It was a terrible war, my friend. And if Tereza hadn't organized those prostitutes from the Street of the Soft

Chancre into a fighting battalion, there wouldn't be any-body in the whole district of Muricapeba left to tell the tale. The folks who lived there couldn't even run away; that privilege was reserved for the rich farmers, storekeepers, and doctors who lived in the middle of town. The doctors were the first ones to scram. They both deserted the battlefield: one run away to the graveyard and the other to Bahia—the little doctor was so wild to get out of there he ran down to the station like a crazy man without even taking any luggage, bawling out that he was going to Aracaju to get help, and then jumped aboard a train going the other way. He 'didn't care where he went, just so it was a long way away.

The smallpox was hopping mad by the time it got to Buquim. It had an old grudge against the place and the people in it, and it went there on purpose to kill. Killing was its business and it killed in cold blood with a bad, ugly death, the most virulent kind of smallpox there is. Before and after the plague, six months before the plague or three years after it—that's how people still divide time on the calendar out there, taking that epidemic for a mile-post. Petrified with terror, Buquim was. Any exceptions? Well, Tereza Batista for one—or if she was afraid she kept it to herself and didn't show it; otherwise she never could have put courage into those lost women and dragged them along with her to do that horrible drudgery, day in and day out, with the pus all around. Because courage, friend, isn't just a matter of starting a fight and trading blows or bullets, however good you are at sticking a dagger or a Pernambuco fishknife into somebody's ribs. Any man above ground can do that if he has to. But if you're going to take care of a person who's down with the smallpox, if you're going to be able to put up with the weeping and wailing, and the stink of the pesthouse, and whole streets rotting away, it ain't enough to be a bully: besides balls, you need a strong stomach and a stout heart. And prostitutes have got both: they don't live the easiest life in the world, and they can't afford to be squeamish. They see enough venereal disease to be used to pus; and the scorn of the neighbors and the higher-ups soon teaches them how little life is worth, or how much. They may be tough and they may talk rough, but they aren't empty and shriveled up and indifferent to other people's suffering

—they're brave, they have boundless courage. Mulheres-
da-vida—*life's women—the name says it all.*

When the smallpox took over, more than one macho
turned into a fairy and hightailed it out of town. It seemed
like the whores had all the manhood then, including the
old woman and the little girl. If the folks in Muricapeba
had enough money and a little more to say about things,
they'd raise a monument in the town square in Buquim to
Tereza Batista and her red-light riffraff, or maybe to
Omolu, the orixá of diseases, especially smallpox, because
some people say it was Omolu who took possession of
Tereza and really won the fight.

I don't like to argue about that kind of thing. Religious
opinions are a question of faith, and I respect them all.
Whether Tereza was her own boss applying the lessons
she learned playing with the country boys as a kid and
learned all over again in the skirmishes of real life—those
we've told about already and the others yet to be told—
or whether she was clothed in the supernatural courage
of Omolu, the spirit of the plague, it was Tereza Batista
who rose up and stared down the smallpox—and don't
you think maybe the bravery of the orixás, the beauty of
the shining angels and archangels, the goodness of God
and the wickedness of Satan may be only reflections of
the bravery, the beauty, the goodness, and the wickedness
of men and women?

C

Cavernous, blind holes for eyes and talons dripping pus,
sores and stench for limbs, the black smallpox got off the
Leste Brasileira freight train in Buquim. It came from
the banks of the São Francisco River, one of its favorite
dwelling places. Those cliffs along the river are a meeting
place where the different kinds of plague and pestilence
hold congresses and sign treaties and agreements. There's
typhus with its deadly kin typhoid and paratyphoid fevers,
malaria and leprosy, a thousand years old and as young
as ever, Chagas's disease and yellow fever, the dysentery
that carries off children, the old bubonic plague, still in
there fighting, tuberculosis and a whole tribe of other

fevers, and illiteracy, patriarch and father of them all. Out there on the banks of the São Francisco, in the outback belonging to five different states, epidemics have powerful natural allies: the landlords, the colonels, the police, the civil guards, the little bosses, the big bosses, the politicians in general—in short, the sovereign government.

The allies of the people can be counted on the fingers of one hand: Good Christ of Lapa and a few saints, a few priests, a handful of doctors and nurses, and a few badly paid primary school teachers: a pitifully small troop to be pitted against the legions of those to whose interest it is to keep pestilence alive and well.

If it weren't for smallpox, typhus, malaria, illiteracy, leprosy, Chagas's disease, schistosomiasis, and all the other plagues that do such fine work out in the countryside, how could those fazendas, some as big as whole countries, be kept up and their borders steadily widened? How could fear be cultivated and respect imposed and the people duly exploited? Without dysentery, croup, tetanus, and starvation too—did you ever think of the hordes of children who would grow up to be adults, tenant farmers, workers, sharecroppers, and whole battalions of bandits —not those straggling bands of old-fashioned highwaymen who have to get out of the way when the trucks blow their horns—grabbing all the land and dividing it up? Plagues are necessary and beneficial. If it weren't for them we'd have to say good-bye to the so-called drought industry, which yields such good profits; some of that money might actually have to be spent on finding a solution for the droughts. If it weren't the plagues, decent. society would fall apart and there would be no holding back the people, the worst plague of all. Just think of it, all those people healthy and knowing how to read. I shudder to think of it.

D

Down by the São Francisco river-banks, by the stony cliffs of Piranhas, the smallpox packed its bags, boarded the train in Propriá, and got off at Buquim. In order to try out its weapons and not waste any time, it infected the lo-

comotive engineer and the fireman, but slowly enough to give them time to die in Bahia and for scare headlines to come out in the papers. A few days later the dispatches from the backlands grew into banner headlines on the front page: Smallpox strikes again.

Why had it returned in such a virulent form? No one ever knew, that is, not with any certainty or real proof. The political opposition attributed the malignant flareup to the deliberately provocative celebration of its extinction. Doubtless one should listen with a skeptical ear to all political statements (especially from the opposition) and take them with a generous grain of salt, but for what it is worth in this prose ballad narrating the memorable fight, we will set down the popular explanation of how the civic commemorations of victory brought on the smallpox. There really does not seem to be any other valid explanation— except the lack of any real preventive measures, the laxness of the public-health authorities, the scant attention given to the problem of rural diseases and epidemics, and the swallowing up of funds by politicians who no doubt had a perfect right to them. But that version has already been denied by the appropriate departments of the state government.

The celebrations in Buquim were organized as demonstrations of public gratitude for the eradication of smallpox, malaria, typhus, leprosy, and several lesser diseases. The festivities centered around an illustrious personage, the visiting State Director of Public Health and his retinue, all in high good humor as they traveled from village to village, visiting health clinics and being treated to banquets.

Banquets, fireworks, bands playing martial music, speeches and more speeches hammering at the same theme: Hip hip hurray, there was no more disease. The whole region had been cleansed of the smallpox. Even the ordinary benignant kind that killed with relative mildness had disappeared from the markets, the highways, the streets and back alleys. Smallpox, malaria, typhus—all of the endemic plagues that, as everyone knows, should rightly be laid at the door of former governments—had been swept away from the sertão *forever. Long live our beloved Governor General, indefatigable defender of the people's health,* viva, viva-a-a-a! *Long live our own Pub-*

lic Health Director, whose brilliant intellect has long been devoted to the well-being of his beloved fellow citizens, so dear to his heart; and last but not least, long live the Mayor of Buquim, Rogério Caldas, the lawyer, who got a smaller share than anyone else of the funds allocated to the struggle against rural endemic disease—bigger, more strategically placed rats had been gnawing at them all along the bureaucratic channels, from capital to outback—even so, the zealous executive got a good big bite.

Of all the eloquent speechifying, the words of his honor the mayor, speaking in the name of the grateful towns-people (that pack of ingrates and skeptical mockers had dubbed him Vaccine-Guzzler), were the most forceful, cogent, and decisive: with the final extinction of these epidemics, the township was entering the golden age of health and prosperity, an apotheosis long overdue. This breath-taking piece of oratory certainly merited the fulsome encomiums which the illustrious Director of Public Health bestowed upon it. Then came the turn of the young and talented Dr. Oto Espinheira, newly appointed director of the public-health clinic which had been set up in Buquim, "completely outfitted and equipped," as he described it, "for all possible contingencies, and staffed by competent and dedicated personnel." The agreeable young man, heir to the traditions and prestige of the Espinheira family, was interested in a political career and had his eye on the next elections to the legislature. Speechifying is hungry work, so on to the next banquet!

Not a week after the patriotic celebration, the black smallpox disembarked from the Leste freight train, and either by coincidence or by design, felled Mayor Vaccine-Guzzler, among the first victims, so called because he had been involved, in exchange for political support and a commission, in a complicated swindle having to do with cattle vaccines diverted from the municipality and sold at a ridiculously low price to neighboring ranchers. The epithet was not inspired, as was alleged, by the fact that the splendidly equipped public-health clinic had no stock of smallpox vaccine at all. That wasn't his fault. Actually, it was nobody's fault. Since smallpox had been totally eradicated and no one in Buquim planned to go abroad to those benighted countries in Europe that still worried about smallpox, what would have been the use of vaccine, can you tell me that?

The day it got off the train, the smallpox felled (in descending order of importance), the mayor, a military policeman, the sexton's wife (the real one, thank goodness, not his mistress), a teamster, two tenant farmers on Colonel Simão Lamego's fazenda, and last and least three children and a decrepit old woman, Dona Aurinha Pinto, who was actually the first to die. One little puff of the smallpox and she keeled over without waiting for the pustules to break out on her face, hands and feet, and poor weak chest; she was too smart to lie on her bed and rot away in agony. The pus bubbled up in her coffin instead, an ugly thing to see.

E

Eradicated, my eye! The black smallpox rode victorious over town and countryside. This was no anemic milkpox, no common varioloides, the kind that's the people's constant companion on the farms and in the streets, the kind that's given away retail and wholesale in the marketplace. And when the pustules dry, the disease is more contagious than ever; the crusts ride the wind with Brother Smallpox, down the roads, in the markets, in the streets, in the squares; he's a permanent feature of the landscape in the backlands.

The danger from the milkpox, the varioloides, is limited since it does not kill many adults. Oh, it does kill a few, of course, to do its duty as a disease; but it's been around so long that people have come to terms with it and found a modus vivendi. The victim's family doesn't get vaccinated, doesn't get alarmed, doesn't call a doctor, just treats it with household remedies and leaves picked in the woods, just takes precautions with the patient's eyes and doesn't worry much about the rest. In return, this kind of mild smallpox is usually satisfied to mark up its victims' faces, leaving pockmarks in the skin and dealing out a few days of delirious fever. Aside from giving its victims the ugliness of a pockmarked face, a nose half gnawed away, a deformed lip, what the milkpox enjoys most is *eating away the light of their eyes, leaving them totally blind. It's also good at killing children, a great help to dysentery at that sanitizing task. Milkpox is really just a children's disease, not much more dangerous than mumps or measles. This time, though, it wasn't mild, timid milkpox that boarded the Leste Brasileira train on the bank of the São Francisco River—it was black smallpox, and it came to kill.*

The newcomer went right to work without wasting any time. It began to carry out the program it had laid out for itself by engaging in some intensive activity in downtown Buquim, starting at the mayor's house and the parish house where the sexton's family, the legal one, lived. The damnable thing was in a hurry to carry out its whole ambitious plan: to wipe out the whole population of the town and the surrounding countryside, all of it, and not leave a soul alive to sing ballads about what had happened. In a very few days it could show impressive results: wakes, funerals, coffins, weeping, mourners clad in black clothes.

It began with an itching in the victim's body, which was soon thickly covered with blisters that at once turned into open sores. Then came high fever, delirium, and pus that spread and covered the eyes. *Just tell the colors of the world good-bye, it won't be long now; there'll be another corpse ready for a casket by the end of the week; just time enough for a little weeping and praying.* Later, the smallpox did its work even faster and left no time for tears or prayers.

Swiftly, ferociously, the smallpox fanned out like a whirlpool from the center of town to the outskirts. On Saturday it reached Muricapeba, a miserable collection of streets on the edge of the city, home to the poorest of the poor, including the few professional prostitutes who were clustered on Soft Chancre Street. Buquim, a small backward little city with limited resources, could maintain only a scant half dozen full-time professionals; the others alternated work in bed with work in the kitchen and laundry, not counting a flirtatious seamstress and a blonde, bespectacled elementary-school teacher, both of whom were from Aracaju and too expensive for anyone but the notables of the place.

Muricapeba was propitious ground, and the smallpox waxed, fattened, and grew even stronger for the battle *that had just begun. Dogs and children pawed over the mountains of trash on this stinking, garbage-filled, muddy swamp for the leavings from more abundant tables in the center of town. Vultures swooped over the adobe huts where ageless old women searched for lice on sultry afternoons, an exciting diversion and the only one they had. When the wind blew it lifted a pestilent stench into the air. All this was better than a feast to the black·smallpox.*

Soon no more songs were sung in the streets, and the harmonicas and guitars stopped playing. The first corpses from Muricapeba had a decent burial in the churchyard, just like those from the more prosperous downtown streets. Later on it was different.

F

Few people in Buquim were in the habit of seeking medical help from anyone but Agnelo the medicine man, who had a voodoo temple in Muricapeba, and the healer Arduína, both of whom enjoyed a vast clientele and considerable fame. Their only medical rivals were two physicians, Dr. Evaldo Mascarenhas and Dr. Oto Espinheira; Juraci, a practical nurse from Aracaju who couldn't wait to go back; Maximiano Silva, popularly known as Maxi das Negras, a combination male nurse, watchman, and errand boy for the health clinic; and the town pharmacist, Camilo Tesoura, whose tongue was as sharp as his name —scissors—but who had accumulated considerable medical competence over the years and spent most of his time diagnosing farmers' ailments, prescribing medicine, and keeping a sharp eye on everyone in town from the vantage point of his counter in the Farmácia Piedade.

Dr. Evaldo Mascarenhas had already passed his seventy-seventh birthday and was half deaf and almost totally blind, but he still managed to make house calls by dragging himself from house to house. He had limited diagnostic powers, a limited pharmacopoeia, and was in his dotage, so the pharmacist said. When the smallpox got off the train the old physician was not taken by surprise; having lived in Buquim for fifty years, he had heard the government authorities hail the eradication of smallpox more than once, and seen it come back every time, arm in arm with death.

Young Dr. Oto Espinheira had graduated from medical school only a year and a half before and had yet to win the trust of the townspeople. His youth was against him, for one thing (he was not yet thirty and he looked twenty, with his smooth chin and boyish face, almost like a doll's), and so was his single state and the fact that he kept a concubine, these circumstances being thought good qualities in a lawyer but faults in a doctor; it isn't hard to see why. Not that his lack of patients gave him much cause for gloom. He was fairly well off, came from a well-known family—which was probably why he had been appointed a public-health doctor by the state when he was fresh out of medical school—and he had no intention of staying a day over the obligatory six months in Buquim, just long enough to earn a promotion. The clinic held no charm for him; he had set his sights on something higher than a career as a country doctor. In fact, he hoped to be elected to the federal congress, ride south on a wave of power, and live a life of revelry forever after, far from Sergipe, where, according to experienced bons vivants— some educated men, some loafers pure and simple—one simply vegetated.

Oto was panic-stricken when he heard about the first fatalities in Buquim: he had believed the commemorative speeches, and all he vaguely remembered about the treatment and cure of smallpox was a few hazy general precepts from his medical-school lectures. On the other hand, he had a holy dread of disease in general and smallpox in particular. Smallpox was a dreadful disease; it disfigured when it didn't kill. He shuddered as he imagined his face eaten away, that round, pleasingly brown, doll-like countenance which was an essential element of his success with women. Without it he would never be able to attract any woman who was worth the trouble.

He had picked up the habit of sleeping around with pretty girls during his years in medical school in Bahia. And so, when Tereza Batista turned up again in Aracaju after an adventurous artistic tour of Alagoas and Pernambuco, and Oto made her acquaintance (he had escaped from Buquim for a few days on the pretext of discussing local public-health problems with his superiors in the state

*capital), he found that she was available and lost no time
in giving her his usual line. Eneida, the amusing companion in former frolics whom he had imported from Bahia,
had stood the quiet life in Sergipe for three weeks and
then left.*

*Tereza was low and despondent just then and could
find no consolation or satisfaction in anything. Not even
the change of air—the sight of new places and cities she
had never seen, the churches in Penedo, the beaches of
Maceió, the fair in Caruaru, the bridges of Recife—not
even the applause that greeted the Queen of Samba, the
hearts flung at her feet, the impassioned sighs, the propositions, and the declarations of love were enough to cure
what ailed her or bring her out of the doldrums. Nor was
the trouble she sometimes got herself into with her mania
for stepping in when she saw an injustice being done, interfering where she wasn't wanted in her desire to right
other people's wrongs—when she couldn't even right her
own, and the pain in her heart would never let her rest.*

*Sticks her nose in everybody's business, she does; she
might as well be a padre or a revenooer, grumbled
Marito Farinhas, a street brawler in Alagoas, when, finding himself unexpectedly without his fishknife ready to
his hand, he gave in and let his whining Albertina have
the money for the midwife. Tereza God-Almighty she
was jeeringly nicknamed by a bunch of raunchy pot-
smokers from whose vicious impotence Tereza had freed
a foolhardy high-school girl who had gone to spy on them
on a beach in Recife one night. Adolescent curiosity had
soon turned to fear, and in shrieks that lots of people
heard, she had called on God Almighty to come to her
aid. But who was brave enough to face that notorious
gang of hopheads? Better not get mixed up with them,
those guys are dangerous, warned the acquaintances with
whom Tereza was enjoying a night out. She ignored their
advice—as long as she was around to do something about
it, no woman, much less a little girl, was going to
be raped—and she was right to do so, for the slimy delin-
quents were soon reduced to jeers, curses, and futile
insults: Here comes Miss God-Almighty, cuntkeeper,
butch, dyke. Cowards to begin with and stoned into the
bargain, they soon let go of their rash victim and sank
into nausea. None of this, however, was any consolation*

to Tereza in her perennial sadness: trips, excursions, flir-tations, nights on the town—none of it could still the yearning that was eating her heart out. She saw Januário Gereba's shadow on land and sea, dissolving into the dawn. Yes, when Tereza Batista returned to Aracaju she was very low, without enthusiasm or any heart for fun.

Her good friend Flori Pachola, owner of the Gay Paree, was not doing very well either just then, at least not at business: there weren't many customers, every-body seemed to be short of cash, and just then he couldn't see his way clear to hiring two stars to perform on the nightclub's brightly lighted dance floor. Yes, two. Busi-ness might be bad, but the impresario's luck in love had changed: his spirits were high, thanks to the presence of a new artiste, Rachel Klaus, in his cabaret. Rachel's flow-ing red hair and freckled bosom had finally cured Flori of his unrequited passion for Tereza. He had sighed over her for months, rolled imploring eyes at the copper girl, begged, entreated, and implored her, but she had not given in an inch for all her smiles and sweetness. Flori was finally rescued from his anguish at Tereza's implaca-ble resistance and subsequent departure by the arrival of Rachel Klaus the blues singer, a cold-natured gaúcha and a prime candidate for a contract at the Gay Paree and an invitation to warm herself in the arms of its melancholy owner. Cabaret and cabaret owner soared like the phoe-nix from Tereza's ashes. What about her other friends? Saraiva the poet was roaming the sertão, looking for a better climate in which to die; Jenner Augusto the painter had left for Bahia on the road to glory; the famous dental surgeon Jamil Najar was engaged to marry an heiress in whose mouth he had inserted five noteworthy fillings. As for Lulu Santos, best loved friend of all, he had dropped dead with no warning one day in court when he was de-fending a gunman from Alagoas before a jury.

Without friends, without a job, Tereza languished in Aracaju and found herself besieged again by the wealthy man described before, the richest man in Sergipe accord-ing to experts in appraising their neighbors' wealth, and in any case a senator, an industrial magnate, and a woman-chaser. A stubborn man who had been spoiled by always getting whatever he wanted without having to wait for it, he had turned nasty and was threatening to *make life impossible for Tereza if she continued to ignore his propositions, which were, incidentally, very generous. Veneranda, the venerable bawd, gave her no rest: If you refuse this man's protection, you're so crazy you ought to be locked up.*

Maybe she was so crazy she ought to be locked up. She was at odds with life, anyhow, in a black depression; and the good-looking, smooth-talking young doctor appealed to her a little. Determined not to give in to the rich politician (she never wanted to take up with an older man again; she wouldn't run the risk), Tereza decided to accept the little doctor's invitation to accompany him to Buquim. There would be no permanent or stable commitment on either side; they would simply enjoy each other's company until one or the other tired of it.

Although she did not count on ever seeing Januário Gereba again, that fishing-boat captain she had met in the port city of Aracaju and whose warmth had brought her dead heart back to life again only to pierce it like a dagger with hopeless love, Tereza Batista was singularly faithful to him in her way, unwilling to assume any sentimental commitment that threatened to be permanent. She was certainly mad enough to be locked up, Veneranda, but at least she was still free to sail away in a fishing boat if she ever had the chance.

G

Good sport Oto Espinheira had invited her to Buquim in order to protect himself from the engagement and marriage that would inevitably result if he went all alone into the interior, where he would be pounced upon in no time at all by greedy matrons with marriageable daughters. All he promised her in exchange was a peaceful holiday. Hearing her say that she was tired of big cities like Recife, Maceió, and Aracaju and would welcome a trip to the interior, when the time came for him to go back to Buquim he suggested she go with him for a rest cure: Buquim was certainly the place for that; it was as quiet as any place could be; the only events of the day were the two trains that passed through, one going to Bahia, the other to Aracaju and Propriá

If Tereza went with him, he could ask for nothing better in the way of a woman and would be in no danger of getting mixed up with some marriageable girl and finding himself engaged before he knew what was happening—doctors were the best bargain to be found in the meager marriage market in those little towns. He'd be out of danger, too, of going to diseased prostitutes and ending up crippled with a dose of clap; that would be almost as bad as having to stand up before a judge or a priest. The doctor's good-looking brown face and idle, agreeable chatter reminded Tereza of Dan, the first man she had loved and given herself to completely; but Oto wasn't really like him. Daniel was rotten inside, a liar and a chicken-hearted coward who was as false as the stone in the ring Aunt Felipa had taken in exchange for selling her to the Captain. The unhappy memory of Dan made Tereza hesitate about accepting Oto's invitation. But then, aside from his good looks and silly way of talking, Oto Espinheira, with his lively personality, frank manners, and lack of false promises was the other's very opposite. She decided to say yes.

Dan, the pusillanimous hypocrite, had pretended to be good and brave and honest and upright; had sworn eternal love and promised to take her away with him to Bahia to rescue her from being a slave to the rod and the rawhide whip, but all the time he was planning to throw her over without even saying good-bye. She had heard all about it when she was in jail; there were plenty of people to tell her, Gabi being the first. And hadn't Tereza heard when Dan's deposition was read in court? An incredible string of lies, accusing her of every crime under heaven, swearing that it was she, the unregenerate prostitute, who had lured him to the Captain's bedroom with the excuse of letting him dry off from the rain, and then enticed him into bed. Since Daniel was not made of stone, the inevitable had happened, but the cynical woman had sworn to him that she and the Captain had not had sexual intercourse for more than a year and that she was a servant in the house and nothing else. Of course, if he had known she was still Justiniano's concubine, he would have refused her insistent invitation, be-

cause he, Daniel, was a friend of the Captain and a respecter of the homes and property of his neighbors. That was a very hard period in Tereza Batista's life in every way, but the worst among all her hardships was hearing that deposition read. Until then she had never known anyone who was not wicked, but Dan outdid them all. He was even more loathsome than the Captain, if such a thing were possible.

There in jail Tereza had sunk almost into an animal state. She curled up in a corner of her cell, completely withdrawn and trusting no one. When Lulu Santos came up from Sergipe at the Doctor's request, she refused to listen to him; she thought the lawyer was out to do her dirt like everyone else. The world was all hard knocks and cowardice, and no one in it was any good. Three of the Captain's bullyboys in uniform, a corporal and two soldiers from the military police, had got together to take turns beating her as soon as she was arrested. And even when the unlicensed lawyer managed to get her out of jail and into a convent, leaving her in the care of nuns who were willing to try to rehabilitate her—rehabilitate her from what?—Tereza still had doubts as to Lulu's good intentions—so many in fact, that she ran away without waiting for him to do the rest of what he had promised. Out of discretion, the lawyer had not mentioned the Doctor's name.

It was not until she was living with the Doctor (and she hadn't trusted him either, in the beginning) that Tereza began to have confidence in life or people again. Why had she agreed to go off with Emiliano Guedes when he sought her out at Gabi's, took her by the hand and said: Forget everything that happened; you're going to begin a new life today? To escape from the interminable line of customers that grew longer every day? If that were all, she could have done it before; Marcos Lemos had begged her every single day without fail to let him take her out of that life to live with him and be free of the customers and the whorehouse. She had only seen the Doctor once, back on the farm; yet she did not argue or hold back— why not? Because of all the men she had known, he was the most attractive—not with Dan's trivial good looks, but with a virile beauty, an aura from within, something indefinable, inexplicable to Tereza in those days? Because *he was so masterful, so imperious? Tereza never knew why. In spite of her fear of being deceived a second time, she went with him and never had cause to regret it, for she did forget the past and begin a new life, just as he had told her she would; and she learned from the Doctor to judge without prejudice.*

That was how she judged Dr. Oto Espinheira. Unlike Dan, he hadn't used his gift of gab to entrap her, promising her earth and heaven and fond, enduring affection. He hadn't talked about love at all; only held out the idea of a little diversion, just a trip to the interior that might possibly be fun. Since he promised her so little, Tereza decided to accept. She wouldn't be disappointed, because she had no illusions about her traveling companion. He was entertaining company, fun to be with, and he would help her get away from Aracaju, from the captain of industry's encirclement, pleas, and threats—the millionaire suitor who had sent her lengths of cloth from his textile mill and a valuable little piece of jewelry, which Tereza sent back. Doctor Emiliano would not have liked to see her in the senator's hands nor in his bed.

H

Hidden away in Estância was a two-story colonial house, dilapidated from time and neglect but painted a soft shade of blue. One calm afternoon the Doctor had shown Tereza that beautiful piece of architecture, pointing out interesting details of its construction, teaching without seeming to do so, helping her see what she could not have seen and appreciated by herself. He no longer kept her hidden away; on the contrary, he seemed to take delight in being seen with her as she walked by his side.

The industrialist (he had not yet been elected senator at that time), a short, stocky little man, had minced across the street to greet Dr. Emiliano Guedes and kept the conversation going unflaggingly, vivaciously, euphorically, undressing Tereza all the time with his covetous eyes. The Doctor had cut off the conversation by replying in brief, though civil, monosyllables, and had not included Tereza in their talk, as if determined not to let the chunky little

*plutocrat so much as touch her with his fingertips, with
even a phrase, a word, a gesture. When the man finally
took his leave, he remarked with unaccustomed curtness:*

"He's exactly like smallpox; whatever he touches, he
corrupts. When he doesn't kill, he leaves pus. He's as contagious as the black pox."

*Fleeing from contagion by the unsavory captain of in-
dustry, Tereza had come to Buquim as a piece of baggage
belonging to the public-health doctor, when the smallpox,
the real infection, got off the train and made ready to lay
waste the town.*

*Better that sort of corruption and death, though, than to
live with someone for no reason besides money. Being a
prostitute was one thing: it imposed no obligation, implied
no intimacy, left no mark. It was something else entirely to
share bed and board with a man, feign a lover's ardor,
play-act at being mistress and friend. Friend: that sweet
word whose meaning she had learned from the Doctor.
Friends were what they had been, she and Dr. Emiliano
Guedes, and they had lived in perfect friendship. She
couldn't expect that from anyone else, and certainly not
from Oto Espinheira, an insignificant little doctor of limited knowledge and charm. Oh, Januário Gereba, where
are you, my friend, my lover, my love? Why don't you
come for me? Why do you leave me to wither away where
everything corrupts?*

I

*Intimacy? Certainly not, much less love. Tereza Batista's
relationship with Dr. Oto Espinheira did not go beyond a
superficial companionship which was soon shattered by circumstances. It's better that way, thought Tereza; better to
face lethal smallpox on the rampage than suffer in the
wrong bed, neither prostitute's pallet nor lover's couch. Being incapable of licentiousness pure and simple, she needed
deep affection and love to give herself eagerly and taste
sensual pleasure to the full. When she had it, her desire
blazed up like a flame, and there was no woman like her.*

*She must have been very lost and confused in Aracaju
to imagine that she could find pleasure and joy in the little
doctor, with his cute babyface and his cynicism, who didn't*

*touch her heart at all. Her heart hadn't been touched since
the barque* Ventania *had set sail for the port of Bahia with
Cap'n Januário Gereba at the helm. Maybe he looked as
free as the wind, but the sailor wore handcuffs on his
hands and shackles on his feet.*

Tereza had gone with the doctor to get away from the
plutocrat's threats, to avoid his persecution, to keep from
being hunted down and corralled all over again, foolishly
believing in the possibility of a restful season without obligations or serious commitments. She would have done better to go back to Maceió or Recife to ply her old trade; she
had certainly had plenty of offers while she was on tour,
with a whole horde of madams, pimps, and procuresses at
her heels. She had refused all their offers, trying to keep
herself alive with what she earned as a dancer. The trouble was that she earned too little. The nightclubs paid miserable, almost token salaries, because singing and dancing
in a nightclub was only a front for a more expensive, less
open form of prostitution. It was unrealistic to think she
could live on what she made as a performer, when the applause and her name in lights only meant that she could
charge a little more to turn a trick. In Aracaju, Flori had
paid her unusually high wages because he was crazy about
her and hoped to seduce her. Now he did the same for
Rachel Klaus and lost money on her; but at least this time
he was getting what he paid for. When Tereza went on
tour she found that the cabaret owners offered her a pittance for her art, and if she objected that it was too little,
they advised her to eke out her salary with whatever she
could get from the open-handed patrons. After all, the title
of artiste, with her name on posters and in the newspapers,
increased a woman's value, and if she played her cards
right she could be successful and put something away. And
so Tereza had had to shift for herself wherever she went,
until her body was weary; and she was still eating her
heart out.

Why had she imagined she could live happily with the
little doctor, feel pleasure when she lay down with him,
overflow with ecstasy all of a sudden? Had she really imagined that just because she found him attractive, his company could blot out the memory of the fishing-boat captain;
that she could pull the knife out of her breast that way?
Her love was hopeless and she had to get rid of it. Easy to

say, impossible to do; love for him was in her very skin, in her heart, wrapping her around so that she was impervious to any other feeling or desire. What a featherbrained idiot she had been to think it could ever be any other way.

When she went to bed with the little doctor in Buquim, when he took her in his arms, she felt cold all over, with the same layer of ice that covered her in her prostitute's bed, keeping her whole and distant from the act, so that all she sold was her beauty and competence, nothing more. What an idiot she had been, to think she could amuse herself and feel pleasure rising from the tips of her fingers, ripening in her womb and her bosom, making body and heart forget the salt taste and keel chest. Foolish, featherbrained girl, three times idiot.

Her cold, distant body, so tightly closed it was almost hostile, was that of a virgin again, and little Oto appreciated her all the more. He was almost hallucinating—I never saw such a tight woman, no virgin can hold a candle to you, you're too much! For Tereza it was the same tiresome exercise that it always was. Idiot! Why had she thought it would be different this time? Oh, Januário Gereba, you've locked up my breast, my heart, and my cunt forever!

J

Just can't stand the little doctor forever after me, she thought. He gave her no rest but dragged her off to bed at any hour of the day or night, in the firm conviction, no doubt, that she was as eager as he and reached climax just as often. It was almost as bad as living with the Captain as a slave, always at his beck and call. Since there was nothing else to do in Buquim, the new director of the public-health clinic could hardly be blamed for being always ready and willing—come on, you gorgeous creature you, let's have some fun. Night would have lasted all day if the little doctor had had his way, and they would have lived in bed, with no appetite or occupation except the one urge and activity which Oto imagined Tereza shared, when actually everything that he enjoyed so much was only a duty to Tereza.

Still, how could she tell him she was leaving, that nothing kept her there and she was tired of acting, mortally tired, that it had been a mistake for her to come with him, that she was a fairly good prostitute but that it was no use trying to be a friend and lover? How could she, when she had come of her own free will and he treated her kindly and even rather tenderly? Concupiscence had softened his cynicism and made him a little less cocky, almost grateful. How could she up and leave him in that dull little town where there was nothing to do, no way to fill the time? And yet she had to; she couldn't wear that suffocating mask on her face any longer.

She wore it four days, long enough for the pustules to fester in the doomed invaded town.

K

K TE ESPERO, said the primitive signboard over the door. It was nothing but a piece of wood with the words scrawled in black ink, but it was all the little dive deserved. It did not even boast electric light, but made do with a smoky oil lamp. A few men sat around drinking rum and chewing tobacco. Two women were sitting there too. They looked like grandmother and granddaughter, but they were old Gregória and Cabrita the Kid, a skinny green girl: two hookers waiting for a customer, a nickel, anything they could pick up; they weren't lucky every night.

A strapping young fellow walked through the door and he leaned against the counter, the lamp shining in his face: Zacarias, a sharecropper from Colonel Simão Lamego's nearby fazenda. Missu, the bar's owner, raised his eyebrows questioningly.

"Two fingers of rum, neat."

Missu poured out the cachaça to the customer's measure. Now the lad was inspecting the girl standing against the wall, obviously interested. That was what he had come for, a lay; he hadn't had one in a month, being short of cash. He wiped his mouth with the back of his hand before drinking down the rum. Missu's eyes descended from the customer's face to his hand. As Zacarias raised the thick glass and opened his mouth, the pustules on his lips

*and inside them showed more plainly. Missu had an inti-
mate acquaintance with the smallpox: he had had a bad
case of milkpox which had spared him his life but left his
face and body covered with pockmarks, Zacarias downed
the* cachaça *in a gulp, set the glass on the counter, spat on
the hard earth floor, paid for his drink, and turned to look
at the girl. Missu picked up the nickel and said:*

*"If you don't mind my asking, friend, do you realize
you've got the smallpox?"*

"Smallpox? Smallpox, nothing. Those are just scabs."

*Old Gregória had approached the farmworker expect-
antly; if he didn't like the girl, maybe he would choose her.
Every day it was harder for her to find a mark. Missu's
words made her look sharply at the boy's face. She knew
all about smallpox too; she had seen it break out more
than once, but for some reason she had never got it. No
doubt about it: he had smallpox, and the black kind at
that. She retreated quickly to the door, caught Cabrita's
arm as she passed, and dragged her out the door.*

*"Hey, where are you two going? Come back here, darn
it," Zacarias protested.*

*The women disappeared in the darkness. The farm-
worker turned toward the men who were staring at the
floor, chewing their tobacco, and addressed them as a
group:*

"It's just some scabs. That ain't nothing."

*"I say it's smallpox," retorted Missu. "And if you know
what's good for you you'll skedaddle to the doctor. Maybe
you'll get there in time."*

*Zacarias looked around the little room, at the silent men;
then looked down at his hands, gave a shudder, and was
out the door. Far ahead of him old Gregória was dragging
bewildered little Cabrita along by force, the Kid still wondering why on earth the old woman wouldn't let the boy
pick her up so she could earn a little bread. There was
less of it every day, and this was no time to turn customers away. The swamp stank, the ground was muddy, the
vast sky was filled with stars, and Zacarias slunk hurriedly
along toward the middle of town.*

L

*Laws are made to be obeyed—laws, regulations, schedules.
The schedule of the health clinic was posted right on the
door: 9:00 to 12:00 a.m. and 2:00 to 5:00 p.m. Those were
the theoretical hours, for neither Maximiano nor Juraci
liked being interrupted during the time the former studied
and prepared his list of numbers for bets on the animal
game and the latter composed touching daily letters
to her fiancé. Those hours were sacred. As for the doctor,
he kept no strict schedule but showed up when he felt
like it, sometimes in the morning, sometimes in the afternoon, but never for long; if there had ever been an emergency, all the nurse or the watchman would have had to
do was cross the street—the doctor's residence was right
across from the clinic—and ring the doorbell. Of course,
the doorbell would probably rouse him out of bed, where
if he wasn't dingdonging Tereza he was sure to be sleeping soundly, forgetful even of his political ambitions, his
plans to organize a nucleus of followers for the next
election.*

*Zacarias, tired of clapping and shouting, open up! and
getting no answer, began to pound on the door with his
fists. Tesoura the pharmacist was away in Aracaju, Dr.
Evaldo was on a house call, and he didn't know where
else to go except to the health clinic and the young feller,
the new little doctor. Zacarias, with a lump of fear in his
chest, was threatening to break the door down. A man
turned the corner, quickened his steps, and came up to the
farmworker.*

"What do you want?"

"Do you work here?"

"Yes I do. What's it to you?"

"Where's the doctor?"

"What do you want with the doctor?"

"I want him to give me some medicine."

*"At this time of night? Are you crazy? Can't you read?
Look at the schedule. We're open from . . ."*

"Do you think smallpox cares about schedules?"

*His voice hoarse, Zacarias raised his hands to Maxi's
eye level.*

*"Take a look. I thought they were just scabs, but it
looks like it's smallpox. Black smallpox."*

*Maxi recoiled instinctively. He, too, knew something
about smallpox and at once recognized it immediately for
what it was. It was either an awfully bad case of milkpox
or it was black smallpox. It was ten o'clock, the town was
asleep, and the little doctor was probably having himself
a high old time right now with that little honey of a
cabocla he had brought with him from Aracaju; you
felt like declaring a national holiday when you looked at
her; Maximiano could have done with one just like her.
Was it worth it to wake up the doctor and maybe get
yelled at? Drag him away from his cozy bed when he
might be on top of her? Nobody liked to be interrupted
when he was having a good fuck, and Maxi hesitated.
But what if it was the black smallpox? It sure looked like
it. He took another good look at the sharecropper's face:
yes, the blisters were dark brown, and that was typical of
the damned deadly plague. Maximiano had learned a
few things in the eighteen years he had traveled all over
the interior in his job with the Public Health Department.*

"Come with me, pal; the doctor lives right over there."

*It was the girl, Tereza Batista, who answered the door.
The watchman had heard and remembered her name.*

*"It's me, ma'am; Maximiano. Tell the doctor I'm taking
a man to the clinic with smallpox. Black smallpox."*

M

Medicine is learned through practice, as Dr. Heleno
Marques, Professor of Hygiene in the Bahia Medical
School, used to say when introducing the subject matter
dealing with epidemics that flourished in the sertão. Late
at night in the Buquim health clinic, cold sweat beading
his brow, and his heart in his mouth, Dr. Oto Espinheira,
who had graduated from medical school only months before, was trying to learn through practice what he had
not learned in theory. Practicing medicine was even more
difficult, nastier, and frightening than reading about it in

books. Here was an obvious case of smallpox in its most virulent form, variola major, *commonly known as the black smallpox. You didn't have to study medicine for six years to know that; all you had to do was take one look at the farmer's face and hear his frightened voice:*

"It isn't the black kind, is it, Doctor?"

Was this an isolated case or the start of an epidemic? The little doctor lit a cigarette, the umpteenth cigarette he had lit and thrown away since Tereza had given him the news. The butts were piling up on the floor. Why the devil had he ever agreed to come to Buquim, no matter how much he wanted a promotion and solid grassroots support for a future life in politics? His colleague Bruno had been right when he had told him, speaking from long experience: It would take more than promises to get me out of Aracaju, they'd have to carry me out feet first. Everybody's sick out there in the country, and God, it's boring. Oto, you'll die of boredom. He had outmaneuvered the boredom—successfully too—by bringing Tereza to screw with, and she was sublime. But could he outmaneuver the smallpox? He flung his cigarette on the ground and crushed it underfoot. Then he washed his hands with alcohol. Again.

Shuffling footsteps were heard in the street and a tremulous hand at the latch of the door, and Dr. Evaldo Mascarenhas stumbled into the clinic, carrying a black bag that was worn and shiny from years of hard wear. His failing eyes peered around the room, trying to locate the young doctor, and finally found him.

"I saw lights on, my dear colleague, and came to tell you that Rogério—Rogério Caldas, our mayor, you know—is in the last stages of smallpox. It's a very serious case. He's gravely ill and I'm afraid there's very little hope. And the worst of it is that he isn't the only one: Lícia has it too. Do you know who she is? The sexton's wife, the real one; the other one's name is Tuca. Lícia is in a critical condition too. It's an outbreak of smallpox, and we can only hope there won't be an epidemic. But I see by the fact that the clinic is open at this hour that you must be informed and are no doubt making arrangements to take all necessary precautions. The first one, naturally, is to see that everyone in the community is vaccinated."

Everyone in the community? How many thousand peo-

*ple? Three, four, five thousand, counting the town itself
and the surrounding farms? How big a supply of vaccine
did the clinic have in stock? And where was it kept? He,
Dr. Oto Espinheira, director of the health clinic, had never
laid eyes on a single tube of it. As a matter of fact he had
never asked about the damned stuff at all. Even if there
happened to be a whole lot of it lying around, who was
going to give the injections? He lit another cigarette and
clutched his cold, perspiring forehead. What rotten luck:
he could have been living it up in Aracaju with a good-
looking piece, Tereza with the narrow crack or some other
high-class girl, and here he was trapped, at bay in smallpox territory and scared out of his wits. When smallpox
didn't kill it disfigured. He imagined himself with a pockmarked face, that dark, handsome babyface, just what
women liked best about him, unrecognizably disfigured.
God, he couldn't stand to think of it. Or he might soon
be dead, and all over pus.*

*Dr. Evaldo Mascarenhas shuffled farther into the room,
stopped beside Zacarias, and tried to remember who he
was. Was it the male nurse at the clinic, Maximiano? No,
it was a stranger with his face covered with blotches. He
focused his eyes better and saw they weren't blotches but
scabs. It was smallpox.*

*"Why, this man has caught the damnable thing too.
Well, that settles it, my dear colleague. We're seeing the
beginning of an epidemic, but none of us can be sure we'll
live to see the end. I've already outlived three of them,
but I won't see the end of this one. No one can conquer
the smallpox."*

*Dr. Oto Espinheira threw his cigarette on the floor and
tried to say something but couldn't find the words. Zacarias
asked again:*

*"What shall I do, Doctor? I don't want to die. Why
should I have to die?"*

*Juraci, the nurse, had been sent for by Dr. Oto and
finally arrived at the clinic. She had been dreaming a dirty
dream about her fiancé when Maxi woke up everybody
in the house where she boarded. Annoyance was plain in
her challenging voice:*

*"Doctor, why did you call me at this time of night?"
He had his nerve, lying around in bed all day and then*

waking people up in the middle of the night. "What's the big hurry, anyway?"

The doctor didn't answer. Zacarias's hoarse voice broke out again:

"Help me, Doctor, for the love of God. Don't lemme die." He appealed to Dr. Evaldo, whom everybody knew.

Nurse Juraci had a delicate stomach. Ooh, look at those sores on the man's face! She did not ask again why she had been dragged out of bed at that late hour. Dr. Evaldo repeated in a monotone:

"It's an epidemic, my dear colleague, a smallpox epidemic."

Treating the sick, comforting the dying, helping with funeral arrangements and occasionally even saving someone from death, Dr. Evaldo had come through three epidemics unscathed. Would he come through the fourth? Dr. Evaldo probably didn't care whether he died or not, reflected Dr. Oto Espinheira: he was a senile old dodo and no longer any use to anyone, but he, Oto, had his whole life before him. Be that as it may, nearly blind, half deaf, forgetful, in his dotage if the backbiting pharmacist was right, Dr. Evaldo loved life and fought for it with all the limited resources a country doctor could command. Of all those in the room, only he and Zacarias thought of fighting the disease. Nurse Juraci felt as if she were going to vomit; Maxi das Negras was trying to remember when he had last been vaccinated—it must be more than ten years ago, the vaccine must have lost its effect by now—and Dr. Oto chain-smoked and stewed in his own juice.

A figure appeared in the doorway, asking for Dr. Evaldo.

"Who's looking for me?"

"It's me, Doctor, Vital, Dona Aurinha's grandson. My grandmother just died and I've been all over town looking for you till I thought of trying here. We need you to sign the death certificate."

"Was it her heart?"

"Maybe so, Doctor. She got a kind of a rash like prickly heat all over her, and then a high fever, and then she kicked the bucket before we even had time to call you."

"A rash?" Dr. Evaldo suspiciously asked for more details.

"On her face and her hands, Doctor, on her whole body, all over; she had started in scratching and scratching and couldn't stop, until she just up and died all of a sudden when the fever went up—the neighbor's thermometer showed more than forty degrees centigrade."

The old doctor turned to the young director of the public-health clinic:

"You'd better come with me, my dear colleague. If there's more than one case of smallpox, we can confirm that an epidemic has broken out, and fill out the first death certificate."

Lighting still another cigarette, his brow bathed in sweat, his mouth unable to form words, Dr. Oto nodded his head. What could he do but go? Nurse Juraci offered to go with them: nothing on earth would have induced her to stay in that room infected as it was by that horrible man with smallpox all over his face. She wanted everyone to know that if she, Juraci, should die of the plague the crime was on the head of the State Director of Public Health: persecuting her out of petty political spite and sending her off to exile in Buquim because he knew she belonged to the political opposition and was a virgin besides, and His Excellency could not tolerate either species.

Since his colleague abstained from giving any medical advice, Dr. Evaldo charged Maxi, before they left, with providing Zacarias with permanganate solution to paint his body and aspirin tablets for his fever. Now you go home, young man, paint yourself with permanganate, wrap yourself in banana leaves, keep out of the light, lie down, and wait.

Wait for what, Doctor? Either death or a miracle from heaven, what else?

N

No one but a quietly weeping white-haired woman kept Aurinha Pinto company as she lay on the table in a room that was empty of other furniture or relatives, sleeping the well-known last sleep. She had gone at the first touch of the fever's breath without waiting for the rest; but even so, her poor carcass was not allowed to rest in peace.

Dr. Evaldo, the litle public-health doctor, and Nurse Juraci contemplated the old woman's corpse in silence.

"She died of the smallpox. Yes, we have an epidemic on our hands. . . ." declared Dr. Evaldo in an awed whisper. His age and experience counted for nothing just then: he shuddered and closed his eyes so as not to see.

Not even by dying without a struggle had Aurinha Pinto secured repose for her weary body. The disease was still alive and only subsiding little by little; the rash turned to blisters, the blisters to pustules, the skin rose and fell, bubbling, popping, oozing black, fetid oil. The filthy, unspeakable smallpox gave the dead woman no rest.

Nurse Juraci, with her delicate stomach, threw up in the middle of the room.

O

Oh, no, Seu Maximiano Silva das Negras, don't tell me you can't find it. Did you put it away in such a safe place that even I, the director of the clinic, the man responsible for public health in this community, have yet to lay eyes on a single tube of vaccine when all of a sudden we need it so much? Why didn't I think to look for it before? Well, when I agreed to assume this position, I was assured that Buquim had an unusually healthful climate, that it was an ideal place to rest and practice public health, with voters by the score just waiting to be registered and vote for me; they swore to me that Buquim was an earthly paradise, an Eden lost in the sertão, in a word, that here I could enjoy peace and quiet. Smallpox was a ghost from the sordid past that didn't scare anyone any more, a macabre phantom swept away by progress, eradicated for good —and not just smallpox, but every other kind of epidemic too, hurrah for our ever-watchful government! But they deceived me. Give me the vaccines, Seu Maxi, we have to start injecting people right away while there still are people to inject.

Oh how they fooled you, little doctor, those big shots up there in Aracaju without a worry in the world. There you were, the man-about-town, the pretty little smooth-talking ladies' man, the governor's protégé, sauntering

*around the town and having yourself a high old time—
and then you thought it would be nice to be promoted,
didn't you, so you marched yourself right into the
hoosegow and threw away the key: you came out to
Buquim, this earthly paradise, this godforsaken hole. And
if the smallpox turns up out here in Buquim, what a grand
chance to show off as the jim-dandy medical man and
macho you are. Lemme laugh, doctor, don't mind me, I
can't stop laughing at the way they pulled the wool over
your eyes. They sure as hell fooled you, didn't they? Oh
yes, the vaccines. Well, I guess there's a little bit left
over from the last shipment they sent. It'll be over there in
the medicine cabinet, yes, that one, the one that's almost
empty. Who has the key? Why, Dona Juraci, that dumb,
highfalutin' dame, acts like she had the king in her stomach and a face like somebody that just ate a mouthful of
crap and didn't like it, always saying she's going to complain in writing if you so much as give her a little pat—
she makes so much fuss you'd think she had a real ass
on her and not that measly little thingamajig she's got,
and if you ask me, doctor, what she's got don't deserve
the name of ass at all, but buttocks, 'cause ass is a right
sweet word and a darned sight too good for her, and
buttocks is the ugliest word I know. There was a team of
volunteers came around to vaccinate, it's been more than
a year now, a bunch of high-school kids, all girls, and
they had a real goodlooker for a leader; black, she was,
and don't think I didn't see my chance and take it; after
all, I went with them when they went trooping out in the
fields to vaccinate and gave them a hand when they tried
to browbeat those farmers out there into getting themselves injected. But they're just a bunch of ignorant hillbillies; nobody took the trouble to explain how it worked,
so they wouldn't do it. They were afraid the needle would
give 'em the smallpox, and they dug their heels in and
some of 'em even ran off in the woods. So the little girls
went off, wagging their tails behind 'em. After all, the
Public Health was giving 'em a paid vacation, and they
had the whole sertão to cover before they went back home.
Vaccine? They haven't sent any vaccine out here in
months. Promises, promises, is all we get out of those great
experts in Aracaju, and even that's a lot to ask of those
birds. If they bother to show up at the office at all they*

probably have coffee breaks all day, and here we are slaving away out here in the sticks—the new doctor with that knockout of a cabocla he brought along with him and Miss Shitty Juraci driving us plumb out of our minds with her hysterics and her fee-ahn-say, the poor fish, and then there's me and my nigger gals, when I can catch one. The witch has the key, Dr. Oto.

Hurry up and do something, Dona Juraci, don't just stand there whining and don't you dare have a fainting fit; we've had enough of making faces and throwing up. Just bring the vaccine. And both of you get ready—yes, you, Miss, and His Excellency Maxi das Negras over there —because you're going out and start vaccinating people right now. What do you think you're paid by the state and the taxpayers to do? Take the box with the tubes of vaccine in it and the needles and everything, and get some soldiers to go with you if you have to; we've got to vaccinate everybody, and we'll begin with me, to set a good example and give me courage. The only reason I'm not going with you is because it's my duty to stay here and take charge of operations.

Why you miserable little pipsqueak of a doctor, you put this in your pipe and smoke it: we barely have enough vaccine left to vaccinate the children in the primary school, plus a few of the big shots, and that is all. Roll up your shirtsleeve and I'll give you the needle right now, maybe it's not too late, we'll see; and then, because it's my job, I'll vaccinate that disgusting laborer over there if you insist; he's got his nerve. I don't need to be vaccinated; I did it in Aracaju before I left because my fiancé explained to me that all that talk about the smallpox being stamped out was just a lot of hot air and the Director made it up. He's the one who persecutes me, because my father belongs to the opposition and I'm engaged to be married. I'll go and vaccinate the well-to-do families and the stores downtown, but don't count on me to go poking around those dirty alleys and back streets vaccinating the riffraff, with all their diseases. I'm not the kind of a girl to go around touching people with smallpox and looking at pus; I'm a decent girl from a good family, not a nobody like that drunken tramp you've got living with you, who ought to be back in the brothel where you picked her up and not in a good street like this where decent people

*have to look at her. If you want to vaccinate the rabble,
go ahead and do it yourself, and take your dirty tramp
with you.*

*Oh, for heaven's sake, don't argue with me, Juraci, and
stop complaining. Don't insult me, I don't deserve that;
I've always treated you with consideration, but now I'm
asking you to obey me and follow orders. I'm the doctor.
I'm the director of this clinic, so show some respect and
get a move on; can't you see I'm even more afraid than
you are?*

*As soon as the post office opens, Seu Maxi das Negras,
you run and send an urgent wire to Aracaju asking for
more vaccine and plenty of it. Tell them the smallpox is
here and it's starting to kill.*

P

*Public-health functionary Juraci, Nurse Second Class, was
the first to run away. She had been a receptionist in a
doctor's consulting room and had never taken a nursing
course, had no diploma, and had never practiced; but her
father had been a district party leader for the last government, which was how she had got her state civil-service
job. When the outs were voted in, they took reprisals on
the former party in power and she was transferred to
that end of nowhere, Buquim. Her stomach was much too
delicate to tolerate stench and rottenness, and in a matter
of days the city had begun to rot.*

*By the second night there were definitely seven cases of
smallpox, by the next morning there were twelve, and on
the fifth day twenty-seven people had fallen victim to the
disease. Thus it went, the pus and the statistics increasing
day by day. One could tell which families were afflicted
by the red paper covering the venetian blinds to filter out
the light in rooms where daylight blinded the victim before the smallpox delivered its deathblow. Through cracks
in the blinds there escaped the smoke of burning ox dung,
the poor man's incense for fumigating houses of the pestilent exhalations of the pox.*

*Pious old women prayed in the Cathedral day and
night, watching over the body of the legitimate wife of the*

sexton, now finally at liberty to live with his paramour in peace—that is, if the smallpox didn't carry both of them off as well. The devout women prayed to God to end the plague sent as punishment for the sins of men—lewd, licentious, lascivious, every one of them, with the public-health doctor and his live-in concubine at the head. From this excellent observation post they saw Juraci on her way to catch the train with her suitcase and her parasol, muttering to herself: They can fire me if they want to, but I'm not staying here a minute more, risking my life; let the doctor go vaccinate anybody he wants to, and he can take his fancy whore to help him.

The day after that agonizing night when the first cases of smallpox had been observed, the nurse and Maxi had gone to the elementary school with the vials of vaccine. The teachers made the children get in line. Three pupils were missing and the news was bad: at first their mothers thought they had measles or chicken pox, but now there was no doubt about what kind of wine-colored blisters their children had. The news spread all over town, gathering specific detail and new names of victims as it went. The two public-health employees carried what was left of the vaccine to the main street, the houses of the richest families.

Nurse Juraci hadn't waited for the poor people's turn in the alleys: she was terrified when she realized that she had been in contact with a smallpox victim in the most contagious stage of eruption when they had gone to the house of Squeff the Syrian, a prosperous merchant. Three houses later the thing was repeated. *Fire me, I don't care, but I'm not going to stay here and wait for the smallpox to kill me. Take the box of vaccine, little doctor, and give it to your tramp. Let her take her pustulent life to a pustulent death. I'm virtuous, a virgin, and engaged, and I won't do it.*

Dr. Oto screamed to high heaven when he saw the clinic's personnel reduced by half by the defection of its nurse: *Now what shall we do?* He sent another telegram to Aracaju, this time calling for capable and willing helpers to come by the first train. At home again he washed his hands with alcohol over and over and lit one cigarette after another. He was afraid and discouraged, and he wasn't meant for this kind of life. He was frank with Tereza: *Even if the Aracaju office did decide to send some of its employees, who was going to do the vaccinating? He would need four or five teams as soon as the vaccine he had already requested arrived. They had got along up to now with Maximiano and the nurse, but how could they manage with Juraci gone? He, Dr. Oto, director of the public-health clinic, could hardly go through the streets vaccinating right and left like a mere underling; it was asking a lot of him just to show up at the clinic in the morning and again in the afternoon to give explanations and advice and examine possible victims to make sure they weren't new cases of smallpox, and they always were. Oh Tereza, the pustules! It was horrible.*

Tereza heard him out in grave, attentive silence. She knew he was afraid—panic-stricken, in fact—and only waiting for a hint to follow on the heels of the nurse. What if she said to him, Let's go away, dear, we're too young to die? That was all it would take to give him an excuse to run away: I dragged you here and I'm going to take you away; we have our love to think of. But we don't. No love, no friendship, no real fun in bed.

Dr. Oto Espinheira walked up and down the room, more and more nervous and agitated, working himself into a swivet:

"You know what she said, the bitch, when I accused her of running away from her job? She said I ought to recruit you, just imagine. . . ."

He heard Tereza say firmly, almost gaily:

"Well, I'll go, then."

"What? You what?"

"I'll give injections. The man at the clinic can show me how."

"You're crazy. I won't let you."

"I didn't ask you if you were going to let me or not. Do you need people or don't you?"

The churchmice in the cathedral saw her go by with Maxi das Negras and the vaccination equipment. They raised their heads to see better without, however, interrupting their litany. Their prayers hardly reached the roof of the church, much less Heaven and the ear of God; the pious old women of Buquim did not have the strength in their lungs to cry out loudly enough for that. Where did the little doctor's baggage think she was going with paraphernalia belonging to the clinic?

When it came time to bury the sexton's legal wedded wife, the churchbells began to peal. Louder, vicar, louder; let them ring out, let both bells toll at once, to tell the authorities and God that the plague of the black smallpox is laying waste the city of Buquim. Make the bells toll, vicar, as loud as they can; let the bells toll.

Q

Quite a job it is, old pal, to do a funeral right when you don't know but what you may be next. You look at your hands all the time and keep running over to the mirror to see if your face has broken out in those blisters yet. Because when it does, that's the beginning of the end.

For a decent wake you have to have peace and quiet and devotion and a presentable corpse. To get a nice wake set up, so everything goes right and the one who passed away won't be forgotten, ain't no job to try to do with the corpse already rotten and you scared to death of the smallpox yourself.

When the epidemic first gets going you can still manage to invite a few friends over, feed them something and open a bottle or two of rum. But as the smallpox spreads and there're more and more funerals, it gets harder and harder to do the thing right. You wouldn't feel like doing it, somehow, even if you had the time. Nobody can be cheerful anymore, and it even gets hard to say good things about the dead: even his kinfolks feel too beaten down to sit there for hours, remembering little things about him and laughing and crying. The truth is that when there's an epidemic in town, and especially the black smallpox, even the poor folks can't scrape their pennies together to pay their respects the right way to someone they loved, the way they always manage somehow when things ain't quite so bad.

Where would all the people and all the money come from for all those wakes, two or three a night in every street in town? You'd have to do it wholesale. Besides, you can't keep a smallpox corpse inside the house for very long. It's too rotten and you just have to get rid of it as soon as you can. That's the time you catch the small-

pox easiest—from the corpse. And finally there comes a time when you can't even worry about whether somebody you care about gets put into holy ground. They all just have to make do with a shallow grave scratched out in the mud by the side of the road, or wherever is easiest.

When you're fighting the smallpox and your own fear at the same time, you've got enough on your hands with burning dung, washing away pus, sticking a needle in the blisters one by one, and praying to God. Did you say we ought to hold a wake? Sorry, old pal. That's more than we can do.

R

Rogério Caldas, Mayor Vaccine-Guzzler—the nickname took on a chilling connotation, what with smallpox on the loose in town and the lack of vaccine to combat it with— was buried on a beautiful Sunday afternoon. Due to cir- cumstances beyond anyone's control, Buquim was de- prived of all the pomp and circumstance for which the funeral would otherwise have been the occasion: the band, the big parade, the pupils from the elementary school en masse, the soldiers from the military police post, the members of the local Brotherhood and those of the Masonic Lodge, and the eloquent speeches by prominent citizens extolling the virtues of the deceased (after all, it wasn't every day they got a chance to bury a mayor who died in office). So there were not as many townspeople at the graveside as there would otherwise have been. The president of the town council said in a few brief words that Mayor Caldas had "sacrificed himself to civic 'duty" and described the city official's poignant end. Toward the end he had been extremely unpleasant to both sight and smell, for long streaks of pustulent abscesses ran into one another down the length of his body, great ulcerating sores which formed what was called "tunnel pox," black smallpox at its final, lethal stage. Most people, however, thought of the tunnel pox as an even more virulent form of smallpox, the most terrible of all, the mother of all poxes, black, white, benignant, chicken, and milk. The town council president had it that the deceased mayor was fulfilling his civic duty by trying out the smallpox to make sure it was the real thing before turning the townspeople over to its tender mercies. Now, thanks to him, it had been stamped and certified a number one smallpox, variola major, *tunnel pox, the mother.*

Several days later Dr. Evaldo Mascarenhas became the last person to be given the tribute of wailing, dirges, and a funeral cortege. The deaf, almost blind, half-senile octogenarian did not run away or stay in his house behind locked doors. As long as his heart held out he shuffled through the streets, taking care of the sick, not just his own patients but all the sick people he heard about— some pox victims were kept concealed out of fear of the pesthouse. Never counting the cost, he poured out all the last strength of his worn-out body; he did all he could, though there isn't much you can do about smallpox. It was he who made arrangements for setting up a quarantine hospital, and it was Tereza Batista, the old doctor's right arm in those hectic days before his tired heart failed, who carried them out.

He had just time enough to send Tereza with a message to his colleague Oto Espinheira, director of the public-health clinic: if they don't send more vaccine pretty soon, everyone here will be dead of smallpox. After that he failed for the first time to make his rounds.

S

Since she had already learned many trades in her life—nightclub performer, mistress, prostitute, volunteer teacher to both children and adults, professional troublemaker, according to the police of three states—it took Tereza Batista only a few days to pass the complete nursing course given by Dr. Evaldo Mascarenhas and Maxi das Negras. She was a quick learner—Mercedes Lima, her first teacher, had always said so.

She learned how to disinfect smallpox patients by painting the blisters with permanganate and camphorated alcohol; she learned to give injections, and what was probably more important, she had a way of convincing even the most recalcitrant to be injected, terrified as they

*were of catching the disease from the inoculation. It did
really happen sometimes that a person who was on the
point of catching it would have a violent reaction from
the vaccine, with fever and blisters; but that was a be-
nign form of the disease, hardly worse than chickenpox.
Maxi was always impatient with such fears; he would
have jumped in head first and vaccinated everyone by
main force if he could, and his attitude only caused more
resistance and made the task harder. Patient and smiling,
Tereza explained what they were doing, showing them
the vaccination scars on her own brown arm, and sometimes inoculating herself again to prove there was no danger. The campaign was just beginning to show results,
with people on line in front of the clinic every day waiting to be vaccinated, when the stock of vaccine ran out.
Again a telegram went off to Aracaju urgently requesting
more.*

*Dr. Evaldo, concerned because the disease was literally
spreading like wildfire, had persuaded the local merchants to donate some mattresses for the quarantine hospital so that the most perilously contagious victims, the
most likely to give the disease to others, could be isolated
there. Before they could lay down the mattresses, though,
the place had to have a thorough scrubbing. It was nothing but a slap-up wooden building out in the woods, a
long way from town, as if the townspeople were ashamed
of their pesthouse.*

*Tereza Batista walked down the forbidden pathway
with Maxi dus Negras, each of them carrying Creolina
and water in gasoline drums. The brush had grown high,
and every so often Maxi rested his drums on the ground
and slashed a path for them with an improvised machete.
The pesthouse had been empty for more than a year.*

*The last ones to live in it had been a couple of lepers,
husband and wife perhaps. They would show up at the
Saturday market to beg for whatever people would give
them—a handful of beans and manioc meal, cassava and
taro roots, yams, sweet potatoes, occasionally a coin
thrown on the ground—and every Saturday the leprosy
had eaten more of them away, until they had holes where
their mouths and noses had been, stumps of arms, feet
rolled in burlap. They must have died together or almost
at the same time, for they stopped coming to market on*

the same Saturday. Since no one was interested or brave enough to go to the pesthouse and bury their corpses, the vultures made a meager banquet of their remains, leaving their bones, no longer unclean, on the bare concrete.

Maxi das Negras looked on in respectful surprise as the pretty cabocla, the doctor's sweetie, hiked up her skirts, kicked off her shoes, washed the cement floor, and gathered the lepers' bones in a little heap and dug a grave for them. And no one and nothing had made her do it! While Miss Touch-Me-Not had run off and abandoned the clinic without a thought for duty or consequences— you can fire me, I don't care, I'm not staying here to die —this little gal, with no salary and no special reason to do so, went tirelessly from house to house washing sick people, putting permanganate on blisters, perforating them with orange-wood thorns when they grew into wine-colored pustules, and bringing ox dung in from the corrals to be burned inside the houses. She didn't keep clinic's hours, and if she was afraid she didn't show it. Why, he, Maximiano, to whom the misery of the sertão was an old story, thick-skinned and callous and inured to disease and misfortune, without relatives or attachments, free to come and go as it suited him, and above all, a hired employee, badly paid but still paid at the end of every month— even he had thought more than once during the past few days that for two cents he would throw it all up, declare his independence, like Nurse Juraci, and run for his life.

Knowing nothing about Tereza except that she was a beauty and lived with the director of the clinic, his respect and astonishment were all the greater. When he had gone out vaccinating with her the first day, wondering why the little doctor's fancy woman had taken the place of the runaway nurse, but sensing that the epidemic was creating a subversive climate in which the higher and lower classes could mingle, Maxi das Negras spun a daring plan to himself: he would do that repulsive job at Tereza's side, sharing peril and panic, with him having to keep her courage up, and when the occasion was propitious and God lent a hand, he would take the pretty cabocla in his arms and together they would decorate the clinic director, the good-for-nothing little shrimp, with a pair of lovely sanitary horns—oh, blissful thought!

But he gave up his plan before it was fully hatched—

*for it was she, the little gal, who kept his courage and
willingness up. If Maxi didn't throw up his job and take
to his heels like the nurse it was thanks to Tereza. He
felt ashamed of having wanted to run away from his job
—he, a big strong man who was paid to do it—when that
fragile little creature kept her chin up firmly without complaining even once, giving orders not only to the patients'
families but to him, Maxi das Negras, to the scared little
doctor, and even to old Dr. Evaldo; in fact, she gave orders to everyone in town. He thought she was a marvel.*

*When the vaccine finally came (Camilo Tesoura the
pharmacist had brought it; while he was in Aracaju he
heard that smallpox had broken out and he went on his
own to the Bureau of Public Health, where they gave him
the vaccine and promised reinforcements: Tell Dr. Oto
to manage the best he can with what he's got until we can
get somebody down there; people aren't too keen on risking their lives for the measly salary we're able to pay),
Maxi das Negras's comment was:*

*"It's a shame there ain't a few more around like you,
ma'am. If we had another three or four we could give
that damned thing a run for its money."*

*Tereza Batista raised her face, marked with tired lines
at the corners of her eyes and mouth, and smiled at the
mulatto—he was ignorant and had a dirty mouth, but he
was willing—and a flash, a gleam of copper, drove the
weariness out of her eyes:*

"I know where to get some. You leave it to me."

T

*Tesoura the pharmacist was too late with his message
from the Sergipe Public Health Department: the little
doctor hadn't waited for Dr. Evaldo's burial, and his path
crossed Camilo Tesoura's at the railroad station. If he had
had any sense he would have been a long way off by now.
He should have been on the five a.m. freight train after
that Last Judgment night when Zacarias had showed his
pockmarked face at the clinic. When you really thought
about it, it was all that damned woman's fault. Why the
devil had she felt called upon to run around vaccinating*

people and taking care of smallpox patients? What a crazy kind of woman Tereza was! She wasn't really a woman at all, for all she was so good-looking and had such a narrow crack. She wasn't any better than an animal, something wild out of the woods, absolutely incapable of thinking, or of understanding and appreciating the good things in life. He, Dr. Oto Espinheira, a young man with a fine future before him, was actually in danger of seeing his babyface women liked so much transformed into a hideous mask—that is, if he didn't lose his life.

He came from a politically minded family and had a taste for politics himself. It had seemed the most natural thing in the world to come to Buquim to lay the groundwork for a comfortable political career, and then leave the miserable, pox-ridden North once and for all for the rich, healthy South where there were parties, theatres, lights, fabulous gardens, up-to-date nightclubs, sumptuous international hotels just right for romantic trysts—everything his heart desired, in fact, except a woman as luscious and beautiful as Tereza. But no, he was forgetting; she was a fox woman, the queen of the smallpox. Shut up in his house, washing his hands in alcohol every two minutes, cleaning out his gullet by gulping down rum, chainsmoking, continually wanting to urinate, rushing to examine himself in the mirror and fearfully touching his face to make sure that no pustules were forming, the little doctor was so terrified that in a very short time he lost his veneer of good manners along with political ambition, self-respect, and the ability to work up a hard-on. Neither his ambitious plans to woo the prospective voters of Buquim nor all Tereza's charms—her radiant body, her calm presence, her tight ass he had loved to screw— could tempt him now.

When Tereza took him at his word after he had told her that Juraci had decamped, and he saw that she was actually determined to go out and inoculate people, all the little doctor could do was gape at her. He had told her about the nurse's impudence, hoping she would hint that they should run away too, or at least make some sort of comment, give him a piece of good advice or a kind word; and instead of providing him with an excuse for taking the next train out, in a twinkling the imbecile had taken

*on the role of a Sister of Charity and pointed him toward
the clinic instead of the railway station.*

At the clinic he had had a visit from the president of
the town council, now the acting mayor, who had come
to talk a little and find out what sort of measures the
young clinic director was taking. He was a merchant, a
rancher, and a political boss as well as a friend of the
little doctor's family, and Oto had brought a letter of introduction to him. The man spoke bluntly: a politician,
young man, should act politically even in time of calamity,
and smallpox was the worst calamity there was. It was a
frightful disease which threatened everyone in town; but
it had its good side if you looked at it the right way, if
you were a candidate to political office looking for a rapid
leg up; especially if you were a doctor; particularly if you
happened to be the director of the public-health clinic.
All you had to do was lead your faithful employees into
battle, or whoever you had to lead—a veiled reference
to the fact that he had seen the doctor's mistress giving
vaccinations around town—so as to break the back of
the smallpox and free the community from the pitiless
monster. My dear fellow, you couldn't ask for a better
opportunity to earn Buquim's undying gratitude and votes.
The people always pay their debts, and the people adore
no one so much as a capable and dedicated physician.
Just look at all the prestige Dr. Evaldo Mascarenhas enjoyed, and it was wasted on him; he had never even run
for town council or the legislature, political posts being a
matter of indifference to him. Dr. Oto Espinheira, now,
if he seized this golden opportunity, what with his family's
prestige, once he had driven the smallpox out of town he
could count on some real, indestructible grassroots support
in Buquim and extend it to the neighboring towns where
both smallpox and the doctor's reputation would certainly
spread—so you see, my friend, the epidemic will have
been good for something after all.

Doctor, you should thank God for this opportunity
that's being handed to you on a silver platter and take
real advantage of it: throw yourself into the fray with vim
and vigor; call on the sick, rich and poor, and tend them
well; make the pesthouse your home. If you do catch the
smallpox, that's tough; but people who have been vaccinated don't usually die. You might have the fever for a

few days and come out of it with a pockmarked face, but the voters will love you for it. A doctor with a pockmarked face cannot lose an election. Oh, there is some slight danger of course—it wouldn't be the first time the small-pox carried off a doctor, inoculation and all; but he who does not sow does not reap, my dear doctor. After all, life isn't worth living unless you play for high stakes and pay up when you have to. Having thus counseled his pupil, the mentor took his leave. The doctor's little gal was vaccinating somebody in front of a house down the street. She was so pretty she scared him; a virtuous, God-fearing man like him and happily married, too. As if the smallpox wasn't enough.

U

Unexpected havoc greeted Tereza when she got back that afternoon from her first nursing stint: she found Oto completely demoralized, with a craw full of cachaça, *his mouth hanging open, his speech indistinct. Just after being assured that the voters would love him with a pockmarked face, a man with a pockmarked face had come into the clinic and it had been too much for him. He rushed home where he cowered behind a locked door and downed a whole bottle of rum. He had a bad head for liquor, though he drank like a fish. When Tereza came cheerfully into the room, all ready to tell him about her adventures while out vaccinating, he almost tripped over his own feet to put more distance between them.*

"Don't come near me, if you please. Go wash yourself with alcohol first, all over."

He went on drinking while she took a bath, and later on wouldn't eat, but sank huddled in a chair, muttering to himself. He would not let Tereza come near him until he passed out, when she put him to bed dressed, just as he was. She went out the next morning before he woke up, and from then on they hardly said a word to each other. He never touched her again. The last few nights he stayed there, he slept alone on a couch in the living room, wait-ing for her to take her accusing presence away and leave him alone. Her presence did accuse him, for she left early every morning to help Dr. Evaldo and Maximiano and came back dead tired every night; he spent less and less time at the clinic, where the number of patients seeking permanganate, caffeinated aspirins, and camphorated alcohol grew day by day. The only medicine the doctor believed in was cachaça.

When Tereza woke him from his stupor one day to tell him there was no more vaccine and that he'd have to go out on house calls because Dr. Evaldo wasn't there to do it any longer, the little doctor had an inspiration; he would go to Aracaju with the excuse of bringing vaccine, get sick there—flu, colic, anemia, indigestion, any ache or pain would do—and ask that a substitute director be sent to the clinic in Buquim. By this time he had let himself go altogether: he hadn't shaved, his eyes were bloodshot, his voice was thick, and he had lost his last shred of common courtesy. When Tereza advised him, with some asperity, to put down his bottle and do his duty as a doctor by visiting the sick in their houses and the pesthouse as Dr. Evaldo had done, he yelled at her:

"Get out of here and go to hell, you shitty tramp!"

"No I won't. I have too much to do."

She turned her back on him and wearily went to sleep. At least she was rid of him. Drunk and impotent from fear of the smallpox, the little doctor was no longer tempted by Tereza's charms.

When Dr. Evaldo was stricken and fell—it was his heart that finally failed him, not his courage; in his last hour he was still calling for vaccine—the young doctor didn't even stay for his colleague's funeral. I'm on my way this minute, I'm on my way like a flash, I'm on my way. When he heard the train's whistle blow, he ducked out of his house, ran down to the station without any luggage, and caught the train to Bahia. The train to Aracaju wouldn't come for another four hours and he didn't want to wait. He would have had to be crazy to hang around a single minute longer in that hellhole of black death with that raving lunatic of a girl. The smallpox could have her and welcome.

V

Very wonderful things were seen in Buquim during the time of the black pox. The director of the public-health clinic, a young doctor with a license and all, ran away in such a hurry that he took the wrong train and went to Aracaju via Bahia. You might say he was run out of town by the smallpox. The fugitive's mad flight, described in detail by the pharmacist at the door of the drugstore, where everybody went to get news, made people laugh even as they grieved for their dead. Hi there, young fellow where're you off to in such a hurry? I'm going to Aracaju to get some more vaccine. But that train doesn't go to Aracaju, it's coming from there; it's going to Bahia. I don't care, any train'll do, I don't care where it's going, I'm in a hurry. But doctor, I've brought the vaccines myself, I have them right here, there's enough to vaccinate the whole state of Sergipe and have some left over. You can keep them and welcome. You can keep the Buquim voters, too, and if you have enough money and feel up to the mark, you can keep the girl.

The people of Buquim witnessed marvelous things in those days of the tunnel pox. They saw the Muricapeba prostitutes, an odd, diminutive battalion commanded by Tereza Batista, disperse through the town and the outlying farms injecting the vaccine. Sweet Ass with her colossal rear; skinny Maricota, just right for those who preferred the skeleton type; Fairy Hand, who had been given her nickname by the boys who courted her when she was a young girl, until one of them got tired of her hand and did her the favor; Ball of Fluff, flabby and roly-poly for those who liked fatback or living mattresses (there are those who do); old Gregória, with fifty years of drudgery behind her, a contemporary of Dr. Evaldo, for the two had arrived in Buquim at the same time; and Cabrita the Kid, fourteen years old and two in the business, with her bleating laugh. When Tereza asked them to go out with her the old woman said no, anyone would have to be crazy to go out looking for smallpox. But Cabrita said yes, I'll go. The ensuing argument was a heated one. Be-

sides their lives, what did they have to lose? And what the hell was a miserable starving backwoods prostitute's life worth? Not even death, not even smallpox, would want a life as worthless as that. Wasn't Gregória tired of living on those terms? In the end all six went and were quickly taught by Tereza, Maxi, and the pharmacist how to give inoculations—nothing is hard for a prostitute, believe me. They picked up dried dung in the corrals, washed pus-filled garments, bathed sick people with permanganate, broke pustules, dug graves, and buried the dead. The whores and nobody else.

The town of Buquim was witness to amazing things in the days when the mother-pox ran wild. It saw smallpox victims crawling along the streets and the highways—run off the fazendas, trying to get to the quarantine hospital, and dying on the way. It saw people abandoning their homes for fear of catching the disease, running away with no place to go—Muricapeba was almost deserted before long. Two refugees asked for shelter at Clodô's farm and he ran them off with a gun: Get out of here, go to hell! They wouldn't go away, and the bullets flew: one was killed outright, the other was wounded. What Clodô didn't know was that he had already caught the disease, he and his wife and two children and another one they were bringing up. None survived; the smallpox gobbled them up every one.

Last but not least, the town was amazed to see that Tereza Batista pick up a man with smallpox who lay in the street, stuff him in a burlap sack, and with the help of Gregória and Cabrita, raise him to her shoulder. It was Zacarias, but neither the old woman nor the girl recognized their would-be client of a few nights before, who had been driven off Colonel Simão Lamego's property with three other men down with smallpox. The Colonel didn't want them there, contaminating his land: they could go to the bitch that bore them and die there, but not on his land, where they were a threat to the other workers and the members of his own illustrious family. When Zacarias and Tapioca came down with smallpox, the colonel was away and that was how they had been able to stay as long as they had. Tapioca's death had come quickly, but not before he'd infected three other men with the smallpox. When the patrón came back the game was

*up; the overseer was given strict orders, and the four sick
men dragged themselves beyond the gate with the help of
a pistol at their backs. Three of them went off into the
brush, looking for a place to die in peace, but Zacarias
loved life. Naked, a mass of sores, his face one huge
abscess, marked by the tunnel pox, a vision out of hell, he
put people to flight wherever he passed. When he could
no longer stand, he fell down in the square in front of the
church.*

*Tereza came by, and with the help of the two whores
—for no man in the community, not even Maxi das Negras
was brave enough to touch the farmworker's putrid body
—she stuffed his inert bulk into the sack and lifted it to
her shoulder, carrying it all the way to the pesthouse, in
the company of two country women and a boy who could
still walk and four people from Muricapeba. Zacarias's
pus oozed through the burlap and stuck to Tereza's dress,
flowing stickily down her back.*

W

*"Weekend, he's just gone to spend the weekend in the
capital,"* Camilo Tesoura the pharmacist laughed mockingly as he criticized the little doctor's decampment; his
sharp scissors never stopped snipping, even in the middle
of a smallpox plague. *"Now it's Maxi das Negras who's
the director of the public-health clinic, and the nurses all
graduated from whorehouses."*

But even the sharp-tongued pharmacist put his scissors
away when Maximiano showed up with a pockmarked
face.

Even though he had been revaccinated when the smallpox flared up, he ended by paying his tax. Tereza Batista
assumed exclusive command of the war and installed
Maxi in the little doctor's house and bed, which were
empty since Tereza had gone to live in Muricapeba with
the girls.

Under her orders they vaccinated most of the townspeople and a good many of the countryfolk. Well known
in the place where, after all, they lived and worked, it
was relatively easy for them to persuade the recalcitrant

and the obtuse. Out in the country, Tereza Batista had a brief skirmish with Colonel Simão Lamego, who had forbidden the vaccinating team to set foot on his property —on the heels of the vaccine came smallpox, was the rancher's firmly held conviction. Paying no attention to the prohibition, Tereza went straight through the gate without asking permission, followed by Maricota and Sweet Ass. After a lot of ugly talk and tail-pulling, the Colonel himself agreed to be vaccinated. He wasn't the kind to have a woman bullwhipped, and this woman was like one possessed. Like all she-devils, she refused to budge. She swore she wouldn't leave before she'd vaccinated all the tenant farmers on the place. The Colonel had already heard all about her and how she'd carried a man with smallpox on her own back to the pesthouse; and seeing her ready for anything and facing up to him as calm as if he weren't the great Colonel Lamego himself, he finally realized that his stubbornness wasn't anything but vanity compared to this cabocla's. *You're a limb of Satan, gal, but you win.*

Vaccinating wasn't the hard part. In a few places they ran into trouble, were threatened with a thrashing, or exchanged insults; but there weren't more than three or four real fights that came to slaps or blows. The really hard part was taking care of sick people at the pesthouse or in their own homes. The pharmacist sometimes acted as doctor, but the women did all the rest: swabbing the victims with permanganate and camphorated alcohol, puncturing blisters with orangewood thorns, wiping off the pus, changing the banana leaves placed under and over the patient's body in the bed, for sheets and blankets were worse than nothing: they stuck to the skin and burst the pustules too soon, so that channels were made for the tunnel pox. They brought in staggering loads of ox dung from the surrounding fazendas and stables and spread it in the sun to dry, later to be delivered to houses where someone lay sick. Burned in the family living rooms and bedrooms, the smoke spread through the house, purifying the pestilent air of the miasma of smallpox. In that extremity, ox dung was healing balm.

X

X marks the most miserable spot in Buquim: the tumble-down shack in Muricapeba where Tereza lived with Fairy Hand near the other prostitutes in the poorest, most wretched spot in whoredom. Tereza Batista became a familiar sight in the streets and alleys of Muricapeba, usually wearing her shawl with black and red roses, a gift from Dr. Emiliano Guedes in a remote time of peace, when she had lived in a spotless house and led a happy, uneventful life.

None of the prostitutes were working at their usual profession—not from pride or any abundance of the world's goods, nor because they had shut up shop to fulfill some sort of vow; it was simply that the men were afraid to come near them. They were wells of smallpox, so full of it they could pass through the epidemic unscathed by the disease in spite of confronting it daily in sick people's houses, in the horror that was the pesthouse, in their contact with pustulant sores, in dragging away the dead and burying them.

No one kept count of how many graves those women dug, occasionally helped by some solitary farmworker. Smallpox gave no quarter in that terrible fight; it killed so rapidly and so efficiently that there was no way to get the corpses to the cemetery even if there had been time. The whores dug shallow graves for those who left no survivors and buried those cadavers themselves. Sometimes the buzzards got there before them and left only the bones to be buried.

Two of the women came down with mild cases of smallpox, not the black kind, because Tereza had vaccinated them all before they began operations. Though she didn't die of it, Ball of Fluff was very sick and had to be taken to the little doctor's house, which was now full of patients—a deluxe pesthouse, the sarcastic pharmacist called it. Tereza came morning and afternoon to tend Maxi and her once roly-poly friend—her corpulence all melted into pus, the girl was skin and bones. Sweet Ass, too, woke up feverish one day, and a rash broke out on her body; but it was just a mild case, nothing to worry about, and it didn't even keep her from making her daily rounds of Muricapeba, where the harvest of corpses broke the town record. Sweet Ass was a powerhouse of energy and strength; there was nobody like her for wielding a shovel to dig the graves.

None of the women died. They all lived to tell the tale, but they had to move away from Buquim and go elsewhere to earn a living. Their business there had definitely dried up for good; there were no more customers and would be none for any woman who carried so much smallpox around inside her. They had become untouchables as well as whores. They're around somewhere, walking the world.

Tereza Batista, too, moved away from Buquim when the epidemic was over, though not because she lacked invitations to stay, not at all. Seeing her walk through the downtown streets with the shawl on her head, always busy with her medicine and her syringes, her permanganate and her shovel and her burlap bags, her patients and her cadavers, the righteous president of the town council, interim mayor until the next elections, landed proprietor and department store owner, the man who had the voters in his pocket and an interest-bearing income, the very model of the perfect family man with but one wife and five children, was so touched by all that grace and beauty being thrown away on such low repulsive service, that he found himself wanting to follow the example of others and set up a second household instead of being an exemplar himself. After all, a mayor needs to think of his image, too: a big car, a fat checkbook, and a pretty concubine.

Colonel Simão Lamego, an old hand at illicit affairs, was another candidate; and Tereza also received broad hints from Squeff the Turk, owner of a prosperous bazaar and horny as a goat, and from the pharmacist, that expert at divining his neighbors' secrets and medicine man in his gloomy idle hours.

Tereza a kept woman? Ah, never again. She would sooner have taken up her old trade, with her door open to every man who passed, in some rotten street of Muricapeba where the epidemic had still not run its course. Now, though, it was the white smallpox instead

*of the black; daughter, not mother; just the treacherous
benignant smallpox, the silly backlands disease that blinds
a few people and spends the rest of its time making angels—killing children is really what it's best at; it only
kills an adult every once in a while from a sense of duty,
so as not to forget how.*

Y

*Y's a fine letter, the wise man's upsilon. We say a per-
son's full of upsilons when he's too smart for his own
good, and that's how Tereza Batista, quack doctor, quack
lawyer, and smartypants, got dubbed Tereza Upsilon,
Etc., Etc. But at the* macumba *ceremony she was acclaimed as Omolu's Tereza.*

*During the smallpox scare Arduína the healer got no
rest at all, but her little earnings mounted up as she tirelessly prayed for the afflicted, saving some people from
catching the disease and curing some who already had it
—not all of them, of course, since, as she explained quite
frankly, it was given to her to cure only those in whose
breasts there was no fear, and those turned out to be very
few indeed. As for the spirit guide Agnelo, he never
stopped beating the barrel-shaped drums and calling up
Obaluaiê, even after all the daughters of the temple but
three had either run away or been carried off to the pesthouse. As we already know, the Old One did not fail
him in this emergency: mounted on Tereza Batista, Omolu
banished the smallpox from Buquim and conquered the
Black Death.*

*And so, when a medical team composed of two doctors
and six licensed nurses finally arrived from Aracaju to
weaken the grip of smallpox on the community, they
found that its grip had been weakened already. Although
two patients still groaned in the pesthouse, there had been
no new cases reported for more than a week and no new
dead to bury. This did not prevent the members of the
team's being duly lauded in a eulogistic official commu-
niqué from the Public Health Director's office, for courage and devotion they had displayed in the final (again)
eradication of smallpox in the State of Sergipe. Young Dr.*

Oto Espinheira, too, was duly praised: it had fallen to him as director of the public-health clinic to take the initial, decisive steps which checked the epidemic, and it was thanks to his skill and dedication to duty, as all agreed, that the tireless struggle against the disease had been crowned with success.

"That'll be the day, when Little Doctor Weekend has the guts to show his face around here," muttered Camilo Tesoura the pharmacist; but since he was known to be a contumacious gossip, no one paid any attention to him, and the director of the clinic, who was enjoying a well-earned holiday in Bahia, got his promised promotion. He certainly deserved it.

The father of the hasty Juraci having gone over to the new government, his daughter was promoted too, rising to the rank of Nurse First Class for the important services she had rendered the community during the outbreak of smallpox in Buquim. She married soon afterward, but did not live happily ever after, her sour nature not permitting her to live happily with anyone forever, or indeed at all. The only one who was not promoted was Maxi das Negras. He had his old job back as a watchman and was thankful to have escaped with his life, with some exciting memories and a tale to tell.

The townspeople trickled back to their houses, and dogs and children went back poking in the garbage dumps of Muricapeba hoping to find some scraps of food. Turkey buzzards grew scarcer out in the country, but once in a while some of them would unearth a corpse buried just under the surface and sate their hunger on that.

Two very different religious celebrations of joy and thanksgiving took place. At Agnelo's temple in Muricapeba, Omolu had a party and danced his ritual dance in the midst of his people. First to dance was Ajexé, the pestilent Omolu, dying and being reborn under the stigma of smallpox, the emblematic whisk in his hand, a veil covering his pustulant face. Next was Jagun, Obaluaiê the warrior, wearing his headdress and carrying a wand, both brown like the mark of the black smallpox. Then the two danced together and the people greeted the Old One by raising one hand and repeating: atotô, atotô; hail, father, hail! Both Omolus went over to Tereza and embraced her as one of their own, purifying her body *and closing it to any and every kind of pestilence as long as her life should last.*

The other religious procession started from the cathedral. The vicar and the mayor pro tem walked at its head, town notables bore the litters carrying the images of St. Roque and St. Lazarus—the white man's Obaluaiê and Omolu—and a great throng of people followed. There were firecrackers, prayers, the chanting of hymns, and the merry peal of the bells.

In order to buy a ticket to take her away from Buquim, where there was nothing left for her to do, Tereza Batista had to sell a few of her trinkets to Squeff the Turk, one of the candidates to a liaison if she was interested, but she was not. No more liaisons for her, not even any excursions or adventures for the sake of pleasure or repose. Never again. Death hadn't wanted her; the smallpox had rejected her, but Oh, Tereza was consumed with an inner fever and a knife was buried deep in her heart; she was off to the sea to drown herself, Oh, Januário Gereba, giant condor, where can you be? Not even death would have me when I sought it out in despair, face to face with the black pox—what good is life to me without you, my dearest Janu? I want to be somewhere closer to you at least, where I can follow you in secret, gaze from a distance at your profile like a ship's keel, and suffer when you lift anchor and sail away—oh, what time does the train for Bahia stop here? Tereza is a runaway, too. If only she could run away from her cruel yearning and despair.

The pious old women congregated in the church porch saw Tereza Batista walking toward the station, alone. One of them said—and the others all agreed:

"You just can't kill a weed. So many decent people died and that slut who even went into the pesthouse when it was none of her business escaped with nary a scar. The smallpox might have marked up her face, at least."

Z

*Zacarias got well. He loved life but doesn't know to this
day how he got to the pesthouse—not, that is, unless he
heard some balladeer sing the tale. A lot of stories got
told about that smallpox epidemic and they traveled a
long way. Famous singers made up rhyming ballads about
that sad tale of pus and tears and death. Some got printed
and sometimes you can find one for sale in some marketplace up here in the Northeast. And not a one of them's
truer than this ABC that ends here with life, 'cause there's
no more death to tell.*

*Before I quit, though, I'll tell you again and you'd bet-
ter believe me: it was the whores of Muricapeba, with
Tereza at the head of them all, who fought the rampag-
ing black smallpox to a standstill on the streets of
Buquim. With her filed-down teeth, plus the gold one,
Tereza Batista chewed up the smallpox and spat it out in
the woods, and that chewed-up smallpox lit out for the
station as fast as it could and took the train back to the
São Francisco River—that's where its home is, you might
say—leaving the people to creep back to their empty
houses. It's biding its time, of course, in some dark cave
back there, if we ain't careful it'll come back one of these
days. What'll we do then? Where'll we find another
Tereza of the Black Smallpox to be our general in the
battle and show us how to fight?*

The night
Tereza Batista
slept
with Death

1

Oh, Tereza, moaned Dr. Emiliano Guedes, his lips leaving hers as his silvery head sank back onto his mistress's shoulder. Tereza, still vibrating with ecstasy, tasted blood on her lips, felt the clutch of his hand tightening on her arm; his fallen head touched her shoulder, she saw red froth on his half-open lips, felt his dead weight. It was Death that had embraced Tereza Batista, covering her breast and womb, penetrating between her thighs, making love to her. Death had taken Tereza Batista to bed.

2

Well, ain't that just the way things go in this world? The lame man badmouths the cripple and the man who's naked badmouths the one in rags. Nothin's easier than findin' fault with your neighbor, young man. It's easy enough to say Tereza Batista broke her word and left everybody with his mouth all set—the party ready, the table all spread, and the booze waiting to be uncorked. What takes a little gumption is guessing why she did it.

There's always some meat buried in the pudding, boy; and if you scratch around deep enough you'll find a good piece. Anybody who really wants to know how such a peculiar thing could happen, etcetera, just naturally has to snoop and pry around and buttonhole everybody he sees—just the way you're doin', young fellow. And if you run into somebody who's so rude he turns his back and won't answer when you ask him nice, why, don't you pay him no mind. Just keep on stirrin' up the cornmeal puddin' and stickin' your hand in everywhere, in the nice part and the ugly part, the clean part and the dirty part.

And if you hit on some pus or a pellet of dung—well, don't let that bother you none; it happens pretty often. Just don't believe everything you hear, but take a good hard look at who's talkin'. You can't take it all for gospel, 'cause lots of people love to run off at the mouth and make up what they don't know. Nobody likes to say he don't know, and especially about Tereza they'd all be ashamed not to know all the chapters upside-down and backwards. You be careful now; you ain't lived so long you can't be fooled pretty easy. When you don't fool yourself, that is.

As for me, young fellow, I'll just say this much: I was born on the docks and I grew up listening and trying to understand things; and when it comes to what happened in my own port of Bahia, I can give you a few pointers about Tereza and her troubles. I know about the order to clear out, about the strike, the police brutality, prison, her marriage, and the sea with no gate and no boundaries, fights, things that went wrong, and love that went right. I may be an old man but I'm not too old to make a baby; I've fathered more than fifty, in good times and bad. Sure, I've had money, I've stood here and watched dozens of my own boats crossing that bay. I'm dirt poor today, but when I walk into Xangô's temple, everybody stands up and asks my blessing. I'm Miguel Santana Obá Aré, and I'll put my hand in the fire for Tereza any old time.

No, Tereza never played anybody false. Other people did it to her plenty of times, but she never let it ruin her. She never gave in to bad luck or thought she was hoodooed or whined that somebody'd given her the evil eye. She never really gave up hope. Never? Well, to tell the truth I can't be dead sure of that, young fellow; and that just goes to show how hard it is to be right all the time. Now that I think about it, I guess Tereza did feel pretty down and out after all that business with the strike and didn't much care what happened, what with the bad news from across the sea that made her grieve so; and weariness and indifference are bad ports to take shelter in. Boats left there just rot away to nothing, like the boats I used to have. And when she was so bone-tired and hopeless she couldn't go on any longer, that's when she said all right, she'd get married, and they ordered the wedding feast. Now that's one part of the story I can tell you about from start to finish. I know all about it 'cause she picked me out to give her away. And even being a friend of the other party and all, I think the girl was right not to go through with it. Yes, I do.

Tereza was feeling pretty hopeless then and didn't care much what she did, 'cause nothin' was goin' to be much good. You can believe how sick of everything she was, and how tired of fighting the world, when I tell you that some kid in the street yelled a dirty name at her and she didn't even hear him, much less light into him. She didn't keep on that way very long, though—didn't let herself. The wind started to blow from the Recôncavo and there was Tereza, back to her old self again, smiling, all sails set and ready to go.

I can tell you about the wedding, boy, and the "closed-basket" strike and the protest parade of all the whores in front of the church, and how the police started shooting, and all the rest of it. But how's this for a handsome offer: I'll not only tell you everything I know, I'll stand you to a plate of the best fish stew you ever ate, besides—over there near the Market, at the place Maria de São Pedro used to run before she died. I may be poor now but I was rich once, and I can still treat a friend. The one thing I can't tell you even though you want to know so bad is about Tereza's life with the Doctor and how he died. I only know about that from hearsay. If you really want to know what happened, you'd better go to Estância and try to find out there. It's not far, and it's a pretty place with nice people. That's where the Piauí and the Piauitinga come together to make the Real, the river that divides Sergipe from Bahia.

3

Late Sunday night, at the end of that long, unexpected talk, Dr. Emiliano Guedes whispered:

"If only I were single and could marry you. Not that that would change in any way what you mean to me . . ." The words were soft, lulling music, the familiar voice was unexpectedly shy, and then even shyer as he murmured in her ear: "My wife."

This sudden shyness, like that of some forlorn creature, an awkward adolescent or an anxious suitor, was absolutely at odds with the strong personality of a man used to giving orders, a man who was firm, resolute, and sure of himself, a man who was arrogant when he had to be but cordial, courteous, scrupulously polite at all other times—feudal lord of canefields, great estates, and a sugarmill, and urban capitalist as well: banker, lawyer, board president. No, shyness was hardly the word to describe Dr. Emiliano Guedes, patriarch of the Guedes clan and the real owner of the Cajazeiras Sugarmill, the Interstate Bank of Bahia and Sergipe, and the firm of Eximportex S.A.—Emiliano Guedes, the imperious, generous, daring entrepreneur. It was the tone of his voice, even more than the words, that melted Tereza's heart.

There in the garden full of Surinam cherry trees, with the huge moon of Estância raining gold on the mango, avocado, and cashew trees and the scent of cape-jasmine heavy on the breeze from the Piauitinga River; after he had told her bitterly, wrathfully, with deep suffering, all that he had never thought to confide to anyone—relative, acquaintance, or friend—and Tereza had never thought to hear (although she had guessed at much of it little by little as time went by), he made an end of it by enfolding her in his arms, kissing her on the lips, and saying, in a voice choked with emotion: Tereza, my life, my love, you're all I have in the world.

Then he stood up, a tall statue like a tree: a great leafy tree that cast a welcome shade. During those six years his gray hair and full moustache had turned the color of silver, but the face that was still unmarked, the aquiline nose, the piercing eyes, and ramrod-straight figure did not show the sixty-four years he had lived. Dr. Emiliano looked at Tereza in the moonlight with an embarrassed smile, so different from his usual easy laugh, as though asking her forgiveness for the taste of bitterness, resentment, even anger in what he had told her. And yet all that he told her was said out of love.

Still lying in the hammock, deeply touched, so deeply that her eyes were wet and her heart constricted with tenderness, Tereza had so many things she wanted to say

to him and so much love to express, that in spite of all
she had learned in his company in the course of those
half-dozen years, she could not find the right words, try
as she might. She took the hand he held out to her, rose
from the hammock into the Doctor's arms, and held out
her lips to him again—how could she call him husband
and lover, father and friend, and son, her own child?
Put your head in my lap and rest, my love. She felt so
many different kinds of emotion for him: respect, gratitude, tenderness, love—no, not pity! He was too strong a
rock to want it or take it if it was offered. Love he would
take from her; yes, love and devotion—but how to tell
him so many things at once? Put your head in my lap,
love, and rest.

Under the heavy perfume of the jasmine, Tereza could
smell on the Doctor's chest that discreeter scent, the dry
woodsy aroma she had grown so fond of—everything she
knew he had taught her. After they kissed, she only said:
Emiliano, my love, Emiliano! and that was enough. He
knew how much it meant, for she had always addressed
him formally, never with the familiar *tu* or *você*, and
only in the most ecstatic moments in bed did she allow
herself to say that she loved him. But now the last barriers between them were down.

"Don't ever call me Doctor again. No matter where
we are."

"Not ever again, Emiliano." It had been six years since
the night he had taken her out of the brothel.

In the full force of his sixty-four intensely lived years,
Emiliano Guedes, with no apparent effort, lifted Tereza
in his arms and carried her to the bedroom through the
flood of moonlight and the fragrance of cape-jasmine.

Once she had been carried like that in the rain, in the
Captain's yard, just like a bride on her wedding night,
but the groom had been treacherous and false. Tonight
it was the Doctor who carried her, and this almost nuptial
night of love was preceded by long years of shared tenderness, a bed of delights, a relationship that was perfect.
If only I were single and could marry you. No longer to
be a mistress, a clandestine kept woman, but a wife, the
real one.

In all those six years there had not been a single moment in bed with the Doctor that had not been perfect

bliss and delight, ever since the first night, when Emiliano had gone to Gabi's brothel to get her and had galloped her off with him into the country, straddling the croup of his horse. He was a past master at the refinements of lovemaking, and in his knowing, patient hands Tereza had blossomed into an incomparable woman. But that night when the jasmine was in bloom, that night of limitless trust and intimacy when the Doctor opened his heart to her and cleansed himself of pain by breaking the hard crust of his pride, when Tereza was comfort to his disenchantment, balm to his disillusionment, joy to make him forget sorrow and loneliness, when the clandestine house of his mistress was the home and she the wife that he longed for, on that singular night when both were at peace with life, the tenderness of equals embraced pleasure at last and made it perfect.

For some time they exchanged leisurely, loving caresses, before setting out at a gallop: the cavalier and his steed, Dr. Emiliano Guedes and Tereza Batista. When the Doctor rose up to mount her, Tereza beheld him as she had first seen him on the Captain's farm, long before she came to live with him: riding a fiery, curvetting steed, holding the silver riding whip in his right hand and stroking his moustache with his left, and those gimlet eyes piercing her through and through. Now she realized that she had loved him even then. She had been a terrified slave, and she had dared to notice a man. For the first time.

Without clothes or sheet but only kisses to cover her, panting with desire, she lay as he mounted her and with legs and arms caught and held him against her as they rode off into the endless meadows of desire. Tireless gallop over mountains and rivers, climbing, descending, crossing roads and narrow pathways, burning the distance, twilights and dawns, by shadow and sunlight and yellow moonlight, in heat and cold, in a kiss of eternal love, Oh, Emiliano, my love, together they melted into honey at the same instant. Their tongues intertwined and they embraced each other more tightly as the two bodies opened and melted in ecstasy. Oh, Tereza, her lover exclaimed and fell dead.

4

Tereza jumped out of bed, feeling the weight of death on her breast, in her womb, hearing only her lover's stertorous death rattle, a hollow groan—of pain or of pleasure? Oh, Tereza, he said, and fell dead at the height of their love-making; her companion lay inert by her side, and she still felt all the joy and delight of their incomparable play, was still swooning in nectar when she felt the weight of death on her. She couldn't cry out or call for help; her chest and throat were stricken into silence, and her mouth was filled with blood from his mouth—it was so like the Doctor, too, to choose the right moment to die and be duly discreet about it.

For a moment, Tereza Batista almost went mad, as if she were cursed by having death for a lover, her bed partner and companion in pleasure. Her eyes widened and she stood lost, mute, and immovable beside the bed with its snowy sheets that had been washed in lavender water. Just then she did not see the Doctor whose heart, worn out by disappointments and pride, had failed him at last; she saw only the stark form of death at the moment of climax. And she, Tereza, had held death against her breast, clutched it to her with arms, legs, and thighs, been penetrated by death, had given herself and received death in return.

There was no more joy. All at once it was death, only death, master of the night that had been hers, stretched rigid on the bed, lying coiled in Tereza's womb and her fate.

5

Making a supreme effort, Tereza put on a dress and went to wake up Lula and Nina, the couple who worked in the house. She must have looked like a madwoman, for the servant cried out in alarm:

"What is it, Sia Tereza?"

Lula appeared in the doorway, putting on his shirt. Tereza managed to say:

"Run and get Dr. Amarílio. Tell him to come as quick as he can, Dr. Emiliano isn't well."

The couple scurried away, Lula to the street door, Nina to the back of the house, half-clothed in a nightgown, crossing herself as she went. In the bedroom she touched and examined the sheets stained with semen and with death, and put her hand over her mouth to check an exclamation—why, the old man had died rutting on top of the damned slut!

Tereza came in on slow feet, not yet in complete control of her limbs nor of her emotions. She had still not realized fully what consequences this death would bring. Nina, on her knees at the foot of the bed, had begun intoning a prayer but looked out of the corner of her eye at her mistress's stony face—*his* mistress; I'm the Doctor's servant, not hers. Why didn't the cursed bitch fall down on her knees and pray too? Why didn't she pray to God and the dead man for forgiveness? Nina tried to squeeze out a few tears. She had been a witness to the wealthy old man's juvenile outbursts, and his death in such singular circumstances was no surprise to her. The old goat was bound to die of congestion sooner or later. Nina had told Lula and the laundress over and over again: One day when he's on top of her he'll suffocate and topple right over on her.

Lately the Doctor almost never stayed away from Estância for more than ten days, and when business kept him away longer he would stay twice as long when he came, sometimes a whole week—hanging around Tereza's skirts night and day, suckling at her breasts, loving it up with his fallen woman. Crazy old man, instead of saving his strength, he threw it all away on an insatiable young girl without even looking at anyone else, with all the women who would have been only too glad—Nina herself, for one; but he was bewitched by the sly thing and never gave a thought to the fact that he wasn't getting any younger or to what the important families in town might think. As if it wasn't bad enough to invite the Mayor, the Chief of Police, the Judge, and even Father Vinícius to his mistress's house, he used to parade through the streets with her, arm in arm, and they'd neck on the

bridge over the Piaui River or together in the Golden
Waterfall on the Piauitinga, the girl in a bathing suit
showing everything she had, the shameless thing, and the
old man practically nude, with just a little slip to cover
his balls, corrupting Estância with those indecent habits
he'd picked up in foreign parts. When you saw him like
that in the buff he was still a handsome figure of a man,
no doubt about it; but you couldn't get away from the
fact that Tereza was more than forty years younger than
he was. It couldn't have ended any other way. God is
merciful but God is just, and none of us knows when
retribution will strike.

The old man must have known he was playing with
fire. However strong and healthy he looked, he was still
going on sixty-five; Nina had heard him say day before
yesterday to Dr. Amarílio at dinner: Sixty-five years lived
to the full, my dear Amarílio; I've worked hard and I've
had a lot of pleasure out of life. He said nothing about
sorrows and disappointments, as if he hadn't had those.
A man who wore himself out trying to act like a boy,
playing the fool and the studhorse—when it wasn't in bed
it was on the living room couch or the hammock, any
old place, any old time; he abused his powers intemperately in a rhythm that would have been more appropriate
for an eighteen-year-old who had what old men usually
lack but he still seemed to have, the hardened old sinner.

On moonlit nights, when the moon over Estância
poured down its radiance of gold and silver, after Nina
and Lula had gone to bed, the two depraved sinners, the
shameless woman and the old man in his dotage, would
lay a mat under the centenary mango trees and do everything in the open air, leaving their rosewood bed with its
silk-cotton mattress and fine linen sheets in the bedroom
open to the river breeze. Nina would open the door to
her apartment next to the house a crack, just enough to
catch a glimpse of their two bodies mingling in the moonlight and hear their moans and sighs and scattered words
in the still night. It had to end in cerebral congestion, for
the Doctor had a high temper. He was usually calm and
didn't get worked up over nothing, but when something
did vex or anger him, the blood rushed to his head, his
face turned red, his eyes flashed, his voice became a roar,
and he was capable of any sort of folly. Nina had seen

him like that only once, when a man selling yams or cassava root had talked disrespectfully to him; he seized the fellow by the collar and struck him in the face over and over. A word and a sign from Tereza, however, had been enough to make him set the man down and recover his composure while the rash root peddler had taken to his heels with the marks of the Doctor's fingers still on his throat, leaving his basket on the ground. Tereza had sent Nina for a glass of water, and when the maid brought it she found the two of them kissing and hugging, with the Doctor's head on the girl's lap. A woman with rickets appeared some time later to pick up the cassava roots and apologize for the man's boorishness. He was always giving her trouble, but this time he had been taught a lesson and then some.

Why the devil was Tereza just standing there instead of praying for the dead man's soul? He had been a good man, even an upright man in his way; but he had sunk into mortal sin on top of his concubine, a married man and the father of children. He even had grandchildren. It would take a great many prayers, a great many masses, a great many promises and acts of contrition and charity to save him, and who but that heretic over there ought to be praying to God for him? She ought to be on her knees, praying and repenting of her sinful life with another woman's husband, living in sin all the time and demanding the impossible from the exhausted, used-up strength of the old man. His death by congestion was her fault, hers and nobody else's.

The silly old clown, trying to satisfy her as well as any man could when he might have known it was impossible. She was a hot bitch in her twenties who was always in heat, and she needed a strong young man, maybe more than one. She might at least have had the consideration to get one of the boys in town to court her and save the old fool's strength that way. But no, she was so depraved she kept herself honest and saved up the need and lust and fire that was burning her up for her senile protector. Yes, that selfish flirt of a girl had as good as killed the old man with the demands of the flesh, the worst sin of all, as everyone knew. Maybe she was in a hurry to get her hands on his wad.

Why didn't she go down on her knees and pray for his

sinful soul? It wasn't just that he needed aves and rosaries and litanies and high masses; she had to admit he deserved them. Nina was in the habit of paying attention to the conversations she heard while she swept the house or cleaned up or served at the table. Early that evening as she came into the garden with coffee on a tray, she had heard the Doctor mention a will to his mistress. Why didn't the heretic look unhappy, cover her head with ashes, break out crying and sobbing? Couldn't she even put on an act? No, she just stood there, stock-still, aloof, not saying a word. Couldn't she even show some proper respect for other people while she waited for the will and what was coming to her, money enough to enjoy life in Aracaju or Bahia, throwing away the old stag's dough on some young fellow strong enough to thump a mattress with her all day and all night? She was bound to come in for a pretty big bundle—money the worthless woman had robbed from her protector's children and legitimate wife, who should have inherited everything by right. Now the sly puss was rich and free to do as she liked, and *that* was a sin and a crime!

Oh, she was clever all right, but she had no morals and she had no heart. After she had sucked him dry and made him weaker and weaker until he died, she didn't have a tear for him, not even out of gratitude for his generosity and all the money he had spent on her while he was alive and all the crazy things he'd done for her. In the depths of her dry eyes was a strange light, like burning coals. Nina cursed the old man and the wicked girl as she prayed.

6

When Nina had gone to get dressed and boil water, and Tereza was left alone in the room to wait for the doctor, she sat down on the edge of the bed; taking Emiliano's inert hand in hers she said to him, with love in her voice, all the things she had not known how to tell him earlier that night as they lay in the gently swinging hammock under the trees in the moonlight. That talk had been surprising and unexpected for Tereza, and for the Doctor it had been his last.

Emiliano, always so reserved when speaking of his family, had all at once poured out a tale of seemingly endless sorrows and hurts, the lack of understanding and affection, the dreadful loneliness of a home without love—all in sad, wounded, irate tones. The truth was that he had no family but Tereza. She was the only joy left to one who finally admitted that he was old and tired, without, however, imagining himself at death's door. If he had had an inkling that he was, he would surely not have waited so long to have this talk with her and take the measures he had told her about. Not that Tereza had ever asked for or claimed anything; the Doctor's affectionate presence was enough.

Oh, Emiliano, how can I go on living and know you'll never come again when I least expect you, never run to the garden gate again when I hear your masterful step and lordly voice, never snuggle up against your chest for a kiss, never feel your moustache tickling my lips, and the hot point of your tongue? How can I live without you, Emiliano? I don't care if I go back to being poor, dirt-poor, back to hard work, back to being a whore and having nothing to live for. The only thing that matters is that I'll never see you again, never hear your voice and your rich laugh echoing in the living room, the garden, our bedroom; never feel the touch of your light, heavy hands, your slow, quick hands, because your hands are cold forever now. I'll never feel the warmth of your kiss, the certitude of your trust in me, the privilege of living with you. The other woman may be a widow, but I've been widowed and left an orphan too.

I never knew until today that what I felt for you was love at first sight; but that's what it was. That day on the Captain's farm when I saw the famous Dr. Emiliano Guedes from the sugarmill in Cajazeiras, all dressed in silver, I noticed a man and I thought he was handsome; I had never noticed that about anyone before. Now all I can do is remember. Only remember, Emiliano.

Riding astride a black horse with silver accouterments glittering in the sun, high boots, and masterful gestures—that was how Tereza had seen him ride up to the farmhouse, and although she was nothing but an ignorant little girl, a drudge, and a slave, she had realized how superior and far above other men he was. In the parlor she served him freshly made coffee, and Dr. Emiliano Guedes, standing with the whip in his hand, stroked his moustache while he looked her appraisingly up and down. By his side the terrible Captain was an obsequious servant, waiting for his orders. A spark was lit in Tereza when she felt the landowner's eyes on her, and the Doctor sensed it. Then, when she was going down to the creek with the bundle of washing, she saw him one last time galloping down the road, sun glancing off silver, and that proud picture washed from her eyes all the mean baseness that surrounded her.

Later on, when she met Dan and fell madly in love with him, her head turned by the good-looking, beguiling young student, she had remembered the sugarmill owner and compared the two men without realizing it. But all that had happened at a very bleak time in her life, and in any case, when the Captain burst into his bedroom without warning, wearing his horns and brandishing his rawhide leather whip, Dr. Emiliano Guedes was touring Europe with his family and heard nothing of the events in Cajazeiras do Norte until months later when he returned to Bahia. Beatriz, a cousin of his, had sought him out soon after he landed. She was in despair and appealed to him as the head of the family. The insatiable female, with whom he had lain in the ides of March before she married that simpleton Eustáquio, was now in a panic and begged for his intervention and aid.

"Daniel's got himself into a horrible mess, Cousin Emiliano! That is, it was somebody else who got him into it; a trollop of the worst kind, a serpent. Dan's just an innocent victim."

What she wanted him to do was extricate her son—who really should not have been involved in the business at all—from being tried by that judge who was substituting in Cajazeiras for her husband, and who claimed Dan was an accessory and was putting him in a ridiculous position —it was the same disgusting man who had been a candidate for the vacant judgeship in Cajazeiras and been passed over in Eustáquio's favor—you were the one who arranged it, cousin—and now he's taking it out on the poor boy, the heartless wretch, and insisting that Daniel be indicted as well as that harlot. Beatriz also wanted

Emiliano to get her husband transferred to some other district. He certainly couldn't serve the cause of justice in Cajazeiras do Norte any longer or write sonnets there either—Eustáquio doesn't want to go back and I don't blame him, but he can't stay on leave in the capital forever driving his family crazy, either. Dona Beatriz's last request to her dear cousin was for a clean handkerchief to wipe her wifely and maternal tears away—with troubles like this, cousin, plastic surgery's not a bit of use.

Realizing it was Tereza who was the center of Dona Beatriz's confused tale, the Doctor had taken measures concerning the girl's protection even before turning to family matters. From Bahia he called Lulu Santos in Aracaju. He was a trusted friend, his devotion had been proved more than once, and as an astute practical lawyer he knew where all the interstices were in the net of the law. Get the girl out of jail, the Doctor told him; make sure she's in a safe place, and then get this trial quashed.

It wasn't hard to get Tereza out of jail. As a minor, barely fifteen years old, her imprisonment in a common jail was monstrously illegal, not to speak of the beatings she had been given. The judge was glad to oblige, but he washed his hands of responsibility for any abuse Tereza had suffered: he had never told them to beat her, that was up to the chief of police, and he was the Captain's friend. As for a *nolle pros* on the case, though—nothing doing. Since Cajazeiras do Norte was in the State of Bahia and Lulu Santos was allowed to practice only in Sergipe, the unlicensed lawyer thought it wiser not to insist. Once he had placed Tereza in the convent, he informed the sugarmill owner of the judge's refusal and went back to Aracaju to await further orders.

Not knowing of the Doctor's intervention, Tereza left the nuns and was persuaded by Gabi, who had visited her in prison and said she was sorry for her, to run away from the convent and enter "the life."

7

Dr. Amarílio Fontes, the family physician, had become
an intimate friend of the Doctor in the past six years and
a regular guest at Tereza's lavish and tempting table. A
stout, affable, elderly man and an immoderate eater who
prescribed diets for his patients and himself devoured
everything that was set before him, he looked forward to
Emiliano's visits and the exquisite luncheons and dinners to which he would be invited. The only other table
in Estância at which one ate so well was João Nascimento
Filho's, the lawyer's; but the French wine and liqueurs
the Doctor had brought back from Europe—ah, those
were incomparable! To his delight, the sugarmill owner
visited Estância more and more often and stayed longer
and longer: one day, my dear Amarílio, I'll come here to
stay; for growing old slowly, Estância's the best place I
know.

The doctor clapped his hands at the door perfunctorily
for the sake of good manners but went straight into the
house without waiting for anyone to come. The message
had alarmed him: When these strong men who are im-
mune to infirmities and seem to be made of steel do get
sick, it's almost always something serious. When she
heard the doctor clap, Tereza came out of the bedroom
to meet him. Dr. Amarílio became even more alarmed
when he saw the girl.

"Is it that serious, comadre?" He called her comadre
out of affection; as the family physician he had been
called in for the abortion, and ever since then the familiarity had seemed appropriate.

The muffled voices of Lula and Nina could be heard
from the kitchen. Tereza took the physician's outstretched
hand.

"Dr. Emiliano's dead."

"What?"

Dr. Amarílio rushed into the bedroom. Tereza lit the
lamp with the strong light, next to the comfortable armchair where Emiliano used to sit and read—he had often
read aloud to Tereza as she knelt at his feet. Dr. Amarílio

touched the body and felt the wet sheet, Oh, poor Tereza.
Silent and absent, Tereza remembered, minute by minute, six years that had just come to an end.

8

When he arrived in Cajazeiras do Norte and learned that
Tereza was in Gabi's establishment, the Doctor reacted
with vexation and annoyance. He decided to leave her to
her fate; the silly girl wasn't worth the trouble. He, Dr.
Emiliano Guedes, had taken the trouble to bother a
friend, an astute and capable lawyer, and make him come
all the way from Aracaju to get her out of jail and out of
circulation, to put her in a safe place, and instead of
waiting for him the idiot had gone running to the brothel.
She must have an irrepressible calling to be a prostitute.
Let her be one, then.

In fact, the Doctor was less irritated by the way Tereza
had acted than because he had been mistaken in thinking
of her as worthy of his interest and protection. That day
he had first seen her on Justiniano's farm, he had thought
he had seen a rare and significant gleam of intelligence
in the girl's black eyes. The story of what had happened
to her later, though confused and biased coming from
Beatriz and Eustáquio, had confirmed that first good impression. Well, he had been wrong, incredible as it
seemed, and what's-her-name had turned out to be the
worst kind of trollop. His depraved cousin Beatriz had
recognized her for what she was, and he had been wrong.
The flash in the girl's eyes had been nothing but a passing
ray of sunlight. Patience, Emiliano.

Since the ability to judge people accurately was a basic
factor in the gift for leadership enjoyed by this lawyer,
landlord, banker, and captain of industry, he prided himself in being able to make such accurate judgments almost at first sight; thus it was all the more difficult for him
to conceal from the substitute judge his displeasure with
himself at making a mistake. Searching for someone on
whom to vent his spleen and to get the bitter taste out of
his mouth, he went to look for the judge who was acting
in Eustáquio's place. In the judge's chambers on an upper

floor of the city hall, he found no one but a clerk, who
did everything but ask for his blessing: What an honor
to see you here, Doctor! The judge wasn't there yet but
it wouldn't take a minute to call him; his honor lived right
across the way in Agripina's pension. What was his name?
Dr. Pio Alves, a magistrate for many years and now District Judge in Barracão. While he waited, the Doctor
gazed down through the open window at the dreary court-
house square and his disenchantment grew. He didn't like
to be thwarted, much less to be fooled. One more disappointment. A man was bound to accumulate a good many
in the course of a long life.

With solemn tread, a shadow of worry in his eyes, his
lip working in a nervous tic, the judge *pro tem,* Dr. Pio
Alves, entered the room, his heart bursting with bitterness and resentment. He was a permanent victim of injustice. He always got the short end of the stick. He was
always being pushed out of the way to make room for
somebody's protégé. He was the victim of a plot by the
clergy, the government, and the people united to thwart
him at every step. When sitting on the bench he dealt out
justice with a heavy hand; his sentences were worthy of
that other hanging judge, Lord Coke; he was deaf and
dumb to any argument not based on the letter of the law.
When anyone tried to speak to him of flexibility, understanding, compassion, clemency, and humanitarian sentiments, he would reply emphatically:

"My heart is the tabernacle of the law, and long ago
were writ upon it the words I live by: *dura lex sed lex.*"

Anger and envy combined had made him into an honest man, and honesty was an awkward burden to bear, a
capital that yielded a very low interest. He feared and
hated Dr. Emiliano, whom he blamed for the years he,
Pio Alves, had had to mark time as a lowly magistrate.
He had been a candidate for the position of District Judge
in Cajazeiras do Norte, where his wife had inherited some
good grazing land; but he had been overlooked in favor
of a nobody of a lawyer from the capital, whose only
qualification for the post lay in being the cuckold husband of a relative of the Guedeses. Dr. Pio's nomination
had already been drawn up when Emiliano intervened
and had the cuckold brought in instead. Much later and
by dint of hard effort, he had got himself promoted to

District Judge in Barracão, a community not far away, but his goal was still Cajazeiras do Norte, where he could conveniently keep an eye on his little ranch, turn it into a lucrative source of income, and perhaps make it bigger. When he was sent to Cajazeiras to take Dr. Eustáquio's place in a controversial case where the judge as an interested party could not preside, he had thought the hour of sweet revenge had come at last: If he could have had his own way, Daniel would have been indicted as a principal, not an accessory; but unfortunately, *dura lex sed lex!* it was the girl who had lifted the knife.

The clerk, burning with curiosity, trotted in at the judge's heels. Dr. Emiliano dismissed him with a gesture and the door closed behind him.

"Did you want to speak to me, Doctor? Here I am, at your service." The judge tried to be dignified and solemn, but his lip twitched nervously.

"I'd like a word with you. Have a seat," Emiliano ordered, as if he were the magistrate, the supreme authority in court.

The judge hesitated: where should he sit? In his high-backed chair placed on the platform to establish the proper hierarchy and impose respect on everyone else? That would put him higher than the Doctor, as if he were asking for a fight. His courage failed him and he sat down next to the desk. The Doctor did not sit at all but stood gazing out the window and spoke in a neutral tone:

"Dr. Lulu Santos came here to give you a message from me; didn't you get it?"

"Yes, Mr. Santos came to see me to set forth his reasons, and I did as he asked by seeing that the minor arrested by the sheriff was freed. Mr. Santos signed the bond for her."

"He must not have given you all of the message. I asked him to tell you to bring in a *nolle pros.* Have you quashed the case, judge?"

The twitch of the judge's lip became more pronounced. The Doctor's rages were famous, though rare. He drew courage from resentment:

"Quash the case? Impossible. A capital crime was committed against the person of an important citizen of this district. . . ."

"Important? A despicable scoundrel. Impossible? Why?

A young student related to me, one of Judge Gomes Neto's sons, is involved in the case; I hear you demand indictment."

"As accessory"—he lowered his voice—"although in my opinion he was much more than that; he committed murder, along with the girl."

"I didn't come here as a lawyer, though I have a law degree; what I don't have is time to waste. I won't mince words, Dr. Alves: you must know by now who gives the orders in this district; you've had proof of it before. I've been informed that you're interested in a judgeship in Cajazeiras. Well, it's up to you: I still think Lulu didn't give you the message straight. Just draw up a *nolle pros;* two lines are enough. But if your conscience is going to bother you I'd advise you to go back to Barracão as soon as you can and leave the rest of the proceedings to a judge of my choice and my way of thinking. So it's up to you. Make your choice."

"It's a serious crime. . . ."

"Don't waste my time. I know it's a serious crime. Why else do you think I'm offering you the post of District Judge in Cajazeiras? Hurry up and decide; don't make me waste my time or my temper." He struck the silver mounted quirt on his thigh.

Dr. Pio Alves slowly rose to his feet and went to look for the legal forms and the file on the case. He would gain nothing by being stubborn; if he dug in his heels he would only be transferred back to Barracão and someone else would dismiss the case to get in the Doctor's good graces. As a matter of fact, the proceedings had been illegal from first to last. To begin with, a minor had been imprisoned and repeatedly beaten, then interrogated without a hearing before a competent judge; no lawyer had been designated to protect her interests until Lulu Santos had shown up, and to cap the climax, there was absolutely no evidence and no reliable ocular testimony. If ever a case was full of holes, this was it. Nothing had even been done in the proper order. Yes, there were certainly overriding reasons to forget about the whole affair. Besides, what did the shelving of one more case signify in the wilds of the outback? Nothing, obviously. Dr. Pio had learned world history from the novels of Zevaco and Dumas and he

knew that Paris was worth a mass. Wasn't Cajazeiras do
Norte worth a *nolle pros* at least?

When he finished writing in his careful, minute handwriting studded with legal terms in Latin, he raised his
eyes to the Doctor standing next to the window and
smiled:

"I'm doing this to oblige you and your family."

"Thank you and congratulations, Mr. District Judge of
Cajazeiras do Norte."

Emiliano walked over to the desk, picked up the file,
and skimmed through it. He read a paragraph here and
there, excerpts from the accusation, the interrogation.
Tereza's deposition, Daniel's—disgusting! He threw down
the papers on the desk, turned his back, and said as he
was going out the door:

"You can count on that appointment, your honor, but
don't forget I'm interested in everything that happens
here."

Still in a bad mood, he went back to the mill, but happening to be in Aracaju a few days later for a look at
how the branch of his bank there was coming on, he ran
into Lulu and learned from him that Tereza had not
known about his intervention in the case and his interest
in her. Ah! Then Emiliano had not been mistaken in his
judgment. What he had read of her deposition had confirmed what he'd seen in her eyes; he had been right after all. She was as brave as she was beautiful.

He went back sooner than he had intended, not waiting for the next day's train but hiring a car to take him
to the sugarmill, telling the driver to go faster—in some
places the road was nothing but a track for oxcarts and
packs of mules. He arrived in the evening and set out immediately on horseback for Cajazeiras, as soon as he
had bathed and changed. Dismounting in front of Gabi's
house, he strode in, causing quite a stir since he had never
set foot there before. When Arruda the waiter saw him,
he left his drinks and his customers and went running to
call Gabi. The madam came in so quickly that she was
puffing too much to talk: this was an unheard-of honor, a
miracle.

"Good evening. I believe you have a girl named
Tereza here. . . ."

Gabi didn't let him finish. What a priceless acquisition

Tereza was! She had worked the miracle; her fame had
reached the ears of the Doctor, and here he was as a
client.

"Yes sir, it's true. She's a lovely little girl, less than fifteen years old, brand new, the sweetest thing you ever
saw and yours to command. Would you like to see her?"

"She's coming with me." He took some bills from his
wallet and handed them to the bawd, who was still overcome with emotion. "Go and get her."

"Are you going to take her with you, Doctor? For the
night or for a few days?"

"She won't be back. Please get a move on."

The customers at the tables looked on in silence; Arruda had gone back to the bar but was so dumfounded he
had stopped serving drinks. Gabi swallowed a protest, along with any reasons and arguments she might
have advanced, and took the money, several five-
hundred-cruzeiro bills. She would gain nothing by arguing. All she could do was hope that Tereza would be
back when the Doctor got tired of her and sent her away.
That would not be for a while, but surely she would not
have to wait more than a month or two.

"Sit down, Doctor, have something to drink while I
pack her clothes and she gets fixed up."

"She doesn't need any clothes, just what she's got on
her back. And she doesn't have to fix herself up."

He set her on the croup of his horse and took her away.

9

After examining the corpse, Dr. Amarílio covered it with
the sheet:

"The attack came on very suddenly, didn't it?"

"He said oh and was dead before I knew it." Tereza
shuddered and covered her face with her hands.

The doctor hesitated to ask the next painful question:

"How did it happen? He had a heavy meal at dinner,
didn't he, and then . . . Wasn't that it?"

"All he ate was a filet of fish, a little rice, and a slice of
pineapple. He had had a cinnamon corncake for tea at
five. After dinner we walked as far as the bridge, and

when we got back he sat down in the hammock, outside in the garden, and we talked for more than two hours. It was after ten when we went inside."

"Had anything important been weighing on his mind lately, do you know?"

Tereza didn't answer. She had no right to parade the Doctor's problems or repeat what he'd told her in private, not even to the doctor. He had died suddenly, from illness or vexation, what did it matter? Would knowing bring him back to life? The doctor persisted:

"They say that Jairo, his son, embezzled some money from the bank, a whole lot of money, and that when the Doctor found out about it . . ."

He broke off, for Tereza was standing as rigid as a statue pretending not to hear him as she gazed at the dead man's face. He tried to explain:

"I'm only trying to find out why he had this heart attack. He was in good physical condition, but all of us have our worries and they're what kill us. He told me only day before yesterday that being here in Estância restored his strength and made him forget the things that bothered him. Didn't you think he was different?"

"He was always the same to me, from the very first day," Tereza said to put an end to the conversation, but then, unable to contain herself, she added:

"No, that's not true. He just got better and better. In every way. All I can tell you is that there was never anybody like him. Don't ask me any more."

Silence fell for a moment. Dr. Amarílio sighed. Tereza was right; it would do no good to badger her about the Doctor's private affairs, for this time neither the peacefulness of Estância nor the presence of his friend and beloved had been enough to give his heart a new lease on life.

"I understand, my dear; I know what you must be feeling. If it depended on me, he would stay right here until time for the funeral, and then you and I and Professor João, the people who really loved him, would take him to the cemetery. The trouble is, it doesn't depend on me."

"I know. We never had enough time together, but I won't complain. There wasn't a single minute that wasn't good."

"I'm going to try to get through to his family: his daughter and son-in-law live in Aracaju. If the telephone isn't working we'll have to send someone with a message." Before going out he asked: "Shall I send someone to wash him and lay him out or can Lula and Nina manage it by themselves?"

"I'll do it for him, while he still belongs to me."

"When I come back I'll bring the death certificate and the priest."

Why a priest, when the Doctor didn't believe in God? True, that didn't keep him from going to the parish Saint's Day festivals, or bringing a priest to the mill to say mass on St. Anne's Day. Padre Vinícius, who had studied theology in Rome, had learned to drink wine there too, and was a pleasant addition to the Doctor's dinner table.

10

With Tereza Batista presiding, lively and smart in her new Bahia clothes, the Doctor derived real pleasure from gathering around his dinner table the physician, his friend and classmate in law school João Nascimento Filho, Father Vinícius, and Lulu Santos, who would come down especially from Aracaju.

They discussed everything in heaven and earth: politics, cookery, literature, religion, art, current events in Brazil and the rest of the world, the latest controversial ideas and scandalous fashions, the frightening changes taking place in traditional customs, and scientific progress. On certain subjects—literature, art, and cooking—only the Doctor and João Nascimento really had any opinions. The physician had a horror of modern art, all graceless, senseless daubs; the Father was allergic to most contemporary writers, masters of impious pornography; Lulu Santos swore that there was not a dish in the world that could compare with sun-dried, salted beef with manioc mush braised in milk—and in this, perhaps, he was not altogether wrong. João Nascimento Filho, on the other hand—inveterate reader, frustrated man of letters, a good-natured elderly man who had left law school in the middle of the course to cure his weak chest in Estância and had never left, living on a small income, wisely administered, and teaching Portuguese and French in the local high school to fill up his time—knew all about the latest book and the latest painting and dreamed of eating glazed Peking duck. The Doctor brought him books and magazines, and they whiled away many pleasant hours chatting in the garden. In Aracaju the gossips wondered what on earth induced an important, busy man like the Doctor to waste so much time in Estância talking foolishness with Professor Nascimento Filho and fondling his rustic sweetheart.

When the talk turned to national politics, however, and the lawyer and the doctor were at each other's throats in violent disagreement over some party candidate or electoral intrigue, Dr. Guedes listened indifferently, without comment. Politics to him was a low sort of calling, well suited to inferior men with petty aspirations and rubber backbones, doormats and lackeys at the beck and call of those who held the real power, the legitimate rulers of the nation—those who really did command and countermand, each in his own territory, his own hereditary fiefdom; just as he did, for example, in Cajazeiras do Norte, where no one dared to move a straw without asking his permission. Politics disgusted him and he distrusted politicians: you had to watch them like hawks; they were liars by the nature of their profession, and nothing but liars.

Arguments about religion really caught fire; here was a fascinating theme, an inexhaustible lode. Whenever Lulu Santos had a little bit to drink he proclaimed himself an anarchist, a Brazilian disciple of Kropotkin, when in fact he was nothing but an old-fashioned anticleric who blamed the world's sorry state on Father Vinícius's cassock and was almost a personal enemy of God Almighty. The permanent polemic between him and the young, excitable priest, who had some erudition and skill in a debate, usually ended by drawing João Nascimento Filho into the argument to recite Guerra Junqueiro's verses with Lulu applauding at appropriate times. Dr. Guedes would slowly sip his fine wine, amused at the heated exchange of reasons, objections, and abuse. Tereza listened attentively, trying to make up her own mind, influenced now by one, now by the other; first the solemn, orotund phrases of the reverend father, then the cynical, funny ones of the lawyer, whose mouth was always full of curses and blasphemy. In the end Father Vinícius would raise his hands to Heaven to ask God's pardon for those impenitent sinners who, instead of giving thanks for this heavenly dinner and these wines that were worthy of the vineyards of the Lord, swore and blasphemed and doubted the very existence of God! Assuredly all that would be saved from that well of iniquity were the food, the drink, and the lady of the house, a saint—the others were impious rascals. There was more than one rascal: Professor Nascimento Filho had recited certain verses, and Dr. Guedes had declared that everything began and ended with matter, that the gods and religion were the fruit of men's fear and nothing more.

The night he made that statement, after dinner and the fierce arguments were over, the Doctor said to the priest, with Tereza there:

"Father, you can help me with a little problem if you will. Father Cirilo in Cajazeiras is starting to creak at the joints. He's so stiff with rheumatism he can hardly get around town on St. Anne's feast day, and he certainly won't be able to celebrate the mass that we always have at the sugarmill this year. Won't you come?"

"Why, of course, Doctor."

"I'll have someone pick you up on Saturday. You can say mass Sunday morning in the big house, baptize the smallfry, marry the engaged couples and the couples who are living together, and have lunch with us. You can stay for the dance at Raimundo Alicate's if you want to, it'll be a fine shindig; or if you don't feel like it someone can bring you back."

If he wasn't a believer, why did he give money to the church, why did he slaughter calves and pigs and hire a priest to celebrate mass at the mill? Tereza realized that Lulu's blustering atheism was just that—bluster. No one lived who was more superstitious; he crossed himself every time he entered a juryroom or courtroom. But the Doctor! She was puzzled by this contradiction in a man who was generally so consistent in all his actions.

She said nothing, but he, no doubt, noticed or guessed something—in the early days Tereza had thought the Doctor possessed the gift of divination. When the priest retired in the company of the excellent Nascimento Filho

who was again declaiming a poem by Guerra Junqueiro,
and Lulu Santos, lighting one last cigar, said good-night
and went into his room, leaving them alone in the garden,
the Doctor took her in his arms and said:

"Whenever you're puzzled about something, just ask
me about it, Tereza. Don't be afraid of offending me. The
only way you could offend me is by not being frank with
me. You *are* puzzled, aren't you? You don't understand
how it is that I, who have no religious beliefs, can hire
a priest to say mass at the sugarmill and give a party
into the bargain, isn't that it?"

Tereza, smiling, nestled against the Doctor's chest and
lifted her eyes to his face.

"It's not for my own sake that I do it. I do it for other
people and for what I represent to them, do you understand? I do it for those who believe and think I believe
too. Poor people need all the religion and parties they
can get; they lead a hard life and don't have much fun.
And who ever heard of a sugarmill without a priest to
teach the catechism and say mass, or one without a holiday
once a year when everybody gets baptized and married
and there's a party? I'm just doing my duty."

He kissed her on the mouth and finished what he had
to say:

"Here in this house in Estância, with you, I'm just
myself. But everywhere else I'm a sugarmill owner,
banker, president of a business firm, head of a family;
I'm four or five different people; I'm Catholic, Protestant,
Jew."

Only on their last night together, after their talk in the
garden, did Tereza fully understand what he had told her.

11

Nina brought a basin and bucket, Lula a kettle of hot
water. They were prepared to help her, but Tereza sent
them away: I'll call you if I need help.

When they left her alone in the room, she washed the
Doctor's body with cotton and warm water, dried it, and
perfumed it from head to foot with the English cologne
he had used. When she took the bottle from the medicine

chest in the bathroom she remembered the episode with
the cologne, at the beginning of their relationship; all
she could do was remember, now. Every time she had
thought of it, in those past six years, she had felt excited,
aflame: Oh, but this wasn't the time to think of such
things. Those memories, scents, and delights were finished
forever; they had died with the Doctor. A smoldering
spark, a flame dying down, Tereza could not even imagine
the possibility that someday she might feel again a flicker
of desire.

She dressed and shod him deliberately, one garment
at a time, choosing a shirt, socks, a tie, and his navy
blue suit, combining the sober colors the Doctor liked, just
as he had taught her. She did not call Lula and Nina until
it was time to straighten up the bedroom. She wanted
everything clean and in order. They began with the bed,
and while they changed the pillowcases and sheets they
sat him in the armchair next to the little table strewn
with all sorts of books.

Seated in the chair with his hands resting on the arms,
the Doctor looked as though he was making up his mind
which book to read aloud to Tereza that night.

Oh, never again would she sit at his feet with her head
resting on his knees, never again would Tereza hear his
warm voice leading her over dark roads, showing her how
to see in the darkness, proposing marvels and riddles and
then offering solutions and understanding. Reading and
re-reading when that was necessary so that she could take
possession of the key to the mystery and unveil all its
secrets; raising her little by little to his level.

12

No sooner had he brought her to Estância than the Doctor was obliged to go to Bahia on urgent business, leaving
Tereza under the guardianship of Alfredão and the company of a local servant girl. Wary and suspicious, her body
still bruised by ill treatment and in her heart the painful
recollection of every minute of a recent, degrading time of
beatings and humiliation, of Justiniano Duarte da Rosa
and Dan, of prison and the brothel, living on out of sheer

habit, without hope of anything worth living for, Tereza was not quite sure where she was. She had come with the Doctor because she was feeling overwhelmed by all that had happened to her, and because of the respect he instilled in her. Would respect have been enough? She felt attraction, too, so strongly that she melted into pleasure when he kissed her at the door of the brothel before setting her on the croup of his horse. And so she had come, without knowing what the end of it all would be. When Gabi told her the Doctor was there, she had warned her that this whim of the sugarmill owner was not likely to last very long and predicted a rapid return to the brothel, where the door was always open—this house is your home, dear.

She had assumed the position of the Doctor's female, not of his mistress. In bed, one look at the masculine figure of Emiliano Guedes, one touch of his knowing fingers, was enough to make her burn. In the constant, growing love that she bore him, voluptuousness had come before tenderness, and only with time did the two feelings mingle and blend into one. As for the rest, she acted as if she were still living with the Captain, as if her new situation were identical to the old one. Early every morning she began working to clean that enormous house and put it in order, taking on the hardest, heaviest chores for herself while the maid took it easy, looking at the pots and pans in the kitchen or flicking the furniture in the parlor desultorily with a brightly colored, useless feather duster. Silent, hard-working Alfredão, with his kinky pate beginning to turn white, had been brought from the sugarmill provisionally to take care of the abandoned garden and orchard, do the shopping, and guard the house and Tereza's virtue. Though he thought he could guess what sort of person she was, the Doctor could not be certain, after all, and thought it best to take precautions. But Tereza even did some of Alfredão's work; when he was going to put out the trash he found she had already done it. She ate with him and the servant girl in the kitchen, using her fingers—while the drawers were crammed with silver eating utensils.

Now the house looked like the gem it was: a comfortable mansion set in an ample estate planted with fruit trees, with two big drawing rooms, one a living room, the other a dining room, four bedrooms open to the breeze from the Piauitinga River, an enormous kitchen and pantry, and an annex with bathrooms, servants' rooms, storeroom, and lumber room. What did he want so much house for, Tereza wondered as she gave it a thorough spring cleaning; why so much furniture, and all of it so outsized? It took time, sweat, and hard labor to keep that heavy old rosewood furniture presentable, especially since it was much the worse for wear and neglect. Mansion, grounds, and furnishings—some remaining pieces of English porcelain and the family silver—were the last vestiges of the grandeur of the Montenegro family, shrunken to one old couple. As Tereza learned later, the Doctor had bought the house and everything in it without haggling over the price, which was, as a matter of fact, very cheap. Unfortunately, some of the best things—a grandfather's clock, a prie-dieu, some images of saints—had already gone south with some antique hound in exchange for a trifle.

The Doctor was charmed with the trees and furniture and the situation of the house at the edge of town, far from the bustling center, a calm backwater in which habitually nothing stirred. Habitually, no; but the arrival of strangers brought clusters of the curious of both sexes to the spot. They knew the mansion had been sold, knew who had bought it, and their noses were quivering for fresh gossip to enliven their idle hours, which were many. Some of the boldest clapped at the door in the hope of milking one of the servants for information, but Alfredão's unfriendly face and laconic words soon discouraged the host of gossips and idlers. All they found out was that two maids were engaged in a colossal housecleaning. One was a local girl, whose laziness was proverbial in more than one family in the place, and the other was a stranger, so dirty you couldn't see her face, but she looked like a young girl and a hard worker. The woman for whom all that comfort was being prepared would no doubt stay away until everything was finished and ready.

None of the busybodies, male or female, had the slightest doubt as to what the mansion was intended for: a rich, warm nest, just right for a clandestine love affair, said Amintas Rufo, a young poet reduced to selling cloth in his father's store because his father was a soulless bourgeois. The Doctor had no financial interests in Estância, where he showed up only occasionally to dine with his friend and compadre João Nascimento Filho. No, he had bought the Montenegros' property to install a concubine there, declared the gossips and idlers, basing their opinion on three weighty reasons: the plutocrat's fame as a womanizer, well known in Bahia, Aracaju, and on both banks of the Real; the convenient location of the place, strategically situated between the two places where the Doctor spent most of his time, the Cajazeiras sugar refinery and the city of Aracaju; and, last but not least, the charm of Estância itself. The quiet beauty of the town was the perfect setting for an idyllic liaison, the very place to shelter a great love affair, according to the unjustly treated Amintas.

One afternoon a truck stopped in front of the house and the driver and two helpers began to unload a great quantity of cartons and boxes, some of which bore the word "fragile" stamped or written in ink. Loafers and gossips came running; the street soon swarmed with them. From where they stood on the opposite sidewalk they could identify each item: refrigerator, radio, vacuum cleaner, sewing machine, what a mountain of things, the Doctor wasn't one to count pennies. It couldn't be long now before he came himself with Miss What's-Her-Name. They were continuously on the *qui vive*, the gossips kept watch by turns; but the Doctor, on purpose perhaps, drove in by car very late that night. The last shift of busybodies had gone off duty when the Cathedral bells pealed at nine.

When he woke up at eight the next morning—he was usually up and about by seven, but that night he had been delightfully employed until daybreak—Tereza was no longer between the sheets. He found her wielding a broom, while the maid in the living room didn't move a muscle except to smile and wish him good morning. Emiliano made no comment but only invited Tereza to sit down with him to breakfast.

"No, I had mine earlier. The girl will give you yours. Excuse me, I'm behind in my work—" as she went on with the housework.

Pensively the Doctor partook of his *café au lait*, steamed cornmeal, fried bananas, and thin manioc-flour pancakes, his eyes following Tereza's movements as she swept the bedroom, took out the garbage, came out with the chamber pot in her hand to empty it into the latrine. The maid stood in the kitchen doorway, ogling her master coquettishly and waiting for him to finish eating so that she could take away the dishes. After breakfast, the Doctor, laden with books, went out to the hammock in the garden, coming in a little before noon to take a bath. When she saw him in clean clothes, Tereza asked:

"Can I set the table?"

Emiliano smiled.

"Yes, after you've had a bath and dressed for lunch."

Tereza hadn't thought of taking a bath at that hour, with so much work still to do after lunch.

"I'd rather wait and take a bath when I've finished the housework. I still have an awful lot to do."

"No, Tereza. Go and bathe now."

Always obedient, she went to obey. When she crossed the patio on her way back from the bathroom to the main part of the house, she saw Alfredão carrying bottles out to the garden where a small collapsible table, one of the many things that had come in the truck, had been set up in front of a stone bench. The Doctor was waiting for her there. She went to him in her clean dress and inquired:

"Can I set the table now?"

"In a little while. Sit down here, with me." He picked up a bottle and a little glass. "Let's drink to our new house."

Tereza was not a drinker. One time the Captain had given her a drink of *cachaça* and she had made a grimace at the first sip. Out of sheer perverseness Justiniano had made her drink down the glass and repeated the dose. He had never offered her a drink again—what a ninny, blubbering at the cockfights and gagging on first-class *cachaça*. In Gabi's house, when a customer sitting at the bar treated one of the women to a drink, the girl's obligation was to ask for vermouth or brandy. The brew that Arruda served to the woman in a dark, thick glass was nothing but tea, in no way resembling cognac or vermouth except in color and price. When the customer ordered a bottle of beer instead, Tereza sometimes took a drink or two of it, without enthusiasm. She never really liked beer, not even after she had learned to appreciate the bitters the Doctor was so fond of.

She picked up her glass and heard him say the toast: "To our happiness in this new house."

Remembering the *cachaça*, she barely touched her lips to the clear liqueur, the color of gold. To her surprise, it tasted delicious, and she tried it again.

"Port wine," said the Doctor. "One of the greatest inventions of man, certainly the greatest of the Portuguese. Don't be afraid to drink it; good liqueur is never bad for you. This isn't really the proper time for an after-dinner liqueur, but in this case the hour matters less than the taste."

Tereza did not entirely understand what he meant, but all at once she felt a serenity she had never felt before. She was at peace. The Doctor told her about port and how it ought to be drunk at the end of the meal after the coffee, or else in the afternoon, but not before a meal. Then why had he given it to her at the wrong time? Because it was the king of drinks. If he had given her gin or bitters to begin with, she might not have liked it; but no one could refuse port wine. Emiliano went on talking of different wines and liqueurs. In time she would learn to distinguish one from another—muscatel, sherry, madeira, Málaga, Tokay—her life was just beginning. Forget all that has happened up to now, blot it all out of your mind; you're beginning a new life here.

He pulled Tereza's chair out for her to sit at the table, and since she did not know how to serve he did so, beginning by preparing a plate for the incredulous girl, who couldn't believe that all this was really happening to her. They drank chilled mangaba juice and the Doctor repeated the ritual, passing the first glass to her. Tereza was so embarrassed that she only picked at her food as she listened to his talk of strange culinary habits—Mother of God!—each one nastier than the one before.

Little by little the Doctor put Tereza at her ease, making her exclaim with horror by describing certain foreign delicacies: shark fins, hundred-year-old eggs, grasshoppers. Tereza had heard that some people ate frogs, and the Doctor confirmed the story and even claimed frog's legs were very good. One time she had eaten iguana, killed and stewed by Chico Half-Sole, and had liked it. All game is delicious, said Emiliano, it has a strange, wild taste. Do you want to know, Tereza, which of all the animals in the world is the most delicious?

"Which one?"

"Escargots, that is, snails."

"Snails? Oh, how nasty!"

The Doctor's clear laughter was a happy sound in Tereza's ears.

"Well, Tereza, one of these days I'll cook you a dish of snails that'll make you lick your lips. You didn't know I was a first-rate chef, did you?"

Tereza began to relax, and by the time dessert came she was laughing openly at his description of how the French leave their escargots shut up for a week in a box lined with wheat flour as their only food, changing the flour every day until the animals are completely clean.

"What about grasshoppers? Do people really eat them? And where?"

In Asia, cooked with honey. The Cantonese loved cobras and dogs. For that matter, didn't people in the backlands eat boa constrictors and leaf-cutting ants? That was the same thing. When they got up from the table and the Doctor took Tereza's hand, she gave him a new kind of smile. She was beginning to be fond of him.

When they were back in the garden, sitting on the old stone bench, once covered with tiles, he kissed her lightly on her lips wet with port wine, just another drop to aid the digestion, and said:

"You must learn one thing, Tereza, before you learn anything else. You must get it into this little head once and for all"—stroking her dark hair—"and not forget for a moment, that you are the mistress here, not a servant. This house is yours, it belongs to you. If one maid can't do all the work, hire another one, as many as you need; but I never again want to see you in a filthy dress polishing furniture and emptying chamber pots."

Tereza did not know how to respond to this gentle reprimand. She was used to hearing shouts and commands, to being slapped and struck on the face, to having her ears boxed and her hands beaten with the iron ferule, to being whipped with the rawhide strap when she had so much to do she couldn't get some task done quickly enough. She had slept in the Captain's bed, but that didn't mean she was not the lowest of his slaves. In prison, too, she had been given the job of cleaning the three cells and the latrine. At Gabi's, instead of sleeping until noon like the rest of the women, she was just another servant to lend ancient Pirró a hand in cleaning the rambling old house—to think that old drab had once been the famous Pirró dos Coroneis, and that all the ranchers had fought over her.

"You are the lady of the house, and don't forget it. We can't have you going around dirty, slovenly, badly dressed. I want to see you look pretty. . . . You *are* pretty, even when you're dirty and covered with rags, but I want your beauty enhanced; I want to see you look clean, elegant, like a lady." He repeated the words. "Like a lady."

A lady? Oh, I'll never be one, thought Tereza; and the Doctor read her thought as if he had the gift of reading other people's minds.

"You won't be one unless you really want to be. You will if you're the person I think you are."

"I'll try. . . ."

"No, Tereza, trying isn't enough."

Tereza looked at him, and Emiliano saw the diamond flash in her black eyes that he had seen before.

"I don't rightly know what a lady is, but you'll never see me dirty and raggedy any more, I promise you that."

"As for that maid who let you work while she didn't do a thing, I'm going to send her away."

"But it wasn't her fault, I was used to doing things and I just went on doing them."

"Even if it wasn't her fault, she can't stay. She won't ever think of you as a mistress, because she saw you acting like a servant and she won't respect you now. I want everyone to respect you, Tereza. You're the lady of the house, and over you there is only me and no one else."

13

Tereza was alone in their room with the dead man for a very long time. They had laid him on the bed with his hands crossed and his head on the pillow. Tereza had picked a newly open blood-red rose in the garden and put it in the Doctor's hands.

When he sprang out of the automobile, coming from the sugarmill or from Aracaju, the Doctor would first give her a long welcoming kiss—the caressing touch of his moustache, the tip of his tongue—and then hand her his fine panama hat and silver riding whip to put away while the driver and Alfredão carried portfolios, books, and parcels into the living room and the pantry.

The Doctor habitually carried the silver riding stock around with him wherever he went—not only in the country, when he was riding over the canefields or inspecting his cattle as they grazed, but also in town, in Bahia, in Aracaju, at board meetings in his bank, in the office of the president of Eximportex, S.A. It was his ornament, symbol, and weapon.

It was a weapon to be feared in the hands of the Doctor: in Bahia, by brandishing it he had put to flight two young thugs who mistook the grizzled nighthawk for a helpless old man and his haste for fear; and in broad daylight, in the middle of downtown Bahia, he had made the impudent scribe Haroldo Pera swallow a newspaper article he had written. Hired by some enemies of the Guedeses, the bold pamphleteer, whose pen could be had cheap and who unmade reputations with calm impunity, had written for a weekly scandal sheet a long, violent, diatribe against the powerful clan. Emiliano, as head of the family, came in for the roughest treatment: "impenitent seducer of naive country virgins," "soulless landowner, exploiter of tenant farmers and sharecroppers, land thief," "contumacious smuggler of sugar and *aguardiente*, who habitually defrauded the public treasury with the criminal connivance of the state tax inspectors." His brothers, Mílton and Cristóvão, came in for their share of blame as "incompetent parasites" and "ignorant and good-for-nothing." Mílton was a "sanctimonious pharisee, a hollow saint," and Cristóvão was "forever tippling *cachaça*, a hopeless alcoholic." Not to mention dear Xandô with his "homophilic sexual tastes"—that is, young Alexandre Guedes, Mílton's son, who had been packed off to Rio and forbidden to set foot in the sugarmill because he was "mad about muscular black workers." It was quite an exhaustive bill of indictment, as we have seen, and was much read and commented upon. "There's a lot of truth in it, even if it is written with pus," was the verdict of a well-informed backlands politician, expressed to an animated circle on the steps of the Government Palace. The words were no sooner out of his mouth than he looked around and put his hand up to his imprudent lips: striding across the square from opposite directions were the Doctor, gripping the silver handle of his quirt, and Pera the journalist, walking with the firm step of a notoriously successful man. They met in the middle; there was no time for flight, and the glorious author swallowed his own article, neat, and was decorated across the cheek with a slash of the whip.

Out in Estância, though, when the Doctor went out for his daily after-dinner stroll, he carried a flower in his hand instead of a whip. He had fallen into the habit soon after the beginning of their life together, when dawning tenderness was gradually widening their intimacy, limited at first to caresses only in bed, and giving it a new dimension. At that time the plantation owner did not show himself in the street in Tereza's company but took his evening walk alone, to the old bridge, to the reservoir, to the river port on the bank of the Piauí; for the sake of appearances he kept her clandestine, hidden away, and the two were never seen together in public—"At least the Doctor respects the decencies, unlike some I could name who flaunt their concubines under other people's noses," Dona Geninha Abib of the Telephone and Telegraph Company, a plump and persistent slanderer, said approvingly. Only those who lived in the same house witnessed the growing affection, trust, intimacy, and fondness drawing the pair ever closer together—stocks of love being patiently built up.

It began one night when, after kissing her, he said: So long, Tereza, I'll be right back, I'm just going to stretch my legs and digest my dinner. She ran into the garden and picked a rosebud, an enormous, velvety, deep-red drop of blood, murmuring as she gave it to the Doctor:

"This is so you won't forget me while you're out."

Next day when he was about to go out, it was he who asked her:

"And where's my flower? Not that I need it to remember you, but it's as if I were taking you with me."

From that day on, their repeated good-byes, in the sadness renewed each time he was about to drive off in the car, Tereza kissed a rose and pinned it to his lapel—because Emiliano would be carrying the silver riding stock in his hand.

The quirt in his hand, rose in his buttonhole, the farewell kiss—the moustache that nuzzled her, the point of his tongue touching his lips—and the Doctor went back to his multifarious life, far from Tereza. When would he return to the peace of Estância? He was a guest who never stayed long. Divided as he was among so many dwelling places and so many commitments, interests, and affections, Tereza's portion was the time it took a rose to blossom and die, the secret, fleeting time that is all a mistress can expect.

In the bedroom, after she had placed the flower in her lover's hand, Tereza tried to close his piercing blue eyes that had sometimes been limpid, sometimes cold and mistrustful. They were the piercing eyes of a diviner, dead now but still open and watchful, fixed on Tereza, knowing more about her than she knew herself.

14

From her apprenticeship in liqueurs and spirituous wines, Tereza had graduated to the more difficult branch of table wines, strong distilled liquors, and digestive bitters. The Doctor had improvised a wine cellar in one of the outside rooms and showed it off proudly to João Nascimento Filho and Father Vinícius, with all the ritual of labels examined respectfully and vintages murmured with devotion. Lulu Santos, faithful to beer and *cachaça,* was the butt of mockery, scoffed at as a barbarian with no vestige of a palate, to whom whisky was the peak in good drinking.

Tereza's progress toward connoisseurship was modest. She remained loyal to her initial discoveries—port, cointreau, and muscatel—although she would sometimes take bitters before a meal. As for table wines, she liked the sweet ones best, with a marked bouquet to perfume the mouth.

When the Doctor showed off his noble dry wines, his illustrious reds, every one from a vintage year, the priest and João Nascimento Filho would turn their eyes up and fall all over themselves exclaiming in rapture; but after several such dinners Tereza realized that Professor Nascimento, with all his fame as a connoisseur of refined taste, preferred white wines that were not very dry, lighter and more agreeable to the palate, just as she did, in spite of his extravagant praise of the dry ones and the reds and all his dainty smacking of lips when he was served one. Above all, he preferred spirituous wines to any other apéritif. Tereza never gave away his secret or let him see that she had surprised his snobbish little fraud.

"Professor João, will you join me in a glass of port even if it's not the right time for it?"—and he quickly refused gin, whisky, and bitters.

"With pleasure, Tereza. That business of wrong and right times is just an aristocratic affectation."

Since she was not obliged like Professor Nascimento Filho to possess exquisite taste, and was not given to lying unnecessarily, she revealed her preferences to the Doctor, and Emiliano would smile at her and say: You're sweet as a honeycomb, Tereza.

On hot nights in Estância when there was a pleasant breeze off the river and an outsized moon hanging over the trees in a sky full of countless stars, they would sip leisurely drinks in the garden, she and the Doctor. He would have strong brandies, gin, vodka, cognac, and she would have her port wine or cointreau. Honeycomb Tereza, what sweet lips you have. Oh, my lord and master, your kiss burns me with flames of cognac and live coals of gin. At such times the distance that divided them shrank almost to nothing, and disappeared completely in bed. In bed or there in the hammock swinging gently in the breeze, under the stars, they set off ardently together toward the moon.

Some alterations had been made in the house to make it even more comfortable, since the Doctor was accustomed to the best and he wanted to accustom Tereza. One of the bedrooms was divided and made into two bathrooms, one opening off the master bedroom, the other off the guestroom occupied by Lulu Santos when he came just to visit or on business of the Doctor's. The parlor lost its odor of mothballs and solemnity and stopped looking like a room that was thrown open only on holidays or to receive visitors ceremoniously; the Doctor installed book-cases, a reading and study desk, a victrola, records, and a little bar. The alcove off the living room became a sewing room.

Concerned with finding ways of filling Tereza's time, which was so empty during the prolonged continual absences of her protector, he had bought her a sewing machine and knitting needles.

"Tereza, do you know how to sew?"

"No, not really, but I mended a lot of clothes on the machine that belonged to the woman who passed away, back on the farm."

"Wouldn't you like to learn? That way you'll have something to do when I'm away."

The Our Lady of Grace Sewing and Tailoring School was located in a side street on the other side of Triste Park, and to get there Tereza had to cross the center of town. The teacher, Miss Salvalena (*Salva* from her father Salvador, *lena* from her mother Helena), a strapping young woman with wide hips and a bosom of bronze, a high-stepping filly in fact, but a filly who wore quantities of powder, lipstick, and rouge, had set aside a time in midafternoon exclusively for Tereza and received payment for the whole course, fifteen classes, in advance. On the third day Tereza gave it up, scissors, tape measure, needle, thimble, and all. Ever since the first class the excellent teacher had hinted at the possibility of Tereza's earning herself some pin money by putting out for a few rich gentlemen of the same class as the Doctor, partners in the textile mills, important men in the town, and discreet gentlemen. By the third class the hints had turned into propositions. There was no problem about the locale; the rendezvous could take place right there in the sewing school, in the back bedroom, a safe, comfortable nest, fitted out with a swell bed and a spring mattress, dear. Dr. Bráulio, a partner in one of the mills, had seen Tereza go by in the street and he was willing . . .

Tereza picked up her purse, turned her back on the woman, and left without saying good-bye. Surprised and offended, the celestina of the sewing machine began muttering to herself:

"That snooty bitch—I'd like to be there the day the Doctor kicks her out the door. Then she'll be after me to get her some customers. . . ." The string of insults was interrupted by an uncomfortable thought: would she have to give back the money for the twelve lessons she hadn't given? "I won't give back a penny. Is it my fault the uppity nigger walked out?"

When the Doctor came back, he inquired what progress Tereza had made at the Sewing and Tailoring School. Oh, she had stopped going to class; she wasn't very good at it and didn't really enjoy it, so she had just stayed until she learned enough to get by. The Doctor had the gift of divination; who could sustain the gaze of those limpid, gimlet eyes?

"Tereza, you know I don't like liars; why are you lying? Have I ever lied to you? What really happened? Tell me the truth."

"She propositioned me with a man. . . ."

"I know; Dr. Bráulio. He made a bet in Aracaju that he would sleep with you and put horns on me. Listen to me, Tereza: you'll get a lot of propositions, and if some-day, for any reason, you feel like accepting one of them, just tell me before you do. That will be better for me and especially for you."

"You don't know me very well, or you couldn't think of me that way!" Tereza's voice rose in anger, her chin high, her eyes flashing, but she immediately lowered her head and her voice and added: "I know why you do, though: when you came for me I was living in a whore-house and you know that when I belonged to the Captain, I had another man." Her voice dropped to a murmur. "It's true. I did have another man, but I didn't like the Captain, he took me by force, I was never with him be-cause I wanted to, I only wanted the other one." Her voice rose again: "If that's what you think of me, I'd bet-ter go away right now. I'd rather go back to Gabi's than live here when you don't trust me, worrying all the time about what might happen."

The Doctor took her in his arms:

"Don't be a little fool. I never said I doubted you or thought you were capable of falsehood; at least that's not what I meant to say. I said that if someday you get tired of me, if someone else interests you more, all you have to

do is just come and tell me so. That's the right way to act.
I didn't mean to insult you; I have no reason to do that.
I have every reason to think you do right, and that makes
me happy."

Still with his arms around her he added, smiling:

"I want to be frank with you too, and tell you the whole
truth. When I asked you what happened I already knew,
don't ask me how. Everything is known here, Tereza, and
remarked upon."

That night after dinner, the Doctor invited her to go
out with him on his stroll to the bridge over the Piaui.
He had never done that before. The old man and the
girl walked through the night together, but the Doctor did
not look his more than sixty years and Tereza did not
look barely sixteen; they were a man and a woman in
love holding hands, two unabashed lovers happily taking
a stroll. The few passersby they met on the way, plain
people, did not recognize the Doctor and his mistress but
saw only a couple in love. Far from the bustle of the main
part of town, they aroused little curiosity. Only once an
old woman stopped to see them go by:

"Good evening, my dears, go with God!"

Back in the house after a look at the river, the dam,
and the port with its ferryboats, the Doctor left her undressing in the bedroom and went to bring the bottle of
champagne he had put in the refrigerator to get cold.
When she heard the pop of the cork and saw it rise in
the air, Tereza laughed and clapped, excited as a child.
Emiliano Guedes poured one champagne cup for both
and they drank it together, Tereza discovering the to-her-
unprecedented taste of champagne. How could she even
think of anyone else, rich man or poor, young or old,
handsome or ugly, when she had the most perfect lover,
the most ardent, the wisest? Teaching her something every
day: the value of loyalty and the rapture of champagne,
the longest measure of ecstasy, and the deepest.

"As long as you want me I'll never belong to anyone
else."

Even dizzy from champagne she did not use the familiar
form, but at the climax, when she was melting in honey,
she said in a low, timid voice: Oh, my love.

15

Dressed all in black like a caricature of a witch or a prostitute in a low-class brothel on the night of a party, Nina appeared at the door of the bedroom, walking on tiptoe; ostensibly not to disturb Tereza, actually to catch her unawares and surprise some trace of smugness on her face. The stuck-up tart couldn't hide her glee forever. After all, she had hit the jackpot and could have a ball for the rest of her life, and however false and hypocritical she was, she'd have to show her true feelings sometime. Phony as she was, she hadn't been able to squeeze a single tear out of those dry eyes—and it was so easy, too; anybody could do it. Nina stopped in the doorway and began to cry her heart out.

The couple had been working in the house for almost two years. If the Doctor had had his way they would have been dismissed long ago, not so much because of poor simple Lula as because of Nina, whom Emiliano didn't like:

"I don't trust that girl, Tereza."

"She's ignorant, poor thing, but she's not really bad."

The Doctor shrugged and let it go. He knew the real reason for Tereza's patience with the creature's slovenliness and habitual lying: the children. Tereza looked after nine-year-old Lazinho and seven-year-old Tequinha with maternal devotion. Tereza taught all the neighborhood urchins, just for fun, in a little improvised school where there was much playing and laughter, and was delighted to do it: children, classes, and study filled the interminable time when the Doctor was away. Besides the afternoon class with its games and festive tea party, Lazinho and Tequinha spent a good part of the day following their amateur schoolmistress around. Their preference for Tereza was marked enough to annoy Nina, who was quick to punish and had a heavy hand. When the Doctor was there, the little ones asked for his blessing and then were banished to the orchard or to play in the street with their schoolmates when there weren't any classes. Time was all too short for the joy and cheerful bustle consequent on the Doctor's arrival; in that holiday there was no room for children, and when Tereza was in Emiliano's company she needed no other. But in his absence the neighborhood children, especially the two in the house, were the constant companions who lightened the burden of aimless time on her hands and kept the girl from thinking of a future when the absence might be for good, if the sugarmill owner should tire of her someday. It never occurred to her that he might die. Death was something that happened to other people, not to the Doctor.

Because of the children, Tereza put up with the inconvenience of the maid's badly done work and her discomfiting, sometimes overt hostility, and the Doctor, no doubt feeling some twinges of guilt—no, Tereza, I won't have a bastard child!—closed his eyes to Nina's bad manners, her envy, her stupidity, the way she rubbed her flabby breasts against him every chance she had. When he came out of his room in the morning, Emiliano Guedes would see Tereza in the garden kneeling near the flowerbeds playing with the two children: what a picture! A photograph of that scene would win a prize in any contest. Ah, why must all bread in this life be doled out as half a loaf? A shadow would fall across the Doctor's face. When the children saw him they asked for his blessing and ran into the orchard, following strict orders.

Standing in the doorway, Nina tried to calculate how big a share of the old millionaire's will would fall to his mistress. Completely cynical when it came to devotion and affection, Nina gave no credence to Tereza's love for the Doctor. In her mind fidelity, fondness, devotion, were nothing but hypocritical playacting on Tereza's part to get her hands on his estate. Now that she was rich and on her own, Miss Smartypants could do whatever she had a mind to. Maybe she would do something for the children; there might be a little something left over for them out of the treasure trove she had done the Guedeses out of. You never knew. Just in case, Nina's voice oozed sympathy and sentiment:

"Poor Miss Tereza, so fond of him and all . . ."

"Nina, please go away and leave me alone."

You see? Miss Hoity-Toity's already showing her claws and her fangs.

16

One day Alfredão came in to say good-bye.

"I'm going away, Missy Tereza. Misael's come to take my place; he's a good boy."

Tereza knew from the Doctor that Alfredão wanted to go back home. Brought for a month, in an emergency, he had been away from his family and the sugarmill for six. He had always worked at the mill but at no particular job; he was always available for whatever Emiliano wanted, a jack-of-all-trades, and quick on the trigger, too. If it hadn't been for his grandchildren he would have been glad to stay in Estância. He liked the place and its kindly people, and he liked Tereza even more.

"She's a good gal, Seu Doctor, like no other. She ain't very old but she acts like she was; never goes out of the house unless she has to, and she don't flirt with nobody when she's walking down the street. She has her eye on the door all the time, can't wait for you to come back, all the time asking me: You think he'll come today, Alfredão? Yessir, I'll guarantee that little gal deserves all you do for her, Seu Doctor, 'cause all she thinks about besides you is her studies."

A fundamental part of the Doctor's definitive judgment of Tereza were the hard facts provided by Alfredão, his detailed accounts of all that happened during Emiliano's absence: from the sewing teacher's propositions to Comadre Calu's attempts at intrigue, not forgetting the still vividly recollected run-in with Avio Auler the bagman, a kind of Dan in the form of a traveling salesman, a second-class philanderer gleaming with brilliantine and reeking with cheap toilet water. Recently transferred from southern Bahia to Sergipe and Alagoas, he was dazzled at the plethora of pretty girls in Estância, unfortunately all virgins. He was in search of some richer, more succulent dish, real fun in bed with no danger of engagement and marriage, some restless woman with time on her hands—some wealthy man's unengaged mistress, in fact. He heard about Tereza and saw her coming out of a store. Yes, she was a real honey. He followed her down the street telling her silly jokes and paying her foolish compliments, of which he had an inexhaustible stock, each cleverer than the last, he thought. Tereza quickened her step; her swain did the same and jumped out in front of her, blocking her way. Knowing how disagreeable any scandal that drew people's attention to her would be for the Doctor, Tereza tried to avoid him, but the drummer opened his arms and wouldn't let her pass.

"I won't let you get by me until you tell me your name and when we can have a little talk."

Tereza, restraining herself with an effort, took the middle of the street. The youth reached out his hand to catch her, but before he could even touch her arm, Alfredão, who had appeared out of nowhere, gave the intrusive meddler such a shove that it sent him sprawling on the ground. He sprang up and ran straight back to the hotel, where he skulked until it was time to take the bus to Aracaju. What Avio Auler lacked was experience in courting other men's mistresses. For anyone who wants to do that, it is indispensable to know something of the woman's character and the point of view of her protector. While it may be true that most concubines are not averse to the pleasures and risks of adultery, and many protectors are tame and complacent cuckolds, there is a small minority of serious girls who are faithful to their commitments and some lovers with sensitive foreheads, allergic to horns. In this case, as it happened, both lover and mistress belonged to the aggressive minority, and that was the downfall of Avio Auler, traveling salesman for the Stela shoe factory.

Through Alfredão the Doctor learned that Tereza spent whole afternoons poring over her books and practicing penmanship in a notebook. She had gone to school before she was sold to the Captain, and in those two-and-a-half years her teacher, Mercedes Lima, had taught her all she knew, which wasn't much. Since Tereza longed to read the books scattered around the house, she set to work to learn how.

For Emiliano Guedes it was an absorbing task to guide and follow the girl's steps as she struggled to learn rules and methods of analysis. Many and various were the things the Doctor taught his young protégée as time went on, in the garden, in the orchard, inside the house and in the street, at table and in bed; but none so useful to Tereza just then as the lesson plan he made for her. Before he went away he would leave homework for her to do, subjects to study, exercises to work on. Books and paper filled Tereza's idle hours, giving her no time to feel bored or insecure.

It was during that period that the Doctor got into the habit of reading aloud to her, beginning with children's books: Tereza traveled with Gulliver, cried over the little tin soldier, laughed with all her heart at Pedro Malazarte. The Doctor, too, would laugh his frank merry laugh; he liked to laugh. He didn't like his emotions to be deeply touched, but he was moved by Tereza, who had broken through the rigid self-restraint he had imposed on himself.

Tereza did not really have so much idle time as all that. Although the Doctor didn't want her doing housework, she had her part in cleaning, arranging, and beautifying the house. Emiliano loved flowers, and every morning Tereza gathered carnations and roses, dahlias and chrysanthemums, so that the vases were always full; the Doctor might turn up any day, any time. Much of her time was now spent in the kitchen, for since the Doctor was such a gourmet and so particular about the quality of the food he ate, Tereza wanted to be an expert too. Civilized man requires the highest quality in bed and board, said the Doctor, and Tereza, who was certainly first-rate in bed, burned her fingers on the stove but learned how to cook.

João Nascimento Filho had found them a wonderful cook, crotchety old Eulina. She complained constantly about her hard life and was frequently down in the dumps, but what an artist!

"An artist, Emiliano; that's what the old bag is. You could eat her stewed kid for a week and not get tired of it," declared Professor Nascimento. "She has no equal at plain cooking. The divine touch is what she has."

She was a marvel at plain and fancy cooking—the rich cuisine of Sergipe and Bahia, Alagoas mussels cooked in palm oil, hot pepper and coconut, and all kinds of desserts. From her Tereza learned to dole out the salt and mix different flavors, how to know when something was done to a turn, the rules of cooking with sugar and oil, and when to use coconut, pepper, or ginger. When old Eulina's head got too heavy and she felt a tightness in her chest—worthless life, made her feel like trash!—she would throw down her cooking pots and stalk out of the house without a word. Then Tereza would fill her empty place before the big wood stove—for anyone who wants to eat superbly knows there isn't anything as good as food cooked over a wood fire.

"That old Eulina's cooking better every day," said the Doctor helping himself to another plateful of chicken cooked in manioc flour. "Though it's such a seemingly simple dish, 'nursing mother' chicken is one of the hardest to prepare. . . . Well, what are you laughing at, Tereza? Come on, tell me."

She was laughing because the old woman had had absolutely nothing to do with the preparation of either the chicken or the manioc mush; she was feeling so blue she wouldn't lift a finger. She had made the dessert, though, the cashew candy and jackfruit and guava paste; weren't they delicious? Oh, Tereza, since when are you a cook, and why? Right here in our house, my lord, the better to please you. Tereza in the kitchen, Tereza in bed, Tereza at her books.

It was as though Alfredão's return to the sugarmill marked the end of the first and most difficult stage in Tereza's life with Emiliano. In the calm, silent presence of this retainer who was gardener, bodyguard, watchman, and faithful friend in one, the garden blossomed, the trees bore fruit; and in their protective shade the trust, affection and tender mutual concern of the lovers blossomed too. Tereza was used to Alfredão's silences, his ugly face, his loyalty.

When the Doctor was there, the time was never long enough for all the things they loved: apéritifs, lunches and dinners, friends, books, walks, dips in the river, the table, the bed—the bed, the hammock, the matting spread in the garden, the couch in the living room where he looked over documents and dictated orders, the wide cane settee in her sewing and study room, the tub where they bathed together, that wonderful crazy idea of the Doctor's. Here, there, and always wonderful.

17

Dr. Amarílio returned about two in the morning, bringing the death certificate and the results of his call to the Doctor's relatives. In order to locate them at the gala dance at the Yacht Club he had had to wake up half the people in Aracaju until he finally got through to the youngest brother, Cristóvão, his voice blurred with drink. It had taken more than two hours to reach him. Fortunately this time the telephone operator, Bia Turca, had not raised a fuss about the lateness of the hour because she was curious to know why he was calling and the details of Dr. Guedes's death. To tell the truth, the doctor had enlisted her aid by giving her to understand that the Doctor had turned into ectoplasm (Bia Turca was a practicing spiritualist) in rather unusual circumstances. He didn't have to be specific, for Bia Turca, thanks to her profession or her spiritual fluids, had powerful antennae.

"Bia was a great help; got on that telephone and hung on until she got Aracaju on the line. When she finally got through to someone who knew where the family all was, she gave a hurrah. You couldn't hear anything at first, the dance music was so loud, but luckily the telephone in the Yacht Club is in the bar and that's where Cristóvão was, drinking. When I told him the news I think he lost the power of speech because he let go of the receiver and left me on the other end shouting until somebody else came on the line and went to call the son-in-law. He said they were leaving right away and would be here just as soon as they could. . . ."

With the doctor was João Nascimento Filho, sad, shaken, fearful.

"Oh, Tereza, what a terrible misfortune! Emiliano was younger than I am, three years younger, not quite sixty-five. I never thought he'd go before I did. He was always so strong. I never once heard him complain of being sick."

Tereza left the two men in the bedroom and went to fetch some coffee. Lachrymose, dressed in stark black, Nina was carrying on like a mourning relative, some inconsolable cousin or niece. Lula was sitting at the table in the pantry with his head on his arms, asleep. Tereza went to make the coffee herself.

On top of the clean sheets, dressed as if he were about to preside over a board of directors meeting of the Inter-state Bank of Bahia and Sergipe, lay Dr. Emiliano Guedes his clear eyes open, as curious about the world and its inhabitants as ever, fully intending to see and accompany every step of the long wake in the house of his mistress, where he had died at the climax of the orgasm. João Nascimento Filho, his eyelids wet, turned to the doctor:

"Poor Emiliano, he doesn't look dead. Look at his eyes. It's as if he still wanted to boss us around the way he always did, even in law school. And with a rose in his hand. All that's missing is the whip. So stern and so generous, the best friend and the worst enemy anyone could have. Emiliano Guedes, lord of Cajazeiras . . ."

"It was grief that killed him," the doctor repeated his diagnosis. "He never told me but the news got around, you know those things without having to ask. He was such a close friend of yours, João; didn't he ever tell you? Not even day before yesterday? Didn't he tell you about his son, and his son-in-law?"

"Emiliano wasn't the kind of man who goes around talking about his private life, not even to his most intimate friends. I never heard anything about the family from his lips but praise: They were all wonderful, all perfect, the imperial family. He was much too proud to ever tell anyone, even his closest friend, anything that put anyone kin to him in a bad light. I do know that his daughter was the apple of his eye. When she was still a little girl, every time he came here on a visit he'd talk about her the whole time—how beautiful she was, and how smart, and the cute things she did. After she married he didn't talk about her any more."

"What could he say? That she put horns on her husband? Aparecida's just like her father. She has his hot blood, she's sensual and fiery, they say she's a real terror in Aracaju. She goes her way and her husband goes his. He's as bad as she is, and they both live just the way they want to."

"Modern times, incredible marriages," João Nascimento Filho concluded. "Poor Emiliano, so crazy about his family, his children, his brothers, his nieces and nephews. There wasn't a one of them he didn't help. Just look at him, you'd think he was alive. All that's lacking is the whip in his hand. . . ."

Tereza came back with the coffee cups on a tray.

"Why the whip, Seu João?"

"Because Emiliano was never without a rose and the whip, the silver riding whip."

"Not with me, Seu João. Not here." It was almost the truth.

"Tereza, in some ways you're exactly like him. When I look at you I see Emiliano. Living with him you've grown to be like him somehow: the same loyalty, the same pride, I don't know what it is. . . ."

He paused for a moment and then went on:

"I wanted to come and see him now, to tell him good-bye while he still has you with him. I don't want to be here when his family comes. It was because of you, Tereza, that he came here to be with us in Estância and gave us a little of his precious time and his love for life. When he came I was resigned to old age, just waiting for death, and he made me feel young again. I want to tell him good-bye here with you. I don't know the others and I don't want to meet them."

Silence fell again, as the dead man looked on with open eyes. Professor João went on:

"I never had any brothers or sisters, Tereza, but Emiliano was more to me than a brother. The only reason I didn't lose everything my father left me was because he concerned himself with my affairs. And even so, he never told me any of his secrets. Just now I was saying to Amarílio: pride and generosity, the whip and the rose. I came to see Emiliano and to see you too, Tereza. Can I be of use to you in any way?"

"No thank you, Seu João. I'll never forget you or Dr. Amarílio. In the time I've been living here I have even been able to have friends. That was something else he gave me."

"Are you going to stay in Estância, Tereza?"

"Without the Doctor, Seu João? I couldn't."

They sipped the last of their coffee in silence. João Nascimento thought of what Tereza's future might be. Poor Tereza; he knew she had had a hard time of it be-

fore Emiliano brought her here; she had led a dog's life.
The doctor longed for the priest to come so that they
wouldn't have to receive the family alone. By this time
they must be burning the road to Estância—daughter,
son-in-law, brother, sister-in-law, and the whole caboodle.

Dr. Amarílio dreaded the family's meeting with the
Doctor's mistress. It was a delicate situation and he didn't
know how to handle it. Some of Dr. Emiliano's relatives
he hardly knew: but Father Vinícius did, from the times
he had gone to say mass at the sugarmill. . . . Where on
earth was the priest, and why was he taking so long?

João Nascimento Filho gazed at his friend for a long
time, deeply affected and not troubling to hide his tears
and his fear of death.

"I never thought he'd go before I did; it will soon be
my turn. . . . Tereza, my dear, I'm going now, before
those people get here. If you ever need me. . . ."

He embraced Tereza and lightly touched his lips to her
forehead, looking much older than when he had arrived
to see his dead friend and tell him good-bye. Good-bye
for a little while, Emiliano.

18

Haven't you ever felt the touch of the whip, Tereza; his
extreme hardness, his inflexibility? Haven't you ever
touched the other side, the blade of steel?

Did death never enter into you before this night of
vigil over the corpse of the eminent Dr. Emiliano Guedes,
here in this so unsuitable house, Tereza? Did you never
feel it curled inside of you, a real, physical presence, a
rending claw of fire and ice in your torn womb? Never,
Tereza?

Yes, I did, Professor João; it was death that led me
by the hand across the border between affection and love.
Tereza's life with the Doctor was not only lived by the
calendar of the rose; there was at least one time of sorrow
and mourning, at least one funeral, and that death took
place inside of her, in her very womb, on a day of bitterness. She thought she had died too, but she had been
resurrected by her lover: his understanding, his delicate

attentions, his devotion were a miraculous remedy. Death and life, the riding whip and the rose.

You won't hear that story from Tereza's loyal, grateful lips, Professor João; she has placed in the dead man's fingers only the rose in farewell. But whether she wills it or not, memory brings back to lay beside the Doctor's corpse the corpse of one who had no wake and no funeral, one who never was, one whose life was extinguished before birth, a dream dissipated in blood, a child. Now there are two corpses on the bed, two absences, two deaths and both took place inside her. Counting Tereza there are three. She died tonight for the second time.

19

When Tereza skipped two consecutive periods—her menstruation was always exact, twenty-eight days between one period and the next—and found that there were other symptoms, too, she felt her heart stop: she was pregnant! Her first feeling was rapture: oh, she wasn't sterile after all and she was going to have a child, hers and the Doctor's, what boundless joy!

In the Captain's farm, Dona Brígida had never let her be around her granddaughter, not even to take care of her, much less play with the child. She saw in Tereza an enemy who was weaving wicked plots to rob Doris's child of her rights as sole heir to Justiniano Duarte da Rosa's property when the avenging angel descended from Heaven, fiery sword in hand. One Sunday afternoon Tereza had walked with Marcos Lemos over from Gabi's place in Cuia Dágua to the center of town to a Sunday matinee at the movies. When they crossed Cathedral Square she caught sight of Dona Brígida with the child at the door of her own house, the house that Dr. Ubaldo had bought and mortgaged and that she had nearly lost. Now she had it back, and grandmother and granddaughter were all spruced up and looked as happy as could be. No one would have taken them for the crazy old doddering woman and the ragged little girl—the person who said that for some troubles there's no cure like money certainly spoke the truth. On the farm Dona Brígida had forbid-

den Tereza to touch either the child or the doll, the gift
of the child's godmother, Dona Beatriz, Daniel's mother.

It was odd: in the little time she had had with Dan,
when she first awoke to passion and was blindly enamored
of the boy, it had never occurred to her that she might
conceive his child. When the worst happened, fear that
Dan had made her pregnant was added to her other tor-
ments; that time in her life was an unrelieved nightmare.
But the beatings in prison had been so hard that they had
brought on her period; at least the whippings had done
that much good. In that world of cruelty, that blind alley
with no exit, Tereza had decided that she could not have
children. She must be sterile, she would never conceive;
and she attributed the fact to the violence with which she
had been raped.

She had not become pregnant with Dan, when making
love was sheer rapture. In more than two years with the
Captain she had never conceived. No thanks to the Captain if she hadn't, for he took no precautions and never
recognized his paternity. When some girl got pregnant he
sent her away immediately. She could have the child or
get an abortion or do anything else she wanted to; that
was her problem. If one of them dared to come around
with a baby on her arm asking for help, he sent Terto
Cachorro to drive that what-shall-I-call-her away; who
the hell told her to have it? The only child he wanted was
Doris's child, a legitimate child.

I'm sterile and dried up inside, Tereza told the Doctor
when, soon after they arrived in Estância, he recom-
mended precautions and contraceptives.

"I've never conceived."

"That's just as well. I don't want any byblows." The
cultivated voice was cruel and inflexible. "I've always been
against it; it's a question of principle. No one has the
right to bring into the world a human being born with a
stigma, an inferior status. And besides, no one who has
family commitments should have illegitimate children. You
have children with your wife, that's what you marry for.
A wife is for conceiving children, giving birth to them,
and bringing them up; a mistress is for life's pleasures.
When she has to take care of a child she's just like a wife;
what difference is there between them? No byblows; that's
how I see things. I want to enjoy my Tereza at leisure, I

want her to make me happy when I have a few days for myself, not to have the worry and nuisance of children. Agreed, Honeycomb?"

Tereza gazed into the clear eyes that were like a blue steel blade.

"I can't have children anyway. . . ."

"So much the better." The frown on the Doctor's face deepened. "Both of my brothers, Mílton as well as Cristóvão, have bastard children. Mílton's are scattered all over the place, making problems for me; Cristóvão has two families and a whole bunch of natural children, and that's even worse. A wife is one thing, a mistress is another. It can't be the same. I want you all to myself. I don't want to share you with anyone, least of all with a child." He fell silent. When he spoke his voice was gentle and the steel blade of his eyes had turned to clear water again, gazing affectionately and a little sadly at her. "All that and my age, Tereza. I'm not the right age to have a small child. I wouldn't have time enough to make a real man of him, or a real woman of her, as I'm still trying and hoping to do with the others. And I want to keep all the time I have left for you . . ." as he took her in his arms to make love, which is what a mistress is for, Honeycomb.

Since Tereza was sterile, none of this was a problem. If she had been fertile she surely would have wanted the Doctor's child to make her the happiest woman in the world, and since he would not have given his permission, she would have been terribly unhappy. The sugarmill owner, always so courteous and thoughtful, had been candid, brutally candid. She was sterile; therefore the problem did not exist.

But she wasn't sterile after all! The Doctor's child was growing in her womb, alleluia! Once that irrepressible explosion of joy had passed, Tereza began to consider, as she had learned to do in jail: the Doctor was right. To bring a love child into the world was to condemn an innocent to suffer. She had witnessed more than one example in Gabi's house: Catarina's baby had died when he was six months old, of abuse at the hands of the woman who was paid to take care of him; Vivi's frail little daughter was consumptive and spat blood, because the terrible old woman who looked after her spent on *cachaça* the money Vivi gave her for food. All children of mothers who lived in the brothels of that district, or walked the streets, were abandoned children, because they had to be handed over to strangers. The life of a prostitute was bad enough as it was, but worst of all was the anguish of bearing children she couldn't take care of.

Knowing the Doctor would be away for three weeks attending to important business at the central office of the Bank in Bahia, Tereza went to Dr. Amarílio's office. A gynecological examination and a few questions yielded an easy diagnosis: pregnancy. And now what, Tereza? He waited some time for her reply. Tereza's black eyes were meditative and self-absorbed: oh, a son of hers and the Doctor's, growing up handsome and proud, with sky-blue eyes and fine manners, who would want for nothing in this world, an hidalgo like his father! Or a prostitute like her mother, living from hand to mouth, going from one sordid bed to another?

"Doctor, I want an abortion."

The doctor had his own firm point of view and weighty moral convictions:

"I don't approve of abortions, Tereza. I have performed some, but only in special cases when there was a real necessity, to save the life of a woman who should never have conceived. Abortion is always a bad thing, physically and spiritually, for the woman who has one. No one has the right to take away a life. . . ."

Tereza looked hard at the doctor, thinking that such things were easy to say and hard to hear.

"Sometimes you just can't help it. . . . I can't have a child; the Doctor doesn't want me to"—she lowered her voice to lie—"and I don't either."

It was not quite a lie: she wanted to, and she didn't. She wanted it with every fiber of her being, how wonderful that she wasn't sterile! Oh, to have a child that was hers and the Doctor's! But when she thought of the days to come, she no longer wanted it after all. How long could Dr. Emiliano's passion, the whim of a rich man, be expected to last? It might end at any moment; it had gone on a long time already. A mistress is for life's pleasures, for pleasure in bed. When the Doctor got tired of Tereza's arms and decided he wanted a change, all that would be left for her was Gabi's house. The door to the brothel was always open, and she would have to bring up her child in the red-light district, or rather, she would have to watch him grow up neglected and in want. Hand him over to some wretched woman poorer even than she was in exchange for a little money. Know that he would have to do without maternal affection—without *any* affection —without a father, seeing his mother only rarely, doomed before his life ever began. No, it wasn't worth it, no one had the right, Dr. Amarílio, to condemn an innocent child, one's own child, to a life of such misery. It was better to condemn him to death while there was time.

"I won't have a fatherless child. If you don't want to give me an abortion I'll find someone who will; there must be plenty in Estância. Tuca, our maid, has had I don't know how many abortions, practically one a month. I'll just talk to her. She knows all the angel-makers."

A fatherless child—poor Tereza. The doctor was afraid to take the responsibility for that.

"Don't get worked up about it, Tereza, there's no need to be in such a hurry. The Doctor's been gone a pretty long time, hasn't he? He'll be back before long. Let's wait until he gets here before we decide. What if he doesn't want you to have an abortion?"

She agreed to that, desiring nothing more than to hang on to that one shred of hope: oh, to have a child, a baby of her own, and joy of joys, a child of the Doctor's! Emiliano came a few days later, just at lunchtime; but he had missed Tereza so much that although the table was set he took his mistress to the bedroom and they began to play the jewel of games. He told her laughingly: All I'm hungry for is you, hungry and thirsty for my Tereza. He had never seen her so nervous, so intensely happy yet with a flicker of worry. When the first impetus was over and they were relaxing on the bed with his hand on her belly, the Doctor queried her:

"My Tereza has something to tell me, doesn't she?"

"Yes. I don't know how it happened, but I'm expecting . . . I'm so happy, I thought I could never have a child. It's wonderful."

A cloud fell over the Doctor's face, his hand became heavy on Tereza's stomach, and his blue eyes were a cold steel blade again. His silence lasted a few seconds, a universe of time, while Tereza's heart stopped beating.

"You'll have to get rid of it, darling." He rarely called her that, and the endearment was made even more tender by his voice, lowered to a whisper, not wanting to hurt her, but inflexible as steel. "I won't have a bastard child. I've told you why, don't you remember? It wasn't for that that I brought you to be here with me."

Tereza had known in her heart what his decision would be, but that did not make it any the less cruel to hear. A light went out inside her. When she spoke, she held back what was in her heart:

"Yes, I remember, and I think you're right. I've already told Dr. Amarílio that I want to have it out no matter what, but he asked me to wait until you got here to decide. For my part, I've already made up my mind."

So firm and intransigent, almost hostile, was her voice that the Doctor was taken aback.

"You've made up your mind that you don't want my child?"

Tereza stared at him in surprise. Why was he asking her that question when he had been the one who told her, when they first came to Estância, that he didn't want any byblows, that only wives could have children, that a mistress's bed was for making love in, that a mistress was a pastime? Couldn't he see that she was trying to control herself so that she could announce her decision in a steady voice, without her lips trembling? He could read Tereza like a book, inside and out. How could he not know, then, how much she wanted that child and what an effort it cost her to say she didn't?

"Why do you ask me such a thing? You know it isn't true. I'm going to take it out because I don't want any child of mine to go through what I went through. If things were different I wouldn't get rid of it, I'd have it, even if you didn't want me to."

Tereza moved the Doctor's heavy hand from her stomach, got up, and started for the bathroom. Emiliano sprang out of bed, caught her and brought her back. They stood nude and serious, face to face. The Doctor sat down in his reading chair with Tereza on his lap.

"Forgive me, Tereza, but it can't be any other way. I know how hard it is for you, but I can't help it; I have my principles and I told you so before. I never deceived you. I'm sorry too, but it can't be."

"I already knew that. It was Dr. Amarílio who said you might want it and I, like a fool . . ."

A dog whipped by its master, a hurt little thread of a voice, Tereza Batista sat on the Doctor's lap and thought that a mistress had no right to a baby. The Doctor realized how infinitely mournful and desolate she felt.

"I know what you're going through, Tereza, but unfortunately it just can't be any other way. I cannot, will not, have a bastard child. I wouldn't give him my name. You must be wondering if I wouldn't like to have a child who would be yours and mine. No, Tereza, I wouldn't. You are all I want, only you, and no one else. I won't tell you lies, not even consoling lies."

He paused for a moment, as though his next words were hard to say:

"Listen to me, Tereza, and then decide for yourself. I love you so much that I'm willing to let you have the child, if you insist, and to support it as long as I live— but I won't recognize it as mine, I won't give it my name, and our life together will come to an end. I want you, Tereza, by yourself, without a child or anyone else. But I don't want you upset, sad, hurt, or the wonderful life we've shared so far will be spoiled. You'll have to decide, Tereza, between me and the child. You'll lack for nothing, I promise you; the only thing you won't have is me."

Tereza did not hesitate. Putting her arms around the Doctor's neck she gave him her lips to kiss. She owed him more than her life; she owed him the joy of living.

"If I can't have you I don't want anything else."

Dr. Amarílio came over that evening and had a talk with Emiliano in the living room. Then the two of them joined Tereza in the garden, and the Doctor scheduled the minor operation for the next morning, right there in the house. But Dr. Amarílio, what has become of your weighty moral reservations and firm convictions? They've gone up in a puff of smoke, Tereza. A country doctor can't afford to have a point of view or strict principles. He's nothing but a medicine man who takes orders from the masters of life and death.

"Sleep well, Tereza, it's just a simple curettage, the simplest thing in the world."

Simple and sad, Dr. Amarílio. A quick womb today, a dead one tomorrow. The physician understood less

about women every day. Hadn't Tereza Batista gone to
him of her own accord to ask for an abortion, and hadn't
she said that if the doctor didn't do it she would find herself a quack, one of the numerous suppliers of angels
to the celestial court? So why that look of anguish, why
that sorrowful face? Because he had been Tereza's last
hope in her battle for the child; she had thought there
was a chance that the doctor's reservations and firm conviction that no one had the right to end another's life
might shake Dr. Emiliano's principles. She had been mad
to think so; she seemed to have forgotten the mill owner's
intransigence and his immutable rules of behavior. No
byblows, choose between the child and me. Good-bye
precious child I won't ever see, baby I wanted so much,
good-bye.

The simple operation took place without incident, and
Tereza only stayed in bed for a day, on the doctor's advice and Emiliano's insistence. He didn't leave her alone
for a minute; offered her tea, coffee, soft drinks, fruit,
hot chocolate, candy; read to her, taught her card tricks,
made her smile on that long, melancholy day.

In spite of repeated, urgent business calls from both
Aracaju and Bahia, the Doctor stayed for a whole week
with his mistress. He petted and fondled her, gave her
such loving care, such devotion, that Tereza's grief was
washed away and she felt repaid for her sacrifice, happy
to be alive, with no visible mark on her of what she had
suffered.

That was the Doctor—the whip and the rose.

20

Father Vinícius met João Nascimento Filho coming out
the garden gate, and they shook hands and spoke banal
words—"What a terrible thing, our friend looked so well
day before yesterday"; "Well, that's life, you never know
what tomorrow may bring"; "Only God, who knows all!"
—and Professor João went off down the still-dark street.
The priest went into the garden with the sexton, a sly,
skinny old man carrying the portable altar. The physician
came to meet him:

"Thank goodness you're here, Father, I was getting nervous."

"I had a time rousing Clerêncio out of bed, and then I had to go by the church."

Clerêncio ducked into the house; he had been chummy with Nina for years. From the orchard came the nocturnal sounds of crickets, frogs croaking, the hoot of an owl. The stars paled, the night wore on, the first signs of daybreak would soon appear. Father Vinícius lingered in the garden to have a talk with the doctor and make sure of what he had heard while he was still half asleep, when Dr. Amarílio had roused him to tell him the news.

"On top of her, you say?"

"Well, yes . . ."

"Good God, he died in mortal sin!"

"Father, if there was anything sinful about it we're all involved. We were friends of that couple, and we all knew how they lived."

"I fully agree with you, Doctor, but what could we do about it? Only God Almighty has the right to judge and pardon."

"Well, Father, if you want to know what I think, if the Doctor does go to Hell it won't be for what he did here."

They went into the dining room, where the sexton was being regaled by Nina's whispered gossip. Tereza sat in the bedroom in a chair beside the bed, absorbed in her own thoughts. She turned her head when she heard steps.

"My condolences, Tereza," said Father Vinícius. "Who could have dreamed this would happen so soon? But our lives are in God's hands. May He take pity on the Doctor and on us."

Oh, anything but pity, Father! The Doctor would be insulted if he heard you say that; he had a horror of pity.

Father Vinícius felt really bereft and sad. He had been fond of the Doctor, a too-powerful man but a cultivated and amiable one. His death had brought to an end the only civilized evenings in the parish, the pleasant chatter, the lively debates, the fine imported wines, the good company. He might go on celebrating mass at the sugarmill and baptizing children and marrying couples on St. Anne's Day, but it wouldn't be much fun without the

Doctor. He was fond of Tereza too; she was intelligent and discreet and deserved a better fate. Whose hands would she end up in now? There would be no lack of vultures croaking after her, aspirants to her empty bed. Some of them had money and social position, but none could be compared with the Doctor. If she stayed here, she would be passed on from one to another, debased in the hands of half a dozen bigwigs who had nothing to recommend them but their money. Maybe if she went south, where no one knew her, pretty and charming as she was, she might even get married. And why not? The fate of each one of us is in the hands of the Almighty. That of the Doctor was to die there in Estância in the mortal sin of intercourse with his mistress. Lord, have mercy on him. And on her.

The Doctor's sharp eyes were on Father Vinícius, the God-fearing priest racked with doubt; and they did not look like the eyes of a dead man. The physician was right: the Doctor's greatest sin had certainly not been that one. He was unbelieving, impious, pitiless when he thought he had to be, and armored in pride. Having seen him in the bosom of his family, the priest had perceived his loneliness and disillusionment and could understand just what Tereza meant to him—not just the attractive young mistress of an aging, wealthy man, but his friend, his balm and joy. On this great earth of God's, this flawed earth of Satan's, who can be sure of anything?

"God will be your strength, Tereza, in your tribulation."

The troubled eyes of the priest left the sharp eyes of the Doctor and wandered over the room. On the tables were books and many other objects, a silver dagger, for instance; on the wall was a painting showing naked sea nymphs. An enormous, shameless mirror reflected the bed. The dead man's hands held only a rose. The room was empty of the attributes of faith, a desert like Emiliano Guedes's heart; a room to his taste, devoid of funeral ornaments, and Tereza had left it that way. But Tereza, the family will be here any minute, and they're religious people who set great store by the formal trappings of their faith. Are we going to show them the corpse of the head of the family with no sign or symbol of Christianity? For he was a Christian, Tereza, even if one without faith.

He had mass said at the mill and attended himself with his wife, brothers, sisters-in-law, children and nephews, the mill employees and farmworkers, and people from a long way off. He would always stand at the head of them all, setting the example.

"Tereza, don't you think he should have lighted candles at his feet, at least?"

"All right, Father, just as you think best. Have them brought in if you want to."

Oh, Tereza, your lips won't ask for candles, your hands won't light them or put them there! You and your Doctor, both wells of pride, Lord have mercy on them! implored the priest, and called out:

"Clerêncio! Clerêncio! Come here! Bring candles and candlesticks."

"How many?"

The priest glanced at Tereza, again absorbed, distant, indifferent to the number of candles, hearing and feeling only the Doctor and death.

"Bring four."

The sexton hurried off in the shadows as the frogs croaked.

21

There was no mark on her that anyone could see, and except for the Doctor, no one ever perceived the faintest trace of resentment in Tereza's behavior. It was as though she had obliterated the incident from her memory. She and Emiliano never talked about it again. Once in a great while, though, Tereza's thoughts wandered, her gaze became abstracted, and the Doctor saw a shadow that was soon covered by a smile. Oh, what power that invisible being had, though he had never been a real presence but only one foreshadowed in the violated womb from which the physician's forceps had torn him at the mill owner's command.

Never before had Emiliano Guedes been conscious of having committed a villainy. The bloody battles he'd fought in and led, the injustices, outrages, and acts of violence he'd committed, the questionable and reprehen-

sible acts he had been guilty of were without number, but
none had caused him one moment of remorse; he hadn't
remembered them long enough to feel guilty at having
done them or ordered them done. He had to do them; all
were necessary and therefore justified. And in this other
matter of the abortion, what he had done had been in
the interests of the Guedes family and his, Emiliano's,
own convenience, both sacrosanct and completely legitimate claims about which scruples were absurd. Why the
devil, then, did an unformed fetus goad at his memory in
this persistent, uncomfortable way?

Tereza stayed in bed, dry and empty inside, and the
Doctor outdid himself in little attentions until he made
her smile and cajoled her out of her disconsolate mood.
That shadowed, hollow day marked the beginning of a
subtle change in the relationship between the two lovers,
a change imperceptible both to strangers and to intimate
friends: Tereza Batista stopped being to Dr. Emiliano
Guedes a plaything, an expensive diversion, a source of
pleasure, the pastime of a rich old man with a passion for
books and good wine, of a grandee who had taken a notion to transform an untutored backwoods girl, a diamond
in the rough, into a perfect lady with polished manners,
refinement, taste, and elegance. In lovemaking, too, he
had led her from the violent explosion of instinct to the
artfulness of prolonged caresses, the quintessential refinement of pleasure enjoyed to the full every moment, the
discovery and mastery of the infinite gamut of voluptuous
sensation. He had made of Tereza both a remarkably
skilled bedfellow and a true lady. It was a fascinating
pastime but a pastime, a whim and nothing more.

Until that day of ashes, Tereza had thought first and
foremost of her debt to the Doctor. Gratitude occupied a
preponderant place among the feelings that bound her to
the mill owner. He had got her out of jail, had gone in
person to rescue her from the filthy room at the brothel,
made her his mistress, and treated her as if she were
somebody, a real person. He was kind and he was interested in her. He had given her warmth, tenderness,
time, and attention, lifting her out of her humiliation and
indifference to her own fate and teaching her to love life.
For Tereza the Doctor was a saint, a god, someone so far
above everyone else that she was shy before him. She

wasn't his equal, nor was anyone else. Only when they were in bed and she went weak with pleasure was he a man of flesh and blood to her, and even then he was superior to other men in both giving and taking. Whether measured by sentiments or by the senses, the man who could be compared with him simply did not exist.

But when she made her choice between the Doctor and the life swelling her womb, Tereza liquidated all her old debt without realizing it. She could not, did not, hesitate in that cruel, cold moment when she gave up her child and sentenced him to death. In an instant she had to weigh two things of supreme value. She placed woman's love above mother's love, and certainly gratitude played an important part in her choice. Without even knowing it, she paid off her old debt and by so doing won unlimited credit with her lover. They were far closer from then on, and everything was easier.

The Doctor knew that material concerns had not weighed in the decision, for he had promised to support Tereza and the child in comfort and free her at the same time from all duties and commitments. You and the baby will have everything you need as long as I live. The only thing he won't have is my name, and the only thing you won't have is me. Money meant little to her, he knew. Emiliano had to be sure his mistress lacked for nothing since she never asked for anything, never took anything as her due, and never took advantage of his generosity. In the six years of their liaison, Tereza never acted out of mercenary motives, and if she had some money in her purse when she went away it was only by chance. The day before the Doctor died he had given her too much, as he always did, for household expenses and for herself. She had practically no personal expenses; the Doctor brought her everything she could possibly need: stylish dresses, shoes, face cream, perfume, costume jewelry, boxes of chocolate candy to share with the neighborhood children.

Not that Tereza was stupidly indifferent to good and pleasant things money could buy. On the contrary, since she was intelligent, with a mind like quicksilver, she cherished and appreciated fine things at their true worth. It was just that she was not indolent, mercenary, or a slave to comfort. Certain presents, such as a music box, for instance, with a tiny ballerina dancing to the strains of a waltz, thrilled her. She prized each object, each gift, each memento, but she knew she could do without them; tenderness, warmth, constant attention, sweet friendship, and love were all that she would really miss. If she chose her lover when she had to make the choice, she did so because he occupied a place in her heart far above all the other good things of life, even a child: If I can't have you, I don't want anything else.

The day after the abortion, the doctor told Tereza she could get up and walk in the garden, but advised her to let her mind and body rest.

"Now don't you start working, comadre, don't overdo and don't let anything bother you." He called her comadre to buck her up a little and show that he was fond of her. "I want to see you strong and well."

"Don't worry, doctor, I feel just fine. I'm not such a softy as you think. I'm perfectly all right, believe me."

Touched by Tereza's bravery and wanting to hasten her complete convalescence in any way he could, Dr. Amarílio gave Emiliano what he thought was good advice as he took his leave at the garden gate:

"Next time you go to Bahia why don't you bring Tereza one of those great big dolls that talk and walk? It would kind of make it up to her."

"Amarílio, do you really think a doll can make up for a baby? I don't. I'll bring her lots of things, all the pretty things I see, but not a doll. Tereza isn't only young and pretty, my dear fellow, she's sensitive and intelligent too. She's a young girl only in years; emotionally she's a grown woman who has lived enough to have character; she's just given proof of it. No, Amarílio, I would certainly not please Tereza by bringing her a doll. If a doll could take the place of a child, everything would be easy in this world."

"Well, maybe you're right. I'll come back to see her tomorrow. So long, Doctor."

From the gate Emiliano watched the doctor turn the corner, his black bag in his hand. What Tereza had lost, Amarílio, what I took away from her by force, with a trick, by putting her between the devil and the deep blue sea, can only be made up for by kindness, affection, fond

words and tenderness, friendship. It takes love to pay
that kind of debt.

Fond words, affection, kindness, gifts, and money, certainly, are common currency between lovers. But love,
Emiliano? Since when?

22

The sexton lit the candles, two tall candlesticks at the foot
of the bed and two at the head. He crossed himself and
mumbled a prayer as he came in, his libidinous old eyes
on Tereza, thinking what she must have looked like when
the Doctor died, sperm and blood in her belly at the same
time. Had she come too? Probably not; the kind of woman
who takes up with an old man learns how to playact
in bed to deceive the old fools. They save all their fire
for the others, their loverboys, the young ones.

Nina was hardly the kind to absolve anyone, quite the
contrary; and yet she swore the woman was honest as
far as anyone knew and never opened the door to a
stranger or had a lover on the sly. Probably because she
was afraid of being punished; those Guedeses were a
bunch of tyrants. Or because she didn't want to spoil a
good thing when she had it: her comfort, her luxury, the
fat little nest-egg she was no doubt putting aside. Maybe
she was honest, but you couldn't be sure. Those sharp
ones could fool God and the Devil when they put their
minds to it, and they could certainly fool a doting old
man and an ignorant servant.

The sexton's eyes slid from Tereza to Father Vinícius.
The padre, maybe? It was true that he, Clerêncio, the
always watchful sexton, had never caught the padre out,
never seen his foot or his cassock slip. The late Father
Freitas had been a horse of another color. At home he
had his goddaughter, a luscious little piece and outside
his own house he ran after every woman he saw. Those
were happy days for the sexton, when he had acted as
go-between and had access to all the hussies he could
handle. Father Vinícius, young, athletic, with his free
tongue and limited patience with over-pious old women,
had never given occasion for remarks despite the pious old

crones' unsleeping vigilance in sniffing out suspicious females. All his pride and virtue, however, had not kept the priest away from the house where that woman lived —that den of iniquity, that dwelling place of sin—nor from stuffing his belly there with rich food and wine. Only his belly? Maybe. There's one of everything in this crazy world, even virgin priests. All the same, Clerêncio wouldn't be at all surprised to learn that the padre and that woman fed the swallow and the tanager, as the saying went. Put a tart and a padre together and they both went straight to Hell, as Clerêncio, sexton and whoremaster, ought to know.

Tereza sat in the chair by the bed, absorbed in her own thoughts. Clerêncio threw her one last glance: what a nice piece of meat. What fun he could have with her. Not tonight, though, when she was full of death. The sexton shuddered: what a filthy dame. He made the sign of the cross, as did the priest, and the two went out, Clerêncio to continue his interesting chat with Nina and Lula, the priest to wait for the Guedes family in the garden.

Dawn broke in a flurry of rain. It was still night in the bedroom, where the four foolish candles burned with a low, guttering flame and Tereza and the Doctor were equally motionless and silent.

23

Gradually people began to see them on the streets by day. At first it was only in the morning, when they went to swim in the river, a source of great pleasure to the Doctor. After he had installed his mistress in Estância, the planter began to take a dip nearly every day in the pool at the Golden Falls on the Piauitinga River. Alone or with João Nascimento Filho, off he would go to the river, early in the morning.

"These swims are the healthiest thing in the world, Professor João."

The Doctor returned from his first trip after the abortion with a thousand gifts for Tereza, among them a bathing suit:

"So we can go and swim in the river."

"Both of us? Together?" Tereza asked hesitantly.

"Yes, Honeycomb, together."

They crossed Estância on their way to the river, Tereza with her bathing suit on under her dress, the Doctor with a jock strap on under his trousers. Despite the early hour, the laundresses were already beating clothes on the flat stones on the riverbank, their chewing tobacco in their cheeks. Tereza and the Doctor stepped under the hard shower of the Golden Falls, a beautiful little cascade. The place was enchantingly lovely. Rippling over pebbles, shaded by enormous trees, the river opened out farther on in a great clear pool. After their shower they would go there, picking their way among the garments the washerwomen had laid out to dry.

At its deepest point the water came up to the Doctor's shoulders. Holding out his arms to Tereza, he supported her on the surface and taught her how to swim. As the water eddied around them they played games, their laughter pealed out, they kissed under water; the Doctor dived down and caught her by the waist, his other hand in her bosom or impudently inside her bathing suit, a strange fish escaping from his trunks. It was a prelude to lovemaking, desire kindled as they swam in the Piauitinga River. Once at home again, they completed the morning's sunny beginnings in bath and then bed. Alas, those mornings in Estância would never come again.

At first they aroused the general curiosity. The windows were full of old maids decrying the unwelcome change in the Doctor's attitude. Prudent and respectable at first, he had lost his discretion as time went by, playing the clown to satisfy his young mistress's whims. What else did the shameless thing want but to flaunt her rich lover in the townspeople's faces, with no respect for family decency? What shameless immorality to go swimming in the river, the Doctor with practically nothing on. They might as well go to it right there in front of the washerwomen and be done with it. No, not in front of the washerwomen; they couldn't see that far. But they had "gone to it" more than once, Tereza straddling the Doctor, in great haste and fearful that someone would show up any minute—how embarrassing, how lovely! At any rate, the gossips would never have believed that Tereza had held back a little the first time he invited her to go for a swim.

"Together? People will talk, they'll meddle in your private life."

"Let them talk, Honeycomb." Taking her by the hands he added: "That time is gone by. . . ."

What time was that? The first phase of mistrustfulness, of shyness when they were virtual strangers to each other, each guessing what the other was like but still unsure, unbending only in bed and not entirely even then: she giving herself violently in her hunger for affection, he guiding her patiently, little by little? That was the testing time, when Alfredão followed her in the street, overheard her talk and repeated what she said to the Doctor, kept watch at the door and ran off would-be wooers and gossips. At that time Tereza stayed concealed in the garden or the orchard or inside the house, afraid that the Doctor would hold her accountable for each little gesture. Although he treated her courteously and kindly, giving her much attention and increasing affection, she still felt that there were walls and prison bars in that dawning relationship. It was not so much that Tereza's circumspection and the Doctor's sense of what was fitting imposed limitations; the walls were inside them. Tereza was still confused, withdrawn, fearful, and her actions showed how heavily the recollection of the recent past weighed on her mind. The Doctor had discerned in the girl all the necessary raw materials—beauty, intelligence, character, that flame in her black eyes—to the formation of the ideal mistress; a diamond in the rough to be polished, a child to be transformed into a woman. This would be a fascinating distraction, and he was willing to spend time, money and patience on it, but he did not yet feel anything for Tereza but the kind of pleasure an absorbing pastime can give, and passion—the intense, uncontrollable, boundless desire of an old man for a girl. It was a seed time, testing time, a time of walls and iron bars, a hard road to travel.

Which time did he mean? The time when seeds sprouted and laughter rang out? When voluptuousness was tempered with affection, when there were no more tests and the Doctor knew her for an honest woman, worthy of his trust and respect, not only of his interest; when Tereza's doubts were laid to rest and she gave herself unstintingly, body and soul, seeing in the Doctor a god and therefore prostrate at his feet, his lover but not his equal? That was a time of caution and discretion. They went out together occasionally but only at night after dinner, and then took rarely used paths; and only Dr. Amarílio, João Nascimento Filho, and Lulu Santos, their first friend, were invited to the house.

Both of those times ended and another began on the day of ashes and death but not of loneliness. That was the day when either everything would come to an end or the love that was latent would triumphantly burst forth, built on all of their former feelings commingled, transformed into the only thing that was really valuable and eternal.

The Doctor started coming to Estância twice as often as before and staying longer, until that was the house in which he spent most of his time. He began to receive people there, not only friends for dinners, lunches, and evenings of conversation, but important people from the city: the Judge, the Mayor, the parish priest, the District Attorney, and the Commissioner of Police. Finally, he began to summon agents from the Interstate Bank and Eximportex S.A. to Estância to discuss business and settle matters that were pending.

By then Tereza was no longer the awkward farm girl fresh out of jail and the brothel, marked with a branding iron inside and out. The marks were fading; under the Doctor's kind treatment she grew in beauty, elegance, and grace and blossomed into a woman in the splendor of her youth. Withdrawn before, she was again the laughing, open girl she had been; oppressed and wary before, she was happy again.

That was the time of love, when each became indispensable to the other: the love of a god, of a knight errant, of a superhuman being, of a lord, and a country girl, a farm wench elevated to mistress, a young girl cultivated and polished and deeply, passionately in love.

For Emiliano, each parting was harder than the last; for Tereza, the days of waiting seemed longer and longer. Several months before the Doctor's death, one of the bank executives summed up the situation for his close friends and colleagues on the board:

"The way things are going, we'll have to move the head office from Bahia to Estância one of these days."

24

When the Doctor was alive and had that whip in his hand, lieutenant, who'd have had the nerve? Nobody I know has that kind of guts—not even in this whole big fairground where the competition gets worse every day—cram full of folks from the biggest tribe in the Northeast, the tribe of them that makes up ballads and sings 'em. With everybody and his dog writing songs, it sure is getting hard to make a living, captain. You ain't a captain, sir? Well, pardon me, major, you had me fooled. You ain't a major either? You ain't a military man at all? Just a plain civilian? Well I'm glad to hear it, but don't let the word get around. If somebody wants to dress you up in a uniform and put stripes on the sleeves, you just salute, sit back, and enjoy it.

Somehow nobody could make up verses about the live Doctor. You may be pretty brave when a ballad's cookin' in your head and you're prettifyin' up what happened, but all the same there ain't many as likes to be whipped on the face or wants to eat their songs, even with salt and pepper on 'em. A guitar's a fine thing to swing around at parties, but it ain't nothin' to fight a whip with, or a knife or a pistol either. As long as the silver on that whip was still a-flashin' down the roads out back or down the avenue in Bahia—the biggest and best capital in all the Brazils, that is—there weren't no fool crazy enough to go around singin' about the Doctor and his lady-friend. There weren't nobody man enough for that. With him alive I'd just like to have seen the kind of he-man could rhyme beds with Guedes. Or bed with dead.

But when all that happened the news went like lightnin' from one mouth to the next and everybody who could pick a string made a grab for his guitar. Nobody'd had such a ready-made, sure-fire handle to hang a dirty song on in nobody could remember when. All the way from Bahia to Ceará—which is as far as you can get in this world and not fall off—all you heard was:

> The old goat croaked
> on top of his whore
> beggin' for more.

Well, Mr. Congressman, what do you think the Doctor would have done if he could have heard folks callin' him a billy?

How did the tale get round, you ask? How did we know all the ins and outs, you might say? Who was it told us? Well, lots of folks knew. There was the doctor and the padre and the sexton, and the people who worked in the house—none of 'em told us, and yet you might say all of 'em did. Things like that always get around. It ain't a speck of use doin' everything private like, with the corpse laid out and the dead watch all done at home; ain't no use pretendin' a feller died sayin' his prayers and tryin' to fool folks. It don't take many hints to make up a song. You gets the main idea and then you just sort of makes up things to suit the rhymes as you go along.

There were plenty more ballads made up besides those three you told me you'd heard, Mr. Senator. One from *Paríba* was called "The Millionaire Who Died Fuckin' a Virgin." You can tell by the name, chief, that the feller heard the cock crow all right but didn't exactly know where. Why the Doctor isn't even called by his right name —just rich man, millionaire, John Doe, so-and-so. But I wonder how in tarnation a feller out in Campina Grande ever found out Tereza's whole name? Funny, ain't it? Now a dirtier song than that one I don't think I ever did hear, and I've made up some pretty green ones myself in my time. I tell you, Mr. Councilman, I never knew there was so many fuckin' four-letter words. Your Excellency ain't a politician? Not even a city councilman or a senator? Not even runnin' for senator? Well, now, I call that a real shame. You can always count on a politician's spreadin' a little cash around. And that ain't so surprisin', I guess, seein' as how the money they spend ain't theirs but ours.

If Toninho at the bookstore can't get you a copy of "The Tale of the Old Man Who Died When He Came with the Mulata," there's nobody can, for love or money. Heliodoro the blind man made that one up and sang it in Aracaju. He don't put many bad words in it—it's all *pretty and rhymed real nice—but he don't leave out nothin' at all about what they was doin' before he up and kicked off. It's all there so plain you'll run out and grab the first skirt you see and start gettin' your money's worth. He even makes the way the old man died so nice and pitiful you'll want to go the same way. Heliodoro's blind, but he sure sees plenty. Why, you can't believe he wasn't there helpin' 'em when it happened.*

But if you have to miss that one, maybe Toninho can get hold of a few that came out here in Bahia. Maybe "The Old Man Who Did the Right Thing at the Wrong Time"; *that's by a young feller just startin' out in this business and you can tell it the way it don't bump along smooth and it don't rhyme too good. Or the one Master-Singer Possidônio from Alagoas did.* "The Death of the Master on Top of the Maid." *He rhymes good but somehow or other he don't quite hit it off in this one. He's got everything all wrong—the Doctor's a mean son of a bitch of a boss and Tereza's an easy piece; and he's got the boss's wife puttin' her oar in too. She turns up at what ain't a good time and the old man gets such a scare he turns up his toes and dies. I tell you, I don't know what's got into Possidônio that he'd get such a bunch of foolishness in his noodle as that stuff. And he goes on to make a woodcut for it where the Doctor gets him a long billy-goat beard and Tereza's hair is all kinky. I tell you the Doctor's family spent a fortune buyin' up every copy of them two ballads they could lay hands on, but of course the fellers who wrote 'em ain't so dumb they didn't stash away some to sell later on, one at a time. They ain't really worth foolin' with, though. Don't get your stick up and don't make you laugh, neither.*

But I was the one had the bad luck. My ballad called all the spades spades and I didn't stick just to what happened to the Doctor; I rattled all the bones in the Guedeses' closets—horns on the husbands' heads, hot checks, stolen cash, smugglin'; I put in the son and the daughter and the son's wife and everybody else interestin' I could think of. Mine was a whole collection of ballads—a whole family history, you might say. Well, it didn't come as no great big surprise when I got thrown in the clink, but what hurt was havin' to sell all the copies I had for nothin' before they'd let me out. The smart law-

*yer them Guedeses had, and the chief of police, too,
wouldn't take no to bringin' me clear home, and between
the two of 'em they even spotted a few copies I'd hidden
under the mattress just to sell to good friends like you, sir.
And danged if they didn't tear 'em up and take the pieces
off with 'em. They told me they'd stick me right back in
jail again and beat me up too if any more got around. A
songwriter sure leads a dangerous life!*

*What I'm gettin' at is, if you really want to read "The
Doctor's Last Fuck: Death at the Zero Hour," you'll have
to pay me what it costs, plus the risks I'm takin' by sellin'
it to you. If you can pry yourself loose from five hundred
cruzeiros I just might be able to find you a copy—the
very last one. And I'm not lettin' you have it because of
the money. No, sir; it's because I took a kind of shine to
you right off the bat. Now in my song you'll get the whole
story straight, just like it happened. I didn't waste time
with a lot of crap. There's no stuff about how the Doctor
sold his soul to the Devil, or how poor Tereza went crazy
and drowned herself in the river. Some folks say that's
how it was, but I don't. I just tell the truth and nothin'
but the truth: that it was God's own blessin' for the Doctor to die that way but sure 'nuff hard on Tereza. She's
the one got left holdin' the bag.*

*And that's what I wrote 'cause that's what I thought
and that's how I figured it out. I, Cuíca Santo Amaro the
Great, Mr. A Number One, takin' my stand here in
front of the Lacerda elevator, in my frock coat and my
top hat, peddlin' what's in my head and my heart and my
song.*

25

"Gee, that guy looks like Dr. Emiliano Guedes! He's
enough like him to be his twin brother," marveled Valério
Gama, a storekeeper in Itabuna who had emigrated
from Estância when he was a young lad and now, prosperous and fortyish, was back in town to visit his
relatives.

"It's not his twin brother, it's himself, out walking with
his honorable concubine." Loose-tongued Cousin Dadá

was always up on the latest news. "The Doctor's been keeping a mistress here for several years; quite an honor for our little town."

"No kidding!"

"Haven't you ever heard that the waters of the Piauitinga are a miraculous restorer of potency, Cousin Valério? Old men grow young again here." She had a dirty mouth but not a vicious one; Estância was a hospitable, complaisant town where even the old gossips looked on lovers and love affairs with indulgence.

The city slicker quickened his pace to see for himself whether the incredible piece of news his busybody cousin had told him could be true. The Doctor and Tereza walked slowly up the street, enjoying the afternoon breeze. When he came close enough to recognize them, the shopowner's mouth fell open: good Lord, his cousin hadn't made it up, it really was Dr. Emiliano Guedes and not his double, and with him was an appetizing young lady, obviously quite at home in the streets of Estância. Confused and agape, he raised his hand to his hat to greet the banker. The doctor responded to the greeting:

"Hello there, Valério Gama, back for a look at your hometown?" Emiliano never forgot the faces and names of persons with whom he had had any kind of dealings, and Valério was a client of his bank.

"Yes, Doctor, at your service here and in Itabuna."

He looked so foolish that Tereza smiled and remarked on it after he was out of earshot:

"I'm the ghost. Valério had never seen me before except in the bank, wearing a necktie and talking business, and when he came face to face with me in Estância, strolling down the street in a sports shirt with a beautiful woman at my side, it was just too much for him—even for a sophisticated shopkeeper from Itabuna. He'll have a story to tell when he goes back."

"Maybe it would be better if you didn't go around with me so much. . . ."

"Don't be silly, Honeycomb. I'm not about to give up the pleasure of going out walking with you because A or B has something to say about it. I don't care what they say; it simply doesn't interest me. After all, Tereza, they only talk out of envy because you belong to me. If I really wanted to make everyone die of envy I'd take you with me to Bahia or Rio; then there'd really be a commotion!" He laughed and shook his head. "But I'm too selfish to go around showing off anything I really prize, whether it's a thing or a person. I want to keep them all to myself."

He offered Tereza his hand to help her step down from the sidewalk.

"The truth is that I'm being unfair to you by keeping you here in Estância, so isolated behind the walls of a mansion, almost a prisoner. That's the truth, isn't it, Tereza?"

"No, it isn't. I'm happy here. I have everything I want."

Take her out in the world and show her off? For the love of God don't do it, Doctor! The Captain liked to make other men envious by showing off his fighting cocks, his saddle horses, his German pistol, and his necklace of maidenheads. He had taken Tereza to the cockfight to see the foul covetous light come into the eyes of his cronies. But how could the Doctor resemble the Captain in any way?

"I want you all to myself."

Having friends in to dinner, swimming in the Pi-auitinga, the evening stroll or short walk after dinner, the bridge over the Piaui, the port with its ferryboats—that was more than enough for her, and even if she had had to stay shut up in the house she wouldn't have cared. To hear him say that he wanted her exclusively for himself made up for any restrictions in her way of life.

More than once they had planned to take an excursion to some nearby place: take a ferryboat to the delta of the Real, the river that divides Bahia from Sergipe, where they could have seen the sand dunes and the ocean waves breaking on Dry Mangrove Beach, or to visit the fishing village of Saco. But in the end they had never gone. Tereza had never seen the ocean in those days, and though she would have dearly loved to go, she never reminded him of the promise; it didn't really matter. The presence of the Doctor was enough—to have him at home, to talk, laugh, and learn with him, to walk in the street with him, to lie down with him, ah! to lie with him!

Since the Doctor had so little free time, and the time he spent with Tereza was always time stolen from the mill, from the bank, from his business, and family, they almost always spent it alone, hidden away in the mansion. To the Doctor it was a restful pause in his busy routine; to Tereza, it was her life.

The town was now accustomed to the Doctor's continual comings and goings—the scandalous bathing slip he swam in, the flower in his hand, the way he would stand with his mistress in front of some old house or talk with her in Triste Park or hang over the railing of the bridge with her, indifferent to spiteful tongues. Yes, the Doctor had lost all sense of decorum. A rich man, as everyone knows, has a perfect right to set his mistress up in a house and open charge accounts for her—in fact, he almost has an obligation to do so—but if he's married, it isn't the thing for him to flaunt his lady friend in public in defiance of local mores. Great wealth should be kept at home, not ostentatiously flaunted.

As the years went by and the affair ceased to be a novelty, the spiteful tongues lost most of their venom. The volume was turned up again only when the prodigal son returned. Then the once-exciting, now well-worn theme of a thousand conversations and gossip-fests was dusted off again: Dr. Emiliano Guedes and his beautiful, public mistress. The excellent Dadá patriotically lauded the merits and virtues of Estância, its flowery fields and its starry skies, its mad, shameless moon, its generous, tolerant people—the perfect place for a clandestine idyll.

"Don't ask me, cousin, ask Major Atílio. He was at his last gasp when he came here, just a crippled old man, hadn't looked at a woman in years, didn't even remember what one looked like with her clothes off. Well, what with Estância's air and the Piauitinga's water, in less than a month he took himself a girl to live with him and sired himself a son. You ask him; he'll tell anybody who wants to know. The Doctor's girl got pregnant too, but she got rid of hers. I tell you, cousin, Estância water works miracles!"

"Cousin Dadá, the Doctor's girl doesn't need any miracles. One look at her would make a dead man rise out of his grave."

26

The Doctor's wide-open eyes seemed to sparkle with mischief in the mean light of the candle as though they could read Tereza's thoughts. It took no miracle water from the Piauitinga River, no herbs, no answer-stick, no billygoat-beard. All it took was one look, a smile, a gesture, a touch, a knee showing, and they were soon playing the best game of all. In fact, that was how they spent most of the all-too-brief leisure time the banker could spend in Estância.

Emiliano, don't look at me like that; I don't want to remember our lovely games on the night of your death. And why not, Tereza? Where did I die if not in your arms, coming inside of you, loving you? We didn't live two different kinds of love, you know, one for our senses and one for our sentiments; we had just one tender, voluptuous love. If you don't want to remember, I will; I, Emiliano Guedes, past master in the art of pleasure, squeezing pleasure even out of death.

The same mischievous eyes, the same provocative look he used to give her when he showed her the tip of his tongue at a table full of friends at dinner. Ever since that night when they had stood in the doorway of Gabi's house for a moment before he swung her up on his horse's croup, he had been able to make her feel all the weight of his authority simply by opening her lips with the tip of his tongue: when she saw it, even at a distance, Tereza felt as if it were penetrating her inmost being. Everything about Emiliano was precise and orderly, and every step on the road to perfection in lovemaking became a landmark to go back to some other time.

In front of solemn visitors—the Mayor, His Honor the Judge, the District Attorney—the Doctor would scratch the nape of Tereza's neck in an apparently innocent way, and she would have to get a grip on herself to keep from moaning with pleasure at the touch of those lascivious cat's claws. Or he would glance obliquely at her neckline to catch a glimpse of her bosom. One night they were conversing in the garden, where the lights had been dimmed at the behest of the Doctor, so that the moon and stars could be seen. Dinner was over and a heated political argument was in progress between Lulu Santos and the doctor. João Nascimento Filho had said what a beautiful night it was and Father Vinícius had praised the Lord's generosity in creating so much beauty to rejoice the hearts of men on earth. Tereza sat under the cashew tree listening. The Doctor went over to her and bent down in front of her, concealing her from the view of the others. Pretending to give her a sip of brandy from his snifter, he opened her dress and looked at the dark, firm breasts which were perhaps Tereza's loveliest ornament. The loveliest? What about her derrière? Ah, her derrière!

No, Emiliano, don't remind me of such things. Take your naughty eyes off me and let's remember something else. Our whole love affair was idyllic; there's more than enough for us to think about without that. Honeycomb, don't be silly; our love affair was born and died in bed. Just a little while ago, when you were getting me ready for the inevitable meeting with solemnity the death of a *prócer* implies, what were you reminded of when you smelled that men's cologne? Oh, Emiliano, those memories, those aromas, those joys are all over for me. No, Tereza, joy and pleasure are my legacy to you, the only one; I wasn't given time to do more.

Before they had been in Estância very long, though the renovations in the house had been finished and the new bathrooms installed, the Doctor initiated Tereza into the pleasures of bathing, with bath salts and fragrant oils. In the morning it was a brisk showerbath or a swim in the river. At the end of the afternoon or at night, it was the languor of a perfumed bath in warm water. With so many bottles of perfume to choose from, Tereza, who knew no scent but the cheap, strong L'Origan-de-Coty of the whorehouse, had noticed that the Doctor's preference was for a bottle of foreign cologne. Emiliano invariably used that dry, woodsy fragrance after bathing or shaving.

To please him one day, after their evening bath, Tereza picked up the bottle, drenched herself with her lover's cologne and went over to him as he was lying on the bed. Emiliano got up when he saw her coming, and when he smelled the perfume she had splashed on herself he laughed his broad, intoxicating laugh:

"Tereza, what have you done? That's a man's perfume."

"Well, I noticed that it was your favorite, so I thought . . ."

The Doctor turned the slender girl with her pert derrière and her still not quite finished body and held her against himself with her back to him. From the roots of her hair to her toes, from the rose in front to the cruciform gilliflower behind, Tereza's whole body was the Doctor's possession, land of his tillage.

In time Tereza learned all about perfumes and how to use them. When the Doctor shaved it was she who dabbed the cologne on his face, his moustache, and the white hair of his chest. She loved to breathe in that dry, masculine, woodsy scent. Once in a while he would take the bottle from his friend's hand and put a drop on her neck and then turn her about, feeling the quiver of her hips. Each gesture, each word, each look, each scent had its own value.

Oh, Emiliano, don't remind me of those moments now. Let death settle in my womb, before I start gleaning your rich legacy of pleasure and joy.

27

Sometimes the Doctor would tell Tereza a piece of gossip in which they both figured and they would laugh over it together.

The gossips' circle had transformed a mirror on the bedroom wall into a boudoir lined with mirrors hung there for erotic purposes. It was true that the mirror reflected the bed, the naked bodies, the caresses; the Doctor had chosen a large one on purpose and had hung it in the right place. But the sharp-tongued old wives had multiplied that one mirror into dozens. The classes Tereza gave to the children who lived on the same block gave rise to sensational news: about to be abandoned by the plantation owner, Tereza was preparing to earn her living as a primary-school teacher. The gossips, without seeing the contradiction, immediately began to discuss the names of possible wealthy candidates to the Doctor's place in the arms of his mistress when the inevitable happened and he finally got tired of her.

Playfully accusing him of spying on her, Tereza asked Emiliano how he managed to know all these things when he was away from Estância most of the time. Alfredão had long since returned to the sugarmill, but the Doctor still seemed to hear all the gossip.

"Tereza, I know everything about all the people who interest me. Not only about you, Honeycomb. I know all about my family, all about what they're doing and thinking, even when I say nothing and pretend I don't know anything about it."

Was there a trace of bitterness in Emiliano's voice? Tereza tried to make him forget his worries, his business deals, and his bitterness by pretending to be afraid and make him laugh:

"You're picking out so many candidates for me, Doctor, anyone would think you wanted to get rid of me."

"Don't say that, Honeycomb, not even as a joke; I won't let you." He kissed her eyes. "You don't even realize how much I would miss you if you ever went away. Sometimes I worry that you may get tired of living here, always so alone, in this narrow, sad, limited life."

Tereza's derisive voice became serious:

"I don't think my life is sad."

"Don't you, Tereza?"

"It isn't as if I had nothing to do when you're not here: there's the house, and the children, and my lessons, and I try out recipes in the kitchen to fix when you come back, I listen to the radio and learn the songs; I really don't have a free minute. . . ."

"Not even to think of me?"

"I think of you all day long. When you're away for too long, then I *am* sad. That's the only sad part of my life, but I know it can't be any other way."

"Would you like me to stay here always, Tereza?"

"I know you can't, so what's the use of wanting it? I don't think about that; I just try to be happy with what I have."

"Is what I give you too little, Tereza? Is there anything you need? Why don't you ever ask me for anything?"

"Because I don't like to ask for things and because there's nothing I need. You give me too much; I don't know what to do with it all. You know that's not what I meant."

"Yes, Tereza, I know. And do you know that it makes me unhappy too, to be coming and going like this? Listen, Honeycomb: I don't think I could ever get used to being without you. When I'm away from you I can think of only one thing: coming back."

Six years, a lifetime, so many things to remember. So many? Almost nothing, really; that is, nothing grave or dramatic, no sensational episode worthy of a page in a novel; just life flowing peacefully by.

"My life would make a marvelous novel, if it were only written down," asserted Fausta, dressmaker and emissary of the ladies of Estância, with pathos in her voice.

Not so Tereza's life in Estância; it was too calm and happy for the pages of a novel. At the most it would have done for a love song, a romanza. When the Doctor was away there were a thousand little duties to fill the time of waiting; when he was there, it was pure joy. Theirs was a lovers' idyll in which nothing much happened worth the telling, at least on the surface. One day Tereza, laughing impishly, showed the Doctor some verses composed and sent to her by the poet Amintas Rufo, the inspired bard who sold cloth by the yard in the drygoods store of his father, the bourgeois with no ideals.

'I have something to show you, Doctor, if you'll promise not to get mad. I've been saving it for you to look at."

An envelope full of saccharine doggerel had come in the mail addressed to Dona Tereza Batista, Rua José de Dome, no. 7. At the bottom of the second page were the signature and titles of its author: Amintas Flávio Rufo, poet and doomed lover. The Doctor, his head on Tereza's lap, read the cloth salesman's stanzas.

"You deserve better, Honeycomb."

"Well, there are some pretty verses in it. . . ."

"Pretty? Do you think so? Well, if someone thinks a thing is pretty, then it is. Which doesn't keep it from being bad. But these verses are really too bad. What a piece of foolishness." He returned the carefully handwritten pages to her. "Later on, Tereza, we'll take a little walk, go into the store where your poet works—"

"You promised you wouldn't get mad—"

"I'm not mad. But you're going to give him back his poems so he won't do the same trick again."

Tereza said thoughtfully, with the pages in her hand:

"No, Doctor, I won't do that. What harm has that boy done? He didn't send me a letter or a note, he didn't ask me to be his sweetheart or to sleep with him; he hasn't insulted me in any way. Why should I go there in person to give him back the poem? And with you, Doctor, it would be even worse—I'd be insulting him and you'd be threatening him, right there in the store in front of everybody. It wouldn't look well for me or for you, Doctor."

"I'll tell you why. If we don't clip the idiot's wings right now he'll do something more impudent, and I won't have anyone annoying you. Or do you prize those verses so much you want to keep them?"

"I told you I thought they were pretty and I do; why should I lie to you? I don't know enough to tell glitter from gold. But I also told you I only kept them to show you. I'll send them back to him in the mail the way they came to me; that way I won't be offending someone who hasn't offended me."

Free of any trace of irritation, Emiliano Guedes smiled:

"That's perfect, Tereza; you have a better head than I do. I'll never learn to control my temper. You're right —leave the poet in peace, poor devil. I wanted to go to the store to humiliate the poor fellow, but I would have been humiliating myself."

He called out to Lula to bring ice and drinks.

"All because I don't think that anyone has the right even to look at you, and that's ridiculous. Tereza, you've acted like a lady. Now let's have an apéritif to drink a toast to my Honeycomb, muse of the poets of Estância."

A lady? When their liaison had just begun he had said to her that he wanted her to be a lady, and that she could be one if she chose. He had thrown down the gauntlet, and she had picked it up.

She didn't know exactly how a lady should act. Certainly Dona Brígida, the widow of a doctor who had held political office, had cut a fine figure as a lady when her husband was alive. But by the time Tereza knew her she seemed nothing more than a harmless, foolish madwoman. Some nights when Gabi bent the elbow she would boast that she had been a lady, Mrs. Gabina Castro, wife of a shoemaker, before she was Gabi the Priest's Mule and Gabi the Madam. But she couldn't have been a very fine lady, ever.

As for the ladies of Estância, she had seen them only at a distance, peering out their windows at her clothes and the way she walked. Some of their husbands, magistrates and political authorities, came to the house to butter up the Doctor. There were no ladies among the people Tereza knew in the neighborhood, only poor women struggling to bring up their children on their husbands' meager wages. Eventually, however, connections of a certain kind were established between Tereza and the ladies of the upper class.

One morning when the Doctor was away, Tereza had a caller: the well-known and expensive dressmaker Fausta Larreta.

"Forgive me for troubling you, but Dona Leda, Dr. Gervásio's wife, asked me to come."

Dr. Gervásio, the lean and courteous tax inspector, had visited Emiliano several times, and once Tereza had seen his wife in a store, choosing yard goods. She was pert, young, and pretty, with a good figure, and apparently the material in stock was not good enough for her aristocratic tastes.

"No, I don't see anything I like, Seu Gastão. You ought to lay in a better stock of goods."

She was talking to the storekeeper but her eyes were on Tereza. As she went out—I'll be back, Seu Gastão, now don't forget to order that printed crepe de chine from Bahia—Dona Leda smiled at Tereza from the doorway. The smile was so unexpected that it caught Tereza by surprise.

The dressmaker and Tereza sat in the dining room to talk.

"Dona Leda sent me here to ask a favor of you: she'd like to borrow that green and beige dress of yours with the big stitched pockets, you know the one I mean?"

Tereza did.

"She wants to have the pattern copied. She says it's the cutest dress she ever saw, and I think so too. But all your dresses are fantastic. People say all your clothes come from Paris, even your underclothes; do they?"

Tereza began to laugh. The Doctor bought her clothes

in the Bahia boutiques; he had very good taste and took pleasure in seeing her fashionably attired, not only when they went out but at home, as well. She had clothes for every activity and hour of the day, all in the latest style. The closets were full of clothes; he brought more every time he came, no doubt to make up to her for the lack of other distractions. But from Paris? That's what they say; but then you can't imagine the things people say in a little place like Estância.

Tereza started for the bedroom to bring the dress. Fearing a refusal, the dressmaker followed on her heels without asking for permission, her curiosity exploding into exclamations when Tereza opened the doors of the big old-fashioned armoires. Oh, my goodness! Lord in Heaven! No one in Estância had such a wardrobe! She wanted to see everything close up, feel the material, examine linings and seams, read the labels from Bahia boutiques. In one of the armoires some men's suits were hanging. Fausta Larreta turned away modest eyes and began oohing and aahing again over Tereza's clothes.

"Oh, what a darling suit! My customers are going to die of envy when I tell them. . . ."

While Tereza wrapped up the dress, the excited dressmaker let the cat out of the bag. There were some ladies, of course, who bit their lips enviously when they saw Tereza arm in arm with the Doctor and lapped in all that luxury and attention, and their dirty tongues never stopped wagging. There were others, however—Dona Leda, for instance—who liked Tereza and praised her dresses and ways, because they thought her not only attractive and elegant but well-mannered and discreet. Even Dona Clementina Nogueira, two hundred magnificent pounds of religious bigotry and unassailable social position, had good things to say about her, incredible as it might seem. In a circle of high-toned ladies who were deploring Estância's lack of public morality, Dona Clementina had spoken the final word about Tereza's much-debated character: She knows her place and doesn't go where she isn't wanted; don't you think that's something to be grateful for? The haughty *grande dame*, highest in the hierarchy of wives of owners of the biggest textile mill in town, went on to declare, out of her fund of down-to-earth knowledge of the world, that instead of criticizing

the girl they ought to be thankful to her for being satisfied
with swimming in the river and going out strolling with
the Doctor. Didn't they realize that if she asked Guedes
to take her to dances and community functions; to wangle
her a place on the committees that organized the church
festivals, the solemnities for Christmas and New Year and
the Month of Mary, the novenas and thirteen-day prayers,
the Devotion of the Sacred Heart, the Society of Friends
of the Library; to introduce her into the best families—
and if he, with all his money and power and an old man's
fondness, decided to push her forward—didn't they realize who the most important person in Estância would be?
When Emiliano Guedes of the Interstate Bank of Bahia
and Sergipe wanted something, was there anyone who
had the temerity to say no? Didn't the town notables, including even Father Vinícius, fall over one another on the
veranda and in the garden of the Doctor's mansion, el-
bowing each other out of the way to get close to him? If
the lovers weren't seen anywhere and everywhere it was
because Guedes and the girl had some sense of decorum,
and not thanks to any strict canons of morality on the
part of the illustrious ladies' husbands.

Those who were least hypocritical deplored the backward mores of Estância, still so monarchical that society
ladies were not permitted to associate with kept women or
the mistresses of married men. Surely Tereza would understand why the ladies did not come to visit her themselves. When Dona Leda had asked Fausta to be her
envoy, she had declared:

"If this were Bahia I'd go myself, I wouldn't care who
she was. But I can't call on her here; this place is too old-
fashioned."

The loan of the dress was only the first of many—
dresses, blouses, jackets, nightgowns—and not only to
Dona Leda, but to Dona Inês, Dona Evelina with her
two black beauty marks, one on her cheek, the other at
the top of her left thigh, Dona Roberta, and the above-
mentioned Dona Clementina, all the *crème de la crème*.
None of them ever nodded to Tereza in the street, but
Dona Leda made her a present of a piece of drawn work
from Ceará, and Dona Clementina sent her a colored
print of Little St. Tereza of the Child Jesus, a delicate

attention. The card had a printed prayer in verse and granted a plenary indulgence.

"Do you mean to tell me it's my Honeycomb who sets the fashion in Estância?" Emiliano laughed his broad, cheerful laugh when he heard the tale of how the local *haute couture* had repeatedly visited Tereza in the person of Fausta Larreta, the seamstress of the golden thimble and the tragic destiny: there had been a series of financial losses and chronic infirmities suffered by her family, all maintained at her expense; broken engagements; heartbreak upon heartbreak: My life is like a novel; no, not a novel, a ballad of love and duplicity.

"At the New Year's Ball there were five dresses copied from mine—and we won't even mention the unmentionables; they even want to copy the pattern of my panties. I'm not the one who sets the fashion, it's my dressmaker the Doctor."

She showed him the card Dona Clementina had sent her, with its plenary indulgence granted by the Pope to anyone who said the right prayer to the adolescent, virginal saint who was her namesake:

"Now I'm free of sin I won't ever let you touch me again; take your hand away from there, you sinner." As she threatened him with eternal chastity she offered her lips for him to kiss.

She did everything she could to make him laugh the warm and kindly laugh that was like a glass of port wine. He laughed less often lately and was more apt to fall into long, heavy silences. And yet he had never been so fond and affectionate with Tereza; had never come so often to Estância, or stayed so long, to enjoy her in their bed or the hammock and to rest in the lap of his friend.

Some of the old wives tried to get inside the mansion to sniff out details of the liaison and pass on the town's rumors to Tereza, who, polite if possible but invariably firm, shut the door in their faces. She did not like mischiefmakers, and neither did the Doctor.

She had lost her temper with one of them and thrown her out a few days before the end. With the excuse of chattering about next Sunday's church bazaar, for which she had requested and obtained an article to be auctioned off to raise money for building an old people's home, the gossipy woman launched into a spicy chronicle of scandal instead of saying good-bye. Inattentive at first and wondering how to get rid of the scandalmonger without insulting her, Tereza did not immediately realize what the woman was talking about.

"You've heard about it, haven't you? It's simply dreadful, no one in Aracaju talks about anything else, you'd think she had fire on her tail, she can't even look at a man without . . . And her husband—"

"Who are you talking about?" Tereza stood up.

"Who do you think? The Doctor's daughter, that Apa—"

"Shut up and get out!"

"Who, me? Are you telling me to get out? What nerve —a married man's kept woman, a cheap little tart—"

"Get out of here before I throw you out."

One look at Tereza's eyes and the busybody took off like a blue streak. Now Tereza knew something she had not wanted to know. She never would have learned it from the Doctor; he never spoke of such things, but only fell into moody silences that were not at all like him; the laughter that had been so easy and unconstrained was now rare and dispirited. I know everything, even when I say nothing and pretend not to know. Tereza, too, pretended not to know; but in the past few months, comadres, servants, and friends had let slip references to unpleasant things, even scandals. When Father Vinícius came back from celebrating the annual mass at the sugarmill he had spoken of how solitary the Doctor was. Dozens of houseguests from Bahia and Aracaju were there to kick up their heels at the sort of huge party that was never given any more except at the Cajazeiras mill. The Doctor was there, of course, firm at his post, courteous and attentive to all, an incomparable host. But the party hadn't been the same the last few years. It was no longer what it had once been: a country festival with masses, baptisms, marriages, guests and farmworkers alike gorging themselves with food, little boys climbing greasy poles, bets on the sack races, accordion and guitar music, and a grand shindig in Raimundo Alicate's house. There was still a shindig, all right, but now it took place in the big house; the Doctor's children and nephews ran things, and the place looked like a madhouse. As soon as the dance caught on, the priest saw Emiliano Guedes go out by himself and walk through the fields toward the stable, where the black horse neighed joyfully when it recognized its master.

Tereza made herself act festive and playful, even more tender and devoted, even more ardent—to give back to him, if possible, a little of the joy and peace the Doctor had generously lavished on her for six years.

To the comadres she was a little tart, mistress to an elderly rich, married man. To the Doctor she was a lady he had molded to his taste in his idle hours. Tereza did not feel like either one thing or the other, only like a woman grown.

It was always late when the Doctor went to sleep and early when he woke. Not until they were both damp and weary from the long, sweet struggle would he fall asleep with his hand resting on her body. Of late, however, Emiliano stayed awake far into the night even after he had closed his eyes.

Tereza soon realized this. Laying her lover's head on her breast, she softly sang old lullabies, the only memory she had of her mother who had died in the bus crash when she was a baby. She sang to lull her lover to sleep and soothe his heart; sleep, my love, and rest.

28

A beam of sunlight pierced the venetian blinds and came to rest on the face of the dead man. Dr. Amarílio appeared at the door and glanced nervously around the room. Tereza still sat in the same position.

"They won't be long now," the doctor murmured.

Tereza did not seem to hear him. She sat stiffly in the chair, her eyes dry and opaque. The doctor withdrew slowly, careful to make no sound. All he wanted was for everything to be over.

It won't be long now, Emiliano, until we both leave Estância forever. There's no town in the world as friendly and as beautiful as this. Mornings in the river pool and the rapids, the old houses in the sunset, holding hands as we walked these paths, nights perfumed with jasmine and moonlight—oh, Emiliano, never again.

Now the men won't envy the Doctor any more, the lucky dog! The women won't criticize his mistress any more, the lucky little tart! They won't be seen in the street any more, offending local custom by walking calmly by and laughing in delight, the lucky pair of rascals!

All the busybodies will be sorry when there's no more argument about which of the bigwigs from the local mills and ranches will take the Doctor's place in Tereza's bed when he's had his fill.

Don't be afraid, Emiliano. I haven't turned into the kind of lady you had in mind. Maybe I couldn't; maybe I wouldn't. What use is a lady like that? I'd rather be an honest woman who keeps her word. Even if all I've been so far is a slave, a prostitute, and a kept woman, don't be afraid: none of these rich men from here will ever have me, Emiliano! None of them will so much as touch the hem of my dress. Your pride is my legacy too. I'd rather go back to the whorehouse.

Your family will be here soon. They've left the party, they're tearing down the highway, they're coming to take the *prócer* away. Our party's over too; we only had time to watch a rose bloom and die. We loved Estância, Emiliano, but now we must go.

They're coming for you, coming to take away your corpse. I'll carry away your life and your death in my heart.

29

The Doctor arrived on Thursday, toward midafternoon. When she heard the honk of the horn, Tereza came running from the back of the orchard, her face alight with happiness. That was how Emiliano saw her as she crossed the garden—emerging from a mythological forest, half-woman, half-bird—the flash of burning coals in her eyes, laughter like running water on her lips, overflowing with love. His cheerless heart brightened at seeing her.

Tereza could plainly see lines of fatigue on her lover's face, in spite of the effort he made to hide them. She kissed his cheek, moustache, forehead, eyes, his whole face, to wipe away the disappointment, the vexation, the sorrow. There's no room here for nightmares, for inglorious battle, for loneliness, my beloved. When he opened the gate and went into the garden, it was as though he sailed into the magic harbor of a fairytale world where only peace, beauty, and pleasure existed. Life waited for him there in the laughter, the eyes, and the arms of Tereza Batista.

Still kissing, they entered the house, while Lula helped the driver unpack suitcase, briefcase, packages, supplies, and a little bicycle Tereza had ordered for Lazinho, whose birthday was coming soon. They sat down on the edge of the bed for the leisurely welcoming kiss.

"I came straight from Bahia without stopping at the sugarmill; the roads are in an awful state from the rains," he said in explanation of his visible tiredness, but Tereza wasn't fooled.

The Doctor never used to come straight from Bahia. He would always stop at the sugarmill or in Aracaju to see how the work was progressing and to spend some time with his relatives. Now that his son-in-law had taken over the management of the Aracaju branch of his bank, he went there only rarely, whereas before he had gone so often to see his daughter, his favorite child. He was tired of making the long trip and even more tired of the vexations he found there. Tereza took off his shoes and socks. In a long-forgotten time, washing the Captain's feet every night had been one of her painful duties as a slave. The Captain, the farm, the store, the cubicle with the print of the Annunciation and the leather whip, the iron with its bed of coals—all that had vanished into the distance, dissolved to nothing by her life with the Doctor, by the harmonious present, by the pleasure she felt in disrobing a lover who was so handsome, so clean, and so wise. The act was the same, or rather, it looked like the same act of vassalage and subjection. But while she was the Captain's slave, a captive of fear, she was the Doctor's beloved, a slave only to love. Tereza was perfectly happy. Perfectly happy? No, because she saw that he was disappointed and hurt, and she felt and reflected his hurts, however much the Doctor tried to keep them from her. I'm going to run a nice hot bath to rest you after your long trip.

After the bath came bed, and pleasure both deep and wide. He was eager and impatient for her, and their first encounter had the violence of hunger and the urgency of thirst. Oh, my love, this was death and resurrection.

"The old goat's making up for lost time, bringing himself up to date. One of these days he's going to flop over dead on top of the hussy," whispered Nina to Lula as they examined the bicycle, a present for their son. It was the best kind, just like the colored ad in the magazine.

When a breeze sprang up at twilight, Tereza and the Doctor went back to the garden. The soothing night of Estância spread like a mantle of peace over the trees, the old house and those in it. From the kitchen old Eulina, mumbling incoherently to herself, sent out tasty appetizers and prepared stewed possum and manioc for supper. Lula brought out the table, the bottles, and the ice. After serving the drinks Emiliano stretched out in the hammock, in his own home at last.

Tereza told him about the bazaar, without referring to the malicious gossip the woman had told her:

"It's next Saturday, day after tomorrow. They came to ask for a white elephant, and I thought that was just the chance to get rid of that lamp made of painted shells that you couldn't stand, the one someone gave you in Aracaju, remember?"

"I certainly do remember the hideous thing. It was a customer at the bank who gave it to me, a tradesman. He must have paid good money for that monstrosity, too. I never saw anything uglier in my life."

"*You* think it's ugly, but everyone else thinks it's just lovely." She teased him to make him laugh. "You're just an old sourpuss, Doctor, you find fault with everything. I don't know how you ever came to care about a useless little nigger like me."

"Honeycomb, when you say that you remind me of my first wife, Isadora. I never told you, did I, that I almost had a quarrel with my father before he'd let me marry her. He was against it because she was a poor girl from an ordinary family, a seamstress. Her mother made desserts and cookies for parties and she had never seen her father. I had just graduated from college when I met her. It was a short engagement. As soon as I clapped eyes on her I liked what I saw. This girl is worth the trouble, I thought to myself. In less than two months I did her the favor, fell in love with her, and married her. It meant I had to go to work for the old man at the sugarmill and give up the plans I had made, but I never regretted it; Isadora was worth it. My father adored her too, before long; she was the one who closed his eyes on his deathbed. She was kind and devoted and a darling, and everyone loved her. When we had been married ten years, she caught the typhus and died in a few days. She never conceived, and that's why she used to say, I'm a good-for-nothing, useless wife to you, Emiliano; what did you go and marry me for? She wanted so desperately to have a child. I took her to doctors in Rio and São Paulo, but they couldn't help her, neither the doctors nor the macumba healers. She was so anxious to have a baby she made ridiculous vows, had spells cast in Bahia, wore scapulars around her neck, drank any kind of medicine they gave her, poor thing. She died begging me to marry again, because she knew how much I wanted a child. Yes, she was worth loving, Isadora was, and so are you, Honeycomb."

He seemed to be in doubt as to whether to go on or not. He shook his head to chase away the ghosts and changed the subject.

"And so on Saturday there's a church bazaar in Cathedral Square? Would you like to go, Honeycomb?"

"What would I do there, all by myself?"

"Who said anything about going all by yourself?" Now it was his turn to tease her, as if remembering Isadora had soothed him. "Why, I wouldn't think of letting you go all alone with so many country bumpkins after you. . . . No, I'm inviting you to go in the company of your humble servant."

Tereza was so surprised she clapped her hands like a child.

"Go, the two of us? Really? How can you ask!" But the prudent woman soon took the place of the enthusiastic young girl. "We'll be talked about too much, it isn't worth it."

"Do you mind if they gossip?"

"Not me; I'm only thinking of you. As far as I'm concerned they can gossip all they want to."

"I feel the same way, Tereza. And that being the case, why not give the good people of Estância, who are so kind and hospitable and who have so little to talk about, a spicy dish they can chew on for a while? Listen, Tereza; I want you to know once and for all that I have no more reason to keep you hidden from anyone at all, and that's the end of that. Let's have a drink to celebrate."

"No sir, that's not the end of that. Isn't Saturday the day Seu João and Dr. Amarílio and Father Vinícius are coming to dinner?"

"We'll invite them tomorrow instead. They'll want to go to the kermis too, the Father especially. We can send Lula with the message."

"Oh, I'm so happy."

After he kissed her and filled their glasses again, Emiliano lay back against Tereza in the wide hammock and told her his news.

"Tereza, do you know what? This time I've brought a wine that will bring tears of joy to João Nascimento's eyes, a wine of our youth. It was still sold in Bahia when we were young but then it disappeared completely. Its name is Constantia, and it's an aromatic wine produced in South Africa. And now, would you believe it? A fellow who imports wine for me found two bottles on board an American freighter docked in Bahia to load cacao. You're going to see old João shaken to his roots. . . ."

At dinner next day Tereza watched the Doctor make an effort to be the perfect host he always was, to keep a cordial, lively conversation going. The dinner was excellent, the wines select, the lady of the house beautiful, elegant, and attentive; everything was of the best, but Emiliano's contagious joviality and vigor and *joie de vivre* were missing. This time Tereza had not been able to take the Doctor's mind off his problems and troubles and vexations, or make him forget that there was another world outside Estância.

It was only after dinner was over, coffee had been served, cigars were lit, and it was time to pour the liqueurs and brandy and digestive wines, that he grew really animated and laughed the ringing laugh of a man who is satisfied with life. He had left the room for a minute and came back carrying a bottle, mischief in his clear eyes and laughter on his lips:

"Professor João, get a tight grip on yourself so you won't keel over. I have a surprise for you. . . . Do you know what it is I have in my hand? Look: a bottle of Constantia, the Constantia of the old days."

João Nascimento Filho's voice was suddenly youthful:

"Constantia? I can't believe it!" He stood up and reached out his hand.

"Let me see it." With trembling hands he put on his glasses to read the label, gazed lovingly at the old gold color of the wine against the light, and breathed:

"Emiliano, you're a devil. Where did you get it?"

In his friend's emotion the Doctor at last seemed to have forgotten his depression. As he filled the glasses, he and Professor João talked on about the wine, absorbed in a world of memory. Emiliano knew that the wine served at his christening had been Constantia. Balzac's heroes all drink Constantia in the *Comédie Humaine,* recalled Nascimento Filho, who had worn his eyes out reading. Frederick the Great couldn't do without it, added the Doctor. Neither could Napoleon, or Louis-Philippe, or Bismarck. The two old men were tasting their youth in the thick, dark wine. The priest and the doctor listened in silence, with their glasses full.

"Your health!" cried Emiliano. "And ours, Professor João!"

João Nascimento Filho closed his eyes, the better to savor the familiar taste: he remembered himself as a young man in Bahia, studying law and full of literary ambitions before he got sick and had to give up his studies and his bohemian life. The Doctor, too, drank slowly, savoring each sip: he remembered the rich lad, the mistresses and carousing, and how he couldn't make up his mind between law and journalism but knew he was cut out for a brilliant career. He had sacrificed those hopes and plans for Isadora and had never regretted it. His eyes sought out Tereza and found her looking at him tenderly, touched because he had finally forgotten his troubles and was laughing with his friend. He walked over to her. What right had he to make her share troubles and sorrows that were his alone? All she had given him was joy, all she deserved was love.

"Do you like the Constantia, Honeycomb?"

"Oh, yes, but I still like port better."

"Port is the king, Tereza. Isn't it, Professor João?"

He set his glass down on the table and encircled his mistress's waist with his arm. No one who had Tereza could feel empty and sad. He scratched the nape of her neck with his fingernail in a quick flicker of desire. Later on they would drink one more glass in bed.

On Saturday night the animation in Cathedral Square was at the boiling point. The important ladies of the town had organized a bazaar to raise money for the old people's home and the charity hospital, and the booths were manned by young people from the best families. There were two improvised bars with soft drinks and beer, sandwiches, hot dogs, rum sours, peanuts, granadilla and tangerine juice, and all kinds of sweets, and João Pereira had set up his whole amusement park with a merry-go-round, snap-the-whip, flying boats, and a ferris wheel. When the fun was at its height, the Doctor and his mistress strolled into the square, arm in arm. For a moment everyone stopped whatever he was doing to look and stare. Tereza was so lovely and so well turned out that the grandest ladies were obliged to admit that no one in Estância could hold a candle to her. The silvery old man and the copper girl walked through the crowd and began to stop at the booths.

The Doctor was having as much fun as a boy. He bought Tereza a blue balloon, won some prizes in the shooting gallery—a card of pins and a thimble—drank some *mangaba* juice, bet and lost at the roulette wheel, and then saw that a white-elephant sale was in progress. Hearing an offer of twenty cruzeiros for the object just then being auctioned off, he made a bid of a hundred without looking to see what it was and immediately found himself holding that hideous lamp with the painted shells on it. Tereza burst out laughing when the auctioneer took the money for the generous bid and handed over the object with a reverential bow; she couldn't help it. She had been a little ill at ease at the sidelong glances of the ladies and the gossips, and the way a little throng of nincompoops kept gaping at them from a distance. But now that she was breathless with laughter, she stared down the glances and the whispers, indifferent to the stares of the curious, arm in arm with the Doctor, happy as could be.

The Doctor, too, had shaken off his troubles and his heartaches in the surprise he had given Professor João the night before, his friend's happiness in the shared memories of their youth, and later on in bed, the voluptuous nocturnal refinements in Tereza's arms, the improvised loving cup of Constantia; and then the swim in the river and their morning fun, the lazy afternoon, the sweet company of his mistress. The town aristocrats eyed the shameless pair from a distance, calculating the price of her dress and wondering if her ring and earrings were real stones or paste. Tereza's laugh, at least, was priceless.

Before she knew it, she found herself asking for something out loud for the first time—well, not really asking even then.

"You know, I always wanted to ride on a ferris wheel some day."

"Haven't you ever ridden on one, Honeycomb?"

"No, I never happened to have the chance."

"Well, you will today. Let's go."

They waited their turn in line and sat down in one of the bucket seats. They rose higher little by little, as the wheel stopped to let people off and new ones on. Tereza, her heart palpitating, took the Doctor's left hand in both of hers; his free arm circled her waist. At last there came a moment when they stopped at the highest point and saw the whole city below them. There was the crowd having fun, the confused sound of laughter and talk, the multicolored lights on the booths, the merry-go-round and the outline of the square. A little farther on were the old houses rising up in the darkness. In the distance, the two rivers flowed and murmured over the stones to mingle in the old port, on their way to the sea. Above them was the vast starry sky and the outsized moon of Estância, bigger than any other moon in the world. Tereza let go of the blue balloon and the wind carried it away toward the port, perhaps to the faraway sea.

"Oh, how wonderful!" Tereza murmured, deeply moved.

From the bazaar down below a few stubborn imbeciles were still gawking up at them. A few of the ladies and old gossips, too, risked dislocating their necks to see them.

The Doctor pulled Tereza closer to him and she rested her head on his shoulder. Emiliano stroked her black hair, touched her cheek, and kissed her on the mouth: a long, deep, public kiss—a scandal, audacity, splendor, delight. Ah, the lucky pair of rascals!

30

In the shadowy silence of the bedroom Tereza heard the sound of cars in the street. How many? More than one, certainly. Your kinfolk are coming, Emiliano. Your family, your folks. They'll take your body away with them. But as long as you're here in this house, here I will stay. I have no reason to hide from anyone in the world, you told me so. I know you don't care if they see me, and I know that if you were alive and they turned up you would say to them: This is Tereza, my wife.

31

That Sunday in May went by in contented, peaceful serenity. They came back from their early-morning swim at a run, for it began to rain, flurries of water washing the face of the sky. They stayed in the house the rest of the day until after dinner, the Doctor as lazy as a convalescent, going from the bed to the couch and the couch to the hammock.

In the afternoon the mayor came to ask for Emiliano's support for a budgetary request the town wanted to make to the state government: a word from such an eminent citizen of Estância—we consider you one of our own! —in the governor's ear would do the trick, there was no doubt at all about that. The Doctor received the mayor in the garden where he was resting and fondling Tereza. The girl got up to leave, thinking they would be more at their ease without her, but Emiliano caught her by the hand and would not let her go. He called Lula himself and sent him for drinks and fresh coffee.

If not completely recovered, he was at least convalescing. His old animation had returned and he was laughing, talking, discussing the mayor's projects and giving advice as if he had put weariness and heartache behind him. Those few days spent in Estância with his mistress had been enough, seemingly, to heal his wounds and lessen his grief. The morning showers had washed the sky clean and there was a steady breeze on that luminous, peaceful Sunday. Tereza smiled happily at supper: a calm, restful day had followed the unforgettable evening of the bazaar and the ferris wheel, a fantastic, absurd evening, the best of her life.

It had been unforgettable for the Doctor too, not just for her. After supper they strolled as far as the bridge and the old port, and Emiliano remarked:

"I haven't had so much fun in years as I did yesterday. Honeycomb, you have the gift of truly enjoying life."

That had been, one might say, the beginning of that final long talk. When they were standing on the bridge Tereza remembered how the Doctor had pretended to stumble in the street on the way back from the bazaar, letting the lamp with the painted shells fall and shatter on the pavement and declaiming a comic epitaph for it: Rest in peace, you king of bad taste, farewell forever! But now Emiliano wasn't laughing. He was upset again, his face looked strained, his head was full of distress and anxiety again.

Now he was deep in heavy silence, and for all Tereza's efforts to make him laugh and forget his worries, she did not succeed. The light, happy mood of the evening before, which had lasted until the beginning of that Sunday evening in May, had broken.

Well, she would make one last-ditch attempt: in bed. Love without hindrance, the giving over of their bodies to desire and pleasure and infinite delight, might pull him out of his opaque sadness and make his burden lighter. Oh, if Tereza could only take that weight of despondency and vexation onto her own shoulders! She had always had to cope with the worst side of life. The Doctor, on the other hand, had always had everything he wanted, just the way he wanted it; those around him had obeyed him, respected him, carried out his orders; he had grown old enjoying the best things in life. It was harder for him. In bed, inside of Tereza, his pain might be eased.

When they went through the gate into the garden, however, Emiliano said:

"Tereza, I want to talk to you. Let's stay here in the hammock for a while."

On Thursday he had been on the verge of opening his heart to her, when he spoke about his first marriage with Isadora. The burden had become insupportable for even the Doctor's pride; now it was time to divide it and relieve himself of some of its weight. Tereza went to the hammock: I'm ready, darling.

"Lie down here next to me and listen," said Emiliano.

Only very rarely did he use the most familiar form when addressing her; only at times when he wanted to emphasize and deepen the intimacy they had grown to share: *Tu*, my Tereza, my Honeycomb.

There in the garden of Surinam cherry trees, with the enormous moon of Estância gilding the fruit on the trees and the scent of cape-jasmine borne on the breeze, he poured out his heart to her. He told her of the disappointments, the failures, the loneliness of his life with his family. His brothers were incompetent fools, his wife an unhappy wretch, his son and daughter calamities.

He had misspent his life working insanely for the benefit of the Guedes family, for his brothers and their families, but even more for his own wife and children. Dr. Emiliano Guedes, patriarch of the Guedeses of Cajazeiras, had formed hopes, made plans, dreamed of triumphs and joys to come, and to those burning hopes, those eagerly made plans, those illusory triumphs he had sacrificed more than his life, he had sacrificed others, everyone who stood in his way, even Tereza herself.

He had ignored the rights of others, trampled on justice, ignored any good cause that would not benefit the Guedes clan. But were the Guedeses a clan or a gang? Eternally unsatisfied, always demanding more and more, they had looked on as Emiliano fought for them implacably, his silver-handled whip in his hand. Hired thugs, politicians, tax inspectors, judges, mayors, every authority bent to his will by hook or by crook, with shotguns and bribes, with arrogance and scorn—all for the sake of the Guedeses, first and foremost for Jairo and Aparecida, his children.

Ah, Tereza, none of them was worth the cost; it had been a high price he'd paid. Neither his brothers, nor their families—not a one of them worth killing!—nor his own wife, nor his children. He had wasted his time, thrown his energy away, labored in vain. All his efforts, interest, affection, friendship, love, had come to nothing. The injustices and outrages he had committed were futile, and the violence, the tears of so many, the despair of many more, the blood he had shed—I even shed your blood for their sake, Tereza; I tore your womb to kill our child. And for what, Tereza, for what?

32

Dr. Amarílio's voice, unctuous with relief, ushered them into the room:

"Come this way, please."

Framed in the doorway stood a dark-haired young man who was almost as tall as the Doctor, handsome and arrogant like the Doctor, but at the same time utterly unlike him. There was a crafty light in his rapacious eyes and a scornful sneer on his mouth. Though he was tough he looked weak; he was vulgar, passed himself off as an aristocrat, but feigned frankness. Clad in an expensively tailored tuxedo, his whole figure was redolent of luxury, parties, and the *dolce vita*.

Half-hidden behind him, the doctor made the introductions:

"Tereza, this gentleman is Dr. Tulio Bocatelli, the Doctor's son-in-law."

Yes, Emiliano, you were right; you can take one look at him and tell he's a fortune-hunter and an opportunist. Tereza had never seen one of that kind from high society, but whatever circle they moved in they all had something in common, an indefinable stamp that was easy for a former prostitute to recognize.

"*Boa noite. . . .*" he said in a plaintive Italian accent.

His eyes, those of a bird of prey, lingered on Tereza, calculating her value and price. She was prettier, much prettier than they had told him she was, a half-caste madonna, a remarkable female; the old devil had certainly known how to pick them and had taken good care of her once he had got her: no wonder he had kept her hidden away in Estância. He glanced over at his father-in-law. The corpse looked alive with those open eyes. The Doctor's eyes were a sharp-edged blade that could bore into people's thoughts; Tulio had never been able to fool him. Emiliano had always treated him with elaborate courtesy but had never granted him the slightest intimacy, not even when he turned out to be a born entrepreneur with a talent for running the business and making money. From the day they met, the son-in-law had never seen anything in the Doctor's eyes but contempt and dislike. Clear, blue, pitiless eyes. Threatening eyes. Tulio had never felt quite safe at the sugarmill: what if the old *capo* had him rubbed out by one of those backlands outlaws who talked so softly and had killed so many men? Even now, his father-in-law was looking at him with disgust. Yes, disgust was the word.

"*Sembra vivo il padrone.*"

Yes, the *padrone* looked alive, but he was dead. Tulio Bocatelli was rich, filthy rich, at last. It had cost him patience, cynicism, and plenty of nerve, but now he was where he wanted to be.

From the living room came the sound of men's and women's voices, Father Vinícius's among them. Tulio came into the bedroom, leaving the doorway free for Aparecida Guedes Bocatelli to pass through. The low neck of her evening gown displayed her vigorous white breasts and plunged to her tailbone in back. Apa was the picture of her father, with the same sensual face and strong, almost aggressive beauty. Her mouth was as eager as Emiliano's, as covetous; more obviously so, for Emiliano's bushy moustache had covered the greed with silver. Aparecida was not very steady on her feet. She had drunk little at the dance—she had been more interested in her dancing partner, Olavo Bittencourt, a young psychoanalyst and her newest heartthrob; Apa liked variety—but had put away most of a fifth of scotch on the way to Estância.

She came in leaning on Olavo's supporting arm, but when she saw her father's body in the dim light of the four guttering candles and the uncertain glimmer of dawn, she

fell to her knees beside the bed, next to the chair where
Tereza was sitting.

"Ai, Papi!"

You had no mercy on her, Emiliano, even if she was
your daughter; you called her what she was: a whore.
But you didn't put the blame on her but on your blood
and genes. Ah, if at least she had been born a man!

Aparecida burst out sobbing, Oh, Papi! She reached
out both hands and touched her father's corpse: You've
been unhappy lately, you never took me on your lap any
more or stroked my hair, or called me your queen and
watched over my sleep, my sleep and my fate. Oh, Papi!

The young expert in complexes and the subconscious
bent over her sympathetically, ready to come to her aid
with a sleeping pill, a tranquilizer, an injection, a squeeze
of the hand, an amorous look, a furtive kiss. Tulio observed Aparecida's emotion with interest from his corner of the room but refrained from interfering. It was not
that he was indifferent to his wife's suffering, but his instinct as an experienced man of the world told him that a
doctor or a lover was more useful and more consoling
than a husband at such a time. All the more so if doctor
and lover were combined in one dancing partner, a poor
fool who thought himself irresistible. When it came to
delicate matters like these, Tulio Bocatelli was the soul of
courtesy and tact.

All the same, when Aparecida raised her tearful eyes
beseeching help and security, it was her husband she
looked at, not her lover. If anybody in the family was
capable of keeping the ship from capsizing, of taking
over command and making sure the party didn't stop, that
person was the son of the doorman at Count Fassini's
palace in Rome, Tulio Bocatelli and no one else. He
smiled at Aparecida. They were bound together by self-
interest—almost as strong a bond as love.

A noisy argument with the priest was going on in the
dining room. A feminine voice rose in a high screech
above the rest:

"I'm not going in there until that woman leaves the
room. It's an insult to poor Iris and to all of us for her to
be there with him."

"Keep calm, Marina, don't get so upset," said a hesitant,
almost inaudible man's voice.

"You go in if you want to; you're used to dealing with prostitutes, but I'm not. Father, get that woman out of there."

That was Cristóvão's wife, no doubt. Her husband was an alcoholic, and she spent all her time going to fortune tellers and persecuting her husband's mistress and his natural children, putting hexes on them, writing anonymous letters, spitting out insults over the telephone—that was what she lived for. A vile, insignificant woman, Tereza, a woman of the lowest sort.

Tereza rose to her feet and bent a face of stone over the bed: Good-bye, Emiliano. She touched his eyelids with her fingers and closed his eyes, then threaded her way among his relatives and left the room. Apa lifted her head to look at her father's famous mistress. Tulio covetously bit his lower lip: *Carina!*

Now at last it was the body of a dead man lying on the bed and nothing more: the corpse of Dr. Emiliano Guedes, once the lord of Cajazeiras, whose eyes had now closed forever. *Ai, Papi!* moaned Aparecida. *Il padrone e fregato, evviva il padrone!* Tulio Bocatelli, the new *padrone* of Cajazeiras, drew a deep breath of relief.

33

"And Tereza, what was the use of it all?"

Tremulous with shame, vibrating with anger and unrestrained emotion, the Doctor's voice died away into frustration and indifference. Indifference? No, Tereza. Disgust.

The golden moon poured its light onto the old man and the girl, and the river breeze was a caress. It was a night for fond words and vows of love, a night for an idyll. They knew it, but came to it only after trudging through the desert, with its sands of hate and bitterness. It was a hard road for Tereza to walk. On a soft May night in Estância, scented with cherry blossom and cape-jasmine, life and death fought without quarter for possession of the old cavalier's heart. Tereza bled beside him, defending him with a shield of love. They reached the gardens of Elysium, but only afterwards.

Now there was only wrath and sorrow and the inmost secrets of a sore heart revealed.

"Do you know how I feel? Dirty, as if I were covered with filth and mud."

Dirty, and he was so scrupulously clean. Even when dealing out violence or outrage. It was terrible to hear him speak of his family with such cold accuracy, such crudity of expression, such desolate, pitiless, inexorable bleakness.

"I've torn them out of my heart, Tereza."

Was it true? Could anyone do that and go on living? Wouldn't it be as fatal as tearing your own heart out of your breast?

"That doesn't mean I've stopped working and fighting for them. I may look like their master, but I'm really their slave. Even though my heart is empty it still beats for them. Even against my will."

Dr. Emiliano Guedes, the patriarch of the Guedeses of Cajazeiras do Norte, was still doing his duty. Was that all? Even against my will my heart beats for them. Was it only the duty of a clan leader or the love of a father and brother that overcame disappointment and disgust and somehow survived? How large a place, Emiliano, does pride have in this arid account of suffering and loneliness? Tereza's body was shaken with chills and fever as she painfully crossed the deserts of sorrow and wickedness.

The only thing his two brothers were good for, besides spending money, was lending their names to the boards of the family firms and the Interstate Bank as eternal and useless vice-presidents. The Guedes name was worth more than they were. You couldn't even say they were bad; they were simply incompetent.

There was Mílton, out at the sugarmill, playing the squire by covering all the country girls, without even taking the trouble to look at them first. He didn't care what they looked like; he slept with them all and made them all pregnant. The one son he had had with his wife Irene, a relic who spent her life eating chocolates and praying, had been destined by his mother for the priesthood. In the Guedes family one male in each generation had been dedicated to the service of God; the last had been Uncle João Carlos, a distinguished Latinist who had died in the odor of sanctity at the age of ninety. That whale tied the future priest to her apron strings to keep him away from the bagasse dump and bagasse rum, from the common millhands' children, and from sin.

"Well, he didn't turn into a priest, he turned into a fairy. I had to send him to Rio before poor Mílton caught his son behind the dump. It was I who caught him there, Tereza!" His voice vibrated with indignation and fury. "I, with my own eyes, I saw a Guedes being mounted like a woman. I lost my head and I think I would have beaten the wretch to a pulp if he hadn't screamed so loud that Iris and Irene came running out and took him away. My hand still aches from that beating and I feel nauseated every time I think of it."

On another occasion, Emiliano noticed a lively, pretty little girl at the mill, just at the most tempting stage of ripeness, and led her to the snug room at Raimundo Alicate's. She followed him in obedient silence and let him do as he wished, grateful for the Doctor's interest, perhaps; she turned out to be a virgin, a lump of sugar. When they were resting, Emiliano tried to find out a little about the girl.

"I'm your niece, Dr. Emiliano; Dr. Mílton's and my mother Alvinha's girl."

How many of Mílton's illegitimate daughters had been thrown down in the bushes, and how many were plying their trade in Cuia Dágua, in Cajazeiras do Norte, and the red-light district of Aracaju? The natural sons were farmhands, planting and cutting sugarcane and drinking *cachaça,* and ostensibly had no father. Cristóvão's did know their father and asked for his blessing. They earned minimum wages as errand boys, doormen, and elevator boys at the bank. His two legitimate sons, on the other hand, both had degrees from law school and supposedly worked as legal advisers, one to Eximportex and the other to the bank, to justify in part the exorbitant salaries they were paid. One was married, the other single, and neither had a talent in the world except for living an easy life.

"Tereza, once I horsewhipped a scoundrel in the street and made him swallow an article he had written against me and my kin. It took a hard beating and a lot of tears to choke it down; it was a long article. A long one and a truthful one, Tereza."

What desolation! Tereza shrank against the suffering breast of her lover as malarial winds invaded Estância and a murky cloud covered the moon.

34

As Tereza's form disappeared into the alcove, Marina flung herself into the bedroom with her husband behind her.

"Emiliano, my poor brother-in-law, what a misfortune!" She fell onto her knees by the bed, shrieking like a paid mourner, sobbing with a will and beating her breast. "Oh, Emiliano, poor, dear Emiliano!"

Cristóvão stared at his brother, still shaken by the news, hardly able to believe that the man lying before him was dead. Only his thick voice revealed how drunk he had been. He was sober enough now, and scared. He felt like an orphan with Emiliano gone; he had depended on Emiliano ever since their father had died when he was a boy. What would happen now? Who would take the place he had left empty, who would take command? Mílton? He didn't have the energy and he didn't know enough. If there had been only the sugarmill, he might have managed. But of banking, business, importing and exporting, freight and shipping, Mílton knew absolutely nothing. Neither did Cristóvão and neither did Jairo. All Jairo understood was horses, and in his hands the Guedes fortune, however vast it might be, would not last very long. Jairo? Never. And Emiliano, better than anyone, knew why.

"Oh, my poor dear brother-in-law!" By uttering piercing shrieks, Marina, relative by marriage, was doing her family duty as she saw it.

Tulio walked by Cristóvão and left the room. Apa was still kneeling at her father's feet, leaning her head against the bed sleepily; she had had too much to drink.

35

Emiliano Guedes the outlaw went to town and turned into a city gangster. What might have been a virtue in the wilds of the backlands degenerated on the city streets, and the great Guedes family of Cajazeiras has sunk into depravity, the lampoonist Haroldo Pera had written in his indigestible pasquinade. That malicious phrase had given the Doctor much food for thought.

"Maybe I should never have gone to Bahia to live. But when the children were born I got it into my head that I ought to make more money for them, more wealth for the family. Where they were concerned, no plan was too great for my ambition."

Emiliano had married again in middle age, choosing his bride from an important family this time, a family of wealthy landholders. Iris, the heiress, brought new wealth to add to her husband's fortune and gave him two children, Jairo and Aparecida.

The Doctor had tried to forge a bond of affection and intimacy, if not love, with his wife, but had not succeeded. He had to be satisfied with providing comfort and luxury, which was all she seemed to want. For her part she gave her husband little except the two children. It cost her no effort or sacrifice to be faithful, since sexual pleasures meant nothing to her. Emiliano could not even remember when the last time was that he had had her in his arms, inert. She was impregnated and gave birth and that was all. Apathetic and indolent, Iris had no real interest in anything, not even her children. It was Emiliano who assumed all the responsibility for them: I'm going to make them a commander and a princess.

Ah, the children! A permanent source of joy and the goals of all the dreams for which the Doctor lived and struggled.

"I have killed for their sake, Tereza, and I've almost killed myself too."

How his dreams had collapsed! Jairo had graduated from law school like his cousins, but not content with the diversions Bahia offered, he sailed for Paris on the pretext of taking a course at the Sorbonne. He never set foot in the University but soon knew every casino and race track in Europe by heart. From whom had he inherited his passion for gambling? He squandered so much money that Emiliano finally got sick of it and made him come back. From several options open to him, Jairo chose to be manager of the São Paulo branch of the Bank. A year later, it was discovered that he had embezzled millions and spent them on the horses, baccarat, and roulette. Then checks drawn on other banks began to bounce and he lost his credit completely. The scandal was hushed up, but no one could keep the news from going around. If the Bank had not been solid, the wave of rumors would have shaken its prestige. It had shaken the Doctor, that fortress of enthusiastic vitality.

"Tereza, I can't find the words to tell you what I felt, it's impossible. . . ."

Jairo had been banished to the sugarmill, where he listened to records all day except when he went off to Cajazeiras to the cockfights.

"What shall I do with him, Tereza? You tell me."

Aparecida, his favorite, was the worst of all. She married in Rio without her family's knowledge or consent. Her parents learned the news from a telegram she sent asking them for money to go to Niagara Falls on her honeymoon. The social columns noted the nuptials of a Bahia millionairess with an Italian count, and even the apathetic Iris was thrilled at the thought of blue blood from the Italian peninsula in the family.

When Emiliano made it his business to find out who this surprise son-in-law might be—where he came from, what family he belonged to and how he made his living—he learned that Tulio Bocatelli had indeed been born in a count's palazzo, where his father doubled as doorman and chauffeur. While still a child he abandoned the damp cellars of the old house to seek his fortune and never looked back. It hadn't been easy, and he had spent some time in jail. Three girls walked the streets to keep him clothed and fed by the time he was eighteen. He worked as doorman and bouncer in a nightclub, guided tourists to blue movies full of lesbian orgies, then graduated to gigolo to elderly American ladies. His handsome face brought him a pleasant, easy life, but it was not enough. He wanted the security of real wealth, not just a trickle of money that he couldn't count on. At the age of twenty-eight he took the plunge and came to Brazil on the trail of a cousin of his named Storoni, who had hit the jackpot by marrying a rich girl in São Paulo. To make his poor relatives envious, this cousin sent photographs of his coffee fazenda and prize zebu herds, and São Paulo skyscrapers, and newspaper clippings about the parties and dinners he gave. Here indeed was the *dolce vita* of Tulio's dreams, the real fortune and security, the plantation, the cattle, the houses, the money in the bank. He booked a third-class passage to Brazil and landed at Santos with two suits of clothes, his face, and a count's title. When he had been in Brazil for six months, his cousin's wife introduced him to Aparecida Guedes at a party in Rio de Janeiro. Flirtation, engagement, and marriage followed in the twinkling of an eye. It was about time; Storoni wasn't willing to support a bum any longer, even if he was a fellow countryman and a cousin.

When they stopped off in Bahia on their way back from the United States so that his wife's family could meet him, Tulio gave up his pretensions to blue blood and his title as a count—though all Romans are noble, as the saying goes. His nerve failed him when Emiliano looked at him; those eyes made chills run down his spine. He introduced himself instead as an unassuming young man, poor but hard-working, who only wanted an opportunity to make good.

"I had decided to have him killed at the sugarmill. But seeing my daughter so happy, and thinking of Isadora, so poor and so deserving, I decided to give the macaroni a chance. I told Alfredão to put away his gun, but that the job had just been postponed; that was in case he behaved badly to Apa and made my daughter unhappy."

The first to behave badly was Apa; she began to put horns on her husband right and left. He paid her back imperturbably in the same coin. Both did exactly as they pleased, but oddly enough they remained friends and got along just fine, lived in the most perfect harmony, in fact —the world was coming to an end! Emiliano could not understand it no matter how hard he tried.

"How can he be a studhorse and a tame cuckold at the same time?"

If his son-in-law was a cuckold, what was his daughter
Apa, his only daughter, his pet? I'm going to make Jairo
a commander and Aparecida a princess. The commander
was a thief and the princess a whore. She had been debased by a dissolute, immoral scoundrel without a shred
of decency. Should he have him done away with? What
for, if his daughter deserved no better and they were
happy together? After all, they had a great deal in common: the children, two little boys; their interest in money;
and their brazenness.

And besides, if he killed him, who would be left to
pilot the ship after the Doctor was dead? The macaroni
was no fool. He understood business and knew how to
give orders; it was a pity he was rotten to the core and
had corrupted Aparecida. Corrupted Aparecida? Wasn't
her own blood corrupt?

"Oh, Tereza, how low the Guedeses of Cajazeiras have
sunk!"

Nausea succeeded anger in his broken voice, and the
cold cutting edge of his eyes reflected only weariness. Tomorrow not even the Guedes name would be left. Tomorrow there would be no Guedeses, only Bocatellis.

"My blood is corrupt, Tereza. Rotten."

36

In the dining room Nina served scalding hot coffee and
kept her ears pricked. She recognized a *patrón* in Tulio's
manner and tone. The husband of the Doctor's daughter
was a handsome boy. She rubbed up against him as she
passed, eyes downcast.

With the physician as guide, Tulio had been almost
all over the house to make an estimate of how much its
contents were worth. The only rooms he had not entered
were the parlor and the alcove; when he had seen those,
the inventory would be complete.

"Was it bought or rented?"

"The house? Bought. The Doctor bought it with the
furniture and everything it had in it. Afterward he made
some improvements and brought all these things." Dr.
Amarílio sank into reminiscence. "The automobile was al-

ways loaded down with the things he brought. All kinds of things. This house was the apple of his eye. Do you see that prie-dieu over there? I discovered it in a little hole a few miles from here, in a farmhouse where the owner was sick. When I told Emiliano about it he insisted on going straight over there. We rode over the next morning, on horseback. The owner was a poor simple fellow who didn't know how to set a price on it. It was just a piece of junk in a corner to him. He left it up to the Doctor to say how much it was worth. Emiliano paid a ridiculously high price for it."

No matter how much he had paid, it was cheap at the price. That prie-dieu would be worth a fortune in any antique shop in the South. In fact, all of this furniture would. Tulio saw his father-in-law's hand in every detail. Neither the manor house in Corredor da Vitória in Bahia nor the big house on the sugar plantation reflected so plainly the presence of Emiliano Guedes. Luxury prevailed in the mansion in Bahia, where the Doctor's austere good taste had foundered on Iris's ostentation and the extravagance of Aparecida and Jairo. As for the house at the sugarmill, only his own wing had that difficult mixture of refinement and simplicity. In the family rooms and the innumerable bedrooms, Mílton's untidiness and Irene's carelessness reigned. In the house in Estância there was not a single false note: Emiliano's perfect taste was complemented by the careful neatness of the mistress of the house. Tulio could see that it was more than a comfortable, delightful, even elegant house—it was a home, that mystic refuge that Tulio had heard about ever since he was a child. An uncle of his, a miniaturist at the Pitti Palace in Florence, had a house a little like that; an intimate house with the personal touch that made it a home.

"When did their relationship begin, do you know?"

Dr. Amarílio considered, then said thoughtfully:

"More than six years ago . . ."

Not until the end of his life, then, had the old *capo* had a home—his only real home, and maybe his only real wife. Tulio hoped he would never feel the need for a home, for the restful quiet and peace that were almost tangible here, even in death. As for women, he was perfectly satisfied with Apa, who gave him wealth and security and was a gay companion. Live and let live was Tulio

Bocatelli's motto. Except in one thing: from now on he would have to control how much money went out. It was all right for the *capo* to throw money away. He had been born rich, his great-grandparents had been landowners and slave-owners and he had no idea what poverty was like. But Tulio had gone hungry and he knew what money was worth. He would keep a firm hand on the reins.

"In whose name is the deed to the house? His? Hers?"

"In the Doctor's. I was one of the witnesses. Professor João was the other. . . ."

"It's a fine house. It must be worth something."

"Real estate is cheap, here in Estância."

If it had been closer to Aracaju it would have been perfect for rendezvous. Here in Estância it was useless. The best thing to do would be to sell the house, or rent it, and take the furniture to Bahia. Tulio thought that he might furnish a house in Bahia with it. He was done with Aracaju.

Dr. Amarílio handed over the death certificate and Tulio put it in his pocket.

"Did he die in his sleep?"

"In his sleep? Well . . . he was in bed, but he wasn't exactly asleep."

"What was he doing then?"

"Well, what a man and a woman do in bed."

"Chiavando? You mean he died on top of her? Lucky man!"

The death of the just, the death of God's favorites. It was awfully hard on the woman, though. In his pimping days Tulio had heard of a case like that; the woman had gone mad and had never been the same again.

"Poveraccia . . . What did you say her name was? Tereza what?"

"Tereza Batista."

"Do you think she intends to stay on here?"

"No, I don't think so. She said she was going away."

"Do you think that two or three weeks would give her time enough to get out of the house? The family will naturally want to sell it or rent it as soon as possible so that people here in Estância will stop talking about it."

"I think that would be time enough. I can ask her."

"I'll ask her myself."

They went into the living room which the Doctor had

turned into a study. The old alcove where Tereza kept her books and other things opened onto this room, and Tereza was there packing her suitcase. Tulio stared at the girl and again appraised her admiringly—she was quite a woman! Who would inherit this legacy of the old *capo?* He went over to her.

"Listen, *bella.* This is just the beginning of May, you can stay in the house until the end of the month."

"I won't need to."

The black eyes flashed; they were every bit as hostile as the Doctor's cold blue ones. Tulio's habitual self-possession was shaken for a minute, but he soon recovered his equanimity; this one couldn't very well have him ambushed on the plantation. Now it was Tulio Bocatelli who would both propose and dispose.

"Can I help you in any way?"

"No."

He gave her another long, appraising look and smiled at her. Both the look and smile were laden with implications.

"Well, come by to see me at the bank in Aracaju just the same, and we'll have a talk. You won't be wasting your time."

Before the words were out of his mouth the door to the alcove slammed in his face. Tulio laughed:

"A wild one, that *bambina!"*

The physician lifted his hands in a vague gesture. He hated everything that was happening that night, it was all a nightmare. If only the ambulance would come soon and take away the corpse. Dona Veva, his wife, was waiting up for him at home so he could tell her how the story ended. Dr. Amarílio wearily accompanied Tulio to the garden, where the psychoanalyst, Olavo Bittencourt, was asleep in in the hammock.

In the dining room, Marina, almost beside herself with excitement, was jabbering in a whisper with Nina. The servant was saying:

"And the sheet all dirty—If you want to see it I can show you, I kept it to wash afterwards."

While she went to get it, Marina ran to the door of the bedroom and called her husband:

"Cristóvão, come here quick."

Spreading the sheet on the dining-room table, the

woman pointed to the stains of dried semen. Marina flicked one with her fingernail.

"How disgusting!"

Cristóvão and Father Vinícius came in from the bedroom.

"What's this sheet doing here?" The priest did not wait for an answer; what other sheet could it be? He ordered indignantly: "Nina, take that sheet away. This minute!" He turned to Marina. "For goodness' sake, Dona Marina . . ."

Hearing their voices, Tulio and Dr. Amarílio joined the group. "What's the matter?" the Italian asked.

Marina was palpitating with excitement. She was in her element.

"Did you know he died right on top of her? What dreadful depravity! Have you seen the mirror in the bedroom? How can we get these people to keep their mouths shut and keep everyone else from finding out? It would be a fine thing, wouldn't it, if the news got around! Emiliano Guedes dying at the moment of—"

"If you don't stop screeching about it like a crazy woman the whole town will find out about it from you." Tulio turned to Cristóvão. "*Caro,* get your wife out of here. Take her into the bedroom, Apa's all alone in there."

It was an order, the first to come from Tulio Bocatelli's mouth.

"Come on, Marina," said Cristóvão.

Tulio turned to the priest and the doctor.

"We can put him in the ambulance as if he had just had a stroke or a heart attack or something; that's up to you, Dr. Amarílio. He didn't die on top of anybody, a man in his position has got to die decently. We can say he died on the way to the hospital, coming from the plantation."

The siren on the ambulance could be heard wailing in the distance. Soon Estância would be wide awake and curious. The vehicle stopped at the door of the house and the male nurses got out and picked up the stretcher.

"Dr. Amarílio, you'd better come with us to Aracaju in the ambulance. It will look better that way."

Good God, wouldn't this nightmare ever end? Then the physician thought what a bill he could send in and assented. He would stop for a second on the way to

soothe the impatient Veva. She would have a long tale to
hear when he got back.

Tulio, Father Vinícius, and Nina went into the bedroom while the doctor and Lula went to meet the interns.
The siren had awakened the children, the neighbors, and
Dr. Olavo Bittencourt, who ran to comfort the forsaken
Apa. How the devil had he happened to fall asleep? He
had just come out to smoke a cigarette and had dozed off
in the hammock. Would he be forgiven? He passed Tereza
in his mad rush through the dining room.

Tereza went into the bedoom, ignoring all the relatives
and in-laws. She walked over to the bed and stood for
a moment in silence, gazing at the beloved face.

"Get that damned woman out of here!" screamed Marina.

"*Finiscela, porca Madona!* Shut your mouth!" Tulio
exploded.

As if she heard nothing and were alone in the room,
Tereza bent over the Doctor's body and touched his face,
moustache, lips, and hair. It's time to go now, Emiliano.
They'll carry away your body, but you will come with me.
She kissed him on the eyes and smiled at him. Then she
walked out of the room, carrying her lover, her protector,
her friend, her love on her shoulders. On the stretcher
the attendants carried the corpse of a sugarmill owner,
bank director, entrepreneur, landowner, and eminent citizen so that he could die decently in the ambulance on the
way to the hospital, of a stroke or a heart attack; that's
up to you, Dr. Amarílio.

37

"Bad blood, Tereza. My blood, and my family's blood, is
corrupt."

It lasted two hours or a little longer; it seemed an eternity of desolation. Emiliano told her everything, harshly
and cruelly, without choosing his words. Tereza had never
dreamed that she would hear the Doctor telling her such
things, hear such expressions about his brothers, his son,
and his daughter. He never spoke of his family in his mistress's house, and when he had referred to them at all

in those six years it was to praise them. Once he had showed her a picture of Apa as a young girl, lovely with her father's blue eyes and sensual mouth. She's perfect, Tereza, he had said fondly; she's my treasure. That Sunday night in May, Tereza realized the full extent of the calamity. It was all much worse than Emiliano's silence and the scattered hints and whispers, friendly and unfriendly, that she had heard had given her to believe. What an enormous effort it must have cost him to remain cordial, pleasant, and smiling, to feign contentment when he was with her and with their friends, and keep to himself the bitterness and gall that were eating his heart out! All at once it was too much to contain and the sick heart overflowed.

"Bad blood, corrupt, degenerate family."

There were only two people who had not disappointed him or betrayed his trust: Isadora and Tereza. It was because he remembered Isadora, the poor seamstress, the exemplary wife, the unforgettable companion, that the plantation owner had decided to cancel the orders given to Alfredão to kill his son-in-law, and instead give him the chance to see what he could do.

"The people's blood is good blood, Tereza. If only I were young enough to have the children it would have been joy to have with you."

Steep roads led to vows of love and a fender idyll. After telling her in bitterness, passion, and wrath what he had never thought to confide to any relative, associate, or friend, the Doctor folded her in his arms and kissed her on the lips, saying regretfully:

"It's too late, Tereza. I should have realized it before. It's too late to have children, but not too late to live. You're all I have in the world, Honeycomb; how could I have been so ungenerous, so unfair?"

"Ungenerous? Unfair to me? Please don't talk like that; it isn't true. You've given me everything. How could I have deserved more?"

"A little while ago, as we were walking toward the port, I suddenly realized that if I were to die today you wouldn't have a thing to live on. You'd be even poorer than you were when you came, because your needs are greater now. In all this time, more than six years, I never gave the slightest thought to that. I never thought of you, only of myself, and the pleasure you gave me."

"Please don't say that, I won't listen."

"Tomorrow morning I'm going to call Lulu and ask him to come right away to put this house in your name and add a codicil to my will, a legacy that will give you something to live on after I'm gone. I'm an old man, Tereza."

"Don't talk that way, please." She repeated: "Please don't, I beg of you."

"All right then, I won't say any more, but I'm going to take steps to do what I can to make up for my injustice, at least in part. You've given me peace of mind, joy, and love, and I've repaid you—how? By keeping you a prisoner, dependent on my convenience, a thing, an object, a captive. I was the master, you the servant; you still call me Doctor. I haven't treated you any better than the Captain. A different Captain, Tereza—clean, starched and polished, but the same thing at bottom. Emiliano Guedes and Justiniano Duarte da Rosa are very much alike, Tereza."

"Oh, don't say that! Don't compare yourself to him! Two men were never more different. Don't insult me by insulting yourself that way. Why would I be here if you were just alike, why would I cry about your family when I don't even cry about myself? When you compare yourself to him, it's an insult to me. All I can say is that you were always good to me; you taught me how to be a woman and how to love life."

Emiliano rose out of the ashes on Tereza's passionate voice.

"In these six years you've come to know me very well, Tereza; you know my good side and my bad side and everything that is in me to do. I reached inside my own heart and plucked my family out of it, but my heart isn't empty and I'm not dead; I survived—because I have you. You, and no one else."

He was deeply affected. In his voice was all the sudden diffidence of an adolescent, a trembling suitor, an unsure nobody who could not have been more different from the man who was used to commanding others, the lordly man who went after what he wanted and never gave an inch, the man who was arrogant when he had to be.

"Yesterday, at the bazaar, our life really began, Tereza. Now our time is our own and the world belongs to us. I won't leave you alone any more; we'll always be together from now on, here and everywhere else. You'll travel with me, too. You won't be a kept woman any more, Tereza."

Before he stood up like a tall tree and took her in his arms, ending the terrible monologue and the loving conversation, Emiliano Guedes said to her:

"If only I were single and could marry you. Not that that would change anything for me. You're my wife."

After their kiss, she murmured:

"Emiliano, my love."

"Don't ever call me Doctor again. Here or anywhere else."

"I won't, Emiliano."

Six years had passed since the night he took her out of the brothel. The Doctor lifted Tereza in his arms and carried her to their nupital chamber. They had crossed the last barriers, Emiliano Guedes and Tereza Batista, an old man of silver, a copper girl.

38

The ambulance left, but the curiosity-seekers waited on the sidewalk in front of the house, talking among themselves. After she had locked the children in, Nina joined them, her tongue flapping.

In the bedroom the sexton picked up the candlesticks and the stumps of the candles. With a last look of envy at the big mirror—those depraved libertines!—he went on his way. The priest had already gone:

"May God be your strength, Tereza."

Tereza finished packing. On Emiliano's worktable she saw the silver-handled riding whip on top of some papers, and thought of taking it with her. But why take the whip? It would be better to take a rose. She covered her head with a red-flowered black shawl the Doctor had brought her on Thursday; his last gift to her.

In the garden she picked the fullest, most crimson

rose; it was like flesh and blood. She would have liked to say good-bye to the children and old Eulina, but Nina had hidden the children and the cook wouldn't come until six.

The suitcase in her right hand, the rose in her left, the shawl on her head, Tereza opened the gate. She passed through the curious crowd unseeingly. Her steps firm, her eyes dry, she went to the bus stop in time to catch the five o'clock bus to Salgado, where the Eastern Railroad had a stop.

Tereza Batista's wedding feast

or

The closed-basket strike in Bahia

or

Tereza Batista dumps death into the ocean

1

Sit right down and make yourself at home here in Xangô's temple, while I fix the table and the shells to see with. Are you in doubt about some little thing you should or shouldn't do? Or do you just want some information? I'll do everything I can for you, coming the way you do with a recommendation from such a good friend of mine. Aside from the spirits, there's nobody who can boss this seer around but a friend.

So you want to know the truth about Tereza's patron saint—who is it who decides what's going to happen to her and protects her? Who her guardian angel is, who rules her head? So you've heard a lot of contradictory stories at every crossroad in Bahia and some of them don't make sense? Well, it's only natural that your different stories from all over don't jibe; they hardly ever do these days, when everybody thinks he knows it all and won't admit he's ignorant, when what you don't know's easy enough made up.

Now, serving the spirits is something mighty different. You give up your whole life to it, and I pity any spirit-mother who finds the job's too much for her and tries to fool the lightning and the thunder, the leaves in the forest and the waves in the sea, the rainbow and the arrow in the air. Nobody in this world can fool the enchanted spirits and if you're not smart enough to pick up the knife at the right time, if the call doesn't find you with the key to the secret and the answer to the riddle, you'd better not mess around with the spirits at all. Spirit business is no joke, and you can die if you're not careful. I could tell you a lot of stories some other time when you aren't in a hurry; right now you couldn't keep your mind on what I say.

*If you've got the hand and the nerve, you can throw
the shells on the table. But if you want to read the spirits'
answer, the message of the shells, you have to know about
light and darkness, day and night, east and west, hate and
love. My name was given to me before I was born, and
I began to learn when I was a little child. When I was
raised up and confirmed I was so scared I whimpered, but
the spirits gave me strength and brought light to my understanding. I learned from my grandmother, from my
old aunts, from the Yoruba priests and Mother Aninha.
Today I'm a big woman and no one raises his voice in
this* axé *but me. The only person I look up to in Bahia is
the* candomblé *priestess of the Gantois temple, Menininha,
my saint-sister, my equal in knowledge and in power, because I look after the enchanted spirits the right way. I
do what they command and I respect their grudges. I walk
through fire and don't get burned.*

*About Tereza, now, it's not surprising that you're kind
of mixed up. Even somebody who knows what he's doing
could find it hard to know what the cowries or the kola
nut mean when he throws them. Plenty of seers have tried
it and don't agree on what they saw. When you go back
a while, it's Yansã shows as her spirit; but do it now and
they'll say it's Yemanjá. You heard her spirit was Oxalá,
Xangô, Oxossi, isn't that so? And Euá and Oxumaré?
Not forgetting Ogum and Nanã and Omolu.*

*But I divided the severed nut in four and cast the
shells, and I reached the heart of the mystery. And I'll
tell you this: never in all my life did I see anything to
equal it, not in the fifty years I've been in the temple
and the twenty I've watched over Xangô.*

*The first spirit to come dawn was Yansã with her golden
scimitar, saying: She's a fighter and belongs to me; her
head is mine and pity the one who does her harm! Then
right after her came Oxossi and Yemanjá. It was Oxossi
who brought her out of the thick forest, the swamps, the
thorny brush, the burning desert backlands; and after all
those battles were over she had Yemanjá's cloak over her
to light up the dawn when she crossed the gulf of the
Recôncavo. She's had to be a fighter all her life, but even
when the fight was at its nastiest, the spirits were helping
her: first and foremost, Yansã, but Xangô and Oxumaré
too, and Euá and Nanã, and Ossain, with his healing*

*leaves. And mightiest of all was Oxolufã, old Oxalá, my
father, pointing out to her the right road to walk with his
scepter of wisdom.*

*And wasn't it Omolu who mounted Tereza's back out
there in Buquim when the black smallpox was raging all
around? Was it Omolu, or wasn't it, who chewed up the
plague with the gold tooth and drove it out of town? Didn't
he name her Omolu's Tereza at the macumba ceremony
in Muricapeba? Well, didn't he? I tell you, Omolu was
pretty excited when he came, all covered with sores, to
possess his steed.*

*You can imagine the commotion when they were all
there at once! I did the best thing I could think of: I
called on my mother Oxum to calm down all those other
spirits, and there she came, gliding into the temple in
her yellow robes, her gold bracelets and necklaces all a-
gleaming, a sight to behold. It didn't take long then for
the spirits to settle down at her feet, every one of them,
loving her, male and female alike, beginning with Oxossi
and Xangô, her two husbands. And of course that meant
they were at Tereza's feet too, because Tereza's a beauty,
with Oxum's honey sweetness and her swaying walk, her
joy in living and her copper color. But there's no denying
that that flash in her black eyes comes straight from
Yansã.*

*When I saw that Tereza Batista was defended and sur-
rounded on every side by the* orixás, *I cast the shells
again and told her: Don't give up and never give in, not
even when you're so tired you want to die and you're in
the worst fix of your life and the hurt seems more than
you can bear; just go on believing in life and keep on
fighting.*

*You're bound to know, though, that a time comes in
everybody's life when it seems like you just can't go on,
no matter how brave you are. You just want to lay down
your spear and give up. It happened to Tereza too, and
you can find out about it if you ask around. I can't tell
you about that; that's a chapter in her life I never studied.*

*If you ask me, though, I'd say it was Exu who led the
drowned man through the alleys of Bahia to where Tereza
was hiding. There is no other spirit who likes to make
trouble so much as Exu. Nobody like Exu to know all
the shortcuts and byways and to want to stop a party in*

the middle. This was one he couldn't stop, though. You might say he turned it into two wedding feasts instead of one. The second was one nobody expected, celebrated out on the ocean with Janaína spreading out her green hair for the lovers.

Now since Pierre Verger was the one who asked me to —did you know he was a wizard?—I've told you all I know about Tereza. Seated on my own rightful throne with my princes around me, I, Lady Mother, Iyá Nassô, spirit-guide of the Temple of Opô Afonjá, the candomblé *Cruz Santa de São Gonçalo do Retiro, where I serve the spirits and gather to my breast the tears of the afflicted, I have told you all I know.*

2

Now this is a delicate subject: Tereza Batista was receiving a marriage proposal for the second time. The first time didn't really count, since the suitor had been a little too intoxicated on that solemn occasion to make the proposal stick. And that really was unfair because Marcelo Rosado was a confirmed teetotaler, but so bashful that he had had to get drunk before he could pluck up the courage to declare his love. Sober, he was more than willing to tie the matrimonial knot; what he lacked was the courage to face Tereza and ask for her hand in marriage. He poured a bottle of *cachaça* down his throat, and that was his undoing; unaccustomed as he was to rum, he vomited his guts out just as he was confessing his passion in Altamira's castle in Maceió, where Tereza occasionally used to meet him (and a few others, too), when she was hard up for money.

Though not insulted, Tereza did not take very seriously the proposal of the bookkeeper for the important firm of Ramos & Menezes. Without troubling to explain her real reasons for refusing him, she carried the thing off as a joke, and that was the end of it. Humiliated by what he had done and his intended's irreverent attitude, Marcelo vanished from sight, taking with him a vivid memory of Tereza, whom he never forgot. The woman he finally married years later in Goiás, where his shame and un-requited passion finally took him, reminded him in manner, laugh, and look of the fiancée he had almost had, the peerless girl who stayed to dance the samba in a cabaret as she passed through Maceió.

Now she was a samba dancer in a nightclub in Bahia, and still a peerless girl who frequented Taviana's discreet and famous castle out of necessity. Sad to say, her success in Taviana's bawdy house was greater than at the Lotus Flower Cabaret, that "dazzling temple of nocturnal entertainment," as its publicity-minded owner, Alinor Pinheiro, called it with debatable accuracy.

Living frugally, for she neither gambled nor kept a gigolo, Tereza went to the castle as little as possible, in spite of constant requests. She was a real professional, a sought-after beauty whose breeding and good manners were much praised; but she was impervious to sexual or sentimental involvements—men simply did not interest her. Her customers were few, all moneyed men, carefully chosen by Taviana from among her oldest, richest clients. Tereza never gave any of them a thought. Some of them proposed exclusive arrangements, exhibited well-stuffed wallets, tried to tempt her with offers of liaisons. She wouldn't hear of it. She had no intention of repeating the mistake she had made when she had tried living with the director of the health clinic in Buquim.

Never since those distant days in Aracaju had she felt her blood beating faster in her veins, never exchanged glances laden with light and shadow, charged with sensual desire. Tereza was dead to love. No, that wasn't true; love burned in her heart, a dagger buried in her breast, cruel longing, last, faint hope. Januário Gereba, sailor on a broad, far sea, where are you now?

All the local lady-killers and pimps tried to ingratiate themselves with her at the cabaret, but Tereza couldn't stand them. With her clients at the castle Tereza made use of her sexual knowledge, her good breeding, Soft-Spoken Tereza; as for the pimps, she ignored them, resorting to indignation when she had to, Tereza Who Fought the Good Fight: Leave me alone, don't pester me, go play your hurdy-gurdy someplace else. She sent at least one irresistible dandy, Lito Sobrinho, running down the stairs from the nightclub to the street, and she stood up to

Nicolau Peixe Cação, the cop with the worst reputation in
Bahia, "Dog-fish," when he started acting like a fool.

When old Taviana, who had been active in the oldest
profession for about fifty centuries, twenty-five of them
as a procuress, and who consequently knew everything
there was to know about prostitution and human nature,
made Tereza's acquaintance, she immediately had a vision of fat profits for herself, her castle, and Tereza as
well. She knew a gold mine when she saw one. Taviana's
plan was to introduce Tereza to her old customers as a
poor but honest married woman whom painful necessity
and tragic circumstances had brought to the castle as a
last resort. Tereza could have her pick of sad stories to
tell: in the oral achives of Taviana's establishment was
an inexhaustible stock, all of them true and each more
touching than the last. That little comedy was bound to
increase the interest and generosity of Taviana's distinguished clients, for surely there could be nothing more delightful, more soul-satisfying, than protecting a needy,
honest, married woman. Doing good and decorating a
husband with horns at the same time—what could be
more satisfying to soul and body?

Silly Tereza had refused to play that game, feeling that
it would make sordid necessity still more painful. In time
the two women became close friends; but Taviana never
stopped shaking her gray head and repeating her first
diagnosis:

"No, Tereza, it isn't any use; you weren't meant for
this life. You were meant to be a housewife and mother.
What you ought to do is get married."

3

Maybe it was on purpose that Taviana introduced Tereza
Batista to Almério das Neves, a friendly, pleasant-spoken
citizen with a bakery of his own in Brotas. Although not
wealthy, he was doing rather well. Old ties of friendship
linked him to the madam, for it was in her castle, fifteen
years before, that he had met Natália, nicknamed Nata
de Leite, Whipped Cream, because of her white skin—
a shy girl, new to the profession, one of those girls that

Taviana would have said were born to be wives and mothers.

Almério, just starting out in business for himself at that time, was toiling day and night to make his first small bakery a success. After a few meetings with Natália he heard from the girl's own lips the pathetic story of how her cruel father had thrown her out of the house when he learned that she had been deceived by her smooth-talking sweetheart. After robbing her of her innocence in his bohemian student garret, he moved away without leaving a forwarding address or telling her good-bye. Almério instantly fell in love with this young and appealing victim of fate and a pair of blackguards. He took Nata de Leite out of the castle and married her, and he could not have found a better wife if he had chosen a nun from a convent. She worked like a trojan and was honest as the day was long. True, she gave him no children; but that was all that marred an otherwise perfect marriage. When life got easier for them as time went on, and Natália was able to leave the cash register in the bakery where she had worked all day until then, the couple decided to adopt an orphan whose mother had died when he was born and whose father, a worker in the bakery, had died six months later of pneumonia. Almério and Natália took charge of the little boy and gave him new parents and a new surname, all legal and official. If their married life until then had been serene and happy, the next two years, as they watched their son grow and develop, glowed with joy. This family idyll was brutally cut short by a car belonging to a young son-of-a-bitch from a rich family. In his mad rush to nowhere, his terrible hurry to do nothing, he ran over Natália in front of the bakery, leaving Almério in despair and the little boy motherless for the second time. The widower sought out his old friend Taviana in hope of sympathy, and that was how he met Tereza.

Tereza came to the castle only at times previously agreed upon, seeing only a select clientele designated by the efficient go-between. But when the session was over and the banker or magistrate sent on his way, she sometimes lingered in the parlor to chat with Taviana. It was on one of those occasions that she was introduced to "my friend Almério das Neves, a person for whom I have had the highest regard since he was a young lad and I was already an old woman." How old *was* Taviana, or was she any age at all?

Almério was a light mulatto, stylishly dressed, plump, peaceable and mild, well spoken too, though a little stilted in his choice of words. Everything about him breathed tranquillity and self-assurance. To please Taviana, Tereza agreed to set aside an afternoon for him three days later.

"Try to console my friend a little, Tereza; he lost his wife not long ago and he's still in mourning."

"I'll wear mourning in my soul for all eternity."

With some flattering and agreeable words after the second act of the matinee (Tereza's usual customers were hard put to it to finish the first and only act), Almério stayed on to tell her a little about himself. He dwelt lovingly on Natália, their adopted son, and his bakery, a new one, much bigger than his first. Now he'd be able to give the Spanish monopolists who'd cornered the market a run for their money. One day, Almério said proudly, my bakery will be an emporium.

"What's the name of it?"

"Panificadora Nosso Senhor do Bonfim."

He had given it that popular name for luck and to honor Oxalá, whose color white he always wore, rain or shine. Tereza learned all this gradually, for the bakery owner became an habitué of Taviana's house. He and Tereza enjoyed many pleasant conversations at the castle or sitting at a table in the Lotus Flower Cabaret. Because Tereza could not reserve more than one afternoon a week for him, Almério began to frequent the cabaret on the second floor of the Rua do Tijolo, where Tereza was currently "the sensual incarnation of the Brazilian samba." According to her verbal contract with Alinor Pinheiro, the owner of the club, Tereza was to come every night at ten and stay at least until two. At about midnight she displayed herself in a brief costume, supposedly a stylized version of the Bahiana dress; but before and after her appearance on the dance floor, she would dance with customers when asked and would sit at certain tables where the liquor flowed freely. Her drink was always vermouth—that is, elderberry tea. Her obligations at the Lotus Flower went no further; she turned no tricks, and when a customer invited her to one of the neighboring hotels she didn't go. From the cabaret she went directly home to the room she had rented in Desterro. Her landlady, Dona Fina, read the cards and prized a reputation as a fortune-teller which she'd built up slowly over many years. Her rooms were clean and decent: have men wherever you want to but not here, I'm an honest widow, Dona Fina had warned her. She was a delightful old woman who loved soap operas on the radio (her eyes were tired after so many years of gazing into a crystal ball) and her cats, which numbered four at that time.

While his bakers pounded the bread dough and heated the oven, Almério would turn up at the Lotus Flower for a samba, a blues, a rhumba, a glass of beer, and a little chat. Often he accompanied Tereza to the door of her pension before going back to the bakery. The girl appreciated his company, his mild, pleasant conversation, his politeness. He had never suggested that they spend the night together in bed, turning their pleasant, rather formal, relationship into a lovers' crush. Bed was a professional affair reserved for a bout once a week at the castle; all the rest of the time they were friendly companions, and Almério was a good friend.

The night before the afternoon when he asked for her in marriage, Almério waited at the Lotus Flower, dancing, talking, and drinking rum sours, until it was time for Tereza to go home. At the door of the nightclub he invited her to go to Brotas with him to see the bakery. It wasn't far by taxi; he could have her home in half an hour. Although she thought the invitation a little strange, Tereza saw no reason to refuse it. He had talked so much about the big oven and the Formica counter that there was nothing left but for her to see them.

With the proprietary pride of a self-made man—I started at the bottom, with a basket of rolls on my head, selling from door to door—Almério showed her the equipment, the clean part of the breadmaking process, the bakers and their helpers kneading the dough, the lighted oven, the huge wooden baker's peels; and then the store itself, four doors opening on the street, all open and lighted up especially for Tereza's visit.

"It'll be an emporium yet. Oh, if only my never-to-be-forgotten Nata were still with me! A man never works so willingly as when he has a woman worthy of his love."

Tereza duly praised the equipment and the counter and smilingly received the tribute of the first early-morning rolls. Then she started toward the taxi, but Almério asked her to come into his house next door for a minute. It was painted blue and white with green shutters and vines running up the window bars; the handkerchief-sized garden showed the loving care of its owners.

"When she was alive, it was a pleasure to see this garden and this house. It's all neglected now."

But he hadn't invited her there to see the vines. They went through the hall to the nursery where a little boy lay sleeping, holding a teddy bear in his hand. The pacifier had fallen onto his little chest.

"This is Zeques. His name is José; Zeques is his nickname."

"What a darling!" Tereza touched the baby's cheek and fluffed his curly hair.

She lingered a moment, touched, gazing at the child, and then went out on tiptoe so as not to wake him. In the taxi she inquired how old he was.

"He's over two years old. Two-and-a-half."

"The crib's too small for him."

"I know it is. I have to buy a bed for him. I'll buy one today. When a child loses a mother's love, there are some things no father can do for him."

Tereza did not understand the reason for all this until the following day at the castle, when Almério lit a cigar after the double feature—mommy and daddy the first time, climbing the palm tree the second—and invited her to go for a walk. At this hour in the afternoon? Yes, he had something to say to her and didn't want to say it here, between the four walls of a brothel.

He had made the very same invitation fifteen years before to Natália, his sweet Whipped Cream, with her snowy skin and shy ways. Now the future bride was copper-colored and fiery. Burning with love, now as then, he spoke the same words he had before:

"I must have Nature to inspire me."

4

Melancholy stole over Tereza as she sat on the wide wall before the hermitage of Monte Serrat toward evening, gazing at the city of Bahia planted on its mountainside, at the calm waters of the bay, at the colored sails of the fishing boats. Almério sat beside her confidently. What spot could be more propitious for a declaration of love than that beautiful, deserted belvedere? It was there that he had asked for and received Natália's hand, and that touching scene was about to be repeated now.

"Tereza, will you consent to let me speak to you of the state of my heart? I find myself at the mercy of a tempest of emotion. No man can control what he feels; love does not wait for permission before entering a wounded breast."

Pretty words, thought Tereza, and true. She ought to know. Love doesn't wait for permission; it appears, it ravishes, it overcomes, and then it's too late. She sighed. To Almério das Neves, the supplicant suitor, that sigh could have one meaning. Encouraged, he went on:

"I love, Tereza, I'm consumed by the fire of love."

The tone of his voice and his attempt to take her hand brought Tereza out of her trance. Turning her eyes away from the landscape and thoughts of Janu, she looked at Almério and saw him enraptured, his adoring eyes upon her:

"I'm passionately in love with you, Tereza. Put your hand on your heart and answer me sincerely: will you do me the honor of becoming my wife?"

Tereza's mouth fell open as he went on to tell her how he had watched her ever since the day they met; how he had been overwhelmed not only by her beauty—You are the loveliest flower in the garden of life—but by her breeding, her good manners. He was sick with love and could no longer contain his sentiments within his breast. Will you make me happy by letting me take you before the priest and the judge?

"But Almério, I'm nothing but a fallen woman."

The fact that she went to Taviana's castle from time to

time meant nothing to him; it was there that he had found his unforgettable Natália, and no man had ever been so fortunate in his wife. Whatever her past had been, it weighed nothing in the balance; a new life would begin for her there, at that very moment. For her, for him, and for Zeques, especially for Zeques. If that was the only obstacle, it was not a problem at all, so that was settled. He held out his hand to Tereza, and she did not spurn it but took it between her own as she replied:

"No, it's not the only one. I'll tell you what the other obstacle is, but first I want to say how touched I am at your proposal. It's as if you had given me a valuable present, something you loved very much; I can't even find the words to thank you. You're a good man and I like you so much. But I can't marry you. Please forgive me, I just can't."

"But why not, if it isn't a secret?"

"Because I love another man, and if he comes back someday and still wants me, no matter where I am or what I'm doing, I'll give it all up and go away with him. So how could I get married, tell me? Only if I were a false woman and didn't care anything about you. But even if I am in the life I have my self-respect."

The baker said nothing but looked sadly off into the distance. Tereza, just as silent and unhappy, gazed at the fishing boats cutting through the bay toward the Recôncavo. What name would its new owner have given the *Waterflower?* Twilight fell over the city and the sea, burning in blood on the horizon. Finally the embarrassed Almério found words with which to break the distressing silence:

"I never realized there was anyone in your life. Is it someone I know?"

"No, I don't think so. He's captain of a fishing boat, at least he was. Now he's gone off in a big ship. I don't know where or whether he'll ever come back."

She still held Almério's hand in hers, and now she pressed it gently in a friendly gesture.

"I'll tell you all about it."

And she told him the story from beginning to end; from their meeting at the Gay Paree in Aracaju the night of the brawl to her desperate search for him in Bahia, how they had lost each other again, and finally the tale

Captain Caetano Gunzá had told her when he came back from a long voyage to Canavieiras in his barque *Ventania*. By the time she had finished, the sun had disappeared under the water, the street lamps were lighted, and the fishing boats were shadows on the sea.

"After he lost his wife he went looking for me and couldn't find me, and by the time I got here he had already left. I decided to stay and wait for him. That's why I'm living here in Bahia."

She gently let go of Almério's hand.

"I know you'll find a woman to be your wife and the little boy's mother, someone as good as you deserve. I can't be the one. Please forgive me and don't hold it against me."

The good Almério, moved to tears, pressed his handkerchief to his wet eyes; but Tereza's eyes were dry; two coals no longer burning. Still Almério did not lose hope entirely; he wasn't out of the race yet.

"I have nothing to forgive you for. It's one of the ironies of fate. But I know how to wait, too. And maybe someday . . ."

Tereza said neither yes nor no. Why wound him, why hurt his feelings? If Janu never came back at the helm of a fishing boat or in the hold of a lugger with a foreign flag, Tereza would wear a widow's mourning in her heart all her life long. She might wear it in a brothel bed, earning her living at a loathsome trade, but never in that of a husband or lover. Why tell him that, though? Why insult a man who had honored her by singling her out?

5

On the afternoon when she refused his proposal of marriage, Tereza Batista repeated to Almério das Neves, almost word for word, the story Captain Caetano Gunzá had told her. Although replete with melancholy incidents, it contained proofs of love and one ray of hope:

"One of these days my comadre'll turn up on the wharf, just you wait and see."

So Captain Gunzá had said as he puffed his clay pipe

on the poop deck of his barque—and Tereza Batista lived
on that hope. Almério das Neves, with his penchant for
heroism and romance, heard her tale with wet eyes and a
lump in his throat: why, it was as touching as a radio
serial! The baker really wanted to marry Tereza Batista:
he was very much in love, hadn't given up—someday,
who knows? But if it had been up to him, Januário
Gereba would have appeared out of the twilit bay that
very moment to take his long-lost, inconsolable beloved
by the hand and lead her to the hermitage of Monte
Serrat, where they would be joined in mystic nuptials
(mystic nuptials! he had heard the expression on the radio and loved it); and Almério would be the first to con-
gratulate them. Just like that generous, unselfish fellow
with the heart of gold that he had read about in a penny
novel when he was young. Almério, too, would be willing
to sacrifice himself for the happiness of his beloved. The
thought of such a magnificent gesture was a consolation
in bitter moments such as these; he was comforted a little.

Tattered phrases blown away by the south wind (it
was going to be a stormy night), sorrows blown toward
the turbulent sea. Where was Januário Gereba, who had
embarked on a Panamanian cargo ship? She had heard
echoes of pent-up emotion in Captain Caetano Gunzá's
voice. He loved his compadre, the friend of his childhood,
candomblé brother who shared the same obligations; his
heart went out to the pretty, brave, appealing girl.

When the masts of the *Ventania* were finally seen as
the vessel crossed the bar one day, Camafeu de Oxossi
wasted no time in sending his nephew with a message to
Tereza. When she finally got it at nightfall, she went running to the Lower Town and saw that the barque had
dropped anchor in deep water at some distance from the
dock. At Agua dos Meninos she put out in a canoe. Captain Gunzá was waiting for her on board; mutual acquaintances had told him that the girl was dying to hear
news of Januário. He was delighted to know she was
alive: so his compadre had been given wrong information
then and she hadn't died in the smallpox epidemic after
all. Well, that was a piece of good luck.

Every day for more than a month Tereza had gone to
the Model Market and the Ramp to see whether the
Ventania had returned from her long voyage. She scanned

the harbor in search of the barque's silhouette, which she could still see in her mind's eye, anchored by the pier in Aracaju loading sugar. About a month and a half before, the *Ventania* had unfurled her sails and headed south to Canavieiras or Caravelas, its hold full of sacks of jerky and kegs of dried codfish. She had no fixed date of return. Sailing ships depend on the cargo, the wind, the tide, and most of all they depend on Yemanjá to give them good weather.

That wait marked the beginning of Tereza Batista's life in Bahia and the first acquaintances she made while seeking news of Captain Januário Gereba and his fishing boat the *Waterflower*. Everyone was as nice as could be; no people in the world could be more polite; but the stories they told didn't fit together. She had come to the capital to find out what she could about Januário, and she asked everyone she met. Here and there she was given a piece of the puzzle, but only Captain Caetano was able to tell her the whole story.

After the smallpox epidemic in Buquim, Tereza had begun to travel slowly south through the backlands, from town to town, from village to village. She had gone from Esplanada to Cipó to Alagoinhas to Feira de Sant'Ana. It was a hard trip and it took her a long time, for she had no money and was forced to ply her trade in the worst conditions. During those months—how many she didn't even know—she finished learning the prostitute's life from A to Z. She touched absolute bottom, but she was determined to reach Gereba's ocean and she kept on fighting until she did.

Feira de Sant'Ana was the only town with a nightclub where she could dance (for almost nothing), but even then she had to raise a hell of a fuss before she got her miserable wages. If an imposing old man with a beard and a staff—he must have been someone very important, and he liked her—hadn't turned up in the nick of time, she would have gone to jail instead of receiving the handful of small change which was barely enough to pay her bus fare and tide her over in Bahia for the first few days. Luckily the old gentleman had added some money of his own. He had liked the girl's grit, and since he was winning at the gambling table at which the owner of El Tango was the banker and where no outsider had ever won before, he not only obliged the fellow to pay what he owed her, but contributed most of his winnings to the pitiful sum. And it was done out of the pure goodness of his heart; he didn't even make her stay and sleep with him, but let her go while he was still enjoying his winning streak, to the bewilderment and consternation of Porteño Paco, the club's owner. His marked cards were no use any more and neither was the rapid sleight of hand that constituted the Argentine's pride and source of capital. It was the first time Tereza had come across that old man in her wanderings, but he treated her as if he had known her for a long time.

Once in Bahia she had begun her search; timidly at first, thinking that Gereba still had a wife. She hadn't come to make problems for him or mess up his life. All she wanted was to find out where he lived so that she could be near him without being noticed. Was that all? Well, she wanted to see the *Waterflower* too, even at a distance. At a distance? Who could say exactly what it was that Tereza wanted and hoped for, when she couldn't say herself? She was just looking for him; he was all she had.

On the Ramp, in the Market, almost everyone knew him and liked him, but no one could give her any news. Or rather, they all gave her some sort of news; no one refused to talk about the fisherman, but none of the news seemed to make sense. One thing was certain, though: Januário's wife had died some time before.

At the Bogun *candomblé* where Januário had held a post as *ogan* or priest for many years, the spirit-mother Ronhoz confirmed the news: Gereba had lost his wife; the consumption had carried her off, poor little thing. The *iyalorixá* looked hard at Tereza and immediately knew who she was:

"You're the girl he met in Aracaju."

After the funeral, Januário had come to the temple to carry out his voodoo obligations to the dead, and also, he had said, to cleanse his body before leaving on a very important journey. Somebody's waiting for me up there in Aracaju, he had added. It was you who was waiting, wasn't it? But he never came back to the temple. She knew, though, that he had come back from that voyage and left on another one.

A voyage? Two voyages? Was he alive or dead? He had disappeared. But where? Tereza had not learned the full truth until the *Ventania* put into port, back at last from the South with a cargo of cacao.

Their talk took place on the poop deck of the barque as it swung at anchor, facing the lights of the city, blown by the south wind whipping the crests of the tame waves of the gulf into whitecaps. It was a dangerous night at sea, a bad night for fishing boats. Janaína had let a storm loose to get her a bridegroom to marry in the depths of the ocean, Captain Gunzá explained, as he wet his fingertips in the water, touched them to his forehead, and pronounced the greeting to the sea siren: *Odóia!* The master of the barque welcomed Tereza affectionately, but he was downcast.

"I heard you were in Bahia and were looking for me. The reason I'm anchored out so far is that tomorrow I have to lay alongside that freighter over there to unload my cargo."

They sat down, the wind blowing Tereza's black hair and the aroma of dry cacao coming up from the hold. Tereza asked fearfully:

"What's happened to Janu? Where is he? I've been in Bahia going on two months now and I don't know much more than I did before. Everybody tells me something different. The only thing I know for sure is that his wife is dead."

"My poor comadre. It broke your heart to see her toward the end, when she was nothing but skin and bones, and such a little bit of a thing. My compadre didn't leave her a minute until it was time to close her eyes. Just a few days before she died, her father turned up to make peace with his daughter and put her in the hospital, but by then it was too late. My comadre wasn't much use as a woman any more, but my compadre felt awful bad seeing her die."

Tereza listened in silence. Behind the voice of Captain Gunzá, broken by the wind and by sorrow, she could hear Januário talking to her by the edge of the sea near the Watchtower: The girl I loved and wanted, the girl I stole from her family, was a healthy, happy, pretty girl. Now she's sick, ugly, and sad but I'm all she has, and I won't leave her high and dry. You're a man, Janu.

"After that he carried cargo on two or three trips to raise some cash, and then he left the fishing boat for me to look after and set off to find you: Compadre, you remember Tereza Batista, that black-haired gal in Aracaju? Well, I'm going back for her, I want to get married again.—That's what he told me."

Captain Gunzá relit his pipe; the wind had blown it out. The barque rose and fell, the waves grew higher, the south wind went mad, calling death in a shrill mournful whistle. Tereza was silent, imagining Janu looking for her, free of his fetters, a soaring bird, ready to bring her home to his fishing boat. Oh, and he hadn't found her!

"He was away nigh onto three months or more, looking for you all the time. He didn't have a plugged nickel when he came back here, had to take him a job as a helper to a truckdriver to get back. It broke my heart to see him so discouraged. He told me where all he had been, way past Sergipe. He crossed Alagoas, Pernambuco, Paraíba, went up to Natal and all the way to Ceará; covered a lot of ground and met a lot of folks, just about everybody but the one he was looking for. He lost track of you in Recife, but he didn't give up till he got to Fortaleza. Then he went back to Aracaju and started inland, and that's when they told him you had died of smallpox. They told him the day and the hour and just what you looked like, there couldn't be any mistake. The only thing they couldn't tell him was the place where you were buried. Seems there was such a passel of corpses there wasn't time for funerals and they just threw five or six dead people in the same grave. That's what they told my compadre, anyway."

Yes, Tereza had gone to look for death and stood her ground when she met up with it, out of despair because she wasn't with Januário; she had tried to forget him too, in the bed of the little doctor, Oto Espinheira, director of the health clinic and king of the yellow-bellies. Death had turned his back on her, though; not even the smallpox would have her. Night came on and the storm grew stronger; Tereza's face was set in stone, Captain Caetano Gunzá's pipe glowed, and the tempest capsized fishing boats. Janaína was calling for a bridegroom, and the whistling wind was her siren song.

"My compadre had changed, he wasn't the man I knew

any longer, didn't even want to mess around on the fishing boat any more. He used to sit right here on the poop of the *Ventania* like a clam, never opening his mouth except to say: How could she have died, compadre? There's a remedy for everything but death, and here I was, thinking all the time we'd live together some day! —That's what he'd say when he did open his mouth, but he had it closed most of the time."

The wind died down suddenly and the fishing boats drifted becalmed and off their course. On the high sea Janaína dragged her bridegroom to his fatal nuptials. Captain Gunzá's voice fell, as he gazed disconsolately at the deck.

"That was when there was the business with the Panamanian vessel, a big freighter. She came into port to land six sailors with rabies and get them to the hospital. A dog on board got sick and before they could kill it, it had bitten all six men. The captain took on some sailors here so he could put out to sea again. Januário was the first to sign up. Before he sailed he told me to sell the *Waterflower* and keep the money for myself, that he had nobody left in the world and he didn't want his fishing boat neglected and rotting away. I sold it, but I put the money in the bank to earn some interest. That way, if he comes back someday he can buy him another boat. Well, I guess that's all I have to tell you."

Tereza only said:

"I'll stay here until he comes back. If he still wants me, he'll find me here waiting for him. But the name of the ship, Captain Gunzá—do you remember what it was?"

"How could I forget? The *Balboa*. And I haven't seen hide nor hair of my compadre nor heard a word from him since the night she left." He puffed at his pipe, the spark glowed, his voice grew warmer and more confident: "One of these days, when we least expect him, my compadre'll turn up on the dock."

6

After her refusal of his suit, the relationship between Tereza Batista and Almério das Neves suffered a sea change, subtle but perceptible. Until then the baker had been to Tereza a client more than anything else. He differed from the others, not only in age (he was only a little over forty, while the others, five in all, were sexagenerians nearing seventy), but also because she was on friendly terms with him outside the discreet walls of the brothel, even at the cabaret where obviously none of those important old men would ever show himself. But there was Almério, telling her how business was, the price of wheat, how he never forgot his beloved wife who had passed away, what clever things the little boy was up to. Tereza listened attentively to this engaging, courteous client who kept an appointment with her once a week.

That twilight hour up on the hill when sorrow had flared over the sea had had its influence on their relationship, making it both more intimate and less so. That may seem contradictory; but such strange and unexpected things occur sometimes in the life of a fallen woman, belying common sense. Less intimate because Almério never took her to bed again, never profited from her erotic experience, never saw her beauty bare, her breasts and buttocks and her secret flower. He was no longer a client. Neither of the two had kept the four o'clock appointment at the castle the following Thursday. Although the matter was never mentioned between them, they both understood that from that day on it would be impossible for them to treat each other as prostitute and client, to deal with each other on a paid, impersonal basis. More intimate, because they had become friends, strong bonds of trust and regard having been forged on that afternoon when they bared their hearts without reserve.

Almério still went to the Lotus Flower often for a beer, a fox-trot, and the pleasure of escorting Tereza to her door. Though still an ardent suitor, he no longer so much as touched the samba dancer's hand, rolled no bedroom eyes; neither did he pester her with pleas or propositions.

He offered only his companionable presence. He kept his passionate love locked in his breast, just as Tereza kept her love for Janu, lost on the high seas where the freighters sailed. Sometimes he would ask her: No news yet, heard nothing from the ship? And Tereza would sigh. On other occasions it was Tereza who would ask her friend if he hadn't found a sweetheart to his taste, a good woman who could fill Natália's place beside the little boy and Almério, in his house and in his bakery, in his bed and in his heart. And the widower would sigh.

He never tried to take advantage of Tereza's obvious loneliness in her long wait, didn't propose himself as a substitute for Januário; but he did try to distract her by inviting her to parties and outings. They went to *candomblé* ceremonies, *capoeira* schools, rehearsals for Carnival parades, together. Without proposing to her again, without talking about love, Almério was always there when Tereza needed him. He kept her from feeling so lonely and abandoned, and she soon felt the warmest gratitude and friendship for him. During that time when she felt so hopeless and discouraged, Tereza sought warmth from a few good friends: Captain Caetano Gunzá, the painter Jenner Augusto, and Almério das Neves. Viviana, Maria Petisco, black Domingas, Dulcinéia, and Anália, all from the zone, were friends of hers too, and so were the people living around the Market Ramp, Agua dos Meninos, and the Lumber Port.

Neither widowhood nor repressed passion could affect Almério das Neves's serene and optimistic temperament or keep him at home for long. He was too fond of a party for that, in spite of his peaceable ways; and whenever he appeared, solid, broad, and smiling, at the Lotus Flower, he had an invitation in his hand. A cordial participant in the popular life of the city, he was on friendly terms with half the inhabitants of Bahia. One night when Tereza started to introduce him to Jenner Augusto, who had come to the nightclub to see her and hire her as a model for a picture he was painting, she was surprised to find that her two friends were already acquainted; were in fact friends, and had gone together to celebrations of the Immaculate Conception on the Beach and Our Lord of Bonfim, to Lady Mother's *candomblé,* and to partake of shrimp and chicken *caruru* on the feastday of Sts. Cosme and Damian.

As long as Natália was alive, Almério's September banquet of *caruru* had attracted dozens of guests, and during the Bonfim festival the baker would rent a pilgrim's house on the Sacred Hill for a whole week and give a party every day. In the miracle room of the Church of Bonfim there was a photograph of the new bakery with all its employees, friends, Father Nélio, Lady Mother, Natália, and Almério, prosperous and jovial. Among the guests was the painter Jenner Augusto.

"Well, Almério, have you forgotten all about me? What about that *caruru?*"

"No, my friend, but I've lost my beloved wife; a terrible tragedy. And while I'm still in mourning it wouldn't be fitting to give a party in the house."

Only then did Jenner notice the black rosette in the lapel of the son of Oxalá's white linen jacket.

"I'm sorry, I didn't know. Please accept my condolences."

He eyed Tereza, thinking he smelled a rat. It would be just like that modest, smiling, imperturbable, cigar-puffing little baker to snatch Tereza from the Lotus Flower and take her home with him just the way he had calmly broken the monopoly of the Spanish bakers, without turning a hair. But would the girl have him? She pretended to be cheerful but was unhappy all the time; he knew there was a sailor in her life. But then again, Almério was just like Mr. Fox: he knew how to sit quietly and bide his time, and time was in his favor. When Tereza was with him she felt secure.

7

She had met the painter again by accident some time before, near the Market, where he was deep in conversation with Camafeu de Oxossi and two odd-looking fellows, one with flowing hair and an enormous moustache, the other with round eyes and a jacket that opened in back. When Camafeu saw Tereza he went over to speak to her; they had been on friendly terms for some time. The painter went over too:

"Why, it's Tereza Batista! What are you doing here?"

That was how he heard about the Lotus Flower, where she visited with the customers and did her dance number, the same one she had danced in Aracaju with a few more flourishes. He turned up at the nightclub alone the first time, then came back with a band of bohemian artists, poor as rats and merry as grigs. Every one of them tried to sweet-talk her into going to bed with him—for free, of course. She turned them all down but none of them held it against her.

She did pose as a model for some of them, adding one more badly paid profession to the many she already had. If you look at the red and blue Yemanjá done by the sculptor Mário Cravo (the moustached fellow)—mistress, wife, mother, strong humanity in living wood, now in the possession of a friend of the sculptor—you can easily recognize Tereza's face and her long black hair. Tereza also gave birth to Carybé's Oxum, which is on display in a bank (Carybé was the other fellow, the one with the round eyes and the coveted jacket that opened in back); you can tell by her posterior and her elegant pose. And who inspired Genaro de Carvalho's *mulatas,* those multiple Terezas with cats and flowers, all with that absent look of a woman gazing out to sea? And didn't shameless little Calá, a prince of good fellows all the same, put together an album of etchings, all based on incidents in Tereza's life? It was at about that time, too, that a certain serenader, who had his eye on her and thought he had some reason for hope, composed a *modinha* for her—a fellow named Dorival Caymmi. More than once when Tereza was in their company she recalled those days in Estância with the Doctor, and the intense joy of living she had felt then.

And so Tereza met a great many interesting people, attended some formal parties, went out to Rio Vermelho where Jenner Augusto lived, and modeled for some of his pictures. At the *capoeira* school Mestre Pastinha taught her Angola samba steps; on board the barque Captain Gunzá told her about the winds and the tides and the seaports along the Recôncavo; Camafeu invited her to dance in a Carnival procession with the Amaralina

Diplomats, but she refused because she wasn't in a Carnival mood. She went to the *candomblé* temples of Gantois, Alaketu, Casa Branca, Oxumarê, and Opô Afonjá where Almério, a friend of Lady Mother, had a place in Oxalá's house.

But Tereza's favorite excursion, day in, day out, was to the Market Ramp, the wharf where the fishing boats tied up, the famed harbor of Bahia. When the *Ventania* was at anchor she would go aboard to visit Captain Gunzá and turn the knife in her wound by talking about Januário Gereba.

The people who lived and worked around the docks were familiar with her anxious, repeated questions. Who had news of a Panamanian ship, the *Balboa*, a black freighter? She had taken on six sailors from Bahia; where were they now?

With Captain Gunzá's help she discovered the *Waterflower*, now the property of an old fishing-boat captain, Captain Manuel. He had rechristened it the *Arrow of St. George* in honor of his wife, Maria Clara, a daughter of Oxossi. Tereza seemed reluctant to get up from where she sat at the helm, touching its wood with her hand. When Maria Clara saw the dark girl so tense and preoccupied, with glazed eyes, trying to see again Januário's look and gestures, to feel the warmth of his hand in the salt-weathered planking, she said:

"He'll come back if you have faith. I'll make an offering to Yemanjá."

Besides a bottle of scent and a big comb to comb her hair with, Yemanjá asked for two guinea hens to eat and a white pigeon flying over the sea.

8

Tereza met a good many hookers at the Lotus Flower and Taviana's castle, and became friends with some of them. Her name began to be spoken with respect after her clash with Dogfish Nicolau, the plainclothesman from the vice squad who was making his pile at the expense of the prostitutes who filled the vast, turbulent red-light zone, the fervid, putrid territory that stretched from

Barroquinha to Pelourinho, from Maciel to Ladeira da Montanha, from Taboão to Carne Seca. Sometimes she had lunch at Anália's house in Pelourinho (Anália was from Estância) or at Black Domingas's and Maria Petisco's in Barroquinha.

Maria Petisco was a firm-fleshed, featherbrained, impulsive mulatto girl to whom laughter came easily, tears even more so, and passionate love at the drop of a hat —she wore her heart on her sleeve and gave it away about once a week—who had been rescued by Tereza Batista from the clutches, or rather the dagger, of the Spaniard Rafael Vedra.

One Tuesday night in the cabaret when business was slow and the giddy girl was talking at one of the tables in the back where the women sat waiting for an invitation to dance or drink, who should enter the nightclub but a passionate Galician just imported from Vigo, still dressed in dramatic black, the picture of jealousy, latest heartthrob of the faithless Moorish girl. The scene was straight out of an Argentine tango, as befitted a rapid, rapacious love affair.

"Perra maldita!"

Rafael raised his dagger, the girl jumped up with a shriek of terror; Tereza jumped up too and there was a scuffle. The poniard, turned aside by Tereza, glanced off Maria Petisco's shoulder, drawing enough blood to cleanse Iberian honor and stay the outraged Spaniard's arm.

Men and women came running up and milled about. On such occasions some tattletale always goes running to call the police, usually someone who has nothing to do with whatever is going on but can't help sticking his nose in, either to show off or because he's a born squealer. Maria was led to one of the rooms on the upper floor where the hookers turned tricks at a fixed price, and the mob trailed upstairs behind them, leaving the dancehall practically empty. Tereza took advantage of this to send the avenger on his way, sobbing repentantly and ready to shit at the thought of cops, jail, and a trial.

"Get out of here, you nut, while you can. Do you have someplace to hide for a few days?"

Yes he did, with relatives living in Bahia. Abandoning poniard and passion together, he flung himself down the stairs and disappeared into an alley. The police arrived

half an hour later in the person of a civil guard. No trace
of the incident could he find; no one could give him any
information about the dagger, the criminal, or the victim.
Some dumb practical joker must have called in to make
fun of the authorities. The owner of the nightclub and
the floor above it opened a bottle of cold beer behind the
counter for the guard.

The rescued victim was later removed to Barroquinha
by Tereza and Almério and treated by a pharmacology
student, reasonably drunk at that hour, with whom she
instantly fell head over heels in love.

"He's a piece of sugarcane," whispered the stabbed
one, rolling her eyes. Maria was a native of Santo Amaro
de Purificação in the sugar zone, and all good-looking
men were sugarcane to her.

Only two days later the saucy girl was seen at the
Lotus Flower, dancing cheek to cheek with the fledgling
druggist. And during working hours too! She really didn't
have a brain in her head.

Rafael had raised his murderous dagger because he
had found evidence that a male had occupied Maria
Petisco's ardent bed just before daybreak, a time for love
and not for work. If certain persistent rumors could be
believed, it was no living man who was putting horns on
the Galician (and on Maria's other sweethearts), but an
enchanted spirit. The story went that the two compadres,
Oxossi and Ogum, would visit Barroquinha at least once
a week to drop in on Maria Petisco and Black Domingas,
their respective devotees. Neither Tereza nor anyone else
ever succeeded in finding out for sure, the two favorites
naturally maintaining discreet silence on the subject.

It was Almério's considered opinion—and he knew all
about such things—that the rumors might very well be
true. After all, it wouldn't be the first time that an *orixá*
had slept in the bed of an adept; or a *iaô* had decorated
a husband or a lover with esoteric horns which were
nonetheless uncomfortable for all that. In some cases
there was even concrete proof. Take Eugenia de Xangô,
a married woman who sold fritters at the Seven Gates.
Xangô, not content to gobble her up every Wednesday,
finally forbade her to have intercourse with her husband
at all, and since there was no appeal from his commands,
the cuckold had to resign himself. Ditinha's story was sad

and funny at the same time: Oxalá fell in love with her and spent so much time in her bed that he neglected important obligations. Poor Ditinha's life became unbearable: no sooner did Oxalá take his leave than his wife Nanã Burokô came down in a jealous rage and beat the poor girl black and blue. Ah! those invisible beatings, you don't know how much they hurt until you've had one, Almério concluded, and he was listened to with attention and respect.

9

Some time after the incident with Rafael, Tereza went to lunch at Maria Petisco's house and found the girl so upset she seemed like a different person. Her shoulder bore only a little scar, but where were the laughter, the lively chatter, the animation, the vitality, all the qualities that made her so popular in the zone? Now she was worried, frowning, and glum; and come to think of it, so were Domingas, Dorotéia and Pequenota, who lived in the same house, and Assunta, the madam, besides. Assunta, who was sitting at the head of the table, pushed aside her food.

"Why, what's the matter with you all?"

"It ain't just us, it's everybody. They're gonna move us all outa here, ain't you heard? By this time next week, if you want to eat with us you'll have to go to hell and back up Judas's ass," Assunta grumbled.

"What are you talking about? I haven't heard a thing."

"The Dogfish came around this morning with Detective Coca. They went to every house in Barroquinha and told everybody: Better get your stuff together, moving day's a-coming," said Maria Petisco.

"We got a week to move. By Monday week we gotta be outa here." Assunta's voice was sharp and weary.

Black Domingas had a husky, nocturnal, caressing voice:

"Gonna move everybody out, that's what they say. First us and then the folks in Maciel, the Carmo Gates, Gallows Hill, everybody in the district."

"But where do they want you to go?"

Assunta's rage was too much for her to swallow:

"That's the shittiest part of the whole deal. To a stinking hole in the Lower Town, somewhere near the Dry Meat district and Codfish Hill, the very filthiest, rottenest part of town. Nobody's even lived there in a coon's age. They've been trying to fix those houses up by plastering on some whitewash. I went to have a look and damn near bust out crying."

The women chewed in silence and drank their beer. Assunta went on:

"Seems like the landlords are some bigshot relatives of Chief Cotias. They should worry. Do you own a slum building in a bad part of town, does it rain inside, is the roof falling in? Just rent it to a hooker and charge what the traffic will bear. That's what they tell 'em up at the precinct."

"Those cops are like buzzards."

"You mean you're going to move?"

"How the hell can we stay? Can the cops push us around? You bet they can!"

"But can't something be done? Can't you complain?"

"Who are we gonna complain to, honey? You think hookers got a right to complain? If you wanna get beat up on, go ahead and complain."

"But it just isn't right, we've got to do something."

"Okay, you tell me: what can we do?"

"Not move. Stay right here."

"Not move, huh? Anybody'd think you never turned a trick in your life. Whores got no right to complain. Whores only got a right to be dumped on."

"Take what you're thrown and be grateful, or you'll get something worse."

"Don't you know that? Ain't you learned yet?"

10

If you don't know it, let me tell you now, once and for all: whores have no rights. Whores are for giving men a little pleasure for a fee, and that's all. When they aren't doing that, they're being abused. By the pimp, the gigolo, the cop, the watchman, the soldier, the delinquent, and the authorities. They're anathematized by vice and virtue alike. They're abused for no reason at all or hauled off to jail. Anybody who wants to can spit in the face of the whore. With impunity.

You, sir, who are a champion of popular causes, who are daily eulogized in the press, will you kindly tell me if you've ever in your life deigned to give a thought to the whores? Except, of course, on those unmentionable occasions when you climb on top of one to regale the flesh, even an incorruptible champion being subject to the urgings of instinct and having to satisfy his carnal needs. Bed of infamy, vile flesh, base instincts, as the whole world has it.

. .Does the dauntless leader know that owning a house with rooms to rent in a red-light district is a very lucrative business? The police can always gerrymander the district a little for political reasons, and some of the gravy can go to relatives and friends. When I say gravy, I mean that a bawdy house brings in a much higher rent than a family dwelling. Is the doughty champion of the underprivileged aware of that little fact? And it isn't only the rent; everything a prostitute gets costs more and comes harder, and everyone thinks that's perfectly all right. No one protests against that injustice, not even the noble defender of the people. You didn't know that? Well, now you know. And here is something else you ought to know: it doesn't take a court order to turn a prostitute out of her house, just a police decision. Any sheriff, any commissioner, any cop on the beat can tell her to move and she's out on the sidewalk. A whore has no right to decide where she'll live and work. Why should she?

When a whore takes off her clothes and lies down to receive a man and grant him the supreme pleasure of life in exchange for a modest fee, is the illustrious battler for social justice aware of how many people get a slice of that fee? Everybody does: from the landlord to the lessor, from the madam to the commissioner, from the gigolo to the cop, the government and the vice rings included. Whores have no defenders; no one stands up for their rights, the newspapers print no columns describing the squalor of the whorehouses; that subject is taboo. Prostitutes are news on the crime page, where they're thieves, disorderly, addicted to drugs, butterflies of vice, tried and sent to jail, accused of all the wrongdoing in the world, and responsible for dragging men to perdition. Who is guilty of all the evil done in this vast world? Why, the whores, sir.

Is the indomitable advocate of the oppressed informed, by chance, of the existence of millions of women who belong to no class and are repudiated by all, cast aside from the honest struggles of life, branded by iron and by fire? With no bill of rights, no organization, no work card, no union, no program for a better life, no manifestos, no banner, no counting time on the job; riddled with disease but with no clinic, no doctor, no hospital bed; hungry and thirsty but with no right to unemployment assistance or a retirement pension or a vacation, no right to have children, no right to a home, no right to love, just the right to be whores and nothing else? Did you know or didn't you? Well, if you didn't I'm telling you now.

To make a long story short, whores are an affair for the police station, the prison, and the morgue. But has the charitable father of the poor ever stopped to think what would happen if all the whores in the world ever got together and called a general strike, refused to take their clothes off and wouldn't go to work? It would mean chaos, the day of judgment, the end of the world, wouldn't it?

The poorest of the poor can find someone to shout and fight for him, but not the whores. I, Castro Alves the poet, dead for one hundred years, now rise from my grave and take the rostrum where I once called for the abolition of slavery in St. John's Theater, since burned down and now the site of a monument to me in the Plaza that bears my name in the city of Bahia. Now I cry out to all whores that the time has come to say: Enough!

11

The firm of H. Sardinha & Co., investments, financing, construction, leases, and general real estate, had purchased an extensive tract of land at the foot of the mountain with a fine view of the bay in order to take advantage of government subsidies for projects aimed at attracting tourists. Imposing plans for the site were drawn up: an architectural grouping of apartment buildings, hotels, restaurants, shopping and entertainment centers, supermarkets, air-conditioning, tropical gardens, saunas, Olympic pools, parking lots—everything, in short, that a city needs to make its inhabitants comfortable and its visitors happy.

Publicity leaflets in full color invited the Bahians to invest in this titanic enterprise by buying shares, dividends payable in twenty-four months. The plan was ideal, the profits were guaranteed, the advantages innumerable. You too can be a co-owner of the Parque Bahia de Todos os Santos, the largest real estate development in the Northeast. Be a tourist without leaving Bahia: each shareholder will be entitled to a stay of twenty days per year at half price in one of the new development's fine hotels.

In the lowest part of the area, on steep little Codfish Hill, four or five old houses were still standing, and next to them half a dozen shacks. Once mansions, the houses had been abandoned years ago and were now a refuge for assorted riffraff, homeless urchins who wandered the beaches, and marijuana pushers. As a first step, the firm ordered the shacks torn down and their inhabitants run off the property.

Inspecting the site with the engineers, old Hipólito Sardinha, the big boss, a man who could squeeze blood from a turnip, according to the consensus of his business associates and competitors, mused for a long time on the fate of those once-fine houses.

An ambitious enterprise like the one in hand takes some time to get under way. Once a company has been organized and plans drawn up, public interest must be aroused and money raised to finance the undertaking, while architects, urban planners, engineers, and landscape designers study blueprints and begin to make the monumental project a reality. The land itself would hardly begin to be touched for another two years.

Two years equals twenty-four months. Old Hipólito inspected the houses. Would they just be sheltering thieves, vagabonds, children, and rats all that time? Or should they be demolished immediately and the whole area cleaned up completely, as one of the engineers wanted to do? They were houses of stone and mortar, in a ruinous condition, true, but solidly built. Old Sardinha couldn't bring himself to give the word to tear them down.

"Unless they were turned into fifth-class cathouses, I can't imagine what earthly use you could put them to," remarked the engineer.

The old man listened in silence. There might be the smell of money even in a careless phrase flung away on the breeze from the bay.

12

The decision to transfer the red-light district from the Upper Town to the Lower was not made quite so suddenly as it seemed to Assunta and her lodgers. Had they been addicted to reading the papers, the order to move, passed on by the Dogfish and Detective Dalmo Coca on their morning rounds, would not have caught them by surprise. The fact was that the crime pages and the social columns gave them a sufficient dose of strong emotions for the day. On the one hand burglaries, murders, violence galore, weeping, and gnashing of teeth; on the other, parties, receptions, banquets, laughter and love, champagne and caviar.

"I'd sure like to have a taste of that caviar some day," said Maria Petisco decidedly after reading about one of Madame Tetê Muscat's dinners as described by the divine Luluzinho, complete with oohing and aahing and exclamation points. "Champagne doesn't mean a thing to me; I've had all of that I could hold."

"Domestic champagne doesn't count, white gal. The only good kind is French, and you'll never dip your snout in that," retorted Dorotéia prissily.

"Have *you* ever had any, princess?"

"Once I did, at Colonel Jarbas's table—he was from Itabuna—at the Palace, when gambling was legal. It's all frothy bubbles, just like drinking wet seafoam."

"Well, some day I'm gonna get me a colonel with plenty of moolah and stuff myself on caviar and French champagne. French, English, American, Japanese. Just you wait and see."

Squabbling over champagne and caviar, scorning the

front page, the big stories, the editorials, they did not realize that the newspaper publishers were suddenly filled with indignation because the red-light zone was located smack in the middle of town.

In Barroquinha, next to Castro Alves Plaza, "not far from the Rua Chile, the commercial heart of the metropolis, where the most elegant shops selling fabrics, garments, shoes, and jewelry are to be found, the degrading commerce of sex goes on." Society ladies out shopping "are obliged to rub elbows with fallen women." From the Hill of São Bento "the sordid picture of scandalous, half-naked prostitutes at their doors and windows" was plainly visible.

Prostitution had spread through the whole center of town: Terreiro, Portas do Carmo, Maciel, Taboão, the whole tourist section. It was a scandal. "Tourists descending the streets and alleys of the world-famous colonial section of Pelourinho witness shameful scenes: scantily clad or completely nude women at the doors and windows, even on the sidewalks; foul language, rivers of *cachaça,* open, unbridled vice and orgies." Did those tourists, perchance, "come all the way from the shores of the South and from abroad to observe such a sorry spectacle, one so unworthy of a civilized center, the tourist capital of Brazil?" No, a thousand times no! thundered the editor. The tourists stream into Bahia "to see and admire our beautiful beaches, our churches embellished with gold, the Portuguese tiles, the baroque architecture, the picturesque popular celebrations and quaint voodoo ceremonies, our brand-new buildings, our industrial progress. They come to see the beauty, not the dirt. They don't want to see our waterlogged swamps and our harlotry!"

There was only one solution: to move the red-light zone to some spot farther away, more discreet. Since it was impossible to put an end to the blight of prostitution, for it's a necessary evil, let's at least hide it from the pious eyes of decent citizens and the curiosity of prying tourists. As a first step, Barroquinha must be cleansed of the infamous presence of prostitutes at once.

The press was really up in arms, no doubt about it— especially about the brothels in Barroquinha, "a cancer that must be extirpated with all possible speed."

The public authorities responsible for safeguarding public morals heard the patriotic clamor and at once made up their minds to move the fallen women bodily from Barroquinha to Codfish Hill.

13

"Thousands of sailors. All paying with dollars. Think about it!"

The speaker's two companions scanned the news item on the front page of the evening paper and liked what they read.

"What are you suggesting, exactly?"

A person coming in for a minute to buy cigarettes or matches at the Elite Bar in Maciel—better known to its large clientele as the Prostitutes' Bar—a person seeing them out of the corner of his eye, three prosperous-looking men in hats and ties in earnest confabulation about the volume of capital, consumer market conditions, the prospects for placing the product and how long the peak demand for it was likely to last, choice of capable assistants, the most strategic locations for selling it, and how much profit it could be expected to make, would have taken them for businessmen absorbed in working out the basis for some lucrative enterprise—and that person would not have been very far wrong.

If that casual customer had stayed to tipple his beer at a nearby table, however, and had watched and listened more attentively to the three entrepreneurs, he would quickly have identified their real profession. Plainclothesmen Dalmo Garcia and Nicolau Ramada Junior and Assistant Bureau Chief Labão Oliveira all had "police" written all over them. Not that that prevented them from turning a nice little business profit when an exceptional occasion presented itself, like the one they were considering now. No less than three American battleships on maneuvers in the South Atlantic were coming to Bahia, where they would be at anchor for several days and nights. Thousands of sailors turned loose on the town, all heading straight for the red-light district to get their fill, all needing prophylactics, all paying dollars for them . . .

how had the Dogfish's little brain conceived of such an excellent idea? That's what love of money can do, thought Assistant Bureau Chief Oliveira, not one to turn up his nose at easy pickings himself: cupidity lights up the dullest brain, lends a glimmer of intelligence to the biggest blockhead in the world.

"Why can't we elaborate on that idea a little?" hinted Dalmo.

"What do you mean, elaborate? You don't mean sell amulets and jew's-harps in the zone, do you? It wouldn't be worth it; the people in the Market do a better job."

The assistant chief couldn't see what the plainclothesman was driving at, and yet it shouldn't have been hard, knowing as he did that Dalmo was an undercover investigator in the Drugs and Narcotics Division.

"Who said anything about amulets and jew's-harps? I'm talking about a certain kind of cigarette. . . ."

"Cigarettes?" The Dogfish made a mighty effort to understand and finally thought he had. "Yeah, I see what you mean; you want to swap condoms for packs of American cigarettes. Say, that ain't a bad idea; U.S. cigarettes are as good as money in your pocket. I know where we can sell 'em."

Obviously, to expect swift, incisive reasoning from the Dogfish would be to expect too much; but Labão Oliveira was an experienced man and an intelligent one. Dalmo wiped his perspiring face and lowered his voice:

"I'm talking about grass. Marijuana."

"Ahh!"

They ruminated on the idea in silence. They couldn't use the same team they had picked to sell prophylactics and aphrodisiacs to sell reefers openly in the street. That particular item was more complicated, more serious, and would have to be dealt with more discreetly. It wouldn't do to discuss the matter out loud in a public place like a bar. Oliveira stood up:

"Let's go someplace else. We better map this thing out from the beginning."

Pushing back his chair, the Dogfish called out to the Galician proprietor:

"Put it on the cuff, José."

That was just one of the little perquisites enjoyed by the watchdogs of law and order and public morals. Thou-

sands of sailors! Oh boy! The Dogfish was so happy he
was almost dancing. On his way out he knocked against
the shoulder of an incoming customer and almost made
him fall. Out of sheer high spirits he laughed in the unlucky man's face:

"Didn't like that? Well you can shove it!"

14

They called him "Dogfish" because it was a notorious
fact that he had eaten his two young daughters as well
as his wife's sister, also a minor. If there had been more
young women in the house he would have had them too;
love of family burned in Nicolau Ramada Junior's breast.
These domestic matters were made public when the sister-
in-law let the cat out of the bag, and soon became the
talk of the town.

"Dogfish, that's what he is! Lies with his daughters!
And he laid me too, right in my own sister's bed."

Ungrateful bitch! To wash all the family's dirty linen
in public and make such a commotion over nothing. And
all because when the girl announced her intention of leaving the family to shack up with a Pooh-Bah at the Department of Agriculture, Nicolau wanted to get something
back in exchange for what he had given his sister-in-
law during the past five years: room, board, laundry, a
high-school education. And what did he have to show in
return for all the money he had spent, all the devotion
and affection he had shown by sleeping with her? Nothing but insults and that nickname hung like an albatross
around his neck. There's nothing like gratitude, is there?

Fiftyish, pasty-white, thick, ungainly, a black hat pulled
down over a narrow forehead, greasy clothing, clam-
digger's trousers, the bulge of a revolver showing under
his jacket to make people respect him—with such a record and such an appearance, where could Nicolau the
Dogfish be of more use than on the vice squad, enforcing
the law and suppressing wrongdoing?

He was one of the little tyrants of the red-light zone,
putting the squeeze on madams, pimps, procuresses, and
owners of the castles, pensions, cabarets, and bars. He ate

and drank without paying, chose women to sleep with, and threatened and persecuted them until they did. Anyone who dared refuse such an invitation from the Dogfish was in for a rough time. That Tereza Batista, for instance, would get what was coming to her one of these days. She had not only spurned the cop's advances; she had mocked him and exposed him to ridicule when the Lotus Flower was full of customers:

"Now you listen to me! When I want to sleep with a pig I'll look for one in a pigsty." Sick and tired of the plainclothesman's threats and propositions, Tereza spoke recklessly, that diamond glitter in her eyes.

Compared to Dogfish, Dalmo "Coca" Garcia was a dandy, a glass of fashion. He was young and wore well-cut, fashionable suits and a gray hat; his gun was not in evidence, and he made his authority felt by his imperious manners and an occasional look from the corner of his narrowed eyes. Aside from these noticeable differences in wardrobe and physique, there was little to choose between them. Despite his youth and elegance Dalmo Coca was thought to be the worse of the two, the reactions of a cocaine sniffer being unpredictable. One night when he was hallucinating he almost strangled Miguelita, a little Paraguayan who was lost in Bahia and had fallen for him. If help had not come in time, the promising career of the docile Indian girl who sang *guaranias* in such a sweet voice would have ended then and there.

As for Assistant Chief Labão Oliveira, it's wisest not to dig too deeply into the chronicle of his long, active, and rather frightening professional career. He had grown rich on a relatively modest salary. As we have seen, he was not one to scorn a good chance to do business. Though twice suspended and his actions investigated, nothing could ever be proven to the discredit of either his personal honor or his professional conduct. He was officially clean, to use an adjective rarely heard in the realm of the police or the whorehouse, the two sides of the stage on which the drama of the closed basket was played—a story we intend to tell here *grosso modo* because our heroine Tereza Batista, never knowing when to leave well enough alone, jumped into it with both feet.

15

No, she never knew when to leave well enough alone. Turning an occasional trick within the discreet walls of Taviana's castle and not in a brothel with an open door, living in a house above suspicion in a family street and not with other prostitutes, Tereza had nothing to do with the moving problem. And yet she jumped right into the fight, and reliable witnesses say that she laid about her with more vim and vigor than anybody else. In fact, Dogfish was firmly convinced that she started it all. There was good and sufficient reason for the cops to vent their rage on her when it was all over.

She had brought with her from the backlands a reputation as a brawler and a street fighter, a hot-tempered virago with a chip on her shoulder. If that wasn't what she was, why did she stick her oar in when nobody asked her opinion? She had a mania for fighting other people's battles and not standing by while injustice was done: a seditious, untamable disposition. As if a prostitute had any right to play the fool by disobeying the authorities, standing up to the police and calling strikes! What was the world coming to?

"Law and order reign again, thanks to the energetic and judicious actions of the police." The adjectives are quoted verbatim from Bureau Chief Hélio Cotias's press conference; and while there may be some doubt as to the judiciousness of the police in this case, no one can say that energy was lacking. There are those who speak of brutal and unnecessary violence and point to the prostitute killed by a bullet in the neck and the wounded of both sexes. "If there were excesses, whose fault was that?" asked Cotias, the law-school graduate, of his colleagues of the working press (he had dabbled in journalism as a law student). "If we hadn't come down with a heavy hand, where would we be now?" This unanswerable question, plus a few shots of the Chief of the Bureau of Gambling and Public Morality—in profile, I photograph better that way—put an end to the press conference and the big story that had inspired a Rio de Janeiro daily to print an illustrated article on the events of the last night of the strike, one of the pictures showing Tereza Batista being overpowered by three cops. There remained only the judge's verdict, certain to be favorable to the plaintiff in H. Sardinha & Co.'s suit against the state for damages done to its property by the mob, fault lying with the authorities for failing in their duty to maintain public order. No question; H. Sardinha would win.

Still, some doubts remain and will never be entirely laid to rest. Where can the curious go to find answers to their queries? The zone of prostitution is vast, blurred, obscure.

How far did the mutually detrimental conflict go between the interests of the highly reputable corporation and those of a recently formed association among three equally reputable police officials—an association to be sure, which, for obvious reasons, lacked a formal name and the initials sanctified by business tradition? Were the assistant chief and the two plainclothesmen so absorbed in their own personal, urgent affairs that they neglected their duty toward society (anonymous) and ignored the strict orders given them by Bureau Chief Cotias? Or was it Cotias himself, carried away by his recent conquest of Bada, the wife of a congressman, lovely, elegant, and gracious, a bouquet of rare virtues, who neglected the sacred cause of home and family (meaning the Sardinhas)? Perhaps it's best not to stir too much the muddied waters of disputes at such a level: two powers-that-be, each jealous of its own authority and rights. Especially not now, when the quarrel is all over. They're all white; let them fight it out themselves, I say.

Was it the press which exaggerated out of all proportion a simple plan to move the Barroquinha brothels to Codfish Hill by claiming that the whole red-light district was being moved, sowing panic and fomenting violence? Would Vavá and Dona Paulina de Souza have appealed to Exu if they hadn't felt personally threatened? On the other hand, how could the press be expected to take up the cudgels in support of transferring a few miserable dens of vice in Barroquinha (only six in all) to Codfish Hill? Appearances count for something, even when you're talking about brothels.

Did the police really issue a warrant for the arrest of a

certain Antônio de Castro Alves, a poet (that is, a bum), a student (that is, an agitator), and comb Barroquinha, Ajuda, the whole blessed zone for him? And the bard in question dead a hundred years and safely tied down with a monument in a well-known public square? Was that story true or just a mischievous hoax on the part of some irreverent reporter bent on making the police look silly? According to the report, the warrant had been issued by Assistant Bureau Chief Labão Oliveira, who was allergic to poets—apocryphal, no doubt, but not entirely without basis. A pale young man with an intrepid moustache and a burning gaze had certainly appeared when the fight was at its hottest and was clearly seen by all to hover over the demonstration. Who could it be if not the poet Castro Alves, dead in his grave these hundred years? What if he is dead, aren't we in Bahia? This is how Maria Petisco described him: A vision of light over the people's heads, more beautiful than I can say. And one final question to wind up with: was the demonstration really nothing but a procession in honor of St. Onofre, patron saint of prostitutes?

That's a lot of questions—more than will ever be answered, even without considering the decisive part played by Exu Tiriri and Ogum, Fish of the Sea. All was confusion, disorder, and anarchy in the closed-basket affair.

"The Closed Basket Strike," that was the title the press gave to the movement. The term came from a pious custom of abstinence on the part of prostitutes, who will have nothing to do with men from midnight on Holy Thursday, when they "shut the basket," until noon on Resurrection Saturday, when with an Alleluia!, the basket is opened again. With this devout custom, scrupulously followed, is Holy Week observed in the red-light zone. This time, however, the question was not a religious one; nor would it have been appropriate in any case with all those Protestant American sailors involved.

16

Hélio Cotias, LL.B., "The Gentleman Cop" in the happy phrase of society columnist Luluzinho (Libidinous Little Lulu, to some), made no attempt to conceal his irritation:

"Well, gentlemen, where have you been and what the devil were you doing?"

Dogfish mumbled some excuse, but Assistant Bureau Chief Oliveira chose to maintain a lofty silence, fixing his chief with a cobra stare which said as plainly as words: You little half-assed law student, you stuck-up papa's boy, you piece of crap. Don't you raise your voice to me or you'll be sorry. Do it and you'll get an answer you won't like; I'll spoil your little game. I'm not your errand boy and I'm still waiting to hear how much I'm going to make out of this deal. His assistant's ophidian eyes, filmed over and blinking, made chills run up Cotias's spine. He softened his tone as he gave his orders:

"I want those women brought here right now. All of them. Requisition the Black Maria and bring them in, and then we'll see whether they move or not."

Oliveira, with Dogfish at his side, turned to carry out the order but began to whistle tunelessly and ostentatiously before he reached the door. The Chief clenched his fists: he was too sensitive to work with such riffraff; but that was just his luck. If it weren't for the compensations . . .

According to a friendly newspaper, the fact that law graduate Hélio Cotias had been named to the post of Chief of the Bureau of Gambling and Public Morality constituted evident proof that the government meant to bring in the best kind of new blood, men worthy of the public trust, to work on the police force. Well born and better married (to Carmen, nee Sardinha), he had been given a furious chewing out over the phone that morning by his wife's uncle. He was still in bed, slowly recovering from a hangover resulting from last night's reception— the only thing that was Scotch about the congressman's whisky was the label—and in no mood to listen to a lecture. But then, the congressman's wife made up for his whisky. She was a goddess, a Tanagra figurine: he had told her so and she had melted. The days to come looked full of rosy promise.

The scornful voice of the old man had left him thoroughly irritated and in need of venting his irascibility on someone. He had started to tell Carmen what he thought of her uncle's disposition, but she had countered him with a stone in each hand: Don't you dare talk that way about my Uncle Hipólito! At headquarters he would have liked to tell that bunch of psychopaths what he thought of them, but he wasn't quite man enough to do it. His assistant's eyes, like something out of the morgue! He was a killer, through and through; it wouldn't do to cross him. Cotias contained his rage intact for the six Barroquinha madams.

The audience lasted only a few minutes. The women were shoved urgently into the Chief's office and given a furious dressing-down before they had a chance to open their mouths. The Chief yelled and pounded the table, just as if he hadn't gone to law school. What in God's name had got into them? Did they think there were no public authorities left in Bahia? They had been given eviction notices and an address where they could lease new quarters and put their deposits down. And there they were, still infesting Barroquinha as if they hadn't heard a word. Had they absolutely gone crazy? Were they out of their minds?

"Those ratholes aren't fit to live in. They're rotting away inside—floors, ceilings, walls, everything. Nobody could live in them or get a man to come there," ventured old Acácia. White-haired and blind in one eye, Acácia was the dean of the madams, the owner of a house where eight women lived and worked. "Conditions there are just too awful."

"I have a report from the Public Health Department right here saying that sanitary conditions in those houses are adequate. Where do you want to live, in a mansion in Corredor da Vitória or Barra or Graça? Who do you think you are?"

"But, *doutor*—" Assunta began.

"Shut up! I didn't call you in here to give me a lot of hot air. There's nothing wrong with the new place, it's been approved by Public Health and the Police Department, so there's nothing to discuss. Now I'll give you until tomorrow to move. By tomorrow night, if there's a single cathouse open in Barroquinha we'll come down on you hot and heavy. Don't blame me if it happens. I've given you fair warning."

17

When he stopped by at Headquarters that night, Chief Cotias tried to find out how moving day was going.

"Where's Oliveira?"

"He's out on a job, Doctor."

"Nicolau?"

"He's not here either. They went out together."

They had probably gone to keep an eye on Operation Moving Day, for which he had made them responsible. Anyway, he had given the women until the next day. Carmen was waiting for him in his car with the special white license plate. They were going to play canasta at the congressman's house with a few other socially prominent couples; the Chief thought of Bada and smiled. He had called her a Tanagra figurine the night before; tonight he would call her an enigmatic Mona Lisa. He would not drink any more of that pseudo-Scotch on any account, but make do with a glass of beer.

Since they were a little late he ordered the driver to take a shortcut to gain time. The car turned down a squalid street where the streetlights shone on women on the prowl for men and others lounging in the doorways of the bawdy houses. Carmen peered out curiously.

"You're the man who bosses all those people around now, aren't you? My little Hélio, king of the hookers. What a joke."

"It's no joke to me. It's an important job and a very responsible one."

The automobile turned into Shoemakers' Lane and headed for Nazaré.

18

Activity was normal in the kingdom of Hélio Cotias, Chief of Gambling and Public Morality. Women waited for marks in the labyrinth of badly lighted streets, offering themselves, calling, inviting, hissing, pleading, naming their specialties. At the doors and windows the merchandise was on display: breasts and thighs, buttocks and vulvas, all for sale cheap. Some of them dolled themselves up, painted their faces, swung their inevitable purses, and walked over to Rua Chile, where farmers and salesmen from the interior took rooms for the night.

In the bars customers mingled with old habitués, and ordered beer, brandy, rum sours, or *cachaça*. Among them were pimps, gigolos, a few artists, and the last poets to seek inspiration from the romantic muse. At Hansen's Flower of São Miguel, the tall, blond, goateed German proprietor sketched figures and landscapes while he chatted with the prostitutes. All of them were his friends, and he knew the life and miracles of each.

Inside the dance halls the dance bands, jazz drummers, and piano players never stopped playing for the couples dancing the fox-trot, the rhumba, the samba, the marcha, and an occasional Argentine tango. Between eleven and midnight the floor show came on: singing girls, dancing girls, and contortionists, none of them very talented. After the applause they waited for invitations for the rest of the night, charging a little more than ordinary hookers; it was a question of status.

The tenderloin came to a boil as the hour grew later. Most customers came between nine and eleven; then business fell off again. Old men and young, solid, mature men, poor men and beggars, an occasional rich man of perverted tastes (rich men usually went to some comfortable, discreet castle when the sea breeze started blowing in the late afternoon), workingmen, soldiers, clerks, students, people of every calling, plus professional bohemians growing old at the tables of the cheap bars and dreary cabarets as they nursed a flame for an incomparable lady of pleasure. Night in the tenderloin meant noise and movement and weariness, and occasionally passion and thrills.

When the pursuit of pleasure was at its feverish height, a few curious society women came slumming with their husbands or lovers. They got a kick out of the lively spectacle of prostitution, the half-naked women, the men entering the brothels, the foul language and insults. Oh, what a thrill it would be to make love in a whore's bed in one of those holes. It gave them gooseflesh to think of it.

In one of the hidden corners of this vast kingdom, on the street the Chief's automobile had taken, men's and women's figures moved on hurried errands. Tereza Batista and undercover agent Dalmo Garcia, coming from different directions, reached the door of Vavá's enormous castle at the same time.

As he crossed the threshold and walked to the main staircase, the detective stopped to glance at the woman: it was that hoofer at the Lotus Flower, a fine brunette piece. Had she started working for Vavá? His colleague Dogfish said she acted high and mighty and thought she was too good to give anybody the time of day; it looked mighty funny for her to be hanging around the biggest bawdy house in Bahia. Something must have happened. One of these days when he had more time, Dalmo "Coca" Garcia would look into that story the Daughter-Eating Dogfish had told him, but right now he was too busy. It was important business that had brought him to Vavá's. He headed for the stairs. Tereza waited a few minutes in the street until he had come out again.

19

What was his real name in full? Probably not a soul in the tenderloin knew it; and yet Vavá had reigned in the zone for close to thirty years. A reporter with literary pretensions and sociological notions, the author of a series of articles about prostitution, had dubbed him "Emperor of the Red-Light Zone," but he hadn't learned anything about his family or where he came from. If he had been an old-style reporter and not so full of himself, he might have taken the trouble to look in the police blotter or his own newspaper morgue, or gone to the records office and found the signature of Walter Amazonas de Jesus, listed as owner of the huge building in which he lived. He bore an honorable and sonorous name, but "Vavá" was enough to get him all the attention and respect he wanted, both in the district and beyond it.

His age was even more of a riddle than his name. He

seemed to have existed forever, holed up in that enormous old house in Maciel, first as a lodger, then as sole owner, not only of that house but of others in the neighborhood. He thought real estate an excellent investment, particularly buildings located in the red-light zone. The reporter had referred to the "streets of houses" Vavá had acquired. That was a manner of speaking, no doubt. Although no one but the old vicelord himself knew exactly how many there were, they probably numbered only four or five buildings in all. However many there were, they brought in a substantial amount each month.

He had his headquarters in a three-story mansion. The ground floor was rented to a grocery store, and the two upper floors housed an immense brothel with each room subdivided into two or more. Respected and feared by all, Vavá saw to his property and ran the brothel from a wheelchair that he maneuvered himself through the living rooms, corridors, and bedrooms. Crippled in both legs, withered by infantile paralysis, hunchbacked, and with a head out of proportion to his body, all the life of his shapeless figure was concentrated in his sagacious, suspicious eyes and his great strong hands: he cracked walnuts and filberts between his knucles. Rarely away from his side was his bodyguard, Amadeu Mestre Jegue, a former boxer, who kept the establishment in order and carried Vavá to the top floor on his daily round of inspection.

From noon until four in the morning the movement was intense and unceasing. There were hordes of women and even greater hordes of patrons; the waiting room where the delicate youth called Greta Garbo served drinks was always full. When he wasn't in the parlor keeping an eye on business, Vavá stayed in his spacious, comfortable quarters on the second floor, his combined office and bedroom. In it was a double bed, a washstand, a desk, a radio, a victrola and records, and a little shrine where Exu Tiriri was enthroned. He performed his devotions to the voodoo spirit faithfully, for Exu had rescued him from many a tight spot. Without Exu's protection, it would have been all up with Vavá long ago, surrounded as he was by envy, greed, and treachery. More than one person had an eye on his wealth.

The police had their eye on it too. In spite of the payoff he made religiously every month to Assistant Chief

Oliveira and a regiment of gumshoes, they were always making his life miserable in one way or another, were always out to exploit him. The police had no sense of decency and couldn't be trusted to keep their word.

One time they had burst into the house, bringing some agents from the juvenile court with them and waving an order from the judge. That time they took away no less than seven girls between fourteen and seventeen years of age. Those crooked cops had known all along that the girls were working there, but they had posed as good family men and put on a fine show of indignation for the representatives of the court. What's more, Vavá had found out later that the bureau had known beforehand that the magistrate was planning to raid his place. Didn't he grease the gumshoes' palms every time he turned around? Was it too much to expect them to let him know? Vavá, you'd better hide those minors who work in your place or you'll be in hot water. What a time he had had reopening the brothel. If he hadn't had some very good friends at court (some of them with a yen for spring chickens), and if Exu were not all-powerful, he would have lost his business and been hauled into jail, slapped with a lawsuit and a stiff sentence on top of it.

Another time, on the basis of a false accusation concocted by the police themselves that drugs were being pushed in the house, they'd turned the place upside down and closed it down for more than a week. Vavá was arrested and held in custody for a day and a night, far from the comforts he was used to. To extricate himself from that trap had cost him five years' savings, hoarded a penny at a time to pay cash for a building across the street that was part of a disputed estate. But that was partly his own fault. Exu had given him strong warnings in plenty of time against that cop and drug addict Altamirando, now fortunately resting six feet under. You don't fool around with Exu Tiriri.

If policemen were wicked, women were worse. Vavá didn't fall in love very often, but when love hit him it hit him hard; he lost his head as well as his heart and was as easily fooled as a child. First he would romance the chosen one with honeyed words and languishing looks; then he would install her in his apartment on the second floor, not let her work any more, and lavish pres-

ents and privileges on her. How many of them had robbed
him? Almost all of them, the heartless tramps. They slept
with him for no other reason than to diddle him out of all
they could. He had almost ruined himself over one of
them: Anunciação do Crato, bronze, slender, haughty,
always with laughter on her lips, exactly to Vavá's taste.
Loving-kindness personified, one would have said. But
one day when Vavá was in bed and couldn't get up without being helped, she announced that she was taking the
train back to the *sertão* that very morning, in just a little
while; just long enough to rob the money in the desk, a
whole day's takings. She laughed in his face and sneered
that it wasn't a bit of use for him to call out at that early
hour in the morning when the whole house slept, even
Mestre Jegue. Vavá watched from the bed as she rum-
maged in the desk. Where did he find the strength to
slide out of bed and creep along the ground? How did
he manage to reach her and seize her by the ankle with
his terrible claw? When Mestre Jegue came running he
had her on the ground and was choking the life out of
her. It was a wonder he didn't kill her. Who gave him
strength for that? What a question! Wasn't Exu sitting
right there in his shrine behind his dish and glass?

"I'd like to talk to you in private," said Dalmo Garcia.

He wants money, thought Vavá. The plainclothesman
was not included on his payoff list. His game was drugs,
and Vavá wanted nothing to do with drugs, junkies, or
pushers. So this was the snowbird they called Dalmo
Coca. Everything that happened in the zone reached
Vavá's ears sooner or later.

20

Of the three partners in the brand-new enterprise established to welcome, protect, and cheer the dauntless defenders of western civilization on their brief visit to Bahia
by safeguarding their health, increasing their potency, and
sending them to dreamland, Coca was by far the most
literate—also the stupidest.

He sat down in the armchair beside the desk and
spilled out his story to the whoremaster without even in-

sisting that Amadeu Mestre Jegue, a witness to the dialogue, leave the room. Street peddlers would be distributed throughout the zone to hawk condoms to the sailors, along with little bottles of an aphrodisiac in the form of an elixir fabricated by Heron Madruga, an acquaintance of Dogfish. For that part of the business he did not need Vavá's collaboration: but for the other, much more lucrative, part he needed it very much indeed; while the prophylactics were being peddled publicly in the street, other discreet, trustworthy vendors would be placed in the brothels to provide the nation's heroic guests with the best quality domestic joints at a reasonable price.

"You want to sell marijuana here, in my house?"

Yes, old fellow, and that's not all. Dalmo, who was responsible for the large quantity of grass that had been ordered and was expected to arrive the next evening, was looking for a safe place to keep it hidden until the time arrived to put it on the market. The fleet was due to arrive any day; no one knew exactly when, because it was a military secret. And the safest place he could think of was Vavá's apartment. Didn't he have a wall safe? Yes he did: he had installed it after the affair with the mulatto girl, Anunciação do Crato. If the safe was too small, a trunk like that one in the corner would be fine; all he had to do was lock it with a key. A huge brothel like Vavá's, with such large-scale, nonstop coming and going of both men and women, was the ideal repository. From there they could easily distribute the product to the agents responsible for selling it. In the midst of the usual hustle and bustle of the place, anyone seeing the pushers going in and out would think they were just customers coming to diddle around and have a fling.

"Keep it in my house? In my room?" Vavá's eyes were almost starting out of his head. "You're out of your mind! I won't have it here and that's flat."

It was fortunate that at that hour Dalmo Garcia's nostrils were not palpitating nervously and uncontrollably and that his reflexes still obeyed his will. Later on it would have been different. Not even Amadeu Mestre Jegue's presence could have restrained the elegant police agent, who was in the habit of slapping anyone who opposed him across the mouth.

Amadeu Mestre Jegue had fought thirty bouts in all,

in both the amateur and the professional class, losing twenty-six on points—a great many points—and winning four by KOs, the only ones in which he had managed to land one on his opponent's chin or rib cage. He had a lethal kick, and he was honestly devoted to Vavá, but would he have retaliated if Dalmo had slapped the boss in front of his eyes? Would he have dared to manhandle a detective? God only knows.

Luckily, this time Dalmo was satisfied with threats. You'd better think twice before refusing to do a little favor for a special agent. Haven't you heard about the order to clear out? This time it's for real; the decision was made at a very high level and it'll all be over in a few days. The women in Barroquinha are moving to Codfish Hill tomorrow. It'll be Maciel's turn next. The brothels here will have to be relocated in those old pigeon roosts in Pilar, and only two or three of them are fit to live in. The whole red-light district is being moved from the middle of town to the Lower Town at the foot of the mountain. Anyone who's in the good graces of the police can count on certain exemptions and privileges, but if you're on the blacklist I pity you! The owner of a big, flourishing enterprise like Vavá's couldn't afford not to be on good terms with the cops. Dalmo Coca would come back tomorrow, sometime in the late afternoon, to work out the details. Maybe he'd bring the grass with him then.

Two packs of American cigarettes were lying invitingly on top of the desk. The plainclothesman slipped them into his pocket and took his leave. Vavá lowered his big head. He was worried and at a loss.

Unlike the women in Barroquinha, he did read the editorials in the newspapers and was aware of the campaign to shift the zone from one part of town to another, but it hadn't really scared him. Whenever there was a dearth of news, the papers fell back to worrying the subject like dogs chewing a bone. He knew, however, that the day before the Chief of Public Morality had set a forty-eight-hour deadline for Barroquinha to be evacuated, and that had alarmed him a little. Now the interview with Dalmo Coca had confirmed his worst fears.

Such a move would jeopardize his whole position, not only because it would be a real calamity to have to move his large establishment, but because the income he received from all the houses and apartments he let out at steep rents to the most reliable tenants in the world, the madams and procurers, would be reduced to a trickle. He would have to lower his rents drastically if he were obliged to lease those houses to ordinary families. It looked as though he would have to agree to keep the marijuana to preserve a little something, at least, from the wreckage of impending bankruptcy. But then, what if the whole thing were nothing but a treacherous plot on the part of the police? They could plant the marijuana in his room and then invade the house, pretend to find it, and ruin his life forever. At a time like this, the only thing to do was ask Exu's advice. He would call in Father Natividade tomorrow.

Greta Garbo appeared at the door of his room:

"There's a female person here to see you. Her name's Tereza Batista, she says."

21

He clapped eyes on Tereza and fell madly in love on the spot. Was this sudden passion love at first sight? You might call it that, since he was seeing her in flesh and blood for the first time, standing in the doorway, smiling with her gold tooth. Then again you might call it something else, for he had longed for her, had searched for her, had seen her in that heavenly vision in a thousand dreams. Now finally she had come, Exu be praised.

He knew Tereza Batista by name. He had heard about the affair of the Toledo dagger, the fury of Rafael Vedra, the Spaniard made a cuckold by Oxossi, and of how Tereza had intervened to save Maria Petisco's life and at the same time helped the jealous man get away—two meritorious actions, according to the code of the tenderloin. He had been informed as well of the reckless retort she had spat in the Dogfish's face, and he had been told that she was comely and attractive, though the description fell far short of the reality. Vavá was so overcome by emotion at the miracle before his eyes that he all but forgot about Garcia's visit and his other worries and vexations. He told Mestre Jegue again to bring Pai

Natividade next day. Now he had a new problem to add
to the others: ever since the Anunciação do Crato business, he had asked Exu's advice about love affairs too.
Vavá, surrounded as he was by envy, greed, and treachery, must be protected on every side.

"Come in and take a seat."

She walked across the room so proudly and gracefully,
God in Heaven! and sat down in the same chair the detective had sat in. The cripple's powerful hands manip-
ulated the wheelchair closer. What could have brought
her there? She couldn't be interested in working in a
brothel that was open to the hoi polloi, not when she
could go to Taviana's place with its rich, select clientele.
She could earn more at Taviana's in one afternoon with
just one john, one polite, generous old man, than any of
Vavá's girls could make in two days and two nights of
hard work, one man after another nonstop.

Tereza, as usual, went straight to the point:

"Senhor Vavá, have you heard they're moving the
zone?"

The warm voice added the finishing touch to the dream
figure that had always vanished at dawn—the flashing
black eyes in a calm face with a touch of melancholy,
hair loose on her shoulders, slim figure, copper color, a
hint of flirtatiousness in her serious manner. There was
an aura about her. . . . Vavá was so distracted he hardly
heard the question. He only realized that she had addressed him ceremoniously. No one in Bahia called him
senhor, not even people who were afraid of him, and
there were a great many. How should he reply? Bahian
rituals of politeness are complex.

"Won't you call me Vavá? That way I can call you
Tereza. What was it you were asking me?"

"All right. I'll be glad to. I was asking if you had
heard that they're moving the zone."

"Why, I was talking about that very thing just now."

"The ones in Barroquinha have to move to Codfish
Hill by tomorrow. Do you know what state those old
houses over there are in?"

"I've heard it's pretty bad."

"Did you know that everyone else is being moved too?
Do you know where Maciel's going?"

"Yes, to Pilar. Now since you're asking me so many

questions, let me ask you one: What's all this leading up to?" He was finding the conversation interesting, both because the subject was important to him and because Tereza's face lighted up at each word. The girl seemed to blaze up in the air like a flame. In his dream he had seen her like that on a cliff, a fiery torch in the blackness.

"The folks in Barroquinha aren't going to move."

"Eh? They aren't going to move?"

This statement contained such a new and revolutionary idea that it shook Vavá out of the romantic cloud that had enveloped him since Tereza had appeared in the doorway. He looked at her inquisitorially, mistrust glimmering at the back of his eyes, and repeated the question:

"How do you mean, they're not going to move?"

"I mean they're going to stay right where they are, in Barroquinha."

"Who told you that? Old Acácia? Assunta? Mirabel? I wouldn't believe anything Mirabel says. You mean old Acácia's not going to obey the eviction notice?"

"That's right. Nobody is."

"The police are going to raise hell."

"We know that."

"They'll come down hot and heavy and drag everybody out by the hair."

"The women won't move even if they do. Nobody's going to those houses on Codfish Hill, not even if they have to camp out on the sidewalk."

"Or in jail."

"They won't be in jail forever. That's why I came to talk to you."

"What for?"

"I've heard that after Barroquinha it'll be Maciel. Please tell me something, if it's not a secret, sir—I'm sorry: Vavá—Are you going to move?"

Vavá stared hard at Tereza with those eyes in which the life of his body was concentrated; scrutinizing, skeptical, divining eyes. Why wasn't she satisfied with being pretty? Too pretty, God in Heaven!

"Not if I can help if, of course."

"But what if you can't help it? Mirabel gave Chief Labão all the money she had, and he just put it in his pocket and it didn't do one bit of good. She has to move just like the others."

"If there's no way to get around it I don't even want to think about it."

"But what would happen if *nobody* moved? Do you think the police can drive everybody out by force if no one obeys the order? I don't."

Disobey the police! What a crazy, ridiculous idea. But how wonderful it would be, if the people in the zone could keep it right where it had flourished for so many years. A crazy, ridiculous idea; a tempting idea. Instead of replying, Vavá asked:

"Tell me something, please: Do you think the police are likely to bother Taviana's castle, with all those big-shots protecting her?"

"I couldn't tell you that."

"Well, I'll tell you, then: They won't. They'll move everybody else before they move Taviana. You know that as well as I do, so why are you mixed up in this? You talk as if you worked in Barroquinha or here in Maciel. Why is that?"

"Because I may be working at Taviana's house today, but I've worked in other places where the door was open and I may have to do it again." She paused for a moment and the lightning flash in her black eyes took Vavá aback. "I've been in some pretty tight spots, and one thing I've learned is that if you aren't willing to fight you don't get what you want in this world. And you don't deserve to."

Resist orders from the police! It was so ridiculous and crazy, it might work. It just might! Exu, father and protector . . .

"I'll think about it and give you an answer tomorrow at noon."

"I'll come back at twelve noon. Good night, Vavá."

"Are you going so soon? Won't you have a little drink to wet your whistle? I have a lovely liqueur made by the nuns from violets and cacao. The night is young; let's talk a little while."

"I have to be at the Lotus Flower soon, and I have some things to do first."

"Until tomorrow then, at noon. Come and have lunch with me. Tell me what you like to eat."

"Thank you, whatever you have."

She got up and Vavá contemplated his vision in the

flesh, oh, God in Heaven! Tereza said good-bye with a
smile. Vavá's hand was a shapeless claw, yet how delicately he touched the girl's fingertips. Not content with
being pretty, she had the most ridiculous ideas. Be careful now, Vavá, don't do anything crazy; remember
Anunciação do Crato. With his breast a raging furnace,
how could Vavá be careful? He had fallen in love, he
was lost to reason.

22

The round prodigy of a mulatto girl called Paulina the
Scuffler or Paulina the Brawler had once been crowned
Queen of the Carnival by the revelers of the Euterpe's
Marionettes Carnival Club and paraded through the city
streets, covered with sequins, on their leading float. Now
she was an imposing madam named Paulina de Souza,
Dona Paulina with all due respect, the monumentally
stout, tremendously well-organized owner and manager of
four bawdy houses in Pelourinho and Taboão. After
Vavá she was the most important person in the tenderloin, her influence reaching vast numbers of people. The
women liked her: Dona Paulina's strict but she'll never
do you dirt, she's not like some others who just want to
suck your blood.

Everyone called her "Dona," and young girls from the
interior asked for her blessing; her four houses were mod-
els of wise management and good order, offering quiet,
safety, and well-spoken, healthy girls. No scandals ever
took place where she ran things, no arguments, scuffles,
robberies, drinking, nor any of the other things so common in bawdy houses. None of her houses had a bar,
and no liquor was sold to the customers. To make up
for that, Dona Paulina provided all sorts of cheap but
effective erotic literature for the curious and the needy:
leaflets with popular ballads illustrated with crude draw-
ings, and sensational photographs for those with a little
more money to spend. This little sideline pleased the customers and was good for business.

Dona Paulina de Souza made her own laws and saw to
it that they were enforced. Goodhearted and a believer

in female solidarity, she never let a woman down who needed help, but she wouldn't be imposed on, either. Any woman who lived in one of Paulina's houses had to behave herself and get it through her head that she was there to make a profit for the house. Bad language, *cachaça*, junk, and other vices—out the door. If the woman didn't like it she could pack her bags and go make a living someplace else.

From her active, fun-filled youth, Dona Paulina kept, besides her memories and some good stories to tell, a fund of energy sufficient to clip the wings of any smart aleck or wise guy or new john who didn't know the rules—most especially the rule that anybody who thought he could hump for free or pay later could go hump his mother. It was worth the price of admission to see Dona Paulina's aggressive, furious indignation in full spate. Agile in spite of all the weight she carried around, she could make a stevedore run for his life.

Dona Paulina lived as the common-law wife of Ariosto Alvo Lírio, municipal paymaster, a polite, well-educated man who was tall, thin, and brown. She had bought a house and some land—in Ariosto's name for legal reasons —in São Gonçalo dos Campos, where she came from, and hoped soon to settle down in peaceful retirement for the rest of her life. In another five years when the municipal official could retire, she would leave her prosperous establishments in other hands (there were plenty of prospective buyers) and go to live in São Gonçalo in the company of her lover, who with luck might be her husband by then.

There were only two things that saddened and irritated Dona Paulina, and one of them was the fact that she was married to Telêmaco de Souza, a barber by trade and a rum-swiller by vocation. The recalcitrant mule had so far escaped from all the successive, powerful spells ordered by his wife, who was great friends with the terrible wizards of Ifa. The figaro had been in two bad automobile accidents: in one three people died, and in the other, two, but Telêmaco, of course, escaped without a scratch. He caught typhoid fever, the doctor said there was no hope, but he showed no respect for the doctor and refused to die. Coming back on the ferry from Itaparica, half seas over in *cachaça*, he fell into the ocean, and, though he couldn't swim, the ungrateful wretch didn't drown. He had been born with a caul and that was the same as being born under a lucky star, for anyone born with a caul is a protégé of Oxalá, Lemba di Lê in Angola. Still, Dona Paulina hadn't given up. If she kept on ordering infallible spells, one or another of them was bound to work someday, and she would find herself a widow and a bride.

The other source of irritation was the good money she had to waste on police payoffs. She ran her business according to the rules—she didn't exploit minors, didn't deal in drugs, didn't allow any roughhousing in her establishments—and it simply wasn't fair that she should be robbed this way, that she herself should be the victim of the most unjust, sordid kind of exploitation and have to dig into the money she was saving up to buy farmland in São Gonçalo dos Campos, just to fatten up a guy like Dogfish, for example, a filthy beast who abused his own daughters.

The pervert had been around that very day to get money from her with the excuse of making preparations for the coming of the American sailors. As if that wasn't enough, he had threatened everybody in sight with that business of the red-light district's being moved. If Paulina wanted to stay in Pelourinho she'd better break her piggy bank and be ready to shell out a hell of a lot of dough—and even then, it might not do her any good. This time, said the gumshoe, trying to get her all worked up, the order came directly from the governor: Get those whores out of the downtown area. It was a promise his wife had made during the electoral campaign: If her husband was elected, he would run the hookers out of town. The Dogfish exulted:

"This is one time I'd like to see your *candomblé* saints do anything to help you. Anyone who wants us to lend a hand is going to have to spend a lot of dough. You'd better start getting used to the idea right now."

Dona Paulina de Souza had met Tereza Batista through Anália, a quiet, smiling girl who sang nostalgic *modinhas* from Sergipe all day long like a bird. Because she was from Estância and always talked about the Piauitinga River, the Golden Falls, and the old bridge, Tereza made friends with her at the Lotus Flower and reminisced with her about the colonial mansions, the Parque Triste, the enormous moon, and days that were dead and gone. The Doctor's name never came up; Tereza hugged those happy, loving memories jealously to herself.

A tenant of one of the ex-Carnival Queen's establishments, the one with the apartments reserved for her highness and consort, Anál019 invited Tereza to lunch, and she went back again and again. Not one to pass up a good gabfest, Dona Paulina became attached to the girl from the backlands, with her distinguished manners and educated way of talking. Tereza talked about the backlands and the cities in the North and told curious tales of animals, people, and haunts. She spoke as warmly of some poor homeless devil of a hillbilly as she did of a distinguished gentleman, a lord of the manor. Dona Paulina was always happy to see her—I've come to mooch some grub off you!—because she knew she would be entertained all afternoon. Anália had told her in confidence that Tereza had been the mistress of a plutocrat up in Sergipe and had lived in the lap of luxury. If she had been less foolish and more fond of money, she could have been independently wealthy by now; the old man was so crazy about her he would have given her anything she asked for.

When Tereza showed up at an unusual hour, Dona Paulina was busy checking up on how things were going in her houses but told her to stay:

"You can just follow me around and tell me what you came for. Is it money you need?"

"No thank you, that's not why I came. Tomorrow the women in Barroquinha have to move."

"It's unfair and a rotten shame. That Dogfish has already been around here today asking me for money because of that move."

"But the folks in Barroquinha aren't going to move."

Dona Paulina de Souza opened her eyes wide.

"You mean they'll refuse to go? And who'll answer for the consequences?"

"Everybody will, if everybody decides not to move. I've had a talk with Vavá and I think he'll go along."

"Tell me what you know, girl, one thing at a time."

Tereza explained once more. It was easy to turn a few cathouses upside down, but how could the police force the whole zone to move if nobody went? In Barroquinha they've already made up their minds: They're not going.

"They won't go? Oh, but the police—"

Yes, the police might resort to violence, make arrests, do anything they liked. The women would refuse to obey them. Not a one would go live in those old tumbledown houses on Codfish Hill. If they couldn't have men in Barroquinha they would work when and where they could, in friends' houses. The madams would have to bear the loss for a few days until the police gave up. They stood to lose a lot more if they had to move.

"Ain't it the truth?"

Well then? The people in Maciel would stay where they were too. Vavá had said he would give her his answer tomorrow, but Tereza was willing to bet that he'd go along. The women in Pelourinho and Taboão would stay too, if Dona Paulina said so. It all depended on her.

"But that's just foolishness! The only thing we can do is pay off the cops. Fill their pockets with money; that's the way it's always been. That beast Dogfish has already started collecting."

"What if it doesn't do any good? Mirabel paid off the cops and she might as well have kept her money."

Ariosto Alvo Lírio, the prince consort, came in while they were talking. He had had a fling at organizing unions when he was a young man and had taken part in a successful strike against City Hall, against a bill that was prejudicial to the interests of public servants. Words came easily to him; he had made speeches on the steps of city hall and been applauded. His memory of the labor movement was that of a jolly good thing. He liked the idea of resisting the eviction order and thought it might bring positive results. His enthusiasm was infectious.

Nevertheless, Dona Paulina de Souza was a woman of common sense who did not like to make her mind up in a hurry, and she was not willing to give the proposal her immediate, unconditional support. Tereza waited, trying not to show her anxiety. If Dona Paulina and Vavá agreed to give the word, no one in the whole tenderloin would move, the Barroquinha women would have a place to work, and refusal to knuckle under to the police would be almost unanimous.

"The sky'll fall in," murmured the madam.

When she was a very young girl, long before she ever became Paulina the Brawler and Queen of the Carnival in Bahia, Dona Paulina de Souza had been made *candomblé* adept by Mother Mariazinha of Agua dos Meninos, in an Angola temple under the protection of Ogum the Fish of the Sea, a spirit held in great awe. Before deciding anything, she would have to ask the advice of her spirit guide. Come back tomorrow, she told Tereza. And as for you, Seu Ariosto, don't you get mixed up in any of this. You just keep out of this mess or they won't like it down at City Hall.

23

Queen of Angola, powerful on earth and sea and in the heavens, Mother Mariazinha gave a warm welcome to her adept Paulina de Souza, initiated in the first boat launched at the *candomblé* temple of Agua dos Meninos by the venerable guardian of the African spirits, in those days herself a novice who had just learned to wield the razor for the ritual shaving of heads. The hour was late, but a spirit-mother has no fixed time for eating, sleeping, or resting; her time is not her own. Paulina hailed the spirits with the ritual clapping, kissed the floor, received a blessing, and poured out her troubled heart. I'm in real trouble, Mother. This move means ruin to me and it hurts me to give the cops the savings it's cost me so much sweat and blood to accumulate.

Ogum the Fish of the Sea has a retiring nature. Even in his own temple he only comes down to dance with the people once a year, in October, and the rest of the time he stays holed up at the bottom of the sea. Well, he thought the problem his afflicted daughter had come to consult him about was so important that, wonder of wonders, he abandoned his own strict habits and instead of answering through the shells, he came in person, gleaming with fish scales and coral. A sudden gust of wind shook Mother Mariazinha and made her tremble. Ogum the Fish of the Sea mounted his steed.

He gave his daughter Paulina a friendly embrace; she

contributed generously to keep up the temple and she was always one of the first to come to the October festivals. He passed his hand over her from head to foot, delivering her from the evil eye and other annoyances. Then, in a surging voice like the lapping of waves, he predicted choppy weather ahead. Paulina was in for trouble and it wouldn't be easy, but if she handled things well the storm would blow over. Nothing ventured, nothing gained. To make his meaning still clearer, he added: If you want something done, go yourself; if you don't, send somebody else and waste your money and your time.

What about the girl, Tereza; could she be trusted? Absolutely! She was a warrior woman, a daughter of Yansã, and behind her Ogum the Fish of the Sea glimpsed an old man with a staff and long white beard, Lemba di Lê himself, Oxalá to the Nagôs.

The spirit took his leave on another gust of wind; Mother Mariazinha shuddered and opened her eyes. Paulina kissed her hand. In the distance, out toward Ribeira, the war drums rumbled.

24

The next evening at the Lotus Flower, Almério das Neves danced with Tereza and sensed that she was worried. It had been four days since he had seen her; he'd had to stay in bed with a bad case of flu but had come to the nightclub as soon as he was on his feet again. Tereza gave him a friendly greeting:

"I haven't seen you around, are you playing hard to get?"

Along with the affectionate joke ran an undercurrent of uneasiness. When they were on the dance floor beating out a rhumba, he asked her if she had had any news of Gereba. No, she was sorry to say she hadn't. She had located the office of the shipping firm that had hired the sailors at the request of the captain of the freighter, and they had promised to try to find out where it was. As soon as they had some information they'd let her know. Why didn't she leave her phone number? She didn't have a telephone, but she would stop by once in a while to see if they had any news. She had been there twice already and they had nothing to tell her. The *Balboa* must have changed its routing; those Panamanian ships had no regular routes but just went wherever there was freight to be picked up. They were gypsies—so Gonzalo the Spanish dispatch agent had told her, staring at her with impudent, covetous eyes. All Tereza could do was be patient and go on living as best she could.

Almério asked what she had been doing since he had seen her last. Oh, such a lot of things! He must not be up on the news, and there was a lot to tell. She was so tense that neither the dancing nor the conversation could soothe her.

"Do you know who I had lunch with today? The best chicken stew I ever ate. I bet you can't guess."

"Who?"

"Vavá."

"Vavá, in Maciel? That guy's dangerous. How long have you been friends with him?"

"Just since yesterday. I'll tell you about it. . . ."

But there wasn't time to tell it. Someone came running up the stairs and shouted from the doorway without stopping for breath:

"There's a riot in Barroquinha!"

Tereza left Almério's arms, ran down the stairs, and was off like a flash down the street. The baker ran after her, not understanding anything of what was happening but not wanting to let the girl go alone. In Ajuda they began to see people milling around, some of them arguing excitedly. In Castro Alves Plaza there were more of them. The howl of police sirens could be heard from Barroquinha. Tereza pulled off her shoes so she could run faster, without even noticing Almério puffing on her trail.

25

A Black Maria full of prisoners passed Tereza Batista; another came after, and two more were still in Barroquinha with people being hustled inside.

Resistance was over. The conflict had been violent but brief. The paddy wagons disgorged a horde of cops and sergeants who closed off the street, invaded the houses, and laid about them with nightsticks, beating a tattoo on the backs of the rebels. Who ever heard of hookers ignoring orders from the police? Beat 'em up, that's all those dumb broads understand, heroically commanded Bureau Chief Hélio Cotias, gentlemanly guardian of public morals. A few men, mostly customers getting their money's worth, tried to stop the violence and were beaten up and hauled off to jail for their pains.

Not many of the women went quietly. Maria Petisco bit and scratched Dalmo Coca, and Black Domingas, who was as strong as an ox, fought until she was overpowered. One by one they were dragged off by the cops and thrown ino the Black Marias. Pickings were good. It had been a long time since that many hookers were picked up in a single raid. Jail would be jumping that night.

As she turned into the street, Tereza saw Acácia being dragged off by two cops. The old woman was struggling and yelling out insults and curses. Tereza ran toward the group, Tereza the Fighter. One of the leaders of the invading troops, none other than Dogfish himself, revolver in hand, caught sight of the hoofer from the Lotus Flower. Aha! Now at last he would have his revenge; the bitch would pay now for her high-and-mighty ways.

A policeman standing near Tereza was ordering the crowd to disperse. Pointing to the girl, Dogfish bawled out:

"Hey! Grab that girl! Don't let her get away! That's the one!"

Tereza whirled her shoes around her head and hit the policeman on the temple with the heels. She ran forward, hoping to reach Acácia before they loaded her into the wagon. Dogfish advanced on her, and Tereza found herself trapped between him and the cop she had hit on the face, who was roaring and foaming with rage: You'll pay me back for this, you damned whore! At that moment a paddy wagon full of prisoners started away and passed between her and the cop. Where had that old man come from who was hiding her from the Dogfish? He was an important-looking old gentleman in a white linen suit, panama hat, and gold-headed cane.

"Get out of my way, motherfucker!" bellowed the Dogfish, aiming his revolver.

The old gentleman paid no attention to him and still blocked his way. The cop gave him a shove, which had no effect. There was just time for Almério to get into a taxi, draw up beside Tereza, and drag her inside. She protested:

"They're taking Acácia away!"

"They've already got her. Do you want to go too? Are you crazy?"

The driver remarked:

"I never saw it as bad as this. Beating up on women —what kind of a man do you have to be?"

Dogfish and his colleague searched in vain for the damned girl: Where in hell had she got to? And where in hell was the old man? What old man? A damned son-of-a-bitch who got in my way. No one ever saw any old man, then, now, or later.

The last Black Maria left Barroquinha, its siren scattering the curious crowd in Castro Alves Plaza.

26

Cops and guards brought a few sticks of furniture out of the houses, some mattresses, linen, articles of clothing, a saint's image, and a victrola, and piled everything up in front of the doors. Later on a police truck picked up these random belongings and dumped them in front of the old houses on Codfish Hill. The symbolic move had been made. It was up to the madams, when they had been freed, to see to transporting the rest of their things, including most of the furniture and objects of daily use. So a triumphant Assistant Bureau Chief Labão Oliveira informed Chief Hélio Cotias when the battle was over. Calm reigns all through the tenderloin: this unthinkable revolt has been put down, the focus of sedition crushed. You can go home and get a good night's sleep if you want to, Doctor Cotias; the assistant chief will see the prisoners, male and female; it will be a pleasure. Doctor, we're gonna have some fun tonight in jail.

27

The valiant Labão Oliveira was a gay deceiver. Calm did not reign in the tenderloin, not by a long shot. The subterranean rumblings grew louder.

Chief Cotias retired to his well-earned rest, the euphoria of victory slightly marred by two uncomfortable recollections: half-dressed women being thrown like sacks into cells, and Labão Oliveira foretasting the fun he was going to have that night. As he crossed Castro Alves Plaza, he saw that Barroquinha, where guards were pacing up and down, was absolutely quiet. It was all over, thank God. The night had been exciting, then depressing. The law-school graduate sighed.

Even as the Chief was preparing for a peaceful night's sleep, the news of violence and arrests circulated swiftly through the streets and alleys, the castles and the cathouses, and penetrated to the cabarets, the bars. Dona Paulina de Souza heard a dramatic tale from one of her clients and remembered Ogum the Fish of the Sea's words of the night before: Nothing ventured, nothing gained. When would it be Pelourinho's turn? For the moment, she told her girls:

"Any of you who see somebody from Barroquinha, you tell them they can come here and work until things settle down."

Vavá, too, was soon aware of what had happened. He waited restlessly for Pai Natividade, whom a taboo had kept in the temple all day, to come and read the shells for him. At lunch the procurer had not been able to give Tereza his promised answer.

"I'm awfully sorry, but it can't be until after midnight. It's not my fault."

The only piece of luck was that the detective hadn't come back with the marijuana, but he might turn up any minute. Dalmo Coca had taken part in the raid in Barroquinha—Vavá had been informed all about that—and he knew the beautiful girl had been there too but hadn't been arrested. It was a miracle she hadn't. Sitting in his wheelchair, played on by conflicting emotions, suspicion and anger, ambition and love, Vavá watched his business and the hands of the clock.

At the Flower of São Miguel Bar, Nília Cabaré, a party girl who was popular in bed and out of it, friend to all and always ready to paint the town red, arrested a thousand times for disrespect and disorderly conduct, was more than a little high. All at once she proclaimed to the four winds:

"Now everybody hear this: Until those girls go back to Barroquinha I'm shutting my basket and I won't let a man come near me. I don't care how much he offers me. Any woman who's a real woman, do like me, lock up your cunt and throw away the key, just like it's Holy Week!"

Hansen the German rose to his feet and kissed Nília Cabaré. Half a dozen women sitting at the tables waiting for customers said they would follow her example. They went out and began knocking on doors to tell everybody. Nília got a lock from the owner of the bar and fastened it to her skirt at exactly the right height. With the women went the German, some poets, a few bums, Anália's pash, Kalil the sketcher—the last bohemians in a world that is fast disappearing in the backwash of conspicuous consumption.

Shut your basket now, a new calendar's begun, the whores' Passion. The penance won't be over until all the girls go back to Barroquinha and shout Alleluia as they unlock their baskets. Because it was spontaneous, their resolution was not to be shaken.

Women at work jumped out of bed, left their johns in the middle of their fun, locked up their cunts, and threw the keys away.

28

When they were safely inside the bakery, Tereza explained to Almério the background of that invasion of Barroquinha by the forces of Gambling and Public Morality. The baker had read some of the calls for relocation of the centers of prostitution in the papers. He didn't think Tereza should go back to the Lotus Flower that night. She was too conspicuous. Hadn't she seen how the Dogfish had it in for her? And the Dogfish was bad news. She'd better stay right where she was and sleep in Zeques's room that night; it was safer than going back to Dona Fina's; the police weren't above dragging her out of her own house. But Tereza refused his offer. After a peep at the little boy asleep in his new bed, she said good-bye to Almério.

"You'll let me take you home in a taxi, at least."

No, because she wasn't going home yet. She needed Vavá's answer, and this was the time, a quarter past midnight, when he had told her she could have it. If no one moves, Almério, the hands of the police will be tied. Wouldn't you love to see the faces of those cops who are so used to pushing everyone around? Almério did not share Tereza's enthusiasm. Why did she want to get mixed up in something that had nothing to do with her? Didn't she have enough troubles already without asking for more? Maybe a new trouble would crowd out the old one: the *Balboa,* the gypsy ship of the Pacific, and beloved Janu, the lost sailor.

"Well then, I'll take you to Vavá's."

When Almério held out his hand to help Tereza out of the taxi in front of the brothel, a group of women came running up, shouting incomprehensibly:

"Shut your basket! Shut your basket!"

Tereza started up the stairs.

"Thank you so much, Almério. I'll see you tomorrow."

Almério, however, did not leave but told the taxi to wait. The women approached. One of them looked like a crazy woman, had a padlock on the front of her skirt. The driver asked what all the hullabaloo was about and was told that the women in the zone had decided to shut their baskets, that was all.

The cabby shook his head as if to say, well, that's a new one; who ever heard of celebrating Holy Week in September? Crazy drunken dames.

29

As he looked at the beautiful girl before him, Vavá could hardly repress the words of love on his lips. Love always struck him like a thunderbolt, but the road to bed was long. Vavá liked to make haste slowly, foretasting each moment, each word, each gesture. His courting was leisurely; he had a timid and romantic heart. In this case, when there were so many other factors besides love to be considered, Vavá did not intend to reveal his feelings until he had consulted Exu. But his eyes betrayed him; he gazed ardently at the girl. Pai Natividade would be here any minute, Mestre Jegue had gone in a taxi to bring him from the temple.

"Be patient just a little while, it's not my fault. I heard you were over in Barroquinha during the riot. What were you doing there? Why do you take so many risks?"

"I got there too late. I should have been there when it started. Wasn't I the one who told them they should stay where they were?"

"You don't have any sense. But that's the kind of people I like: wild and reckless."

"More than twenty women were arrested over there."

"They're probably being roughed up this very minute. Is that what you wanted?"

"Would they have been any better off giving in and moving out to that dungheap? You tell me! The police can't keep them locked up in jail forever, can they?"

From the passageway came unwonted sounds: voices raised, laughter, the hurried footsteps of many people running down the stairs. Vavá pricked up his ears as the noise became louder on both floors. Greta Garbo came running, in a tizzy:

"Vavá, the women are all running out on the men, jumping out of bed in the middle of the fuck-fuck. They say they're shutting their baskets because of what happened in Barroquinha. I just don't know what's gotten into them—" The words tumbled jerkily out of him as he gestured nervously.

Vavá's eyes, heavy with suspicion, went from Greta Garbo to Tereza, seeing treachery and falsehood on every side.

"You stay here, I'll be right back."

He wheeled his chair rapidly toward the waiting room, Greta Garbo beside him.

"What the devil does this mean? Where are you all going?"

Some of the women stopped to explain: they had shut their baskets and were not going to open them again until the women in Barroquinha could go back to their houses.

"Have you gone crazy? Now come on and get back to work. Customers are waiting."

They did not obey him, but went on trooping down the stairs like a band of students at recess. Vavá wheeled himself back to his room. Greta Garbo, hands on hips, asked him plaintively:

"Vavá, do you think I ought to shut my basket, too? Or should I stay out of this?"

"Get out of my sight!"

Back in his own room he glared balefully at Tereza and exploded:

"All this was your idea, wasn't it? It was you who decided it was carnival time!" He shook a deformed, menacing finger at her.

"What do you mean? What carnival are you talking about?"

Vavá's conviction was shaken by Tereza's puzzled face, her surprised expression, her frank, limpid eyes. Could she really be so false and hypocritical as to be putting it all on, or did she honestly know nothing about it? He told her indignantly that his women had all gone mad and were babbling about shutting their baskets. Tereza's face lighted up as he spoke. Without even waiting for him to finish, she sprang to her feet saying, "I'll come back later for your answer," and dashed out the door.

30

For the first time in many years at that hour in the brothel, no sounds of heavy breathing of the sexes could be heard, no mills of pleasure grinding away. In the novel silence Greta Garbo gnawed fingernails in an agony of indecision: should he join the strike, or not?

In Vavá's room Pai Natividade laid out the cowrie shells to be cast. Amadeu Mestre Jegue leaned against the wall and watched. The crippled whoremaster was speaking, trying to put the complicated situation into words:

"Father, I called you in because things are starting to turn ugly around here and I thought I should ask my compadre for advice."

A necklace of black and red beads, the beads of Compadre Exu, hung around Vavá's neck. Doubts assailed him on every side; he had never needed help so much. If the police wanted the prostitutes in Maciel to move to Pilar—which would mean his ruin—should he obey, as he always had before, or should he listen to the girl's advice and stay where he was? Meanwhile, should he take the Barroquinha women in? And what about the marijuana Dalmo Coca wants to put in my room for safekeeping? Should I play along, or would that be dangerous for me? And as if all that weren't enough, there's this business of shutting the basket that just fell on me out of a clear sky; the girls are playing hooky. What does Compadre Exu have to say to that? What should I do? I feel like a babe in the woods.

The last thing I want to ask about is the girl. Is she straight or crooked, can I trust her or is there a chance she'll doublecross me? I've nourished serpents in my trusting breast before; if the girl's a bad 'un, turn me away from her and save me. But if she's as good as she is beautiful—ah, then I'm the luckiest man in the world.

Pai Natividade shook the iron rattle in a salute to Exu, and chanted in a low voice:

> Bará o bebê
> Tiriri lonan

From the little heap of earth in the shrine where the trident was thrust, Exu Tiriri answered gaily:

> Exu Tiriri
> Bará obebê
> Tiriri lonan

Make way, everybody for Exu Tiriri! Exu is just the opposite of Ogum the Fish of the Sea: he's noisy and puts himself forward, loves motion and mischief and best of all a chance to raise Cain.

The cowries jumped out of Pai Natividade's hand,

rolled on the table, and spelled out Exu's words: I don't want any kind of drugs around here, just victuals and *cachaça*. Like living creatures in the hands of the spirit-guide, the shells gave Exu's answers one by one.

I want to see all the baskets shut tight, every one, and the men with their pricks up and no way to let off steam. If all hell breaks loose and blood runs, don't you worry; the grease may sputter but it'll come out all right in the end and nobody in Maciel is going anywhere, Exu won't let 'em. Nobody in Maciel or anywhere else in the zone, if you keep all the baskets shut until the police stop giving people a hard time. It was me, Exu, who ordered the baskets shut, and nobody else.

The spirit-guide read in the cowries the fatal decree: It'll be a black day for any whore who lies with a man before Alleluia Saturday in Barroquinha! A black day for the madam of any house, brothel, or castle who leaves her door open and tries to cheat on the shutting of the baskets!

The girl will rot with disease and her flesh will be eaten away by syphilis and she'll be blind, and crippled and a leper. The procurer or procuress will die before a month is out; a nasty, lingering death.

And what can you tell me about the girl? Her name's Tereza Batista. I want to know if she's a good woman or if there's wickedness in her heart under all that beauty.

Exu Tiriri stopped the words in his mouth. You wash out your dirty mouth before you say Tereza's name again. She's as straight as a die, there's nobody like her in Bahia or anywhere else. But my advice to you is, start forgetting her while you can; she's not for you. Tereza's lost out at sea with a dagger in her breast.

"Is she sick or in love?" asked Vavá.

"In love. And that's the worst sickness there is."

"She might fall out of love, though. . . ." No one had lived as long as Vavá; time in a brothel counts triple.

Exu asked for a goat and twelve black cocks to make everything come out right. Then he told them all to get out of the way and took his leave:

Bará o bebê
Tiriri lonan

Give my regards to the girl and tell her I'm right behind her. Woe betide the woman who doesn't close her basket! His last words from atop his trident were: Woe betide her!

31

Woe betide her!—The curse was repeated by all the women in the zone, from Barroquinha to Carmo, from Maciel to Taboão, from Pelourinho to Ladeira da Montanha, from house to house, from room to room, from mouth to mouth.

Woe betide her!—The threat was put into words and passed on in the name of Vavá, of Dona Paulina de Souza, and of old Acácia, still a prisoner in jail.

Woe betide her!—It was the voice of Exu at every crossroad in the tenderloin; Exu, lord of all roads and owner of the key to every basket.

32

Chief Hélio Cotias woke early and began his day with a long telephone conversation with Hipólito Sardinha. He could not help boasting a little as he proudly told the old man that the move was as good as accomplished, the houses in Barroquinha having been locked up and the furniture transferred to Codfish Hill—not that it had been easy; he had had to use a hand of iron. His wife's uncle meanly retorted that he didn't see that any of that was a cause for self-congratulation. It would have been a whole lot better if the women had gone quietly without a fuss, without a skirmish, without idiotic interviews and news stories in the press, not to mention that shot of the police truck carting furniture away and that column by Jehová. Cantankerous old grouch, thought Hélio; there was no pleasing him.

As might have been expected, the papers had featured the Barroquinha incident on the crime pages. BATTLE IN THE TENDERLOIN, MOVING DAY FOR RED-LIGHT DISTRICT

BEGINS WITH RIOT; POLICE TRUCKS TAKE PROSTITUTES TO CODFISH HILL, were some of the headlines and subheads of these stories, one of which was illustrated with a photograph of an official truck loaded with belongings taken from the brothels. There were no pictures of the ruckus. Only one photographer, the bearded Rino, had turned up to document the heroism of the police as they battled with nightsticks and revolvers against women. His camera was taken from him and the film destroyed, and he narrowly escaped arrest. The guardians of public morals are self-effacing, in addition to their other virtues, and not fond of seeing snapshots of their noble acts of bravery and devotion to the public weal published in the press. They prefer simple, posed photographs taken at police headquarters.

Photographs like the one of a smiling Chief Cotias, taken to illustrate a brief press conference to which accredited reporters had been invited. "We're cleaning up the whole downtown area, clearing out the red-light district as the press has so patriotically urged us to do. We've begun with Barroquinha, and now that we've started nothing's going to stop us—not a single brothel will be left downtown when we get through."

A highly moral and civic statement, no doubt, well worthy of encomiums and applause. Just the same, the Chief's inflexibility and the vastness of the predicted clean-up campaign, which, though barely begun, had already raised such a ruckus, were certainly important factors in the brothel-owners' support of the closed-basket movement.

On the other hand, not all the gentlemen of the press were sympathetic to the gentleman cop. The popular columnist Jehová de Carvalho, who favored the prostitutes' cause and had little love for the police, wrote a rude and racy column about the strong-arm methods used on this occasion. In the last paragraph he asked ironically, "Has the removal of the Barroquinha ladies to Codfish Hill been undertaken as a part of the promotion campaign to make the development a tourist paradise, a phrase we've heard repeated ad nauseam?" The columnist and poet Jehová could hardly have been more explicit. As we all know, it is paid ads, not newsstand sales or subscriptions, that keep a newspaper going.

Seeing her husband's virile pose in the picture in the

morning paper, Carmen, born a Sardinha and a Sardinha still in her tart disposition, remarked scornfully:

"Look at the great big macho! The King of the Hookers chastising his subjects! The police department's good for my dear little Hélio; it's making a man of him."

But none of these disagreeable details was enough to destroy the Chief's sense of well-being. He had reason to feel proud of the firm action he had taken the night before. Bada read the papers too and had run to the telephone. My hero! Weren't you in danger? Will you tell me about it this afternoon? The place we decided on, at four? My Bonaparte!

33

That morning at about eleven, Chief Hélio Cotias got out of his automobile at the Bureau of Gambling and Public Morality. The first thing he did was have the arrested prostitutes brought into his presence.

The men had turned loose at daybreak with some cuffing and protests, two of them clad only in shorts. They had been knocked around a little, just to teach them not to get in the way of the police another time—a few slaps, nothing to amount to much.

A real beating, the kind that makes you swell up and leaves welts, was what Black Domingas got. She had been a little too active during the brawl, had stood up a little too well to the cops; so they beat her lustrous, appetizing face to a dull and ugly pulp. As for Maria Petisco, she had aroused the lust of the elegant Dalmo Coca when she bit him and scratched his face. In the middle of the night the guardian of public morality, high on coke by that time, burst into the detention cell with the firm intention of mounting the girl right there in front of everyone. The only funny scene that night, amid all the ugly thrashings and vengeful punishment, was the snowbird stumbling toward Maria Petisco and not quite making it. The cops laughed and egged the champion on, until they tired of the joke and hauled him off.

Chief Cotias was beginning to get the hang of his job and earn the respect of his subordinates, as we have seen. Even so, the sight of Black Domingas rather took him aback. The girl's dark skin was covered with huge bruises and purple marks. One eye was swollen shut, she had a busted lip, and she could hardly stand on her feet. His assistant looked on scornfully as the Chief's stare wavered. This was a job for a man, not for a pantywaist.

"That one over there's a troublemaker. She was raising a rumpus in the cell and not letting anybody sleep, so we had to give her a lesson; a good beating's the only language they understand." Labão paused, then added: "Don't waste your sympathy on that gang."

He would just have to get used to it, thought the Chief. No, he shouldn't waste his sympathy on that gang. But it was no use trying to steel himself; he didn't have the stomach for it. He ordered the girls to be set free. Now only the madams were left. The young law-school graduate scanned the forlorn group of women, only six in all, and assumed a fierce yet paternal tone.

"You wouldn't go willingly; now you'll have to go whether you like it or not. What do you think you'll gain by holding out? Any one of you who's thought better of it and is ready to move now, step forward, and I'll let you go scot-free right now."

He expected general agreement and congratulations. Only Mirabel made a move, but old Acácia spoke before she could step forward:

"We ain't going. Not even if we spend the rest of our lives in jail. None of us going to that trash heap to rot."

Losing all restraint, the Chief pounded the desk and shook his finger in the old woman's face, looking every inch the great big macho Carmen Cotias, née Sardinha, had called him.

"Then you'll rot here. Have them taken back to the cell."

His assistant, in high good humor, had a suggestion to make:

"How about hitting their hands with a rod a dozen times, at noon and at night, instead of feeding them food? That's a good diet, but they'll be willing to move before very long, you'll see."

Just then the Dogfish, rubbing his hands in glee, burst into the office without even knocking.

"The American fleet's been sighted off Itapoã. It'll be raining dollars pretty soon!"

34

Labão Oliveira was so delighted at the news, and in such a hurry to take private measures of his own, that he forgot to order the turnkey to apply a dozen raps of the rod to each of the madams when he brought them their watery soup and stale bread twice a day. If it hadn't been for Dogfish, ever punctilious in the performance of his duty, the renegades would have been spared this free and efficacious program for losing weight and learning better manners.

On their way out, they rousted out plainclothesman Dalmo Garcia. Startled out of a sound sleep, the elegant Coca heard the great news: the U.S. fleet had been sighted off Itapoã and the battleships were steaming toward Bahia: Every one of them loaded with dollars, old boy, and the exchange rate favorable! Three cheers for the sailors and marines of the great nation to the north, who are coming to honor the city by their presence! May they find beautiful women, capable professionals, gracious hostesses to welcome them. The health and well-being of the invincible warriors will be zealously safeguarded by the local police force, so well represented by our three heroes. Yes, they too were heroes. We mustn't pass up this opportunity to do justice to our homegrown variety too, those humble but equally indefatigable defenders of western civilization against the red and yellow hordes, against immorality and corruption.

How is that other little business of the grass coming along, friend Coca? Well, Camões didn't show up last night; apparently he had run into some unexpected snag in getting hold of the stuff. We have another date this afternoon, and he'd better show up this time! If he tries to weasel out of it again it'll be himself he's outsmarting, not us. I'll have him in stir for pushing drugs so fast it'll make his head swim. All we have to do is revive that old case against him that I got dismissed, and let justice take its course.

Better go look for him righ now, old friend, old partner,

old pal; find the guy's hideout and dig him up and the grass with him, 'cause a chance as good as this to make a little easy money comes just once in a blue moon.

35

The three partners followed good modern business practice by dividing the responsibilities and the work. To Assitant Chief Labão Oliveira, the senior partner and the feared, respected leader, fell the task of masterminding the operation and raising the necessary funds to carry it out.

He came to an agreement with the peddlers and street urchins as to the distribution and sale of the prophylactics and the aphrodisiac elixir. At the São Joaquim market he had bought a whole slew of little straw baskets for almost nothing. Each boy and each street peddler would be given one to carry his merchandise in. How many salesmen would there be? So many he didn't even know the exact number. The zone would be swarming with them, all hawking condoms and little vials of Stiff Prick and swapping them for greenbacks. The operation had been very carefully planned, even to having the hustler memorize a few phrases in English. Naturally, security measures had been taken to avoid pilfering and the diversion of either the merchandise or the profits—although the best guarantee of the salesmen's honesty was their fear of the Assistant Chief, whose innocent-sounding name was enough to make a miscreant's knees knock together. Nobody fooled around when he was doing a job for Labão Oliveira.

Oliveira had a flair for organization and a nose for deals. He told the cop and the detective that he had gone to certain well-known moneylenders to raise the cash to float the operation, and reckoned the high interest they would charge as part of the overhead. The truth was, however, that he had advanced the necessary funds out of his own pocket, and thus stood to earn a little profit at the expense of his two naive supernumeraries.

Things were too hectic that morning for him to leave

his office. He sent policemen he could trust to round up spokesmen for the peddlers and street kids. The great day had finally come.

36

In a filthy sty in Taboão, Nicolau Ramada Junior, the infamous Dogfish, was talking business with Heron Madruga, the illustrious Pernambucan chemist. He had just handed the supplier half the sum agreed on for five hundred doses of Stiff Prick, the Wonder Elixir! One Dose, Five Fucks.

Heron Madruga's scientific acumen had long since spread his fame into the backlands and to more than one state capital. His interest in chemistry and pharmacology had been aroused in Recife, where he had worked in the laboratory of Drs. Dóris and Paulo Loureiro, a highly competent medical team who were also husband and wife. Madruga spent the morning collecting urine, feces, and blood specimens from clients, the late afternoon delivering the results and collecting fees. In his free time he admired the salts and acids mingling in the glass globes, the flasks, the pipettes, the beakers and test tubes. He was fascinated by the strong smells, the strange colors, the wisps of blue smoke; and all the time he was learning scientific formulas and phrases.

His education came to an abrupt end when he overstepped the bounds of caution. Not content with occasionally pocketing the fee for a simple urinalysis, he kept two myelograms to study, was caught, and summarily dismissed to his great regret, for he was fond of his employers and they had treated him well. He soon realized, however, that he could capitalize on the training he had received in chemistry, pharmacy, and medicine and that he was as well fitted as anyone to alleviate the sufferings of humanity and of other living creatures too, for on more than one occasion he practiced veterinary medicine with fair to middling success. Dogs sometimes bit him, horses sometimes kicked him; but after all, a scientist's life can't be all beer and skittles.

Some products concocted by him according to his own

formulas enjoyed unshakable prestige among the rural population and in the little towns of the Northeast, where they were sold at every fair and market. Chest-Cleansing Elixir, for example, was indisputably effective against all kinds of bronchial and lung diseases; it wiped out whole epidemics of flu in Pernambuco and cured many a chronic consumptive in Alagoas. A bottle of Capiberibe Wonder was potent enough to cleanse the body of any and all infections, including cancer and gonorrhea. A sweet-smelling hair lotion called Magnolia Flower cured dandruff, killed nits and lice, and made hair grow on the baldest head, as could easily be seen from authentic testimonials, illustrated with before-and-after photographs. If the distinguished customer doesn't boast a lion's mane by the time the bottle is empty, just turn in the bottle and get your money back (but no one ever did). Just choose the color hair you want from the color of the label. Purchase a blond mane or a black, brown, red, blue, or green one. Green hair is very much in style with society ladies.

As for Stiff Prick, we already know how potent that was. As Madruga himself used to say when touting his meritorious product to his attentive listeners in market squares, a centenarian got up from his deathbed after swallowing the prescribed dose, deflowered a virgin then and there, diddled her four more times, and knocked her up on the fifth try. She had twins and he died happy, of priapism.

The idea of labeling the bottles in English—red letters on a black ground. APHRODISIAC: ONE DOSES 5 FUCKS—came from Madruga and the translation from Dalmo Coca the polyglot, who had already taught the peddlers how to charge a dollar at least for a condom or a little bottle of Stiff Prick. The slum kids didn't need any lessons; they spoke every known language and grinned to beat the band. Those ragged, scrawny, indomitable kids were the real owners of Bahia; its streets had been their turf for immemorial years. Soon Chief Labão would send for the merchandise, the Dogfish told Madruga; the ships had been sighted off the Itapoã lighthouse.

"Will they get here today?"

"They're on their way."

"Do you think the women'll open their baskets?"

"What are you talking about?"

Madruga told him that, feeling an itch in his balls the night before, he had gone to the red-light zone to relieve it. What was his surprise to find castles and brothels empty, bedrooms deserted, doors shut and locked. He thought the lateness of the hour—it was after two in the morning—might explain the scarcity of women. He went sniffing from bar to bar, hoping to find a girl scout ready and willing. When he got to the Flower of São Miguel the room was noisy and full of customers, and a lot of professionals were sitting around, but none would take him home with her. He was informed that all self-respecting whores had shut their baskets until the Barroquinha girls went home again.

Dogfish took the story lightly. Whenever the police arrested a few troublemakers and taught them a lesson, as they had done last night in Barroquinha, that was a sign to other tramps with nothing better to do to get together in the bars to drink and cuss. He pricked up his ears, though, when Heron Madruga mentioned one of the hookers, the most enthusiastic one of all and a pretty gal, by God—he had met her in Recife a few years ago. She seemed to have a yen to hit men, and to tell the truth, she *had* hit more than one and gotten away with it. He, Madruga, had been an eyewitness to one of her exploits; he wasn't just repeating gossip he had heard. Her name was Tereza Batista, nick-named Tereza Foot-in-the-Nuts for obvious reasons.

When he heard her hateful name, Dogfish foamed at the mouth and growled:

"That damned bitch slipped right through my fingers yesterday, I still don't know how; it was like witchcraft. But never mind, she'll pay me back for it; oh, won't she just! I'm glad you told me she's going around sicking the prostitutes on us, the lousy good-for-nothing whore!"

37

That twenty-first of September, a banner headline in the evening paper announced to all Bahia: HOLIDAY IN THE CITY—SPRING AND THE SAILORS ARRIVE TOGETHER.

At the Flower of São Miguel the night before—before

the news that Barroquinha had been invaded by troops from the Bureau of Gambling and Public Morals, before Nília Cabaré's war-cry, before Exu Tiriri's decree—young Kalil Chamas had spoken scathing words against the pack of subservient imitators of European customs who were la-de-dahing about the first day of spring while September rain was falling on their heads—the same bunch of idiots who dressed their children up like rabbits at Easter and put cotton on Christmas trees in torrid December to imitate winter snow.

"The only thing they don't do is put on fur coats and pretend they're freezing to death! Tomorrow we'll have to watch the dear little schoolchildren parading down the street singing 'Welcome, Sweet Springtime.' Pure colonialism. I hope it pours all day."

A social-science student at the School of Arts and Sciences, cashier at his father's antique shop in Ruy Barbosa Street, an amateur artist who dreamed of exhibits, fame, and fortune, and an ardent nationalist—Kalil Chamas was all of these and sweet Anália's lucky flame besides. Sitting at his table in the bar, he waxed indignant at the idiotic importation of foreign habits that simply made no sense in Brazil. Winter in the tropics meant six months of rain; summer was six months of scorching heat; and to talk about spring and fall was ridiculous. Ridiculous! He rose to his feet, one long finger raised to reinforce the exclamation.

"But this is the land of eternal spring," Tom Lívio declaimed. The unemployed actor was always looking for a stage on which to show off his talent and well-modulated voice.

Poems by Telmo Serra, Kalil's bosom friend and according to him a poet of genius—greatly overrated, however, to Tom Lívio's way of thinking—had twice appeared with Kalil's illustrations in the Sunday supplement of one of the newspapers, and on both occasions author and artist repaired together to a bar to celebrate their incipient glory with beer and mutual praise.

In the small hours, the bohemian circle began to melt away, some going home to sleep, others going on to the bawdy houses where the girls had a little time for their own flames, flirtations, and love affairs after a hard night's work. When there were too many customers, Kalil would sometimes have to sit on the steps of the Blacks' Church of the Rosary waiting for the go-ahead sign in Anália's window. As soon as the girl waved a white towel, Kalil would rush to join her.

The night war was declared, Anália left her post early with her colleagues. She and Kalil roamed through the red-light zone, passing on the good word that all baskets should be shut. Anália clapped her hands elatedly:

"This basket-shutting business came at just the right time. Now I can go see the schoolchildren's spring parade tomorrow. I haven't seen one since I don't know when. Did I ever tell you I was in my elementary-school parade in Estância? I was the drum majorette. I sure don't want to miss the parade tomorrow."

"You overgrown kid from an underdeveloped country!" Oh, Kalil, where are your principles and convictions? You must really be in love. "We'll go to the parade together. I hope it's a pretty day."

The banner headline took up half the front page of the evening paper. If he had wanted to tell the whole truth, the editor should have rounded off the phrase: HOLIDAY IN THE CITY—SPRING, THE SAILORS, AND THE WHORES.

38

Dalmo Garcia left the two guys waiting in the car—an old Buick belonging to one of them, the one who was blind in one eye, known in the half-world and the underworld as Joy-Smoke Camões—and trudged up the steps to the brothel. It was hot as hell that afternoon. He found the door closed—that door that was always open after 1:00 P.M. to accommodate the mass of customers who flocked to the biggest whorehouse in Bahia.

He knocked, called, pounded on the door. No one came. As he stood before the locked door, Dalmo Coca suddenly realized that he had seen no women in Maciel at all. It was early yet, but there should have been somebody around: boobs sticking out the windows, hookers strolling down the street swinging their purses to steal a march on their colleagues before the real working day began. Today there was none of that. He saw an occasional passerby but not a single whore. And the bawdy house was closed. Dalmo Coca couldn't understand it. He pounded on the door with both fists and shouted for Vavá. No answer.

He went back down the steps and got in the car.

"Hey, what's going on?" Joy-Smoke Camões asked nervously.

Even in the company of a public servant, a highly trained police detective, he didn't feel quite safe, somehow. In the first place, he was suspicious of Dalmo. Never trust a police agent, not even if he is a junkie. When was he going to hand over the dough he had promised? It had been left that Coca would meet them late that afternoon with the sum they had agreed on, a nice big handful of change. Instead he had turned up right after lunch without a nickel, pretending to be in a big hurry. The ships are coming; where's the stuff? Joy-Smoke Camões felt threatened, pushed to the wall. You better find it quick or you'll be sorry. The pusher began to be worried.

"What's going on, anyway?" he asked again, imagining the worst.

"I don't know. . . . There's nobody there and I don't know what the hell's happened to all the women. Where do you think they can be?"

Blind Belarmino shuffled down the nearly deserted street and settled down in his accustomed lucrative spot to ask for handouts. The boy who was his guide helped arrange his drinking gourd, his newspaper, and the sandwich for his mid-afternoon snack. He picked up his ukulele and began to sing a dirty ditty, thinking that the usual two or three curious passersby might stop to listen and reward him:

> A hen's ass is dirty
> a dame's ass is neat
> the hen lays eggs
> and eggs go with meat.

Joy-Smoke Camões was feeling more and more unhappy. He turned to his partner, the silent pygmy seated in the driver's seat of the old rattletrap:

"Come on, let's get out of here."

Dalmo Garcia settled back in his seat, repeating in a puzzled tone.

"Where the hell do you think those broads went?"

39

Some of them stayed in the cathouses, taking advantage of their holiday to mend their clothes, write letters full of lies to their folks, or just rest. Until further orders, no prostitute could receive a customer or even a lover, in any house, brothel, or castle in the tenderloin district. If a petting party was what they wanted, they'd have to take their la-la's out of the zone. They had tacitly committed themselves the night before, and now they'd have to go the whole hog. None of them would have had the nerve to do anything else. Exu had foretold disease and death, blindness, leprosy, and the morgue for those who disobeyed.

The women let out of jail that morning had tried to go back to the disputed houses, either to go on living in them or to salvage their clothing and other belongings, but the policeman patrolling Barroquinha would not let any of them in. They had had to find refuge in other houses. Dona Paulina de Souza alone took in twelve, four to each house, and she dug into her purse for money to send Domingas to São Gonçalo dos Campos.

"You need a rest, girl. They roughed you up pretty bad."

But the black woman would not hear of leaving Bahia just then, In fact, she and Maria Petisco were really worried; would Oxossi and Ogum, who were so used to coming down in Barroquinha, know where to find them?

"And tomorrow's their day."

"You think the spirits don't know where you are? I'm telling you, Ogum will find a way to hump you here or in São Gonçalo just as easy as Barroquinha."

What most of the women longed for was an outing; they filled the city with laughter, joy, and fun. They could have been working girls, salesgirls, students, housewives, mothers, enjoying a day on their patron saint's day. They went on shopping sprees, to the matinee at the movies, on excursions out to the suburbs, in pairs or festive little groups or arm in arm with their sweethearts, necking and making eyes: a bevy of nice-looking girls, smart young women, and calm, sedate matrons.

Others went to visit their children, left in the care of strangers. For once they could be the loving mothers they were, carrying their offspring or leading them by the hand, indulging them with ice cream, soda pop, and candy, kissing and petting them to their hearts' content.

Some of those out enjoying the first day of spring were old women. Free for one day from the terrible obligation of plastering on makeup to hide their loose skin and wrinkles, from the inglorious struggle for a client, they could relax and just be the tired old women they were.

The women knew a blessed holiday like this wouldn't come along very often, and they made the most of it. They strolled through the center of town, ran barefoot along the beach, sat in the grass in the parks, stood before the cages of monkeys, birds, and wild beasts at the zoo, and visited the Church of Bonfim, where like any other tourist they bought guidebooks recounting the miracles of Our Lord of Bonfim.

At about three o'clock in the afternoon, those who were standing on the hill gazing out over the bay saw three battleships cross the bar.

40

It was not quite four when the fleet admiral's flagship anchored off Bahia and, escorted by his staff, he called on the governor at his palace. After an exchange of civilities, the admiral invited the governor to visit the flagship next morning and lunch with the officers.

Flashbulbs popped and the photographers scurried from one side of the room to the other, asking for a smile or handshake to be repeated. The admiral announced that the sailors would be given shore leave that night, which seemed most opportune.

41

The four o'clock wrapup of the day's news over Rádio Abaeté, the powerful station with the most listeners, featured a detailed report on the American battleships anchored in the harbor. "If you like your news hot off the griddle, listen to Abaeté," "Abaeté brings you the news as it happens," "Abaeté's microphone is the ear of History," the announcers repeated over and over during the programs. "If there's no news, Abaeté will bring you some anyway," the station's competitors gibed.

After describing the admiral's courtesy call on the governor, the compliments exchanged and the invitation that had been extended, the Rádio Abaeté reporter furnished a detailed and precise description of each of the three battleships: name, launching date, number of officers and crew, cannons, firing range, speed, curriculum vitae of commanding officers, and many other enthralling facts. The documentation and research department had lived up to the station's traditions of accuracy, as usual.

The newscast concluded with the information that the sailors would come ashore some time that evening, probably about eight o'clock.

And, oh, yes. Before signing off, there was one more curious news item, connected in a way to the Yankee sailors' shore leave as a protest against the imminent transfer of the zone of prostitution, which had begun the night before with the vice squad's violent incursion into Barroquinha, the women in the trade had decided not to work as long as their companions were kept from returning to the houses from which they had been expelled and the threat of a forcible move still hung over the tenderloin.

42

At about five o'clock, while Bada was taking a quick shower to wash off the sticky perspiration she had worked up on that hot afternoon, Chief Cotias, the gentleman cop, the happy, exhausted lover, switched on the radio and relaxed to the beat of the music.

Rest was what he deserved after an hour of violent exertion: fragile Bada was a firecracker, a powder train, a fabulous female in every way. He had called her Tanagra figurine and enigmatic Mona Lisa; when she was naked in his arms he murmured in her ear: Josephine, my Josephine.

"Why Josephine? My God, what an awful name!"

"Am I your Napoleon Bonaparte or am I not? And wasn't he married to Josephine?"

"I'd rather be Marie Antoinette."

"A historical error, darling, because Marie . . ."

"What do I care?" And she closed his mouth with one of her great sucking kisses.

Neither Josephine nor Marie Antoinette was the right name for her. If Dr. Cotias had had the nerve he would have called her by another: Messalina. They had spent an hour of rapture, if copulating like a windmill was rapture: Bada was a ravening fury, and the Chief had had to make a supreme effort not to let his side down. His sharp-tongued wife Carmen, née Sardinha, always said disdainfully when she sensed his interest in another woman:

"Do the thing properly now; don't make a poor showing and leave me looking like a fool."

It always upset him and made everything harder, which no doubt was exactly what Carmen had in mind. Luckily he had been able to handle Bada, the debauched, insatiable pig. She asked countless questions about the zone, not only about Hélio's triumph of the night before but all about what the whores were like and what they did. Oh, how I'd love to visit a brothel! She bit her lips, grappled with Cotias, and at climax sobbed and pleaded.

"Call me a whore, curse me, hit me, my policeman!"

The apartment was on the upper slopes of Gamboa. Through the window the weary Chief, covered with sweat, smoking a cigarette, listening to the tune of a popular Italian song, could see the three ships anchored in the harbor.

Before it was time to meet Bada, Chief Cotias had dutifully stopped by his office, where Labão had informed him that everything was in perfect order: the sailors would

come ashore about nightfall and he had arranged for reinforcements of MP's to help the cops police the zone to
make doubly sure there would be no trouble. As for the
Barroquinha madams, they still insolently refused to obey
police orders to change their place of residence. A good,
thorough beating would soon change their minds—early
next morning, when the tenderloin was quiet. In the meantime, they could go on being starved and rapped on the
hands. Just be patient for a little while, Chief; those rat-
infested ruins on Codfish Hill will be rented out at a profit
before long. His assistant had actually laughed in his face,
staring at him with those basilisk eyes. This man standing
before me is a criminal, thought the gentleman cop; what
does he mean by that dig about renting the old houses?
Had the corporation promised Oliveira a cut, or what?

Bada shut off the faucet and the sound of the shower
stopped. Still covered with drops of water she came toward
her lover, fixing him with her lascivious gaze. There was
a drop of water on her left nipple. All at once the radio
music was interrupted by the martial theme of a newscast, followed by an announcer's voice: *"Atenção!
Muita atenção!"*

Ignoring the urgent call to attention, Bada flung herself
on the bed on top of Hélio. As she kissed him avidly he
heard the announcer say: "The situation in the zone of
prostitution is causing the authorities concern. The sailors
are due to come ashore at eight o'clock this evening at
the Praça Cayru pier, and so far the brothels remain shut.
Assistant Chief Oliveira, of the vice squad, who has gone
to Maciel to take the measures called for in these unusual
circumstances, has told this station positively that the situation will be back to normal before the sailors come
ashore. He assured us that they won't have to sit and
watch the ships go by, as the saying goes, and added:
What would this mecca of civilization be coming to if anything so ridiculous were allowed to happen? Firm measures
will be taken to ensure that it does not. The police are in
control of the situation. This is Rádio Grêmio, Bahia."

Dr. Hélio Cotias's eyes nearly popped out of his head
as he struggled to free himself from Bada's clutches. What
on earth did the announcement mean? Why was the situation in the zone of prostitution causing the authorities
concern? The crooning music returned to the air waves, a

nostalgic Neapolitan song. Please wait just a minute, darling, the Chief said imploringly, as he was pulled this way and that by his bed partner. He twisted the dial, trying to get another news broadcast, and finally found one: "No disturbances of the peace have been reported since last night, but the ranks of the police have been augmented by the mounted special force to be prepared for any eventuality. The prostitutes are still on strike, and our reporter is on his way there now. We'll be broadcasting directly from Maciel, where the police forces are concentrated, at any moment now. Stay tuned to Rádio Abaeté. We'll be back with the news after this announcement. . . ."

Bada threw the radio on the floor in a pet. The panic-stricken Chief knew he must answer the call of duty. It was no use for her to grab him and try to tease him into a response. Hélio could not respond just then; he had neither the time, strength, nor inclination. He had to go to headquarters and find out what was happening and what that alarming broadcast meant; he had to take command of the situation. That was why he was Chief of the Bureau of Gambling and Public Morality.

"I have to get over there this minute, darling. Let go of me, please."

He hadn't reckoned with his passionate, strong-willed Bada:

"You chicken!"

She threw herself face down on top of him. The Chief gave in and let her do as she liked—she wasn't just a whore, she was a god-damned nymphomaniac. The radio bellowed from the floor: "We're broadcasting directly from Pelourinho. The police have decided to open the brothels by force."

43

Laughing at anything and everything as she clung to Kalil's arm, Anália clapped for the boys and girls as they paraded by in the children's salute to spring, thinking of the days when she too had gone to school, before she went to work in the textile mill and Dr. Bráulio had thrown her out into the world.

They had lunch at the Pôrto Restaurant, which specialized in Portuguese dishes. The student chose May wine
to go along with their codfish à la Braz, and they drank
to eternal love. When they were outside again, he bought
a little bunch of violets and handed it to her with a bow.
They stopped beside the bust of the late lamented journalist Giovanni Guimarães so that she could pin the violets
to the front of her white summer dress; and she let the
boy kiss her in the protective shade of that lovable
chronicler of the city's life and people. He gave her a
sweetheart's kiss. Anália felt happy in a silly, wonderful
way; she laughed at nothing as they wandered slowly
through the streets.

With the excuse of having to go to the University, Kalil
had left his old man by himself at the antique shop and
set aside the whole day for Anália. This was the first time
since he had fallen for her, about two months ago, that
they had ever spent a day together. They usually met
sometime before dawn whenever she could send away the
last customer, and could be in bed together only until
daybreak—when his parents got up Kalil had to be at
home to have breakfast with the family.

Now they walked hand in hand, and no cloud marred
their happiness. They lay on the grass at the Lighthouse
on the Bar, drank coconut juice in Amaralina, enjoyed a
snack of fresh fried beancakes, went swimming in the
ocean at Piatá, and watched the sun set in a burst of color
over the sea. Blissful adolescents!

They heard nothing about the trouble downtown, the
battleships anchored off Bahia, or the police occupying
Maciel, Pelourinho, and Taboão, the zone where, it was
said, the lowest forms of vice flourished. They lingered
on the twilit beach at Pituba until it was dark, then went
off to dine on crab broiled with hot peppers and shredded
coconut, washed down with beer. Before they entered
the Jangadeiro Restaurant, Anália let the old organ
grinder's green parakeet pick out a fortune for her with
his beak:

> When you're choosing a young man
> you should choose him by his bonnet
> if you want a city slicker
> make sure there's no ribbon on it.

They laughed for no reason at all. How happy the day of the closed basket had been! For once spring had obeyed the calendar and come to Bahia on the right day.

44

At vice squad headquarters, Labão Oliveira had just outlined his plan of action to the Chief:

"You just leave it to me. I'll get those whores of bitches back to work if it's the last thing I do. Either they open their god-damned baskets an hour from now or my name isn't Labão Oliveira and I'll get me a new one."

Labão Oliveira was the name that made prostitutes and madams, procuresses, loafers, malefactors, hardened criminals, and innocent civilians—anyone who had ever any sort of contact with the upholder of morality and decency—tremble for their lives. People spoke in whispers of cold-blooded murder done at the police station, of cadavers buried in secret, and other horrors. Certain accusations reached the pages of the newspapers, but where was the proof?

On that particular afternoon even callused cops who had worked with him for years, and sometimes as partners in deals on the outside, got the wind up when they saw the assistant chief in a towering rage, his glare more sinister than ever. Sinister was the word; no other adjective was strong enough. Nervous, sensitive, Dr. Hélio Cotias, whom the policemen despised as a chickenhearted coward, felt ill and laughed wanly as he reluctantly approved the plan drawn up by his competent subordinate. He was sick at his stomach, as if he had swallowed something unwieldy that was trying to work its way back up into his mouth again. It took all his strength to keep it down and get a grip on himself, especially after he had just exhausted himself in bed with that madwoman. In a feeble attempt to lighten the heavy atmosphere, the gentleman cop proposed that the planned operation be given the name of "Heigh-Ho, Heigh-Ho, It's Back to Work We Go." The inspiration was not a happy one. Jehová de Carvalho, the poet and columnist quoted above, commented in a column after everything was all over that he considered the phrase "a sick, monstrous joke, worthy of Hitler and the Nazi death camps."

45

In the Elite Bar or the Whores' Bar (the proprietor doesn't care which name you use), where Labão is giving his staff one last briefing before the rapidly approaching campaign against the rebellious forces of evil, Joy-Smoke Camões, pusher and junkie, is trying to collect the money due him for the huge load of pot he has just delivered. Vavá's disappearance has left Detective Coca with no place to put his explosive merchandise for safekeeping and no one to put the screws on for the fifty percent due the pusher tonight—the rest to be paid once that lucrative night full of sailors and dollars is over. And now the dollars have been put in jeopardy by those damned and doubledamned whores. The assistant chief turns his awesome glare on the nervy bastard, but the one-eyed pusher is not intimidated. Fear can't reach him on cloud nine.

As they were rolling around in the rattletrap Buick, Dalmo Coca had had a bright idea. Why hadn't he thought of it before? He told the driver to head for Codfish Hill, and he deposited the grass in one of the old tumbledown houses. With Camões treading on his heels, he got in touch with the mules in charge of selling joints to the sailors, and ordered them to get over to Codfish Hill and wait for the signal. As soon as things were quiet and the girls went back to work, he'd send a message, and then they were to hightail it downtown and start raking in the dollars. Don't get stoned, for God's sake. Not till your night's work is over and you get your commission in bread and pot. He would have felt pretty good about things if that pest Camões would stop whining about his dough.

"Get the hell out of here!" roared Oliveira.

The junkie was sure he couldn't last another five minutes without a smoke. He knew he had to go back to Codfish Hill, snitch the grass quiet and easy while the

mules weren't looking, put it in the Buick, and take it
back where it came from. Before he did that, though, he
had to have a smoke.

46

While Labão Oliveira prepared to set in motion his program for obliging the brothels to open and the prostitutes
to get back on the job—"Operation Heigh-Ho, Heigh-Ho,
It's Back to Work We Go" was a lovely name; only enemies of the police could see anything wrong with it—
unsettling rumors, almost all based on radio news reports,
raced through the city.

The very popular sports commentator Nereu Werneck,
finding himself short of items for his evening sportscast,
fell back on the closed-basket problem after reporting on
the sports practiced by the sailors of the U.S. fleet and
the featherweight boxing champion among the crew of
one of the battleships anchored in the harbor.

As dramatically as if he were describing a soccer penalty, he speculated on what might happen if the efforts of
the police were unsuccessful, if the prostitutes persisted
in their negative attitude and had no intention of cooper-
ating with the authorities, if the sailors had to sit and
watch the ships go by—to borrow the picturesque phrase
used by Assistant Chief Labão Oliveira. What would be
the outcome? Why, anything at all might happen! Nereu
Werneck was used to making every soccer game sound
like the most dramatic ever played. He knew that the
secret of keeping the fans on the edge of their seats was
suspense.

To concentrate a large body of the military in a zone of
prostitution was to ask for trouble. Blood was almost sure
to be shed. And the danger increased when foreigners
were involved, and the inevitable friction between hosts
and guests degenerated, as it all too often did, into
violence of unforeseeable extent and consequences. He
quoted examples and asked his listeners to remember
World War II.

What will happen, the popular sports announcer asked
with rhetorical eloquence, when the woman-hungry
sailors find no one with whom to slake their natural ap-

petites? What then? Will they go quietly back to the ships, resigned to more months of loneliness at sea? Or will they prowl the city streets in search of women, good or bad? They may even break into decent people's homes in respectable neighborhoods! Let me remind you that it has happened before. His listeners surely remembered that it had happened before.

The ominous threat hung in the air, fear made a path for itself, decent families bolted their doors, and panic ensued.

47

City Councilman Reginaldo Pavão never missed a cue when it came to stepping into the limelight—he wasn't named "Peacock" for nothing. He couldn't see a microphone without making a grab for it. The passion of this smart, shrewd, crooked petty politician was speechifying in a style which was an unholy jumble of the crude and the baroque. When a group of people gathered together for whatever reason, there was Pavão strutting in their midst. On that afternoon when the baskets were shut, where else would he be but in the tenderloin?

Envious rivals claimed that he had gone there for inadmissible reasons, and, unable to find an outlet for his instincts, had taken advantage of the presence of reporters and radio journalists to sling a little bull. Talk about slander! The conscientious alderman was only doing as his conscience bade him; only acting out of selfless devotion to public good, which in this case meant serving both the authorities and the lower-class citizens.

When he got to Pelourinho toward late afternoon, after a city council meeting at which a motion had been passed welcoming the ships of the U.S. fleet, he headed as usual for Dona Paulina de Souza's house, which he preferred for several very good reasons: the women had class, the rooms were clean, the place was quiet, and his friend Ariosto Alvo Lírio backed him and brought in the votes, you scratch my back and I'll scratch yours. Stout Dona Paulina explained the predicament they were in. Their good friend would just have to forgive them; it was none of their doing, but today the baskets were closed.

With the madam was the dancer from the Lotus Flower Cabaret, a Venus, a divine creature with flashing eyes. Taking up where Dona Paulina left off, the beauty declared that all the baskets were closed, and closed they would stay until the madams of Barroquinha, who had been arrested and beaten up in jail the night before, could go back to their invaded houses and the prostitutes who had been driven out of them could return to their beds without having to worry about being dragged out of them again the next day. Eager, impassioned, and obviously spoiling for a fight, the rare beauty would have made a good orator and councilwoman herself. It was up to the Barroquinha women to decide when to cry Alleluia! Reginaldo Pavão decided to go around to the Lotus Flower more often when the club reopened. Why, the girl was a vision.

Next the councilman let himself be seen walking purposefully through the zone, through Pelourinho, Taboão, Maciel, entering the bars to chat with both customers and police. From there he went to vice squad headquarters, where Hélio Cotias listened to him politely, even cordially. However, the Chief would not budge an inch from his fixed purpose of moving the Barroquinha brothels to Codfish Hill. The move had been accomplished for all practical purposes the night before, except that the madams had yet to resign themselves to obeying the measures taken by the police for the common good. There's not a thing I can do about it now, my dear fellow; those orders come from very high up—underlining the words with a vague gesture.

As to ways and means, that's up to my assistant; his job is to make the prostitutes go back to work again. He'll have to be quick about it, too, because the sailors are coming ashore at eight o'clock tonight.

48

By nightfall the tenderloin looked like a city occupied by enemy troops. Police cars unloaded the reinforcements the assistant chief had asked for, and the entrances to streets and alleys were strategically blocked by paddy wagons and shock troops on wheels. The Mounted Special Forces and MP's went up and down Pelourinho and patrolled Maciel. A curious crowd collected in the Terreiro de Jesus and milled about waiting to see what would happen. Only a few stubborn customers stayed in the blockaded stronghold, downing beer and arguing heatedly in the bars.

There was not a working professional to be seen. Those who weren't out having fun were enjoying a restful evening indoors. Labão's henchmen presented these seditious women with an ultimatum: you have exactly half an hour to open up and take your posts in doorways, windows, and parlors, or to come out and start walking the streets. No answer.

The bars were still open, but that was all. Houses, castles, cheap hotels were shut, locked and dark. The usual animation was missing. No gutter language, no lewd laughter, no hissed invitations or dirty, tempting offers, no men eyeing half-dressed women up and down, only the echo of horses' hooves on the black cobblestones. The calendar had gone crazy and Holy Week had come in mid-September.

Even Blind Belarmino, with his more than twenty years in the same place before Vavá's busy establishment, which he only left on days when there was a big church festival, had got tired of hearing no coins drop into his plate and had hied himself to the cathedral steps. He had a suitable repertory for each begging spot:

> Hail the Christ Child
> So meek and so mild
> Saint Joseph our lord
> whom our faith doth guard
> And the Holy Virgin bright
> in her halo of light.

In Maciel, Labão Oliveira drew his revolver and ordered the defenders of public morality to march forward. In Pelourinho, a minute late because that watch he had picked up off a smuggler kept such lousy time, the Dogfish advanced, followed by cops and civil guards.

The battle is joined!—proclaimed Rádio Abaeté; where there's news there's Abaeté, through water and fire, in war and peace. Pandemonium in the red-light district!—the microphone vibrated with the voice of Pinto Scott, golden larynx of Rádio Grêmio of Bahia.

49

The doors to the bawdy houses and hotels were broken down as the police shouldered and kicked their way in. Cops invaded the houses, grabbed the women and shoved them outside. Nightsticks and rubber truncheons flailed about their heads; some of the agents wore brass knuckles. Amid blows, shouts, and curses the women fled out of doors. Those who resisted were dragged out. It was the first step in Operation Heigh-Ho, and the forces of legality enjoyed it.

In a few instances, however, the agents' task was both more difficult and more unpleasant. The plumbing in Ceres Cocksucker's place had been out of order for the last twenty-four hours, and the women had had to resort to using chamber pots; piled up at the back of the house, they turned out to be very good weapons in a fight. With full pots in their hands, the prostitutes stood up to the invaders and put them to flight. Plainclothesman Dalmo Coca, in command of that battalion, received the contents of one receptacle full in his face and all over his light gray suit. As luck would have it, it was the one in which a new girl, Zabá, who was struggling with a fierce bout of dysentery, had relieved herself a great many times, and the elegant detective was soon reeking with crap, urine, and hate. He ordered drastic reprisals and himself set the example.

Assistant Chief Oliveira, revolver in hand, went in person to take charge of the assault on Vavá's brothel. He climbed the steps at the head of a group of his trusted men, told them to break the door down, and stepped across the threshold. Not a living soul did he find on either of the two top floors of the enormous house. The cubicles were deserted, the silence complete. Where was the whoremaster? Ah, when Labão laid hands on him he'd soon make him talk out of the other side of his mouth. He had counted on Vavá, as a matter of fact. Vavá's word was law in that district, and if he said the word for the baskets to be opened, then victory was in the bag. Where had the son-of-a-bitch of a cripple holed himself up?

At a sign from Labão the cops broke down the door of the paralytic's private room. Not a sign of him. In their rage they ripped the sheets off the bed, destroyed personal possessions Vavá had used and loved, pried open the lock of the desk, scattered papers and tore them up, and tried to open the wall safe but failed.

Remembering the golden days when the *candomblé* rites had been suppressed, when he had still been a lowly plainclothesman at the start of a brilliant career, doughty Assistant Chief Labão Oliveira, who feared nothing in heaven or earth, went over to the shrine, the *peji,* and began to pull it to pieces. Alírio, an undercover man who had never balked at murder in cold blood, cried out aghast:

"Chief, are you crazy? Don't touch Exu!"

"Chicken-shit! What are you scared of? I'll crap on your Exu!"

The sacred iron trident, spear, and emblem were sent flying, the heap of earth which was Exu's throne was scattered, and the offerings of food and drink—the goat stew with garlic and pumpkin seeds and the heads of twelve black roosters—were flung around the room. The cops could only watch in silence as Labão smashed the *peji* to smithereens and then spat at them irately:

"Why the hell are you standing around like bumps on a log? Go make some of those whores go back to work, you chicken-livered bums. Or are you scared of the women too?"

He looked at his watch: it was almost time for the sailors to come ashore. He'd better get a move on.

50

Once they were dragged out of doors, the women took to their heels, fled down alleys, disappeared. The mounted police tried to round them up but it wasn't easy; the hunt covered too wide an area.

The customers in the bars, with Hansen the German in the lead, threw empty bottles under the horses' hooves in protest against the brutality of the police. Over Rádio Grêmio, the poet Telmo Serra called it "sheer vandalism."

The zone of prostitution is catching fire! This phrase spoken by one of the radio announcers added to the general panic, for many listeners took it literally and began to circulate the rumor that fire had broken out in several places. Photographers' flashbulbs caught prostitutes in attitudes of terror or rage. Covered with feces and urine and stinking to high heaven, Dalmo "Coca" García gave up the good fight.

51

Councilman Pavão stepped to the microphone installed by Rádio Abaeté "in the heart of the battle zone," where "this popular personage in local politics has come to face danger beside us in a praiseworthy attempt to find a way out of a situation that is becoming graver by the moment," and began to appeal to all the thousands of his fellow citizens who were glued to their sets.

The stentorian voice of the wily vote-catcher boomed out over the airwaves into almost every house in Bahia. Not even from the forum of the city council, not even from the platform at a monster rally, had he ever had such an audience. Radios were turned on all over town; no one left his set for fear of missing some new development in the epic struggle of the closed baskets.

His "heart heavy" within him, Reginaldo Pavão addressed "the listeners of Rádio Abaeté, the people of Bahia, and the population outside its walls," described the "Dantesque spectacle" unfolding before his eyes "obfuscated by emotion" and compared it to spectacles that had taken place "in the Rome of the Caesars, of which sublime Universal History tells us." The airwaves thrilled with his words: "My voice is choked with tears."

He directed a moving appeal to the prostitutes: "I have faith in the patriotism of my dear fellow countrywomen whom the storms of existence have caused to stumble and fall, only to be washed up on the dismal shores of prostitution. It is impossible for me to believe that these fallen sisters will persist in the discourtesy of leaving the heroic sailors of the invincible South Atlantic fleet of the great American nation—" How to put it? "High and dry?" Why not say "to watch the ships go by," dear councilman; why not use Chief Labão's *bon mot,* now a household word, thanks to the radio announcers concealed in doorways in Maciel and Pelourinho? "No, I shall never believe they will leave those brave boys who daily risk their lives so that all of us—including you, gallant Magdalenes, good Bahians all—may reap the joys and blessings of civilization, with no recourse, those brave lads, but to watch the ships go by. Your untimely abstinence threatens to provoke an international incident. I beg of you, my dear sisters in sin, I beg of you: heed, oh heed, my words."

It was a pity that this speech full of patriotism and pathos, which so moved Rádio Abaeté's listeners, never reached the ears of Councilman Pavão's sisters in sin, who were too busy being hit on the head by the police or trying to run fast enough to keep out from under the horses' hooves to listen to the radio.

Reginaldo Pavão's final appeal was addressed to His Excellency the Governor, "with all due respect for the eminence of a great man placed by the voters at the helm of a ship of state outward bound toward a glorious future," and appealed to his "Christian sentiments and time-tested capacity as a statesman." The sailors were about to land, the prostitutes were resisting the orders of the police, the red-light district was one great powderkeg, and the present riot might well spread to the point where it threatened the decent families of Bahia. The honest public servant exhorted the noble Governor to "issue orders immediately, Your Excellency, to free the brothel owners who still languish in jail and allow them to reopen the houses from which they were dislodged by the overzealous police in their haste to move the women from Barroquinha to Codfish Hill." Governor, we are in a state of emergency! Suspend the order to move, put an end to the conflict "which is still restricted to the zone of prostitution but which may at any moment assume the proportions not only of a statewide but even a national or—God forbid—an international catastrophe!"

Now Bahia was really in an uproar. Whole families shut themselves inside their houses and bolted their doors, and the telephones at the government palace and police headquarters never stopped ringing. The people were calling on their authorities to act.

52

Inside the Buick hidden in a dense patch of woods, Camões and his pal heard Councilman Reginaldo Pavão's impassioned speech. They had turned on the radio to provide themselves with a pleasant musical background for their trip. Camões pricked up his ears:

"Well, the deal just went *pfft*. We'd better go get our stuff before it's too late."

"Yeah." Joy-Smoke's squat friend, almost a dwarf, was a man of few words.

He got behind the wheel and drove the Buick down the ruinous avenue that led up Codfish Hill. The two partners were not by any means too stoned to pick up their merchandise and take it back where it had come from. From the very beginning, nothing about this deal had gone well.

Inside the house, once the precious stuff had been divided up under the capable orders of Cincinato Gato Preto, the pushers lounged around, thinking it was a hell of a note that they had been told to keep watch over that pile of grass and not smoke any.

Most of the furniture brought from Barroquinha the night before in the police truck and dumped in front of the houses had been "liberated" that day by an assorted collection of beggars and bums. The few mattresses left were dragged into the main room of the house and the boys stretched out on them to wait. The wait turned out to be a long one, and the vision of pot became irresistible. After a brief discussion they agreed unanimously that Dalmo Coca's prohibition was patently absurd. Who would lose out if they lit up a joint or two while they waited? What harm was there in that? Obviously, none. Cincinato Gato Preto, who had a reputation as a man who kept his promises, finally gave in. He felt the need of a smoke as much as anyone.

Reclining voluptuously on the mattresses, they smoked and dreamed until Joy-Smoke Camões and his half-pint pal burst into the room. Cincinato Gato Preto liked a calm, peaceful trip. He lifted his head, stared at the interlopers, and recognized their faces. They must be here with the message from Chief Coca.

"Is it time to go?"

Camões explained that the detective's plan had fizzled out. At this very minute the red-light zone was an inferno of beatings and running and shooting. Not even a lunatic straight from an asylum would be crazy enough to try to sell grass with the place full of police on foot, on horseback, and on wheels throwing everybody in the lockup. They had just heard about it over the car radio. Skeptical Cincinato did not believe a single word of Camõe's rigmarole, least of all his concluding statement:

"They haven't passed us a nickel, so we've come to take the stuff back."

"The hell you will!" Gato Preto made a mighty effort, sat up on the mattress, and repeated: "The hell you will."

Joy-Smoke Camões was the soul of valor when stoned. "I'll send you to hell right now, you piece of shit."

A few of the boys struggled to their feet and a free-for-all began. The pygmy pulled out a switchblade knife and charged. A lighted joint rolled across a mattress with holes in it and fell onto dry straw. Smoke filled the room, then flames leapt to the roof.

53

In Pelourinho, where the armies of morality and law went on the offensive under the command of Nicolau Ramada Junior, the picture was much the same as in Maciel: women being beaten, dragged from their houses, rounded up, penned into the square, and chased by the mounted police. In Pelourinho it was harder to find a hiding place or get away, because the streets leading into the Terreiro de Jesus and Shoemakers' Hollow were blocked by police cars. Cudgels thudded and blows rained down upon the women. The order was not to let up until the criminals went back to "the life" and opened their baskets. It's Back to Work They'll Go!

The invasion of Dona Paulina de Souza's main establishment, which Dogfish directed himself, added something new to the battle: barricades. Not trusting to locks, the renegades had blocked the doors with heavy furniture, obstructing the police still further in the performance of their duties and enraging the already angry plainclothesmen beyond words.

Finally they got the door open. Dogfish ran down the hall, and who did he see in front of his very eyes? That no-good troublemaker, that dame who liked to shoot her mouth off, Tereza Batista herself. Tereza Foot-in-the-Nuts just then, her foot in Führer Dogfish's nuts with all the weight of her fashionable square-toed shoe, a gift from her friend Mirabeau Sampaio, who had painted her as Our Lady Suckling the Infant Christ.

"Arrrrrgh!"

The plainclothesman's strangled bellow paralyzed the invading troops. Tereza darted past the police and out the door, some of the other women at her heels. Dogfish flopped on the ground with his hands on his balls. The pain at that moment was so great that he wasn't even thinking of revenge. Not until several minutes later, when he had struggled to his feet with the help of two of his colleagues, did he mingle heartfelt curses with his roars of pain.

With the slow, majestic tread of a carnival queen and a bawdy-house madam, Dona Paulina de Souza paraded with her guard of honor—two cops before her and two behind—to the Black Maria, where she settled down with those of her subjects who had been arrested a little earlier. She told them to keep calm and not to worry; Ogum the Fish of the Sea had told her everything would be all right—nothing ventured, nothing gained.

Surrounded by troops of the Special Forces, Tereza escaped between the horses' legs, ran up the steps to the Blacks' Church of the Rosary, and flattened herself against a door. Other women followed her example. The horses could not climb the stairs, but the cops came running to drag them away.

The door at Tereza's back opened halfway, and as she slipped inside she just caught a glimpse of an imposing old man with a long beard and a staff disappearing behind an altar. Was he the sexton, maybe, or a priest, or a saint? Even the whores have a patron saint, St. Onofre. Was it St. Onofre who had helped her, or one of the *orixás* from Tereza's court? On the Long Night of the Battle of the Closed Baskets—the title given by Jehová de Carvalho to a long, impassioned poem in which he sang the deeds and tribulations of that night—many inexplicable things took place, which no one but poets understood.

Women were precipitated from the Pelourinho brothels; some were hurled to the sidewalk by the cops and detectives. Others escaped to the church, where they were joined by women from Maciel and Taboão in search of a haven of safety. Little by little the nave filled with prostitutes, some of whom fell on their knees and began saying the Lord's Prayer.

54

After their softshell crabs and ice-cold beer, Anália and Kalil took a bus to Cathedral Square. Dona Paulina de Souza had told her girls to be back early to avoid possible unpleasantness with discontented customers. But when the bus stopped at Castro Alves Plaza, Kalil slapped his forehead and made Anália get off:

"I was just about to forget for the third time."

"Forget what, honey?"

"The St. Onofre for Dona Paulina."

St. Onofre, not content with favoring business deals and helping his devotees earn money, is the official patron saint of women in the life. Every self-respecting bawdy house has an image of the saint in its dining room, smothered with flowers and votive candles, his niche often having as a neighbor a *peji* where a powerful *orixá* sits enthroned.

For a long time Dona Paulina had been looking for a good-sized image of the protecting saint to enthrone in the little oratory along with the statues of Our Lord of the Navigators and Our Lady of the Immaculate Conception

which were already there. Learning that Kalil's father
dealt in saints' images as well as all kinds of other antiques
she asked the boy to reserve her a large St. Onofre in
good condition, one that wouldn't cost her too much. She
hadn't found a single one for sale, old or new, in the shops
that sold religious articles.

The saints that old Chamas sold were usually worth a
fortune, even those in bad condition, with missing arms,
heads, or legs. They were museum pieces, collector's
items. But occasionally, in a batch of images from the interior of the state, there would be some of recent work-
manship, effigies that had no place in an antique shop;
and these they got rid of at once, selling them for whatever they could get. If a St. Onofre like that turns up,
Dona Paulina can have it and it won't cost her a thing;
that's little enough return to make for her hospitality. One
had turned up day before yesterday, a big plaster statue,
almost new, but Kalil kept forgetting to bring it.

Leaving AnálIa on the corner, he ran off to get the
saint and came back with it under his arm, wrapped in
newspaper. They walked the rest of the way, climbing up
Rua da Ajuda on foot.

55

After the event it came out that a few of the brothel keepers in Maciel and Pelourinho, afraid of the violence of
the police on the one hand, and reckoning up how much
money they would lose if the girls weren't working when
the sailors rolled into town loaded with dollars, had seriously thought of breaking the agreement and putting
pressure on their girls to open their baskets.

News of this threat of treason was brought immediately
to Vavá in the place where he had gone to lie low
(the police never found it, and most of the people who
live in the zone still have no idea where it was). He sent
an urgent message to the lukewarm. Woe to any woman
who breaks her commitment and disobeys Exu's orders!
There'll be no place for her in the zone; she can't even
stay in Bahia; she'll have to move right away—if she has
a chance to move, that is, before dying an ugly death.

She can die here tonight or in some other whorehouse within a month. It was Exu Tiriri who decreed the death sentence, and woe to the woman who tries to flout it! Once the matter was put in those terms, the union stayed strong to the last, and every basket was closed.

Or should one say that there was, indeed, one open basket?

All at once, in the middle of the fracas, a tall, gangling strumpet appeared out of nowhere with a purse in her hand, a blond wig, very high heels, and a blue organdy dress. She sashayed down the street swinging her purse, the classic street-walker looking for a man. The delighted cops hurried up to safeguard the one professional who was willing to cooperate in the Back to Work We Go movement.

When the cops came closer, they saw—oh cruel deception!—that it was only Greta Garbo, the waiter at Vavá's brothel, who had been in an agony of soul-searching since the night before. Should he close his basket too? Did the order apply to him (her) or not? He wavered indecisively for hours, but desire to take advantage of this rare opportunity—ah, a city full of sailors and empty of women! —had finally won out.

He was arrested and thrown in the paddy wagon, where the girls who were already in there started hitting the poor fairy, victim of an overweening though laudable ambition to take on the U.S. Navy all by himself.

56

In strict obedience to the instructions given by assistant Chief Oliveira, senior partner in the touristic enterprise set up for the benefit of the visiting sailors, scores of peddlers and street boys invaded the tenderloin district at about eight in the evening, each with a basket on his arm full of condoms and vials of Stiff Prick—One Dose, Five Fucks.

At exactly the moment when the police forces, under the supreme command of the assistant chief, prepared to round up all the women and make them go back to work, a crowd of peddlers and ragamuffins entered on stage, hawking their wares in English and adding to the confusion of the scene with their infernal din.

The Special Forces, who had been told nothing about the little arrangement, flung their horses against the unexpected sea of new lawbreakers in an attempt to clear them from the streets and reduce the chaos by that much, at least. For their part, the street vendors had expected a crowd of eager customers, nice sailors chewing gum, passing out cigarettes, buying prophylactics and paying for them in dollars, all under the indulgent gaze of the vice squad—since everything had been arranged. Instead of sailors and girls, here were mounted police running them down on horseback and forcing them off the streets. The kids scattered and ran through the first open door they saw. Baskets rolled in the street, scattering thousands of condoms on the paving stones. Bottles broke, and Heron Madruga's miraculous elixir was spilled in the gutter.

The women accepted the rain of bottles as heaven-sent weapons to use against the cops; and as Chief Labão Oliveira brandished his revolver in a vain attempt to save some part of his crumbling organization from the general bankruptcy into which all his scheme had fallen, the wailing siren of fire engines was heard rising high above the pandemonium.

57

When Anália and Kalil reached Cathedral Square, they realized that something very serious was going on in the zone. They heard people talking excitedly, relaying the latest rumors in the Terreiro de Jesus. Only a few had the courage to walk into the battle zone, keeping pace with the police cars. The girl and the young man skirted the school of medicine and walked down the hill to Pelourinho Square. There Anália took the image of St. Onofre from Kalil:

"You can't come home with me today. The basket's shut."

As they walked on together for a few steps, they suddenly found themselves in the middle of a turbulent crowd and hemmed in by police. A cop headed for Anália;

Kalil stepped in and the girl started to run away but didn't know which way to run. All at once she heard a masculine voice, like a voice from Heaven, murmur in her ear:

"To the church, quickly, fair daughter of the Piauitinga."

The high-flown words, the melodious voice, floated on the night breeze, sweet and imperious at the same time. Anália obeyed it and went running to the church, but the steps were full of cops to keep the women from going up or down. How could she get past them? She never knew how she did it, but she did.

She felt herself lifted in the arms of a handsome young man whom she thought she recognized—but where was it she had seen him? Who was he? In a twinkling they were on the other side, she and the image of St. Onofre, safe and sound before the half-opened door of the church. She looked down and saw Kalil struggling in the hands of two policemen, who were carrying him to a Black Maria. She would have run back down again to her lover but the other women stopped her and dragged her into the church, holding up the image in triumph. The weeping Anália sought refuge in the arms of Tereza Batista.

"Don't cry, child, everything's all right," said Tereza consolingly. "He won't be in prison very long. Dona Paulina's there, and a whole lot of other people. But the baskets stayed shut."

58

In Castro Alves Square, Edgard the old cabby dozed in his taxi. There were hardly any customers at that hour when everyone was home eating, talking, listening to the radio, getting ready to rest or go out. What with the women from Barroquinha not around and the closing down of the bawdy houses the night before, the flow of customers to the neighborhood had dwindled to nothing. It was still too early for the Tabaris Cabaret to open its doors and the place to liven up.

Edgard was alone at the taxi rank just then, the other cabbies having knocked off for supper. Half-asleep as he was, he managed to prop his eyes open just long enough for a look around the plaza to make sure he wasn't missing a customer. Breadfruit Jacira was at the stand near the bus stop with her tray of cornmeal and tapioca, but almost no one else was in sight.

He put his head back to rest his neck and his jaw fell open. Where was the poet Castro Alves's statue? It wasn't there where it always was, standing on its tall pedestal, arm outflung toward the sea in an oratorical gesture, demanding justice for the people. Who had taken it, and why? To be cleaned, maybe? But they had always cleaned it right where it was and never had to move it before. Something must have happened to it. Well, he'd read all about it tomorrow in the paper.

Edgard went back to his catnap. As he dozed off he was thinking of how different the square looked—smaller, somehow, and diminished—without the statue.

59

When the governor was made to understand how grave the situation had become, he left the room where whisky was being served before the banquet honoring the U.S. admiral and his staff, to have a word with Councilman Pavão. The Peacock was unquestionably an indefatigable worker for the governor's party, but he was also a shameless and unmitigated rascal. It was impossible to snub him, but the governor managed to maintain a discreet distance between the fiery vote-and-status seeker and himself, while making use of his undoubted shrewdness and political acumen. Born in poverty on the bank of the São Francisco River, he had risen in office by dint of audacity and practical knowledge learned in the school of hard knocks and turned to good account. Reginaldo was extremely useful in certain circumstances, but he had to be handled with care; he was as bumptious as he was illiterate. Still, the political aide had whispered horrors into the gubernatorial ear. His Excellency excused himself in his best English and rose to his feet. In the next room he heard a sad tale and a heartfelt cry for help.

Bathetically, with a catch in his voice, Reginaldo Pavão alluded to Greek tragedy. Why Greek, wondered His Excellency; had the councilman read Aristophanes? But it was not the right moment to pull his leg. He merely asked him to wait while he took the necessary measures: "You wait right here, my dear Pavão, and you'll have some good news to pass on to our—What was it you called them? That lovely expression you used? Oh, yes!—our sisters in sin."

"They may be prostitutes, Your Excellency, but they're voters."

From his office the governor telephoned the chief of police.

"What's this I hear about your moving the prostitutes by force? Who ever heard of strumpets going on strike? Only in Bahia, and only during my term of office! And my dear fellow, what's to be done about the sailors?"

The explanation he heard was neither very clear nor very convincing; the chief of police was soon hopelessly entangled in his own arguments. Fooling a politician as smart and experienced as the governor wasn't easy. You say it's a routine operation? Then why did the police come down with such a heavy hand and provoke this disturbing wave of rumors? His thoughts ran ahead of the conversation, and he brusquely cut short the confused rigmarole stammered out by the chief of police. The important thing now was to nip the panic in the bud, and the only way to do that was to stop the riot in the district. That would keep the sailors from being disappointed, too, as that impudent rascal Pavão had put it with such unexpected quaintness. He dictated restrictive orders to curb the police.

Tomorrow when he wasn't so rushed, he would get to the bottom of the thing and find out what had really happened. There was something fishy, something very suspicious, behind that hasty transferral of the zone. Who could say—maybe the harlots would provide him with the good excuse he so badly needed to name another chief of police and force this one to resign. His Excellency understood how to follow the strait and crooked path; if he hadn't, he could never have endured politics and the solemn and utter stupidity of petty men. He loved to catch them by the toe when they had one hand in the cookie jar.

He returned to the room where the councilman was

totting up the possible advantages he might extract from the situation, and smiled. Reginaldo was just a little gutter rat, after all; his most secret thoughts were transparently reflected in his rogue's face. It occurred to His Excellency that the Peacock was the ideal emissary to take a message of peace to the whores.

"My dear Pavão, I've ordered the women who were arrested last night to be set free and all removal orders rescinded. Why don't you go and tell them the good news? You can look in at the vice-squad headquarters and relay my orders to the bureau chief in person, if you like"—a little maneuver to make the chief of police lose face—"and then escort those poor women back to their houses in Barroquinha and put those little votes in your vest pocket as a present from me to you."

"Anyone who votes for me will vote for Your Excellency too! That's a promise!"

60

Still digesting the governor's rebuke and seeing black clouds piling up on the horizon—If I don't do some fast footwork I'll find I'm a fifth wheel before long—the chief of police called the chief of the Bureau of Gambling and Public Morality and passed on the governor's order that the Barroquinha brothel keepers be released and allowed to go home and stay there until further notice.

On the other side of the wire his subordinate was evidently putting up an argument. The police chief rubbed his chin and said regretfully:

"There are times when you just can't do as much for a friend as you'd like to. Now we're right back where we were before. Or rather, we're worse off than we were before. So turn the women loose, tell them you won't bother them any more, and get our men out of the zone. Don't leave anybody but the regular patrolmen."

He impatiently broke in on Cotias's continued urging:

"The order came straight from the governor, I tell you; there's not a thing I can do. Don't worry about old Sardinha, I'll take care of him. Just leave it to me. I'll talk to him myself. And don't forget to give me some news once in a while. I have to keep the governor informed."

Hélio Cotias, LL.B., replaced the receiver. Oh, yes, you'll take care of the old man; and who'll take care of Carmen? His wife and her uncle between them would make life impossible for him. What he really wanted to do was throw it all up, resign, tell them all to go jump in the lake, and then go home, shut himself up in his bedroom, and sleep. He was utterly exhausted.

He had saved at least one thing from the debacle: Bada, a prize that should put him automatically in the upper ranks of lady-killers, those successful in winning the favors of hard-to-get-married women. Well, Bada was married all right, but hard-to-get? A nymphomaniac, that's what she was, and the easiest lay in town. He was only the last in a long line of men who had had her in their arms. A regiment, no doubt. Job, family, mistress, the source of so much envy, the tangible appurtenances of fame and glory, in reality meant only unhappiness and frustration. The abused women, that black one with her face beaten to a pulp, her split lip, the bruises all over her. Labão Oliveira's murderous eyes. And all that, for what? To let the women go in the end, and rescind the order to move.

The radio on the edge of the desk interrupted its broadcast of the battle of the closed baskets to announce a big fire in the Lower Town. Flames were consuming the old houses on Codfish Hill at that very moment. Cotias put his hand over his mouth and ran out of his office, past an astonished guard. He barely had time to reach the men's room before vomiting bitter green bile.

Grave, polite, but rather distant, as befitted an envoy from His Excellency the Governor, Councilman Reginaldo Pavão walked into the empty office of the Bureau Chief for Gambling and Public Morality.

61

A raging fire is destroying the old mansions on Codfish Hill!—announced Rádio Abaeté, as the news caught fire. The old houses designated by the police as new quarters for the prostitutes who were moved from Barroquinha yesterday are being rapidly devoured by flames. Firetrucks are on their way to the scene of the fire; our microphones are with them. The cause of the fire is still unknown, but it has been established that furniture and other property belonging to the prostitutes was taken there yesterday by police trucks and dumped. This suggests that there may very well be some connection between the fearful fire blazing opposite the harbor and the increasingly serious situation in the tenderloin, where the forces of public safety have so far been unable to persuade the prostitutes to go back to work. On this twenty-first day of September, the first day of spring, the city is uneasy, even alarmed. The boats are on the point of being lowered to bring the American sailors ashore. In these circumstances, no degree of precaution is too great. We urge our listeners to remain in their homes with doors and windows securely locked, at the least sign of trouble. Deposit your savings in the Interstate Bank of Bahia and Sergipe and sleep peacefully. Stay tuned to Rádio Abaeté. We'll be back with more sensational news after this announcement.

Several ladies fainted, and an old woman suffered a heart attack and had to be rushed to the Emergency Room of the hospital. Old maid Veralice sighed as she resignedly obeyed her sister-in-law's admonition to shut the doors and windows: if only there *would* be an invasion of lustful, woman-hungry sailors! She'd know what to say to a blond, lusty Yankee sailor: Here I am, come and get me!

62

While Chief Hélio Cotias was vomiting his guts out just before giving orders that old Acácia, Assunta, and the other Barroquinha madams be set free, the doors of the Blacks' Church of the Rosary in Pelourinho opened wide and the scores of women who had fled to it for refuge came slowly out.

Reporters, photographers, and radio announcers ran up from all directions and began popping flashbulbs and broadcasting their first reports in a machine-gun staccato. Little by little the women filled the church porch at the top of the steps, St. Onofre in the lead.

Prostitutes begin a protest march! March of the Closed Basket!—bawled the Rádio Abaeté announcer. Unwilling to yield first place to his rival, Pinto Scott, the golden voice of Rádio Grêmio of Bahia, simultaneously released the sensational news: Protesting prostitutes march on the governor's palace!

Placed on a litter they'd found in the sacristy, the image of St. Onofre was borne on the shoulders of four women, including Black Domingas, her face still badly swollen, and Maria Petisco, as unquenchable as ever. From the four corners of the famous old square came cops, detectives, secret police agents, brandishing truncheons, rubber nightsticks, guns, hatred, rage. The mounted troops posted themselves in readiness to trample the parade, religious procession, protest march, or whatever the devil it was, under the horses' hooves.

Still leading the forces of law and order, Assistant Chief Labão Oliveira, with his adder's eyes and venomous heart, couldn't take a step without treading on envelopes full of condoms and crushing under his boots the little glass bottles once filled with the precious aphrodisiac Stiff Prick. And with every envelope and every bottle, he was trampling underfoot his own capital and all his profits. That mess had cost him good money out of his own pocket, money that should have produced a miraculous harvest of greenbacks. And now—look how those goddamned bitches had ruined all his well-laid plans and dreams of wealth. Nicolau Ramada Junior hobbled after him, stifling his groans; he too was a ruined man in more ways than one. Dalmo Coca having vanished in a cloud of dung, Oliveira and the Dogfish were still in happy ignorance of the fate of the marijuana, their last hope for recouping something from their financial debacle. Like the dollar, they thought, grass is never devalued.

All of the women paused for a moment at the top of the steps. Old Granny—who would have been a churchmouse at the cathedral in Cruz das Almas if she hadn't been a whore in Bahia—raised her cracked old voice in a litany:

> Ave, ave Maria
> Ave, ave Maria

The women joined in the chant and as the image began to move toward the steps, Granny's tired voice continued to lead the prayer:

> Dressed as an angel
> in Heaven she sings
> the colors of Heaven
> shine on her wings

The women stood ranked behind the image. And there, right in the front row, was Tereza Batista. When he saw her, the Dogfish forgot how his balls hurt and made a lunge for her. At exactly the same moment, the Flower of São Miguel Saloon debouched a noisy phalanx of customers. There was Tom Lívio, our stage star with the promising future; Hansen the German, who gouged out woodcuts showing the life and hard times of the whores he knew so well; Telmo Serra the poet— all the eternal bohemians who sit up arguing about the fate of the world until dawn, the guardians of men's dreams who save mankind from total catastrophe and annihilation. In the engraver's powerful hands was a poster showing gaunt, disheveled, half-naked female figures in the act of breaking the chains that bound their wrists, each with a padlock on her cunt. An inscription in large letters read POWER TO THE PUTAS. Labão Oliveira yelled out orders to the cops and soldiers to break it up, make arrests, use violence, kill if they had to.

A charge of mounted police broke up the procession; the cops laid about them with truncheons, and the plainclothesmen aimed their revolvers. The effigy of St. Onofre was deposited carefully on the ground, still erect. Beside it Granny went on singing her litany in a high, feeble voice. Anyone looking at her wrinkled, foolish old face and toothless mouth could see she had lived at least a hundred years and been a whore for a thousand, but she still loved to fight and praise the saints:

Ave, ave Maria
Ave, ave Maria

Assistant Chief Oliveira ran toward her to stop her
by force, caught his foot in a hole, fell, rolled over, and
didn't get up. He fired from where he lay prostrate on
the ground. The old woman stopped in mid-note, the
song ceased, and silence came over the square. Next to
the image of the saint lay Granny's worn little body. She
had died praying, she had died fighting, so she must
have died happy.

Cops ran over to help Labão Oliveira to his feet, but
both legs were broken and he was unable to stand. Detective Alírio flung himself on the ground in terror and
beat his head against the paving stones. And he had
warned him, too! Chief, don't be a fool, don't touch Exu.

The police wagons rumbled off to headquarters,
crammed with women and barflies. Practically everybody
in the zone was thrown in jail. Dogfish lingered for a
few minutes to direct the final cleanup, but he was in a
hurry—Tereza Batista, under heavy guard, was waiting
for him in the clink.

She was going to be given a new lesson in respect and
obedience. Dogfish rubbed his hands at the one bright
prospect before him in a night of calamity.

63

When the American sailors walked into Pelourinho
Square, they admired the old colonial houses and looked
around for the beautiful, fun-loving women they
expected would be there to welcome them. There was
only one woman in sight, and she was just a useless old
hag—even if she hadn't been dead, stretched out stiff
as a board next to St. Onofre, patron saint of whores.

While they were still speechless with surprise, strict
orders came to return to the pier on the double. Bahia
was in a state of panic, and shore leave would have to
wait.

64

Too many miracles, you say? Maybe you just can't swallow so many whoppers in one night. Orixás butting in all the time with their magic spells; a bearded old man with a staff turning up out of nowhere to open church doors and shunt the police off the track; a poet who's been dead a hundred years saving damsels in distress; Ogum the Fish of the Sea telling them to cheer up; Exu giving that assistant bureau chief a shove that laid him flat on the ground and broke both his legs, when he was already mad as a wet hen before; St. Onofre keeping a death watch over Granny's body when there was nobody else around—I know it's a stiff dose for a practical man and a materialist to swallow, and I know you said you wanted the truth and nothing but the truth, minus magic and witchcraft.

I don't doubt a bit that you've totted up the score right and know just how many times I've told you magic came in to save the day; but don't forget that all this happened in the city of Bahia, east of the world, the land of black and white magic and voodoo spells. If you've lived here awhile like you say, you ought to know by now that strange things happen in Bahia all the time; they're all in a day's work, as you might say, and people here wouldn't think of telling fibs, especially about something everybody saw with his own eyes.

If you don't believe me, answer me this: how could a bunch of ignorant whores without a penny to their names or anything to fight with have stood up to the police and won the Closed-Basket War if they hadn't had the saints and orixás to help them, and the poets and the witch doctors too? Just tell me that if you're so smart and have such a good imagination.

No, I'm sorry, but I can't explain it either. I'm only telling it to you the way it happened because you wanted to hear about it so bad, and a cabby owes his customers a good jaw at least, to make the trip a little shorter. Anybody who thinks he can explain all the things that happen in this world by chopping them into neat little

*facts and figures and then tying up all the loose ends—
well, you'll excuse me, friend, but he's nothing but a
false materialist, a half-pint know-it-all, a short-sighted
historian, a buttinsky, and a fool.*

*Now I'll give you one last dose to make your cup run
over. This is a thing that happened to me, Edgard
Rogaciano Ferreira: and anyone in Bahia can tell you
I'm a sober man and no teller of tall tales. I've already
told you how I saw the statue of Castro Alves missing
from its pedestal that night, in Castro Alves Square where
I park my cab. Well, I must have slept for a pretty long
time, but when the sirens woke me up as the police cars
were carting off the women at the end of the fight, I
look up at the monument and what do I see? The poet's
statue, right in the same place it's always been, with his
arm pointing out to sea and a torn poster in his hand
with some naked women on it and some kind of crazy
slogan—*POWER TO THE PUTAS, *how do you like that?*

*Explain away that one if you can. Well, a pleasant
evening to you, and watch out for Exu.*

65

Next day there was rejoicing in the tenderloin. At twelve
noon the Barroquinha women gave the Alleluia shout
and opened their baskets. The prostitutes who had been
arrested the night before were let out of jail beginning at
dawn, along with their bohemian followers.

That morning old Hipólito Sardinha, head of the big
real estate corporation that had launched the grandiose
tourist development known as Parque Bahia de Todos os
Santos, was seen among the ruins of the mansions on
Codfish Hill, now burned to the ground. With him was
the firm's chief legal adviser, a smart lawyer if ever
there was one. The fire had saved them the cost of
demolishing the buildings but deprived them of the
chance to rent the old houses out to the prostitutes for
two lucrative years. Too bad; prostitutes pay higher rents
than anybody else and they pay on time.

Even so, they might not have to write those houses off
as a loss. They might wring some profit from them yet.

The distinguished attorney and his canny old boss were in complete accord in holding that the State's negligence in maintaining public order had resulted in the fire. Since the old houses were technically a part of the zone of prostitution, which had been the scene of continuous riot and sedition during the afternoon and evening of the Closed-Basket Strike, there was no reasonable doubt that they had been set on fire as a consequence of those disturbances, and it was up to the State to reimburse the proprietors for the losses they had suffered due to the incompetence of the responsible authorities.

And so the fire on Codfish Hill was no loss to anyone, unless one counted Cincinato Gato Preto, who was lying with his throat cut, burnt to a cinder in the pot-smokers' fire.

The only prisoner still in jail was Tereza Batista. The police could not have freed her with the others even if they had wanted to; after Dogfish's visit she was in no state to be seen in public. Though not in top form because of the persistent pain in his balls, the plainclothesman had helped four of his subordinates administer a thorough, paternal thrashing.

66

During the days that followed the epic battle of Pelourinho, Almério das Neves ran desperately to and fro, pulling every string at his command to get Tereza out of jail. The American battleships had steamed away from the port of Bahia after three days and three nights, and with them spinster Veralice's last best hope of being ravished by a blond Yankee with a tool a foot long; ancient Granny, the devout and disorderly Vovó, was lying forgotten in a common grave in Quintas Cemetery; the closed-basket polemic had disappeared from the daily press—and Tereza was still in stir.

Not even Jenner Augusto the painter, who had powerful friends in the government, could get the authorities to turn her loose. As soon as he found out she was in jail he moved heaven and earth to get her out, as did the other artists for whom she had posed as a model and who were now her friends. They got nothing but promises for their pains: she'll be out today, don't worry. The promises meant nothing. Tereza was Detective Nicolau Ramada Junior's personal hostage, a prisoner to be disposed of at his pleasure, and in prison, therefore, she would stay until the hero of Barroquinha was back in peak sexual and physical condition and the swelling in his balls went down.

He was far from satisfied with the punishment dealt out to Tereza on the night of the riot. Even though it had been quite a beating, with four men taking turns not counting him, the Dogfish's performance had not been up to snuff; his nuts were hurting him too much. Now that his strength was back he wanted to give her the beating she deserved, but even more than that, he wanted to see her defenseless, at his mercy, and make her swallow the insult she had shouted out at him at the Lotus Flower Cabaret, along with his prick and balls.

Tired of being given the runaround, the painter got his dander up and handed the case to a lawyer friend of his, Dr. Antônio Luis Calmon Teixeira, known in underwater-fishing circles as the record-breaking Chiquinho. The lawyer saw that it was a clear violation of the right of habeas corpus, but just as he was ready to take the case to court, Tereza was set free. Several public officials at once claimed the palm, as well as her friends' gratitude, for having been the one to get her released.

The truth was that Tereza owed her freedom to Vavá. He had gone into action, too; but he had gone about it the right way, by getting in touch with the vice squad. He spent a lot of money before he was through, the lion's share going to the assistant chief. Labão Oliveira drove a hard bargain from his bed of pain, his two legs in casts sticking straight up in the air (where they would stay for another two months, the doctors told him). Determined to reduce his losses on that ill-fated deal in any way he could, he demanded a hefty sum to make him forget Vavá's crimes and let that trouble-making broad out of jail. After all, Vavá had to remember that she was booty, a part of his friend and colleague's spoils of war. Vavá paid up without a murmur.

He paid without a murmur, with love in his heart but

no hope, for Exu, back in his shrine for the ritual celebration had told him again that Tereza was not to be a tidbit for the cripple's mouth. Besides, from his own sources of information, he had learned about Almério das Neves waiting quietly in the wings and Captain Januário Gereba lost at sea. Nevertheless, he did not leave the girl to rot in jail while she waited for the second half of her lesson in good behavior. Intermediaries came and went. Finally, one day the door to Tereza's dungeon was unlocked and she saw the light of day.

Amadeu Mestre Jegue was waiting for her at the prison door and escorted her to Vavá's apartment, where Taviana, another acquaintance who had approached everyone she could think of on Tereza's behalf, waited with her heart in her mouth. Tereza had lost a little of her color and was very thin, and she still had ugly bruises on her thighs and breasts from the rough treatment of her first night in jail. Otherwise she was just the same: cheerful, grateful, happy at the way the fight had turned out, Closed-Basket Tereza.

Vavá did not take advantage of these propitious circumstances to so much as breathe an insinuating word. He kept his eyes off Tereza—she's not a morsel for your mouth. Someone else would come along sooner or later and he'd fall in love again. But she wouldn't be as beautiful as Tereza, and she wouldn't be as straight.

67

Taviana sent a message to Almério with the good news— she hadn't told him sooner because she was afraid Oliveira might have given Vavá the runaround. The baker went running to the castle as soon as he received the glad tidings. Tears came to his eyes when he saw Tereza, and he couldn't say a word. She went over to him and kissed him on both cheeks.

"What she needs is to rest up for a while. She's a walking skeleton; those dogs ate her flesh," said Taviana indignantly, and added: "The best thing to do is keep Tereza out of circulation for a few days. Dogfish is going to have an attack when he hears she's out of jail, and I wouldn't

put it past him to try another of his tricks. That's not a
person; it's a pig." She spat scornfully and ground the
sordid individual into the dust with the sole of her shoe.

Tereza saw no reason to go into hiding. She wanted to
go back to the Lotus Flower dance floor that same night
and start working at the castle as soon as she got her copper color back and put on a little flesh. But Almério and
Taviana wouldn't hear of it. Do you want to get thrown in
jail again and make more trouble for your friends when
they're worried and upset enough already? Just get that
idea out of your head.

"I know where I can hide her," Almério spoke up.

He took her to the voodoo temple of São Gonçalo do
Retiro, the Opô Afonjá Axé, and left her in the care of
its priestess, Lady Mother.

68

While Tereza Batista lay sleeping in Oxum's house,
where the *iyalorixá* had put her, she had a dream about
Januário Gereba and awoke in great distress. In the dream
she saw him on a rock in the middle of the ocean where
enormous waves were beating. Foam and great fish were
all around. Janu held out his arms to her and Tereza
walked toward him on the water as if she were walking
on dry land. Just as she was about to reach him a divine
apparition rose out of the sea, a woman who was half
fish, half mermaid. She wrapped Januário in her long green
hair—so long it covered her scaly tail, so green it was like
the bottom of the sea—and took him away with her. Just
before the mermaid and the sailor went down into the
water, Tereza caught a glimpse of the apparition's face
and saw that it was not Yemanjá as she had thought, but
Death. The face was a skull and the hands were two
withered claws.

Tereza said nothing about her dream, but she could not
conceal her distress from Lady Mother.

"What's gotten into you, daughter?"

"Nothing, Mother."

"Don't ever lie to Xangô."

Tereza told her the dream and Lady Mother heard her

out attentively. She saw no immediate solution to the riddle.

"We'll have to cast the sacred nut. Has anybody ever done that for you before?"

"Not that I know of."

Their conversation took place in Xangô's house, where the country calm of housework followed the morning rituals observed at dawn. Lady Mother went to the *peji*, prostrated herself at the feet of Xangô, and asked him for a boon: the light of understanding. From a dish placed before him she took a kola nut and went into the room where she received visitors and gave advice. Sitting down at a table made of lianas twisted together, she cut the nut into four pieces with a little knife, first paring away a little at the top and bottom. With the four pieces in her hand she made a fist, touched it to her forehead, and pronounced the magic word in Nago to begin the game.

She began her throws, and each time the pieces of kola nut rolled on the crocheted tablecloth she glanced over at the girl in wonderment. Even though Tereza tried to remember, and did remember, the Doctor's skeptical words and the lessons about life and matter that he had taught her in Estância, Tereza felt a tremor at her heart, an old ancestral fear from the ages before she was born. She said not a word but waited tensely for what might be a sentence of death.

Three or four spirit-daughters were in attendance, and beside the *iyalorixá* sat an important visitor renowned for his unquestioned wisdom: Nezinho, priest of the Muritiba temple. He, too, raised questioning eyes to the girl several times. Finally Lady Mother's face lit up. Leaving the four parts of the kola nut on the table, she lifted her hands, palms upward, and exclaimed:

"*Alafía!*"

"*Alafía!*" Nezinho said after her.

"*Alafía!*" The word of joy and peace, echoed by the adepts, rang through the temple.

They all clapped their hands to show their satisfaction. Priest and priestess looked at each other, smiling, and simultaneously nodded. Only then did Lady Mother speak to Tereza.

"You can leave your cares behind you, daughter. All is well and there's no danger on the horizon. Have faith;

the *orixás* are powerful and they are near you. I never saw so many together in my life."

"Neither did I," added Nezinho. "I never saw a human being so well protected."

Once more, as if to make sure she had been right, Lady Mother took the pieces of the sacred nut and threw them on the table after touching them to her forehead in her closed fist. Again she and Nezinho smiled at the same time. The priestess of São Gonçalo do Retiro handed the kola nut to the priest of Muritiba with a bow. Nezinho turned and hailed Xangô: *Kauô Kabiecie!* Then he cast the pieces on the table and the result was the same. Nezinho looked fixedly at Tereza and asked:

"Haven't you ever found an old man with a staff near you when you're in danger?"

"Yes, I have. Never the same one, but they all looked alike."

"Oxalá looks after you."

Lady Mother reassured Tereza again that no danger threatened her.

"Even when you're most troubled in your mind and you think everything's all over, have faith and courage; don't give up."

"But what about him?"

"Don't be afraid for him or for yourself. Yansã is powerful and Januário is her steed. There's nothing to be afraid of. Go in peace. *Axé.*"

"*Axé! Axé!*" repeated all in the house of Xangô.

69

A few days later Tereza thanked Lady Mother for her hospitality, took her leave of the *candomblé* temple, and went back to her room in Dona Fina's boarding house in Desterro.

In the samba dancer's absence, the Lotus Flower's owner, Alinor Pinheiro, not having any idea how long she would be away, had hired two new attractions, a contortionist and a singer who went by the odd name of Patativa de Macau, although she hailed from Rio Grande do Norte and not the Orient as some imaginative customers believed. Tereza found herself without a job, but she was soon approached with an offer to perform at the Tabaris, the most elegant and fashionable cabaret in Bahia. Always lively, always full of well-dressed customers, the Tabaris was the heart of the city's night life. Now this was a dazzling and unexpected offer! It had never even crossed Tereza's mind that she might be given a chance to show what she could do on the stage of the Tabaris, whose performers were all either foreigners or professional entertainers from the South. She didn't know that Vavá was the majority stockholder in the holding company that owned the nightclub. They told her she would have to wait a little while, though, until the Argentine dancer Raquel Pucio's contract expired and she could take her place. What did that matter! She would wait as long as she had to. A job at the Tabaris was a sure road to fame and fortune.

She could afford to wait. Dona Paulina de Souza had lent her some money through Anália, to pay back whenever she could, and Taviana had offered to lend her what she needed for expenses. But Tereza never set foot on the stage at the Tabaris.

One afternoon Camafeu de Oxossi's nephew came looking for her with an urgent message: Cap'n Caetano Gunzá wanted to speak to her, and it was urgent, because the barque would weigh anchor that evening for Camamu. Tereza felt her heart stop. She knew beyond a doubt that it was bad news. She covered her head with the shawl the Doctor had given her before he died and went down with the boy on the Lacerda elevator.

She saw Camafeu at the entrance to the Market, but he swore he didn't know what the message was. He just knew there was one, that was all; but the *Ventania* wasn't anchored far, just out by the Sea Fort. Tereza heard a tremor in the voice of her friend, whom she had addressed as compadre ever since one St. John's Eve party Almério had taken her to, where she had jumped over the bonfire with Camafeu and his wife Toninha. They had been good friends ever since. But now Camafeu wouldn't look at her but gazed out to sea, and every word he said seemed dragged out of him. The most good-humored fellow in the world was gloomy and morose that afternoon. Feeling

more and more like a condemned woman, Tereza took a
canoe out to the barque.

Captain Gunzá's ravaged face told her the truth before
he said a word. In a toneless voice, Tereza said:

"He's dead."

Cap'n Caetano said he was. The *Balboa* had been shipwrecked off the coast of Peru in a great storm, the beginning of a tidal wave, and the crew had drowned. There
were no survivors, according to sailors from two other
ships who had tried to come to the rescue but couldn't
even get close to them, the storm was so bad. They had
seen the *Balboa*'s lifeboats, full of sailors, being swallowed
up by the waves.

He held out a newspaper. Tereza looked at it but
couldn't read it. Cap'n Caetano recited the story, which
he had learned by heart in a few dreary hours. It had
been a tragic night on the Pacific. Besides the *Balboa* another ship, an oil tanker, had been sunk. Anyone who
earns his livelihood from the sea is subject to storms and
shipwrecks; what else could he say to her? There *is* no
consolation for death. The newspaper had published a
list of the crew members taken on in Bahia, and Tereza
made out Januário Gereba's name. Her eyes were dry,
two coals that had been extinguished, and her throat was
so constricted she couldn't swallow.

The dead men Tereza carried on her shoulders had
always weighed her down. It was a heavy load to carry,
but until then she had shouldered it cheerfully and never
despaired. She carried three deaths on her back and had
been resuscitated from death three times. But Janu was
too heavy, and his death was more than Tereza could bear.
Januário Gereba the sailor, my beloved Janu, your death
is mine, and I can't go on any longer.

70

What was the point of going to the office of the shipping
company just to hear Señor Gonzalo confirm the news,
present his formal condolences, and appraisingly eye her
beauty and her black dress? Wasn't he the one who had
given the list of names to the press? To drive the knife-

blade deeper into her heart; to know that all hope was lost. There, in the uninviting waiting room of the maritime firm, the Spaniard read her the telegram informing him that all the *Balboa*'s crew were dead, including the Bahians. Why had she come? To drive the dagger even deeper into her heart, if that was possible. Tereza Batista was no more.

On her head was the flowered shawl the Doctor had given her. She had worn it when she was happy, worn it when she was fighting mad. Now it was a widow's veil, a tatter from a shroud. Her eyes were black, opaque, and empty, her lips pale. She walked aimlessly to the Xarriô elevator and rode in it to the Upper Town. In Cathedral Square she came face to face with Dogfish. When he caught sight of her the cop shouted:

"You dirty bitch! You shitty whore!"

He hoped she would give him as good as she got so that he would have an excuse to arrest her and taste the revenge he'd been balked of; but Tereza only looked through him and walked on. That one look was enough to stop the plainclothesman in his tracks. She had stared at him like a dead person, a corpse wandering the streets.

71

Maria Clara and Cap'n Manuel welcomed her aboard their fishing boat and took her for a long, leisurely voyage around the Recôncavo. It was Tereza's farewell to the city, the harbor, the sea, the bay, the River Paraguaçu. She had decided to leave Bahia and go back to the *sertão* where she had been born. In Cajazeiras do Norte, Gabi still spoke of her incomparable beauty and had told her: Come back whenever you want to, you have a home here.

Before she left, though, she wanted to follow the sea paths Janu had sailed. She would go aboard the *Arrow of St. George,* which had once been called the *Water-flower* and had belonged to Cap'n Januário Gereba, with the handcuffs on his wrists and the fetters on his feet. She wanted to see the old wharves he had described to her in Aracaju as they stood on the Emperor's Bridge.

Cachoeira, São Feliz, Maragogipe, Santo Amaro da Purificação, São Francisco do Conde; the lost islands, the
canals, a whole sorrowful geography. Why recapture
those memories, why learn those landscapes by heart, why
listen to the wind in the sails, when he wasn't there and
would never come again?

Cap'n Manuel was at the helm. Maria Clara, standing
beside him, sang Janaína's songs, songs of the sea and
death, of Inaê sailing on the breath of the storm winds,
of Yemanjá covering the body of a drowned mariner
with her scattered hair, as green as the depths of the
ocean.

When the night was almost over and the moonlight
died away at the edge of dawn, when the sails were furled
and the fishing boat rested at anchor at the mouth of the
Paraguaçu, Cap'n Manuel, thinking Tereza was asleep,
lay down beside Maria Clara and the sound of their lovemaking quieted the wind and the water.

Moans of love flew like birds over Tereza where she
lay sleepless on the deck, her dry eyes filled with emptiness, a dagger thrust into her dead heart, one hand touching the mingled waters of the river and the sea, beloved
Janu's river-sea.

72

By the time the fishing boat lowered anchor at the Market
Ramp, Tereza was ready to leave the port of Bahia and
go to earth in the *sertão*. The good Almério was waiting
for her on the dock. Her poor friend would be heart-
broken at the news, but she wasn't strong enough to stay
there, following Janu's footsteps everywhere, gazing at
the sea that had been his home, touching the wooden
tiller of the sailboat where he used to set his hand.

Despair was written on Almério's face, and his voice
was choked with tears:

"Tereza, Zeques is very, very sick. It's meningitis. The
doctor says he may not pull through—" A sob escaped
from his chest.

"Meningitis?"

She went straight home with Almério and didn't stir

from the little boy's bedside for ten whole days, scarcely taking her eyes from the child long enough to eat or sleep. After all, she had been given her nursing degree by the smallpox. Black Smallpox Tereza had struggled against death so many times and won. Now, when she was dead herself, she fought for the orphan's life.

After several days the young pediatrician, Dr. Sabino, smiled for the first time. When Almério thanked him, he pointed to Tereza sitting next to the convalescent's bed.

"He owes his life to Dona Tereza, not to me."

Seeing them side by side and both so concerned about the child, Dr. Sabino, with the unthinking impertinence of the young who rush in where angels fear to tread, remarked:

"If you're both free and unattached, why don't the two of you get married? That's what the kid needs most: a mother."

With this remark he went away, leaving the two face to face. Almério raised his eyes, fearfully opened his lips, and took the plunge:

"Well, why not? . . . For my part, it's what I want most in the world."

Tereza Batista, burdened down with dead men, dead herself, surrendered at last:

"Give me a little time to think about it."

"How much more time do you need?"

Maybe she could be a good companion to him and take good care of the house and the little boy. But in bed? What could she be there but a competent professional? And since she was Almério's friend and was grateful to him and fond of him, it would be all the more painful and difficult to let him make love to her; much more of a hardship than it ever could be in a backlands brothel with an open door, like Gabi's house in Cuia Dágua, Cajazeiras do Norte. Would she be able to put on a good enough act? In a whore's bed it wasn't so hard, but in the nuptial bed it would be a difficult task, a thankless obligation.

But Almério wasn't even asking for love; he was sure he could win her love in the course of time. All he wanted was friendship, a companion for him and the child, lovemaking like the kind he enjoyed at the castle, and someone who was interested in him. She couldn't give him happiness, because she had none to give. Ah, she wasn't strong enough to fight any longer. Tereza Batista, Home from the Wars.

"Well, if you'll take me the way I am . . ."

Almério rushed over to the bakery to tell his employees the good news.

73

Can I offer you some wild cherry or mangaba sherbet, a nice cold drink of cashew-fruit juice, or passionflower or genipap? You can have your choice of fresh fruits in syrup, too: we have jackfruit, mango, sliced banana, or guava. Or would you rather have pineapple rind or ginger? Will you have a beanpaste-and-pepper cake? Plain, or wrapped in a banana leaf? Nobody makes beancake like our Agripina. Now eat a little something, do; it's a pleasure to serve you. For a really good talk you need a little something to eat and drink along with it, don't you think?

Yes, I know her; she's been right here in this house. You wouldn't believe it, but people come here from all over the world. Poor men, rich men, experienced old men and wild young men, painters of pictures and painters of walls, abbots from monasteries and voodoo priestesses, modest wise men and conceited fools—they all come and shake my hand and I talk to them all, in whatever language it is, it doesn't matter, I get along all right. God made languages to help us understand one another, not to make it hard for people to know each other and be friends. I give everyone the same kind of welcome, because that's how we do in Bahia, and I tell them about things I know and things I've learned in these eighty-eight years I've had the good fortune to be alive.

You ask me who Tereza Batista reminds me of? Life had been too hard on her, she was too tired and had such a long row to hoe, but she kept on going just the same. With all those dead men weighing her down, she still had enough grit left in her to grapple with death and bring a little boy back to life. I'll tell you who she reminds me of.

Sitting on this veranda and looking out over Rio Vermelho where it meets the ocean away off, and at those trees, some of them a hundred years old but most of them planted by me and my folks, with these hands that picked up a rifle in the woods in Ferradas when people fought over cocoa plantations, remembering my deceased husband João, such a good man, and a good-natured one too; with my three sons, my treasures, around me, and my three daughters-in-law, my daughters and rivals; my grandsons and granddaughters and great-grandchildren and all my kinfolk and their families, I, Eulalia Leal Amado, Lalu to the people who love me (and there're lots of them)—I tell you, sir, that Tereza Batista is just like the people, that's who. The Brazilian people, who've had to suffer so much and never know when they're beaten. When you think they're done for and dead, that's the time they hop right out of the coffin.

Won't you have some ciruela juice or hogplum ice? If you'd rather have whisky, you're welcome to it but I don't think much of your taste.

74

Tereza Batista's marriage feast was talked about and praised all over Bahia for months. Rodolfo Coelho Cavalcânti immortalized that convivial and truly unforgettable occasion in a ballad.

One of the most unforgettable things about it was the four big tables heaped with all the glorious food Bahia can offer. On one table were all the palm-oil and coconut dishes, the delicious peppery stews of chicken and rice and shrimp, the grilled fish and fried chicken and beans seasoned with herbs. The other tables groaned under the weight of roast beef and roast pork, chicken and green beans, roast ducklings, turkeys and guinea hens, forty pounds of haggis, a kid and two suckling pigs; great platters full of all kinds of meat, and more in the kitchen. And the desserts? Better not begin on them; when I tell you there were five kinds of coconut candy alone—! Liquor flowed by the case, by the barrel, on the same grand scale as the victuals: beer and ale, all kinds of rum sours, gallon bottles of Capelinha wine, whisky, vermouth, brandy, good Santo Amaro *cachaça* and the usual soft drinks—plus a dozen bottles of champagne reposing on ice in one of the crowded kitchen cupboards, a gift from Dr. Nelson Taboada, President of the Manufacturers' Association, to his esteemed business associate, to toast the bride and groom in after the marriage vows. The ovens of the Panificadora Nosso Senhor do Bonfim worked all day, not to serve the population of Brotas but to make bread and rolls exclusively for the wedding feast. Wasn't it Almério das Neves, the happy bridegroom, who owned the prosperous establishment, soon to be an emporium? Lady Luck's favorite, he must have been born with a caul; a self-made man, he had every right to celebrate his second marriage with pomp and pageantry.

Practically everyone in Bahia got an invitation to the feast, and those few who had been forgotten crashed the party anyway. The wedding banquet took place in Almério's house, but as the night wore on, the dancing spilled over into the bakery next door and swirled around the ovens. To the Kings of Sound Jazz Band from the Lotus Flower Cabaret goes the credit for keeping the party lively, but the delirious climax came shortly after midnight, when the Electric Trio pranced out into the street and the party turned into a carnival.

The breadmakers' guild, all the Spanish monopolists and their Brazilian competitors, turned out *en masse*, and so did Almério's *compadres*: friends from the Confraternity of the Church of Bonfim and from São Gonçalo do Retiro, where he held an honored place in the house of Oxalá. Lady Mother was seated in a high-backed armchair, surrounded by her court of princes. The other *candomblé* temples were well represented, too. There was Little Mother Creusa, Mother Menininha de Gantois, Olga of Alaketu in all her finery, Eduardo of Ijexá, Master Didi and Nezinho of Muritiba, who had made a special point of coming for Tereza's sake. There were the artists Tereza had posed for—Mário Cravo, Carybé, Genaro de Carvalho, Mirabeau Sampaio—and those still waiting their turn, which alas! would never come: Emanuel, Fernando Coelho, Willys and Floriano Texeira, who because of his name and because he came from Maranhão and had a gift of gab, always reminded Tereza of her friend Flori Pachola of the Gay Paree in Aracaju. With the artists came the literati, as snobbish as they were extravagant, guzzling whisky after looking carefully at the labels: João Ubaldo, Wilson Lins, James Amado, Ildásio Tavares, Jehová de Carvalho, Cid Seixas, Guido Guerra, and Telmo Serra the poet. Hansen the German and architects Gilbert Chaves and Mário Mendonça listened attentively as Mister Calá recounted for the thousandth time the true story of the whale who headed up the Paraguacu River and swallowed a whole field of sugarcane. Anyone who has the good fortune to meet Calasans Neto the printmaker and admire his bucolic huts and capering goats should ask him to tell that story. If you haven't heard it, you don't know what you've missed.

Anyone reading the list so far might think there were too many men at the party and not enough women, but it wasn't so: every one of those men brought a wife with him and some more than one. Dona Zélia brought perfume for the bride, from Lalu, and a pretty piece of costume jewelry, a ring, from herself. Dona Luiza, Dona Nair, and Dona Norma brought flowers. And what about the women in the life; don't they count? The madams— Taviana, old Acácia, Assunta, Dona Paulina de Souza on Ariosto Alvo Lírio's arm—were grave, almost solemn, very ladylike and discreetly dressed. The girls were modest, retiring, some hardly more than shy children, some with their sweeties by their side. Black Domingas, Ogum's favorite, looked like a princess.

In a corner of the living room, almost hidden by the window curtain and by Amadeu Mestre Jegue, sat Vavá in his wheelchair. Tereza had asked him to be her witness before the judge, along with Dona Paulina and Toninha and Camafeu de Oxossi. Before the priest she wanted Jenner Augusto the painter and his wife, a noble lady from Sergipe with real family titles and, miracle of miracles, no class prejudice. Almério's witnesses were the banker Celestino, who gave him credit and good advice, the lawyer Tibúrcio Barreiros, and Dr. Jorge Calmon, publisher of the afternoon paper *A Tarde*—all top-drawer witnesses. For the religious ceremony the groom kept the same sponsors who had presided at his first wedding: Miguel Santana, a prince of the Opô Afonjá Temple, a

first-class singer and dancer and a patriarch who had once
been a very rich man and had helped Almério in the
early days when he was sometimes short of cash; and
Taviana, madam at the castle where he had twice found
a bride. Why change godparents, when his marriage to
Natália had been such a happy one? Little Zeques, now
well on the road to recovery, would be ring-bearer.

They had asked Dom Timóteo, a lean, ascetic Bene-
dictine priest who was also a poet, to officiate at the religious ceremony. For the civil ceremony they had chosen
Judge Santos Cruz, who was still on the family court at
that time.

There was Dorival Caymmi with his guitar. Surely he'd
sing for the bride; hadn't he composed a lovely song just
for her? With him were two young fellows who already
looked like musicians, one named Caetano, the other Gil.
As for the toast to the newly wedded pair, who but the
nonpareil councilman, Reginaldo Pavão? When it came
to making speeches at baptisms and weddings, nobody
could touch him.

The only friends who were missing were Cap'n Manuel
and Maria Clara—the *Arrow of St. George* was away in
Cachoeira just then—and Cap'n Caetano Gunzá. The
barque *Ventania* was taking on cargo off Agua dos
Meninos, but its captain wasn't much of a partygoer. The
sea and the stars were all the party he wanted.

No groom was ever so happy. Almério looked splendid
in the best new white suit of English goods that money
could buy, a suit worthy of Oxalá's favorite son. A little
before four, the time set for the wedding, a messenger
came with an urgent message from Tereza, begging Almério to run over to Dona Fina's house, where she was
dressing for the ceremony.

75

Maria Petisco and Anália were helping Tereza Batista
dress and fix herself up at Dona Fina's. Whoever saw a
bride so down-in-the-mouth on her wedding day? Was it
her wedding she was dressing for, or the wake at her own
funeral?

Anália upbraided her friend for not knowing how lucky she was. Oh, how I wish it was me! I'm sick of this whore's life, hopping in and out of bed all the time, one man after another, selling my body and wasting love on la-las who just throw me over after a while. Didn't you see what happened with Kalil? Oh yes, such a nice boy, but he gave me up to marry his cousin, the beast. Not that Anália blamed him. She'd give up a silly sweetheart to get married any day. Oh, if I could only have a home and children, and a husband all to myself who could have me all to himself. Oh, Tereza, if I were in your place I'd be dancing for joy and grinning all over my face. Maria Petisco was only partly in agreement. She didn't find it easy to be faithful to a man, especially with the spirits swooping down on her bed all the time without bothering to ask whom the mattress, the pillow, and the person sleeping on them belonged to.

When Tereza was dressed and combed, Maria Petisco hung around her neck a dazzling necklace like Yansã's, a necklace with a charm on it, a symbol of victory in her war against the dead. It was a present from Valdeloir Rego, jeweler to the *orixás,* and it had been washed by Lady Mother in the temple. Anália led Tereza to the mirror to look at her beautiful, unhappy self.

While her friends primped, Tereza gazed deeply at her reflection in the polished steel. That vibrant crimson necklace, those beads like drops of blood—she wasn't fit to wear them. She was defeated. She was through. She felt old, battle-weary, dead inside.

People and incidents crowded into her mind: people who had died, things that had happened long ago. The Doctor, the Captain, Lulu Santos, the baby torn out of her womb, murdered before he was born. The time when she had lived in chains, her days in the brothel, the years in Estância, the places she had seen, the bad and the good, the rawhide leather whip and the rose. Which birthday was it that had come a few months ago while she was in jail, a prisoner abused by the vice squad in Bahia? It was the twenty-sixth. But that was impossible. She must be a hundred and twenty-six years old, a thousand and twenty-six, or even older. Age doesn't count when you're dead.

The sound of voices raised at the front door startled

Tereza out of her reverie; Dona Fina's voice contradicting someone, then a reply and a laugh. Tereza shivered, and her heart beat wildly. Whose was that unforgettable voice that held the lapping of waves and the sound of the conch shell?

"She's being married. you say? Well, maybc shc is, but to me."

Trembling, not believing her ears, she rose to her feet and walked step by step down thc hall, gazing fearfully before her. At the street door, determined to come in, was the giant condor, alive and whole. Then Tereza Batista broke down and wept convulsively. Still weeping, she flung herself into Januário Gereba's arms.

76

"The wedding is off!" Maria Petisco announced, jumping out of a taxi at Almério's front door.

She had left Tereza in Cap'n Gereba's arms. But hadn't he been shipwrecked? Wasn't he dead after all? Dead nothing, he was alive and well, a hunk of man to make a girl smack her lips, a sweet hunk of sugarcane for Tereza, the lucky thing. The *Balboa* had foundered more than three months after he and Toquinho, one of the other Bahians, had quit and started for home. They had taken the long way around and seen the world. He had just got back and Compadre Caetano Gunzá had told him what had happened. Almério, my friend, I'm awful sorry but it looks like your wedding is off.

At first Almério was very disappointed, of course. After all, it came as a shock to him, with the papers drawn up and the banquet spread and all. But as an insatiable comic-book reader and soap opera fan, he was used to identifying himself with the melodramatic heroes of those stories, and once over the initial shock he begged for details. Incredible as it may seem, in less than half an hour he was alight with enthusiasm. Maria Petisco had come on ahead to tell the wedding guests the news and arrived at almost the same time as the judge and the priest. The magistrate went away again, but Dom Timóteo waited for Almério, thinking the poor man might be in need of consolation.

"And what's going to happen to all the victuals?" asked old Miguel Santana, who had eaten a light lunch to leave plenty of room for the banquet.

"Oh, damn, now there won't be any party!" groaned Domingas, who had been all set to samba all night long.

Almério das Neves, who came into the room just then with Anália, heard the protests and flung up his hands to show it wasn't his fault. Well, folks, he said, the wedding's come a cropper. I'm sorry for myself but glad for Tereza. The sweetheart she thought was dead has landed just in the nick of time. It would have been a lot worse if he'd got here too late; then we all would have been in a fine fix. Almério was the generous lover incarnate, ready to sacrifice his own happiness without a murmur for the sake of his beloved and his fortunate rival.

"Well, if that's the way things are, we ought to celebrate," proposed Dorival Caymmi, a man who never gave bad advice.

Almério looked around the crowded room, the people spilling out into the passageway, the great tables spread, the bottles on ice, the jazz band. A smile dawned on his lips, clearing from the placid face of the ex-bridegroom the last trace of disappointment. In a burst of heroic altruism he spoke in a loud voice for all the guests, for all Bahia, to hear:

"There won't be a wedding, but that's no reason why there shouldn't be a party. Let's break out Dr. Nelson's champagne!"

"Now that's the kind of talk I like to hear," said Miguel Santana approvingly, making for the dining room.

And so Tereza Batista's wedding feast, sans wedding, was celebrated throughout the night with song and dance. The wedding guests ate and drank their fill, to the last crust of bread and the last drop of champagne. It was the kind of blowout you don't find anywhere but in Bahia, and not very often even there. The jazz musicians never stopped playing except to down a glass of beer and snatch a mouthful from each dish, and the dancers were still going strong the next morning, hopping up the street after the Electric Trio. By the time the party was half over, Almério, a little high by then, and Anália—that girl wasn't meant to be a prostitute—had become inseparable, and she had confessed that she adored children. Now isn't that like something right out of a novel?

77

Sails unfurled, the fishing boat sliced through the gulf of Bahia. The late-night breeze blew softly over the bay. Tereza Batista, splashed with sea water, tasting of salt, smelling of sea and salt both, black hair loose on the wind, was reborn, Alleluia! She snuggled close to Januário Gereba's chest. As he stood at the helm, Cap'n Janu mused aloud about the good points of the boat he was thinking of buying. If she's strong enough for long trips, I'll buy her and pay cash on the nail. Compadre Gunzá put my money in the bank to earn interest; now I call that the right kind of compadre to have. What should we call her, do you think? Before giving thought to a name for the fishing boat, Tereza said:

"I killed a man, did you know that? He was too bad to live, but I've been carrying him around on my back all this time."

Januário put away his clay pipe.

"Well then, let's throw him overboard right here and now. If he was bad let the sharks have him; they're a mean race of fish. That way, you'll be rid of him."

He smiled into the dark and the sun came up. Well, that's one of them gone but there's more, Janu.

"A man died inside me, just after he came. I don't know if other people would say he was good or bad, but he was the best man in the world to me, a husband and father both. I carry his death around in my guts."

"If he died when he came he went straight to Heaven. Anybody dies that way, it's a sign of God's love. Throw the just man's corpse to the eagle rays and you'll be shut of his death, but hang onto everything good he gave you."

The sea opened and closed, and Tereza sighed with relief. Gereba asked:

"Have you got any more of 'em? If you have, this is a good time to throw 'em overboard. It was right around here I unloaded my poor wife's corpse."

Tereza thought of the one who had never drawn a breath of life but had been torn out of her before he had a chance to be born. She laid her hand on that of Januário Gereba, her beloved Janu, to make him turn the fishing boat into a little inlet among the bamboo thickets on the shore of the bay, a quiet, hidden nesting place. Then she lay down on the deck.

"Come make me a baby, Janu."

"Well now, that's a thing I do very well."

There between night and morning, river and sea, *riomar.*

THE END
Bahia, March to November, 1972

GLOSSARY

axé—Voodoo temple. Salute to the spirits.

babalorixá—"Spirit father," high priest in *candomblé* rituals.

caboclo, -a—Half-white, half-Indian person, or one from the backwoods; copper-colored and straight-haired mulatto; acculturated Indian.

cachaça—Firewater, white rum.

candomblé—Afro-Brazilian voodoo religion or place of worship.

capoeira—Anglo leg wrestling, with many stylized feints requiring both agility and skill.

conto—One thousand cruzeiros.

Exu Tiriri—Most mischievous of the voodoo spirits; often represents the Devil.

figa—Clenched-fist fertility symbol, a popular amulet in Brazil.

guaraná—Popular soft drink made from jungle fruit of the same name.

iyalorixá—"Spirit mother," high priestess in *candomblé*.

macumba—Voodoo ceremony with singing, dancing, and drums.

modinha—Simple art song, folk song, or popular song.

odóia—Salute to the sea goddess, Yemanjá.

ogan—One possesssd by a voodoo spirit; that spirit's "steed."

Ogum—Warrior god of iron.

Omolu—Spirit of disease, especially smallpox.

Orixá—African voodoo spirit. Many *orixás* in Brazil are syncretized with Christian saints.

Oxalá—Supreme voodoo deity; syncretized with Our Lord of Bonfim.

Oxossi—Yoruba forest deity, god of the hunt; syncretized with St. George.

Oxum—Alluring river divinity, wife to Xangô and Oxossi.

sertão—The backlands, the dry, scrubby outback of northern Brazil.

Xangô—Powerful voodoo thunder-god.

Yansã—Female warrior divinity who receives the dead, Xangô's principal wife; syncretized with St. Barbara.

Yemanjá (also *Janaína, Inaê*—Sea goddess, "Mother of Waters"; sometimes syncretized with Our Lady of the Immaculate Conception.

(*X* in these words is pronounced "*sh*")

 **BARD BOOKS**

DISTINGUISHED
LATIN-AMERICAN FICTION

BETRAYED BY RITA HAYWORTH
Manuel Puig
36020 2.25

THE FAMILY OF PASCUAL DUARTE
Camilo José Cela
11247 1.45

**THE EYE OF THE HEART: SHORT STORIES
FROM LATIN AMERICA**
Barbara Howes, Ed.
20883 2.25

GABRIELA, CLOVE AND CINNAMON
Jorge Amado
18275 1.95

HOPSCOTCH   Julio Cortázar
20487 2.65

THE GREEN HOUSE   Mario Vargas Llosa
15099 1.65

LEAF STORM AND OTHER STORIES
Gabriel García Márquez
35816 1.95

NO ONE WRITES TO THE COLONEL
Gabriel García Márquez
32748 1.75

ONE HUNDRED YEARS OF SOLITUDE
Gabriel García Márquez
34033 2.25

62: A MODEL KIT   Julio Cortázar
17558 1.65

Where better paperbacks are sold, or direct from the publisher. Avon Books, Mail Order Dept., 250 West 55th St., New York, N. Y. 10019. Include 25¢ per copy for postage and handling; allow 4-6 weeks for delivery.

BLA 9-77

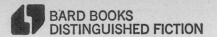

BARD BOOKS
DISTINGUISHED FICTION

Finally, in one paperback volume...the finest
writers in all of Latin America are represented
in an anthology which Jorge Luis Borges has
called *"quite impressive. All of the important
writers are there and the stories are all good...
Such a book will certainly be valuable...I know
nothing like it now."*

THE EYE
OF THE HEART
EDITED BY BARBARA HOWES

Outstanding short stories by Llosa, Fuentes,
García Márquez, Donoso, Borges, Asturias,
Amado, Cortázar, Paz, and thirty-three
others

0672

20883/$2.25